BATTLES, BETRAYALS, AND BROTHERHOOD

Early Chinese Plays on the Three Kingdoms

Battles, Betrayals, and Brotherhood

Early Chinese Plays on the Three Kingdoms

Edited and Translated,
with an Introduction, by

WILT L. IDEMA
and **STEPHEN H. WEST**

Hackett Publishing Company, Inc.
Indianapolis/Cambridge

Copyright © 2012 by Hackett Publishing Company, Inc.

16 15 14 13 12   1 2 3 4 5 6 7

For further information, please address:
  Hackett Publishing Company, Inc.
  P.O. Box 44937
  Indianapolis, IN 46244-0937

  www.hackettpublishing.com

For information regarding performance rights,
please email us at Permissions@hackettpublishing.com

Cover design by Abigail Coyle
Text design by Stephen H. West and Meera Dash
Composition by Carol Pierson
Printed at Data Reproductions Corporation

Library of Congress Cataloging-in-Publication Data

Battles, betrayals, and brotherhood : early Chinese plays on the Three Kingdoms /
edited and translated, with an introduction, by Wilt L. Idema and Stephen H. West.
     p.   cm.
  Includes bibliographical references and index.
  ISBN 978-1-60384-813-8 (pbk.) — ISBN 978-1-60384-814-5 (cloth)
     1. Chinese drama—Translations into English.   I. Idema, W. L. (Wilt L.)
II. West, Stephen H.
     PL2658.E5B38 2012
     895.1'2008— dc23   2012004760

Contents

Preface

In this collection we present the translations of seven early plays on the saga of the Three Kingdoms. These plays cover the major episodes in this saga, from the famous scene of the oath in the Peach Orchard, when Liu Bei, Guan Yu, and Zhang Fei swear brotherhood, until the moment many years and many battles later when Guan Yu and Zhang Fei have been killed and their souls travel to Chengdu to appear to Liu Bei in his dream, calling for a bloody revenge. In each case we have based our rendition on the earliest available edition; in some cases we additionally provide a translation of a later version if that version departs in important aspects from the earlier version.

This collection is first of all an anthology of early Chinese drama, presenting a number of plays that in and of themselves are important as representatives of *zaju* as it was performed in the urban theaters of the Yuan and on the palace stage of the Ming. Together these plays are also representative of the stage of the development of the Three Kingdoms saga in the centuries immediately before the saga was written up by the end of the fifteenth century as the *Sanguo zhi tongsu yanyi* (*The Popular Elaboration of the Records of the Three Kingdoms*), commonly known as the *Romance of the Three Kingdoms* (the earliest extant edition dates to the early sixteenth century). From the same centuries (1250–1450) we also have a prose account of the saga entitled *Sanguo zhi pinghua* (*Records of the Three Kingdoms in Plain Language*). In an appendix we have provided a detailed summary of the contents of this work, together with complete translations of the corresponding episodes for each of the plays we have translated (in another appendix the corresponding text is from the *Hua Guan Suo zhuan*). These supplementary accounts should provide the reader with a fuller picture of the many shapes of the popular saga in the period 1250–1450, and demonstrate how the demands of the different genres informed each adaptation.

There already exist translations of the major historiographical accounts of the civil wars at the end of the Han that resulted in a tripartition of the empire on the death of Cao Cao. The *Romance of the Three Kingdoms* also has been available in an excellent English translation now for quite some years. Together with the materials presented in this collection, these materials should make it possible now to design undergraduate courses that trace the development of the Three Kingdoms materials from fact to fiction and from history to myth. The contrastive readings of these materials provide a unique opportunity for students to become aware of the conflicting demands of the academic and the performance traditions, as materials move from the scholar's study to the popular stage, and are (at least partially) recovered for Confucian morality by the *Romance of the Three Kingdoms* to become China's "greatest story ever told."

The saga of the Three Kingdoms has lost little of its appeal to Chinese audiences in modern times. The novel has been repeatedly adapted as multi-episode television dramas that were hugely successful, and it has inspired one of China's most popular video games. As we become more and more aware of many of the underlying continuities of Chinese culture despite the huge challenges and changes of the last two centuries, we hope that these translations will provide one more stimulus to our colleagues to teach the saga of the Three Kingdoms from its very beginnings to its many manifestations in contemporary culture.

For their help in the preparation of the manuscript for publication, we would like to thank Kimberly Harui as well as Rick Todhunter, Meera Dash, Abigail Coyle, and all of their colleagues at Hackett Publishing Company. Stephen West would like to thank the American Council of Learned Societies for a fellowship that allowed him to work full-time on the project.

Cambridge, Massachusetts, and Tempe, Arizona, 2012
Wilt L. Idema and Stephen H. West

Introduction

The Three Kingdoms

No cycle of historical tales has enjoyed greater or more enduring popularity in China than stories of the Three Kingdoms. This cycle encompasses the legendary accounts of the civil wars (c. AD 180–220) that assured the destruction of the Han empire; the tripartite division of the old empire among contesting lords who founded the states of Shu-Han (221–63) in the west and southwest, Wei (220–65) in the north and northeast, and Wu (220–80) in the area south of the Yangzi; and the eventual reunification of the realm under the Western Jin in 280. The names of the major characters in these tales, such as Liu Bei (161–223), his sworn brothers Guan Yu (d. 219) and Zhang Fei (d. 221), his adviser Zhuge Liang, and his crafty adversary Cao Cao (155–220), are still uttered in both conscious and unconscious contexts as part of the quotidian language of millions of Chinese households worldwide. From the early sixteenth century on, the mainstay of this popularity has been the one-hundred-twenty-chapter novel now generally referred to as the *Romance of the Three Kingdoms* (*Sanguo yanyi*), originally titled *The Popular Elaboration of the Records of the Three Kingdoms* (*Sanguo zhi tongsu yanyi*). This text, which springs first to Chinese and Western minds when the Three Kingdoms are mentioned, is in fact a late addition to a collective body of works about the era—for six hundred years before its appearance, actors, storytellers, and writers had already brought the exploits of the Three Kingdoms to literate and illiterate audiences alike. In recent years, television series, movies, and most recently computer games have continued to hold sway over the minds and emotions of new generations of audiences.[1]

---

1. For studies of various aspects of this Three Kingdoms culture in premodern and contemporary China (and Korea), see Besio and Tung 2007. Kim 1993 is more modest in scope but more systematic in its treatment. Most available English-language scholarship focuses on the novel, which is available in a complete translation in Roberts 1991. Hsia 1968, pp. 34–74, provides a very useful general introduction to the development of the legend and analysis of the novel, discussing the major characters at length. For a more detailed analysis of the construction of the novel, see Plaks 1987, pp. 361–495. Also see Chang 1990. Little is known about Luo Guanzhong, to whom the novel is usually ascribed, beyond the fact that he is listed as an early-Ming dramatist. See Liu 1980, which tries to determine which other historical novels, also ascribed to Luo, actually may be his works. The novel circulated in a number of different editions in the sixteenth and seventeenth centuries. McLaren 1985 and 1995 discuss these editions and their intended audiences. From the later decades of the seventeenth century onward, the novel was usually printed with the

As has been shown by the recent (2009) supposed discovery of Cao Cao's tomb and the heated debate about its authenticity that immediately inundated the Internet, the Three Kingdoms is an era that is extremely important to the national psyche of China. But it is also one in which the claim to truth is hotly contested. Web sites are flooded not only with scholarly articles on the period, but also with movies and computer games that present variant forms of that ancient world to the modern public. Critical discussion and reviews of the historical accuracy of these fictional and even fantastical products—by a range of people from teenage gamers to scholars from various countries—betray a deep-seated (and ultimately unattainable) desire to learn the "truth" of what went on in that century of turmoil, betrayal, and violence.

Canonical Historiography and Popular Traditions

These latest retellings of the Three Kingdoms stories are the most recent iteration of a historical process in which the tales have been told and retold by succeeding generations; furthermore, the events narrated and the characters involved depart more and more from earlier canonical accounts, which themselves were compiled decades or more after the events they describe and include more rumor and legend than most modern scholars are willing to admit.[2] The major canonical account is a text now called the *Records of the Three Kingdoms* (*Sanguo zhi*), a historical account of the major personalities between AD 184, the first year of the Zhongping reign of Emperor Ling (r. 168–88) of the Han, and 280, the year in which the Western Jin completed the unification of the Chinese world by its conquest of the southeastern state of Wu.[3] The original accounts of the three kingdoms of Shu-Han, Wei, and Wu were created independently. Chen Shou (233–97), the author, had originally been in service to the Shu, but when he compiled the records as a private history, he was in service to the Western Jin and had to promote the Wei, founded by the Cao family, as the link in the "orthodox succession" (*zhengtong*) of dynasties between Han and Jin. Chen had at his disposal earlier historical sources for the Wei and Wu, but was

---

literary commentary of Mao Zonggang. The opening essay of that commentary has been translated and studied in Roy 1990. Basic reference works in Chinese are Guan 2009, Shen and Tan 2007, and Zhu and Liu 1983. Zhang and Wei 2006 is primarily focused on Peking Opera dramatizations of episodes from the Three Kingdoms saga.

2. For a convenient survey of the events that resulted in the collapse of the Han and the foundation of the Three Kingdoms by a modern historian, see Mansvelt Beck 1986.

3. Both dealing with the founders of the Three Kingdoms and taking the story down to the conquest of Wu by the Jin, the *Records of the Three Kingdoms* partly overlaps on one side with the *Documents of the Later Han* (*Hou Hanshu*), and on the other side with the *Documents of the Jin* (*Jinshu*), which were both compiled at a later date.

left to create a small number of chapters on the Shu-Han alone. His text is noted for its spare language and the way in which it closely ties historical events to moral evaluations.

After Chen Shou died, a memorial remarked of the *Records of the Three Kingdoms* that "its language admonished [the reader to goodness] and forewarned them [about bad actions]; it was clear about successes and failures [of various courses of action], and was beneficial to moral edification." Such praise should warn us that the text is not a completely transparent recounting of the facts, but one that makes a judicious selection of events that are meant to exemplify moral qualities in action. There are also clearly places in Chen Shou's accounts where he expressed his personal resentments through pejorative statements or outright omission, or those in which he settled accounts with old enemies for injustices done to him or his family.[4] Moreover, working in an environment so close to the end of the period, Chen had to suppress certain facts about the ruling family of the Jin, and write an account that would be acceptable to them, including their descent in the line of orthodox succession. He was criticized in later times for not using the correct dynastic name for the Shu-Han, "the Han," but he was writing before the advent of official state-sponsored history and before Confucian ideals demanded the use of this name. The fact that he is always singled out as "the one historian" who refused to use the preceding dynastic name is a peculiarly ahistorical and anachronistic criticism levied from the retrospect of state-sponsored historiography.

Although Chen Shou originally compiled his historical account as three separate works—the *Record of Wei*, the *Record of Wu*, and the *Record of Shu*—by the end of the Western Jin, these chronicles were combined into a single text called the *Records of the Three Kingdoms*. In the fifth century in the state of Song in the Southern Dynasties, Pei Songzhi (372–451) wrote a commentary to the individual texts. In doing so, he used more than 240 texts then extant about the era, drawing on a wide variety of sources with varying values of veracity. Pei's work has been criticized for its lackluster language and for the indiscriminate selection of sources, but his expanded version not only highlights the quality of Chen's writing by comparison; it also fleshes out the spare texts of the original. The earliest printed edition we know of the *Records of the Three Kingdoms* was published in 1003, and the work would repeatedly be reprinted throughout the following centuries.

---

4. The modern Chinese polymath Miao Yue (1904–95) had a stout rebuttal of some of these criticisms and an even more robust assessment of why Chen suppressed or distorted what he did. Still, no matter the reason, these alterations to fact and the rationale of selection remain as matters to consider when considering the veracity of accounts. For a careful discussion of the text of the *Records of the Three Kingdoms*, see William Gordon Crowell and Robert Joe Cutter, "Records of the Three States," in Cutter and Crowell 1999, pp. 61–81. Also see De Crespigny 1970.

In contrast to other so-called dynastic histories, which divide their information over annals, treatises, tables, and biographies, the *Records of the Three Kingdoms* consists only of biographies. Some chapters provide biographies of single subjects whereas others group comparable characters together in collective accounts. Cao Cao, Liu Bei, and Sun Quan each have their own individual chapters, but the biographies of Guan Yu and Zhang Fei are included with those of Ma Chao, Huang Zhong, and Zhao Yun in a chapter devoted to "The Five Tiger Generals." The *Records of the Three Kingdoms*, therefore, does not provide a single continuous narrative. A detailed chronological account of the events from 180 to 280, largely based on Chen Shou's work and the sources preserved by Pei Songzhi, was provided by the Song-dynasty statesman and historian Sima Guang (1019–86) in his *Comprehensive Mirror for Aid in Government* (*Zizhi tongjian*), which covered Chinese history from the fifth century to 960 BC.[5] This huge work gave rise to many abridged versions in later centuries.

Various Tang dynasty (AD 617–906) sources suggest that tales of the Three Kingdoms were extremely popular with adults and children during these centuries, but they do not indicate that there was yet a body of professional storytellers who specialized in Three Kingdoms stories. For that, we have to wait until the eleventh century, when Gao Cheng states in his *Record of the Origin of Things and Events* (*Shiwu jiyuan*), "In the reign of Renzong [r. 1023–63] there were people in the marketplace who could recount the stories of *The Three Kingdoms*." This is the earliest record we have of the performance of the cycle of Three Kingdoms stories in the capital. At approximately the same time, the noted Song writer Su Shi (1037–1101) remarked in an entry in his *Forest of Stories of Dongpo* (*Dongpo zhilin*), entitled "Little Children of the Alleyways Listen to Stories of the Three Kingdoms,"

> When little children of the alleyways are naughty and their families tire of dealing with them, they give them a bit of money and tell them to join their friends and go listen to tales of old. When it comes time to tell stories about the Three Kingdoms, they all wrinkle up their faces and some weep when they hear of the defeat of Liu Bei. But when they hear of Cao Cao's defeat they are all happy and pleased. From this we can know that the influence of a gentleman or a small man will not cease after a hundred generations.

We know that by 1117 these storytellers were a specialized guild, and along with actors, were a mainstay of the capital cities (first Kaifeng, then Hangzhou) of the Song dynasty (960–1279). The cycle had become popular with puppet players as well. It is listed together with the more recent stories of the Five Dy-

---

5. De Crespigny 1969, 1989, 1996.

nasties as one of the favorite topics of the storytellers specializing in historical subjects in Kaifeng during the early decades of the twelfth century. Capital diaries written about these years actually list the names of prominent "storytellers of the three-part division" in their records of entertainments in the capital. During this time, the process of legend formation can only have accelerated, providing ever more richly embroidered oral traditions that came to stand alongside written sources.

During the last millennium of imperial China, no period of dynastic change could rival the enduring popularity of this tale of the collapse of the Han and the rise of the three competing kingdoms, but this story-cycle had to compete against others about both earlier and later periods of dynastic change. Authors of plays and ballads on episodes from the Three Kingdoms saga often avoid anachronistic references to later periods of dynastic transition such as the collapse of the Sui dynasty (581–618) and the founding of the Tang dynasty (618–907), or the collapse of the Tang, the quick sequence of the short-lived Five Dynasties (907–60), and the founding of the Song, but they often refer to the events and personalities of the founding of the Zhou (eleventh century BC), and to the wars and characters connected with the collapse of the Qin dynasty (221–207 BC) and the founding of the Han dynasty (202 BC–AD 220). On stage, this latter period enjoyed an equal popularity with the Three Kingdoms saga during the Yuan and early Ming dynasties.[6] The story was often referred to as "Chu-Han," as this story-cycle had come to focus on the competition between on the one side the hegemon-king of Western Chu, the supremely self-confident Xiang Yu (232–202 BC), who was undefeatable in battle, and on the other side the Prince of Han, the lowborn and wily Liu Bang (256 or 247–195), who achieved final victory because he surrounded himself with expert advisers and fine generals. The Chu-Han story-cycle also stressed how a suspicious Liu Bang, following his final victory, killed off his three most meritorious commanders (Han Xin, Peng Yue, and Ying Bu) because he thought they might threaten his own regime. It was widely believed in late imperial China that the eventual tripartition of the Han empire more than four centuries later was a direct form of retribution for these callous murders by its founder (and his wife, Empress Lü), and the main characters involved in the demise of the Han were seen as reincarnations of personalities involved in the founding of the dynasty.[7]

---

6. Idema 1990a.

7. This story forms the opening paragraphs of the *Records of the Three Kingdoms in Plain Language* (see next section). The story also circulated independently in a work entitled the *Causes of the Three Kingdoms* (*Sanguo yin*).

The Colloquial Tradition: 1250–1450

When the colloquial literature that flourished in the period 1250–1450, such as Northern drama (*zaju*), plain tales (*pinghua*), and a performance genre of alternating prose and recited poetry, called *chantefables (cihua)* appeared in print in the late thirteenth and early fourteenth century, the accounts they provided were a world apart from the earliest canonical sources—not only because they neglected all aspects of political administration and the elegant literature of writers of those years in favor of military action, but also because they reveled in mayhem and magic, unbridled violence and bloodthirsty revenge. Among these earliest colloquial texts, we include here seven dramas that date from the fourteenth century to 1616 as well as selections from the *Records of the Three Kingdoms in Plain Language (Sanguo zhi pinghua)* and the *Tale of Hua Guan Suo (Hua Guan Suo zhuan)*.

The *Records of the Three Kingdoms in Plain Language* has been preserved in two editions: one, from 1294, carries the title of *A Short Account of the Tripartition (Sanfen shilüe)*, whereas the better known version, from the years 1321–23, is entitled *The Records of the Three Kingdoms in Plain Language* (hereafter the *Records in Plain Language*).[8] As the anecdote above by Su Shi demonstrates, by the time these texts were printed, Liu Bei was considered the rightful heir to the Han, and the text of the plain tale focuses on the adventures that he and his sworn brothers Guan Yu and Zhang Fei encounter. A *chantefable*, the *Tale of Hua Guan Suo* most likely dates from the period 1250–1450. Discovered in the tomb of the wife of a lowly official, the text is a printed edition from the Chenghua period of the Ming dynasty, 1467–87. This ballad focuses on the heroic life and death of Hua Guan Suo, a son of Guan Yu.[9] Its presentation of the Three Kingdoms saga departs significantly from the account of the *Records in Plain Language* in many details. Both works have been preserved in extensively illustrated editions, with the upper one-third of each page reserved for continuous illustrations.

---

8. The *Records in Plain Language* was published by the Yu family of Jianyang along with at least four other works of the same nature (including titles devoted to the founding of the Zhou and Han dynasties). Together these works are known as the *Five Completely Illustrated Plain Tales (Quanxiang pinghua wuzhong)*. The set has repeatedly been reproduced in photographic reprints. See for instance *Quanxiang pinghua wuzhong* (1956), and *Quanxiang pinghua Wuwang fa Zhou shu* (1971). For a modern typeset edition of the *Records in Plain Language*, see *Sanguo zhi pinghua* (1959); a critical and annotated edition is provided in Zhong 1989. On *pinghua* as a literary genre, see Idema 1974, Breuer 2001, and Lu 2009.

9. For photographic reproductions of the original printing, see *Ming Chenghua shuochang cihua congkan* (1973; reprinted 1979). A modern typeset edition is provided in Zhu 1997. Also see Inoue 1989. A full English language translation is provided in King 1989.

The *Records in Plain Language* is divided into three *juan*, or "scrolls." The first of these focuses on the adventures of the three sworn brothers Liu Bei, Guan Yu, and Zhang Fei in Northern China where they first establish their merit for the house of Han by fighting the Yellow Turbans; later they contribute to the downfall and death of both the incredibly fat usurper Dong Zhuo (who had moved the imperial court from Luoyang to Chang'an) and his adopted son, the dashing young warrior Lü Bu. During this period, when they still are small players in the political arena, they come to enjoy the support of Cao Cao (who moved the imperial court back east to Xuchang). But by the beginning of the second scroll, they join up with the last Han Emperor to fight Cao Cao. This results in their defeat, dispersal, and quick move to Hubei. Once the three sworn brothers are reunited in Old City, they move on to Xinye, where Liu Bei serves as prefect. Liu Bei now manages to attract Zhuge Liang (also known as Zhuge Kongming, 181–234), a brilliant tactician, as his main adviser and Field Marshal. Liu Bei concludes an alliance with Sun Quan, who controls the Jiang-nan area (south of the eastern stretch of the Yangzi), and they successfully ward off the attempts of Cao Cao to extend his control into the south. This is all due to the superior tactics of Zhuge Liang and Sun Quan's adviser, the young and talented Zhou Yu, who soon dies of jealousy when he realizes that he will never be able to match the brilliance of Zhuge Liang. The third scroll focuses on Zhuge Liang's attempts, following the deaths of Liu Bei, Guan Yu, and Zhang Fei, to maintain the Shu-Han dynasty in modern-day Sichuan, and provides detailed accounts of Zhuge Liang's campaigns, first against the southwestern barbarians led by their king Meng Huo, and then against the Wei dynasty in modern-day Shaanxi. In this last scroll, the center of activity is Sichuan. Appendix 1 in this volume provides a detailed summary as well as translations of selected passages of the *Records in Plain Language*.

The *Records in Plain Language* lays great stress on Liu Bei's descent from the imperial house of the Han, even though at the beginning of the story he is in reduced circumstances, making a living by plaiting straw sandals. Liu Bei is a fine fighter himself, but the anonymous author of the *Records in Plain Language* prefers to stress Liu's qualities as an administrator: each time Liu serves in an administrative position, the population is said to benefit greatly from his rule. His sworn brothers Guan Yu and Zhang Fei are primarily characterized as formidable warriors. Both men have impressive physiques—one is tall and the other stout—but whereas Guan Yu is the very embodiment of virtue, Zhang Fei is an impetuous drunk who brooks no authority. If Guan Yu has a fault, it is his overweening self-confidence and irascibility, whereas Zhang Fei wins our sympathy by his love of an honest fight and his horror at the tactics of mass destruction that Zhuge Liang and Zhou Yu employ, such as the use of fire and water.[10] In the *Records in Plain Language*, Zhuge Liang is very much portrayed as a Daoist wizard who combines his superior tactical and strategic insights with a variety of magical skills.[11] The humility with which Liu Bei seeks Zhuge Liang's assistance is offensive to Zhang Fei, whose resistance to the newcomer, however, is skillfully broken by Zhuge Liang.

Cao Cao, who quickly rose to become the most powerful warlord on the North China plain and who also controlled the late Han imperial court, is distinguished by his ruthless quest for power, even though at times he displays an unexpected magnanimity.[12] All of the generals who serve under him pale in comparison to his bravery and cunning. Each of these personalities, in turn, looks down equally upon Sun Quan because of his lowly background. The successive members of the Sun family are all based in Jinling (modern Nanjing) and from there securely dominate the Jiangnan region (in the third century still a relatively underdeveloped part of the country).

Events in these narratives are closely linked in terms of action to the same incidents in contemporary and later theatrical versions of the cycle. However, due to the use of fixed role types in drama, one must be careful when comparing characterization across genres. For instance, Cao Cao's very able general Xiahou Dun is turned into a fool on stage, not because he was a fool, but because he happens to be cast in the role type of the clown (*jing*), who plays only evil or foolish characters.[13]

Episodes from the saga of the Three Kingdoms were popular on stage from an early date. A list of farces (*yuanben*)[14] from the Jin dynasty (1115–1234) lists such titles as *Liu Bei in Full* (*Da Liu Bei*), *Skewering Dong Zhuo* (*Ci Dong Zhuo*),

---

10. The character of Zhang Fei in early drama has been studied in Besio 1997. Most studies on Guan Yu have focused on his divine career. From the late sixth century, Guan Yu was revered as a deity, and eventually he would become one of the most powerful divinities of both the official and popular pantheon in late imperial China. Guan Yu is still widely revered throughout the Chinese world. See Diesinger 1984 and Duara 1988. The extensive studies by the Russian sinologist Boris Riftin on the later traditions concerning Guan Yu (and the Three Kingdoms in general) are available in Chinese translation. See Li 1997a and 1997b. For Chinese studies of the development of the legend of Guan Yu, see, for instance, Zeng 2003, pp. 509–28; Liu 2004; and Wang 2007, pp. 207–364.

11. For a study on the earliest reputation of Zhuge Liang, see Henry 1992; for studies on later changes in the evaluation of Zhuge Liang, see Tillman 1996, 2002, and 2007.

12. The evolving characterization of Cao Cao has been studied in Kroll 1976. For an evaluation of the historical Cao Cao, see De Crespigny 1990a and 2010. The historical Cao Cao was, like his sons Cao Pi and Cao Zhi, a major poet. See Diény 2000.

13. See West and Idema 2010, pp. xvii–xviii, for a discussion of role types.

14. While the majority of the titles listed as *yuanben* indeed must have been short farcical plays, the genre also included a sizable number of longer melodramatic plays.

Cursing Lü Bu (*Ma Lü Bu*), *Meeting at Xiangyang* (*Xiangyang hui*), and *Carnage at Red Cliff* (*Chibi aozhan*).[15] The continued onstage popularity of the Three Kingdoms saga during the Yuan and early Ming dynasties (1250–1450) is attested by the fact that three of the thirty *zaju* preserved in print editions from that period, part of the later collection *Yuan Zaju in Thirty Editions* or *Thirty Yuan Plays* edition (*Yuankan zaju sanshizhong*), deal with episodes from the Three Kingdoms. Two of these plays—*The Great King Guan and the Single Sword Meeting* (*Guan dawang dandao hui*) and *In a Dream Guan and Zhang, A Pair, Rush to Western Shu* (*Guan Zhang shuang fu Xi Shu meng*)—are attributed to Guan Hanqing (late thirteenth century) in our earliest catalogues; the third of the *Thirty Yuan Plays*, *Zhuge Liang Burns the Stores at Bowang* (*Zhuge Liang Bowang shaotun*), is an anonymous work that may date from a considerably later period. *Burning the Stores* dramatizes Zhuge Liang's first victory in the service of Liu Bei and tells how Zhuge Liang establishes his authority over Liu Bei's sworn brother Zhang Fei.[16] *Single Sword Meeting*, which features Liu Bei's other sworn brother, Guan Yu, during his final feat of arms, and *Dream of Western Shu*, which features the ghost of Zhang Fei newly murdered by his own subordinates, show remarkable structural similarity and may well originally have been written as a pair.

We provide complete translations of these three plays. In the case of *Burning the Stores* we also include a translation of the final act of a late Ming manuscript version of the play from the Maiwang Studio collection to illustrate some of the changes these plays underwent when they were incorporated into the palace repertoire of the Ming dynasty. This manuscript probably is a script of the play as it was performed in the sixteenth century at the imperial court and helps the reader of the truncated *Thirty Yuan Plays* edition envision how the complicated stage action of the final act may have been performed. For the *Single Sword Meeting*, which has enjoyed continuous stage popularity in various versions down to modern times, we have provided a complete translation of an early Ming manuscript from the Court Entertainment Bureau (perhaps in Nanjing before the Ming capital was moved to Beijing). It is also from the Maiwang Studio collection. *Dream of Western Shu* is not known from any later edition, probably because the play hinges on the appearance of Zhang Fei's apparition to Liu Bei, who by this time had assumed the title of emperor, and laws prohibited the portrayal of emperors on stage during the Ming—a prohibition that seems to have been strictly followed at the imperial palace. Another reason may have been that the plot is different not only from historical sources, but also

---

15. Guan 2009, pp. 146–47.
16. Besio 2007.

from the way the deaths of Guan Yu and Zhang Fei are recorded in both the *Records in Plain Language* and the novel. We provide translations of the parallel passages for these three plays from the *Records in Plain Language* (in the case of the *Single Sword Meeting* and *Burning the Stores*) and the *Tale of Hua Guan Suo* (in the case of *Dream of Western Shu*). These supplemental texts should not necessarily be considered as direct sources of the plays, but they provide narrative accounts from roughly the same period that may help to facilitate an understanding of the action of the plays and highlight the originality of the dramatic adaptations of the same episodes. They also serve to show that the totality of the story-cycle is not captured by any one work, or for that matter by any one genre. In all three plays, the characters often refer to earlier incidents in their careers. Rather than summarizing these incidents in our own words, we have preferred to provide our readers with translations of the relevant episodes in the *Records in Plain Language*.

Another early *zaju* about Guan Yu that has been preserved in a contemporary edition is *Guan Yunchang's Righteous and Brave Refusal of Gold* (*Guan Yunchang yiyong cijin*) of 1416 by the playwright and royal prince Zhu Youdun (1379–1439).[17] This play shows Guan Yu in the service of Cao Cao when the fortunes of war separated him (and Liu Bei's wives, who were under his care) temporarily from his sworn brothers. Guan Yu wants to repay Cao Cao for an earlier favor, and in Cao Cao's campaign against his last rival for power in North China, Yuan Shao (d. 202), Guan Yu single-handedly kills Yuan Shao's general, Yan Liang, who earlier had defeated Cao Cao's subordinate general, Xiahou Dun. Once Guan Yu learns the whereabouts of Liu Bei, however, he leaves Cao Cao, despite all the presents and honors the latter offers him in order to entice him to stay. In this play, Guan Yu displays not only his famous martial valor, but also his undivided loyalty to Liu Bei and his scrupulous virtue—in refusing the lavish presents of Cao Cao, and in taking care of his sworn brother's wives without trying to take advantage of the situation. The play also shows a new concern for historical truth as Zhu Youdun tries to square the account provided by the evolving legend with the account provided by canonical historiography. In the years that followed Zhu's death, however, this concern was not shared by other *zaju* composers, even if they were active at the imperial court.

Plays in Palace Manuscripts and in Late Ming Printed Editions

A few other Three Kingdoms plays from the period 1250–1450 by known authors have been preserved, but only in versions from the late Ming dynasty, and

---

17. On Zhu Youdun as a playwright, see Idema 1985.

all show signs of heavy editing. We include a translation of *Liu Xuande Goes Alone to the Xiangyang Meeting* (*Liu Xuande du fu Xiangyang hui*). This play, preserved in the Maiwang Studio collection, dramatizes Liu Bei's first meeting with Liu Biao in Jingzhou and Liu Bei's flight across Sandalwood Creek, followed by an account of the activities of Xu Shu, Liu Bei's Field Marshal before Liu had attracted Zhuge Liang to his cause. The modern scholar Yan Dunyi suggested that this play, which lacks a strong unifying plot, may have been composed by actors at the Ming court out of elements of earlier plays, including an earlier play with a very similar title by Gao Wenxiu, a playwright who was a contemporary of Guan Hanqing.[18] Gao Wenxiu also authored a second play on the Three Kingdoms, *Zhou Yu Visits Lu Su*, of which only fragments have been preserved. Two Yuan dramatists, Zheng Dehui and Zhu Kai, are credited with the authorship of *Yellow Crane Tower* (*Huanghe lou*), which deals with Zhou Yu's failed attempt to kill Liu Bei at a banquet at the famous landmark of the title. Whereas the extant play may be traceable back to a work originally written by Zheng Dehui, Zhu Kai's work of the same title is extant only in fragments. Multiple dramatizations of the same story are quite common in *zaju*, which can have as many as three plays by different authors bearing the same title. For example, the same Maiwang Studio collection of manuscripts that included versions of *Burning the Stores, Single Sword Meeting, Xiangyang Meeting*, and *Yellow Crane Tower* also includes *Thrice Battling Lü Bu at Tiger-keep Pass* (*Hulaoguan sanzhan Lü Bu*), which is ascribed to Zheng Dehui by the collator Zhao Qimei, but it should be noted that Zheng Dehui's contemporary, Wu Hanchen, was also credited with a play featuring the same title, of which only fragments survive. The attributions to particular authors are often an arbitrary conjecture on the part of later compilers and collators. These multiple titles may lead to confusion in terms of identifying authorship, but they also demonstrate just how popular these episodes from the Three Kingdoms cycle were.

The Maiwang Studio collection contains a total of seventeen plays that take their subject matter from the Three Kingdoms saga. The majority of these plays, however, are anonymous works that are classified by modern Chinese bibliographers as works of the "Yuan or Ming dynasties."[19] But, in their current incarnations, they are best considered scripts of the sixteenth-century Ming palace repertoire. In all likelihood, most of these plays were written at the palace over the course of the fifteenth and sixteenth centuries. Taken together, they provide

---

18. Yan 1960, pp. 78–85.

19. This convention started with Wang Jilie (1873–1952), who provided modern typeset editions of a selection of plays from the Maiwang Studio collection as *Guben Yuan Ming zaju* (1942; reprinted 1958).

a remarkably full account of the cycle from the brotherhood oath of Liu Bei, Guan Yu, and Zhang Fei down to the battle of Red Cliff and its immediate aftermath. There are a relatively large number of plays that deal with the early careers of Liu Bei, Guan Yu, and Zhang Fei, and many of them assign their main role to Zhang Fei. No doubt the martial antics of this "heavy" made for great entertainment. As an example of these plays, we provide a translation of *Liu, Guan, and Zhang: The Tripartite Oath of Brotherhood in the Peach Orchard* (*Liu Guan Zhang Taoyuan san jieyi*).

What is remarkable too is the relatively small number of plays dealing with episodes from the decades of the Shu-Han dynasty in Sichuan—just two plays dramatize further victories of Zhuge Liang over Cao Cao. There are two possible reasons for this. One is that Liu Bei had at that time assumed the imperial title, which made it impossible to portray him on stage. Perhaps the Ming court also was not amused by plays featuring his successor—a silly child-emperor— and an overbearing Field Marshal. A second is that the earlier plays focus on the personal bonds of loyalty (primarily between the three brothers, but also between the three and Zhuge Liang and Xu Shu), on pivotal battle scenes such as Tigerkeep Pass, or on the schemes and machinations of people trying to kill one of the three brothers. Once the three sworn brothers have passed from the scene, the possibility of exploring the conflict between the particularistic ethics of personal loyalty and friendship and the allegiance to a universal ethical order that is the basis of political rule also dies away.

None of the manuscripts of the Three Kingdoms plays in the Maiwang Studio collection went into print in the final decades of the Ming, when publishers were scrambling to find plays to print. The only Three Kingdoms plays to be included by Zang Maoxun in the prestigious *Selection of Yuan Plays* (*Yuanqu xuan*) of 1615 and 1616, which includes one hundred *zaju*, are the anonymous *Plan of Interlocking Rings* (*Jinyun tang anding Lianhuan ji*), which dramatizes the old and wily minister Wang Yun's successful scheme to create dissension between the military dictator Dong Zhuo and his finest general Lü Bu by means of the beautiful Diaochan, and the equally anonymous *Duel of Wits across the River* (*Ge Jiang douzhi*), which dramatizes one of the failed attempts of Zhou Yu on the life of Liu Bei, by having the latter marry Sun Quan's younger sister. These plays well may have merited their inclusion in *A Selection of Yuan Plays* because of their romantic interest. *A Duel of Wits across the River* is also one of the rare Three Kingdoms plays in which the arias are assigned to a female lead.[20] We include in Appendix 3 a translation of Zang Maoxun's edi-

---

20. Liu Bei's first wife, Lady Gan, has the singing role in *Guan Yu Travels a Thousand Miles Alone* (*Guan Yunchang qianli duxing*), and other anonymous plays preserved in manuscript in the

tion of *The Plan of Interlocking Rings*. This play had also been printed in the earlier *Anthology of Northern Dramas New and Ancient* (*Gujin zaju xuan*), which would appear to represent a printing that captured an earlier phase in the development of the text. In the copy of this latter printed edition as preserved in the Maiwang Studio collection, the main text of the play is followed by a handwritten list of the costumes for each actor per act, which clearly shows that this play too was once part of the Ming imperial palace repertoire.[21]

Some modern scholars set the total number of Three Kingdoms plays from the Yuan and early Ming at twenty, whereas others come up with the number of forty. By including every preserved or lost play, the action of which is set in the period of 180 to 280 AD, others reach the number of sixty.[22] Apart from the many anonymous lost plays in these lists, we also encounter the names of playwrights as diverse as Wang Zhongwen, Wang Shifu, Li Shouqing, Li Qujin, Yu Boyuan, Shi Junbao, Zhao Shanfu, Jin Renjie, Wang Ye, and Hua Li Lang ("Tattooed Young Li") as authors of lost plays. In early bibliographies, Wang Zhongwen, Wang Shifu, and the actor-playwright Hua Li Lang are each listed as having two plays on the Three Kingdoms. The two lost plays ascribed to Hua Li Lang may well have been composed as a pair, as they would appear to have dealt with two closely related episodes. His *Lord Cao Interrogates Ji Ping at the Chancellor's Office* (*Xiangfuyuan Cao gong kan Ji Ping*), of which two songs survive, dramatizes Ji Ping's attempt to poison Cao Cao as part of a secret plot ordered by Emperor Xian and engineered by Dong Cheng, and in which Liu Bei also participates. Ji Ping dies without naming any of his co-conspirators. The second lost play ascribed to Hua Li Lang is entitled *Rude and Rash Zhang Fei Creates a Disturbance at the Chancellor's Office* (*Mang Zhang Fei danao xiangfuyuan*). This play most likely dramatizes the events at the "Meeting for the Evaluation of Heroes," which takes place a few days following the interrogation of Ji Ping and at which Cao Cao announces to Liu Bei that he considers him his only true opponent, scaring Liu Bei so much he drops his spoon and chopsticks while eating. Whereas Zhang Fei is not mentioned in this connection in either the *Records of the Three Kingdoms* or the *Records in Plain Language*, it would not be difficult to imagine a play in which, at this moment in the action, Zhang Fei would burst onto the scene to protect Liu Bei against Cao Cao. Actually, a play about the meeting along these lines, *Rude and Rash Zhang Fei Creates a*

Maiwang Studio collection. See Ross 1977 for an English translation of Acts 3 and 4 of that play. A full translation of the play is found in the University of Texas dissertation Ross 1976.

21. For the development of this episode, see Wang 2007, pp. 63–206. Also see Hu 1993. On the relationship of clothing to narrative, see Besio 2007, pp. 77–78.

22. Guan 2009, pp. 148–51.

Disturbance at the Pomegranate Garden (*Mang Zhang Fei danao Shiliu yuan*), is one of the anonymous works preserved in the Maiwang Studio collection.

Zaju emerged in Northern China and remained, despite some inroads into the big cities of the south during the first half of the fourteenth century, very much a Northern genre throughout the period 1250–1450. But the saga of the Three Kingdoms also was popular with the playwrights of the south who wrote "play texts" (*xiwen*), a term used for a Southern form of drama. Unfortunately, all of these plays have been lost except for minor fragments. *Xiwen* granted all actors a singing role and often focused on romantic interests, so we should perhaps not be surprised to encounter a somewhat different emphasis in the preserved titles, which include *Diaochan* (*Diaochannü*), *Zhou Yu Flirts with the Younger Qiao Sister on a Moonlit Night* (*Zhou Xiaolang yueye xi Xiao Qiao*), and *Bronze Sparrow Courtesans* (*Tongque ji*). These titles all would appear to focus on those rare episodes in the story-cycle in which women play a significant role. One of the few titles that does not show this tendency is *Former Lord Liu Jumps across Sandalwood Creek* (*Liu Xianzhu tiao Tanxi*), which must have dramatized an episode that also is treated in Act 2 of *Xiangyang Meeting*. By the sixteenth century, *xiwen* had evolved into *chuanqi*, plays of forty to sixty scenes that might take two days to perform. As a result, each *chuanqi* could cover a much larger segment of the tale of the Three Kingdoms than one *zaju*, but we still have the titles of twenty-three Ming dynasty *chuanqi* for episodes from the tale. Many of these plays are anonymous, which makes it difficult to suggest a date. Of these twenty-three plays, only six have survived. Moreover, once the *Romance of the Three Kingdoms* had been printed, most playwrights relied on it for source materials, and the earlier tradition represented in Northern *zaju* and the *Records in Plain Language* fell away.

Conventions, Editions, and Translations

All plays included in this selection are *zaju*. This genre of musical theater emerged in the large cities of Northern China in the second half of the thirteenth century. According to one tradition, *zaju* drama was created by Guan Hanqing. *Zaju* rely on a limited number of role types, the most important of which are the "male" (*mo*), "female" (*dan*), and "clown" (*jing*). In contrast to *xiwen* and all other later forms of traditional Chinese theater in which all actors (and actresses) are expected to sing, all songs in each *zaju* are assigned to a single actor, either the "leading male" (*zhengmo*) or the "leading female" (*zhengdan*). Perhaps not surprisingly in view of the subject matter, all plays translated in this volume are *moben*, that is, plays in which the arias are assigned to the "leading male."[23] The backbone of a *zaju* consists of four suite-length sets of songs. These four sets, each in a different musical mode, usually consist of eight to twelve songs. A "wedge" (*xiezi*) consisting of one or two songs may also precede any of the sets of songs, although most often this demi-suite comes before Act 1, 2, or 3. As some of the plays in this collection demonstrate, the leading male does not have to play the same part throughout the play but can switch from role to role with each set of songs. On the basis of the sets and wedges, later editors formally divided the plays into four acts and one or more wedges. Also, the final act might be followed by another small group of songs, which with the surrounding dialogue and stage action would make for a final demi-act. Like other forms of traditional Chinese musical drama, *zaju* is technically a form of ballad-opera, as the playwrights use preexisting melodies for their arias. All *zaju* make use of the same repertoire of roughly four hundred songs.[24] While costuming might be lavish, the stage often was almost bare, and the stage action quite likely highly conventionalized. For a detailed look at how these conventions are represented in our translation, please see Conventions below.

  Zaju flourished for two centuries in Northern China (and those southern cities with a large population of northerners) from 1250 to 1450, and was adopted by the Ming dynasty upon its foundation as its court drama. At court, *zaju* continued to be performed well into the sixteenth century.[25] We do not know whether the first generations of *zaju* playwrights wrote out the complete text of plays, or whether they limited themselves to composing the arias and cue lines of the male lead or female lead. The thirty *zaju* that survive in fourteenth-century editions provide the readers with only the arias, or the arias and the cue lines of the lead. The first playwright to have his plays printed with full dialogues and stage directions was the Ming prince Zhu Youdun. At the Ming court, full texts (including every repetition and every lame joke) were de rigueur as the script of a play had to pass the scrutiny of court censors before it could be performed in front of the emperor. When, from the sixteenth century onward, *zaju* were increasingly collected and read as literature, they also were increasingly printed once again. These printed editions often appear to have been based on the palace manuscripts of the plays. One of the largest collections ever of manuscript *zaju* and printed plays was put together by the late Ming bibliophile Zhao Qimei (1553–1624) in his studio the *Maiwang guan*.

---

23. For a concise introduction to the genre characteristics of *zaju*, see West and Idema 2010, pp. xii–xix.

24. For a detailed study of the musical organization of *zaju*, and the characteristics of each of the roughly four hundred songs in the repertoire, see the study by Dale Johnson 1980.

25. For a large collection of contemporary descriptions of stages, actors, and performances, see Idema and West 1982.

The most influential of the printed anthologies of the late Ming was the lavish *Selection of Yuan Plays*, an anthology of one hundred *zaju*, edited and published by Zang Maoxun in 1615 and 1616. Zang believed himself to be the ultimate connoisseur of *zaju* and heavily edited the plays he printed in order to make them more acceptable in form and content to the upper-class reading public, which he targeted with his editions.[26]

With the exception of the manuscript version of *Single Sword Meeting* from the Maiwang Studio collection[27] and the *Selection of Yuan Plays* version of *Interlocking Rings*,[28] none of these plays has been published in an English translation before. In the hands of their translators, the two that were rendered into English have suffered excision of key scenes and the collapsing of several arias into three or four lines, and have been shorn of any scene that refers to famous incidents that would have demanded long explanatory notes. They are thus paraphrases, not translations—simple literary summaries of complex episodes, the language of which, filled in the original with comic irony and startling metaphors of violence and desire, is uniformly dampened.

In this volume we have arranged the plays we have translated according to the chronological sequence of the tale of the Three Kingdoms. By chance, this has resulted in an arrangement in which the examples of the latest editions come first and the examples of the earliest printings come last. It also has the unwelcome result that arguably some of the finest plays in this collection, Guan Hanqing's *Single Sword Meeting* and *Dream of Western Shu*, appear at the end.

---

26. See West and Idema 2010, pp. xxvii–xxxi. Also see Idema 1996 and West 2003.

27. In Yang and Yang 1979, pp. 160–85.

28. In Liu 1972, pp. 225–79. This play was also rendered into German in Forke 1978, pp. 109–85.

Table of Dynasties

SHANG c. 1460–1045 BC

ZHOU 1045–256 BC
  Western Zhou 1045–771 BC   Eastern Zhou 770–256 BC
  Spring and Autumn 722–421 BC   Warring States 480–221 BC

QIN 221–207 BC

HAN 202 BC–AD 220
  Western Han 202 BC–AD 9   Eastern Han 25–220

THREE KINGDOMS
  Wei 220–65   Wu 220–80   Shu-Han 221–63

WESTERN JIN 266–316

EASTERN JIN 317–420

NORTHERN AND SOUTHERN DYNASTIES 386–589
  Northern 386–581
  Northern Wei 386–534   Eastern Wei 534–50   Northern Qi 550–77
  Western Wei 535–57   Northern Zhou 557–81
  Southern 420–589
  Song 420–79   Qi 479–502   Liang 502–57   Chen 557–89

SUI 581–618

TANG 618–907

FIVE DYNASTIES 907–60
  Later Liang 907–23   Later Tang 923–36   Later Jin 936–47
  Later Han 947–50   Later Zhou 951–60

SONG 960–1279
  Northern Song 960–1127   Southern Song 1127–1279

LIAO 916–1125

JIN 1115–1234

YUAN 1260–1368

MING 1368–1644

QING 1644–1911

Conventions

As the Introduction indicates, there is a great disparity among the physical formats of the actual texts of the dramas that we have used. Consequently, there will be some inconsistencies in their presentation in translation. A typical *zaju* drama, stripped to its skeletal form, has a title, a wedge (optional), and four acts, and concludes with a "title" and a "name." Each act consists of a suite of songs in a single mode arranged in order, written to the same rhyme, sometimes concluded by a coda (*wei*, or *sha*). For instance, in the Xijizi edition of *In the Hall of Brocade Clouds: The Beauty and the Story of the Interlocking Rings*, the structure looks thus:

In the Hall of Brocade Clouds:
The Beauty and the Story of the Interlocking Rings

Act 1: XIANLÜ MODE:
- (*Dian jiangchun*)
- (*Hunjiang long*)
- (*You hulu*)
- (*Tianxia le*)
- (*Houting hua*)
- (*Nezha ling*)
- (*Que ta zhi*)
- (*Jisheng cao*)
- (*Jinzhan'er*)
- (*Coda*)

Act 2: NANLU MODE:
- (*Yizhi hua*)
- (*Liangzhou*)
- (*Gewei*)
- (*Sikuai yu*)
- (*Ma yulang*)
- (*Gan huang'en*)
- (*Caihua ge*)
- (*Xu hama*)
- (*Muyang guan*)
- (*Gewei*)
- (*Ku huangtian*)
- (*Wu ye ti*)
- (*Huangzhong Coda*)

ACT 3: ZHENGGONG MODE:

   (*Duanzheng hao*)
   (*Gun xiuqiu*)
   (*Ban dushu*)
   (*Xiao heshang*)
   (*Gun xiuqiu*)
   (*Daodao ling*)
   (*Kuaihuo san*)
   (*Baolao'er*)
   (*Shua hai'er*)
   (*Second from Coda*)
   (*Coda*)

ACT 4: SHUANGDIAO MODE:

   (*Xinshui ling*)
   (*Zhuma ting*)
   (*Bubu jiao*)
   (*Hushiba*)
   (*Yan'er luo*)
   (*Gua yugou*)

TITLE: At the Gate of the Silver Dais, Lü Bu stabs Dong Zhuo.

NAME: In the Hall of Brocade Clouds: the beauty and the story of the inter-locking rings.

We identify cases where the original edition signals the end of a scene by leaving the remainder of the line blank and skipping to the top of the next line to begin the new scene with the following symbol:

❇❇

We use brackets for several purposes: (1) to add information that the Chinese infers but does not state, (2) to indicate a missing subject, or (3) to indicate a a missing object:

[ZHANG FEI] *speaks:*
WANG YUN *speaks* [to DIAOCHAN]
No one can say [about him] . . .

A play is composed of three basic kinds of text: stage directions, plain speech, and lyric songs or arias (translated as blank verse). In our edition, role types appear in small capital letters, stage directions are in italics, arias are inset three spaces, and padding words are inset six spaces in reduced type. Poems are centered. Rhymed text from other forms of performance (for instance, Guan Ping's recited lines in the Ming palace edition of *The Great King Guan and the Single Sword Meeting*) is inset two spaces and left-aligned. Tune titles are in italics, and the mode to which the suite is written is in small capitals, as in the following passage from *Interlocking Rings*:

LI SU *enters, leading* SOLDIERS, *and speaks:*   ← ROLE TYPES and *stage directions*

The top of Mount Tai has been ground down by blades
    I have sharpened;
The waves of the Northern Sea have been drunk dry by
    my warhorses;
If a man of thirty has yet to establish his name,
Then it's for naught that he is a strapping great man.

Recited doggerel, entrance and exit rhymed verse

I am Li Su. Wang Yun gave Diaochan to my father as a wife. Who would have expected that that little beast Lü Bu would have such bad intentions, and take advantage of my father? He doesn't have any sense of hierarchy—his behavior is unacceptable by any accounts! He knocked father down on the ground. Father sent me out with a cavalry troop of one hundred thousand, had me put on my battle robes and wriggle into my armor, stick arrows in my quiver, and bend my bow to go out and capture Lü Bu so that this hatred can be cleansed away. I'll have to catch up to him.

Spoken text: dialogue, monologue.

Exits.

MALE LEAD *enters and speaks:* I am Wang Yun, and I set up this plan with Diaochan, but I still don't know how it is going. *Sings:*

    (SHUANGDIAO MODE: *Xinshui ling*)   ← MODE and *tune title*
        In vain I
    May have used my heart's clever designs in   ← Lyrics
        double-trap plans,
        But it all was because
    I have labored so hard all my life for the rivers
        and mountains of Han.
        Unhappily tonight   ← Padding words
    The jade lotus leisurely drips
    And the hoary moon is slow to rise on the
        window's silken screen.
    I pace back and forth;
    Whatever comes to pass will be because of her
        ability.

MALE LEAD *speaks:* It's almost midnight. Why is there no news? [*Sings:*]

    (*Zhuma ting*)
        Grand Preceptor Dong
    Was set for a tryst of swallows and orioles.

There are some additions and exceptions to these rules. The *Thirty Yuan Plays* editions and some of the print and manuscript editions do not separate stage directions with parentheses. Sometimes the text is inconsistent in the use of parentheses. In the *Thirty Yuan Plays* edition and some of the early Ming manuscript, stage directions are set apart by large spaces. In this volume, we use long dashes to separate these stage directions, as in the opening to *Single Sword Meeting*:

> EMPEROR *and entourage enter, open, stop.* — EXTRA MALE *enters, makes a formal request, stops.* — EMPEROR *speaks.* — EXTRA MALE *speaks, stops.* — MALE LEAD, *costumed as* QIAO GUOLAO, *enters, opens, stops.* — EXTRA MALE *speaks. Speak as if pondering a question:* The tripartite partition is already set now; I fear pulling out shield and spear will cause the people's lives more bitterness. You group of ministers should remonstrate with the Son of Heaven.

In the *Selection of Yuan Plays* edition of *The Plan of Interlocking Rings*, Zang Maoxun has added the phrase "continues in speech" (*daiyun*) to indicate the continuation of a thought in stylized speech:

> (*Sings:*)
> Who would have ever thought that right here, in my house,
> I would come up with this beautiful charmer?
> And on the day when we set the feast,
> In that bevy of rouge and powder a battle campaign will be secretly
>   hidden away.
> How could he ever escape
> This crafty plan?
>> (*Continues in speech:*) Diaochan,
> I will have husband and wife be whole and complete,
> Forever reunited.

We have annotated the text primarily with students in mind. By the time these texts were created, many of the gems of Chinese poetry had entered the colloquial lexicon and had become standard, even cliché, parts of ordinary speech. Unless a poem has special significance in the text, we have merely identified these passages by putting them in quotation marks. They function as a form of speech the Chinese call "set phrases" (*chengyu*) or "colloquial sayings" (*suyu*), which are handy aphorisms that are spoken to capture the moment linguistically as a precise category of behavior or feeling. These colloquial and set phrases are also enclosed in quotation marks. These are most often folk sayings, as in "Our mistake of a single day turns into a mistake for an entire generation," "Men bring disaster upon themselves," or "A single branch completely leaked all of the news of spring."

I

Liu, Guan, and Zhang:
The Tripartite Oath of Brotherhood
in the Peach Orchard

Anonymous

Few episodes in the tales of the Three Kingdoms are more iconic than that of Liu Bei, Guan Yu, and Zhang Fei swearing brotherhood in the Peach Orchard. Starting from that moment, the story-cycle primarily follows the adventures of the three sworn brothers as they try to make a name for themselves and achieve a position, are separated and united, fight their way all over China, and end up as the rulers of Shu-Han in modern Sichuan. The essential tale of the Three Kingdoms begins with the oath in the Peach Orchard and ends when Liu Bei, against the advice of Zhuge Liang, goes to war against the kingdom of Wu in order to avenge the death of his sworn brother Guan Yu. That campaign will end in disaster and Liu Bei will die. Since Zhang Fei is already dead by that time, the many decades that are still to follow in the tale are simply an epilogue as Zhuge Liang continues to campaign against the Cao family and their generals.

The oath in the Peach Orchard brings together three unlikely friends. In the *Records of the Three Kingdoms in Plain Language*, Guan Yu is a fugitive from the law, Zhang Fei a rich local landlord, and Liu Bei a student who, despite his noble background, is so impoverished that he has to make a living by weaving mats and plaiting sandals in order to support his mother. In the play we have translated here, Zhang Fei has metamorphosed from a landlord into a butcher. In premodern China the trade of a butcher was a necessary but lowly job, and butchers were often considered the dregs of society. The three friends are united by their love of the martial arts, their concern for the state of the country, and their urgent desire to make a career. Although this play, the *Records in Plain Language*, and the *Romance of the Three Kingdoms* locate the oath of brotherhood at the Peach Orchard, there existed another early tradition, preserved in the *Tale of Hua Guan Suo*, that places the oath at the temple of Jiang Ziya, the god of war. Similarly, the brothers sacrifice a white horse and a black ox, and "they only seek to die on the same day; they do not wish to be born on the same day." But the unconditional nature of their bond is stressed when Liu Bei points out that he is the only one who is single and voices the distrust that his two sworn brothers may regret their oath because of their wives and children.

To solve that issue, Zhang Fei kills Guan Yu's family, and Guan Yu massacres Zhang Fei's, as shown in the following excerpt (not elsewhere in this volume):

From *The Tale of Hua Guan Suo*

Guan, Zhang, and Liu Bei became sworn brothers. In the temple of Jiang Ziya they made an oath with Heaven as their witness. They slaughtered a white horse in sacrifice to Heaven and killed a black ox in sacrifice to Earth. They only seek to die on the same day; they do not wish to be born on the same day. If the elder brother would be in trouble, the younger brothers would rescue him, and if a younger brother was involved in a fight, the elder brother would side with him. If they did not act according to this vow, Heaven would not cover them and Earth would not carry them; they would be banished to the backside of the mountain of shade,[1] never to be reborn in a human body! Liu Bei said, "I am single, but you two have parents and children who weigh on your mind, so I am afraid that you may have regrets." Lord Guan said, "I will kill my parents and children and then follow you." Zhang Fei said, "How could you do such a thing, killing your own parents and children? You, elder brother, will kill my parents and children, and I will kill yours." And Liu Bei said, "Right!"[2]

Zhang Fei promptly sets out for Xieliang, where he kills eighteen members of Guan Yu's household but saves the lives of Guan Yu's wife and their young son Guan Ping.

Liu, Guan, and Zhang: The Tripartite Oath of Brotherhood in the Peach Orchard (*Liu Guan Zhang Taoyuan san jieyi*) is one of several anonymous Three Kingdoms plays preserved in the Maiwang Studio collection. Although modern scholars often classify it as a work of "the Yuan or the Ming," we can conclude from the format of the manuscript and its language that it should be dated to the Ming dynasty. The play repeatedly refers to Ming emperors only in an oblique manner when the reigning emperor is described as the "sagely bright" (*shengming*) ruler. The work betrays its origin in the palace workshops when our heroes insist, "we must keep to our station as we bide our time" (*daishi shoufen*). That is, they should not take the initiative to collect a militia to fight the Yellow Turbans, as they do in the *Records in Plain Language*, but rather wait until they have been properly appointed as officials by the imperial court to take action. There was no possibility that the Ming emperors would sanction the raising of an army that would operate outside the umbra of the imperial aegis. As is the common practice in Ming palace plays, this *zaju* starts with long scenes all in prose, here devoted to Guan Yu's execution of a local official who

---

1. The deepest layer of the underworld.
2. Shanghai bowuguan and Shanghai wenwu baoguan weiyuanhui 1973, p. 2.

is contemplating rebellion, further underlining by contrast the proper behavior of our heroes. And whereas the *Records in Plain Language* includes in its description of Liu Bei the fact that Liu Bei as a child used to play at being the Son of Heaven, the play omits any mention of such a potentially scandalous detail.

Tripartite Oath is a regular *zaju* consisting of four acts. The four sets of songs are assigned to the male lead, who plays the part of Zhang Fei throughout. In view of the structural similarity between the account provided in the *Records in Plain Language* and the play, it seems quite likely that the play is based on that work. If that is so, our anonymous playwright(s) have gone to considerable effort to enliven the rather undramatic action of its source where, after the three friends are only too eager to swear brotherhood, there is no dramatic conflict to speak of once Guan Yu has murdered his local prefect at the beginning of the play. The playwright has stressed the superhuman strength of both Zhang Fei and Guan Yu by having them move a thousand-pound rock in Act 1, and in Act 4 Liu Bei, Guan Yu, and Zhang Fei each demonstrate mastery of a weapon of their choice. Both of these scenes will have contributed to the spectacle of the play.

Most of the liveliness of this *zaju*, however, is generated by the introduction of the character of the butcher, a younger colleague of Zhang Fei who tries to talk some sense into his buddy to no avail. The young butcher also tries, unsuccessfully, to be included in the sworn brotherhood, and he eventually makes a fool of himself when he tries to handle the weapons of our heroes. This character of the butcher, played by a clown, derives from China's rich tradition of farce. As is the case with Shakespeare's fools, much of the humor of the clown's speeches derives from punning and bawdy insinuations. One telltale sign of the connection of this role to the tradition of farce is the presence of "commentary from backstage" when the clown is speaking. Such "commentary from backstage" is otherwise only encountered in farces that are included as such in *zaju*.

In the later novel, *Romance of the Three Kingdoms*, the oath in the Peach Orchard is described in the very first chapter. There, the oath is a reaction of Liu Bei, Zhang Fei, and Guan Yu to the emperor's edict recruiting volunteers to fight the Yellow Turbans. The novelist highlights Liu Bei's primacy among the brothers by describing him first, and only then introducing Zhang Fei and Guan Yu. Zhang Fei is now described as both a rich local landowner and a butcher. Liu Bei, Guan Yu, and Zhang Fei are accompanied by three hundred troops, who, one trusts, will have been sufficient in number to consume the meat of the sacrificial animals. Whereas the buffalo is quite common as a sacrificial animal in the Chinese tradition, the horse is actually quite rare, even though we do have a reference to Liu Bang sacrificing a white horse when he swore that only members of the Liu family would be enfeoffed as princes under his dynasty. The Red Scarves, one of the anti-Mongol movements at the end of the Yuan dynasty, practiced horse and buffalo sacrifices, but they actually may have done so in imitation of the oath in the Peach Orchard.

Dramatis personæ in order of appearance

Role type	Name and family, institutional, or social role
Opening male, extra	Guan Yu, Yunchang
Clown, extra, official	Zang Yigui, a local prefect
Zhang Qian	Zhang Qian, prefectural clerk
Clown	Pi Han, a head clerk
Male lead	Zhang Fei, Yide
Clown	Butcher, a younger associate of Zhang Fei
Clown	Innkeeper and wine seller
Extra	Liu Bei, Xuande
Extra	Huangfu Song, a high government official
Soldiers	Soldiers

Liu, Guan, and Zhang:
The Tripartite Oath of Brotherhood in the Peach Orchard

Act 1

OPENING MALE, AN EXTRA, *enters, costumed as* GUAN YU,[3] *and speaks:*

> I once studied the *Three Strategies of the Yellow Lord,*[4]
> But for many years have been stuck here in this village.
> Constantly I practice my martial arts without interruption;
> I love to read *Zuo's Commentary to Springs and Autumns.*[5]

I am Guan Yu, also known as Yunchang. I hail from Xieliang in Puzhou. Since my youth I have been brave and fierce. I have the eyebrows of a divine being and eyes of a phoenix. My beard hangs down in three braids. I am nine feet, two inches tall. Throughout my life I have been straight and proper, stubborn and strong. I fully command both the civil and the military arts, and my favorite reading is *Zuo's Commentary to Springs and Autumns.* Whenever I read about rebellious vassals or evil sons, my heart is filled with a furious rage. I employ a Green Dragon crescent-moon blade. But alas, the right moment for me has yet to come, and I have not yet achieved merit and fame. At present, Emperor Ling of the Han has ascended the throne and stalwart warriors have arisen on all

---

3. The designation of role types and roles in this play departs in some respects from more common usage. The "opening male" (*chongmo*) refers to the actor who first appears on stage, but he is usually not identified as an "extra" (*wai*). This actor is said to be costumed as "the male role Guan," which we translate for convenience's sake as "Guan Yu." Likewise, the actor playing Liu Bei is said to be costumed as "the male role Liu."

4. The Yellow Lord (*Huanggong,* also known as *Huangshi gong*) was the mythical teacher of Zhang Liang, one of Liu Bang's main advisers. In later centuries the Yellow Lord was considered the author of a handbook on military tactics entitled *Three Strategies* (*Sanlüe*).

5. *Springs and Autumns* (*Chunqiu*) is a dry-as-dust chronicle of the main event affecting the state of Lu from the eighth to the sixth century BC. *Zuo's Commentary* (*Zuozhuan*) covers the wars and other events of those same centuries in great detail. It may have originated as an independent work, but is has been preserved as a commentary to the *Springs and Autumns.* This work, with its commentaries, was counted as one of the Five Classics, and from an early date its authorship was attributed to Confucius, who is supposed to have expressed his moral judgment of events and personalities by his subtle wording.

sides, creating chaos and confusion. That's why I live in hiding here in this village where I bide my time and keep to my station. Because the official and clerks of this prefecture covet money and love kickbacks, they grievously harm the common people, and I am constantly filled with frustration. Today I have nothing else to do, so let me go out for a walk on the main street for a leisurely stroll and to see if I can find any wise and good men.

> My ambition reaches to heaven; my courage is lofty;
> Loyal and righteous throughout my life—that's not just boasting!
> I hope to remove threats, pacify disturbances, and bring peace to the world;
> Sincere in my devotion to the state, I support the house of Han.

Exits.

CLOWN, *costumed as* EXTRA, OFFICIAL, *enters with* ZHANG QIAN,[6] *and speaks:*

> As magistrate of prefecture or county I display my dirty tricks
> And levy tax on grain and hay and on fields and plots alike;
> Because of my power and might, people are frightened and scared:
> The black-haired multitudes call me the Marquis of a Hundred Miles.

I am Zang Yigui, and I have been appointed as Prefect of Puzhou. At present Emperor Ling of the Han dynasty has ascended the throne. Throughout the empire stalwart warriors have arisen, each a hegemon of his own domain. The common people flee in all directions so the grain in the fields is left unharvested, resulting in terrible hunger and starvation and great deprivation. Only in our Puzhou do mulberry trees and fields of hemp bake in the sun, and wheat and millet stretch to the horizon, so the people are happy and prosperous. This must all be due, I believe, to my blessing! That is the reason why winds are mild and rains timely, and the black-haired masses are enjoying their life. So why should I not rise in rebellion and raise troops? This Puzhou of mine has a broad and extensive territory, the provisions are ample and the fodder is plentiful, the soldiers stalwart heroes all! Why shouldn't I rise in rebellion and sow confusion? Why shouldn't I become a liege lord instead of a prefect? In my staff here I have a clerk by the name of Pi Han. This person is very capable. Let me call him over to discuss this with him. Zhang Qian, go and invite Clerk Pi Han. ZHANG QIAN *speaks:* Yes, sir. *Acts out inviting, and speaks:* Clerk Pi, where are you? His Excellency is calling for you. CLOWN *enters, costumed as* HEAD CLERK, *and speaks:*

> As a clerk I am in power,
> A model for the magistrate!

---

6. Zhang Qian is the conventional name of an official's servant.

> Dirty tricks of the officials
> All depend on my decision.

I am Pi Han, also known as Neire.[7] I am a clerk here in the prefectural office of the Puzhou Prefecture. I'm not bragging, but this brush in my hand controls everything! All large and small affairs in this office have to be discussed with me and depend on my decision. Just as I was reading the *Story of the Western Wing*[8] in my room, some underling has to come and tell me that His Excellency has called for me. I don't know what for, but I'll have to go. No need to announce me, I'll go in there by myself. *Acts out greeting, and speaks:* Your Excellency called for me. What would you like to discuss? OFFICIAL *speaks:* I have something very important I want to discuss with you. At present stalwart warriors are rising up everywhere. The common people flee in all directions and the grain in the field is left unharvested, resulting in terrible hunger and starvation. Only in our Puzhou do mulberry trees and fields of hemp bake in the sun, and wheat and millet stretch to the horizon, so the people are happy and prosperous. This must all be due, I believe, to my blessing! That is the reason why winds are mild and rains timely, and the black-haired masses are enjoying their life. So why should I not rise in rebellion and raise troops? This Puzhou of mine has a broad and extensive territory, the provisions are ample, the fodder plentiful, and the soldiers are stalwart heroes all! Why shouldn't I rise in rebellion and sow confusion? Why shouldn't I become a liege lord instead of a prefect? So I have called you to discuss this. CLERK *speaks:* Your Excellency, even before you raised this issue, I had already considered it for a long time. Long ago that Exalted Ancestor of the Han[9] also was only a common citizen of Fengpei. When he grew up, he became a post station chief at Sishang. Because the Great Wall was being constructed,[10] he escorted corvée laborers to Mount Li, and he served as the headman. But many of these corvée laborers escaped and fled. When he arrived at Mount Mangdang, he beheaded a white snake.[11] But he was much indebted to the clerk Xiao He, whom he appointed as general manager for rising

---

7. Pi Han (*pihan*) literally means "cold skin," and Neire (*neire*) literally means "hot inside."

8. The *Story of the Western Wing* (*Xixiang ji*) was China's most famous love comedy. Its most popular version was the five-*zaju* dramatization by Wang Shifu (late thirteenth century), which circulated widely in print, often in illustrated editions. In traditional times, the *Story of the Western Wing* was often condemned as "a book that teaches lechery." See West and Idema 1995, pp. 3–5. Pi Han's interest in this text must of course be seen in contrast to Guan Yu's more edifying readings. And of course, this is highly anachronistic since the play was not written until the fourteenth century.

9. Liu Bang, founder of the dynasty.

10. In traditional times the construction of the Great Wall by the First Emperor of the Qin was usually condemned as an act of folly and tyranny.

11. The white snake represents the Qin dynasty.

in rebellion and raising troops, hiring soldiers and buying horses, staking up hay and storing provisions in order to complete the great enterprise. Your Excellency, when I look at your features and actions, you may be compared to Liu Bang. But I, Pi Han, am certainly no less gifted than Xiao He in terms of tricks and plots, wisdom and insight! OFFICIAL *speaks:* You are right. This is exactly my idea. Do you have any other suggestions? CLERK *speaks:* Your Excellency, if you are like Liu Bang and I am like Xiao He, then we still lack a Grand Marshal like Han Xin. I will recommend someone to you. OFFICIAL *speaks:* Whom will you recommend? CLERK *speaks:* In this locality lives a fine fellow named Guan Yu—also known as Yunchang. He can read *Zuo's Commentary to the Springs and Autumns.* He combines in one person both wisdom and courage. He is the right person to be given the seal of marshal. In those days Xiao He recommended Han Xin, and today I, Pi Han, recommend Yunchang! Your Excellency, what do you think about it? OFFICIAL *speaks:* Master Pi, how could your proposal be mistaken? The most important thing is to achieve this grand affair.[12] Tell someone to invite this Guan Yunchang. CLERK *speaks:* I will have someone invite him. Hey, you, Zhang Qian! At the order of His Excellency you must go and invite Guan Yunchang. ZHANG QIAN *speaks:* Invite whom? CLERK *speaks:* Invite Guan Yunchang! ZHANG QIAN *speaks:* And where does this guy live? CLERK *speaks:* I will explain it to you, but you have to remember it well. When you go out through the gate of this office, go to the east. Turn and cross the main street and enter that little lane. It's the house to the north of the crossing, to the southwest of the vegetable market, left of the police post, across the street from the brewery, and next to the baked bun seller. ZHANG QIAN *speaks:* I have no clue! CLERK *speaks:* Now hurry and invite that Guan Yunchang! ZHANG QIAN *speaks:* Yes, sir! So I go outside through the gate of the office, pass through the main street, go to that short lane, and have arrived there. This house must be it. Mr. Stoutfellow, are you at home? GUAN YU *enters and speaks:*

> My ambition reaches beyond the clouds, my courage is lofty:
> A phoenix helmet, golden armor, and a brocaded battle coat.
> This red heart, blazing and bright, is filled with proper loyalty:
> I exhaust my strength and risk my life for this sagely dynasty.

I am Guan Yunchang. I had just bought some books in the market and was reading them in my study when someone called at my door. Let me go and have a look. Here I am outside. Sir, what brings you here? ZHANG QIAN *speaks:* Stout fellow, you and I will go and visit His Excellency. While we are talking, we have already arrived in front of the office. You wait here and I will announce you. *Acts out announcing, and speaks:* Your Excellency, Guan Yunchang has ar-

---

12. "Grand affair" (*da shi*) refers to the establishment of a new dynasty.

rived. CLERK *speaks:* Your Excellency, just look at the fellow I recommend to you. Let's not talk about his inner talents; just look at his outer appearance. With these features and actions he'll attract more attention than others! OFFICIAL *speaks:* Ask him to come in. ZHANG QIAN *speaks:* Yes, sir. Please come in. GUAN YU *acts out greeting, and speaks:* Your Excellency, why have you summoned me? CLERK *speaks:* Guan Yunchang, His Excellency has invited you because he has something he wants to discuss with you. Your Excellency, please tell him. OF-FICIAL *speaks:* The only reason why I have invited you is this. At present stalwart heroes arise everywhere. The common people flee in all directions and the grain in the fields is left unharvested, resulting in terrible hunger and starvation and deprivation. Only in our Puzhou do mulberry trees and fields of hemp bake in the sun, and wheat and millet stretch to the horizon, so the people are happy and prosperous. This must all be due to my blessing! So now I want to rise in rebellion and raise troops. But I still need a Grand Marshal. Clerk Pi has recommended you as someone who combines civil and military arts in one person. You will receive the seal of commander—how about that? GUAN YU *speaks:* Your Excellency, I am just a poor scholar. What do I know of weapons and armor? How could you make the mistake of appointing me? I wouldn't dare! CLERK *speaks:* Don't be so modest! I recommended you! Once His Excellency becomes the liege lord of the region, you won't have to worry about a high position. GUAN YU *speaks in an aside:* This scoundrel is quite daring. But there is no other way now. OFFICIAL *speaks:* Soldier, bring it here. General, do you see this? This sword I will hang at your waist. Today is an auspicious day, so I appoint you here and now as commander. Hang the sword from your waist! GUAN YU *speaks:* In accordance with your command I have hung this sword from my waist. OFFICIAL *speaks:* Grand Marshal, when will you start your campaign? GUAN YU *speaks:* Your Excellency, today is an auspicious day, a propitious hour. As you employ me as your Grand Marshal, I will not hesitate or tarry, and start my campaign this very day. It's rightly said, "Troops have no discipline without executions, and generals maintain no order unless they are strict." So broadcast this order of the general: act in accordance with orders—whoever disobeys will lose his head! OFFICIAL *speaks:* Grand Marshal, you are right! Officers and soldiers, obey the orders of the general! GUAN YU *acts out grasping his sword, and speaks:* I now hold this sword in my hand. Officers and soldiers, listen! This sword will behead whomever discloses military secrets, falsely assumes fake titles, or does not honor the commands of the court. Prefect, is someone calling you? OFFICIAL *speaks:* Where? GUAN YU *acts out beheading him, and speaks:* Get a taste of my sword! OFFICIAL *acts out dying.* CLERK *speaks:* How could he commit such an act? This doesn't look good. I'll have to run for my life! GUAN YU *acts out grabbing him, and speaks:* Where are you off to? "One swipe of the sword makes two halves." CLERK *acts out dying.* GUAN YU *speaks:* I have killed off everyone in this prefectural office, so I should grasp this opportunity and fight my way out. All of you lackeys! Whoever opposes me will die; whoever blocks me will be wasted. So be it! I cannot stay here any longer. I will have to go into hiding in some other prefecture and district.

> With sword in hand I met my enemy and I leave the prefectural office:
> Corpses are strewn across the field and lie in the sandy dust.
> I set out on my journey to go into hiding at another place,
> Whether it is at some corner of the sea or the edge of the sky.

Exits.

OFFICIAL *and* CLERK *struggle up; they don't say a word but act out making faces and hand gestures, and exit.*[13]

MALE LEAD, *costumed as* ZHANG FEI, *and* CLOWN, *costumed as* BUTCHER, *enter together.* MALE LEAD *speaks:* I am Zhang Fei, also known as Yide. I hail from Fanyang in Zhuo Prefecture. From youth I have practiced the martial arts. I thrust the lance and cock the crossbow. I strike and hammer with whip and mace. There is no skill I do not possess; there is no skill I cannot master. But alas, my time has not arrived, so I engage in some petty trade, make a living by selling meat, and ply my blade as a butcher. Zhang Fei, when will you rise to glory? *Sings:*

> (XIANLÜ MODE: *Dian jiangchun*)
> My character and personality are stubborn and strong,
> My knowledge[14] and schemes are broad and capacious:
> Very much a stalwart hero!

BUTCHER *speaks:* Brother, you seem pretty uninterested in our business lately. You only want to twirl your lance and swing your cudgel. How come? MALE LEAD *sings:*

> Through practice have I perfected broadsword and long lance.

BUTCHER *speaks:* Brother, what you say makes no sense to me. You don't have even the inclination to use your knife to make a living as a butcher. Go ahead and practice your broadsword and long lance, but even if you master them, what'll you use them for? MALE LEAD *sings:*

> I hope to support the altars of the state
> And become a military commander.

---

13. Usually, actors playing characters who are killed or die are said to "exit unobtrusively." The precise nature of the stage direction here is unclear, although it may refer to their actions as ghosts; the interlude is probably farcical.

14. Here, specifically military knowledge and know-how.

BUTCHER *speaks:* Brother, you are surely mismatched! *Commentary from backstage:*[15] You mean "mistaken"! BUTCHER *speaks:* Shit! It's "mistaken." You are uninterested in this business, but now you want to sell floss and soy sauce! *Commentary from backstage:* He means "military commander"![16] BUTCHER *speaks:* Brother, according to me, your younger brother, even if we are not in it for the money, we have wine and meat to eat every day, and even if we don't have meat, we still have more liver and offal than we can finish! MALE LEAD *sings:*

> (*Hunjiang long*)
> At present I "live in a narrow alley,"[17]
> And each day I busy myself uselessly, meticulously slicing thin little skins.

BUTCHER *speaks:* Brother, you are really stupid. That great sage Confucius has said: If you do not suffer the greatest suffering of all suffering, you cannot top the men on top.[18] Just listen to me and get beyond it! Our line of business may be the lowest of the low, but it still manages to set out the plates! But you never take care of the shop. Tell me which day you don't drink yourself into a stupor? It's all rising early and late to bed! MALE LEAD *sings:*

> Constantly it is "under the stars, by the light of the moon."[19]
> Each and every day I "lie in the snow and sleep on the frost."[20]

BUTCHER *speaks:* Brother, because you had to grasp the lance and swing your cudgel, our business has really slowed down the last couple of days. MALE LEAD *sings:*

---

15. The use of "Commentary from backstage" is only known from farces; here it is an artifact of the cliché role of the butcher as played by the comic in earlier farce skits.

16. "Military commander" and "floss and soy sauce" share the same pronunciation (*rongjiang*).

17. A comic reference to Yan Hui, Confucius' perfect disciple, who lived in utter happiness amid his poverty. *Analects* 6.11 (trans. Slingerland 2003, p. 56): "The Master said, 'What a worthy man was Yan Hui! Living in a narrow alley, subsisting on a basket of grain and a gourd full of water—other people could not have borne such hardship, yet it never spoiled Hui's joy.'"

18. Akin to the modern cliché, "You have to eat the bitter in the bitter before you can be man atop others!" (*chide kuzhong ku fang wei renshang ren*). This is an oblique reference not to Confucius, but to *Mencius* 15.2, "Hence, when Heaven is about to bestow a great responsibility on a particular person, it will always first subject one's heart and resolution to bitterness, belabor one's muscles and bones, starve one's body and flesh, deprive one's person, and thwart and bring chaos to what one does. By means of these things it perturbs one's heart, toughens one's nature, and provides those things of which one is incapable"; and *Mencius* 15.5, "Only in these ways do we know that we live through adversity, but die through ease."

19. Constantly busy.

20. Daily hardships.

On top of that, how can I stand this desolate livelihood, encounter-
    ing hardship;
A life of insignificance full of fortune's constant change?

BUTCHER *speaks:* Brother, because our fated lot is no hundred and twenty percent joy, we need to make what we have richer. MALE LEAD *sings:*

It's all because our fortune stinks
And the devils are against us.

BUTCHER *speaks:* Brother, I will be honest with you. I have suffered such un-
happiness these last few years. Look how my hair has all turned white from
sorrow. MALE LEAD *sings:*

To no avail he's suffered till his dark hair turned hoary;
All in vain we've spent the fleeting light of years and months.

BUTCHER *speaks:* Brother, I will be honest with you. Yesterday I cooked up a
blood sausage and I bought a bottle of fine wine. I had hoped that you would
come and drink yourself into a stupor, but who could have known that you
would not come? Now it was fine that you didn't show up, but all through the
night I have been pestered by my boatman—oh no, it's "by my wife"—who told
me that I was no good. Just look at my face. I'm still ashamed today. MALE LEAD
speaks: Younger brother, don't blame me; I had some urgent business to attend
to. BUTCHER *speaks:* Brother, I wouldn't dare blame you! If I blamed you, I'd be
the son of a whore! But—what kind of business was it? MALE LEAD *sings:*

(*You hulu*)
Every day I link up with heroic warriors for idle discussions.

BUTCHER *speaks:* I don't know what kind of business you are engaged in but
make sure not to involve me! MALE LEAD *sings:*

I am not involved in some shady business;
I only want to discuss military matters—how to rule the world.

BUTCHER *speaks:* You and I are only butchers. What do we understand of military books, battle tactics, or the martial arts? Do you know about the hat that
was three *zhang* tall? *From backstage:* What do you mean "the hat"? BUTCHER
speaks: Well, it was completely empty inside! I just don't believe you! MALE
LEAD *sings:*

I study the *Six Tactics*[21] and *Three Strategies*—that's no lie!

---

21. The *Six Tactics* (*Liutao*) is yet another handbook of military matters. Its authorship was
attributed to Lü Shang, an adviser to King Wen and King Wu, the founders of the Zhou dynasty.
Also known as Lü Wang, Jiang Shang, Jiang Taigong, or Jiang Ziya, he was a hermit who spent

BUTCHER *speaks:* Even if you mastered the *Six Tactics* and the *Three Strategies,* where would you employ them? MALE LEAD *sings:*

> I want to extend the borders, expand the land, and expel traitorous
> cliques.

BUTCHER *speaks:* Brother, isn't it said, "Without a club in your hand, there's no point in wrestling with a tiger"? So let's not say there are no traitorous cliques— even if there would be traitorous cliques, you don't have any weapons. What are you going to do? Bite them? MALE LEAD *sings:*

> With this bamboo-node whip dangling from my wrist
> And this eighteen-foot lance held in my hands
> I want to support those in danger, rescue those in trouble, be true to
>   my word,
> And even more I want to support the royal house,
> Promote those loyal and good!

BUTCHER *speaks:* We brothers enjoy a brisk trade; food and clothing just seem to flow in and all our needs are met. So don't talk this nonsense. Ply your honest heart and mind, and just get on with selling liver and tripe. MALE LEAD *sings:*

> (*Tianxia le*)
> Oh, don't let this place bury heroes![22]
> I imagine those capable men of ancient times
> And ponder my own case.

BUTCHER *speaks:* Brother, how many of the ancients did not stick to their ancestral place? Give me a list! MALE LEAD *sings:*

> Just think of the misfortunes suffered by Han Xin and Yue Yi.
> But later Grand Marshal Han established ten great merits,[23]

---

his days angling in Pan Creek until he was brought to court at the age of seventy by King Wen of the Zhou. At the age of eighty, Lü Shang assisted King Wu in his conquest of the Shang and the establishment of the Zhou dynasty. It was only in imperial times (i.e., after 220 BC) that he was credited with the authorship of this military handbook. His biography is found in translation in "T'ai-kung of Ch'i, Hereditary House 2," in Sima Qian 2006, pp. 31–46.

22. The character *fang* (work district, area where work is carried out) is used in the term *difang* (this place of work), which may be a simple mistake for *difang* (place); but the invocation itself seems to suggest that it is the place—and its associated hereditary occupation that determines social status—that will "bury" heroes out of sight. In this sense, Zhang Fei is complaining that no one would think of looking in the butcher stall for a hero, but also referring to the fact that many of the great military heroes of the past came from low positions (including Lü Shang, purported author of the *Six Tactics*).

23. His ten great military exploits began with building a trestle road to move his army across the Chenqiang Mountains and ended with him forcing Xiang Yu to commit suicide at Rook

And Yue Yi's achievements for Yan were extensive.[24]
They both received gifts and glory,
And became famous for all eternity.

BUTCHER *speaks:* Brother, when you explain it this way, I sort of get it. Brother, you told me yesterday that you had some urgent business today. Why haven't you left yet? MALE LEAD *speaks:* Younger brother, I will go to visit relatives. This rock out in the fields weighs about a thousand pounds. I rolled it over with both hands and put this knife under it. If someone comes to buy meat, no matter how much, if he can take out this knife, he can have the meat for free. Don't ask him for any money. Just ask for his name and where he lives. When I come back, I have my own plan. BUTCHER *speaks:* Brother, I know this rock weighs a thousand pounds. Even if I ate another twenty years worth of rice, I couldn't budge it. I'm afraid that nobody has this kind of strength. Don't worry! Of course I would like to gobble up this piece of meat, but I don't have the strength in my body to move this rock. If I were to exert heart and lungs[25] at the same time, I would waste my liver, my life![26] Brother, you have so much in your heart,[27] but tomorrow it will turn into a rotten stomach![28] Brother, you just go! MALE LEAD *speaks:* Younger brother, remember what I said. Now I am off to see my relatives.

Exits.

BUTCHER *speaks:* Brother has left. I'll keep standing here in front of this meat table to see who may come. GUAN YU *enters and speaks:* I am Guan Yunchang. After I killed the Prefect of Puzhou, I came here to Fanyang in Zhuo Prefecture, and am staying at a merchants' inn. Let me go to the main street and buy some new snacks to eat as I drink my wine. Hello, can you help me? BUTCHER *speaks:* Sorry, sir! *Acts out looking at him from head to toe, and speaks:* Wow, this man has a fine physique. And this early in the morning he has already drunk so much that his face is all red. Sir, what would you like to fart? *Commentary from*

River. When Kuai Tong was trying to get Han to rebel against Liu Bang, he listed these ten great merits as his "ten major wrong acts."

24. When the state of Yan had almost completely been occupied by the state of Qi, it offered great rewards for capable men who would come to its rescue. One of these who responded was Yue Yi. In 284 BC he led the army of Yan in a campaign that freed the country and conquered seventy cities in the state of Qi.

25. "Heart and lungs" is a common term for one's "authentic feelings" or "good heart." Used here, of course, in a double sense, "to exert all my very being."

26. There is a nice pun to follow "heart and lungs" here. The Chinese sentence reads *kebu ganhua le wode ming. Ganhua* is written as "liver lobes," but it is exactly the same pronunciation as "to waste in vain."

27. I.e., "you think too much."

28. I.e., "you'll suffer from it."

backstage: It is: "to buy"! BUTCHER *speaks:* I mean: to buy! GUAN YU *speaks:* I would like to buy two hundred coins worth of fresh snacks. BUTCHER *speaks:* Sir, I have the meat, but I don't have a knife. My brother has gone off to see his relatives, and when he left he put his knife under this rock. He said that if anyone came to buy meat and could move the rock to take out the knife, it did not matter how much meat it was, but I should let him take it away for free. Old fellow, I'm not just making this up. This is a bamboo basket, and these are almonds. But if you can move that rock to one side and take out that knife, then you can cut off as much meat as you like and I won't ask you for any money. GUAN YU *speaks:* If that's the case, I will lift this rock with both hands, set it aside, and pick up this knife. Sir, here, you have the knife. Now cut off some meat for me. BUTCHER *speaks:* Wow! That is some guy! With both hands he picked up that rock and lightly put it aside. What a guy! So I'll take this knife and cut him some meat. Sir, this meat is free. We don't want your money. Just take it with you. GUAN YU *speaks:* How is that possible? If you will not take my money, I cannot take this meat. If you take my money, I'll leave with the meat. BUTCHER *speaks:* You are an honest man. So be it! You leave your money here and take the meat with you. Sir, what is your name, and where do you live? GUAN YU *speaks:* I am Guan Yu, also known as Yunchang. I am staying here at the inn. BUTCHER *speaks:* That inn isn't far. It's just around the corner. Sir, take your time. GUAN YU *speaks:* Well, then I'm going back to the inn with my meat. *Exits.* BUTCHER *speaks:* That red-faced fellow has left. My brother should be back soon. MALE LEAD *enters and speaks:* I've just come back from a visit to my relatives. Let me go and see my younger brother. Brother, did anyone come to buy meat? BUTCHER *speaks:* Brother, there you are! Someone came to buy meat: a tall guy with a red face who wanted two hundred coins worth of meat. I told him that the knife was stuck under the rock and that if you can move that rock and take out the knife, we don't want your money. No matter how much, you can take the meat for free. That fine fellow picked up the rock with both hands and put it aside. Then he picked up the knife and cut off a slice. But he was an honest fellow and said, "Keep the money and I'll take the meat and be on my way, but if you don't keep the money, I won't take the meat." I offered it to him for free a number of times, but he stubbornly refused to accept it. Only after I took his money did he take the meat and go. Brother, I think he is even stronger than you! He is a fine fellow! MALE LEAD *speaks:* Indeed he must be! BUTCHER *speaks:* I'm not lying! In case you don't believe me, isn't that the rock pushed to one side? MALE LEAD *sings:*

> (*Zui fu gui*)
> He must be, I believe, awe-inspiring and brave, rich in talents,
> His know-how and strength out of the ordinary!

BUTCHER *speaks:* Brother, this man abides by righteousness! I didn't ask him for money, but he forced me to take it. This man talks straight, displaying loyalty and trust. By the looks of it, he is not some ordinary fellow. MALE LEAD *sings:*

> His loyalty and trust, honesty and ability abide by ethical norms;
> On top of that, his actions show extraordinary signs.
> If the two of us would meet face to face by the side of the street,
> Just observe how I would act the modest one,
> And yield to him with all humility.

Speaks: Did you ask him his name and where he is staying? BUTCHER *speaks:* When I asked him, his name was Guan Yu, also known as Yunchang, and he is staying at the inn. MALE LEAD *sings:*

> (*Jinzhan'er*)
> You say that he is living at the inn,
> Staying with the merchants,
> That his name is Guan Yu,
> Also known as Yunchang.

BUTCHER *speaks:* That guy looks quite strange. The three braids of a fine beard hang down on his breast. MALE LEAD *sings:*

> His beautiful beard in triple strands is tossed by the wind.

BUTCHER *speaks:* Brother, he has a face like purple jade. MALE LEAD *sings:*

> His cheeks are like purple jade;
> A heroic energy stuffs his breast.

BUTCHER *speaks:* Awe-inspiring and majestic, he looks just like a living god! MALE LEAD *sings:*

> His body is awe-inspiring;
> His face is oh so majestic!

BUTCHER *speaks:* Brother, by the looks of his figure and his face, this is the greatest hero of the world! MALE LEAD *sings:*

> This man's heroic talents are rare in a world of dust,
> Without a match throughout the known realm!

BUTCHER *speaks:* Brother, why do you keep asking about this fellow? MALE LEAD *speaks:* Younger brother, come with me to the inn to find that hero. BUTCHER *speaks:* Brother, I'll come with you. The charisma of that man means he is no common fellow. Let's go and find him. MALE LEAD *sings:*

(*Coda*)
You aren't really needed, so don't tarry or dawdle!
I have to go there in person and be filled with respect.

BUTCHER *speaks:* Brother, walk a little bit slower! MALE LEAD *sings:*

I have just taken a step,
But now hesitate and deliberate for a while.

BUTCHER *speaks:* Brother, there's no need for doubt. In my opinion this fellow
is no liar. He definitely is staying at the inn. We will visit him there. MALE LEAD
sings:

If I am lucky enough to meet a real friend when I make this visit . . .

BUTCHER *speaks:* Brother, you seem to have been in turmoil since you heard his
name. We'll have to see what happens once you have met him. MALE LEAD *sings:*

I would be happy if we could become as attached as Chen and Lei.[29]
And I should not act slowly.
I'll see to it that my heart and guts are like iron and rock,
To ensure that our feelings are unfettered, our ambitions eternal.

BUTCHER *speaks:* Brother, here in the city of Zhuo Prefecture I've never seen a
man like this. MALE LEAD *sings:*

If I, here in this Fanyang in Zhuo Prefecture,
Can find a friendship that pleases me,
For all eternity I will support the court with loyalty and
    righteousness.

Exit together.

Act 2

GUAN YU *enters and speaks:*

My nature composed of loyalty and directness, my ambition unshakable,
    My physique awe-inspiring, my energy vigorous,
With all my heart I support the dynasty with valor and righteousness
    To ensure the prosperity of the nation for ten thousand years.

I am Guan Yunchang. I just came back to the inn from the main street and have
ordered someone to prepare a meal for me. I'll just sit here and see who may

---

29. Chen Zhong and Lei Yi are exemplary friends from the Eastern Han dynasty. They were
said to be as attached to each other as glue to lacquer.

come along. MALE LEAD *and* BUTCHER *enter.* MALE LEAD *speaks:* Younger brother, come with me to the inn to find that stout fellow surnamed Guan. BUTCHER *speaks:* I will help you find him. But you don't know this man. Why can't you get him out of your mind? MALE LEAD *speaks:* Younger brother, how could you understand? *Sings:*

> (YUEDIAO MODE: *Dou anchun*)
> I want to associate myself with stalwart heroes,
> Handle weapons and employ my martial skills.
> I hope to exert both my strength and true sincerity
> To pacify the borders and stabilize the land—
> To distance myself from my base livelihood,
> And set myself apart from companions in the world of dust.

BUTCHER *speaks:* Brother, as soon as you open your mouth you offend people. You want to eat fish and still complain about its stench! You haven't yet shed the name of "butcher" and you already call it "a base livelihood"! Well, fine! Which martial arts have you mastered? MALE LEAD *sings:*

> On the basis of my strong ambition and ability
> And my rash courage and bravery,
> I wager my name will be listed in the Yellow Pavilion,[30]
> More famous than anyone—past or present!

BUTCHER *speaks:* Well, as for me, I am not the equal of that man. Let's also not talk about my meat-selling skills. But when it comes to my blood sausage, I do make more money than anyone else. If you want to reject me as unworthy, I'll have a look at which people you do want to befriend. MALE LEAD *sings:*

> (*Zihua'er xu*)
> I seek a trusted friend who knows my heart,
> A good companion who shares my ambition,
> A poor scholar willing to slice his throat.[31]

BUTCHER *speaks:* Brother, you'd be better off emitting a foul odor than talking! You all too easily make up your mind to reject your old acquaintances. The friendship between the two of us is at least on the level of Guan and Bao.[32] MALE LEAD *sings:*

---

30. The name of the prime minister's office in Han dynasty times.

31. The term translated here as "to slice their throats" is often used in expressions denoting double love suicides.

32. Guan Zhong and Bao Shuya are exemplary friends from ancient times. When Guan Zhong took more than his fair share of the profits of a common trading enterprise, Bao Shuya did not complain because he knew that his friend had to take care of his ailing mother. Guan

I call to mind those former worthies Guan and Bao:
Their loyalty and filial piety were for real!
Yet I silently think of how in the beginning
They prized righteousness and rejected yellow gold like it was dung
    and dust.
We have to imitate great men from the past!

BUTCHER *speaks:* What kind of men? According to me, we should take care of our trade and make some money to take care of our wives, our parents, and our children. When the little kids get up in the early morning and are sitting there on the *kang*[33] and want some baked buns to eat, now brother, if you ask me about my feelings, how can I bear to say no? Of course I buy some for them!
MALE LEAD *sings:*

What do I care about shedding a family inheritance,
Or the glory or poverty of my wife and children?

BUTCHER *speaks:* Brother, here we are at the inn. It's that big fellow over there.
MALE LEAD *speaks:* That's quite a big fellow indeed. I will go up to him and ask him a question. Stout fellow, pardon me. GUAN YU *speaks:* Please, please, please. It's quite all right. MALE LEAD *speaks:* Stout fellow, are you the man who bought some meat a while ago? GUAN YU *speaks:* Yes, I did. Do I perhaps still owe you some money? MALE LEAD *speaks:* Stout fellow, I didn't come here for the sake of money. *Sings:*

(*Jin jiaoye*)
I came because of your sincere character, your pure and capable
    innards,[34]
Your lofty ambition, your manly might, and your heroic valor.
You imitated the hegemon-king of Chu, whose heroic fame lasts
    forever:
He lifted that thousand-pound tripod with all the strength in his
    body!

GUAN YU *speaks:* So why have you come here? MALE LEAD *speaks:* This is the reason why I came: in front of my meat table there is a rock that weighs about

---

Zhong would later serve as the prime minister of Duke Huan of Qi (r. 685–643 BC). Thanks to the policies of Guan Zhong, Duke Huan became so rich and powerful that he became the first of the Five Hegemons. Later this reference to Guan and Bao comes to mean a friendship that accepts the idea that one person is due more than the other and that equality is not at issue.

33. The *kang* is a raised platform in the houses of Northern China that is heated by the smoke of the family stove, and on which families sleep at night.

34. We have maintained the play on these offal puns; the term "innards" (*feifu*) figuratively means "what is in the bottom of your heart."

a thousand pounds. I placed my butcher's knife under that rock and left to see my relatives. I told my younger brother that if anyone came to buy meat and took the knife from under the rock, he could keep both his money and the meat. Who could have known that you would come and get the knife? But you also insisted on giving us the money. This means you are an honest man. So I have come straightaway to visit you. GUAN YU *speaks:* What virtue do I have that I have bothered you to come all this way? MALE LEAD *sings:*

> (*Xiaotao hong*)
> From earliest youth, my character has been out of the ordinary:
> I love to befriend true heroic personalities.

GUAN YU *speaks:* Sir, so you love to make friends, and that's why you come to seek me out. MALE LEAD *sings:*

> I hope you'll be so kind as to share a cup with me.

GUAN YU *speaks:* I wouldn't dare. I am just an ordinary citizen of the streets. MALE LEAD *sings:*

> I have not miscalculated!

GUAN YU *speaks:* By the looks of it, sir, you have practiced the martial arts. MALE LEAD *sings:*

> I have practiced martial arts, but why?

GUAN YU *speaks:* Which martial arts have you practiced? MALE LEAD *sings:*

> Even though just the long lance and broad axe . . .

GUAN YU *speaks:* What use will you put them to? MALE LEAD *sings:*

> To find a viable way to establish myself.

GUAN YU *speaks:* What proof do you have for that? MALE LEAD *sings:*

> Of course you know: "A gentleman is decisive about his beginnings."

GUAN YU *speaks:* Sir, may I ask what your name is? MALE LEAD *speaks:* I am Zhang Fei, also known as Yide. Since my youth I have practiced archery and riding. I use a one-*zhang* eight-foot-long steel-tipped lance. But alas, my time has yet to come, and I make a living by selling meat. May I ask where you are from and what your name is? Please let's exchange names. GUAN YU *speaks:* I hail from Xieliang in Puzhou. I am Guan Yu, also known as Yunchang. I love to read *Springs and Autumns* and *Zuo's Commentary* and I have practiced the martial arts. I employ a Green Dragon crescent-moon third-of-the-length

偃月刀

Fig. 1. Guan Yu's "Green Dragon" crescent-moon, third-of-the-length blade knife

blade.[35] Because the Prefect of Puzhou did not honor the emperor's command and wanted to be the liege lord of one of the regions, I killed Puzhou's officials and clerks to remove this danger to the people. Now I have come to Zhuo Prefecture but I never thought I would meet such a gentleman. This is a truthful statement—please forgive me for any offense. MALE LEAD *speaks:* You are a true man of valor! Come on. I don't care who is older or younger. I honor virtue, not age. Elder brother, please be seated and accept these eight bows of your younger brother, Zhang Fei. GUAN YU *speaks:* How would I dare? What virtue or ability do I have? MALE LEAD *acts out bowing.* BUTCHER *speaks:* Let me return this honor! MALE LEAD *sings:*

(*Tiaoxiao ling*)
Here I bow and bow again

Acts out bowing. Sings:

In front of the steps.

---

35. Guan Yu's blade is mounted on a staff twice the length of the blade. See Fig. 1.

Acts out bowing. GUAN YU *acts out bowing in return, and speaks:* Please, don't!
MALE LEAD *sings:*

> I, your younger brother, am shallow in wisdom, poor in talents, too
> stupid by nature.

Acts out bowing, and sings:

> I never expected to meet you here.

Acts out bowing, and sings:

> It's not that I, this rude and rash Zhang Fei, am so brave that nothing
> frightens me.

Acts out bowing. GUAN YU *speaks:* I cannot accept this. Please rise! MALE LEAD
sings:

> But you have studied the *Springs and Autumns* and *Zuo's
> Commentary,*
> And are so well versed in battle tactics and military writings.

Acts out bowing. GUAN YU *speaks:* Please rise! You must have heard, "Bestow
kindness on a man before he has met his time, and befriend a man when he is
living in dire poverty." This testifies to that. BUTCHER *speaks:* The Sage has said,
"Zhao, Qian, Sun, and Li may well be strong, but you also have to bow to
Zhou, Wu, Zheng, and Wang."[36] But I have said too much. Sir, don't blame me
for being so modest in my studies. But if I would be too modest, I'd be sired by
a cat.[37] MALE LEAD *sings:*

> (*Tusi'er*)
> As friends our feelings are deep, our intentions complete;
> Our characters are in accord, capable of sharing a house.
> We have only to be firm and unyielding in our actions, and our
> behavior will be fine.
> It's not that by devious schemes
> I seek to humor and flatter you.

GUAN YU *speaks:* What kind of virtues and abilities do I have that you honor
me as your elder brother? I cannot live up to this. BUTCHER *speaks:* There is no

---

36. "Zhao, Qian, Sun, and Li; Zhou, Wu, Zheng, and Wang" are the first eight surnames
listed in the *One Hundred Surnames* (*Baijia xing*), a compendium of common surnames in rhym-
ing four syllable lines, which was widely used as a primer in premodern China.

37. This is perhaps a reference to the expression "cat and rat sleeping together," which has the
meaning of high and low collaborating in crime and sin.

need to be too modest. For you, the elder will come first, and little old me will be Number Three. MALE LEAD *sings:*

> (*Sheng Yaowang*)
> Elder brother, your ambition is extraordinary,
> A truly great man!
> Throughout your life your heroic valor has found no equal.
> Your younger brother has a boorish personality,
> His talents and insight are lacking,
> And there is none in the world who knows less than me about past
>   and present.
> You must make the best of this doltish, boorish fellow.

GUAN YU *speaks:* Younger brother, now we have become united as siblings, I hope you will accept my invitation to provide you with a simple meal in an inside room and offer you some crude brew so we can drink a few cups at will. MALE LEAD *speaks:* Elder brother, how could I not accept your kind offer? BUTCHER *speaks:* Right! For celebration wine, three cups is exactly right.[38] I will help out, raise the bottle, and strain the wine. I will be the cook and carry the plates, invite the guests and tend the fire, bring in the good water to replace the muddy, and sit at the table and play guessing games[39]—all of these jobs will be my responsibility! GUAN YU *speaks:* Brother, let's have some wine in an inner room. MALE LEAD *sings:*

> (*Coda*)
> Let's drink today as much as we can without any sorrow or worry.
> I, this Zhang Yide, may be foolish and stupid, rough by nature;
> Before I met my time, I was an idle man,
> But when my ambition is achieved I'll support the sagely bright
>   ruler!

Exit together.

---

38. "Celebration wine" (*xijiu*) is a term normally used for a wedding banquet. It is surely meant in a satirical sense here.

39. "Guessing games" (*caimei*) is a drinking game where one person holds a seed, chess piece, or other object in the hand, and the other person has to guess what it is.

Act 3

EXTRA, *costumed as* LIU BEI, *enters and speaks:*

> My ancestors laid the foundation and created a solid land of emperors;
> The age of Restoration[40] was a world of chaos, each a power unto himself.
> But the house of Han was reestablished, annihilating vile rebels,
> And I tarry here around Zhuo Prefecture, living in Lousang.

I am Liu Bei, also known as Xuande. I hail from Lousang in Dashu. I am a seventeenth-generation grandson of Emperor Jing of the Han, and a descendant of Liu Sheng, the Quiet Prince of Zhongshan. Because Wang Mang monopolized power, he was able to supplant the house of Han. It was later reestablished during the Restoration, when Mang was annihilated and rebels were captured. When Emperor Guangwu occupied the throne, the empire was stable once again. At present Emperor Ling has ascended the throne, mighty warriors have arisen everywhere, and the Yellow Turban bandits have rebelled. Our Liu clan is incapable of maintaining its inherited enterprise. I am just a common citizen and make a living by weaving mats and plaiting sandals. I have studied both the civil and military arts, but so far have been unable to display my heroic talents. I bide my time and keep to my station. Today I have nothing else to do, so let me go for a walk down the main street.

> Buried away in this red dust for so many years:
> A real man's stalwart ambition rises up in heaven's void.
> One day I will take off and ascend that road to the clouds,
> And then people will know I am a man, a true hero!

Exits.

CLOWN, *costumed as* INNKEEPER, *enters and speaks:*

> I operate a wine house here,
> But I swear I don't care for customers:
> One jug of wine is as sweet as honey,
> But the next, sour as vinegar.

I am a wine seller. Everyone who engages in trade and passes by on the road comes to my place to drink. I have cleaned out the compartments and hung up a bundle of straw,[41] so now I will heat up the wine warmer and see who comes along. GUAN YU *enters with* MALE LEAD, *and speaks:* Since Zhang Fei and I have

---

40. The "age of Restoration" here refers to the years of civil war following the collapse of the Xin regime (AD 9–23) of the usurper Wang Mang.

41. A bundle of straw or a flag was a sign that the wine house was open for business.

become sworn brothers, I am very happy indeed. My younger brother is strong and unyielding in his attachment to what is right and proper and has a character like a raging fire. Today we have nothing to do and have gone for a walk here on the main street. Younger brother, just look at how these Yellow Turban rebels create chaos—this is the right moment when men of right are needed. When will come the moment we brothers make our career? MALE LEAD *speaks:* Elder brother, even though you are right, we have to keep to our station as we bide our time. *Sings:*

> (ZHONGLÜ MODE: *Fendie'er*)
> Calling to mind those heroic stalwarts before they made their
>   names—
> At the end of their ropes, drifting through the four directions—
> They too suffered frustration for half their lifetime.

GUAN YU *speaks:* For instance, the Great Duke[42] was angling in Pan Creek, but later he established the Zhou dynasty that ruled the empire for eight hundred years. And he also was awarded a fief. MALE LEAD *sings:*

> You mean Ziya who angled on the banks of the Wei in Pan Creek,
> And later supported the establishment of the Zhou dynasty,
> Acquiring signal merits in helping make the ancestral temple secure.
>
> (*Zui chunfeng*)
> If it weren't the case that "Jiang Shang met King Wen,"
> He would have remained buried in the red dust until his death.

GUAN YU *speaks:* Men like us have stuffed their bellies with strategies and tactics through their studies. There must be a place for us to find employment. MALE LEAD *sings:*

> Who is our equal in heroic talent and limitless courage?
> When will this come to an end?
> To an end!
> We're fully trained in the martial arts,
> Have an imposing air, a dashing courage,
> And tricks, schemes, tactics, and strategies.

GUAN YU *speaks:* Here we have arrived on the main street. Let's just let our feet take us where they will. LIU BEI *enters and speaks:* I am Liu Xuande. Here I have arrived on the main street. Look at all those people engaged in selling and buying. It's quite a bustling crowd. GUAN YU *speaks:* Younger brother, do you see

---

42. The Great Duke here refers to Lü Shang; see note 21.

that gentleman over there? MALE LEAD *speaks:* Elder brother, where? Let me have a look. *Acts out looking.* MALE LEAD *speaks:* That man has an exceptional physique! GUAN YU *speaks:* Younger brother, let me tell you. His earlobes hang down to his shoulders and his hands hang beyond his knees. He has an aquiline nose and a dragon face. He truly has the aura of greatness. This man must have blessings in store. MALE LEAD *speaks:* True. *Sings:*

> (*Hongxiuxie*)
> His features are awe-inspiring and impressive;
> I linger on him to observe every little detail.
> On top of that, that aquiline nose and dragon face cannot be faked.
> In the future he will rise to high position
> And in due time enjoy great power and wealth.
> And more than that, his intentions are honest and sincere,
> His heart good and great.

GUAN YU *speaks:* Younger brother, let's invite him to the wine house and have a few cups with him. MALE LEAD *speaks:* Elder brother, you are right. Let's go meet him. GUAN YU *speaks:* Sir! Please. LIU BEI *speaks:* Oh! Please take no offense, you two stout fellows! GUAN YU *speaks:* We brothers would like to invite you to this wine house to have a few cups. We hope you will accept our invitation. LIU BEI *speaks:* I wouldn't dare! What kind of virtue or ability do I have that I can bother the two of you to do me this honor? But the proverb says: "Within the four seas all men are brothers." So let's enjoy ourselves and have a few together. GUAN YU *speaks:* Here we have arrived in front of the wine house. Hey, wine seller, brings us two hundred cash worth of wine. INNKEEPER *speaks:* Gentlemen, please be seated. This compartment is nice and clean. There's wine! Drink all you want for two hundred cash. GUAN YU *speaks:* Serve the wine! Sir, allow me to toast to you. Drink this cup to the full! *Acts out offering him wine.* LIU BEI *speaks:* I wouldn't dare. You drink first. MALE LEAD *speaks in an aside:* To judge by his bearing, this man is no commoner! *Sings:*

> (*Shiliu hua*)
> I see that his outward appearance is right and proper, with no false
>   pretense.
> By accident we meet to drink a fragrant brew,
> And he is so mild and respectful, humble and modest, right on
>   point.
> We only met each other a moment ago,
> But already we're like lacquer and glue.[43]

---

43. See note 29.

LIU BEI *speaks:* What kind of virtue or ability do I have that you two gentlemen do me this honor? GUAN YU *speaks:* Please! MALE LEAD *sings:*

> Everything he says or speaks is exceptional and marvelous!
> I could never expect that we'd make his acquaintance.
> I am so unrefined and stupid—don't laugh at me.

LIU BEI *speaks:* How would I dare? What kind of virtue or ability do I have? MALE LEAD *sings:*

> Really, I lack all politeness,
> Am just too stupid and muddled.

LIU BEI *speaks:* You two gentlemen are too kind in treating me generously. GUAN YU *speaks:* Please have another cup of wine. LIU BEI *speaks:* Yes, I will. *Acts out drinking, and speaks:* Sir, please drink this cup to the full! GUAN YU *speaks:* Yes, I will. *Acts out drinking, and speaks:* Sir, please drink one more cup! LIU BEI *speaks:* Yes, I will. *Acts out drinking, and speaks:* This is enough wine for me! MALE LEAD *sings:*

> (*Dou anchun*)
> The proverb says: "When you meet a true friend, a thousand cups are
>   too few."

GUAN YU *speaks:* Bring more wine! This cup is for you, younger brother! MALE LEAD *speaks:* Elder brother, you drink first! GUAN YU *speaks:* Younger brother, you drink! MALE LEAD *sings:*

> I have no intention to refuse and with reciprocal feelings, reciprocal
>   feelings, we pour each other a cup.
> Elder brother, you are so sincere and shirk no trouble.
> How could your younger brother deserve all this?

Acts out drinking, and speaks: Elder brother, you drink this cup! GUAN YU *speaks:* Yes, I will. *Acts out drinking.* LIU BEI *speaks:* I am only a poor scholar and yet you two stout men show me such great honor! GUAN YU *speaks:* Please. MALE LEAD *sings:*

> We only wish that our bond will last as long as heaven
> And earth,
> But we also fear that this karmic affinity may be light and our lots in
>   life too limited.

GUAN YU *speaks:* Sir, where do you live? LIU BEI *speaks:* I am from this prefecture and I live in Lousang in Dashu. GUAN YU *speaks:* And what is your name? LIU BEI *speaks:* I am Liu Bei, also known as Xuande. GUAN YU *speaks:* What do you do for a living? LIU BEI *speaks:* I make a lowly living weaving mats and plaiting sandals. Please don't look down on me for this. GUAN YU *speaks:* I wouldn't dare! Sir, you are mistaken; many of the sages of antiquity engaged in lowly trades when they were still living in obscurity. MALE LEAD *sings:*

> (*Shang xiaolou*)
> Ning Qi once upon a time sang his song, beating the horns of his ox;[44]
> Yi Yin once upon a time plowed and hoed his wheat and rice.[45]
> As for Fu Yue who built up walls,[46]
> Maichen who carried firewood,[47]
> And Wu Yun who played the flute—[48]
> They all later rose to glory in the Eight Residences,[49]
> Became famous throughout the four seas,
> And achieved dazzling glory for themselves
> As they received that one vermilion edict sealed with purple wax.

LIU BEI *speaks:* You have spoken right! Bring in some more wine! Let me propose a toast to you. Stout fellows, please drink! GUAN YU *acts out drinking wine, and speaks:* Sir, you should also drink one cup! LIU BEI *acts out drinking wine,*

---

44. Ning Qi attracted the attention of Duke Huan of Qi when he was singing a song of frustration while beating out the tempo on the horns of his ox.

45. Yi Yin eventually served as prime minister under Tang, the founder of the Shang dynasty.

46. Fu Yue was a slave in the area of Fuyan (modern Shanxi), where he worked on constructing walls of rammed earth (he is often wrongly credited as the inventor of the form system for these walls). According to the *Records of the Grand Scribe*, the Shang thearch Wuding dreamt of obtaining a wise sage:

> At night Wuding dreamt of attaining a sage, who was named Yue. Based on what he had seen in his dream, he looked at the assembled ministers and hundred clerks of his government, but none of them matched. At that point he sent his hundred officers to seek him in the wilds, and he obtained Yue from the precipices of Fu. At this time Yue was a slave, forming walls in the precipices of Fu, and when Wuding saw him, he said, "This is he." He got him and conversed with him, and indeed Yue was a sagely man, so he was raised to be minister and the state of Yin was grandly governed. Therefore, he consequently bestowed on him the surname Fu because of the precipices of Fu and called him Fu Yue.

47. Zhu Maichen (d. 115 BC) was a poor scholar who continued reciting his books even while he was carrying firewood. His wife divorced him because of his poverty, but he later rose to high office.

48. Wu Yun (also known as Wu Zixu; d. 484 BC) had to survive by begging, playing the flute, after he had fled from Chu. He later would achieve high office in the state of Wu.

49. The Eight Residences are a collective designation for the highest offices of the bureaucracy in Yuan dynasty times.

and speaks: My stout man, may I ask your name? GUAN YU *speaks:* I am Guan Yu, also known as Yunchang. I hail from Xieliang in Puzhou. LIU BEI *speaks:* And you, this stalwart fellow? Please also drink this cup of wine to its full. MALE LEAD *acts out drinking wine, and speaks:* Sir, please drink a cup too. GUAN YU *speaks:* Bring it on. I also will drink another cup. It's true indeed: "When one meets true friends, a thousand cups of wine are too few." *Acts out drinking.* [LIU BEI] *speaks:* And may I ask this hero for his name? MALE LEAD *speaks:* I am Zhang Fei, also known as Yide. I hail from Fanyang in Zhuo Prefecture. LIU BEI *speaks:* If I look at the might and energy of the two of you, your physiques are awe-inspiring and your appearances are majestic, without equal in this world. It is truly my good fortune to have met you two today. MALE LEAD *sings:*

> (*Manting fang*)
> This meeting of ours here today is the greatest!
> We truly are eminent men of this world,
> Not little kids playing in the courtyard!
> Each and every one a heroic talent, hiding the way of the former
>   kings in his belly.
> With stalwart energy and dashing courage
> We're exactly like the fierce tiger on the plains, disporting its claws,[50]
> Or the divine *jiao* dragon retracting its scales in the mud.[51]
> In fact we are ospreys at the edge of sky,
> Quite unlike the swallows and sparrows under the eaves!
> One day we'll soar to the highest layer of heaven.

GUAN YU *speaks:* Younger brother, we must keep to our station as we bide our time. Sir, please drink another cup. LIU BEI *acts out being drunk, and speaks:* I've had a few too many. I'll have to sleep off this wine. Let me lean on this table and rest for a while. *Acts out sleeping.* GUAN YU *speaks:* Younger brother, Liu Xuande is into his cups. As we were talking, he has fallen asleep. Wow! Little brother, did you see that? He is lying on one side and a little red and white snake is coming out of his mouth and going into his nose. Wow! It is coming out of his eye and boring into his ear! Younger brother, let me tell you, this is called "the snake boring through the seven openings." This means that this man is predestined for a lofty position in the future. We will wait until he wakes up and then honor him as the eldest brother, irrespective of actual age. What's your opinion? MALE LEAD *speaks:* Elder brother, you are right. That was also my idea. We'll do as you

---

50. The tiger is normally in the deep mountains. Here it means "to be out of place." They are biding their time until they are properly used.

51. The *jiao* dragon is a ferocious type of dragon that can display its true power only in deep water. The couplet speaks to the great and unrealized ambition of these three men.

say. GUAN YU *speaks:* Don't startle him! He's waking up! LIU BEI *acts out waking up, and speaks:* That was a good sleep! You two stout fellows, please don't take offense; forgive me. GUAN YU *speaks:* We wouldn't dare! Xuande, may I ask you, who are your forebears? LIU BEI *speaks:* Just common citizens. GUAN YU *speaks:* Don't be so modest! You must be the descendant of a noble house of former times! LIU BEI *speaks:* I will be honest with you. I am a seventeenth-generation grandson of Emperor Jing, and a descendant of Liu Sheng, the Quiet Prince of Zhongshan. GUAN YU *speaks:* Younger brother, did you hear that? I told you he was not of common stock. He is a distant scion of a former emperor! However old you may be, we will honor you as our eldest sibling and swear brotherhood. Please allow your younger brothers to perform eight bows. GUAN YU *and* MALE LEAD *act out performing their bows.* MALE LEAD *speaks:* Eldest brother, please be seated. LIU BEI *speaks:* How could I dare to accept this honor? Please rise. *Acts out bowing in return.* MALE LEAD *sings:*

> (*Shi'er yue*)
> We must bend our bodies then fall on our knees,
> Crook our backs and lower our waists:
> We are only commoners from among the people,
> Whereas you are a scion of the Han dynasty!
> It's not that we are prattling in front of the cups,
> And don't think we are flattering or boasting!

LIU BEI *speaks:* What kind of virtue and ability do I have that the two of you should honor me in such a way? GUAN YU *speaks:* Elder brother, your younger brothers honor virtue, not age. MALE LEAD *sings:*

> (*Yaomin ge*)
> Oh,
> Even though we, orphaned and destitute, bereft of virtue, may be
>   your elder in age,
> You definitely are branch and leaf of a noble house, not to be
>   disesteemed.
> We live at present in a "lowly lane,"[52] in impoverished circumstances,
> But truly in this shallow water of a muddy pool[53] we've encountered
>   a leviathan.
> If I consider things carefully,
> Our courage and bravery throughout our life,
> Were all because of the Way that is Heaven!

---

52. See note 17.

53. An emperor-to-be is often called "a submerged dragon" who can hide in the water of a horse's hoof print. When he takes the throne, the dragon assumes its real form and soars into the heavens.

LIU BEI *speaks:* Now we have become sworn friends, we honor each other as brothers. There is a peach orchard outside the walls of Zhuo Prefecture. Let's choose an auspicious day and a propitious hour, slaughter a horse in sacrifice to Heaven, kill an ox in sacrifice to earth and swear this oath with Heaven as our witness: We don't seek to be born on the same day, but we vow to die on the same day, to bind ourselves in friendship in life and death. Younger brothers, what do you think about it? GUAN YU *speaks:* Elder brother, we'll do as you say. We will choose an auspicious day and a propitious hour, prepare the objects of sacrifice, and offer them up to the gods.

> We must learn from Guan and Bao, and how they divided gold,[54]
> And later we will assist and aid the house of Liu to restore the empire.

MALE LEAD *sings:*

> (*Coda*)
> Of a mind to swear our brotherhood in the Peach Orchard
> When the sun is high at the propitious hour on the auspicious day
>   we choose
> We will butcher this ox and slaughter this horse and announce to
>   blue heaven:
> We desire only to share life and death as long as we live.

Exit. LIU BEI *speaks:* Who would have thought that today I would have sworn brotherhood with my younger brothers. This is no ordinary joy!

> Majestic physiques, courage and energy strong:
> Unmatched in this world are my younger brothers Guan and Zhang.
> Just look at the brotherhood we swore in the Peach Orchard:
> For all eternity this will spread the fragrance of our names.

Exit together.

Act 4

EXTRA, *costumed as* HUANGFU SONG, *enters with* SOLDIERS, *and speaks:*

> Straight and right and firm of heart: so I establish my place in history;
> For the sake of the people and the benefit of the state I use my powers.
> Removing the cruel and evil, I bring back the power of kingly
>   transformation;[55]
> Ensuring the longevity of the imperial house I ensure great peace.

---

54. See note 32.

55. That is, the power of a king of virtue to transform his people through his own ethical actions.

I, this official, am Huangfu Song. At present Emperor Ling of the Han has ascended the throne. Because I am incorruptible and able, pure and capable, I have been appointed as Prefect of Beidi. Now in the first year of the reign period Zhongping[56] there was a certain Zhang Jiao from Julu who respectfully served the Yellow Emperor and the Old Master.[57] He instructed his disciples in magical techniques that he called the Way of Great Peace. He consecrated holy water to cure people of their diseases, and the masses revered him like a god. Zhang Jiao dispatched his disciples throughout the four directions to spread their lies and lead people to delusion. After more than ten years he had amassed over a hundred thousand adherents. The people from the Eight Regions—Qing, Xu, You, Ji, Jing, Yang, Yan, and Yu—all were in his thrall. In total they formed thirty-six dioceses. A big diocese had more than ten thousand people, and a small diocese counted six or seven thousand people. One of Zhang Jiao's disciples, Tang Zhou, sent up a petition to him, whereupon Zhang Jiao ordered all dioceses to rise in rebellion. They wrapped their heads in yellow turbans as a symbol, so people at the time called them the Yellow Turban rebels. Within a few weeks the whole empire had responded and the capital itself was shaken. The Sage convened his ministers for a conference. Together with the Palace Attendant-in-Ordinary Lü Qianghui, I stated, "The festering evil of the prohibition of cliques[58] has created resentment and grudges among the people. If we do not declare an amnesty, these people may collaborate with Zhang Jiao and the adverse consequences may be even worse, and what can be done then? If these three proposals of ours are accepted, the Yellow Turbans will disappear all by themselves." When the Sage asked us which three proposals, I replied:

> The first is to proclaim a general pardon throughout the subcelestial realm. The second is that if there are bandits and highwaymen who have rebelled and gathered in mountain forests, from there to threaten and attack walled cities, kill and harm duly appointed officials, plunder and rob granaries and storerooms, or wound and harm the common people—if they are willing to exterminate the Yellow Turbans, they will be recognized as good citizens of the state. The third is that if people do not take off their yellow turbans, they will be killed and their whole family annihilated.

The emperor followed the proposal and pardoned all clique members throughout the empire. The only one not to be pardoned was Zhang Jiao. The emperor

---

56. AD 184.

57. Laozi, the "founder" of Daoism.

58. A failed attempt in 166 by some officials to curtail the power of eunuchs at court resulted in a "prohibition of cliques," and persecutions of "clique members" in 169 and 176, creating widespread resentment.

next ordered me to take these edicts of appointment with blanks for the names and pearls and jewels and all kind of treasure, and attract heroes and stout fellows to our cause. I have arrived here in Zhuo Commandery. I have often been told that this place has three heroes—one is called Liu Bei, also known as Xuande; one is called Guan Yu, also known as Yunchang; and one is called Zhang Fei, also known as Yide. These three men are sworn brothers. I've learned that today in the Peach Orchard they will slaughter a white horse in sacrifice to Heaven, and kill a black ox in sacrifice to Earth. They don't seek to be born on the same day, but they vow to die on the same day—if one lives, three live, and if one dies, three die. These truly are outstanding men in the human realm. So I will spur on my horse and go straightaway to the Peach Orchard to enroll these three men. Let me get going—what's to stop me?

> The four seas are in utter confusion, battle horses so bold!
> Right now the house of Han is rising again.
> The huge blessing of the "sagely bright" partakes of heaven and earth;
> It is within my power to have rebels and bandits beheaded.

Exits.

BUTCHER *enters and speaks:*

> Butchering oxen and slaughtering horses is my living;
> They completely depend on the butcher for their affairs.

I am the butcher. Today is an auspicious day. Brother Zhang Fei has acquired two sworn brothers. One is surnamed Liu and one is surnamed Guan. That one surnamed Liu has a white face, the one surnamed Guan has a red face, and my brother has a black face.[59] I wanted to become Number Four, but they said that my face is too blotchy[60] and rejected me. Well, that is fine with me too. *Commentary from backstage:* How is that fine with you? BUTCHER *speaks:* It's because my "way of color"[61] is not right. Today they want to swear brotherhood in the Peach Orchard, and they ordered me to prepare the sacrificial items. I have just slaughtered the ox and killed the horse. The incense, candles, flowers, and fruit are all laid out. They should be here soon. LIU BEI *enters together with* GUAN YU *and* MALE LEAD. LIU BEI *speaks:* My younger brothers, today is a lucky day and a good hour. The sacrificial items have been prepared.

---

59. A black face is a dark, sunburned face of someone who has to do physical work under the scorching sun.

60. The word used here, flower (*hua*), can mean "blotchy, multicolored, variegated" and it can also refer to a pock-marked face.

61. The Chinese word for color (*se*) also is the common word for sex—hence the reference to pock marks.

Here in the Peach Orchard we will swear brotherhood. Let's light the incense.
MALE LEAD *speaks:* I never thought I would experience this day! *Sings:*

> ([SHUANGDIAO MODE:] *Xinshui ling*)
> Today we will swear brotherhood in the Peach Orchard, united in
>   purpose,
> Because my two elder brothers are magnanimous and tolerant.
> They base themselves in talent and ability—they have no peer—
> And rely on virtue and behavior—can be harsh or mild.
> When I think of the past and the springs and autumns I so emptily
>   passed:
> Such true and sincere fellows as us
> Will never dissemble or lie!

LIU BEI *speaks:* We have already arrived at the Peach Orchard. Have the sacrificial items all been laid out properly? BUTCHER *speaks:* My three elder brothers have arrived. Forgive me, your younger brother, for the crime of not welcoming you at the proper distance.[62] Elder brothers, I have laid out everything most properly so the three of you may conduct your sacrifice. *Acts out kneeling down, and speaks:* My three elder brothers, please take into consideration how hard I have worked. There's nothing to be done about that, but please, in one way or another add my name to the sacrificial statement. I'm happy to be Number Four! GUAN YU *speaks:* Elder brother, please raise your incense. LIU BEI *speaks:* My two younger brothers, please. GUAN YU *speaks:* I wouldn't dare. Elder brother, please raise your incense. LIU BEI *acts out raising the incense. The three of them act out kneeling down.* LIU BEI *acts out reciting the prayer text, and speaks:*

> Liu Bei from Lousang, Guan Yu from Xieliang, and Zhang Fei from Zhuo Commandery devoutly and sincerely bow in prayer, and present here, in sacrifice to the deities of the heavenly court, incense and candles, flowers and fruits, a white horse and a black ox, and various delicacies. Liu Bei and the others swear to become brothers, seeking not to be born on the same day, but vowing to die on the same day—as long as one is alive, may the three of us be alive, and as soon as one of us dies, may the three of us die. Together we will support the universal rule[63] of the house of Liu, and collectively we will contribute to the foundational enterprise of the Han dynasty. We have prepared these gifts with a devout heart, and pray in this way to the Lord of Heaven. May the divinities scrutinize this with care!

---

62. It is customary politeness to wait at a distance from any gathering site to escort one's guests to that place.

63. More literally: (the area inhabited by) the Chinese (*hua*) and barbarians (*yi*).

Act out bowing together. MALE LEAD *sings:*

> (*Zhuma ting*)
> All together, with folded hands and lowered heads,
> We gaze afar at the divine welkin and repeatedly kowtow.
> The incense burns in precious animals,[64]
> As we, with a devout heart, slaughter a horse and butcher an ox.
> Green ants[65] spurt their fragrance as we lift the golden goblets.
> May the divinities in their jade palaces faraway accept our gifts!
> The brilliant light shimmers
> As we light the painted candles;
> The finest delicacies, flowers and fruits are all readied.

BUTCHER *speaks:* This sacrifice to divine heaven, I say, has all been laid out by me. What a joy! They drink their three goblets. You swear brotherhood, but what is in it for me? LIU BEI *speaks:* My two younger brothers, let's each get our weapon and try it out. GUAN YU *speaks:* Yes, let's do so. Bring in our weapons. *Acts out setting out a pair of swords, the Green Dragon blade, a steel-tipped lance, and a finely polished whip.* LIU BEI *speaks:* Younger brothers, you may not know this, but I have practiced all of the eighteen martial arts, and I excel in the use of a pair of swords. This is no boasting on my part!

> I support the universal rule of the Han with full determination,
> Daring to engage in battle with any general.
> Once these hands lift aloft that pair of swords,
> I'll have corpses cover the field and blood collect in pools.

GUAN YU *speaks:* A pair of swords like yours, elder brother, is unique in this world! BUTCHER *speaks:* What's so special about that? I can do the same. *Acts out dancing with swords, and speaks:* It's not as much fun as twirling a pinwheel of fire! MALE LEAD *sings:*

> (*Chuan bo zhao*)
> I see how he displays his fierce force;
> Truly, he's rich in insight and strength.
> I gather he's well versed in the martial arts.
> His divine eyes bulge out,
> His sword so sharp and keen it howls like a cold wind.
> In truth here applies: "His heroic fame has no match."

---

64. "Precious animals" are animal-shaped incense burners made of precious materials.
65. Green ants is a common designation for newly brewed ale.

LIU BEI *speaks:* Eldest younger brother, what about you? GUAN YU *speaks:* My Green Dragon crescent-moon blade weighs nine times nine, eighty-one, pounds, and I have a valor that ten thousand men cannot match.

> With this Green Dragon crescent-moon third-of-the-length blade
> I display my heroism on the battlefield as I rein in my horse.
> With a loyal heart I requite the state and remove evil cliques—
> My only desire is to defend the Han dynasty with my life.

LIU BEI *speaks:* Bravo! You truly have no match in the way you handle your blade! BUTCHER *speaks:* What's so special about that? Let's see who can handle it better, me or him. *Acts out grabbing the knife but being unable to move it, and speaks:* Aiya, damn it! Even if I would eat rice for another twenty years, I would be unable to pick up this blade. But I'll say it's not that I can't handle this blade, just that I can't lift it. If I could lift it, I could wield it better than him! MALE LEAD *sings:*

> (*Qi dixiong*)
> Your know-how and schemes extend far and wide; your valor is like a
>   young tiger;
> When you lift your third-of-the-length blade, it moves with a natural
>   grace.
> Just lightly twirl it and the breath of death hisses coldly.
> Strong as a god, you never wrinkle your brow to frown!

LIU BEI *speaks:* Second younger brother, what about your steel-tipped lance? BUTCHER *speaks:* Now my brother's lance has engaged in quite some underhand business! MALE LEAD *speaks:* Elder brother,

> It's not that I, Zhang Fei, want to brag or boast,
> But with lance athwart the saddle I spur my horse to be at the very front.
> This one-*zhang* eight-foot divine spear always comes out first—
> All I want is to support the house of Liu for hundreds of years!

BUTCHER *speaks:* My brother was busy all the time selling meat, so he neglected his practice. You haven't seen what I can do with the lance! *Acts out handling the lance, and speaks:* Three quick stabs! Three slow strokes! Two hands folded! Scattering flowers over the rooftops! Encircling the waist! *Acts out stumbling and falling down, and speaks:* Bah, I just had some fun with this lance despite my busy schedule. How does it compare to my elder brother? MALE LEAD *sings:*

> (*Meihua jiu*)
> How could my strength contain this divine spear eighteen feet long?

My fierceness surpasses that of the *jiao* and *qiu!*[66]
My insight and strength are both complete.
When I meet with enemy troops, I will engage them in battle;
When I run into rebels and bandits, I will never let them off.
My energy pierces the skies, transfixes Dipper and Buffalo.[67]
If you want to grapple with me, I need no excuse—
I covet profit and fame, and the title of liege lord!

GUAN YU *speaks:* When will we ever stop just wasting time? MALE LEAD *sings:*

(*Shou Jiangnan*)
Ah,
I want with all my heart to share the sorrow of our king—
How can I earn enough glory to have an imperial audience at the
Phoenix Tower?
Isn't that better than throwing on a straw cape and wearing a bamboo
hat on a fishing boat?
Let me make something of nothing—
In the arena of merit and fame I dare fight for the prize!

LIU BEI *speaks:* Today Liu, Guan, and Zhang, swearing brotherhood in the Peach Orchard, offer sacrifice to divine Heaven. We have laid out this banquet in celebration. Now listen to me:

As sworn brothers we are united in purpose:
Confronted with danger we will die and enter our graves together.
Here in the Peach Orchard we sacrifice to Heaven and Earth,
Our only wish to protect the state's borders for all eternity!

LIU BEI *speaks:* Look over there! Someone is coming! HUANGFU SONG *enters with* SOLDIERS, *and speaks:* I am Huangfu Song. I am on my way to the Peach Orchard to visit these men. Let me be on my way! Here I am there already. Servants, take my horse. You there, inform Liu, Guan, and Zhang that they should come and receive the imperial edict! BUTCHER *speaks:* Yes, I will. You three gentlemen can let go now! Outside the gate there is a man who orders you to receive the imperial edict. LIU BEI *speaks:* An imperial edict has arrived. The three of us should go and receive it. *Acts out greeting, and speaks:* Your Excellency, please come in. HUANGFU SONG *speaks:* You three kneel down facing the palace and listen to His Majesty's command:

---

66. Both the *jiao* and the *qiu* are ferocious dragons.
67. Dipper is the Chinese name of Ursa Major. The Buffalo Star is Altair.

Because the Yellow Turbans have rebelled and there is no one to stop them, and because you three brothers have sworn brotherhood in the Peach Orchard and have excellent martial skills, the three of you are appointed as generals to defeat and annihilate the Yellow Turbans. Express your gratitude for Our Grace.

All speak: We are deeply moved by His Majesty's grace! MALE LEAD *speaks:* Elder brother, how can we repay the grace we brothers have received from the emperor? Whenever a military situation arises from now on we must display our loyalty and exhaust our strength! LIU BEI *speaks:* We may have received these official appointments today, but I'm afraid our martial skills are too limited to live up to our task. MALE LEAD *sings:*

> (*Dianqian huan*)
> I just want to lead the bravest troops
> And display my loyalty as I share the king's sorrow.

LIU BEI *speaks:* Second younger brother, don't boast! MALE LEAD *sings:*

> Elder brother, don't fret and worry.
>> *Speaks without interruption:* Whenever there is a military situation,
>> *Sings:*
> I will ready my spear!
> This is the season for a real man to achieve his ambition.
> This single eighteen-foot lance of mine cannot be stopped.
> Whenever someone who needs to die engages me in battle,
> I will root him out to the west, exterminate him in the east,
> So my name will be recorded in history books.

HUANGFU SONG *speaks:* After the three of you have defeated the Yellow Turban bandits, you will of course be promoted and rewarded. Now listen:

> This is all because that rebel from Julu creates havoc in the cosmos,
> Covets money and goods, enslaves and plunders the good citizens,
> And teaches them the heresies of the Yellow Emperor and Laozi,
> Curing peoples' disease like magic with tallies and holy water.
> He has gathered a million disciples in rebellion—all evil scoundrels
> Who wrap their heads in a yellow turban which serves them as a
>   sign,
> The imperial command orders you to wipe out and remove these
>   local bandits—
> You will be promoted in rank and title, have many tripods, layers of
>   carpets!

Today you have received the vermilion edict of official appointment.
Express your gratitude with a bow while you face the imperial palace.

TITLE: Heroic fellows in Zhuo Prefecture: twice well met.

NAME: Liu, Guan, and Zhang: the tripartite oath of brotherhood in the
Peach Orchard.

2

In the Hall of Brocade Clouds:
The Beauty and the Story of the Interlocking Rings

Anonymous

The Story of the Interlocking Rings, also known as *The Plot of the Interlocking Rings* (*Jinyun tang anding Lianhuan ji*), is a well-known fictional story about how the minister Wang Yun creates a rift between Dong Zhuo, the tyrannical usurper and power behind Emperor Xian of the Han, and his adopted son, the general Lü Bu, the two most powerful men at the end of the Han. The rift itself is a historical fact, but *Interlocking Rings* introduces the figure of the beautiful Diaochan, whom Wang Yun cleverly betroths to both men to create a triangle of desire. The earliest extant source for the story of the plot, which becomes much more elaborate in the *Romance of the Three Kingdoms*, is the *Records of the Three Kingdoms in Plain Language*. In fact, this latter work, if not the source of the story of both Diaochan and her place in the plot, is surely drawn from the same popular legend as the drama. There are two extant versions of the drama (as we will discuss later in this introduction) that have different versions of the actual plot, but they are the same in staging this triangle of desire as the reason for Lü Bu's willingness to kill Dong Zhuo.

Background and Historical Sources

In the turmoil following the suppression of the Yellow Turban rebellion, He Jin (d. 192), whose half-sister was Emperor Ling's empress, was in charge of the army in the capital of Luoyang. Together with Yuan Shao (d. 202), another powerful figure, He Jin drew up plans to exterminate the powerful eunuchs who held control at the court. Twelve of these eunuchs (two of whom were so close to Emperor Ling that he called them "daddy" and "mommy") held extraordinary power. Yuan Shao suggested to He that he enlist generals stationed at the border, including Dong Zhuo, to help with the suppression of the eunuchs. Dong Zhuo entered the capital and for all intents and purposes seized complete control of the court. When Emperor Ling died in 189, the eunuchs, along with the newly installed Emperor Shao, fled the capital out of fear, but Dong Zhuo intercepted them and brought the emperor back to the capital. In 190,

Dong Zhuo deposed Emperor Shao after a year on the throne, and installed a mere child of the royal clan, Emperor Xian, and Dong Zhuo took for himself the title of Grand Preceptor. A few years later, Yuan Shao finally massacred the eunuchs, and Dong Zhuo was subsequently left without a significant check on his power at court. Regional warlords, however, soon began to rise in power, particularly in Shandong. Fearful of their strength, Dong Zhuo burned Luoyang, looted graves for valuables, and moved the new emperor to Chang'an, where he also constructed for himself a fortified city called Mei on the north bank of the Wei River to safeguard his family and friends. Dong Zhuo's biography in the *Documents of the Later Han* is full of repugnant episodes of orgies, rape, and murder committed by Dong Zhuo, but it is difficult at this remove in time to determine the veracity of these stories.

Dong Zhuo installed Wang Yun as chief minister in 190, and later made him minister of instruction, which ranked as one of the three highest offices in the Han. According to the "Biography of Dong Zhuo" in the *Documents of Wei*,

> In the fourth month of summer [in the third year of Chuping, May 192], the Minister of Instruction Wang Yun, the Vice-Director of the Department of State Affairs along with Shisun Rui and Zhuo's general, Lü Bu, plotted together to execute Zhuo. At this time, the Son of Heaven was newly recovered from an illness and held a great convention in the Weiyang Hall. Bu ordered Commandant of the Cavalry Li Su, who was from the same commandery, and others to bring ten or twenty of their private guards, have them falsely don the robes of the imperial guard, and keep watch at the side gate. Bu had an edict in the bosom of his robe. When Zhuo arrived, Su and others stopped him. Zhuo, startled, called out to find out where Bu was. Bu said, "There is an edict." Thereupon he slew Zhuo and exterminated his three clans.

Wang Yun and Lü Bu then jointly shared power, but they soon lost the good will of other officials. This had in large part to do with Wang Yun's desire to execute Cai Yong (132–92), the great historian and scholar, for expressing grief over Dong Zhuo's death. Eventually, the former generals who served under Dong Zhuo and were expecting a pardon that never came joined together to sack Chang'an. Lü Bu fled, but Wang Yun remained and was executed, his body left exposed in the marketplace. He was fifty-six.

The historical record is never quite clear about how Lü Bu was persuaded to kill his foster father. Under Dong Zhuo's suggestion, Lü Bu had killed his first foster father, Ding Yuan, called Ding Jianyang in the dramas, so it was completely in keeping with his character. The reasons are spelled out fairly clearly in Lü Bu's biography in the *Documents of the Later Han*. The following occurs just after a passage relating how Dong Zhuo persuaded Lü Bu to kill Ding Yuan and join their two armies together:

Zhuo then made Bu Commandant of Cavalry, and by oath bound them as father and son, and [Zhuo] deeply loved and trusted him. He then raised [Bu's] rank to Leader of Court Gentlemen, and enfeoffed him as the Marquis of Duting. Zhuo knew that he was, himself, quite violent and unrestrained, and he was constantly in a suspicious and paranoid state, so no matter what he did he used Bu as his personal guard. [Bu] once displeased Zhuo and Zhuo plucked out his hand axe and threw it at him. Bu managed to avoid it by parrying it quickly and he changed countenance, turned to look at [Zhuo], and apologized. Zhuo's anger also went away. From this time on, Bu carried a secret grudge against Zhuo. Zhuo also sent Bu to guard his inner apartments, and [Bu] had a private affair with one of the maidservants and became even more ill at ease.

Consequently, he went to see Minister of Instruction Wang Yun, and related the events about how Zhuo had almost killed him. At that time, Yun and Vice-Director of the Department of State Affairs Shisun Rui had secretly planned to kill Zhuo, and they reported this to Bu and asked him provide an [armed] response from the inside [for their attack from outside]. Bu said, "What about being father and son?" Yun said, "You are surnamed Lü and were never his own flesh and blood. If you are in a constant state of anxiety about dying, how can you speak of 'father and son'? When he threw the hand axe at you, what feelings of 'father and son' were there then?" Bu subsequently assented to it and thereupon stabbed Zhuo to death at the gate.

The illicit affair between Lü Bu and the servant girl certainly provided the motive for including Diaochan in the later folk stories. The bond of father and son as well as Dong Zhuo's paranoia also explain why, in the drama, Lü Bu lives in a separate apartment close to Dong Zhuo in the grand preceptor's private residence. But neither drama mentions the incident of the hand axe, since it would take away from the emphasis on lust and love as the center of the interlocking rings.

The Popular Tradition

Pei Songzhi's commentary to the third-century *Records of the Three Kingdoms* includes many clearly fictional episodes, including one that has been adapted into Act 2 of the drama. The *Record of Heroes* (*Yingxiong ji*), attributed to Wang Can (177–217) in early bibliographies, records an incident in which a popular song circulates about Dong Zhuo, and a second incident in which a Daoist master shows Dong Zhuo a piece of cloth with the character for "mouth" on either end (see *Interlocking Rings*, n. 37–39), which materially and graphically spells out the name of Lü Bu. The drama conflates these two events, but in doing so it generally paraphrases the *Record of Heroes*:

At that time there was a popular ditty that said,

> A thousand miles of grass
> Oh green, so green,
> Ten days of prognostication
> It still won't grow.

And there was the song of Dong Tiao. There was also a Daoist master who wrote the character Lü on a piece of cloth in order to show it to Zhuo, but Zhuo did not understand that it meant Lü Bu. Zhuo had to attend the grand conference, and he put in order his foot and horse soldiers, going from his encampment to the palace. Escorts in court dress walked among them. When his horse stumbled, Zhuo thought it uncanny and wanted to stop. Lü Bu urged him to go on, then he revealed his armor inside of his robes and went in. Once Zhuo was slain, the sun and moon became clean and clear, and not the slightest breeze arose. Min, Huang,[1] and all of Zhuo's family, young and old, were in Mei[2] and when they returned, they were hacked to death and shot by their underlings. Zhuo's mother was ninety at the time, and she walked to the gates of the fortress and said, "I beg to escape my death." She was immediately beheaded.

The members and old clerks of the Yuan clan [later] changed the burial place of all who had died in Mei, and they gathered together the corpses of the Dongs at the side and burned them. They exposed Zhuo's corpse in the marketplace. Zhuo had been obese for a long time, and the fat ran out of his body and into the ground, staining the grass the color of cinnabar. At dark, the soldiers guarding the corpse made it into a huge candle, placing [a wick] in Zhuo's navel to make a lamp. It stayed bright clear through to the morning. It was like this for days on end. Later, Zhuo's old soldiers gathered up the ashes that were left from the burning of the corpses and put them all in a coffin, burying it at Mei. There were two or three hundred thousand catties of gold in Zhuo's fortress, seventy or eighty thousand catties of silver, and the pearls, jade, brocade, fine silks, rare items, and other things were heaped in mounds high as mountains. They could not even be counted.

The rest of the passage clearly is based on the same material used almost a millennium later to compile the *Records of the Three Kingdoms in Plain Language*.

Since the drama we include in this chapter and the *Selection of Yuan Plays* version in Appendix 3 are both Ming compilations, and it is impossible to judge how much they changed earlier dramatic versions on which they may have been

---

1. Dong Zhuo's younger brothers.
2. Dong Zhuo had built a small fortress here on the north bank of the Wei River.

based, we must resort to two sections found in the *Records in Plain Language*—
"Wang Yun Offers Diaochan to Dong Zhuo" and "Lü Bu Stabs Dong Zhuo"—
as the earliest known version of the story in colloquial writing or performance
literature (these incidents are incorporated into "The Story of Diaochan and
the Interlocking Rings," Appendix 1, item 4). There is also, in a list of titles of
farces performed during the Jin (1115–1234), a playlet called *Stabbing Dong Zhuo*
(*Ce Dong Zhuo*). We have no way of knowing if this was related to the story of
"interlocking rings," but it does demonstrate that there was already a separate
dramatic tradition at a time that the *Records in Plain Language* was circulating.
Reading the *Records in Plain Language* and the dramas together, moreover,
clearly shows that the dramatist and the compiler of the *Records in Plain Language* were both drawing on the same reservoir of popular traditions found in
the early medieval period.

The drama makes some significant changes, however, to create a much more
interesting story. The character of Wang Yun, for instance, is considerably
fleshed out in the drama (as he is the only singer, this is to be expected), and is
portrayed as a much more complex personality. He is limned out as one who
is capable of planning and scheming but at the same time is clearly unwilling to
act alone. Both *The Anthology of Northern Dramas New and Ancient* (*Gujin zaju
xuan*) edition and that of *A Selection of Yuan Plays* stress that the plan is carried
out by "a group of officials" (*zhongguan*) under the leadership of Wang Yun and
Wu Zilan in the former or by Wang Yun and Yang Biao (who does not appear
in the *Records in Plain Language*) in the latter. Moreover, in the dramas the plot
to kill Dong Zhuo originates with Cai Yong, a figure who also does not appear
in the *Records in Plain Language* or in any historical materials in this connection. The plot involving the interlocking rings is much more complex in the
drama, unfolding through several acts and relying on a much more fully articu-
lated Diaochan, who is portrayed as a beautiful yet responsible and loyal wife
who is willing to sacrifice everything—honor, self-respect, and even her life—
out of a sense of gratitude to Wang Yun. While her status in Wang's household
is unclear, we must remember that she is a token or instrument to be exchanged
between men: the emperor to Ding Yuan, Ding Yuan to Lü Bu, and Wang Yun
to Dong Zhuo and Lü Bu again. For Diaochan to have any subjective agency,
we have to wait until Luo Guanzhong's recreation of her in the later *Romance
of the Three Kingdoms*.

The *Records in Plain Language* also has no equivalent for the scene in Act 4
in which Cai Yong and Li Ru claim different readings of the portents warning
Dong Zhuo about going to his final court audience. This scene is found in a
muted form in the *Record of Heroes* in Pei Songzhi's commentary on the *Records
of the Three Kingdoms* and, like the story of the Daoist and the piece of cloth, is
clearly a popular legend of considerable antiquity. Its absence from the *Records
in Plain Language* is worth noting, but we must consider the nature of the *Re-*

cords in *Plain Language* as a text. For one thing, it shows considerable influence from other forms of performing literature (the *cihua*, for instance) and as a single printed text it represents only one version of events that had been ladled out of a huge reservoir of possible stories and combinations of stories and given shape by the vessel that was used to present it to a reading audience. The same would have held true for oral performance for a listening audience as well. Therefore, we should not consider the *Records in Plain Language* as an authoritative account of circulating popular stories, but as a single possibility among many. That this scene is missing from the printed text does not mean that it was missing from the body of stories that circulated as popular history of the Three Kingdoms, but simply that it was not chosen by the compiler.

The drama has taken greater liberty with the portrayal of Cai Yong, presenting a completely unhistorical depiction. In the historical sources Cai Yong is drafted into Dong Zhuo's government and serves in several high positions. But, he had been coerced into serving in the first instance—Dong Zhuo reminded him that he had the power to exterminate whole clans—and at least once thought about fleeing to Shandong. But after Dong Zhuo was assassinated by Wang Yun and Cai Yong was in attendance to Wang Yun, Cai refused to discuss the issue of Dong Zhuo's death, which visibly pained him. Wang Yun accused him of "perhaps being a co-conspirator" and had him thrown in jail. Cai pleaded to have his face branded and his feet cut off so that he could finish his history of the Han instead of lingering in prison, but it was to no avail. Cai was enormously talented, and many of Wang Yun's colleagues and other leading figures of the day all pleaded for his release. Before the situation was resolved, Cai died in prison. The sympathetic portrayal of Cai may reflect a revision of the story in the popular mind to rescue him from opprobrium. Certainly, this sympathetic portrayal is in the background of the account of Cai's life in the *Documents of the Later Han*.

Later Traditions

Two major works appeared at the end of the fifteenth century and beginning of the sixteenth. Probably the first to be compiled was *The Popular Elaboration of the Records of the Three Kingdoms* (commonly referred to as *Romance of the Three Kingdoms*), the earliest extant edition of which was published in 1522 but bears a preface dated to 1494. Authorship of this novel is attributed to Luo Guanzhong, who probably lived in the middle and later fourteenth century. We know this because he is mentioned in the *Continuation of the Register of Ghosts* (*Lugui bu xubian*) as being alive in 1364. As the name of the novel suggests, it stayed closer to historical sources. In the novel,[3] Diaochan is not Lü Bu's wife

---

3. The plot of interlocking rings is found in chapters 8 and 9.

and is clearly identified as a singing girl who had been a favorite of Wang Yun's for so long that he began to consider her a daughter. Her character is much more fleshed out in the novel, and she enters into the stratagem willingly, flirting with both Lü Bu and Dong Zhuo to lure them into the plot. As the center of this action, she is both calculating and intelligent. The modern scholar Zhong Linbin has written about how skillfully she uses her eyes, first flirting with Lü Bu ("sending him autumn waves" = amorous glances), then seeing him in the garden and spying on him, and finally covering the tears in her eyes to signal her disgust at having sex with Dong Zhuo and thereby inflame Lü Bu.

The novel makes no mention of Cai Yong in the plot itself but reports on the nature of his relationship with Wang Yun. The reading of signs is left to Li Su, who assumes in the novel the role played by Cai Yong in the *zaju* drama. Li Su goes to Meiwu to fetch Dong Zhuo to court, explains away the broken wheel on the cart and the broken reins of the horse, and lures him into court. It is only after Dong's death, when Cai Yong is found weeping over his corpse in the marketplace, that he is brought to court for punishment.

The novel also expands the role of Li Ru, who is portrayed as an evil psychopath who carries out Dong Zhuo's grisly decisions to the end. Li Ru is not mentioned at all in the *Records in Plain Language*, and though he does appear in this *zaju*, he is less well-defined than in the novel, where he appears as the public face of Dong Zhuo's clique. His cunning in the novel is shown quite clearly by the fact that he is the only person to see through Diaochan's manipulations to create a rift between Lü Bu and Dong, but his advice goes largely unheeded.

Around the same time that the 1522 edition of the novel appeared, Wang Ji (1474–1540) wrote a Kun drama entitled *The Plot of the Interlocking Rings*. The earliest text of this drama at our disposal is a Qing dynasty manuscript, but a work written in 1521 cites "Wang Ji's *Plot of the Interlocking Rings*," so we can place its composition before that date. The play is in thirty acts and draws its material from chapters 3 through 9 of the novel as well as the *zaju* we have translated here. It begins by describing how Dong Zhuo moves the capital to Chang'an in anticipation of seizing the throne, which causes Ding Yuan and his adopted son Lü Bu to attack Dong. Dong dispatches Li Su with gifts to persuade Lü Bu to surrender and join forces. Lü, described as "brave but without any plans, greedy but without righteousness" (*yong er wu mou, tan er wu yi*), kills his adoptive father Ding Yuan, becomes Dong Zhuo's adopted son, and is enfeoffed as Marquis of Wen. Wang Yun, who wants to remove Dong Zhuo, concocts a plan with Cao Cao to kill Dong, but the plot is detected and Cao Cao does not carry through. The scenes then switch to the interior of Wang Yun's household, where he gives his favorite singing girl, Diaochan, a set of jade interlocking rings, telling her to keep them safely stored away. A few days later Diaochan sees Wang Yun moping in the rear garden and prepares incense to wish for the quick disposal of Dong Zhuo and salvation of the state. Wang Yun overhears her loyal desires and then concocts the plan.

When Wang Yun hears that Lü Bu has lost his precious cap while doing battle with Zhang Fei at Tigerkeep Pass, he has a new hat made and sent to Lü Bu. The courier arrives just as Dong Zhuo is roundly berating Lü Bu, and the latter, overcome by Wang's kindness, goes to Wang's house to thank him. A feast is arranged where Lü Bu is presented with Diaochan. Lü Bu gives her a phoenix head ornament as a betrothal gift and she gives him the interlocking rings in return. At a second banquet, Dong Zhuo sees Diaochan and, overcome by her beauty, claims her as his own. When Lü Bu returns to Tigerkeep Pass, Wang Yun sends Diaochan to Dong Zhuo. Upon Lü Bu's return, Wang Yun shows him the injustice done to Diaochan, and Lü goes to see her. He finds her as she is putting on her makeup and they make a tryst at the Hall of Phoenix Mates. Diaochan describes how painful Dong Zhuo's sullying had been and tries to commit suicide by leaping into a pool. Lü Bu stops her, but at that moment Dong Zhuo discovers them and hurls a short axe at Lü, who parries the blow and flees. Dong Zhuo sends Li Su to track him down at Wang Yun's residence where, as in this *zaju*, Wang Yun changes Li Su's mind. They then entice Dong Zhuo to come and ascend the throne, and Li Su slays him.

Since every actor in Southern drama sings, this form of the play gives a much more complex picture of the political intrigue of the time and expands its characterization of ancillary figures. Lü Bu's inconsistency and indecision, Cao Cao's craftiness, and Dong Zhuo's violence and sexual appetite are as roundly written as Wang Yun's ability to scheme. Diaochan has a much clearer understanding as to whom her loyalty belongs (that is, Wang Yun) and has a far greater grasp of political intrigue, which she remarkably demonstrates as she manipulates both of the men to whom she was betrothed. Many of the scenes of this drama are still in the standard repertoire of Kun drama, Peking Opera, and other forms of regional opera, and the story of Diaochan has been dramatized in movies and television in China, Hong Kong, and Taiwan from the 1950s to the present.

Editions: *The Anthology of Northern Dramas New and Ancient* and *A Selection of Yuan Plays*

There is one edition of the *Story of the Interlocking Rings* currently found in *The Anthology of Northern Dramas New and Ancient (Gujin zaju xuan)* of 1598. Only a single copy of this print edition survives. It is found in the Maiwang Studio collection, in which it bears Zhao Qimei's annotations and colophon as well as a list of costumes and properties used in the court production of the play. This suggests that Zhao had access to a court play that he used as a basis for collation. His notes, quite meager, terminate after only a few annotations are inserted. This leads one to ask whether the court edition and the printed edition were completely alike, or whether he gave up on collating the text because the differences were not that significant or somehow detracted from the quality of the print edition. Minimal differences would suggest that he was working with a manuscript edition that was the basis for the commercial print version.

A second version of the play is printed in *A Selection of Yuan Plays* (*Yuanqu xuan*), where it is entitled *The Plan of Interlocking Rings*. It is significantly different than the *Anthology of Northern Dramas New and Ancient* version translated here,[4] and seems to be based on a different court play. We can tell this by the fact that the few insertions that Zhao Qimei makes in the printed text are not found in the arias of the play in *A Selection of Yuan Plays*.

The *Anthology of Northern Dramas New and Ancient* is often called "the Xijizi edition" because the text bears a preface by the unknown compiler (for whom the name Xijizi is a sobriquet), dated 1598. Other plays found in *The Anthology of Northern Dramas New and Ancient* that exist in both Yuan editions and in *A Selection of Yuan Plays* demonstrate a closer affinity with the earlier Yuan texts, revealing that they are probably based on earlier Ming court texts that had been copied from Yuan materials. This edition uses smaller characters for spoken passages, which are set two character spaces from the top, as well as smaller characters for the padding words—extra-metrical words that are spoken in a heightened stage manner (not ordinary speech) as lead-in phrases or intrusive phrases in the songs (see Fig. 2).

The *Story of the Interlocking Rings* is a regular *zaju* in four acts. It has two intrusive performances, both in Act 2. The first is a poem composed spontaneously during a zither performance in the garden. The second is a free lyric (*sanqu*) delivered by Diaochan at the banquet for Lü Bu. Both intrusive songs are matched to their specific occasion by genre. The first is akin to traditional Chinese poetry, which is supposed to express one's refined moral subject; the second is a performance piece here used to narrate events from Diaochan's and Lü Bu's life prior to a recognition scene. Otherwise, the play uses the standard rules for *zaju*.

---

4. For a discussion of this version and its differences with the edition we are using here, see Appendix 3.

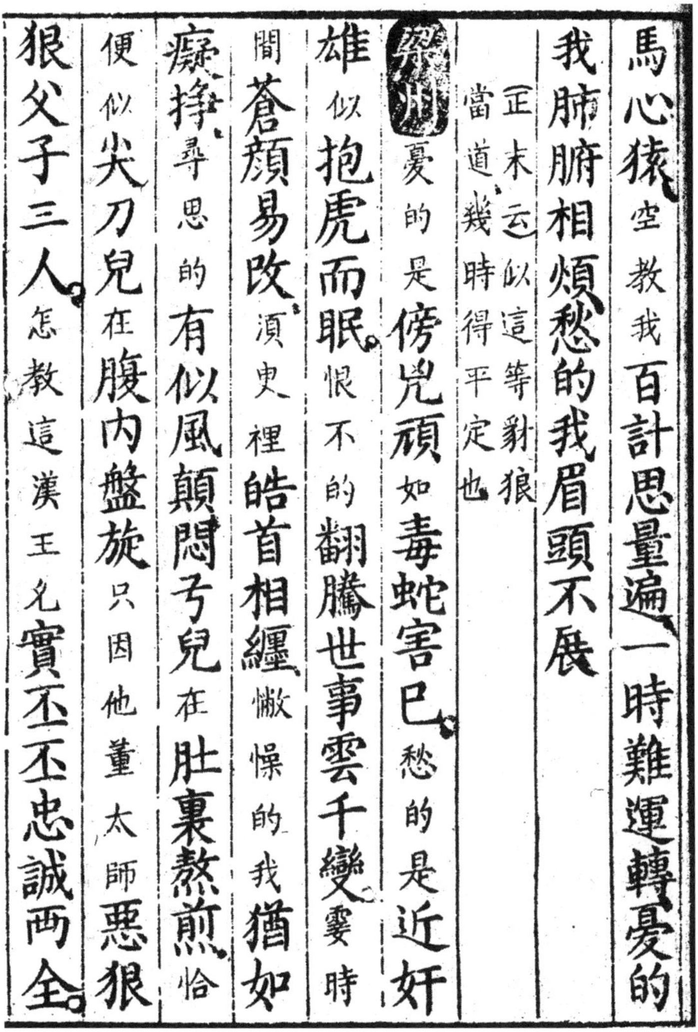

馬心猿空，教我百計思量遍，一時難運轉憂的

我肺腑相煩愁的我眉頭不展

（正末云）似這等豺狼當道幾時得平定也

【梁州】憂的是傍兒頑如毒蛇害已。愁的是近奸

雄似抱虎而眠。恨不的翻騰世事雲千變要時

蒼顏易改。頃史裡皓首相纏懶惰的我猶如

癡掙尋思的有似風顛悶弓兒在肚裏熬煎恰

便似尖刀兒在腹內盤旋只因他董太師惡狠

狼父子三人。怎教這漢王兄實丕丕忠誠兩全

FIG. 2. Page 9a from the *Anthology of Northern Dramas New and Ancient* edition of *In the Hall of Brocade Clouds: The Beauty and the Story of the Interlocking Rings*

Dramatis personæ in order of appearance

Role type	Name and family, institutional, or social role
Opening male, clown	Dong Zhuo
Attendant	Attendant to Dong Zhuo
Extra	Wu Zilan, Defender-in-Chief
Attendant	Attendant to Wu Zilan
Male lead	Wang Yun, Minister of Instruction
Li Ru	Li Ru, adopted son of Dong Zhuo
Li Su	Li Su, adopted son of Dong Zhuo, general
Zhang Qian	Zhang Qian, household attendant to Dong Zhuo
Extra	Great White, a Daoist deity
Extra	Cai Yong, Grand Academician
Houseboy	Wang Yun's houseboy
Female	Diaochan
Meixiang	Meixiang, Diaochan's maid
Clown	Ji Lü
Lü Bu	Lü Bu, adopted son of Dong Zhuo, commanding general
Soldiers	Accompanying Lü Bu
Servants	Wang Yun's servants
Attendant	Attendant to Dong Zhuo
Generals	Dong Zhuo's personal guard
Soldiers	Accompanying Li Su
Soldier	Wu Zilan's aide
Soldier	Member of Dong Zhuo's personal guard
Soldiers	Part of the emperor's guard

The Northern Drama

In the Hall of Brocade Clouds:
The Beauty and the Story of the Interlocking Rings

Act 1

OPENING MALE, CLOWN, *costumed as* DONG ZHUO, *enters, leading* ATTENDANT, *and speaks:*

> My office sealed with the Nine Bestowals,[5] my position among the Three
> Dukes,[6]
> When running I catch up with fleeing horses in a display of heroism.
> All the officials, civil or military, are frightened when they hear of me,
> My own desire is to not grow old in the Han court.[7]

I am Dong Zhuo, known as Zhongying, and am a man from Lintao in Longxi.[8] From youth I have owed my success to the great general He Jin, who recommended me to court where I have held several positions. I am now the Grand Preceptor and have been awarded the Nine Bestowals. *These nine bestowals are:*[9] (1) horses and carts, (2) a full set of gowns, (3) musical instruments, (4) vermilion gates, (5) inset steps,[10] (6) a bodyguard, (7) axes and broadaxes, (8) bows

---

5. Originally the "nine bestowals" were provided by the Han emperors as the highest favor granted to an official. By the post-Han, however, the use of the term was changed because of Wang Mang's receiving of the nine bestowals as a prelude to usurping the Han dynasty. After the Wei era, the term came to describe the as-yet-unrevealed desires of a high minister to seize power and initiate a new dynasty.

6. The three highest positions in the Han bureaucracy.

7. By deposing the Han and establishing his own dynasty.

8. In modern Gansu.

9. The text has handwritten emendations by Zhao Qimei, which we are entering in the translation in italic script. These notes give supplementary text and emendations not found in the *Selection of Yuan Plays* version, and are probably based on another edition (most likely the palace manuscript, which also provided the list of costume items required for each actor in each act, copied by Zhao at the end of the play).

10. These were cut into the foundation and therefore under the eaves of halls to allow venerable ministers to enter and exit while being protected from the elements.

and arrows, and (9) sweet sacrificial wine. When I go out, a personal guard surrounds me; when I come back, they clear the road in front.[11] For proclamations, I send out imperial edicts; for sending down commands, I call them imperial orders; for discussions, I call them imperial proclamations; and for reports, I call them imperial rescripts.[12] Each time I go into court I allow this precious sword at my waist to show four fingers of its blade, making all the officials civil and military blanch with fear. *I am known throughout the world and my power is felt to the far reaches. Under my command now are* Lü Bu and Li Su and the eight strong generals—all perfect in insight and bravery—as well as hundreds of thousands of unsurpassed crack troops. Because of this I am known throughout the world and my power is felt to the far reaches. As I see it, there's only that old miscreant, Wang Yun, who's set against me with his whole heart. No matter what he does—walk, stop, sit, or lie down—I have someone follow him, lest he come up with some other evil idea. I was sitting in the Prime Minister's office doing nothing today when a servant came to tell me that when he left court that old miscreant had gone out of the palace gate and went straightaway to Wu Zilan's house instead of going home. Afraid they might be cooking up some plan, I'd best go straight to Wu Zilan's house myself and put an end to that old miscreant's plan.

Exits.

EXTRA, *costumed as* WU ZILAN, *enters, leading an* ATTENDANT, *and speaks:* This old man before you is named Defender-in-Chief Wu Zilan. Right now the Sage of the Han is on the throne, but that Dong Zhuo has usurped his power and suppresses all the court officials and squelches the liege lords. All of the officials tremble in fear and dare not look him straight in the eye. Alas, because of this the Sage is anxious and depressed. It is truly said, "The ruler's anxiety is the shame of the minister; if you do not share the anxieties of your ruler, how can you complete the way of the minister or son?" I want to get rid of the evil, eliminate the violent, and exterminate those treacherous braves. But that household slave of his, Lü Bu, is more heroic and brave than anyone else. I am thinking that this needs the Minister of Instruction, Wang Yun, who is full of plans and strategies and is someone I can work with. I've asked him to come and discuss this with me. I sent someone to invite him earlier, but it doesn't appear he is here yet. Servants, keep watch at the door, and if Minister Wang arrives, report to me. ATTENDANT *speaks:* Understood. MALE LEAD, *costumed as* WANG YUN, *enters and speaks:* I am Wang Yun. From the time that I passed the

---

11. Usually done only for emperors.
12. That is, he sends these out under the emperor's name. He is the real power.

Advanced Scholar examination I have served in several positions.[13] I am thankful for the favor and love of the Sage, who has awarded me the rank of Minister of Instruction. But that Dong Zhuo is manipulating authority, putting the house of Han in peril; all of the officials are terrified and in awe and dare not ask "Who?" or "Why?" Defender-in-Chief Wu Zilan sent a servant to summon me. I don't know why, but I'd better go. I am ashamed to be so old and useless, eating off my salary and giving nothing in return!

(XIANLÜ MODE: *Dian jiangchun*)
   At the present I
Pass my springs and autumns for nothing,
Force myself to endure the nights and days,
And linger here to no avail.
   For nothing I enjoy
Fat horses and light sables.
   But in these days
Anxiety and worry have burdened me until I'm worn and thin.

(*Hunjiang long*)
   It's all because our
Universe of the Han
   Makes my
Two thin brows lock away the sorrows of the dynasty.
   It's just like
An opening blossom encountering rain,
   That never sees
The autumn leaves drop to depart forever.
   It's just like
Looking casually at flying floss tossed on the river's dike
   Uselessly turn into
Floating duckweed on flowing water—when will it end?
   I have asked for this
Important position in the imperial house, but it's hard to enjoy,
   And if for one morning
I can employ a plan to settle this state,
   I will have earned
A name to endure for a ten thousand epochs.

---

13. This is completely anachronistic. There were no Advanced Scholar examinations in the late Han dynasty. These examinations, first established in the Tang, were the prerequisite for joining the civil bureaucracy.

Speaks: I've reached his gate. Servant! Report that I am here. ATTENDANT *acts out reporting.* WU ZILAN *speaks:* Tell him he is welcome. ATTENDANT *speaks:* Please go in. *Act out greeting each other.* MALE LEAD *speaks:* Defender-in-Chief, you have asked me over. What do you want to discuss? WU ZILAN *speaks:* I have asked you, Minister of Instruction, for the express purpose of discussing something I've been thinking about: four hundred years or more have passed from the time that Chu and Han were locked in struggle and our state was established. It has not been easy for it to last this long, and now Dong Zhuo monopolizes all authority and bullies and suppresses all of the officials at court. There's no plan we can use yet. I have asked you, sir, to discuss how we can come up with a plan. What do you think? [MALE LEAD *sings:*]

> (*You hulu*)
>> Consider
> Chu and Han contested in battle, first spring then autumn,
> Lord and minister were all full of wise plans.
>> Who doesn't know
> To divide the empire in the middle they pointed to Goose
>> Channel?[14]

WU ZILAN *speaks:* If it weren't for those worthy officials and ministers who raised up the house of Han to run its course for four hundred years, it would be all over today! MALE LEAD *sings:*

>> We owe everything
> To the persuasive rhetoric of Zhang Liang of the Han,[15]
>> And we trusted to the end
> Marshal Han Xin's innate ability to grasp battlefield
>> circumstances.[16]
> Marshal Han was able to do battle with the enemy,
> Zhang Liang was able to perfect plots and plans:
>> Those two
> Were such help that all succeeding generations of the Han found
>> success;
>> Truly—
> They shared and thereby destroyed the worries of their emperor.

---

14. Goose Channel (Honggou) was a waterway in Anhui that was agreed to be the boundary between Han and Chu. The term is still used today to mean a line, a gap, or a gulf that divides two parties.

15. Literally, "a mouth that discusses heaven and talks about earth" (*shuotian tandi kou*).

16. Literally, "a hand that can grab fog and take hold of clouds" (*wowu nayun shou*).

WU ZILAN *speaks:* Now Dong Zhuo monopolizes authority. I think about when the Sage sent out his edict—the liege lords from every place controlled an army of a million men yet never attained the smallest success. How can we ever root out this kind of violent power? [MALE LEAD *sings:*]

> (*Tianxia le*)
>> I just fear this:
> "Problems will come from sticking your nose in where it does not
>> belong,"[17]
>> Think of those eighteen circuits of
> Liege lords—
>> Just bringing it up
> Fills my face with shame.

WU ZILAN *speaks:* If it had not been for the fact that Liu, Guan, and Zhang had smashed Lü Bu once, how could all of the liege lords get to take their soldiers home? MALE LEAD *sings:*

>> Back then, I think,
> Tigerkeep Pass was hard to control.[18]
> And up to now that one with power, ever growing, cannot be
>> stopped.
>> For they are now used to that guy's
> Unrestrained freedom and total control.

WU ZILAN *speaks:* Dong Zhuo is in complete control now. I have received the Sage's order to summon you here to discuss coming up with a plan by some means to capture Dong Zhuo. MALE LEAD *speaks:* Defender-in-Chief, that treacherous official Dong Zhuo is a man of much power and authority. What ability do I have? Summon all of the officials to discuss how we might get rid of him together? WU ZILAN *speaks:* In that case, what shall we do? Let's just discuss this in detail. Servant, stand guard at the door and if anyone comes along, inform me. ATTENDANT *speaks:* Understood. CLOWN, *costumed as* DONG ZHUO, *makes a sudden entrance and speaks:* I am Dong Zhuo. I've come directly to Wu Zilan's house today to catch this old devil. Servant! Report that Grand Preceptor Dong is at the gate. ATTENDANT *speaks:* Understood. *Acts out reporting:* Master, Grand Preceptor Dong is here. WU ZILAN *speaks:* The Grand Preceptor is here! What shall we do? Tell him to come in. ATTENDANT *speaks:* Understood. Please come in. DONG ZHUO *acts out greeting them and speaks:* Wang Yun,

---

17. Literally, "forcing oneself to stick out one's head" (*qiang chutou*).

18. I.e., because each of the liege lords held different aspirations and could not agree to advance; so they never advanced and, in the end, wound up fighting each other.

what have all of you been discussing here? WU ZILAN *speaks:* I never said anything! DONG ZHUO *speaks:* Wang Yun—could it be that you are discussing ways to bring me some harm? MALE LEAD *speaks:* We had no such idea, Grand Preceptor.

> (*Houting hua*)
>> Not at all; we just want to allow you,
> Grand Preceptor Dong, to control the great authority.

DONG ZHUO *speaks:* And when I have this great authority, what office shall Lü Bu have?

> And Lü Bu, the Marquis of Wen, will be head of all generals.
> Right now we are all engaged in a discussion . . .

DONG ZHUO *speaks:* And what are you discussing? [MALE LEAD *sings:*]

> We wanted to pick out a propitious day.

DONG ZHUO *laughs and speaks:* Ha ha ha. What you are saying precisely matches my heart. [MALE LEAD *sings:*]

>> I see that we
> Are on the same page.

DONG ZHUO *speaks:* If I carry off that grand affair,[19] just say what you want and I will act accordingly. [MALE LEAD *sings:*]

>> What he said was,
> "I will go by what you propose."
>> But I fear,
> In his heart he will not be so easily swept along.[20]

DONG ZHUO *speaks:* Wu Zilan, let me ask you, from ancient times to the present, has there ever been anyone who has humbly yielded the throne? WU ZILAN *speaks:* Grand Preceptor Dong, from the past we know that Yao, Shun, Yu, and Tang[21] all possessed the way and yielded the throne. There is an ancient saying, "If one house is benevolent, the whole state will give rise to benevolence; if one house yields, the whole state will yield." DONG ZHUO *speaks:* Wang Yun, since

---

19. The grand affair refers to his investiture as emperor.
20. These last two lines are spoken in an aside, here signaled by a switch momentarily to a third person pronoun.
21. Yao ceded the throne to Shun, and Shun ceded the throne to Yu, who established the Xia dynasty and was succeeded by his son. Tang founded the Shang dynasty.

there is going to be a ceding of the throne, and since so many officials are here, it is better to act quickly and not delay. MALE LEAD *speaks:* Grand Preceptor, the common saying goes, "Things done at ease will be as perfect as you please."

> (*Nezha ling*)
>> If you
>
> Know proper moral standards and effect just laws,
> You can follow old precedents and endure a long time.
> Bring security to the black-haired masses, hold to a true heart—
> Actualize sincerity and hold firm to it,
> Put the mainstays of ethics in order, establish a true self,
> Be a bit more modest, and don't curse at others.

DONG ZHUO *speaks:* If I carry off this grand affair, I will act like I want and do what I want. If anyone dares cross me, I'll let him see fresh blood flow in front of his eyes. [MALE LEAD *sings:*]

> If one is dignified in bearing one's whole life,
> There will be nothing left undone,
> But you have to separate the good and evil, the strong and weak.

DONG ZHUO *speaks:* In my opinion, only I am revered both inside the court and out. Should anyone confront me, I'll bring him disaster and misfortune in a snap, his life and his family will be hard to protect, and none of the nine mourning grades of his family shall be left.[22] Wang Yun, since there is going to be a ceding of the throne, how will you persuade your many officials here? It's better to act quickly and not delay. [MALE LEAD *sings:*]

> (*Que ta zhi*)
>> With all your heart
>
> You strive to take this on—
> Open wide your eyes:
>> How can you not see
>
> The heavenly signs and the four stars of Dipper's bowl?[23]
> Good luck is flowing all around them.

---

22. There are several theories of what these nine relations or nine grades of mourning were. One was that it was the patrilineal clan four generations before ego and four generations after ego; another was that it was four generations of the patrilineal clan, three generations of the matrilineal, and two generations of the wife's clan. The Ming codified the punishment as four generations before and after ego, and laterally to include brothers, cousins, and second cousins.

23. This constellation, composed of the four stars of the Dipper's bowl, is used as a metaphor for power, authority, or the imperial throne itself.

DONG ZHUO *speaks:* I will rely on those under my command: Lü Bu, Li Su, Lu Ru, those eight strong generals, and hundreds of thousands of soldiers. When I do act, it will be as easy as turning over your hand. [MALE LEAD *sings:*]

> I don't want
> Your bravado nature to put your eccentricities on display or expose
>   yourself to ridicule,
> Your brutal and stupid heart to hack away at political strategy.[24]

DONG ZHUO *speaks:* All you officials need to do is to support me, nothing else. [MALE LEAD *sings:*]

> (*Jisheng cao*)
> That will turn auspicious omens to disaster,
> Change grace and glory into vengeance.
> The true Way is put into effect by responding to Heaven's aid with
>   moral governance,
> The mandate's authenticity awaits a single morn's proper moment.
> If the position is venerated, then ten thousand miles of rivers and
>   mountains are resplendent.[25]

DONG ZHUO *speaks:* How do you think I should carry this out? [MALE LEAD *sings:*]

> We just want you
> To act in accord with the harmony of people: "a musk that has a
>   natural odor";[26]
> We don't want you
> To go against the mind of Heaven—"Without its blessing, who can
>   accomplish it?"[27]

DONG ZHUO *speaks:* Brother, if all of you officials can support me and support my children, I will handsomely reward everyone with rank and money. MALE LEAD *speaks:* Grand Preceptor, give us three or four days; we will pick out a propitious day and the host of high officials will come to welcome you. DONG ZHUO *speaks:* Since we've settled this, once you have decided a time, come and tell me. I am going back to my residence now. There's no need to go over everything in excruciating detail. "If it is settled with a single word, cling to him for

---

24. These lines are clearly spoken in an aside.
25. "Rivers and mountains" is a metonymy for the state.
26. I.e., it is naturally attractive; it does not need a wind to carry it to others' noses.
27. No one wins against the will of Heaven.

ever; if there be a disagreement of a single word, behead him with your sword." You two think it over carefully, but don't delay.

Exits.

WU ZILAN *speaks:* Dong Zhuo is gone. This guy lacks all decency! With all his heart he wants to wrest away the empire of the house of Han. Minister, what are we going to do about this? [MALE LEAD *sings:*]

> (*Jinzhan'er*)
> Originally I
> Was just a single layer of sorrow,
> But now it's become
> A double layer of sorrow!
> Only now do I believe
> "Those who understand the ways of the world are slow to open their
> mouths!"

WU ZILAN *speaks:* Minister, how can we set a plan to capture this miscreant so that we can secure the rivers and mountains of the Han? [MALE LEAD *sings:*]

> You want me
> To painstakingly search through all my secret plans and divine
> strategies—
> Am I knowledgeable enough
> To become a Jiang Lü Wang and attack the state of Zhou[28]
> Or a Zhang Liang who could establish the fiery Liu's rise?[29]

WU ZILAN *speaks:* Minister, I believe you are the equal of former worthies in employing plots and laying out snares. [MALE LEAD *sings:*]

> How can we
> Root out Preceptor Dong?
> By what method
> Shall we deal with Lü, the Marquis of Wen?

WU ZILAN *speaks:* In this we must rely completely on the plan you choose. MALE LEAD *speaks:* Rest easy.

> (*Coda*)
> To get control of this episode of difficult turmoil
> I've brought some idle torture on myself—

---

28. Zhou, the evil last ruler of the Shang dynasty.

29. The Han dynasty, founded by Liu Bang, was associated with the phase of fire in the theory of the Five Phases.

We can't avoid
Three or four nights of "haggard face and hoary head."[30]

WU ZILAN *speaks:* When will our vexation ever cease? [MALE LEAD *sings:*]

Only now do
I believe "A human life is a hundred years of worry."
What I fear is that
I will have to search throughout the four great areas of the
heartland.[31]
To find a clever plan to put in action,
I will search in my own heart—
These rivers and mountains that extend for tens of thousands of
miles will always be sorrow.

WU ZILAN *speaks:* Minister, you must plan this early, and you must get it right!
[MALE LEAD *sings:*]

Well then, let
That raven fly and the hare run,[32]
For I have seen
This contest of dragons and battle of tigers:[33]
It has taken
A heavy draw-weight bow and dragged it across
my
heart.[34]

[*Exits.*]

WU ZILAN *speaks:* Once he leaves here he'll employ a trick to capture Dong
Zhuo and protect the empire of the house of Han. I'll now go secretly to reply
to the Sage and be done with it. *Recites in verse:*

---

30. Deep worry.

31. The term here (*si da shenzhou*) in Buddhism means the four great worlds that make up
the world of being. In more common parlance in Chinese, it means the four of the nine traditional areas (*jiuzhou*) that make up the Chinese world that comprise the Central Plain, the heartland of Chinese civilization.

32. The sun is inhabited by a three-legged metal raven; the moon is the home of a jade hare
that is pounding out the medicine of immortality.

33. Usually, the ruler is a dragon and his generals and ministers are tigers. Here the phrase is
used figuratively to mean "everyone contesting for control of the empire."

34. The term *mengong* originally meant a bow with a heavy draw-weight. It was used as a
metaphor for a problem that was difficult to solve. In chess, *mengong'er* is a term that means to
put someone in an intolerable position.

A virile presence so strong and powerful, displaying proud aspiration,
Dong Zhuo's power and authority cannot be withstood;
Wang Yun, employing his plots and using his ploys,
Will raise up the house of Han with all his heart.

Exits.

[Act 2]

DONG ZHUO *enters with* LI RU, LI SU, ZHANG QIAN, *and speaks:*

My power and might are imposing; my authority suffuses heaven;
The jade steps and vermilion gate are linked by brocade.
Rewards and punishments stem from me alone,
And all day long songs and ditties delight in harvest and crops.

I am Dong Zhuo. Damn, Wang Yun and the other assembled officials are so disrespectful. They said they would discuss the grand affair and then tell me. How come I haven't seen him yet? Servant, keep watch at the gate, and if Wang Yun and the other officials come, let me know. ZHANG QIAN *speaks:* Understood. EXTRA, *costumed as* [SPIRIT OF] GREAT WHITE,[35] *enters and speaks:* Laymen of the world, follow me and leave your homes, and I'll make each and every one become a transcendent, and all of you, person by person, come to know the way! This humble Daoist is Great White Star from the upper realm. Born to reside in the territory of metal, I issue forth from the western quadrant. I make no mistakes when I observe the good and bad among the world of men and I discriminate high and low, honor and riches, noble and base. I was coming back from a feast in heaven, and I looked down and saw Dong Zhuo manipulating power in the lower realm as a way to scheme for the empire of the Han house. The Upper Welkin[36] was exercised in its anger, and all of the spirits were unhappy, so they sent me down to convert this person by a hint, and see if he can get the message. Here's Dong Zhuo's house. *Acts out weeping three times, laughing three times, and speaks:* Grand Preceptor Dong, you will soon die! *Acts out weeping and laughing.* ZHANG QIAN *acts out reporting in a panic and speaks:* I

---

35. In the Five Phases theory, the west is coordinated with the element of metal, the season of fall, with death, destruction, and Venus, which is known in Chinese as "Great White" (*taibai*). It was considered the "essence of metal in the western quadrant" (*xifang jin zhi jing*), the son of the White Emperor (*baidi zhi zi*), and a Daoist god. In popular literature of late imperial China, Great White is a divinity who is often sent down to earth by the Jade Emperor in order to help deserving persons. On earth, he often will appear in the guise of an elderly Daoist priest. Here he appears in the guise of the holy fool well known from deliverance plays.

36. Where Buddhist and Daoist immortals dwell.

want to report to the Grand Preceptor that there is a crazy priest at the door who looked inside the gates of the residence and laughed three times then wept three times, so I've come to report it to you. DONG ZHUO *speaks:* This priest has no decency at all! Let me go out and take a look myself. *Acts out looking.* GREAT WHITE *speaks:* Dong Zhuo, you will die this year, this month, this day, this hour! Ha ha ha! DONG ZHUO *speaks:* This is truly some crazed Buddhist monk or lunatic Daoist priest! Soldiers, arrest him! ZHANG QIAN *acts out being unable to catch him.* DONG ZHUO *speaks:* I'll catch this guy myself! GREAT WHITE *acts out taking a cloth and beating him, and exits.* DONG ZHUO *acts out avoiding the blows and speaks:*[37] Aiya! He beat the hell out of me! How did he disappear? What was it he beat me with? So it's just a piece of cloth, with two mouths, one on each end,[38] and two lines of writing in the center, which read, "A thousand miles of grass oh green, so green, / Prognostication says that ten will live forever."[39] Li Ru, can you figure it out? LI RU *speaks:* Father, your son cannot figure it out.[40] DONG ZHUO *speaks:* What to do now? Who can understand its meaning? LI RU *speaks:* Father! Only Academician Cai Yong can comprehend it. DONG ZHUO *speaks:* You are right. Have someone go and fetch Cai Yong for me. LI RU *speaks:* Academician Cai, the Grand Preceptor is calling for you.

EXTRA, *costumed as* CAI YONG, *enters and speaks:*

> In the Pavilion of Silk and Ribbon the documents are silent,
> In the Tower of Bell and Drum the clepsydra is endless.
> Sitting alone in semi-darkness—who is my companion?
> Purple crepe myrtle flowers face the man clad in purple.[41]

---

37. Zhao Qimei has inserted these two stage directions.

38. The cloth that has struck him has two mouths (口口), which, rearranged, make the character *lü* (呂), the surname of his adopted son, Lü Bu; the son's given name is the same word as "cloth," so the implication of this phrase is that "Lü Bu beat the hell out him," foretelling what will happen.

39. The first three characters of line one are thousand (*qian* 千), mile (*li* 里), and grass (*cao* 草). Thousand and mile combine to make the character *zhong* (重), which are then combined with the grass radical (艹) to render Dong Zhuo's surname, Dong (董). Likewise the first three characters of line two—prognostication (*bu* 卜), says (*yue* 曰), and ten (*shi* 十)—are combined to create the character for Dong Zhuo's personal name, Zhuo (卓). Thus the lines can be read as, "Dong will always remain alive, Zhuo will live forever."

40. This story may ultimately derive from an anecdote in the *Documents of the Later Han*, related in Dong Zhuo's biography: "At that time Wang Yun, together with Lü Bu and Sun Rui, plotted to kill Zhuo. Someone wrote the character 'Lü' on a piece of cloth and wore it on his back as he went through the market, singing 'O Bu.' Someone reported it to Zhuo, but he did not get its meaning." The word for "back" (*bei*) also means "to rebel," so a "cloth on the back" (*bei bu*) is homophonous with "rebelling Lü Bu."

41. This is a poem by the Tang dynasty poet Bai Juyi (772–846), written in the summer of 821 when he was serving in the capital Chang'an as Director of the Bureau of Receptions and

This minor official is Cai Yong, also known as Bojie, and my hereditary home is Chenliu.[42] I now hold the post of Academician. I was just sitting at ease in my private home when the Grand Preceptor summoned me. I don't know for what reason, but I'd better go. Here I am, there already. Zhang Qian, go and report that Cai Yong has arrived. [ZHANG QIAN] *acts out reporting.* DONG ZHUO *speaks:* Tell him to come in. ZHANG QIAN *speaks:* Understood. Please come in. CAI YONG *acts out greeting and speaks:* Grand Preceptor, for what reason did you summon me? DONG ZHUO *speaks:* Cai Yong, I was just sitting quietly in my residence when a crazed priest looked inside my door and wept three times, then laughed three times. I went out to take a look at him, and he cursed me, saying I would die. I punched him once, but he struck me with something that he was carrying. I ordered people to catch him but he had already disappeared in a shaft of golden light on a fragrant breeze. I don't understand what this thing means, so I've called you to take a look. CAI YONG *speaks:*[43] If that's it, let me have a look. So it's a piece of cloth, ten feet in length, with two lines written on it: "A thousand miles of grass oh green, so green, / Prognostication says that ten will live forever." There must be a hidden meaning in here. Underneath the character "thousand" is the character "mile" and on top of the character "thousand" is a grass radical. Isn't this the character Dong?[44] Under the character "prognostication" is the character "speak," and under "speak" is the character "ten." Isn't this the character Zhuo? So it conceals the name of Dong Zhuo. This piece of cloth is ten feet in length and has the character "mouth" on either end—if you put them together side by side, that doesn't make for any character, but the two characters one on top of another make for the character Lü. This conceals the name of Lü Bu.[45] *Acts out speaking in an aside:* This old miscreant will die by Lü Bu's hands in the future. I can only handle it this way. [*Turns back and speaks:*] Grand Preceptor, this piece of cloth has two lines of verse, "A thousand miles of grass oh green, so green, / Prognostication says that ten will live forever." Underneath the character "thousand" is the character "mile" and on top of the character "thousand" is a grass radical. Isn't this the character Dong?[46] Under the character "prognostication" is the character "speak," and under "speak" is the character "ten." Isn't this the character Zhuo? These lines conceal your

---

charged with the drafting of imperial proclamations. The Pavilion of Silk and Ribbon is the place where imperial edicts are drafted, from the following lines in the *Book of Rites* (*Liji*): "The king's words are like silk; they emerge like a ribbon."

42. Located just south of modern Kaifeng.

43. Here, he clearly speaks to himself.

44. The lines would be read vertically on the cloth.

45. The personal name of Lü Bu is written with the same character as the word for "cloth" (*bu*).

46. The lines would be read vertically on the cloth.

honorable taboo name.[47] This piece of cloth is ten feet in length and has the character "mouth" on either end, and when you fold them, doesn't it make the character Lü? This conceals the name of Lü Bu. Grand Preceptor, please accept my congratulations! Thanks to Lü Bu's heroic bravery, you will succeed in the grand affair! DONG ZHUO *speaks:* You've got it right, sir. If I am successful in carrying off this grand affair, the position of Prime Minister of the Left is yours to occupy. CAI YONG *speaks:* I'm just afraid you will forget, Preceptor. DONG ZHUO *speaks:* You are absolutely right. The common saying is, "Important people often forget things." You take this cloth with you, and if I complete this grand affair, bring it back out and this office of Prime Minister of the Left is yours. CAI YONG *speaks:* Many thanks, Grand Preceptor. I am leaving now. Here I go out the door. I don't dare linger any longer. I'm going secretly to Minister of Instruction Wang's residence to discuss this with him. Here I go.

Exits.

DONG ZHUO *speaks:* Cai Yong is gone. Well, this just tickles me to death! Having nothing else to do, I'll go into my private chambers and have some wine in celebration.

Exits with group.

MALE LEAD *enters and speaks:* I am Wang Yun. This morning an edict of the Sage ordered me to come up with a plan to arrest Dong Zhuo. But when I think about it, he has enormous authority and power, and relies on Lü Bu's power, so it is impossible to take him. I have no plot that will work. It's getting dark and I should close up my compound gate. Then I will sit down to see who may come. CAI YONG *enters and speaks:* I am Cai Yong. It's already late. Here I am at the house of Minister Wang Yun. All around there is no one in sight, so I'll call out at the door. *Acts out calling out at the door.* MALE LEAD *speaks:* Who's calling at the door? CAI YONG *speaks:* It's me, Cai Yong. MALE LEAD *speaks:* Well, well, well! So it is the Academician. Please come in. *Acts out opening the door, acts out greeting, and speaks:* Why have you come, Academician?[48] CAI YONG *speaks:* Minister, I wouldn't have come if I didn't have something important. That miscreant minister Dong Zhuo was sitting at ease at his home when suddenly outside a mendicant priest looked inside the gates and laughed three times then wept three times. When Dong Zhuo asked him what he meant by that, that priest didn't answer him at all, so Dong Zhuo was enraged and or-

---

47. Taboo, because in normal course of conversation Chinese never use the given name of a person; in the hierarchical system of social and bureaucratic structure, the given name of a superior can never be used.

48. The text here writes *xuesheng* (student), which must be a mistake for *xueshi* (academician).

dered his people to grab him. That priest remained totally unperturbed, but got out something and hit Dong Zhuo with it. When Dong Zhuo panicked and leaned to one side to avoid the blow, that priest transformed into a shaft of golden light and disappeared. When Dong Zhuo picked up that thing to check it out, it turned out to be a piece of cloth, on which the following two lines of verse had been written, "A thousand miles of grass oh green, so green, / Prognostication says that ten will live forever." MALE LEAD *speaks:* Academician, what do these two lines mean? CAI YONG *speaks:* "A thousand miles of grass oh green, so green"—Minister, just give it some thought. If you add the character "mile" to the character "thousand" and put a grass-head on top, doesn't that make for the character Dong? "Prognostication says that ten will live forever." Add a character "says" to the character "prognostication" and add the character "ten" at the bottom: isn't that the character "Zhuo"? Isn't this the name "Dong Zhuo"? MALE LEAD *speaks:* But why this piece of cloth? CAI YONG *speaks:* How come it is not nine feet long or not eleven feet? It is exactly ten feet. This means that Dong Zhuo's number is fulfilled and that he will die at any time.[49] If you place the two "mouth" characters on the cloth on top of each other, it must be the character "Lü." So this makes for the two characters "Lü Bu." Minister, within a few days Dong Zhuo will die by the hand of Lü Bu. MALE LEAD *speaks:* You are mistaken. That slave Lü Bu is Dong Zhuo's adopted son—would he be willing to kill his father? CAI YONG *speaks:* What is Dong Zhuo compared to Ding Jianyang?[50] Sir, as Prime Minister, how can you stand beneath the one man, sit above the ten thousand, "mix perfect fixings in the tripod,"[51] "put yin and yang in proper order,"[52] and still not understand a trifling matter like this? I have little talent, but I want to offer up a plan. It consists of the five characters "A beauty and a plot of interlocking rings." It's already late though, and I must go home.

> This time around make every effort to work your schemes and plots
> To remove the wicked and depraved and restore the Han dynasty.

Exits.

---

49. I.e., it has reached ten of ten, ten being the ideal number of a virtual quota.

50. When Emperor Ling died in 189, He Jin tried to remove the powerful eunuchs at court. He summoned both Dong Zhuo and Ding Yuan (Ding Jianyang) to help him. He Jin was assassinated before Ding or Dong arrived in Luoyang. Ding Yuan had earlier been prefect of Bingzhou, where he took Lü Bu under his wing. He essentially became an adoptive father for the young military hero. Later, Lü Bu was seduced by gifts and promises of power to join Dong Zhuo. In doing so he beheaded Ding Yuan.

51. "You govern by making everything work in harmony," a metaphor for a wise minister.

52. Regulate government by making sure everything works by abiding by the synchronic tie between cosmic forces and human affairs; to aid the emperor in governing.

MALE LEAD *speaks:* The Academician is gone. He did have a good point. He's left me with a something I can't even guess at. This just drives me mad!

(NANLÜ MODE: *Yizhi hua*)
> In this moment of pressure,
> Nothing goes according to my wishes:
> I cannot redeem the grace of our sovereign,
> I cannot annihilate that Grand Preceptor Dong,
> I cannot establish the mountains and rivers of the Han.
> It drives crazy
> The horse of my will, the monkey of my mind,
> And in vain sends me
> Through a hundred different plots—
> All, alas, hard to unravel at a moment's notice.
> It has made me so anxious that my lungs and bowels are in up-
> roarious battle
> And made me so sad that furrows crisscross my brow.

MALE LEAD *speaks:*[53] With these kinds of wolves and jackals in power, will I ever be able to pacify them?

(*Liangzhou*)
> What I'm anxious about is that
> Associating with such violent villains
> is like
> harming yourself with poisonous snakes;
> What I sorrow over is that
> Being next to these cunning braves
> is like
> sleeping next to a tiger.
> I cannot begrudge
> Those flying and tumbling human affairs, a thousand transforma-
> tions of clouds—
> Or that in a moment's time
> A ruddy face is easily transformed,
> Or more so, that
> A hoary head becomes our curse.
> It irritates me so much
> I am struck dumb—

---

53. To this point, Zhao Qimei has put parentheses around stage directions. Like the punctuation he sometimes puts in the arias, they are part of the practice of reading, and not of collation, hence they will not appear in our translation.

Come to think of it—
Just as if I had lost my senses.
A heavy draw-weight bow
          lies
                    simmering and bubbling in my heart,
          Just as if
A knife tip
          were
                    twisting and turning in my belly.
          Because of this Grand Preceptor Dong,
And this utterly evil threesome of fathers and sons,
          How can Wang Yun of the Han
Find full measure to keep loyalty and sincerity whole?
          When this Marquis Lü of Wen,
Filled with pride, can be both general and minister?
          Here have I
Laid plaint to Heaven that is so distant;
But the Lord of Heaven is not inclined to grant us ease.
          If you could only
Find a scheme that would get me what I desire,
          I would rely on
My concentrated vermilion heart,
          that is as
                    solid as iron or stone,
          But for now
I cannot sleep by day or night.

MALE LEAD *speaks:* My heart and mind are troubled and tired. I'll go into the
rear garden for a while to wile away some time. Here I am at the pavilion in the
rear flower garden. Houseboy, bring me my zither. HOUSEBOY *enters, acts out
handing him the zither, and speaks:* Here is the zither. MALE LEAD *acts out strok-
ing the zither and speaks:* This old man laments the house of Han about to collapse. Let me play my zither by moonlight, and sing a tune. *The song says:*

The house of Han is about to collapse and traitors rise up;
Dong Zhuo monopolizes power; the liege lords lie low.
He depends on Lü Bu to rob us of our house and state
While Emperor Xian is weak and has no one upon which to rely.
I am advanced in years and am incapable of action;
In the wind I voice my lament, searching for a far-reaching strategy;
By moonlight I strum the zither, seeking an excellent plot.
After more than four hundred years all depends on me;

After twenty-four emperors we have reached this day!
When will we restore the house of Han once again?
When will we annihilate the miscreants once again?
I ask Heaven to slaughter that dragon—
Let my hand grasp the curved rainbow!
May the sun and the moon in the sky be polished once again—
When will they shine again on the ten thousand miles of the
cosmos?

FEMALE, *costumed as* DIAOCHAN, *enters, leading* MEIXIANG, *and speaks:*

My frowning eyebrows knit spring hills in an artful manner;
My heavily powdered cheeks set off my ruby lips.
All because of this charming face of mine,
I was inducted into the imperial palace to serve His Majesty.

I am Diaochan. After my man Lü Bu left me, I have no idea where he went. I never thought I'd wind up here.[54] Now I have led Meixiang out into the rear garden to burn incense. Here we go. MEIXIANG *speaks:* Sister, move it! MALE LEAD *acts out rising hastily.*

(Gewei)
I would have said that,
Rustling and swooshing, a bird going to roost was slipping
through
the flower's shadows,
But it turned out to be
A charming and winsome beauty gliding along the bamboo path.
Let her
Tread over this jade dew and green moss.

MEIXIANG *speaks:* Sister, this side of the peony garden is fine. [MALE LEAD *sings:*]

I will hide behind this
Taihu rock,[55]
While she walks over there by
The peony patch.

FEMALE *acts out sighing.* [MALE LEAD *sings:*]

---

54. The status of Diaochan in the household of Wang Yun is never made clear. Although she is treated like a daughter and addresses Wang Yun as "father," she probably was acquired by Wang Yun as an entertainer and a concubine.
55. Rocks with large holes in them, often used for decoration in gardens.

I see her
Seek support or her hand against the lilac tree and heave a sigh.

FEMALE *speaks:* Meixiang, bring the incense here. MEIXIANG *speaks:* Understood. I will bring the incense and candles over. Sister, aren't these the incense and candles? Sister, please raise the incense. FEMALE *speaks:*

> Pond's bank keeps apart double-stemmed lotuses;
> Pair after pair have been separated for over a year.
> For two single winged birds to fly alone is no easy task,[56]
> With this one stick of pure incense, I pray to Heaven.

I, Diaochan, was Lü Bu's wife from my youngest years. Since I was separated from my husband at Lintao Prefecture, I have wandered to Minister Wang's residence, where I have had the fortune of being treated like his own daughter. Unfortunately, I do not know where Lü Bu is. Now that evening has fallen, I will burn this stick of nighttime incense in the rear garden and pray to Heaven. I want us—husband and wife—to be whole again and together soon.

> Willow shadows and flowers' shade—the moon shifts its palace,
> The censer beast's incense breath is dispersed by the wind;
> So many heartbreaking feelings in my heart,
> Are expressed to the full in these two deep, deep bows.

MEIXIANG *speaks:* I'll burn another stick on your behalf, sister. Heaven, I pray that sister and her husband will be reunited as soon as possible. People all say, "Among men it's Lü Bu; among women, Diaochan." They rightly make a fine couple. If they can be a pair soon again, let them also take Meixiang along.[57] [MALE LEAD *sings:*]

> (*Sikuai yu*)
> I only thought she
> Was suffering some illness,
> But all the time she was
> Overcome by "boudoir resentment."[58]

---

56. "Single winged bird" is our translation for the *jian*, a bird with one wing and one eye, which must join with its opposite in order to fly. An inseparable pair, they represent a husband and wife making their journey through life together.

57. This last phrase, "take Meixiang along" (as a concubine), is a nearly verbatim quote of Hongniang (Crimson) in the famous scene in the *Story of the Western Wing* in which Yingying (Oriole) prays in the rear garden. This scene, generally, seems indebted to the *Story of the Western Wing*. See West and Idema 1995, pp. 81–83, 209–16.

58. Lovesickness.

Now I admit,
"Desire for sex has always been as great as heaven!"

FEMALE *acts out weeping.* [MALE LEAD *sings:*]

Just look at
The tear tracks dissolving the ruined makeup on her cheeks.
How could I
Rule the family and rule the state like that,[59]
Respect the foolish, not respect the wise,
Look to the past, and not look to the future?

MALE LEAD *speaks:* Diaochan, what are you doing there? Do you dare to be so bold as this?[60] MEIXIANG *speaks:* It's all over! Father has heard everything. FEMALE *speaks:* Father, I never did anything; I just came to burn some incense because I am not feeling well. MALE LEAD *speaks:* Silence!

(*Ma yulang*)
I don't want you to
Change your seductive and clever words according to the occasion!
Just a moment ago you
Burned incense and prayed to blue Heaven,
There, you
Sincerely and reverently personally professed an oath.
Because your
Heart was devout as this,
Your intent so firm,
Your
Body knew no exhaustion!

FEMALE *speaks:* Your child had no other oath. Seeing it was such a fine night, my whole intent was to burn incense to celebrate the moon. I never said anything wrong! [MALE LEAD *sings:*]

(*Gan huang'en*)
No, you said you wanted
To tie the marriage knot once again and
Put the silken strings in order once more.
After being scattered

---

59. As head of the household he has a duty to protect Diaochan; as a minister his duty is to sacrifice her for the higher good. Also, as Diaochan's owner he is not supposed to pimp her, but that is the expectation associated with his function.

60. That is, be out alone at this time of night and express her love for another man.

Like embroidered mandarin ducks—[61]
> You were kept apart in life
As a pair of flying swallows—
> After cutting down
The double-headed lotus,
> By which
Your longtime distress was stirred,
> You were then
Led around by your passion.

FEMALE *speaks:* I never did such a thing. [MALE LEAD *sings:*]

> What you said was,
"We encountered separation,
And another year has passed since we parted."

FEMALE *speaks:* Your child is living deeply hidden in painted pavilions and scented halls. Your child prayed to the moon and burned incense only to relieve my depression. That was truly the only reason. [MALE LEAD *sings:*]

> (*Caihua ge*)
> Because of
The injustice in your belly,
The words in your mouth
One after another pray, "Let us be reunited again!"

MEIXIANG *speaks:* My sister never said such a thing. If I am lying, then I'm as lonely and lost as a dog's bone. FEMALE *speaks:* Father, your daughter never said such a thing. [MALE LEAD *sings:*]

> You said,
"Lü Bu is the most handsome and elegant among men,
And Diaochan the most gorgeous in all the world."

FEMALE *speaks:* Father, your child really didn't say anything. MALE LEAD *speaks:* Diaochan, how could you say, "I pray that husband and wife will be reunited as soon as possible"? Which one is your husband? Tell me the complete truth. If you don't tell me, I will have someone get a thick cudgel ready. DIAOCHAN *kneels and speaks:* I beg you, father, still your anger and stop your rage, set aside for a moment your tiger and wolf-like might, and listen to your child slowly tell you all. I am not from here, but a person from Mu'er Village in Hanyan in Xinzhou,

---

61. Mandarin ducks were thought to mate for life, hence they are a symbol of a married couple.

the daughter of Ren Ang, and my child name was Hongchang. Because Emperor Ling of the Han made a thorough search for women for his seraglio, I was selected and sent to the palace, where I became Lady in Charge of Sable and Cicada Hats.[62] Emperor Ling gave me to Ding Jianyang, and in those days Lü Bu was Ding Jianyang's adopted son. Ding then arranged for me to marry Lü Bu. But during the chaos of the Yellow Turban revolt, we were separated from each other. I wound up in your house, father, where you treat me like your own daughter. This is truly an act of grace, and I am incapable of repaying it correctly. Yesterday mother and I were on the Loft for Watching the Mainstreet, and we saw the head of a ceremonial guard prance by, and it was surely Lü Bu on Red Hare, his steed. This is why I was burning incense and praying to heaven. MALE LEAD *speaks:* My child, is this the truth? FEMALE *speaks:* Father, I would not dare lie to you. MALE LEAD *speaks:* Hai! Academician Cai, you are truly a capable man. So this is the plot of the beautiful girl and the interlocking rings. I've got it!

> (*Xu hama*)
> This is truly a case of "the Way of Heaven
> Changes to accommodate man";
> My loyal heart
> Will completely succeed in its objective.
> In secret
> I am overcome with happiness—
> There's no need to search out another expedient plan,
> There's no need to calculate other exigent changes.
> I need not face off with him;
> I need not do battle with him.
> This
> Marvelous plan of mine will last forever;
> This
> Marvelous plan of mine will be long effective.
> The common folk will be released from their dire straits,
> And family and state can again be called good and virtuous.
> That rebellious official Dong Zhuo manipulates authority—
> His whole family will be exterminated, masters and slaves.
> Heaven and Earth protect and save the altars of the state,
> Let sun and moon brilliantly shine on our mountains and rivers.
> By an imperial edict of His Majesty, you can be sure,

62. These hats were made out of sable tails and cicada wings. Tortoiseshell cicadas, silver flowers, and sable tails were hung on a square frame made of woven rattan that was lacquered.

You definitely will eventually be reunited in wedlock.

    I worried so much, so much

My thinking was muddled, my feelings turned upside down,

And my heart seemed to be fried in seething oil.

    Who would have ever thought that right here, in my house, I would
      come up with this

Beautiful girl and the interlocking rings?

    When

Tomorrow we set a feast,

    In

That bevy of rouge and powder a battle campaign will be secretly
hidden away.

    When I

Execute my plans,

    How can he

Ever escape

This crafty plot?

    Diaochan, I'll have you two,

Husband and wife, be whole and complete,

And for all eternity reunited again.

MALE LEAD *speaks:* Child, if you can just do as your father tells you this one time, I will unite you and your husband. FEMALE *speaks:* Father, not one, but ten things would I do for you. I will comply, but what is it? MALE LEAD *speaks:* I was just thinking that back in the Spring and Autumn era, there was the wife of a certain Zhuan Zhu[63] who had the strength to help her husband and aid him in the completion of his great success, and the wife of Gongsun Sheng reacted to a dream and recommended her own husband, and he thus acquired the greatest luster of his age.[64] Once we have outwitted Dong Zhuo, I will see to it that you and your husband are reunited forever. Child, don't be concerned about a moment of "spring's defilement" from that fat Dong Zhuo but win for

---

63. Zhuan Zhu was an assassin of the fifth century BC. He is most famous for his trick of hiding a knife in the belly of a fish and using it to assassinate King Liao of Wu for Duke Guang. His biography can be found as "Chuan Chu," in Sima Qian 1994, pp. 320–21. According to the text of *Springs and Autumns of Wu and Yue*, Wu Zixu ran into Zhuan Zhu on the road just as Zhuan was about to fight someone he was angry at. Zhuan's wife called him back, and Wu questioned him about why a man so full of rage would simply break off his attack at a single sound of his wife's voice. Zhuan replied that he might submit to one person, but he would excel above ten thousand others. Wu Zixu then considered him worthy and recommended him to Duke Guang.

64. Gongsun Sheng is another name for Zhao Sheng, who is better known as Pingyuan jun. He was one of the most conspicuous statesmen of the Warring States period. We have failed to locate the anecdote of his wife recommending him to office in reaction to a dream.

yourself an eternal name, vaunted for rescuing your emperor. FEMALE *speaks:* Father, I will do as you say. What is it you want me to do? MALE LEAD *speaks:* As it is going to be this way, child, return to the rear chambers for the moment. FEMALE *speaks:* Understood. I have nothing else to do, so I will return to the rear chambers.

Exits.

MALE LEAD *speaks:* The sky is turning bright.

> "You can wear down iron shoes and still not find it,
> But when you get it, it comes without effort."

Ji Lü, where are you? CLOWN, *costumed as* JI LÜ, *enters and speaks:* I am no one else but the major domo of Minister Wang's house, Ji Lü. The minister has called me, and I don't know why, so I have to go and see the minister. Here I am, there already. *Acts out greeting him and speaks:* What use do you have for me, minister, now that you've summoned me? MALE LEAD *speaks:* Ji Lü, give orders to prepare a feast to lavish on our guest. Then go and ask Lü Bu to come. JI LÜ *speaks:* Understood. On the one hand I will give orders to prepare a feast, and at the behest of minister I will go and invite Lü Bu.

Exits.

MALE LEAD *speaks:* Ji Lü is on his way. I reckon that Lü Bu will certainly come to the feast. When he gets here, I have an idea of what to do. Let me go back to my private rooms.

Exits.

LÜ BU *enters, leading* SOLDIERS, *and speaks:*

> Awe inspiring my power and might, all due to my dashing courage,
> My sword reaches Buffalo and Dipper; my rage bursts through the skies.
> A real man, I exerted myself to fulfill my lifetime's ambition:
> My fame has spread through the world since the battle at Tigerkeep Pass.

I am Lü Bu, also known as Fengxian. I once drove the army of eighteen liege lords into retreat at Tigerkeep Pass; my might shook the empire and I was enfeoffed as the Marquis of Wen. I now am an aide in the house of Grand Preceptor Dong. I am his adopted son. I am just sitting at ease here in my private quarters, so let's see if anyone comes. JI LÜ *enters and speaks:* I am Ji Lü, and at the behest of the minister I've come to invite the Marquis Lü of Wen. Here I am already. Doorkeeper, please report that Ji Lü is here. SOLDIER *speaks:* Understood. *Acts out reporting.* LÜ BU *speaks:* Tell him to come in. SOLDIER *speaks:* Understood. Come inside. [Ji Lü] *acts out greeting.* LÜ BU *speaks:* Ji Lü, why did you come? JI LÜ *speaks:* I am bearing the command of Minister of Instruction

Wang, who respectfully invites the commander to have a few drinks. LÜ BU *speaks:* I have to say that this old fellow is not to be bested! Go ahead. I will come later. JI LÜ *speaks:* Understood. I will go back and report to Minister Wang about inviting Lü Bu, so here I go.

Exits.

LÜ BU *speaks:* Ji Lü has left. Servants, saddle up my horse, and I will go off to Wang Yun's residence for a banquet.

> Now His Excellency, full of kind feelings, has set out a feast,
> I cannot but go to the banquet and gulp down what is inside those
> chalcedony vessels.

All exit.

MALE LEAD *enters, leading the* CLOWN JI LÜ, SERVANTS, *and speaks:* I am Wang Yun. In the morning I had someone invite Lü Bu. By this time he should arrive. Servants! Keep watch outside the door and report to me when he is here. JI LÜ *speaks:* Understood. LÜ BU *enters and speaks:*

> My heroic reputation is the greatest throughout this age:
> My power subdued the liege lords as the empire has learned.

I am Lü Bu. Minister Wang invited me to a meeting, so I have to go. Here I am, there. Report that Lü Bu has arrived. JI LÜ *acts out reporting.* MALE LEAD *speaks:* Tell him to come inside. JI LÜ *speaks:* Understood. Please come in. MALE LEAD *acts out greeting and speaks:* If I knew earlier you were coming, I should have met you at a distance from the house. Please don't hold me at fault for this lack of proper reception. LÜ BU *speaks:* You are an elderly person, so why do you need to be so formal? MALE LEAD *speaks:* I wouldn't dare! Servants, bring out the table. SERVANTS *act out bringing the table and speak:* Understood. MALE LEAD *acts out offering wine and speaks:* Bring the wine. Marquis, please drink this cup to the full. LÜ BU *speaks:* What virtue or ability do I have that can make you, elderly minister, set out wine and spread a banquet? How could I be worthy of this? [MALE LEAD *sings:*]

> (*Muyang guan*)
>> When I consider
> How insignificant my office is,
> How shallow my talents and arts,
> How do I earn the visit of "A man of rank coming to my feast?"[65]

---

65. From the phrase, "A stout man goes into battle: if he doesn't die, he is injured. A man of rank goes to a feast; if he is not drunk, he is full to the brim." Here, it is used to vaunt Lü Bu's martial skills, the unspoken half of the quote.

LÜ BU *speaks:* Old Minister, what was on your mind when you invited me?
[MALE LEAD *sings:*]

> I hope that the Marquis of Wen's
> Household will be given an escort of a thousand soldiers.
>> I hope that the Marquis of Wen's
> Status will be invested with tax rights to eight districts.
>> I hope that the Marquis of Wen
> Soon controls the Field Marshal's seal of office,
>> I hope that the Marquis of Wen
> Will soon be summoned by the emperor.
>> I hope for the Marquis of Wen
> That a black parasol will fly above his head.
>> I hope for the Marquis of Wen
> That vermilion robes will be aligned before his horse.[66]

LÜ BU *acts out laughing and speaks:* Minister, what virtue and ability do I have that you show me such kindness and set out this banquet? MALE LEAD *speaks:* Nothing in particular, but I'm afraid the Grand Preceptor is about to ascend the exalted position, and I am just hoping that the Marquis of Wen will then raise me, Wang Yun, to a high position. LÜ BU *speaks:* Minister, don't worry. If the Grand Preceptor carries off this grand affair in a few days, at the very least a post like Prime Minister of the Left is yours. MALE LEAD *acts out pouring him wine and speaks:* Thank you! Thank you! Please, Marquis, drink this cup to the full. LÜ BU *speaks:* This is too much wine too soon. Let me drink several cups at a leisurely rate. MALE LEAD *speaks:* It is well said, "If there is no music at a feast, then it does not become a happy affair." Servants, send my words to the rear chambers and please ask the young lady to come out. JI LÜ *speaks:* Understood. MALE LEAD *acts out rising.* FEMALE *acts out entering, leading* CLOWN, MEIXIANG, *and speaks:* I am Diaochan. My father summons me, so I have to go. Here I am, there already. *Acts out greeting and speaks:* Father, why did you call your daughter? MALE LEAD *speaks:* My child, Lü Bu is now out in the front hall, drunk. You should pretend that you don't recognize him. Give him a cup and then sing a song, and let's see what he says. FEMALE *speaks:* Understood. MALE LEAD, FEMALE *act out greeting* LÜ BU. MALE LEAD *speaks:* My daughter, greet him properly. FEMALE *acts out bowing and speaks:* My lord, myriad blessings! MALE LEAD *speaks:* My child, offer the Marquis of Wen a cup of wine. FEMALE *acts out offering the wine and speaks:* Bring the wine. MEIXIANG *speaks:* Here is the wine.

---

66. These lines represent carefully graded symbols of office, assigned through sumptuary rules to various high officials. Many of these are completely anachronistic for the period in which Lü Bu lived.

FEMALE *speaks:* Marquis, please drink this cup to the full. LÜ BU *acts out drinking the wine and speaks:* Minister, forgive me for my lack of manners, but that's enough wine. MALE LEAD *speaks:* Marquis, please relax, enjoy yourself, and drink. FEMALE *speaks:* Let me sing a song. FEMALE *sings:*

(SHUANGDIAO MODE: *Zhegui ling*)[67]
> Once long ago
In my early youth we were united as a phoenix couple,
> But because of our separation
We mandarin ducks were divided and scattered.
Halfway through
> we met
> > great danger,
And for three years we were unfortunately
Driven to two places far apart.
> I remember how in the beginning
Men and horses were in a panic;
Buckler and spear caused commotion,
> While now at present,
In years of great peace, the black-haired people are safe and
> prosperous.
> I kept on hoping for
A beautiful fulfillment as a pair once again,
So we could pay our thanks to that arching welkin.
> Now we have managed
Today to meet face to face;
> How could you
Forget your Hongchang?

LÜ BU *acts out recognizing her and speaks:* Isn't this Diaochan? How did she get here? MALE LEAD *speaks in an aside:* So her story was true. That guy has fallen for my plan!

(*Gewei*)[68]
> One of them
Transmits her feelings with her eyes
> And
> > covers her hibiscus face in embarrassment with her
> > handkerchief;

---

67. This is an inserted performance text (like zither lyrics, poems, etc.), and is not the beginning of a new suite.
68. The normal suite continues after the interlude.

> One of them
>
> Cannot sit still, and finds it hard to keep from picking at the tortoise-
> shell mat!
>
> I on my side
>
> Feign drunkenness, pretend to wash my hands, and take my time to
> return.

LÜ BU *speaks:* Old Minister, I am really feeling not well.[69] Please forgive me.
[MALE LEAD *sings:*]

> Please, general,
>
> Be at ease.
>
> What
>
> Mess is there to speak of?

(MALE LEAD *speaks:*) Marquis of Wen, please sit back down. I will take care of
this matter. *Sings:*

> I,
>
> While speaking,
>
> Will withdraw further
>
> and further
>
> away.

Exits unobtrusively.

LÜ BU *speaks:* The old minister has left. Diaochan! FEMALE *speaks:* Yes! LÜ BU
speaks: My wife, how did you come to be here? FEMALE *speaks:* I drifted to the
minister's residence after we were separated at Lintao. I never thought I'd have
to wait until today to see you. Fengxian, you have caused me so much pain.
FEMALE *acts out weeping.* LÜ BU *acts out weeping and speaks:* Diaochan, don't
make me pine so much it hurts. MALE LEAD *rushes on and speaks:* What are the
two of you talking about? LÜ BU *speaks:* Aiya, daddy has overheard us! The two
of us were not talking about anything specific. LÜ BU, FEMALE *act out kneeling.*
[MALE LEAD *sings:*]

> (*Ku huangtian*)
>
> My prying eyes have already discovered you.

LÜ BU *speaks:* We never said anything! [MALE LEAD *sings:*]

> You truly are
>
> Too willful because of love.

---

69. The *Selection of Yuan Plays* version of the play specifies here that Lü Bu vomits.

FEMALE *speaks:* Father, your child did not dare say anything! MALE LEAD *speaks:* Silence! (*Sings:*)

> You, base woman, have no dowry to offer!

LÜ BU *speaks:* She's innocent in this! MALE LEAD *sings:*

>> Silence!
>> You, a new bridegroom, want to save your money.[70]
>>> You
>> Look on me as if I were as insignificant as a blade of grass,
>>> Whereas I
>> Laid this banquet with all good intentions.
>>> But you
>> Strode in and flaunted your charms to get her in the sack.
>>> You
>> Really have stepped in it this time,
>>> yes, you have,
>>>> Lü Fengxian!

LÜ BU *speaks:* Minister, you don't understand. Let me explain it to you in all detail. She's originally a girl from Mu'er Village in Xinzhou, the daughter of Ren Ang, and her child name is Hongchang. She was selected for Emperor Ling's seraglio, where she was Lady in Charge of Sable and Cicada Hats, and so was called Diaochan. Later Emperor Ling gave her as a gift to Ding Jianyang. I was his adopted son in those days, and he gave Diaochan to me in marriage. We were split apart in the battles of the Yellow Turban revolt, and I didn't know that somehow she ended up in your house. Just now I accidentally met with her. Minister, please take pity on us and ensure the reunion of husband and wife. Until my dying day I never will forget that favor! [MALE LEAD *sings:*]

>>> You and she:
>> "A single thread cannot make a string."
>>> I will make your
>> Waning moon whole again!

> (*Wu ye ti*)
>>> This couple of
>> Mandarin ducks will not be locked up in palaces of gold.

MALE LEAD *speaks:* This is not my private residence. LÜ BU *speaks:* If it isn't your private residence, then what is it? [MALE LEAD *sings:*]

---

70. In traditional marriages, the money that the male's family pays to the bride's family as a "bride price."

Who would have thought that
Liu Chen of the Han would stumble into his Peach Blossom
    Fount?[71]
That the beauty would be done reciting the "Rhapsody of Long Gate
    Palace"?[72]
    The two of you should,
Hand in hand, shoulder pressed to shoulder,
Side by side, sleep on a shared pillow.
    How could I
Separate the double-stemmed lotuses on the blue waves,
Tear apart the swallow pair among the painted beams?
Ahead lies a beautiful road
Of a new marriage bond—
    Let all those
Spring winds enter into the courtyard dwellings,
And let the night moon shine on their balustrades.

MALE LEAD *speaks:* If you hadn't said anything, Marquis, how would I have
known? I could never have found such a match as proper as this. I will select an
auspicious day, and will also provide a dowry of three strings of a thousand
cash to make Diaochan your wife. How does that sit with you, Marquis? LÜ BU
speaks: Many thanks, minister. Diaochan's father is my father. Such grace as
this must be repaid with equal weight. MALE LEAD *speaks:* There is just one
thing, Marquis, I just fear that if the Grand Preceptor should find out, won't he
see it as an offense I've committed? LÜ BU *speaks:* This is not a problem. When
my father knows, he'll even be happier. MALE LEAD *speaks:* If this is the case,
then have no worries, general. I will invite the Grand Preceptor tomorrow and
lay out another banquet. On the one hand we will be able to discuss the grand
affair, and on the other bring up this marriage business to see what he thinks
about it. LÜ BU *speaks:* Father-in-law, you exercise your mind to such extent to
aid your child! I will never forget this favor until the day I die. I've had enough

---

71. Liu Chen and Ruan Zhao were herbalists who had gone into the Tiantai range in 63 and
did not emerge again until 384. They said that they were dying of hunger when they spotted a
peach tree high up on the mountain. After they struggled to get to it, the fruits of the tree slaked
their thirst and did away with their hunger. Later they met two ladies, who enticed them with food
and sex. They stayed with a bevy of young beauties for ten days and then were escorted out of the
mountains. But when they returned to their village, they discovered they had been gone for three
hundred years, the news relayed to them by one of their seventh-generation grandchildren.
72. When Emperor Wu of the Han's childhood sweetheart Empress Chen lost his favor and
was banished to the "cold palace," she had the poet Sima Xiangru (179–117 BC) write the "Rhapsody of Long Gate Palace" (*Changmen fu*) to give expression to her undying love for the emperor
and win back his favor.

wine, so I'll take my leave. MALE LEAD *speaks:* Forgive me for any breaches of protocol, general. LÜ BU *speaks:* I dare not presume![73] I'm out the door now and on the way back to my private residence.

> Unexpectedly today we met once again
> Just as if I were having a dream of the Southern Branch.[74]

Exits.

MALE LEAD *speaks:* Lü Bu has left. Ji Lü, go straightaway to the Grand Preceptor's residence again and say that Wang Yun especially invites the Grand Preceptor to a banquet. If he will not come for that, tell him that I am inviting him to discuss the grand affair. JI LÜ *speaks:* Understood. So today I will go and invite the Grand Preceptor to a banquet.

Exits.

MALE LEAD *speaks:* Ji Lü has left to invite the Grand Marshal to a banquet.

> (*Huangzhong Coda*)
> Tomorrow, I'll arrange a
> Peaches of Immortality banquet of the Queen Mother with Zhou
> Qiongyi[75]
> And so prepare
> A feast like that of Empress Lü with its traps for catching
> phoenixes.[76]
> I'll use my innate cleverness,

---

73. These last two lines are formulaic utterances for departing a feast.

74. In a famous classical tale of the Tang dynasty, a man lives through a brilliant career in Nanke (Southern Branch) to find out when he wakes up that it had been a career in the kingdom of ants under the acacia tree in his courtyard.

75. The Queen Mother is the Queen Mother of the West who rules all female immortals from her abode on top of the mythical Kunlun Mountains in the far west. The peaches of immortality that grow in her garden ripen once every three thousand years, when she invites all immortals to a sumptuous banquet to enjoy the fruit. Zhou Qiongyi is one of the highest-ranking female immortals in her establishment. In one dramatic version of the legend of Liu Chen and Ruan Zhao, Zhou Qiongyi is the name of one of the two female immortals who welcome the men into their hidden paradise and into their beds.

76. This is more than likely a general reference to the evil of Empress Lü, the wife of Liu Bang and the person responsible for the deaths of men who had supported Liu Bang in his rise to power. If it has a specific reference, it is to a feast she held with the weakling Emperor Hui and his elder brother, the Prince of Qi. She had been affronted by the seating arrangements and had the prince's wine spiked with poison. She offered a toast, but Emperor Hui seized Prince Qi's cup and was about to drink in response. The empress overturned his cup. The prince, suspecting that something was afoot, dismissed himself from the banquet. "A feast with Empress Lü" has come to mean a banquet that is fraught with danger.

Employ shrewd plans.
These expedient tactics
Must be clever and facile.
We will look for results:
Forget "praise and blame."[77]
I set out beakers and mats:
Lay out a tortoise spread.[78]
We'll play the ocarina and sing:
Set out pipes and the strings.
The flowers will seem like embroidery
And the wine will flow like rivers.
        I
Will be even more humble,
Act the meek and good one.
Grand Preceptor Dong
Is a fool when he's drunk—
Seeing that beauty
He will certainly fall in love.
        At that time I will then
Offer him that beautiful face of Diaochan as a gift
And secretly pronounce a vow to Heaven.
        In my vow I wish to
Quickly exterminate this rebellious minister,
        And let the
Sagely brilliance shine for all to see.[79]

(*Exits with* JI LÜ *and* SERVANTS.)

FEMALE *speaks:* Father has left. Who could have thought that I would see my husband Lü Bu again today? I'm so happy! MEIXIANG *speaks:* Who could have known that today I would see the young lady's husband again. What a handsome figure! I'm so happy too! FEMALE *speaks:* I've nothing else to do here, so let's go back to the rear chambers.

---

77. Confucius is believed to have adjudicated "praise and blame" by his subtle choice of words in the *Springs and Autumns* (*Chunqiu*), a dry-as-dust chronicle of his native state of Lu. Here the term refers to the later judgment of historians.

78. A banquet laid out on a mat decorated with tortoiseshell.

79. The term *shengming* is nearly always used in reference to the emperor. There may be a bit of wordplay here, as in modern *xiehouyu*, in which the second line of a common quote, "a sagely brilliant ruler must have ministers who are loyal and worthy" (*shengming zhi jun bi you zhongxian zhi chen*), is omitted but understood as what is intended.

Today my husband and I saw each other again:
It seemed as if phoenix glue[80] had repaired a broken string.

Exit together.

Act 3

DONG ZHUO *enters, leading* ATTENDANT, *and speaks:* I am Dong Zhuo. Wang Yun and these officials have discussed the grand affair, but have not reported to me. Servant, keep watch at the gate. If anyone comes, inform me right away. ATTENDANT *speaks:* Understood. JI LÜ *enters and speaks:* I am Ji Lü, and I've been entrusted with a message from the Prime Minister, who has sent me to invite Grand Preceptor Dong. Here I am, at his residence already. Doorkeeper, please report that Ji Lü, messenger from Minister of Instruction Wang is at the door. ATTENDANT *acts out reporting:* I want to report that Ji Lü, messenger from Minister of Instruction Wang, is at the door. DONG ZHUO *speaks:* Tell him to come in. ATTENDANT *speaks:* Understood. Enter! JI LÜ *acts out greeting.* DONG ZHUO *speaks:* Ji Lü, why have you come? JI LÜ *speaks:* My Prime Minister has ordered me, Ji Lü, to come and invite the Grand Preceptor to a banquet. DONG ZHUO *speaks:* Ji Lü, I am totally occupied by thoughts of the grand affair, which I want to discuss with the ministers and high officials. I couldn't care less about that banquet of yours! You go back and tell that old geezer that I am not coming. JI LÜ *speaks:* Grand Preceptor, my Prime Minister said, "Think about it: what is that banquet for?" For no other reason than to discuss the grand affair with the Grand Preceptor. DONG ZHUO *speaks:* Oh, he's here to invite me to discuss the grand affair. Ji Lü, go back first, and I will come later. JI LÜ *speaks:* Understood. Having bid the Grand Preceptor adieu, I dare not tarry or delay, but go back and report to the Prime Minister.

Exits.

DONG ZHUO *speaks:* Ji Lü is gone now. Servant, follow me to Wang Yun's residence to attend a banquet. If something untoward happens at the banquet, then I'll just finish that old fellow off.

Exits.

MALE LEAD *enters, leading* ATTENDANT, *and speaks:* I am Wang Yun. I sent Ji Lü off to the Grand Preceptor's residence to invite Dong Zhuo. I wonder why he

---

80. The glue made of the bones of the mythical *luan* bird (a kind of phoenix) was said to be so strong it could even mend broken strings.

isn't here yet. Servant, keep watch at the door and if someone comes along, then report to me.

(ZHENGGONG MODE: *Duanzheng hao*)
Depending on my talent and capacity to think,
There will be no need to stir broad swords and long lances;
> I'll just arrange

Red skirts and kingfisher green sleeves like a wind screen—
> And take

Those tables, cups, and serving dishes and set them out.

(*Gun xiuqiu*)
In the censer I will burn precious seal-script incense;[81]
For wine I will pour a liquor of liquid jade.
During the playing of pipes and singing, the sound of the music will
> be crisp and concordant;
> In today's

Painted hall will be a special atmosphere.
It might seem like a land of brocade and embroidery,
But it secretly conceals a battlefield,
But one without tiger-mighty generals who fight to win—
At the tortoiseshell mat I shall lead out one who is rouged with red.
> I just want to set out

Hidden bows and poisoned arrows to shoot the wolves and tigers
And to snare the phoenix with snares unrolled and nets stretched
> tight.

It will be no ordinary feast.

MALE LEAD *speaks:* Servant, keep watch and when Ji Lü comes, report to me. JI LÜ *enters and speaks:* I am Ji Lü. I'm coming back to report to the Prime Minister. *Acts out greeting.* MALE LEAD *speaks:* Ji Lü, how did it go? JI LÜ *speaks:* I used your exact words to go and invite the Grand Preceptor and then came back. MALE LEAD *speaks:* Ji Lü, go and keep watch at the door, and when you see the Grand Preceptor's outriders far off in the distance, you come quickly to inform me. JI LÜ *speaks:* Understood. CLOWN, *costumed as* DONG ZHUO, *enters,* [*leading* GENERALS,] *and speaks:* I am Grand Preceptor Dong. Wang Yun has invited me to a banquet today. Generals—station yourselves and your men outside the door. If that old miscreant is half a second late or a makes a little mistake, I'll trample his residence flat! Servant, go and report that Grand Preceptor Dong

---

81. That is, coiling threads of incense resembling the complicated and curving forms of archaic seal-script characters.

has arrived. GENERALS *act out responding affirmatively.* JI LÜ *speaks:* Understood. *Acts out reporting and speaks:* I want to let you know, Prime Minister, that Grand Preceptor Dong has arrived. MALE LEAD *speaks:* I'll go out personally to greet him. *Acts out kneeling, speaks:* I have troubled the Grand Preceptor's noble feet to tread on this base ground; please pardon Wang Yun's faults. DONG ZHUO *speaks:* Wang Yun, you've got such a high rank, Prime Minister of the Left; people outside will see you kneeling in the street and think it is vulgar. Get up. MALE LEAD *speaks:* This humble official should act in this way! I early on wanted to invite you here today; if we had put it off four or five more days, then the Grand Preceptor would already have taken the imperial position and you would not be willing to visit my humble home. Please! Please! Come in. Servant, bring out the table. JI LÜ *speaks:* Understood. *Acts out bringing out the table and snacks.* MALE LEAD *speaks:* Preceptor, please drink this cup to the full. DONG ZHUO *speaks:* Stop! I want to drink and I want to say clearly what I have to say. Why have you arranged this banquet today? If you explain it clearly, I will drink. MALE LEAD *acts out handing him wine and speaks:* Grand Preceptor, you will complete the grand affair soon. Please drink this cup to the full. DONG ZHUO *speaks:* Wang Yun, everything about this affair is important. If the grand affair is completed in three or four days, it will still be you, Prime Minister, who does it. [MALE LEAD *sings:*]

> (*Ban dushu*)
> I am clear about your words, Grand Preceptor,
> And they make me wisely surrender.
>> If the Grand Preceptor
> Quickly takes control of power and prospers well,
> The hundred officials, civil and military, will each be raised in rank
>   and rewarded.
>> I desire
> That you do not incline toward either new emotions or old feelings!
>> I desire
> You live a long and happy life without end.

DONG ZHUO *speaks:* Minister, if I carry off the grand affair, I will make certain that your grade is at the highest level and your position is above that of all of the liege lords. All of you officials here will be raised in rank and rewarded. If you have anything you want, then now is the time to express it all! [MALE LEAD *sings:*]

> (*Xiao heshang*)
> I desire that the Grand Preceptor ascend the hall of the Son of
>   Heaven toward evening.

DONG ZHUO *speaks:* If this day should happen, what office should Li Su be given? MALE LEAD *sings:*

> Li Su should be made Vanguard General.

DONG ZHUO *speaks:* Good. And my son Lü Bu? What rank should we give him? MALE LEAD *sings:*

> Lü Bu should sit in a lotus-blossom tent with a golden peak.[82]

DONG ZHUO *speaks:* Good. It should be so. What position do you want? [MALE LEAD *sings:*]

> I don't want to be an Attendant Gentleman,[83]
> And I don't want to be a Manager of Governmental Affairs.[84]

DONG ZHUO *speaks:* Even so, what position do you really want? [MALE LEAD *sings:*]

> I hope the Grand Preceptor
> Will make me the Top Minister.

DONG ZHUO *speaks:* I would say that the reason you invited me was because you wanted this position all along. No matter. If I complete this grand affair in a few days, the office of Prime Minister of the Left is yours to take. MALE LEAD *speaks:* Many thanks, Grand Preceptor. Servant, bring out more wine. ATTENDANT *speaks:* Understood. MALE LEAD *acts out presenting him wine and speaks:* Grand Preceptor, please drink this cup to the full. DONG ZHUO *speaks:* Stop! The wine is coming too fast. The weather is really hot and I'm feeling tired right now. Let me rest a bit. *Acts out nodding off.* MALE LEAD *speaks:* The Grand Preceptor is feeling the effects of the wine. The weather is really hot. Send Meixiang to carry this report and bring Diaochan out to fan the Grand Preceptor. JI LÜ *speaks:* Understood. *Acts out summoning her.* Meixiang, take this report to the rear quarters and ask missy to come out. FEMALE *enters holding a fan, acts out greeting, and speaks:* I am Diaochan. I was just sitting glumly in the rear quarters. Father, why did you call me? MALE LEAD *speaks:* Child, Dong Zhuo is now passed out in hall and is sleeping. Go fan him! FEMALE *speaks:* Understood. [MALE LEAD *sings:*]

> (*Gun xiuqiu*)
> Make
> Your chignon, brushed with oil, shine,

---

82. The tent used by the Field Marshal, the highest military post.
83. I.e., the second highest of three ranks of court gentlemen (*lang*).
84. This is an anachronistic title (used from the Song dynasty onward) for court dignitaries picked to serve on the Grand Council.

Your newly made up face fragrant and
Drawn in the new fashion of curved-moon brows.
> Now I believe the saying,
"When lotus threads are soft and new, they weave immortals' skirts."
> If this
Girl, gorgeously made up
Urges on the jade goblets—
I want you to pour out cups to the brim, and sing in a low voice—
> He won't be able to resist
Those ten fingers that reveal springtime bamboo shoots, long and
   delicate.
> I simply want you
To get rid of this "illness" in the Han emperor's heart—
> You will be
That special prescription from the magic isles that will cure this
   traitorous treachery;
It needs no discussing![85]

FEMALE *acts out fanning him;* DONG ZHUO *acts out reviving and speaks:* Aiya!
This cool breeze penetrates to the very bone. Who is fanning me? DONG ZHUO
acts out seeing FEMALE *and speaks:* What a fine girl! The human world seldom
sees such a face as this. Just like an immortal! A fine girl! A fine girl! Come
closer, and let's drink a few cups together. FEMALE *acts out being embarrassed.*
MALE LEAD *speaks:* You old miscreant; you are already in the trap!

> (*Daodao ling*)
> I see Dong Zhuo
Bend down and set the wine cups down with a clatter.

DONG ZHUO *speaks:* What a beautiful woman. On her head is a put-up chignon
of the blackest clouds; on her body she wears clothes of brocade and embroidery. She looks just like that Chang E[86] in the moon! [MALE LEAD *sings:*]

> Now he
Examines her charming and gorgeous form from head to toe.[87]
> I see Diaochan
Flustered and embarrassed, with nowhere to escape.

---

85. I.e., it will work like a charm.

86. Chang E is the beautiful goddess of the moon, where she escaped with the elixir of immortality, only to live her life alone in the Palace of Broad Cold.

87. The verb used here is *xiang,* which has the meaning "to physiognomize," in the sense of
assessing either someone's fate or the quality of animals that one is going to purchase. It clearly
has this second usage here.

DONG ZHUO *trembling, speaks:* What a fine girl! [MALE LEAD *sings:*]

> That old man's
> Drooling eyes furtively gaze at her.

DONG ZHUO *speaks:* What a fine girl! Come nearer. MALE LEAD *sings:*

> This miscreant has already
> Fallen into my trap,
> Into my trap.
> Right now
> I will make an excuse about giving orders in the kitchen and leave
> this feast.

DONG ZHUO *speaks:* I look at this girl, who has a countenance to make fish sink to the depths and geese fall from the sky, a face to outshine the moon and put flowers to shame. Oh, what a fine breeze. Aiya! What a fine girl. Missy, come closer and fan a little harder.

> FEMALE *acts out trailing the fan on the ground [and exits].*

DONG ZHUO *acts out running after her and speaks:* Wang Yun! Who was that young girl just fanning me a minute ago? MALE LEAD *speaks:* That's my daughter, whom I've yet to grant in betrothal. DONG ZHUO *speaks:* Oh, so it turns out to be your daughter. Minister, after completing that grand affair in a few days, all I will lack is just such a fine wife. Minister, if you are willing to give her to me, then you'll be my esteemed father-in-law—then won't both of us fulfill our desires? *He acts out kneeling.* MALE LEAD *speaks:* Grand Preceptor, please rise. If you don't find my little daughter's ugly face with its unkempt makeup too offensive, I would very much desire to give her to you as a wife. DONG ZHUO *speaks:* Thank you very much, minister. Today is hard to compare with days past. Now that you have given me your beloved daughter as wife, you will later on become an imperial relative and elder of the state. I will be your son-in-law, which is the same as a son, so you are my father. Father, please sit and receive your son's obeisances. I have something to say, but dare I say it? Since you have granted me your daughter, wouldn't it be great if you summoned my wife back out here to pass about a round of wine? MALE LEAD *speaks:* Of course. Servant, summon Diaochan. FEMALE *enters and speaks:* I am Diaochan. Father has called me, so I have to go. Here I am, already. I'll go on in. Father, why have you summoned me? MALE LEAD *speaks:* Child, please pass a cup of wine to the Grand Preceptor with the utmost respect. FEMALE *acts out passing the wine.* DONG ZHUO *speaks:* If this wife were to send the wine cups about, I'd drink it whether it was wine or sewer water. Bring out a large flagon, and if you don't have a large flagon, a foot-washing basin will do. What a fine girl! What a fine girl! She gets finer and finer. Father, today is different than earlier times. I've drunk enough already, I can't drink anymore. I judge that tomorrow will be an auspicious day, so send your precious daughter over "to cross the threshold."[88] I will be sitting in the Grand Preceptor's residence, just waiting for you to bring my wife across the threshold. Wife, please return to the rear quarters now. FEMALE *speaks:* Understood.

Exits.

DONG ZHUO *speaks:* I've had enough wine now. Father, I have been treated very well by you, and I thank you. I will rely on you. When do you think this marriage might happen? MALE LEAD *speaks:* It won't be long, Grand Preceptor. Tomorrow is an auspicious day. I will bring my daughter to your residence, and throw in a dowry of three thousand cash. DONG ZHUO *speaks:* I will wait in my residence for the "crossing of the threshold" and wait there for you to bring Diaochan. Many thanks for the kindness and concern you have shown me, father. I will go back now.

The face of Diaochan outshines the moon and shames the flowers,
And tomorrow she becomes my wife.

Exits.

MALE LEAD *speaks:* Dong Zhuo is gone. Ji Lü, prepare my cart. Tomorrow, when the cows and sheep have entered their pens, we'll take Diaochan to the Grand Preceptor's residence.

Exit together.

DONG ZHUO *enters, leading* LI RU, *and speaks:* I am Dong Zhuo. Li Ru, put the banquet in order. Father is bringing Diaochan today to be my wife. I didn't sleep all night. I've already prepared the gifts for the ceremonies of "making obeisances in the ancestral hall"[89] and "crossing the threshold." Everything is in proper order. They should be here soon. MALE LEAD *enters, leading* FEMALE, *and with drum music being played.* MALE LEAD *speaks:* We've reached the residence gate already, with drums and music playing. Li Ru, go and report to the preceptor that Wang Yun is at the door. LI RU *speaks:* The Grand Preceptor has been waiting a long time! You remain here and I will go report. LI RU *speaks:* Grand Preceptor, Minister Wang is at the gates. DONG ZHUO *speaks:* Invite him in. *Act out greeting.* [DONG ZHUO *speaks:*] Father, you are a man of your word and I confess you are a good man. Where is my wife now, father? MALE LEAD *speaks:*

88. That is, to "enter my house as a bride."
89. The new couple make an offering to Heaven, to their ancestors, and to their parents.

She's in the cart. DONG ZHUO *speaks:* My wife, please go on into the back rooms. Servant! Bring out the wine. Today is different than earlier days. You are now my esteemed father-in-law. Here are a few snacks. I beg you to drink three cups. *Acts out passing the wine and speaks:* Father, please drink this cup to the full. MALE LEAD *speaks:* I dare not. Please, sir, you drink first. DONG ZHUO *speaks:* Father, please! MALE LEAD *speaks:* I have drunk now. Please, Grand Preceptor, drink a full cup. DONG ZHUO *speaks:* Bring it here. In the future, I'll drink round after round and flagon after flagon and eat until dawn. I'll arrange a banquet on some other day. Today, I have a little bit of business to attend to. MALE LEAD *speaks:* The wine has been sufficient. I will return now. DONG ZHUO *speaks:* Please don't take offense, father. I'll invite you on another day to drink. Goodbye. Li Ru! Set out wine in the rear compartments and I will go and drink the "exchange cups" with my wife.[90]

Exits with FEMALE *and* LI RU.[91]

LÜ BU *enters and speaks:* I am Lü Bu. Minister Wang said that he was going to bring Diaochan today to present to me as a wife. I didn't expect that when they got here, the little cart, the carrying poles loaded with boxes, the drum music, and Wang Yun himself would already have gone inside [the Grand Preceptor's residence]. Could that old miscreant have done something so wrong? I'll just wait here at the gate and if Wang Yun comes out, I'll see what he has to say! MALE LEAD *speaks:* The Grand Preceptor has gone back into the rear chambers, so I might as well go home.

(*Kuaihuo san*)
I see Dong Zhuo
Welcome that jade girl like the spring breeze,

MALE LEAD *acts out going out the door.* LÜ BU *speaks:* Old minister, I've been waiting here a long time. [MALE LEAD *sings:*]

Silence! In vain you
"Wait for the moon at the Western Wing."[92]
Father and son both want to be new grooms,
And both lean against the door to gaze afar with hope.

---

90. Two cups of wine held together by a red thread. The bride and groom drink and then exchange cups and drink again.

91. Wang Yun remains on stage.

92. This is a direct and partial quote of the Chinese of one of the titles by which the *Story of the Western Wing* was known, *The Story of Oriole Cui Waiting for the Moon at the Western Wing*, as well as a citation from a line in an aria describing Student Zhang waiting for Oriole to make her appearance. See West and Idema 1995, pp. 57–60, 215.

Lü BU *speaks:* It was *my* wife who had wound up in your residence. You personally granted her to me at the banquet. What is she doing today going into the Grand Preceptor's residence? [MALE LEAD *sings:*]

> (*Baolao'er*)
>> You
> Cross your hands and bow, talk about right and wrong,
>> But that
> New bride was on the cart.
>> It's just like
> "The mute wife who poured out the cup yet was the one who suffered misfortune."[93]
> You roundly curse Minister Wang!
>> All in vain have you
> Actualized your loyalty, exhausted your integrity,
> Established the state, made the country secure.[94]
>> How sad
> Those jade fingers like spring's onion roots
> And the pliant willow of her supple waist
> Have been wrongly matched to a magical bird.

Lü BU *speaks:* Old minister, in truth, what has happened? MALE LEAD *speaks:* You can't know, Marquis, that yesterday when I invited your father to a feast to bring up this affair of the wedding, he was extraordinarily happy and said, "Call the girl out and let me have a look at her." I should never have called Diaochan out to bow to your father four times. Your father saw that Diaochan was a beauty, and who expected that old miscreant to do such an inhumane thing? Today when the cart arrived, your father sent out a group of people to force Diaochan into the back chambers of his household. Marquis, this makes it moot that you are a husband—if you can't even protect your own wife, what use are you? When has a father ever taken an intended daughter-in-law and forced her to become his concubine?[95] Bah! This makes me so embarrassed. Lü

---

93. Half of a common couplet in *zaju*, "A plowing ox works for its master but gets the whip; a mute wife pours the cups but receives the misfortune." I.e., she is beaten when her husband gets drunk, but she can't complain. The phrase has come to mean to become the target of revenge after performing an act of kindness.

94. This is rather ambiguous. It could be a sarcastic taunt to Lü Bu, or perhaps a lamentation about himself.

95. The one very apt example is King Ping of Chu, who, despite the protests of his councilor Wu She, took the woman Meng Ying, who was destined to be the wife of the crown prince, as his own. The same person who persuaded the king to take the woman also hounded Wu She to death. Wu She's son, Wu Zixu, later fled to Wu and launched five punitive invasions against

BU *speaks:* If you hadn't said something, minister, how would I have known? That this old fellow would carry out such an inhumane act—this really infuriates me. MALE LEAD *sings:*

> (*Shua hai'er*)[96]
>> I see you,
> Marquis of Wen, as having always been a model among men;
> Sparkling, shining clear, your name is renowned in the four
>> directions.
> At Tigerkeep Pass you displayed your heroic valor—
> A stern and powerful face, not of the ordinary kind.
>> You have always been
> A pillar holding up heaven in your support of the altars of state,
> A beam arching across the ocean that secures the peace of the
>> cosmos.
>> You
> Have benevolence and righteousness,
>> but he
>>> has no sense of yielding or concession—
>> If you are willing to exterminate that treacherous minister
> And restore the house of Han
>> You'll earn a
> Fame that lasts forever.

LÜ BU *speaks:* Minister, that boorish Dong Zhuo has no sense of shame. Diaochan and I were a husband and wife who had been matched from youth. Dong Zhuo is my adoptive father. How can there be such a family tradition as this? [MALE LEAD *sings:*]

> (*Second from Coda*)
>> This child
> Moved through the main halls with slow steps—
> Who had ever visited her in her hidden apartments?
>> But she

Chu. When his armies finally occupied the Chu capital, Wu Zixu dug up the corpse of King Ping and whipped it three hundred times.

96. The cartouche bearing the name of the song has been effaced; however, it could be *banshediao shua hai'er*, which would render the title BANSHE MODE: *Shua hai'er*. This is probably a simple mistake, which would explain why it was effaced. In *sanqu* songs of the time, this was the favorite mode for writing songs in this title.

Worked her clever plans that sold her charms—a feigned
   appearance.[97]
        In the beginning
You met in Wang Yun's fore hall,
        But today
Have been put into two separate wings of the residence by Dong
   Zhuo.
        You truly are:
"A home that is not ordered has nothing good to offer."
        And never think:
"A minister can repay the state."
        It's all about
"The foundational bond between husband and wife!"

LÜ BU *speaks:* Old minister, don't worry. If sometime tonight I get to see Diaochan, I will ask her the reason for all of this. I cannot say that I will let that old miscreant off. [MALE LEAD *sings:*]

(*Coda*)
        If you are willing
To turn toward Heaven's court,[98] there will be no calamity or peril;
To support our illustrious ruler, there will be exalted glory.
        If you
Display the radiance of your power, it will become your reputation;
        But what is necessary is that
Your jeweled sword must leave its case to exterminate the treacherous clique.

Exits.

LÜ BU *speaks:* This old miscreant is completely off base. You have stolen away Diaochan and I will see it done and over with. I'll go straightaway into the rear chambers and find that old miscreant.

Exits.

---

97. The referent of this line is ambiguous. We have translated it as if it were in reference to Diaochan. But it is also possible that it refers to Dong Zhuo and that Wang Yun is using it to taunt Lü Bu. In either case, it implies that Diaochan was not totally innocent. The term "sell a winsome appearance" (*maiqiao*) refers usually to women, and occurs frequently in such phrases as "sell a winsome appearance in order to carry out something treacherous" (*maiqiao xingjian*), which would fit well with either case.

98. The emperor's court.

CLOWN, *costumed as* DONG ZHUO, *enters, leading* FEMALE, *and speaks:* I am so happy I could die. Little ones, bring out the table. Wife, pass me a cup and I'll drink a full one. FEMALE *acts out passing wine to him.* DONG ZHUO *speaks:* I'll have another cup. Wife, you have one too. Take the table away and spread the bedding! I'm going to rest awhile with my wife. *Acts out falling asleep.* LÜ BU *enters and speaks:* I am Lü Bu. It's late now; how can I get Diaochan to come out? Everything will be better if I can see her once. FEMALE *speaks:* This old miscreant is drunk. I've heard people say that there is a little corner gate in the rear garden that leads to Lü Bu's private residence. I'll go have a look. There really is a gate here! Let me open it up. LÜ BU *speaks:* Isn't that Diaochan coming here? I'll call her name. Diaochan! FEMALE *speaks:* Aren't you Fengxian? *Act out meeting.* LÜ BU *speaks:* Aren't you Diaochan? FEMALE *speaks:* Lü Bu, this embarrasses me to death. When my cart reached your residence gate, I was whisked away into the preceptor's residence by a bunch of people sent by him. When has a man's father ever taken his son's betrothed? What kind of principle is this! Fengxian, you are a real man, with heaven above and earth below, teeth in your mouth, and hair on your head. But if you cannot even protect your own wife, then what use are you? Bah! Aren't you embarrassed? *Recites:*

> I am only a young girl in the spring of her youth,
>   And now I have told you what happened;
>   Even if you scooped out all of the water from the three rivers,
>   Damn! It would never wash away the embarrassment on your face today.

LÜ BU *speaks:* Wife, I already know the whole story. Just turn inside this gate and my private residence is right over there. Let's go there and talk. FEMALE *speaks:* No problem. I'll hide here by this shadow wall.[99] DONG ZHUO *acts out waking up and speaks:* Wife! Diaochan! Why don't I see her? Where did she go? Why is this corner gate open? Could she have gone in this direction? Let me see if I can find her. Diaochan, where are you? FEMALE *speaks:* Fengxian! Isn't that the old miscreant coming? LÜ BU *speaks:* No problem. I'll hide beside this shade wall and see what he says. I'll give him a taste of my fist! DONG ZHUO *speaks:* Diaochan! Why are you talking to Lü Bu? Was it because that little beast dared do something inhumane? Lü Bu, don't run. Get a taste of my sword. LÜ BU *acts out striking* DONG ZHUO *and speaks:* Go on! I've knocked down this old miscreant. This is no good. I have to flee, flee, flee!

Exits.

---

99. A wall, usually placed at the entrance of door or gate to prevent a view inside of the residence, built on a platform base and sometimes moveable to create shade.

DONG ZHUO *acts out falling.* FEMALE *acts out hurriedly helping* DONG ZHUO *rise and* DONG ZHUO *speaks:* Aiya! That little beast gave me a whipping. Where is Li Su? LI SU *enters and speaks:* I am Li Su. It's really late, deep in the watches of the night. I wonder why father called me? DONG ZHUO *speaks:* Li Su, for some reason this beastly Lü Bu has completely overstepped what is proper. Diaochan is *my* wife. This little beast did something improper and then knocked me down to the ground. He's fled now. Go nab that little beast for me. Be careful, and make haste. LI SU *speaks:* I have received your orders. Now I have an order from my father and I'll take some foot and horse soldiers and go nab Lü Bu now.

Exits.

DONG ZHUO *speaks:* Li Su has gone off to nab Lü Bu. When he comes, tell me. My whole body aches from falling down. Wife, please help me back to the rear chambers. FEMALE *speaks:* Fortunately you came in time, Grand Preceptor, before that fellow could sully me. You just take care of yourself now, preceptor.

Exits with FEMALE.

Act 4

LI SU *enters, leading* SOLDIERS, *and speaks:*

> The top of Mount Tai has been ground down by blades I have sharpened;
> The waves of the Northern Sea have been drunk dry by my warhorses;
> > If a man at thirty has yet to establish his name,
> Then it's for naught that he is a strapping great man.

I am Li Su. Wang Yun gave Diaochan to my father as a wife. Who would have expected that that little beast Lü Bu would have such bad intentions, and take advantage of my father? He doesn't have any sense of hierarchy—his behavior is unacceptable by any accounts! He knocked father down on the ground. Father set me out with a cavalry troop of one hundred thousand, had me put on my battle robes and wriggle into my armor, stick arrows in my quiver, and bend my bow to go out and capture Lü Bu, so that this hatred can be cleansed away. I'll have to catch up to him.

Exits.

MALE LEAD *enters and speaks:* I am Wang Yun, and I set up this plan with Diaochan, but I still don't know how it is going. *Sings:*

(SHUANGDIAO MODE: *Xinshui ling*)
> In vain I
> May have used my heart's clever designs in double-trap plans,

But it all was because
I have labored so hard all my life for the rivers and mountains of
    Han.
            Unhappily tonight
The jade lotus[100] leisurely drips
And the hoary moon is slow to rise on the window's silken screen.
I pace back and forth;
Whatever comes to pass will be because of her ability.

MALE LEAD *speaks:* It's almost midnight. Why is there no news? [*Sings:*]

(*Zhuma ting*)
            Grand Preceptor Dong
Was set for a tryst of swallows and orioles.
            Overjoyed he was,
A new groom whose flesh weighs in at a thousand pounds!
            Lü Bu, the Marquis of Wen,
Was an orphaned simurgh and lonely phoenix cock,
            Driven to distraction
Over a former winsome wife whose passions are now split in two.
            And the girl Diaochan:
Teary pearls drip until they fill the purple golden cup.
            Lü Bu, the Marquis of Wen's,
Anger blew apart a mandarin-duck rendezvous.
            And because of all of this
I fell asleep most slowly,
            For I feared
A "single branch completely leaked all of the news of spring."[101]

MALE LEAD *speaks:* I'm going to close the door, sit here sullenly, and see who comes along. LÜ BU *enters and speaks:* I am Lü Bu. I knocked that old miscreant down with a single punch, and he's surely sent someone to capture me. I'll hide out for the time being in Minister Wang's residence and talk it over with him. I will have to kill that old miscreant before my life's ambitions are fulfilled. Here I am, already. Let me call out. Open the gate! Open the gate! MALE LEAD *speaks:* That sounds like Lü Bu calling at the gate. That guy has fallen into my plan. [*Sings:*]

---

100. A clepsydra carved with decorations of white lotuses.
101. I.e., he is worried that something has happened to give the whole plan away, just as the early blooming of a prunus branch can signal the spring that is to come.

(*Bubu jiao*)
> Just hearing
> The sound of knocking on the residence gate, I say, "Thank god!"
> Here I
> Am secretly overjoyed and with panting breath—"Who is it?"
> And now it's
> So quiet at midnight, "Who can it be?"
> Let me ask for the true facts.

MALE LEAD *speaks:* I'm opening the door. Let me see who it is. LÜ BU *speaks:* Minister, it's your son, Lü Bu. [MALE LEAD *sings:*]

> All down and distracted,
> He stands, half leaning against the door.

MALE LEAD *speaks:* Marquis, please come in and we can talk. Why have you come here now? LÜ BU *speaks:* Because that old miscreant was so inhumane, I knocked him down with a single punch, and I've come to tell you about it. This kind of treacherous official and miscreant is of no use to anyone. I have come to see you to especially discuss how, for better or worse, I can take vengeance on him. [MALE LEAD *sings:*]

> (*Hushiba*)
> According to what I think,
> I will express Fengxian's anger on his behalf:
> "To no avail did you help him and support him.
> No one in all the world is as ignorant as him;
> To act in such a way shows the so-called
> Intelligence of a donkey or a horse.
> This is what comes from working so hard,
> Working so hard for him."

LÜ BU *speaks:* Rest easy, minister. That old miscreant must die by my hand. MALE LEAD *speaks:* Marquis, let's talk it over a bit longer and see who comes. LI SU *enters and speaks:* I am Li Su, and bearing the order of the Grand Preceptor I gathered a cavalry troop of one hundred thousand to capture Lü Bu. I've chased him, but he's suddenly disappeared. Let me have a look here. This is Minister Wang's personal residence; he must be hiding here. I'll call out at the door. Minister! Open the gate! Open the gate! LÜ BU *speaks:* Minister, isn't that Li Su calling at the gate? *Acts out greeting.* MALE LEAD *speaks:* It's not a problem. Hide here behind the arras and let me go open the door. *Acts out going out and meeting him.* LI SU *speaks:* Minister Wang, what were you thinking? If you gave your daughter to the Grand Preceptor, then give her to the Grand Preceptor. If you are going to give her to Lü Bu, then give her to Lü Bu. Not clarifying who you were giving her to caused father and son to fight it out all night long. Lü Bu knocked the Grand Preceptor down, and it took a long time for him to get up again. I am now bearing the Grand Preceptor's orders to capture Lü Bu. I've been close behind him, and I can see that he's gone into your house. Hurry up and hand him over. If you don't, I won't spare you. MALE LEAD *speaks:* You don't recall at all that your ancestor Li Tong gathered together twenty-eight generals at Cloudy Terrace,[102] and executed Wang Mang on Jian Terrace, thereby restoring the Later Han and its twelve emperors. The last two hundred years of the empire owes a great debt to your ancestor Li Tong. You are the progeny of loyal officials; what are you doing in the employ of that treacherous official? When you later are the object of foul cursing from ten thousand generations, won't that also tarnish the fame your ancestor Li Tong earned for loyalty and filial piety? Won't everyone be stained? Consider that Diaochan was originally Lü Bu's wife, but Dong Zhuo, seeing she was a real looker, took her in as a concubine by force. General, if your wife was forcibly snatched away by Dong Zhuo, how would you react? LI SU *speaks:* If you hadn't explained it, minister, how would I have known? How could I know that it was this old miscreant all the time who was the one without shame, or that elder brother Lü Bu was the good one? If it were me, the white-robed Li Su, that old miscreant would have been dead a long time. If I could just see big brother Lü, then I'd give him a hand and go kill that old miscreant together. MALE LEAD *speaks:* Marquis, if you haven't come out yet, what are you waiting for? LÜ BU *greets him and speaks:* Brother, why didn't you know the circumstances? LI SU *speaks:* Brother, I didn't know that all the time it was this old miscreant who was completely out of order. I'll lend you a hand and we'll go kill him ourselves. MALE LEAD *speaks:* General, since you are thinking this way now, go with me to see the Sage.

Exit together.

WU ZILAN *enters, leading* A SOLDIER, *and speaks:*

Rooting out danger and settling rebellions, I actualize my loyalty and integrity,
And by that, reveal that autumn[103] when a real man gets his ambition.

---

102. The portraits of twenty-eight generals who helped Emperor Guangwu kill Wang Mang and reestablish the Han (as the Eastern Han) were painted on the walls of Guangde Hall on Cloudy Terrace.
103. I.e., "the crucial time."

I am Wu Zilan. All because Dong Zhuo has monopolized power I cannot sleep day or night, and body and mind are both uneasy. I'll sit here in a funk today, and see who comes along. MALE LEAD *enters, together with* LÜ BU *and* LI SU, *and speaks:* I am Wang Yun, and I am going with Lü Bu and Li Su to see Wu Zilan. Here we are, already. Servant! Go report that Wang Yun, Lü Bu, and Li Su are at the gate. SOLDIER *speaks:* Understood. *Acts out reporting and speaks:* I am reporting to you, master, that Wang Yun, Lü Bu, and Li Su are at the gate. WU ZILAN *speaks:* Tell him to come in.[104] SOLDIER *speaks:* Understood. Please go in! *Acts out greeting.* WU ZILAN *speaks:* What have you come this time to discuss, minister? MALE LEAD *speaks:* Now Lü Bu and Li Su are willing to go together to capture Dong Zhuo. I have come precisely to discuss this with you. The two generals are at this moment outside the gate. WU ZILAN *speaks:* Ask them in. SOLDIER *speaks:* Understood. Please go in! LÜ BU *and* LI SU *act out greeting.* WU ZILAN *speaks:* You two generals have such loyal and righteous hearts. If you are willing to capture Dong Zhuo, your names will be marked in the historical record and you will establish a merit that will never ever decay. I will immediately report it to the Sage, and reward and higher rank will naturally follow. LI SU *speaks:* Now that is this way, please rest assured, sir. This old miscreant is inhumane, and brother Lü Bu and I will go and nab Dong Zhuo.

Exits with LÜ BU.

WU ZILAN *speaks:* Minister, this plan is really marvelous, but how can we get Dong Zhuo to come to court? MALE LEAD *speaks:* We can ask Academician Cai Yong to ask him. This man will not suspect anything. WU ZILAN *speaks:* Servant, quickly go and summon Academician Cai Yong. SOLDIER *speaks:* Understood. Academician Cai Yong, please go in. CAI YONG *enters and speaks:*

> Cleverly setting the "plot of trailing the knife,"[105]
> With joined hearts we root out evil ministers.

I am Cai Yong. The grand one has summoned me and I must hasten there. Here I am, already. Go report. SOLDIER *acts out reporting.* WU ZILAN *speaks:* Tell him to come in. SOLDIER *speaks:* Understood. Please go in! *Acts out greeting.* CAI YONG *speaks:* Why have you two distinguished officials summoned me? WU ZILAN *speaks:* We have asked you here specifically to discuss taking Dong Zhuo into custody. You can ask Dong Zhuo to come to court and then lure

---

104. Wang Yun is asked in alone.

105. A plot, usually attributed to Guan Yu, in which the knives of soldiers are trailed on the ground as they retreat. The enemy, reading it as a defeat, chases them, but the soldiers suddenly turn around and mount a counter charge.

him inside the court gates. If we nab him, you will earn rank and reward. CAI
YONG *speaks:* Rest easy, sir. First we must ask the Sage to write out an edict,[106]
and then I'll rely on the three inches of my glib tongue and persuade Dong
Zhuo to enter the court. There will surely be no problems. WU ZILAN *speaks:*
This is an excellent plan. Academician, be careful. Go quickly and return soon;
don't hesitate or tarry. We will go and report to the Sage. We are very happy
that you are willing to go and invite Dong Zhuo. We should inform the Sage
about what is going on, so that he can disseminate the edict. It cannot be
delayed.

Exits with MALE LEAD.

CAI YONG *speaks:* I'm going out the door, and as I've been talking, I reached the
gate of the Grand Preceptor's residence. I'll call out at the door. Is anyone there?
DONG ZHUO *and* LI RU, *leading* SOLDIERS, *enter.* [DONG ZHUO] *speaks:* Li Ru,
who is calling at the door? CAI YONG *speaks:* It's Academician Cai at the door.
DONG ZHUO *speaks:* Since it is Cai Yong, Li Ru, open up this corner gate and
let him in. LI RU *speaks:* Understood. I'll open the door. Academician, please
come in. *Acts greeting.* DONG ZHUO *speaks:* Cai Yong, why have you come now?
CAI YONG *acts out kneeling and speaks:* Grand Preceptor, the group of officials
has deliberated and the officials have decided this is the auspicious day. All the
officials who fill the court are waiting at the Gate of the Silver Dais, and we
sincerely invite the Grand Preceptor to enter the court and complete the grand
affair. DONG ZHUO *acts out laughing and speaks:* Good! Good! Good! I will
award all of you with high office. Bring my court robes. LI RU *speaks:* Understood. Bring the court clothes. Oh, oh. Father, you can't go to court today. These
court robes have all been chewed to pieces by bugs and mice. This is very inauspicious. There will be certain disaster if you go to court. DONG ZHUO *speaks:*
Cai Yong, I won't go to court. These court robes of mine have all been chewed
to pieces by bugs and mice. I can't go. CAI YONG *speaks:* Preceptor, this is the
time to establish the new and discard the old. DONG ZHUO *speaks:* What does
that mean? CAI YONG *speaks:* This means you'll go to the Gate of the Silver Dais
in the clothing of an official, but when you're there you have "those clothes."
This is what is meant by establishing the new and discarding the old. DONG
ZHUO *speaks:* You are right. Cai Yong was right; Li Ru was wrong. Servant,
open the central gate. LI RU *speaks:* Understood. A calamity, father! A spider's
web has sealed up tight the whole residence gate! If you go this time, I fear you
will encounter the disaster of being trapped in a net. DONG ZHUO *speaks:* Cai
Yong, I'm not going. There must be something dishonest afoot right now. CAI
YONG *speaks:* Preceptor, this is also called establishing the new and discarding

---

106. I.e., to authorize the execution of Dong Zhuo.

the old. Once you complete the grand affair inside the Gate of the Silver Dais, then you shall cover the empire as a net.[107] DONG ZHUO *speaks:* You are right; Li Ru is wrong. Servant, bring out my cart. LI RU *speaks:* One of the wheels on this four-in-hand is broken. This is a very inauspicious event. Grand Preceptor, you cannot get on the cart today. You might leave on this trip today, but you will not come back. CAI YONG *speaks:* The general has it wrong. When the Grand Preceptor's cart reaches Gate of the Silver Dais, all of the high officials will greet you, and you will mount the imperial chariot. Why stop with this four-in-hand? This is also called establishing the new and discarding the old. DONG ZHUO *speaks:* You are right; Li Ru is wrong. Say one more thing and your head will roll. You leave here! LI RU *speaks:* Enough! Enough! Enough! Father, you will not heed any of my warnings. When you go to court, you will wind up dead. Don't say then that I did not warn you! What is the point of my life? I will bid you adieu today, father. It's better to die by banging my head against the cart. *Acts out dying.*

Exits.

SOLDIER *reports and speaks:* I am informing you that Li Ru smashed his head against the cart and died. DONG ZHUO *speaks:* Huh? Li Ru smashed his head against the cart and died? Li Ru, my son, you are so unlucky! Cai Yong, through which gate are we entering? CAI YONG *speaks:* All of the officials, civil and military, are waiting inside the Gate of the Silver Dais to receive you. DONG ZHUO *speaks:* Good! Good! Good! Let's walk to the Gate of the Silver Dais. Why don't I see anyone here to greet me? CAI YONG *speaks:* Everyone is waiting inside the Gate of the Silver Dais to receive you. Let me go ahead and announce you, then bring out the minor officials to welcome you. DONG ZHUO *speaks:* Right, right. You go on ahead. CAI YONG *speaks:* I'm going through this door. Servant, close the gate.

Exits.

DONG ZHUO *speaks:* Why did Cai Yong go in and then have the gate closed? This affair has taken a turn for the worse. This is no good! I'll go back for the time being. MALE LEAD, WU ZILAN, CAI YONG *enter, leading* SOLDIERS. MALE LEAD *speaks:* Dong Zhuo, you traitorous official, where do you think you're going? Do you understand your crimes? DONG ZHUO *speaks:* Wang Yun, what have I done wrong? MALE LEAD *speaks:* Cai Yong, you read out that edict in a loud voice, and you, you traitorous official, you listen. CAI YONG *reads the edict aloud and speaks:* The edict of the August Emperor reads:

---

107. I.e., he will no longer need his residence.

From the time of the Han's burgeoning, We have controlled the August Foundation, relying on our forefathers to overcome and force the four barbarians to submit. Completely relying on officials civil and military, in hereditary line We have assumed the precious throne. Now that treacherous official Dong Zhuo has seized power and bullied us, we who are so young. He has extensively slain civil officials and let evil acts loose on the land, plotting to rebel. His Highness orders the Middle Esquire Generals Lü Bu and Li Su to execute the traitorous official Dong Zhuo, in order to warn those who would come after him. This is why this edict is proclaimed.

DONG ZHUO *speaks:* This is not right! I had better flee and save my life. Flee! Flee! LI SU *enters, leading* SOLDIERS, *and speaks:* Where are you going, you old miscreant? Eat my spear. DONG ZHUO *speaks:* Good Li Su, how dare you stab me? Where is my son, Lü Bu? LÜ BU *rushes on and speaks:* Don't flee, you old miscreant! Eat my halberd! LÜ BU *acts out using the halberd to stab* DONG ZHUO, *who acts out stumbling and falling down and speaks:* Damn! What bad luck to have. LI SU, LÜ BU *act out binding* DONG ZHUO. THE GROUP *all act out striking the drum of victory.* WU ZILAN *speaks:* Today we have punished Dong Zhuo. Ten thousand years of peace for our Sage! Now the house of Han is as stable as a massive boulder, and there will be glory for ten thousand generations. This is all due to the old minister's miraculous plan. [MALE LEAD *sings:*]

> (*Yan'er luo*)
> He had the guts, but you had them too;
> But you are righteous, and he was not.
> "A man does not have a desire to kill the tiger,
> And the tiger, no intent to kill the man!"

WU ZILAN *speaks:* That we were able to slay Dong Zhuo today was all due to your plan, minister. [MALE LEAD *sings:*]

> (*Gua yugou*)
>   Simply for the benefit
> Of the rivers and mountains of the Han did I exert all my strength,
>   And it's all due
> To all you heroes strong.

WU ZILAN *speaks:* How did Diaochan ever wind up in your household, minister? [MALE LEAD *sings:*]

>   Who could have ever expected
> That my adopted daughter Diaochan was truly Lü Bu's wife?

He[108] never should have flirted with her.
> Lü Bu has

A prestige that rises above his age,
> And Li Su,

A courage that assails Heaven itself.
> So today

We have exterminated this treacherous miscreant
And allowed ten thousand miles of radiant light to *shine like fire*.[109]

WU ZILAN *speaks:* We owe all of the thanks to Wang Yun for devising the plan by which we have killed Dong Zhuo today and brought security to the empire. All of you officials face the imperial palace and kneel. Heed now the order of the Sage. THE GROUP *kneels*. WU ZILAN *recites:*

Dong Zhuo monopolized power, flaunted his power and strength;
He turned his back on his ruler, bullied the officials, and plied his evil mind.
His treacherous mind, by unhappy fortune, grew even wilder
And took children and wives for his own use, cutting asunder Heaven's intent.
His whole household, noble and base, shall be completely slaughtered,
His corpse hacked into a myriad segments, his head hoisted on a pike.
Lü Bu turned to the good and established loyalty and goodness.
He is enfeoffed as a prince and shall guard and defend the Liao borders.
Diaochan exercised to the utmost the heart of womanhood.
Her name shall be entered in the historical record for three thousand generations.
For Wang Yun, the highest rank that a thousand stone in salary brings,[110]
> It was not in vain

To settle the state and secure the land: The Story of the Interlocking Rings.

---

108. I.e., Dong Zhuo.

109. Zhao Qimei has added two characters to the end of the printed text, *guanghui*. This has changed the grammar of the original line, which would have read, "And both [the prestige and bravery] will shine brilliantly for ten thousand miles."

110. Salary was granted in the form of grain.

TITLE: At the Gate of the Silver Dais, Lü Bu stabs Dong Zhuo.

NAME: In the Hall of Brocade Clouds: the beauty and the story of the
         interlocking rings.

The End

Editorial note:[111] *Collation begun on the morning of New Year's Day in the forty-third year [January 29, 1615] and finished while waiting for the clepsydra at the court celebration.*[112] *The Daoist of Clarity's Constancy.*

---

111. By Zhao Qimei

112. The court celebration was held on the the fifteenth of the first month (February 12, 1615), on the first day of the lantern festival known as "First Prime."

3

Newly Compiled:
Guan Yunchang's Righteous and Brave Refusal of Gold

ZHU YOUDUN

Zhu Youdun (1379–1439) is easily the most productive playwright of the first half of the fifteenth century. He wrote no fewer than thirty-one *zaju*, all of which he had printed during his lifetime. He was able to do so because he was a member of the imperial house. His father Zhu Su was the fifth son of Zhu Yuanzhang, the founder of the Ming dynasty, known as the Hongwu Emperor. Zhu Su had been enfeoffed by his father as Prince of Zhou in Kaifeng. When Zhu Su's brother Zhu Di, the Prince of Yan (a great patron of drama), rebelled in 1399 upon the death of their father against his nephew, the Jianwen Emperor, Zhu Su was suspected of complicity and removed from his position, but he was returned to Kaifeng in 1402 as Prince of Zhou when his brother had succeeded in usurping the throne, inaugurating the Yongle or "Eternal Joy" reign. Zhu Su reciprocated by capturing a *zouyu*, a mythical animal in the shape of a white tiger believed to manifest itself only during the reign of a sagely ruler. Zhu Youdun's first play of 1403 was written to commemorate this auspicious event. As his father's eldest son, Zhu Youdun also inherited his father's title upon the latter's death in 1425. When Zhu Youdun himself died, he received the title Exemplary Prince of Zhou (*Zhou Xianwang*).

Zhu Youdun's plays may be divided into roughly two equal groups. On the one hand, he wrote court pageants for performance at annual or other festivals. These included a number of deliverance plays written for performance first at his father's birthdays and then later at his own. He also wrote a number of plays to be performed at flower-viewing parties. Some other pageants are best characterized as scripts for rituals such as the end-of-the-year Nuo exorcism and the New Year's Day Lion Dance. Most of these dramas require a large cast, spectacular costumes, elaborate props, and special effects. They may also include grandly staged song-and-dance numbers. Some of these plays depart from the traditional conventions of *zaju* music by having more than one singing character or by including choral performances. On the other hand, Zhu Youdun also wrote a substantial number of "regular *zaju*," works that require a limited cast and abide by the common conventions of the genre. Presumably these plays were to be performed by both court troupes and regular *zaju* companies outside the princely palace. In many of these plays, the central theme is loyalty as exemplified by a courtesan. Professionally expected to betray her patrons for money, a courtesan's willingness to remain loyal, even if it meant her own death, proves to Zhu Youdun that loyalty is an innate virtue. Apart from these glorifications of loyalty, he also wrote a number of comedies satirizing dishonest craftsmen and disloyal courtesans or detailing the deeds of highwaymen.

Zhu Youdun's printings of his own plays are innovative in that they are the earliest known editions of *zaju* that provide readers with an approximation of the full text of a *zaju*. Zhu Youdun was very much aware of the novelty of his printings in this respect, and each title is followed by the two characters *quanbin*, meaning "with the complete dialogue." Zhu Youdun not only provides the full dialogues for all his characters; he also provides extensive stage directions for all of them. He carefully distinguishes between the stage directions and the prose of the dialogues. The titles of tunes are printed in a cartouche, and in the arias the main words of the songs are carefully distinguished from the "padding words" (*chenzi*). Zhu Youdun's carefully prepared printings are a world apart from the thirty printings of plays that have been preserved from the fourteenth century.

Guan Yunchang's Righteous and Brave Refusal of Gold (*Guan Yunchang yiyong cijin*) is somewhat of an exception among Zhu Youdun's regular *zaju* on loyalty. Whereas those plays dramatized materials from earlier fiction or from contemporary events, this play is based on history, as the author stresses in his own 1416 Introduction to the Play (included here), which praises Guan Yu as the embodiment of undiluted loyalty and righteousness. The episode chosen to exemplify Guan Yu's loyalty is his stay with Cao Cao, the period in his career when his loyalty would appear to be most compromised. Following the failure of Emperor Xian's plot to have Cao Cao murdered, a plot in which Liu Bei participated, Cao Cao had turned on Liu Bei and chased him from Xuzhou. In the ensuing mêlée the three sworn brothers Liu Bei, Guan Yu, and Zhang Fei are separated: Zhang Fei has become a highwayman in Old City, Liu Bei ends up staying with Cao Cao's adversary Yuan Shao, and Guan Yu finds himself in charge of Liu Bei's wife Lady Gan and her infant son. Under these circumstances Guan Yu, who does not know the whereabouts of his sworn brothers, is convinced by Cao Cao's general Zhang Liao to join Cao Cao. Guan Yu does so, but only on three conditions: the house that will be provided to him will be divided into two separate apartments; he will surrender to the Han and not to Cao Cao; and once he learns the whereabouts of Liu Bei, he will join him again. Cao Cao, who dominates the Han court as prime minister, agrees to these three stipulations and treats Guan Yu, whose martial qualities he greatly admires, most generously. Once Guan Yu has obtained information about the whereabouts of Liu Bei, he does not immediately leave, because, he says, he first wants to repay Cao Cao for his excessive kindness. He does so by killing Yuan Shao's redoubtable warrior, Yan Liang. When he finally does depart, he leaves behind all of Cao Cao's earlier gifts.

According to the brief account of this sequence of events in the *Records of the Three Kingdoms*, Cao Cao acquiesced to Guan Yu's departure because "each man serves his own lord." According to the later tradition, however, as reflected in the *Records of the Three Kingdoms in Plain Language*, Cao Cao tried to prevent Guan Yu from leaving by having his generals catch up with Guan Yu and offer him a fine robe as "a farewell gift"—should Guan Yu dismount to accept the gift, that would provide the immensely strong "Equal to Nine Oxen" Xu Chu with the opportunity to grab him. The smart Guan Yu, however, saw through the trick, refused to dismount, picked up the coat with the tip of his sword, and continued on his journey. Zhu Youdun fused these two versions of events by having Cao Cao grant Guan Yu's departure, but also by having Cao Cao's general Xiahou Dun try to kill Guan Yu against the express orders of Cao Cao. Zhu Youdun's Guan Yu also has to tread a fine line in defending his loyalty to Liu Bei because Cao Cao, despite all his power, never deposed the legal Han Emperor.

Zhu Youdun's *Refusal of Gold* is not the only dramatic treatment of this crucial episode in the career of Guan Yu. Among the anonymous plays included in the Maiwang Studio collection we find a play entitled *Guan Yunchang's Lonely Trek of a Thousand Miles (Guan Yunchang qianli duxing)*, which provides an elaborate dramatization of the events from Cao Cao's attack on Xuzhou to the reunion of the three sworn brothers at Old City, where Guan Yu proves his loyalty to Liu Bei to a suspicious Zhang Fei by killing Cai Yang, a general who has been dispatched by Cao Cao to capture the "fugitive" Guan Yu.[1] A *Formulary of Correct Sounds for an Era of Great Harmony (Taihe zhengyin pu)* of the early fifteenth century lists in its catalogue section a title *Traveling a Thousand Miles Alone (Qianli duxing)*, but that most likely does not refer to the play in the Maiwang Studio collection, which shows all the signs of being a Ming palace production. A more likely candidate is the equally anonymous *Traveling a Thousand Miles Alone* of which the sixteenth-century aria anthology and formulary, *Songs of Happy Peace (Yongxi yuefu)*, has preserved the full set of songs of the first act. But because these songs from the first act describe Guan Yu's journey and his arrival at Old City, this play must have started at the point in the story where Zhu Youdun's *Refusal of Gold* left off. Fragments of an anonymous early play entitled *Beheading Cai Yang (Zhan Cai Yang)* have also been

---

1. A full translation of that play is available in Ross 1976. The translation of the last two acts of the play was published in Ross 1977.

preserved, but nothing remains of the anonymous play entitled *Guan Yunchang's Reunion with His Brothers at Old City* (*Guan Yunchang gucheng juyi*), which at one moment was included in the Maiwang Studio collection but has not come down to us.

Zhu Youdun's *Refusal of Gold* is in practically all respects a regular *zaju*. It consists of four sets of songs that are assigned to the male lead who plays the part of Guan Yu in Acts 1, 2, and 4, and that of a messenger reporting Guan Yu's victory over Yan Liang to Cao Cao in Act 3. Act 4 is preceded by a wedge. The "messenger act" is often a convenient device to deal with scenes of violence that may be difficult to enact on stage,[2] but in this play Act 2 is devoted to dramatizing Guan Yu's victory over Yan Liang, so at first sight this act might appear superfluous. Zhu Youdun, however, would appear to have been greatly attracted to the aesthetics of the messenger act, with its alternation of descriptive arias to be sung and descriptive passages in parallel prose that were recited. Seven of his thirty-one plays feature a messenger act of some kind. The contemporary Taiwanese scholar Tseng Yong-yih has praised Zhu Youdun's songs in Act 3 in the following manner: "Through the mouth of the messenger, he [i.e., Zhu Youdun] narrates the battle. In an unhurried style he depicts Guan Yu's vigorous and forceful spirit vividly evoking his haughty self-confidence on the battlefield." It should also be pointed out that the messenger act here also has the dramatic function of impressing on Cao Cao Guan Yu's superior qualities as a warrior.

A unique feature of the messenger act in *Refusal of Gold* is that the entrance of the main messenger who will sing the set of songs is preceded by the entrance of a group of four messengers who sing in unison to the tune *Dou anchun*, the opening aria of the set. The unique opening of this act follows the unique ending of Act 2, in which the clown, playing the part of Cao Cao's general Xiahou Dun, sings a comic song to the tune of Guan Yu's coda, immediately after the male lead has left the stage. Another remarkable but not exceptional aspect of Act 2 is its farcelike opening, consisting of a dialogue between the clown and the added male, which relies for its comic force on punning. It should perhaps also be pointed out that the two songs used for the wedge are not songs typically used in a wedge—actually, they are more typically used in a final demi-act, in this way stressing perhaps that this moment in the plays marks the end of Guan Yu's stay with Cao Cao.

The importance of Act 4, which portrays a Guan Yu who has left Cao Cao, is underlined by its special musical structure. The main body of its set of songs

---

2. See Act 5 of Zhu Youdun's *Black Whirlwind Li Spurns Riches out of Righteousness* in West and Idema 2010, pp. 385–88, for a good example.

consists of songs to the nine variations of the tune *Huolang'er*. These so-called *Zhuandiao Huolang'er* or *Jiuzhuan Huolang'er* occur only in one earlier play, the anonymous *The Peddler: A Female Lead* (*Huolang dan*), in which these songs are used to provide the heroine of that play the opportunity to perform an extensive narrative of her misfortunes in front of a high official who eventually turns out to be her son. In *Refusal of Gold*, the suite is more tightly integrated into the action but still retains a strong narrative emphasis, allowing Guan Yu to recount his background and career to Xiahou Dun and his companions. However, Guan Yu then proceeds to sing elaborate songs in which he spells out the moral duties incumbent on officials at the present moment and provides Cao Cao with a number of honorable alternatives. One can only surmise that *Zhuandiao Huolang'er* made great demands on the singing abilities of the actor or actress concerned.[3]

Zhu Youdun's *Refusal of Gold* has also been preserved in a 1558 printing in an anthology of ten plays entitled *Ten Strips of Brocade Northern Dramas* (*Zaju shiduanjin*). This printing is largely identical to Zhu Youdun's own, but one aspect of the later printing deserves mention. During the Yuan and early Ming actors representing characters on horseback rode bamboo horses on stage. In *Refusal of Gold*, Zhu Youdun is very specific in specifying which actor is riding or dismounting his bamboo horse. By the early sixteenth century, this stage routine must have gone out of fashion, as the *Ten Strips of Brocade* edition of the play contains no reference to the use of the bamboo horse. The *Ten Strips of Brocade* also omitted the clown's coda song at the end of Act 2 but maintained the choral singing of *Dou anchun* by the foursome of messengers at the opening of Act 3.

Because the plays of Zhu Youdun have been rather inaccessible since the final decades of the Ming, they have attracted little critical attention. *Refusal of Gold*, however, is an exception, one surmises, as much because of its theme as because of its literary qualities. Qi Biaojia, the official and drama critic who would commit suicide out of loyalty to the fallen Ming dynasty in 1645, had the following to say:

> Not only are the righteousness and courage of Lord Guan displayed right before our eyes for all eternity, but also the tricks of A'man [Cao Cao] to ensnare the hero are shown on the spot. I had always regretted that Lord Guan had no fine biography, so I greatly rejoiced upon discovering this play.

---

3. On the metrical system of *Zhuandiao Huolang'er*, see Dale Johnson 1980, pp. 169–74. The suite from *The Peddler: A Female Lead* has been translated in Idema and West 1982, pp. 278–98.

And, writing in the 1930s, when Japan was increasingly encroaching on Chinese territory, the modern scholar Zheng Zhenduo declared that the play "gives full expression to the loyal and brave spirit of a great hero."

It should be kept in mind that in the Ming and Qing dynasties Guan Yu had grown into one of the most popular and powerful divinities in the Chinese pantheon. If Jesus was tempted by the Devil before he set out on his preaching, Guan Yu likewise rejected the temptations of the devilish Cao Cao before rejoining Liu Bei and assisting him in fulfilling his preordained mission. According to the *Analects*, Confucius once stated that he had never met a man who loved virtue as much as sex. Guan Yu is the hero who rises above all temptations of money and sex. Not only does he reject Cao Cao's gifts of money and comely maidens, but he also behaves with exemplary propriety toward his sister-in-law, despite the opportunities potentially provided by her dependent position during the shared stay with Cao Cao and during the "lonely trek of a thousand miles." Guan Yu's conspicuous display of "loyalty and righteousness"— a phrase used frequently throughout the play—still fascinates his Chinese audiences.

In the later *Romance of the Three Kingdoms*, Guan Yu's stay with Cao Cao and his eventual departure are treated in a number of scenes in chapters 25 through 27. These chapters further develop Cao Cao's generosity to Guan Yu and mention that Cao Cao presents Guan Yu with Red Hare, a magnificent steed that once belonged to Lü Bu and becomes Guan Yu's favorite mount. The novel also describes not only Guan Yu's victory over Yan Liang, but also that over Wen Chou.

Dramatis personæ in order of appearance

Role type	Name and family, institutional, or social role
Extra, added male	Zhang Liao, general under the command of Cao Cao
Male lead	Guan Yu
Female	Lady Gan, the wife of Liu Bei
Child	Infant son of Liu Bei and Lady Gan
Females	Ten beautiful maidens presented by Cao Cao to Guan Yu
Clown	Xiahou Dun, general under the command of Cao Cao
Extra clown	role unspecified—Adjutant to Xiahou Dun?
Added male	role unspecified—Messenger?
Extra	Yan Liang, general under the command of Yuan Shao
Troops	Common soldiers
Extra	Cao Cao, also known as Cao Mengde
Messengers	Messengers
Male lead	Messenger
Clown	Xu Chu
Clown	Innkeeper and wine seller

Introduction to the Play Guan Yunchang's Righteous and Brave Refusal of Gold

In a man's life, loyalty and filial piety are simply the greatest virtues for all time, and the way of loyalty and filial piety is necessarily established through sincerity. I observe that from ancient times those persons who are highly famed for their great virtues have been sincere in their loyalty and filial piety. People record them in books and writings, and they leave their renown to posterity so that each and every one of them may be counted. Not only do they leave their renown to posterity; their undiluted and sincere energy rising up becomes a divinity, and descending determines disaster and happiness, so they are for all eternity recorded in the sacrificial canons.

Therefore the loyal vassals and filial sons of ancient times who would practice the way of loyalty and filial piety based themselves on sincerity. Now, if one faces the caitiffs as a single horseman,[4] alleviates thirst by praying to a well,[5] lies down on the ice on behalf of one's mother, or grabs a tiger to save one's father,[6] this certainly isn't because the thirst of people, the cruelty of caitiffs, the cold of the ice, or the fierceness of a tiger are things one can avoid with a happy smile! But they all pursued their vow and achieved loyalty and filial piety. Basing themselves on their undivided sincerity, they were daring in their loyalty and daring in their filial piety.

Whenever I read history and come to the scene of Guan Yu leaving Cao Cao and returning to Liu Bei, I cannot but close the book and sigh thrice, convinced that the sincerity of Yunchang's loyalty and righteousness reached the divinities and permeated heaven and earth. Now, Cao Man was a crafty brave with a vicious and cruel mind. He was of a different order than tigers and caitiffs! But if

---

4. A reference to Guan Yu's beheading of Yan Liang as described in this play.

5. When the first-century general Geng Gong was campaigning in Central Asia, he on one occasion was besieged and cut off from water supply. He then had a deep well dug, which yielded water upon his sincere prayers. "Geng Gong prayed to his well" is one of the common stories found in elementary primers.

6. Two well-known cases in the *Twenty-four Exemplars of Filial Piety*: Wang Xiang lay down on the ice in order to melt it with his body so he would be able to provide his cruel stepmother with the carps she demanded, while Yang Xiang attacked the tiger that had captured his father. Needless to say, Wang Xiang got his carp and Yang Xiang managed to free this father.

Cao could not bring himself to kill Yunchang when the latter, in the end, was capable of pursuing his vow of loyalty and righteousness, it wasn't because Cao had the magnanimity of a hero of the kind displayed by Gaozu of the Han[7] or Taizong of the Tang[8] in their actions. It was brought about by the undiluted sincerity of Yunchang's loyalty and righteousness, just like that tiger and those caitiffs were incapable of bringing themselves to kill him. Fitting it is that later generations list Yunchang in the canons of sacrifice and that he determines disaster and blessing! His proper and straight energy will forever survive throughout heaven and earth!

Because I admired his behavior, I made this play in order to broadcast his great virtues of loyalty and righteousness, and so I wrote this introduction.

Written on the first day of the eighth month of the *bingshen* year [August 23, 1416] of the Yongle reign.

---

7. Liu Bang, the founder of the Han dynasty.
8. Li Shimin, the actual founder and second ruler of the Tang dynasty.

Newly Compiled

Guan Yunchang's Righteous and Brave Refusal of Gold
With the complete dialogues

EXTRA, *costumed as* ZHANG LIAO, *enters, opens, and recites:*

> The state of Han divided into three: Wei, Shu, and Wu;
> Heroes, standing in contention like a tripod's legs, ply their crafty schemes.
> He who preserves loyalty during a lifetime's fierce fighting
> May truly be called a man among men.

I am Zhang Liao, General of Cleansing the Realm of Bandits under the command of Lord Cao. Lord Cao has conducted a campaign in the east since the fifth year of the Jian'an reign [AD 200]. After he obtained Liu Xuande's tiger-like general Guan Yunchang, he appointed him deputy general and treated him most generously. This fierce general has only to give out one furious yell, and a combined force of ten thousand common men cannot match his courage. His heart is set on virtue and righteousness, and he is determined to maintain his unwavering loyalty.[9] Today Lord Cao has set aside wine and food, soup and rice, and he has selected ten beautiful maidens and a hundred yi[10] of gold, and has ordered me to take them over and visit him. During the banquet I will try to change his thinking with a few well-chosen words. If he is willing to serve Lord Cao with all his heart and forget about Liu Xuande, then the empire will be pacified without trouble. I'd better go on.

Exits.

MALE LEAD, *costumed as* GUAN YUNCHANG, *enters and speaks:* I am the Han general Guan Yu, also known as Yunchang. I hail from Xieliang in Hedong. From the time General of the Left Liu Xuande and I became sworn brothers, in the camp we have slept in the same bed and eaten from the same table. Unfortunately the city of Xiapi was overrun in the last few days, and I arrived here

---

9. Literally, a loyalty that cannot be created by demands of others; it is actualized solely within his own nature.

10. One yi equals twenty-four ounces (*liang*). Roughly equal to two troy pounds.

in Xuchang bringing my sister-in-law, Lady Gan, together with my little nephew. We live here in a single house divided into two courtyards. Lord Cao treats me most generously and has appointed me deputy general: his favor and trust are unmatched. But in my opinion a loyal vassal does not serve two lords. On that day in the Peach Orchard I committed myself to serve Xuande; I am unwilling to serve anyone else! But my sister-in-law does not understand my true intentions and says that I have truly gone over to Lord Cao. When I see my sister-in-law again, I will explain the situation to her, so she will understand my loyalty. I imagine how difficult it must have been long ago for Emperor Guangwu to establish the state and restore the Liu![11] MALE *sings:*

(XIANLÜ MODE: *Dian jiangchun*)
> I only want
The state's good fortune to endure and last,
Our current court to flourish and prosper.
> I desire to
Drive troops forward to serve my king with all my might,
> So in a distant future
My portrait will be depicted on Cloudy Terrace![12]

(*Hunjiang long*)
> Ever since
The Yings of Qin[13] were destroyed by Heaven.
The two founders of the Han, Gaozu and Guangwu,
> In protecting and guarding
The embroidered brocade of mountains and rivers,
> Have relied on
Walls of metal and moats of boiling water.
> In the past
China and Barbaria adhered to the orthodox succession for four
hundred years,[14]
> But later

---

11. Emperor Guangwu (Liu Xiu) reestablished the Han dynasty in AD 25 after many years of warfare following the interregnum of the Xin dynasty.

12. Cloudy Terrace had been established by Emperor Mingdi (r. 58–75) and displayed the portraits of twenty-eight generals who had achieved merit in the establishment of the Eastern Han.

13. Ying was the surname of the royal family of Qin. Ying Zheng proclaimed himself First Emperor of the Qin dynasty in 221 BC. Following his death in 210, the empire quickly descended into chaos.

14. Counting the Western Han (206 BC–AD 9) and the Eastern Han (AD 25–220) as one dynasty.

Recalcitrant warlords laid down the rules of the court.
> Barely had

Eunuchs[15] and favorites been removed,
> When favors were lavished on

Relatives by marriage and women of the pepper chambers.[16]
> Barely had

That violent Dong Zhuo been executed,
> When we ran into

That crafty and treacherous Cao Man!
> All because

Dong Cheng and Zhong Ji spilled the secret plan,[17]
> This stirred up a

Secret edict hidden in a belt to increase our misery.
It induced the heroes to chase the deer,[18]
> And leaves me uselessly

All alone [to patch up the fence] after losing the sheep.[19]

FEMALE, costumed as LADY GAN, enters, leading CHILD — acts out greeting MALE. — MALE acts out offering wine. — FEMALE speaks: Dear brother-in-law, by any chance have you found out where Liu Xuande is? — MALE speaks: — I just learned that after our troops dispersed he has been staying with Yuan Shao, the Warden of Jizhou. Yuan Shao treats him very generously, so, sister-in-law, you don't have to worry! — FEMALE speaks: — I've also heard people say that he died, so I don't know what's true yet. — MALE speaks: — Sister-in-law, don't believe it! The ancients said: "The true king will not die." And they also said: "The lucky man has heavenly features." My elder brother cannot have died because his body is seven feet tall, his hands reach below his kneecaps, he is magnanimous and virtuous, he nurtures gentlemen and seeks out the wise, and he cultivates and manages his royal inheritance—and the fighting has only just

---

15. On the suppression of the eunuchs in Emperor Ling's reign, see the introduction to *Interlocking Rings*.

16. These were empresses and royal consorts, and by extension their families. The "pepper chambers" were bedrooms whitewashed with a mixture that included Sichuan pepper (*fagara*). It was supposed to produce warmth, fragrance, and by virtue of its many "seeds" (*duozi*) induce fertility for the women who occupied them.

17. Dong Cheng was the father-in-law of Emperor Xian (r. 189–220) who at one moment gave him a secret edict to kill Cao Cao. Zhong Ji was also involved in this plot. The plot was discovered, and Cao Cao killed Dong Cheng and Zhong Ji along with many others. As Liu Bei had also been involved in the plot, Cao Cao turned against Liu Bei at this moment.

18. I.e., to engage in warfare in order to become emperor.

19. Trying to restore order to things after the bad act has already occurred.

started. There is no way he has died. Sister-in-law, let me explain it to you. —
MALE *sings*:

> (*You hulu*)
> He who subdues others by virtue will flourish in this world—
> How could he pass away?
>> My elder brother has
> A body seven feet tall—
> A face so impressive;
> Energy so full and extraordinary:
> The image of a hero to command the age!
> Modest by nature, he has great magnanimity to win over the masses.
>> My elder brother is
> Pure in his love and righteousness,
> Long in wisdom and foresight.
>> From his birth he grew till
> His hands reached below his kneecaps—an extraordinary
>   characteristic!
>> He is bound to
> Achieve the position of Prince of Hanzhong![20]

FEMALE *speaks*: — My dear brother-in-law, then why have you surrendered to Lord Cao if our Liu Xuande has such virtue? — MALE *speaks*: — Dear sister-in-law, you absolutely do not understand that real heroes pledge themselves to each other on the basis of righteous friendship in order to make a name in this world. How can they be compared to the ordinary men who commit suicide and die unknown in some ditch? If I wanted to kill Lord Cao and escape, I imagine, that would be no problem at all. — FEMALE *speaks*: — If you say it is so easy, why haven't you yet killed Lord Cao and made your escape? Wouldn't that have been better? — MALE *speaks*: — Not necessarily so. If a real hero acts, he does so with great fanfare, clearly for all to see like the sun and moon! How could I be a fellow who commits a murder in secret and flees for asylum some-where? Sister-in-law, listen to me explain it! — MALE *sings*:

---

20. When Liu Bang and his troops had outraced Xiang Yu and his army and had been the first to arrive at Xianyang, he was not enfeoffed with "the lands within the passes" (the Wei valley of Shaanxi province) as had been promised to him, but with the much poorer and very isolated area on the upper reaches of the Han River as Prince of Hanzhong. From this base, however, he would proceed to defeat Xiang Yu. When shortly before his death Cao Cao forced Emperor Xian to elevate his title to that of Great King of Wei, Liu Bei would assume a similar title of Prince of Hanzhong. As the historical Guan Yu died in 219, before Liu Bei assumed the title of emperor, this may well be the highest possible title of Liu Bei that Guan Yu could have imagined.

(*Tianxia le*)
  Such a
Secret murder does not count as brave:
  Even if I
Killed him,
  It would display no
Superior degree of insight.
  How could I agree to
Commit the vile acts of robbers or assassins?
  All I wish is
To spread my heroic fame through eternity,
To establish a fragrant name to be bandied about for a hundred ages,
  By relying on my ability
To capture heroes galore like turning my hand!

FEMALE *speaks:* — Brother-in-law, as you have reliable information about Liu Xuande, I am less worried. — EXTRA *enters with* FEMALES, *carrying boxes, and speaks:* — I, Zhang Liao, accompanied by these beautiful maidens and yellow gold, and bringing some tea and rice, have arrived outside the gate of General Guan. Gatekeeper! Go announce us. — FEMALE *speaks:* — I will go back inside now that people from Lord Cao are here.

FEMALE, CHILD exit.

EXTRA, MALE *act out greeting each other.* — EXTRA *speaks:* Ever since our Lord Cao obtained your services, general, he has been extremely pleased, just like a dragon finding clouds[21] or a tiger sprouting wings. He is worried that there is no one to serve you in your inn and that you lack the daily necessities. He hopes to express his sincere appreciation by sending these ten beautiful maidens and this hundred *yi* of gold. He very much hopes you will accept these gifts. — MALE *speaks:* — I am very much aware that ever since I joined Lord Cao after I lost Xiapi, he has treated me most generously, far more generously than others. He also has appointed me deputy general. I've received plenty of favor from him. How can I dare accept these beautiful maidens and this yellow gold? Please, sir, take these back in order to keep my loyalty and righteousness untarnished. — EXTRA *speaks:* — Everybody knows of Lord Cao's desire to cherish capable men. Because you have no family with you, he has now selected these beautiful maidens as a present. Why do you insist on refusing them? — MALE *speaks:* — You say that Lord Cao cherishes capable men? Listen to me explain! — MALE *sings:*

---

21. The Chinese dragon can rise into the sky only with the aid of the moisture of the clouds.

(*Nezha ling*)
>   I think that if Lord Cao
> Cultivates men of worth,
> It's to capture bandits and chase robbers away!
>   If Lord Cao
> Establishes virtue,
> It's to order the Three Mainstays and Five Norms.[22]
>   If Lord Cao
> Exhausts his loyalty,
> It is to assist his king stabilize the state.

EXTRA *speaks:* Lord Cao's red heart of loyalty is burning brightly; he would never dare neglect proper protocol. As you are both servants of the Han dynasty and Lord Cao greatly loves you, why do you, general, refuse to accept these gifts? — MALE *sings:*

>   Why do I
> Display my red heart and refuse these fine maidens?
> Reject his gracious gift and decline this yellow gold?
>   It's all to
> Add further luster to Lord Cao's spectacular favor!

EXTRA *speaks:* Our Lord Cao: his schemes are subtle, his wisdom broad; he is good at scrutinizing; he knows people; he recognizes and promotes exceptional, talents, pays no heed to base status or poor background; if his troops have yet to eat, he will not speak of hunger; if his troops have yet to bivouac, he will not retire to his tent. He treats his officers like his trusted friends, shares good and bad with conscript troops. At court he holds—as general and minister—all power, in the empire he leads—as hero and brave—all other leaders. So, general, why are you so suspicious that you intently reject his gracious gifts? — MALE *sings:*

(*Que ta zhi*)
>   Don't so
> Insistently beseech me!
>   You and I
> Should discuss this well.
>   You want me

---

22. The bases of social order: three mainstays are the relationships between ruler and minister, father and son, and wife and husband; the five norms are those three relationships and two others: elder and younger brother, friend and friend. This is a metonymy for good government and the social order that it brings.

To drink without restraint this wine sealed with yellow,[23]
And drunkenly cuddle those made up red.
>   You only want
To wag your three-inch pointed tongue, its devilish skill,
And loquaciously natter on about black and yellow.

EXTRA *speaks:* General, I wouldn't dare come here to persuade you to do something. But a banquet has been laid out, and I invite you to drink a few cups or so. — *Acts out offering wine.* — BEAUTIFUL MAIDENS *act out singing together.* — MALE *sings:*

>   (*Jisheng cao*)
>   Silk and gauze in a row: a fine banquet has been laid,
>   Surrounded by panpipes and songs here at the painted hall.
>   Green ants,[24] new and unstrained, and cups made out of glass,
>   Are filled to the brim with jade liquor, fermented from grapes.
>   How high they lift the spring colors, bejeweled beakers!
>   But I am only
>   A lonely traveler here at the inn, a drifter roaming about,
>   So let that fact
>   Dampen the splendor of their song before the cups of bamboo
>   leaf![25]

EXTRA *once again offers wine.* — MALE *speaks:* That's enough of wine; let's all go back. Please express my gratitude to Lord Cao for his kind intentions. — MALE *sings:*

>   (*Zui zhong tian*)
>   Let me tell you:
>   "When the wine is finished, warm no more;
>   After you're drunk, be a meek lamb led away."

EXTRA *speaks:* General, have one more cup! — MALE *sings:*

>   Don't just
>   "Point out the silver bottles and ask to taste the wine."
>   Many thanks, Chancellor Cao!

MALE *speaks:* — And please take these one hundred *yi* of yellow gold back with you. —EXTRA *speaks:* Lord Cao offered those to you without any ulterior motive, so please take them for your use. — MALE *sings:*

---

23. Wine designated to be drunk by Cao Cao alone.
24. A designation for newly brewed ale.
25. A conventional designation of fine ale.

Why do I need yellow gold to fill my coffers?

MALE *speaks:* — And these ten beautiful maidens have to go back too. — EXTRA *speaks:* Lord Cao only sent you these ten girls because you had nobody to take care of you, so there's absolutely no need to refuse them! Please keep them as a gesture toward Lord Cao. — MALE *sings:*

> Just because I am
> A traveler far away from home,
>> Don't think I will
> Engage in any amorous match!

EXTRA *speaks:* — General, if you don't want those girls, that's fine. But this gold is money, so how could it soil your fine virtue to accept it? — EXTRA *acts out kneeling down and offering the gold in both his hands.* — MALE *sings:*

> (Jinzhan'er)
> I weigh this out minutely
> And mull it over carefully:
> Three times, five times—it's hard to counter!
> What's the harm in accepting a bit of fame, a tiny profit?
>> If I simply
> Guard my sincerity and long for my former ruler,
>> I see no problem in
> Accepting an empty position here in this court.
>> How it makes me
> Sigh that my unwavering loyalty follows the sun's setting,
> And grieve that separation's bitterness is as endless as the sky!

MALE *speaks:* Fine then! I will accept this gold and be done with it. — *Acts out accepting the gold.* — EXTRA *speaks:* — General, your name is feared through-out the empire. Today you have accepted Lord Cao's great kindness and thus, on the basis of righteousness, one great man assents to another. Although it is the General on the Left, Liu Xuande, who is bound close to you by oath, for you two generals it is quite a bother to come and go between two states, and it is not the right solution. Why not "shun that and side with this" as a technique to ensure your position? If you fail to achieve final merit and fame and meet with unpropitious times, what would you do then? Will you still cling to your old companions and claim that a life-and-death friendship has to be on the basis of loyalty and righteousness? Will you not, then, forget how it all started? You have to give it some thought. General, you should make your choice. — MALE *speaks:* — I am very well aware that Lord Cao treats me with utmost sincerity, and I am deeply grateful for his intentions. But in the past I have received the favors of Liu Xuande, and I have sworn to share his life and death. I cannot betray him. Let me explain it to you. — MALE *sings*:

> (*Zui fu gui*)
> When I became the sworn brother of Pingyuan's magistrate,
> I never thought we once would turn into Shen and Shang.[26]
>> But our
> Friendship in life and death cannot be forgotten—
> The oath we swore remains and cannot be denied.
>> Uselessly it makes me
> Gaze to heaven's edge: clouds of sorrow and my home village
> All pinched together on my sad brows.

EXTRA *speaks*: General, if you don't intend to stay here for long, why don't you take your leave from Lord Cao and go and seek out Liu Bei? — MALE *speaks*: — I have received Lord Cao's great kindness. I must establish some merit. I must repay him. Then it will be time to go. — EXTRA *speaks*: — At present the heroes and braves of the empire each occupy a separate region. At which place do you want to establish your merit to repay Lord Cao? — MALE *sings*:

> (*Jinzhan'er*)
>> It's not the case that I
> Brag about my strength,
> But I dare take on the fight.
>> Just wait until I
> Establish merit and fame in order to repay Minister Cao:
> Rumblingly, brilliantly, I will display my eagle's might.
>> Just look at my
> Golden lance shimmering in the morning sun,
> And my precious sword, cleaving autumn's frost.
>> I don't care whether
> Zu Shou is encamped at Yan Ford;[27]
>> I'm not afraid of that
> Yan Liang, now stationed at Official Ford.

MALE *speaks*: — As a vassal I will exhaust my loyalty, all for the sake of the empire of the Lius of Han. Liu Xuande and Lord Cao may each lead their troops and conduct their campaigns, but they both are vassals of the house of Han. MALE *sings*:

---

26. Shen and Shang are two stars that never appear in the sky at the same time.

27. Zu Shou was one of the officers in the army of Yuan Shao. Captured by troops of Cao Cao, he refused to surrender and was killed.

(*Zhuan Coda*)

> Relying on my
> Merit in supporting and upholding the altars of the state,
> A magnanimity that holds within it the whole universe,
> This one heart of mine is clear as the sky, bright as the sun.
> I am different from those
> Recalcitrant warlords and crafty braves, all black-hearted!
> I only want to
> Establish merit and honor; strictly adhere to the norms of the court;
> Maintain loyalty and virtue so green staves[28] can transmit my fame.
> As the manliest of men, my authority and my courage are unyielding.
> For the moment I am
> Temporarily staying here at Xuchang,
> And my mood and feelings are muted by unhappiness,
> Consumed by fear that,
> Trapped in the dust, my Ganjiang[29] will get rusty.

MALE *exits.* — EXTRA *speaks:* — At this banquet I have tried for a full day to make General Guan change his mind, but to no avail. He also has refused these beautiful maidens. I will have to go back and report to Lord Cao.

EXTRA *exits.*

[Act 2]

CLOWN, *costumed as* XIAHOU DUN, *enters and recites:*

> Arranging troops and disposing formations, I've never been victorious;
> When in a face-off with opposing fortifications, I'm scared witless.
> If some enemy country wants to know my name and surname,
> I am that
> Xiahou Dun who fears the blade and runs from arrows.

I am Xiahou Dun, and I serve under the banners of Lord Cao as the Might-Establishing General. When joining the battle in the campaign against Xuzhou, my left eye was done blinded[30] by Lü Bu's arrow. When I joined the battle while defending Puyang, my left leg was done crippled by Zhang Liao's lance. So when

---

28. Until the invention of paper in AD 105, books were written on bamboo strips or narrow wooden tablets; newly stripped or worked, they appeared green.

29. Ganjiang is the name of a famous sword of legendary antiquity. It is also the name of the sword smith who produced the sword.

30. The words translated here as "done" are all pronounced *dun*, meaning strike or hit. It has the same pronunciation as the Dun in the name of Xiahou Dun.

I now go into battle, my greatest fear is to be "done." — EXTRA CLOWN *speaks:* — But why are you done called Xiahou Dun? — CLOWN *speaks:* — If I'm done done on top by anyone else, then I done do them on the bottom.[31] — ADDED MALE *enters and speaks:* — At present the Warden of Jizhou, Yuan Shao, is encamped with his infantry and cavalry at Official Ford, and his superior general, Yan Liang, challenges us to battle. — CLOWN *acts out panicking.* — CLOWN *asks:* What kind of weapons does that Yan Liang use? — ADDED MALE *recites:* —

> In his hands he holds a twelve-foot lance tipped with steel,
> And on his body is hung seven-star[32] raven-black oiled armor.
> On his head he wears a triple-crossed cap of purple gold,
> Around his waist is tied a lion belt studded with jewels.

ADDED MALE *asks:* General, which weapon will you wield? — CLOWN *speaks:* He's of no use! He's of no use at all! What kind of stalwart hero is he if he has to wear so much stuff? Dressed like this, he must be afraid of getting wounded when going into battle. I'm not scared in the least! Just listen to me. — CLOWN *recites:* Now as for my troops,

> They wear no battle gowns or chain-mail armor,
> Wear no leather helmets or steel visors;
> They use no gongs or drums, flags, or banners,
> And employ no lances or swords, bows, or arrows.
> For us no facing off with opposing fortifications,
> No fierce struggle or cruel carnage;
> I will raise a hundred thousand troops, and I will give
> Each and every one a garlic plant!

ADDED MALE *asks:* — How come you will not fight with him but give them a plant of garlic? — CLOWN *speaks:* — You don't understand strategy; you've never read your *Master Sun Wu. Master Sun* writes, "He who has many plants[33] will be victorious, and he who has few plants will not be victorious—the less so he who has no plants whatsoever!" Doesn't this mean that the one with the most garlic will win? *Beat and stop.*[34]

[*Exit.*]

---

31. *Xia* (bottom) has the same pronunciation as the element *xia* in the surname Xiahou.

32. The seven stars of the stars of the Dipper (Ursa Major), China's most potent asterism, here symbolically imparting its power to the armor.

33. "Plans" (*suan*) and "garlic" (*suan*), here transplanted as "plants," have the same pronunciation in Chinese.

34. The opening scene of this act would appear to be based on a traditional farce, which would be concluded by a physical altercation between the clown and the added male (*fumo*).

EXTRA, *costumed as* YAN LIANG, *enters and speaks:* I am Yan Liang, a superior general under the command of Yuan Benchu. Today I have arrived here at Whitehorse at the head of a great army to fight against the Cao's army. Send your strongest general out to meet me! CLOWN *enters and acts out confronting the enemy — acts out being defeated and running off.* — MALE *enters and speaks:* — I have been informed that Yan Liang has defeated Xiahou Dun. I'll go up to the front to have a look. — CLOWN *enters, running in a panic, and speaks:* — Great Prince Guan! Great Prince Guan! If you kill Yan Liang and chase his troops away, I will prepare for you a *suovitaurilia*[35] that includes a pig's head! — MALE *speaks:* How can you be in such a panic? In my eyes Yan Liang doesn't count for much. — MALE *sings:*

(SHUANGDIAO MODE: *Xinshui ling*)
In my opinion, that Yan Liang is no "match for ten thousand men."
    When confronted with my
Third-of-the-length blade,[36]
    I'm sure I will turn him into
Someone as fragile as a bent onion green!
    Here I
Rejoice as I use my martial tactics,
Banter and laugh as I explain military tricks.
    I want to relieve
This double siege of Whitehorse
And stand alone in front of my troops.[37]

(*Zhuma ting*)
    There's no need
To mass in the rear and lead in the front.
    I have prepared
A battle robe dyed in simian blood,[38] a banner of flaming fire,
    And I just want
To be one man on one mount.
    I am fitted out with
Armor of vermilion red, a helmet of gold leaf,
A precious carved saddle on a crimson ferocious beast,
A spear with ruby tassels, wound about with silk ribbons.

---

35. A sacrifice of three animals: a pig (*sus*), a sheep (*ovis*), and a beeve (*taurus*).

36. See *Tripartite Oath*, n. 35.

37. I.e., in both senses: to stand alone and unvanquished at the head of his troops, and to establish his merit alone.

38. The blood of the orangutan was believed to make a brilliant red dye.

> If I
> Display my manly might,
>> Then even
> Iron-tipped mountains will be shaken down into level plains!

MALE *speaks:* —I need no other soldiers; I will go alone to the front to have a look. — CLOWN *speaks:* — Oh no! That won't do! My millions of troops were defeated by him, so how could you go there as a single man on a single mount? — CLOWN *acts out being frightened.* — MALE *smiles and speaks:* — You really have no courage at all! — MALE *sings:*

> (Qiaopai'er)
>> The way you speak
> Lacks all courage;
>> In my eyes
> This is a relatively easy matter.
>> Even though he has
> Ten thousand battalions of fierce warriors, what's their use?
>> How many of them
> Can face off with me,
> Or stand against me?

MALE *speaks:* — Look: they have already set out their battle formation. Most likely Yan Liang will be with the central troops. — MALE *sings:*

> (*Pingsha zou kaige*)
>> I see how
> Lances and swords are arranged, as regular and even as the wings of
>> geese;
> And battle horses are aligned, stacked like the scales of a fish.
> Orders are shouted to the soldiers in the voice of fierce tigers;
> The front battle lines are arrayed in the formation of the long snake.
> Boom! Boom! They beat the battle drums;
> Whoosh! Whoosh! They wave the signal flags.
>> I don't care whether
> Their commander is surrounded by a thousand troops;
>> Here I will
> Display my general's might to all eight directions.

CLOWN *speaks:* He is right in the middle of a million troops! You are going to rush in there alone. Do you really dare do it? — MALE *sings:*

> You should not
> Hesitate in the slightest:

> Just watch as I
Display my martial arts in the midst of many battalions!

CLOWN *acts out being afraid.* — MALE *sings:*

> There is no need
To be frightened or in doubt:
> I will make sure your
Whole army goes back singing a song of victory!

> [*They exit unobtrusively.*]

EXTRA *speaks:* I am Superior General Yan Liang. I defeated Cao's army this morning in a single encounter. At present I cannot but line my troops up for battle once again and wait for Cao's troops to challenge them to battle. — MALE *rushes on stage* [*with accompanying troops*] *and acts out skewering* YAN LIANG — *act out fighting.* — TROOPS *act out giving out one yell and dispersing.* — MALE *sings while making the round of the stage while raising a helmet:*

> (*Gu meijiu*)
I entered into the massed battalions of Yuan's army
And skewered Yan Liang—as easy as a child's game.
> I take
In my hand this battle helmet smeared with blood and raise it high:
Just one man on one horse,
I return to our base camp.

> (*Taiping ling*)
> Because of my onslaught,
Their troops are defeated and slain.
Shimmering, reflecting bright, lances and swords fill the field
All cast away: in confused and chaotic disorder, gowns and armor
> piled in heaps.
Those who run for their lives: in still and soundless silence they hide
> away in the forest;
Those who surrender: with the quaking trembling shakes, they kneel
> before our horses.
> As quick as you can,
Report the situation
So the army may celebrate.
Now I have paid back Lord Cao for all his kindness.

CLOWN *speaks:* My congratulations, General Guan! In the midst of a million troops you have skewered Yan Liang and you have ended the siege of

Whitehorse. — ADDED MALE *asks:* And what did you do? CLOWN *speaks:* I performed even better! He may have skewered Yan Liang, but all he did was kill one superior general. But the army in its totality is commanded by me, Xiahou Dun. And with our big and small arrow tips we've done[39] them in until they ran! — MALE *sings:*

> (*Chuan bo zhao*)
> This very moment your face is all smiles—
> Even a wax-tipped lance[40] doesn't sink as low as you.
> > When you heard
> The battle cries and the waving flags,
> The roaring boom of the war drums,
> The battle horses' incessant whinny,
> And the thunder of the signal explosions,
> > Oh, then you were so scared
> That your faced turned as yellow as wax.
> > But at present
> You quickly talk about your military genius.

MALE *speaks:* — The most important thing now is to gather our troops and return. We also have to take the captured maps and registers, provisions and stores, wagons and carts, and weaponry of Yuan Shao with us to our camp. — MALE *sings:*

> (*Qi dixiong*)
> Don't tarry;
> Gather things up,
> And urge on the troops!
> > Take
> The maps and registers, the provisions and stores to our camp.
> > Play
> One song of martial strain on drums and fifes to rouse our might,
> > And let those two
> Fine sounds report our victory—our horses fast as flying stars!

MALE *speaks:* — Soldiers, congratulations! Today we return in victory. It happens to be the springtime of the third month. What fine scenery along the road! — MALE *sings:*

---

39. The word translated as "done" is again *dun*.

40. A "wax-tipped lance" or a "tin-tipped lance" is only good for show and not for actual fighting, so it is a common designation of a *miles gloriosus* or boasting soldier of the Falstaffian type.

(*Meihua jiu*)
Leading the soldiers I return victoriously,
At a moment close to Cold Food Festival.[41]
We race forward on the official road,
Just when the weather is most pleasant.
Willows let droop golden threads, heavy;
Grasses grow into carpets of emerald green, level.
I hear yellow orioles warbling amid the trees,
See swallows squabble over mud beneath the flowers.
Outside a lonely village the road is lost in pleasant mists,
Next to a little bridge the water runs level with the dike.
Leaning on my carved saddle, drunk on spring's radiance,
I discard battle gown and armor, and change into an unlined gown.

(*Shou Jiangnan*)
I look afar to the supreme commander's precious stronghold so
    imposing in its power!
We return, "whips striking metal stirrups, singing a song of victory."
        Ah, the
Heroic energy in my bosom spurts out to make a colorful rainbow!
        Within the state
I did away with peril and danger,
        My only desire to find
Great peace without warfare and the end of battle flags.

MALE *speaks:* Even though I displayed my courage and insight by beheading
Yan Liang, I keep thinking about my brother Xuande, who is now with Yuan
Shao. When will we be able to meet? — MALE *sings:*

(*Litingyan Coda*)
Heroes naturally have heroes to match—
How can I forget kindness once it has been bestowed?
        Involuntarily
I find myself in turmoil—
This unwavering loyalty forever ties my heart.
Remembering Xuande, I weep in vain,
So I want to inform Lord Cao of my departure.
        Today I have

---

41. Cold Food was celebrated on the 105th day following the winter solstice. This day often
falls in the early days of the third month.

Beheaded a superior general, lifted a double siege:
>> That's my way to
Repay his great kindness and establish stellar merit!

MALE *exits.* — CLOWN *speaks:* Even though I have been defeated. I also want to sing a little bit. CLOWN *sings:*

(*Litingyan Coda*)
>> He may say:
"Heroes naturally have heroes to match."
>> But I say:
Braggarts always have the tendency to be braggarts.
>> They pursued me to such an extent
That I ran fast as flying.
Holding the head of an underworld judge,[42] I kept panting without end,
And when my life was saved, happy tears coursed down.
Sabache[43] and let me declare:
>> I'll never dare again
Done do their lower end with iron door-bars;
>> Let them go ahead and
Shoot my head with leather-barbed arrowheads.[44]

Exits.

[Act 3]

EXTRA, *costumed as* CAO MENGDE, *enters and opens:*

My short armor and battle mantle are light upon my body;
My war saddle and small mud deflectors carry red tassels.
Military messages from my commanders are carried through the night,
So now let me listen at the gate of the camp for voices reporting victory.

---

42. Clowns played a major part in the Nuo ceremonies held at the end of the year to exorcise demons from the community before the beginning of the New Year. Underworld judges (*tongpan*) that were featured in these boisterous parades would be wearing large heads. As a clown, Xiahou Dun is said to be carrying such a head instead of a helmet and visor.

43. *Sabache* is a Mongol term meaning roughly "to drink without restraint."

44. The text is quite indistinct here and the translation of these last two lines consequently is very tentative. "Done" is again *dun*; the first line ends with the phrase *xiatou dun,* which is obviously a pun on his name, Xiahou Dun.

I am Cao Mengde. I have been appointed as Awe-Inspiring General and War-den of Yanzhou. Now the Warden of Jizhou, Yuan Shao, has ordered his superior general, Yan Liang, to lead his troops in an attack on Whitehorse. I have dis-patched my Might-Establishing General, Xiahou Dun; the bandit-extirpating general, Zhang Liao; and the deputy general, Guan Yu, to go and rescue White-horse from the siege. I am sure they were victorious. So I am waiting here for the messengers reporting victory. — *[Actors,] costumed as* FOUR MESSENGERS, *enter, riding bamboo horses, and speak:* That was a great battle! *They sing:*

> (YUEDIAO MODE: *Dou anchun*)
> Sounds of victory like a sudden torrent of rain;
> Messengers' horses resemble shooting stars:
> Soiled with mud are our army uniforms;
> Loosened up, the straps of our iron armor.
>> We have run so hard
> Smoke comes out of our mouths,
> And our bodies are covered in sweat.
> Men are exhausted,
> Horses worn out.
> Right now we have arrived at the gate of the precious camp,
> To be questioned slowly about the battle, about the fight!

MESSENGERS *dismount from their horses and speak:* — The messengers report-ing victory have arrived! — EXTRA *speaks:* — Suddenly appear four riders, rac-ing like stars, speeding like rain, and on all sides banners and clouds are furled by the wind and sent flying away. Now you tell me whether that is urgent or not! — ADDED MALE *speaks:* How can you see that this is urgent? — EXTRA *speaks:* Look at the horses they are riding; their bodies are covered in blood and sweat! They resemble moisture-dispensing dragons rising on clouds as they emerge from the bottom of the sea. The officers in the saddle shake their shoul-ders and grasp for breath—they are the equals of the Four Heavenly Kings descending from the clouds with drawn swords. You four lookouts, first regain your breath! Over there, there's still another messenger coming. — MALE LEAD *enters riding a bamboo horse and speaks:* Our victory in this battle was largely due to Guan Yunchang. What a fine general! — MALE *sings:*

> (YUEDIAO MODE: *Dou anchun*)
>> I've run so fast
> My strength is exhausted and my tendons quiver;
>> My horse has sped so fast
> It is splattered with mud and dust.

I just left
The sandy arena of that bloody battle,
    And have already reached
The headquarters of the commander in chief.
    Those
Soldiers who clashed
    as numerous as
        drops of rain;
The rolls of the drums
    resounding like
        roaring thunder.
    Here we are
A victorious army;
    There they
Are defeated troops.
Those who were defeated: they paid no heed to their lives;
Those who were victorious: they vied to be first to happily look on.

MALE *dismounts from horse and speaks:* — Sir! All messengers reporting victory have arrived. — EXTRA *speaks:* — Messenger reporting victory, first take time to regain your breath, then tell me exactly how we engaged the enemy and met them in battle—which side was victorious? Which side was defeated? Narrate it from the very beginning. — MALE *speaks:* —An excellent general this Guan Yu is! — MESSENGER(S) *sing(s)*:[45]

(*Zihua'er xu*)
    Relying on
The valor and courage of this one man
    Who dashed into
An army camp of ten thousand battalions!
    This far surpassed
"A hidden ambush on all ten sides."[46]
    After I saw him,
Filled with energy, displaying his martial arts,
Overwhelmingly brave, he executed his artful plans.
    Calling out angrily,

---

45. Most likely only the main messenger (the male lead) sings this aria, but the stage directions allow for the possibility that all five messengers sing.

46. Han Xin, one of the most outstanding generals in the founding of the Han dynasty, eventually brought down Xiang Yu with "a hidden ambush on all ten sides." The "ten sides" refer to the four main directions, the four directions in between, and above and below.

Half-seated in his carved saddle, his body one that could tangle with
    tigers,
        He
Looked lightly on the enemy troops.
        There he
Hastily raised his golden whip,
Hurriedly drove his dragon courser on.

EXTRA *speaks:* Tell me how General Guan was fitted out when he entered the
fray. Narrate it in detail. — MALE *speaks:* Before we saw Yunchang's martial
arts, we first observed Guan Yu's outer appearance. A red face and green[47] sideburns: the lord of the beautiful beard. His eyes are long and shapely like those
of a phoenix. A handsome build that rises above everyone else in the realm, a
hero who is the greatest of his age. His body is seven feet tall, and his energy
resembles a rainbow. He truly is a beam that can span the oceans and support
the sky! — MALE *sings:*

(*Xiaotao hong*)
        He wore
A brocaded helmet with gold-threaded phoenix wings,
And iron armor protected by a simian mantle.
His long lance of wrought iron was coated in tempered bronze;
He rode a dragon courser
That can roil rivers and seas, spurt out clouds and mists.
His carved bow was made of patterned birch,
His steel whip was inlaid with silver,
And from a precious sheath he drew his Kunwu sword!

MALE *speaks:* — The outfit of General Guan is truly manly! — EXTRA *speaks:*
— How manly? Explain it once again to me in great detail. — MALE *speaks:* — I
saw the two armies display their banners and arrange their troops. Our Might-
Establishing General, Xiahou Dun, was the first to sally forth and fight with Yan
Liang, but he was defeated after only a few bouts. General Guan was there at the
front of the troops, holding his horse in check and observing the situation from
afar. He saw how Yan Liang chased Xiahou Dun in such a way that the jade belt
around Dun's mantle was loosened and his helmet dropped its red tassels. When
the jade belt loosened, his sweat sprinkled all around him, and when the red tassels fell, his hair flowed down over his back.[48] After General Guan saw this,

---

47. "Green" refers to the green sheen of oiled hair.

48. Upper-class Chinese men would wear their long hair in a topknot on their head; this
topknot was covered by a scarf and a helmet or cap. Only shamans and madmen let their long
hair freely hang down.

He suddenly became angry,
Then promptly flew into a rage.
He furiously became upset,
And his face began to brightly burn.
He tightly cinched his carved saddle,
Hastily fastened gown and mantle.
                    I just saw—
A golden-phoenix helmet
As glistening as snow,
Metal chain-mail armor
Knitted in mottled pattern,
A crimson brocade mantle
Dyed with simian blood,
And his Kunwu sword
Unsheathed autumn's frost;
A bow of magpie birch[49]
With strings of red,
Eagle feather arrows
Tipped with steel;
A Green Dragon blade
The shape of the crescent moon,
His horse Red Hare
A rogue dragon.
                    I just saw
Him stretch out his tiger arms to stroke his beautiful beard,
With silkworm eyebrows, phoenix eyes, and cheeks of red.
                    He was
A true and proper god in service to heavenly officers,
An authentic and heroic brave for all times in the world of men.

MALE *sings:*

> (Jinjiaoye)
>   He took this
> Green Dragon blade and without hesitation lifted it up,
>   Dashing into
> The commander's tent inside seven circles of guards.
> One time he roared, his might resembling a tiger's,

---

49. *Quehua gong,* "a magpie birch bow," is what the text writes, but it is probably a mistake for the homophonous expression *quehua gong,* a common term meaning "a bow adorned with pictures of magpies." The magpie was considered to be a lucky bird.

And took
One blood-smeared human head to bring back!

EXTRA *speaks:* How wonderful, this Guan Yunchang! As he had beheaded Yan
Liang in the midst of a million troops and taken his head, I gather that those
troops must have been just like . . . — EXTRA *recites:*

> As chaotic as ants and crickets carried away by water—
> Gongs and drums kept silent, their armor turned dark,
> Last night after the Banner Star fell to earth,[50]
> And the headquarters lost a trusted commander!

How did our victorious troops kill off those defeated troops once they had lost
their superior general? — MALE *speaks:* I only saw

> Men shout and horses whinny in that disordered camp,
> Defeated battalions discard their armor and trail their swords.
> Those who ran for their life threw away boots and jackets;
> Those who wanted to surrender begged to be spared.
> Explosions echoed until they alarmed the heavens;
> Gongs were drummed until they shook the earth.
> Iron helmets had their rims flattened,
> Armor strings were snapped from the plates.
> A dark miasmic fog covered the earth;
> Pitch-black clouds rose high into the sky.
> Banging and beating, the drums were wild with noise;
> Flapping and snapping, the flags waved and fluttered.
> Clattering and banging, helmets dropped,
> Ringing and clanging, swords were put to work.
> Swift and sudden blood spurted out,
> And roiling and running, turned into moats.
> There have always been hot-pitched battles!
>> But never like
> This one in front of Whitehorse slope!

MALE *sings:*

> (*Tiaoxiao ling*)
> When all of a sudden I looked out,
>> On the other side
> Their troops had panicked,

---

50. Either the banner constellation of fixed stars or a comet, a symbol of the vanguard of an
army.

And all I saw was
Murky and hazy yellow dust obscure the great void.
General Guan on horseback often looked back,
And his
Embroidered battle-coat was blotted and smudged with blood.
When Xiahou Dun in front of the troops saw this sight, he sighed,
And he said:
"If the six Ding spirits[51] were to see him, they too would submit in
defeat!"

EXTRA *recites:*

Warhorses whinny amidst the noise of gongs and drums;
Armor flashes and shines in the shadows of banners and flags.
The general achieved his victory but hurries not to return;
All smiles, he sits in his saddle and brandishes his sword.
A red padded jacket,
Brocade battle robe—
Pursuing those who fled, chasing the defeated, as the sun goes down.
It's just as if
Three million jade dragons had withdrawn from battle:
The scales of the defeated and maimed filled the plains in piles.

MALE *sings:*

(*Tusi'er*)
They all threw away
Their strong bows and stiff crossbows,
And had dropped
Their padded jackets and battle gowns.
On our side
A mêlée of horse tracks pursued the defeated caitiffs:
Each and every one
Had sunk away to hide: near wooded slope or into deep rushes.

(*Sheng Yaowang*)
I only saw
The clouds spread over
The obstructed ravines:

---

51. The six Ding spirits of the sexagenary cycle: *dingmao, dingsi, dingwei, dingyou, dinghai,*
and *dingchou*. These are six yin spirits, envisioned as fearsome warriors who are dispatched by the
heavenly thearch when summoned by Daoist talismans to dispel evil influences.

The clothes and armor that filled the streams were a confusion of
    brocade!
They cried out in pain—
Hit by arrows!
            How different from
"A body covered by flowers' shadows—supported by pretty girls"!
            And it deeply shamed
Yuan Shao, who pouted with pursed lips.

EXTRA *speaks:* — So they had achieved victory. Military handbooks state:
"Don't pursue desperate bandits!" This is out of fear that they might risk their
lives and counterattack. Have you gathered the troops? — MALE *speaks:* Our
three great generals know no fear. They have pursued them till they scattered
like stars and dispersed like the mist. [The enemies] don't even dare rescue the
dying or assist the living. Would they dare come back to face us? Please listen
to me. MALE *sings:*

(*Malang'er*)
Those who were lightly wounded hid themselves in commoners'
    homes;
Those who were severely hit lay strewn about on the empty wastes.
Those who achieved victory brandished their spears, jumped, and
    danced;
Those who were defeated and maimed lost their souls.

EXTRA *speaks:* Did they capture money and treasure? — MALE *sings:*

(*Reprise*)
They transported provisions and stores to the imperial storehouse;
They captured valuable goods, and also maps and registers.
Having collected plenty of things from his camp
They returned as one, singing songs of victory.

MALE *speaks:* They pursued those defeated troops until no trace remained of soldiers or officers. And they gathered their troops only when dusk fell. MALE *sings:*

(*Huang qiangwei*)
Waving banners and pennants, they hastily gathered into their units;
Striking metal gongs, they gathered soldiers for the count.
The "hill of corpses"[52] was high and filled a field of a few *mou*,
And the common people who surrendered are now at peace.

---

52. It was a practice to gather the bodies of the defeated, mound them up, and cover them
with earth as a symbol of victory.

(*Qing Yuanzhen*)
> Here at this

Precious tent in the middle of the army they'll present their captives;
But to discuss merit and distribute rewards, it must be in the
  imperial capital.
> Still, the

Merits of Yunchang stand at the fore.
> He has

Excellent strategies—
His martial arts are seasoned.
His heroic courage has no equal in this world!

EXTRA *speaks:* — The messengers have come and reported victory, and they have explained everything very clearly. The messengers will be awarded a hundred *liang* of gold, ten herds of sheep, and twenty bottles of wine. They may go home and take their rest. I further order that tea and wine be prepared and gold and silver be made available to give as reward to the troops, and that a special bonus be given to Yunchang! — MALE *sings:*

(*Coda*)
> Should they come again and

Hear that General Guan will join the battle,
The troops of Yuan will quickly tremble with fear.
> Never again will they

Trust their power and might, flaunt their power, or vaunt their
  martial skills.
> If they once more encounter

His Green Dragon blade, his Red Hare horse,
His yellow-gold armor, or his crimson gown,
> They're sure to

Furl their flags, pull back their troops,
Fold their hands, and lower their heads:
They'll quickly submit to the Lord of Great Brightness.[53]

[*Exit.*]

[Wedge]

CLOWN *enters and speaks:* I am Xiahou Dun. In that battle of a few days ago I did not even win a single battle, and it had to happen to me that that red-faced

---

53. *Shengming,* "sagely brilliance," is here neutrally translated as "great brightness" and may also be understood as "great Ming."

bearded fellow skewered Yan Liang and relieved the siege of Whitehorse. Today Lord Cao will hand out rewards on the basis of merit. I am really upset about this, and I'll make certain to slander that bearded fellow just to make sure Lord Cao kills him. Then the greatest ambition of my life will be fulfilled.

Exits.

EXTRA, *costumed as* LORD CAO, *enters and speaks:* Guan Yu has established great merit today. He not only has relieved the siege of Whitehorse, but he also has beheaded one of their superior generals. I think that this guy is longing for his old lord Liu Xuande and won't be willing to stay here for long. Now he has accumulated great merit and I will reward him all the more handsomely. I'll decide what to do when I see what he's going to do. — CLOWN *enters and acts out greeting* EXTRA. — CLOWN *speaks:* — My lord, you are going to reward Guan Yu, and that man has great capabilities indeed. But he constantly thinks of Liu Bei and definitely is not willing to stay here for long. If he suddenly runs off, it would be just like releasing a tiger—you bring harm only on yourself! The best would be to do away with him as soon as possible right now, so you will not have to regret your actions later. — EXTRA *speaks:* — Absolutely impossible! If he wants to leave and join Liu Bei, that only means that "each man serves his own ruler." He is a loyal and straightforward man. How could I bring injury to him? Call him in for me, and I will reward him.

CLOWN exits.

EXTRA *speaks:* Today I will give him one hundred catties of yellow gold, one thousand ounces of silver, and a hundred thousand strings of big cash. And I will ennoble Guan Yu as Marquis within the Passes. [*Stage hands*] *act out carrying on stage the props for the rewards.* — CLOWN *enters together with* MALE. — CLOWN *speaks:* General Guan, you are greatly indebted to me for the credits of your merit. Only after I had provided a full account to Lord Cao, did he decide to reward you. The Prime Minister is waiting, so let's get moving. — MALE *acts out greeting* EXTRA. — EXTRA *speaks:* — General, you have not considered Us unworthy and have courageously established great merit in battle. You penetrated deep into the camp of the caitiffs to behead their superior general, and subsequently relieved the siege of Whitehorse. Your trust and loyalty are conspicuously brilliant, and I deeply, deeply admire you. So I have here some paltry gifts as a small token of appreciation for your rich virtue. — MALE *speaks:* — Ever since Xiapi was overrun and I came here to serve you, my lord, I have had no opportunity to exercise my loyalty and devotion to repay your great kindness. How dare I accept this high title and these extensive rewards? MALE *sings:*

(*Houting hua* followed by *Liuye'er*) (*A wedge*)
In my opinion

Repaying your great kindness with such a slight display of loyalty
> Does not merit

These gifts of gold and silver or a noble title.
> I only wished

To fully exercise my loyalty toward Your Excellency,
Establish great merit for the imperial court,
And broadcast the seeds of integrity.
> All I wish is that

Shields and spears will not be raised,
That campaigns will be stopped, warfare brought to an end.

MALE *speaks in an aside:* Even though I have accepted the noble title and these great rewards, he does not know the troubled feelings in my heart. MALE *sings:*

> They make

Pearly tears spill as I am moved by my old vexation:
I recall Liu and Zhang—when will we meet again?
> Indeed,

"Dreams can travel a thousand miles over passes and mountains."
Ever since our separation, I've seen no trace,
> And so to no avail

I stare at the lonely cloud and the returning geese right where my
gaze ends.

Exit.

[Act 4]

FEMALE, *costumed as* LADY GAN, *enters with* CHILD. — FEMALE *speaks:* Since I followed my brother-in-law here to Xuchang, more than half a year has passed. Every day we try to obtain information about Liu Xuande but have never had solid news. Brother-in-law just defeated Yuan [Shao's] army, and he got hold of one of the soldiers. Once he interrogated him, we were fully informed. Xuande is still with the army of Yuan Shao and is now heading for Ruying. Brother has sealed the storerooms and returned Lord Cao's presents. We will leave Xuchang together to find Xuande. But I am also afraid that when Lord Cao learns of this, he will send people after us to block our progress. Let me wait until brother-in-law gets here and talk it over with him. —MALE LEAD, *costumed as* GUAN YUNCHANG, *enters and acts out greeting* FEMALE. — FEMALE *speaks:* Brother-in-law, you now want to get things ready to go find Xuande. But I am still afraid that Lord Cao may come to learn of it and will have people stop us and kill us all! What should we do? — MALE *speaks:* — Sister-in-law, don't worry. Everyone says Lord Cao is a crafty brave. He may have many tricks up his sleeve, but he would not dare kill a loyal man. My trust and righteousness fill heaven and earth and reach to the intelligent gods. Even though he may be a crafty brave of some insight, he definitely dare not kill me. Listen as I, Guan Yu, will explain it. MALE *sings:*

(ZHENGGONG: *Duanzheng hao*)
Relying on wisdom and power
> they
> > collect eminent talents;[54]
Feigning love and righteousness
> they
> > win the people's hearts.
Each displays his heroic valor, his martial excellence:
In confusing chaos they occupy land and scheme for the highest
> achievement,[55]
> > Exactly resembling
The buzzing swarms of flies that vie for blood.

MALE *speaks:* In ancient times it was said: "Now Qin has lost the deer[56] and the whole world chases it, those of great talent and fleetness of foot will make the catch." The current situation is the same. Yuan Shao occupies the north, and Liu Biao occupies the south. It's not just one corner of the empire where each of these heroes occupies land.[57] Today I find my old lord and go back to him. If Cao Cao is wise, he definitely will not try to keep me here. If he is stupid, I don't fear him at all. MALE *sings:*

(*Gun xiuqiu*)
If he is wise, he's smart enough to let me leave;
If he is stupid, he will not dare provoke me.
When we go, that will satisfy the greatest desire of my life:
Fame and integrity for a hundred years!
> I want to leave behind
A letter to Cao Cao in which I take my formal leave.

---

54. This song appears to be a general description of the warlords, not specifically of Cao Cao, although the first two lines could be read in reference to him alone.

55. I.e., founding a new dynasty.

56. This refers to the collapse of the Qin dynasty following the death of the First Emperor in 210 BC. "Losing the deer" is a metaphor for the Mandate of Heaven, from which stems the right to rule.

57. Liu Biao occupied Jingzhou. Yuan Shao had asked Liu for help at the battle of Official Ford (the battle described in this play), and Liu refused. Cao Cao then mounted a campaign against Liu Biao, but Biao died before Cao Cao reached there.

MALE *acts out taking brush and paper.* — MALE *sings:*

> Here I
> Take this cloud-patterned letter-paper and fold it into lines,[58]
> Dip in the ink the frost-hair brush[59] to write true characters.
> In full detail[60] I will explain my sincere feelings—
> Flowers of ink are new as I set dragons and snakes in motion.[61]

FEMALE *speaks:* — Brother-in-law, if Xuande and Zhang Fei have gone to Runan, that's a journey of a thousand miles. How can you take us there all by yourself? — MALE *sings:*

> Just because I
> Have received no letters from my brothers for half a year
> > Doesn't mean that I fear
> The long trek on a road that runs a thousand miles over passes and
> hills.
> How could I dread the difficulty of foot travel and fords?

MALE *acts out writing the letter.* — MALE *speaks:* — I've finished writing my farewell letter to Lord Cao. — FEMALE *speaks:* — Please read it out to me. — MALE *reads aloud:*

From Han Deputy General Guan Yu
To Han Warden of Yanzhou and Prime Minister Cao

Just as the sun stands in the sky, the heart is at the center of the human body. When the sun stands in the sky, it universally illuminates the ten thousand regions. As the heart is at the center of our body, it displays red-hot sincerity, and this red-hot sincerity is trust and righteousness.

When some time ago you accepted my submission, I explained to you: "If my lord has passed away, I will support you, but if my lord has survived, I will return to him." I have newly received your exceptional favors, Lord Cao, but for a long time I enjoyed the gracious kindness of Lord Liu. The recent favors of Your Excellency versus the old friendship with Lord Liu—favors have to be repaid, but friendship cannot be cut off.

Recently I have received information about my lord. Watching the form, one establishes the image,[62] and looking for deeds I sought merit, so I skew-

---

58. I.e., in creased segments so it will guide his hand as he writes, from top to bottom, from right to left.

59. The best brushes were made from the hairs of hares caught in autumn.

60. Literally, star by star—both in detail and describing the ink as it is put to paper.

61. These are conventional similes for the appearance of handwritten Chinese characters.

62. The meaning of this line in the context of this letter is unclear to us.

ered Yan Liang at Whitehorse, and executed Wen Chou at Southern Slope.[63] The generous kindness of Your Excellency has now been fully repaid. I have always preserved the riches you have given me, and they may all be found in the storerooms, properly sealed.

I very much hope you will show me compassion and judge this matter dispassionately.

Yours sincerely,

Guan Yu

MALE *speaks:* — All the precious goods and gold and silver that Lord Cao has given me I have sealed and left in the storerooms to return to him. I will place this letter here in the main hall and then we can leave. — MALE *sings:*

> (*Tang xiucai*)
> I give this letter to Lord Cao to bid a formal adieu!
> I have sealed the storerooms oh so tightly.
> Honorable sister-in-law, dear nephew, please get on the cart;
> Far away I seek out my goose companions[64]
> And here jump out of this den of tigers and wolves—
> Guan Yunchang is gone!

MALE, FEMALE, CHILD *leave unobtrusively.* — EXTRA, *costumed as* CAO, *enters and speaks:* Now Guan Yunchang has established such merit; that man definitely will not be willing to stay here much longer. I now had a set of clothes made for him: a crimson mantle, a white jade belt, a far-roaming cap, and a pair of black boots to give to him at his departure. — ADDED MALE, *costumed as* ZHANG LIAO, *and* CLOWN, *costumed as* XU CHU, *enter with the letter, and speak:* Guan Yu has left the city together with the wife of Liu Bei. By now they must have made more than ten miles! He left this letter, and the gold and silver in his storerooms had all been sealed—he didn't even take a single speck! We have come here to report. We should pursue him with troops and horses and bring him back—we cannot allow him to escape! — EXTRA *speaks:* You fellows really don't understand! If you had been in the service of Liu Bei and if he had treated you most generously, would you still care for Us? — ADDED MALE *and others speak:* —Your Excellency, we have received your great kindness. Even if it were a matter of living or dying, how could we turn our backs on you? How could we think otherwise? — EXTRA *speaks:* If that is the case, "Each man serves his own lord." So why would you want to capture him and bring him back? — ADDED

---

63. See Appendix 1, item 7.
64. Lines of geese are an oft-used simile for brothers devoted to each other.

MALE *and others speak:* — Our wisdom really does not measure up to this. —
EXTRA *acts out reading the letter, finishes reading, and speaks:* — Such men are
rare in this world! Now I have here a set of clothes I had made. The two of you
and Xiahou Dun take a farewell banquet with you, catch up to him, and give
him these clothes. After you have shared some wine, see him off on his southward journey.

EXTRA, ADDED MALE, CLOWN exit.

MALE, *riding a bamboo horse,* FEMALE, CHILD, *seated in a cart, enter.* [MALE]
speaks: We have traveled all morning. Over there I see Eight-Mile Bridge! —
MALE *sings:*

> (*Zhuandiao Huolang'er*)
> The season of coolness—autumn breezes of the eighth month:
> Slowly the cart creaks, going slowly along to the open fields.
> A faraway gaze to distant hills is obscured by morning clouds.
> The forests of liquid ambar trees turn red,
> The rows of geese are slanted[65]
> As we strain our eyes to watch far away to the horizon.

FEMALE *speaks:* This autumn scenery beyond the city walls is so distressing! It
really affects one. But where does the road go from Eight-Mile Bridge? — MALE
speaks: Past Eight-Mile Bridge we go east. East of this lake lie autumn wilder-
ness slopes without human habitation. — MALE *sings:*

> (*Erzhuan*)
> Flashing, shining bright, dazzling clouds reflect the light;
> Limpidly, pellucidly clear, cold waves go on and on.
> Softly, subtly swirling, wind blows, felling leaves that float away;
> Drily scraping and rubbing, withered lotus leaves turn sere from
>   frost.
> Deeply, heavily silent, a broad plain of grasses that link to Heaven,[66]
> An endlessly honking annoyance: a lost swan goose pitifully cries out.
> Hastily, anxiously in a hurry, our hearts follow the falling sun far
>   away.

MALE *speaks:* Here we have arrived at Eight-Mile Bridge. There are quite a few
houses on both sides of the bridge. Let's rest here for a while. I will get some
drink and food for sister-in-law and my little nephew. — MALE *sings:*

---

65. A reference to the inverted "v" of the formations of migrating geese.
66. At the horizon.

(Sanzhuan)
> I only see,

Shady and shadowy green, willows weep on both sides.
Dismounting from my warhorse, slowly hesitating, not disposed to
    act.
> After I've inspected

The several tens of thatched houses along the winding stream . . .
As soon as the cart comes to a halt.
I quickly hitch the jade bridle.
> At

The inn I have them clean up a room.
Only then do I loosen the saddle;
I still have no moment of idleness,
As I myself select the jade kernels,[67]
And then invite my sister-in-law and nephew to enjoy a fine meal.

MALE, *putting down the food,*[68] *speaks:* I have prepared some dried provisions I
brought along on horseback for sister-in-law and nephew to eat. I haven't seen
the innkeeper come out. — MALE *acts out calling for the innkeeper.* — CLOWN,
costumed as innkeeper, enters and speaks: — I am a citizen of Xuchang who is
running a wineshop here at Eight-Mile Bridge. Who might be calling for me?
— CLOWN *acts out greeting* MALE, FEMALE, CHILD. — MALE *speaks:* — Bring
me two hundred cash worth of good wine if you have it. — CLOWN *speaks:* —
Coming right up! — *Acts out warming wine.* — *After one scene of attending the
wine warmer and pouring out wine* — CLOWN *presents wine to* MALE. — MALE
accepts the wine, acts out lifting it up high and giving it to FEMALE *to drink.* —
FEMALE *speaks:* This wine is still a little too cold. Innkeeper, could you warm
this wine a little bit more? — CLOWN *acts out flirting with* FEMALE *and speaks:*
Sister, let's heat this wine in that little pot of yours. — MALE *acts out being enraged and beating up* CLOWN. — MALE *sings while administering a beating:*

(Sizhuan)
> I'll beat this guy who,

With slippery, slimy tongue, flirted with indecent language,
Whose blabbering and rattling mouth lacked all common decency.
I've clenched both fists to beat this foul scoundrel
> Who has riled up

---

67. White rice.
68. The text here actually reads, "gets off his horse." If this were correct, all of the actions
above would have been potential actions in the future. He would also have inspected the grains
of rice while still on horseback.

My boiling rage!
> You have

Bumped into an evil spirit,
Dug up the very star of disaster.[69]
> I'll beat you until you

Can't bear it any more,
Can't take it any more,
And fall down on the ground all curled up in a coma!
I will bash your skull
And snap your thighs.

CLOWN, *collapsed on the ground, speaks:* — Your strength can kill me! — MALE *speaks:* Who told you to flirt with someone else's wife? MALE *sings:*

This is your way to "invoke the power of Guanyin."[70]
Any harder, you'd really have a hard time getting up.
You shit-head,
If you act once more like this,
> Don't think

The Han general Guan Yunchang will forgive you.

Exits unobtrusively.

CLOWN *shouts out and speaks:* So you are that Han general Yunchang! You are that Great Prince Guan who skewered Yan Liang! You are just a spy for Liu Bei! I will not forgive you for this! I will lodge an accusation against you with the authorities!

Exits unobtrusively.

EXTRA, ADDED MALE, *and others enter, and speak:* — We've been carrying this meal and these clothes and chasing Guan Yunchang, but we still haven't seen him. Who knows how far he has gone? Let's rest for a while in this wineshop. — CLOWN *enters, acts out greeting* EXTRA, ADDED MALE. — *Acts out submitting an accusation.* — EXTRA *speaks:* So Yunchang is here. Ask him to come and see us. — MALE *enters and acts out greeting them.* — EXTRA *speaks:* — General, upon learning that you had left today, Lord Cao has ordered us to bring you this banquet and these clothes as farewell presents. — MALE *speaks:* After I

---

69. This is literally "dug up." Yuan Haowen's tales of the uncanny, *A Continuation of the Tales of Yi Jian,* has several stories about people who dig up lumps of flesh from the earth and die from eating them. They were considered an incarnation of the "Year Star," Jupiter's shadow star, which caused calamity and disaster. A bully was often called "a living Year Star."

70. According to the *Lotus Sutra,* those who are attacked by enemies but with a devout mind pray to the bodhisattva Guanyin will see the evil plots of their enemies turned back against them.

announced my departure, I did not take the trouble to say goodbye face to face, so I am guilty of the crime of laxness and arrogance. How can I bother Lord Cao even more by sending this farewell banquet and extravagant gifts? — MALE *sings:*

> (*Wuzhuan*)
> I'm very grateful for this generous gesture of farewell wine,
> And it also will be my honor to keep this set of clothes.
> > Here
> On this long journey frost falls as we encounter the autumn,
> > And it very much seems
> A goose-down cloak can withstand the cold.
> Since you press these gifts on me, I can only accept them.
> I am deeply moved by his gracious kindness,
> And looking toward the north, I bow down.
> > As for you,
> My generals, I thank you for seeing me off on my trip.
> But why is there need for another toast before the send-off banquet?
> > But if I would not accept,
> It would only go to show that Yunchang cannot get along with
> > people.
> So let's banter and joke with each other;
> Let's urge each other on and fill the cups:
> One after another we pour out five or six beakers of finest wine!

FEMALE *acts fearful and speaks:* Brother-in-law, why do you drink that wine? What to do if it turns out to be poisoned? — MALE *speaks:* — No problem. Lord Cao knows my trust and righteousness. Do I fail to understand his Lord Cao's feelings? He definitely would not try it. — MALE *sings:*

> (*Liuzhuan*)
> Broad magnanimity can accept minor disagreements;
> Only extensive planning can make a great minister:
> Setting out a banquet to enjoy ourselves, we arrange the fragrant
> > beakers.

EXTRA *acts out offering wine.* — MALE *speaks:* — I'm drunk! — MALE *sings:*

> When I'm drunk, ever so lightly spurt some water on me;
> > I'm going to
> Close my eyes and doze off for a while.

EXTRA *speaks:* — General Guan is drunk. Let's help him to lie down so he can rest. — CLOWN *speaks:* Brother, you really don't know to make the most of the

situation! Now he is drunk; we should act. — EXTRA *speaks:* — Impossible!
Lord Cao did not give you such an order. We don't dare kill him! — CLOWN
speaks: Fuck him! I will take the responsibility and do it myself! — CLOWN *acts
out stepping forward and being ready to strike.* — MALE *opens his eyes and gives a
shout.* — MALE *sings:*

> A fine man you are, Xiahou Dun:
> Your heart is poison and hatred!

MALE *acts out drawing his sword, and sings:*

> I can't help it; my rage towers, anger springs up, giving rise to fury,
>> And I'll have that
> Dripping, dropping bloody head of yours—that seat of Yang
>> ethers—
> Sully this glittering and sparkling bright blade of steel.
>> Only that would be
> Repayment in full!

MALE *tightly grabs* CLOWN. — CLOWN *acts out kneeling down.* — MALE *speaks:*
Xiahou Dun, you don't know Guan Yu's fame. You wanted secretly to murder
me! Listen as I will tell you from the very beginning! CLOWN *kneels down in a
panic, begging for forgiveness.* — MALE *sings:*

> (Qizhuan)
> I, Guan Yu, came from Hedong to gather with friends,
> And fled to Zhuo Prefecture where I joined my old ruler.
> Whenever troops clashed or faced each other, I never lost—
> Wherever my horse went, they submitted!
> From the time Xuande was magistrate of Pingyuan,
>> Zhang Fei and I
> Together kept that district inviolate.
>> He and I
> Are bosom friends, a perfect match.
>> He trusted me
> To lead the soldiers
> To attack Pi City,
> Execute Che Zhou,[71]
> And occupy Qing[72] and Xu[73]—
> I dared display my might

---

71. See Appendix 1, item 6.
72. Roughly the area of modern Shandong.
73. An area roughly equivalent to modern Huaibei: parts of Shandong, Jiangsu, and Anhui.

And was able to illumine my martial valor!
But you had to hide your bitter heart behind sweet words,
And foully and violently repugnant, you became deeply jealous,
>   With the result that
My face has turned red, and my heart is on fire—
In a towering rage my anger and fury increase,
>   So I now
Grasp the precious sheath at my waist
And in one swoosh pull out Kunwu.

After MALE *releases* CLOWN — CLOWN *acts out bowing, thanking, and getting up.*
— MALE *sings:*

>   If it were not for momentary consideration of Lord Cao's great
>   kindness,
>>   I would have your
>   Rotten life finished and in no time at all splatter the ground with
>   your blood.

MALE *speaks:* I had wanted to kill you, but I will spare your life for the moment and let you go. You thought that as soon as Guan Yunchang was drunk, you could murder him! — EXTRA, CLOWN *act out being afraid.* — EXTRA *speaks:* General, still your rage! We will take our leave and go back. — MALE *speaks:* — When Lord Guangwu of the Han dynasty established the enterprise and expanded the borders, that was no easy achievement. Now various heroes each occupy a single region. This is precisely the time to earn merit. When you go back and report to Lord Cao, tell him what I now say. — MALE *sings:*

>   (*Bazhuan*)
>   In the time when the Fiery Han[74] weakens and wanes,
>   Every man who is a vassal must exhaust the duties of his office.
>>   Remember when,
>   Restoring the dynasty, the Guangwu emperor ascended the throne,
>   He united ten thousand miles under his sway;
>   Ten thousand miles!
>   He promoted heroic worthies and incorruptible men and established
>   the mainstays of government,
>>   Which later
>   Emperors Ming and Zhang[75] were able to inherit and continue:

---

74. According to the theory of the Five Phases, the Han dynasty is aligned with the phase of fire.

75. Emperor Ming (r. 58–75) and emperor Zhang (r. 76–88).

They celebrated bountiful harvests, oh yes,
During a period of great peace, oh yes!
From the east to the very west
Wells were dug, fields cleared:
They enjoyed peaceful harmony;
The common people were so happy,
Yes, so happy!
       But more recently,
When we come down to Emperors Heng and Ling,[76]
Treacherous traitors were employed,
And the mainstays of the court were not maintained.
Factions and cliques arose, oh yes,
Official positions were sold, oh yes,
       And because of this,
That tumultuous, clamorous chaos of heroes seethed in this tripod.[77]

MALE *speaks:* I have received generous gifts from Lord Cao. I've heard that the ancients said, "When gentlemen part from one another, they each make a gift of words." I here have some words of encouragement and remonstrance for Lord Cao. You generals, please tell them to Lord Cao upon your return. — MALE *sings:*

(*Jiuzhuan*)
Who is willing to establish unwavering loyalty and straight rectitude?
There's not one who is pure like ice, unblemished like jade!
I repeatedly implore Lord Cao to ponder these matters.
May he listen to these words of loyalty and honesty
And honor the imperial house—don't overstep the bounds of your
    office!
       Our
Liu Xuande may be weak and timid,
But in the end he is still branch and leaf, a scion of the house of Han.
Now I've explained this carefully to you in all detail,
You should be able to grasp each and every sentence.
       Right now
Both fishes and dragons enter the sea, a mixed up mess of the brave
    and eminent.

---

76. Emperor Heng (r. AD 147–67) and Emperor Ling (r. AD 168–88).

77. While "seething in the tripod" usually means a very unstable situation, here it certainly carries the second meaning of the "three-part division like a tripod's legs" used to describe the Three Kingdoms period.

Who is willing
To establish a fine reputation, build on integrity?
To follow Confucius, who honored the ethical king and despised the
   hegemons' power to create meritorious acts?[78]
To learn from Duke Huan of Qi, who assembled the liege lords nine
   times, and sealed their oaths with blood?[79]
Or follow Yi Yin and the Duke of Zhou,[80] loyal and sincere ministers
   who never had other thoughts?
I've listed a number of possibilities, leaving it to you to choose.
       Don't take this as
Ill-considered small talk, not worth remembering.

MALE *speaks:* Goodbye! I am leaving. — MALE *sings, astride his bamboo horse:*

(*Coda*)
Sorrow follows the misty willows—thousand of threads[81] tied in
   knots;
Depression presses in on the cloudy forests, myriad feet layered on
   high.
As I reach this desolate land beyond the city, this open plain,
I sigh and grieve, affected by pain.
My straining eyes are blocked by mountains:
We are already on the road with its pavilions every ten miles![82]

TITLE: Cao Mengde, a crafty brave, treats a worthy man well:

NAME: Guan Yunchang's righteous and brave refusal of gold.

Newly Compiled: *Guan Yunchang's Righteous and Brave Refusal of Gold*

---

78. Confucius' lifetime ambition was the restoration of social order as it had prevailed in the
first century of Zhou-dynasty rule, before the rise of the feudal states into independent powers.
   79. Duke Huan of Qi (d. 643 BC) was the first of the so-called Five Hegemons, powerful
local rulers who imposed their authority on the other liege lords and so ensured peace throughout the world.
   80. Both of these men were in a position to take power, but neither did. Yi Yin was the prime
minister of Cheng Tang, the founder of the Shang dynasty. Yi Yin exiled Tai Jia, the grandson of
Cheng Tang, because he was "without the way." Tai Jia was rehabilitated and restored by Yi Yin to
the throne. The Duke of Zhou was a younger brother of King Wu, the founder of the Zhou
dynasty, and served as regent for the latter's son and successor King Cheng.
   81. The word for thread (*si*) used here is homophonous with the word for "thought, longing"
(*si*).
   82. I.e., the official post roads from one end of the empire to the other.

4

Liu Xuande Goes Alone to the Xiangyang Meeting

ANONYMOUS

Liu Xuande Goes Alone to the Xiangyang Meeting (*Liu Xuande du fu Xiangyang hui*) is a complicated drama, the contents of which are only partly indicated by its name. The four acts and two wedges of the play relate four major events:

In Act 1 Liu Bei sends his trusted messenger Jian Yong to Jingzhou[1] with a letter to Liu Biao, requesting the loan of a walled city to use as a base. Liu Biao invites Liu Bei to a banquet to celebrate the *Shangsi* festival, an ancient ablution rite that had devolved into a communal gathering to celebrate spring. Liu Bei arrives alone, and Liu Biao sends his two sons Liu Qi and Liu Cong to the meeting to express Liu Biao's desire to give his seal of office to Liu Bei so that the latter might assume control of Jingzhou and all that it encompasses. Liu Bei refuses the offer and says that Liu Biao's elder son, Liu Qi, should inherit the position. Liu Cong, the younger son, gets angry and plots with Cai Mao and Kuai Yue to kill Liu Bei. Liu Cong sends Wang Sun to steal Liu Bei's horse, Rogue (*Dilu*). Liu Qi finds out and secretly tips off Liu Bei about the plan.

In Act 2, Wang Sun, played by the male lead, tries to steal the horse, but Liu Bei catches him and persuades him to help him. Wang Sun leads him out of the city to Sandalwood Creek, where Liu Bei makes a miraculous escape. In the first wedge, Liu loses his way in the Deergate Mountains and encounters two Daoist masters, Sima Hui and Pang Degong, and the latter offers up a son for Liu Bei to adopt and recommends another Daoist, Xu Shu, to be his Field Marshal.

In Act 3, Cao Cao sends his sons Cao Ren and Cao Zhang to capture Liu Bei, Guan Yu, and Zhang Fei in Xinye, and Xu Shu dispatches various gen-

---

1. In the Eastern Han, the province of Jingzhou covered roughly the area of the modern provinces of Hubei and Hunan. Traditionally the capital of Jingzhou was Jiangling on the Yangzi River, but Liu Biao had moved his residence northward to the city of Xiangyang on the Han River. Xiangyang is therefore the city referred to here and in the following play, in contrast to the *Single Sword Meeting*, where Jingzhou refers to the city of Jiangling as residence of Guan Yu.

erals to repel the attack and capture Cao Zhang. The second wedge is primarily taken up with battle sequences as Cao Cao launches his attack against Xinye and his adopted son, Cao Zhang, is taken captive.

In Act 4, Liu Bei sets a feast for Xu Shu and hands out rewards to all.

A handwritten entry under the title of the drama as we have it in the copy of the court manuscript in the Maiwang Studio collection attributes the play to Gao Wenxiu. There is no way of knowing who has inserted this, since the manuscript passed through many hands to its present condition, but we assume that Zhao Qimei wrote it there when he collated the text in 1615. The attribution to Gao stems from Zhao's usual practice of checking the titles of the Ming court edition against the bibliographies in *A Formulary of Correct Sounds for an Era of Great Harmony* and less often in *The Register of Ghosts*. The *Register*, depending on the edition, lists a play under Gao Wenxiu's name variously as simply *The Meeting at Xiangyang* (*Xiangyang hui*) or in longer form as *First Ruler Liu and the Meeting at Xiangyang* (*Liu xianzhu Xiangyang hui*). There are three variant editions of *The Register of Ghosts*. One is a Ming manuscript edition that includes a series of elegies written by Jia Zhongming sometime in the early fifteenth century as well as notes to the simple three-syllable titles (e.g., *Xiangyang hui*) that are found in the other editions. While several of Gao's short titles have full "Titles" (*timu*) and "Names" (*zhengming*) appended to them, *Xiangyang hui* does not, which may mean that Jia never saw the play. This is a strong possibility, since Gao Wenxiu was probably deceased by 1320. And while he could have written the play, or parts of, it seems more likely that the play represents a script that was prepared at court for presentation.

Whoever wrote the play took its basic plot from the *Records of the Three Kingdoms in Plain Language*. A version of this narrative had been in print since 1294, so it does not rule out Gao, but the actual quality of the arias in the play does. The second wedge and the fourth act in particular seem hastily contrived to stage the spectacle of a battle and bring the play to a proper close that is both suitable for performance before an imperial audience and written to have the rewards stream from a set of ethical criteria that support the emperor's authority. The name of the male lead in Act 2, Wang Sun, is a misreading on the part of the playwright(s) of a poem by Hu Zeng (ninth century) found in the *Records in Plain Language* (see Appendix 1, item 8) in which he or they either simply misread or playfully reinterpreted the term "grandsons of princes" (*wangsun*) as a name, Wang Sun, to add a note of irony about the travails of someone destined to be emperor.

Both the drama and the *Records in Plain Language* make use of the hearsay and fabrications that are found in Pei Songzhi's notes to to the earlier *Records of the Three Kingdoms*, in particular the "Biography of the First Ruler." *The Records of the Three Kingdoms* recounts how Liu Bei, after being attacked by Cao Cao, seeks out Liu Biao, who is Prince of Jing and Warden of Jingzhou:

> Biao welcomed him in the area outside of the city walls, and treated him with the rituals due to an honored guest as he augmented his army, and sent him on to occupy Xinye. The powerful and brave of Jingzhou who turned their allegiance to the first ruler increased daily; Biao began to have doubts about [Liu Bei's] intentions and wanted to secretly ward him off. He sent him to repel Xiahou Dun, Yu Jin, and others at Bowang.

Pei Songzhi inserts a note from the *Conversations from the Wei and Jin Eras* (*Wei Jin shiyu*):

> Liu Bei was occupying Fancheng. Liu Biao treated him courteously but had fears about how he acted and did not employ him with any trust at all. He once invited Bei to a feast, where Kuai Yue and Cai Mao wanted to take the opportunity to seize Bei. Bei became aware of it, pretended to go to the privy, and sneaked away. The horse that he was riding was named Rogue, and he fled on Rogue, but fell into Sandalwood River on the west side of Xiangyang. He was drowning and unable to escape. Bei quickly said, "Rogue, we are in deep distress now; it's time for you to show your stuff." Rogue then leapt thirty feet in a single jump [to return to the original bank], and then they got onto a raft to cross the river. They were midstream when the pursuers caught up, and they bid him goodbye, relaying Biao's concern, saying, "Why did you leave so fast?"

As in *The Story of the Interlocking Rings*, these "unofficial" versions of the Three Kingdoms' stories are reworked in both the *Records in Plain Language* and the drama.

Liu Xuande Goes Alone to the Xiangyang Meeting is often criticized because the story deviates considerably from the title of the drama, and the action is spread out in four different locations. The last two acts come under considerable disparagement as being a fabrication by court actors. Modern scholar Yan Dunyi thinks that the first two acts could possibly be from an earlier drama—perhaps by Gao Wenxiu—and that the last two are by court actors. In his opinion, the final two acts of the original may have been compressed into the two wedges. That is, in his reconstruction the third act should have had either Pang Degong or Sima Hui as the singer, and the last act would probably have Zhao Yun as the lead. He continues, "The part of the play about Xu Su and Cao Ren occupies more than half, and it is unavoidable that the *Xiangyang Meeting* we have today was tinkered with by actors, who had to drag material in to patch up things that were incorrect or missing in the story; or perhaps there was nothing that they could copy at all and they simply compiled a story of the Three King-doms, faithfully relying on the *Records of the Three Kingdoms in Plain Language* and *The Romance of the Three Kingdoms*, and by accident used a title that was the same as Gao Wenxiu's play." What is more likely to us is that the story is a faithful replica of a narrative that, like a modern television serial, tells in con-densed form a series of events that take Liu Bei from a position of weakness and danger to one in which he has defeated the strongest brave in the empire.

In the later *Romance of the Three Kingdoms*, Liu Bei's appeal to Liu Biao for support and his association with Xu Chu are the subject of a number of epi-sodes in chapters 31 through 36, which offer a far more complicated story.

Dramatis personæ in order of appearance

Role type	Name and family, institutional, or social role
Opening male	Liu Bei
Zhao Yun	Zhao Yun, general under Liu Bei
Male lead Guan	Guan Yu
Zhang Fei	Zhang Fei
Jian Yong	Jian Yong, general and negotiator under Liu Bei
Liu Cong	Liu Cong, younger son of Liu Biao
Soldier	A soldier in service to Liu Cong
Kuai Yue	Kuai Yue, father-in-law of Liu Biao, conspirator with Liu Cong
Cai Mao	Cai Mao, father-in-law of Liu Biao, conspirator with Liu Cong
Liu Biao	Liu Biao, Prince of Jing, distant relative of Liu Bei
Male lead (Act 1)	Liu Qi, elder son of Liu Biao
Male lead (Act 2)	Wang Sun, personal general to the Prince of Jing
Sima Hui	Sima Hui, Daoist master
Acolyte	Sima Hui's servant
Pang Degong	Pang Degong, Daoist master
Acolyte	Pang Degong's servant
Kou Feng	Kou Feng, later Liu Feng, Liu Bei's adopted son, and general
Old woman	Madam Chen, Xu Shu's mother
Male lead (Acts 3, 4)	Xu Shu, Daoist master and Liu Bei's Field Marshal
Acolyte	Xu Shu's servant
Cao Cao	Cao Cao
Soldier	Soldier, Cao Cao's aide
Cao Ren	Cao Ren, Cao Cao's son and general
Clown	Cao Zhang, Cao Cao's adopted son and general
Mi Zhu	Mi Zhu, general in Liu Bei's army
Mi Fang	Mi Fang, general in Liu Bei's army
Xu Chu	Xu Chu, general in Cao Cao's army
Gong Gu	Gong Gu, general in Liu Bei's army
Group of generals	Various generals in Liu Bei's army

Liu Xuande Goes Alone to the Xiangyang Meeting
Gao Wenxiu of the Yuan[2]

First Act[3]

OPENING MALE, [*costumed as*] LIU BEI, *enters with* ZHAO YUN, *speaks:*

> A layered covering, stratum by stratum—sunset clouds that penetrate
> the blue,
> "Plaiting sandals and weaving mats"—so I made my living;[4]
> Should someone come to ask of my ancestors and forefathers,
> "Four hundred years ago we were a house of generals and ministers."

I am Liu Bei, also known as Xuande, and am a man of Lousang in Dashu. In
the Peach Orchard I bound myself in righteousness to two brothers: Guan Yu,
known as Yunchang, a man of Xieliang in Puzhou, and Zhang Fei, known as
Yide, from Fanyang in Zhuozhou. I lost contact with my brothers in Xuzhou
more than three years ago, and none of us expected to wind up together here in
Old City. I want to kill Cao Cao out of vengeance, but I don't have a wall or a
moat to my name,[5] so I've stayed in Old City for a month or more. I want to
have a discussion today with my brothers and officers. Summon Yunchang and
Zhang Fei!

MALE LEAD GUAN, ZHANG FEI *enter.* — GUAN *speaks:*

> A sound or two from the marshal's drum or gong of brass,
> Outside and inside the headquarters' gate, heroes line up;
> One inch of brush tip or three feet of iron—
> Together we aid the state and protect the very cosmos.

---

2. This notation appears to have been added by Zhao Qimei to the text; we believe the play
to be by an anonymous author.

3. Like other palace editions, the text uses the ordinal phrase "first act" (*touzhe*) rather than
the later editorial convention of the cardinal phrase "Act 1" (*diyizhe*).

4. A common aphorism to capture the early part of Liu Bei's life, from the line, "when the
First Ruler was young and without a father he made his livelihood with his mother by plaiting
sandals and weaving mats," found in his biography in the *Records in Plain Language*.

5. That is, a walled city surrounded by a moat to use as a base of operations.

I am Guan Yu, known as Yunchang, a man from Xieliang in Puzhou. The third brother is Zhang Fei, Yide, from Fanyang in Zhuozhou. And there's my elder brother from Lousang in Dashu, Liu Bei, known as Xuande. We have finally gathered again in Old City after being split up in Xuzhou. I don't know why elder brother has summoned me today, but I'd better go find out. Here I am, already. Sergeant, report that Guan Yu and Zhang Fei are here. — SOLDIER *speaks:* Understood. Oyez! I would like to report to you, Grand Marshal, that Guan Yu and Zhang Fei are here. — LIU BEI *speaks:* Tell them to come in. — SOLDIER *speaks:* Go on in! — *Act out greeting.*[6]

GUAN *speaks:* What do we have to discuss? — LIU BEI *speaks:* Brothers, I just want to discuss this one matter: after we crossed swords with Cao Cao in Xuzhou, we brothers were split apart; we're here in Old City now, but that's not a long-range plan. Should Cao Cao launch another campaign against us, unfortunately Old City is too cramped, and we have no grain or fodder. How can we withstand an attack? — ZHANG FEI *speaks:* — Elder brother, my idea is this: we lay in fodder and stock up on grain in Old City, enlist an army, and purchase horses. What do you think? — GUAN *speaks:* — That won't work, brother. When you consider that Cao Cao has a million brave soldiers at hand, along with a thousand seasoned generals, he'll trample Old City into level earth if he brings an army here. It'll be too late for regret then. — LIU BEI *speaks:* That's right, brother. I have a plan that I want to discuss with you. I want to send someone to the Prefect of Jingzhou with a personal letter from me. Liu Biao is related to me on my father's side, and he's in charge of occupying and protecting the nine provinces around Jingzhou and Xiangyang. I will ask him for the temporary loan of a walled city, which we can use as a base to station our army. Then if we gather together some men and horses, it won't be too late to take out our revenge on Cao Cao. What do you think of this plan? — GUAN *speaks:* — I think you have it right, brother. But who will go? — LIU BEI *speaks:* Go summon Jian Xianhe[7] for me. — SOLDIER *speaks:* Understood. — JIAN YONG *enters and speaks:*

---

6. The text is very consistent about starting new paragraphs for new scenes. We have followed the practice in our translation.

7. Jian Yong (c. 180–220). Jian had been an acquaintance of Liu Bei's from youth. He followed Liu Bei in Liu's campaign against the Yellow Turbans, and stayed with him through the campaign for control of China. He was mostly noted as a very successful negotiator. In 211 Liu Bei went to Yizhou (modern Chengdu) to help Liu Zhang, and Liu Zhang and Jian Yong became good friends. Conflict between Liu Zhang and Liu Bei erupted in outright warfare, and Liu Bei besieged Liu Zhang in Yizhou. He sent Jian Yong to negotiate Liu Zhang's surrender, which he did successfully, and he was awarded with the high title General of Brilliant Virtue (*zhaode jiangjun*).

When I was young I worked hard at the martial arts.
On campaigns to the south and bandit suppressions to the north, I displayed
my heroism;
When approaching an army, I could count the enemy's number by their
clouds of dust.
I am the first among all the heroes within the four seas!

I am Jian Yong, known as Xianhe, and on the civil side I thoroughly understand
the *Three Strategies*, and comprehend the *Six Tactics* on the military side. I am a
general now under the aegis of Noble Xuande, whom I aid. Noble Xuande has
summoned me for something, and I'd better go. Here I am, already. Sergeant,
go report that Jian Yong is at the gate. — SOLDIER *speaks:* Oyez! I would like to
report to you, Grand Marshal, that Jian Yong is at the gate. — LIU BEI *speaks:*
Tell him to come in. SOLDIER *speaks:*[8] He said go on in. JIAN YONG *acts out
performing greeting rituals and speaks:* Why did you summon me? LIU BEI *speaks:*
I have called you because now I want to take vengeance on Cao Cao, but, alas,
we have no grain or fodder here in Old City. I have just written a letter, which
you should take directly to the Prefect of Jingzhou. When he reads it, he'll
know what to do. Set out on this long journey today! JIAN YONG *speaks:* Understood. I shall not tarry or stay but be on my way, under general order of Xuande,
and take this letter off to Jingzhou.

Receiving the command for a personal mission, I am now under restraint,
I respectfully give the posthouse mount its head, dash off on this noble steed;
A sword of tongue and lances of lips will turn into merit and ability.
No day or night for me—off to Jingzhou.

Exits.

LIU BEI *speaks:* Jian Yong is gone now. If I can borrow a walled city, then we can
begin the campaign of vengeance against Cao Cao again. Let me know when
Jian Yong returns.

Exits.

LIU CONG *enters and speaks:*

In the middle of the river, a single boat;
Up on the bank, eight trackers;

---

8. At this point the scribe briefly abandons the practice of centering the smaller stage directions and separating them each other and from speech with an extended space and has begun
placing them on the right side of the column in further reduced size, leaving no extended spaces.
See Fig. 3.

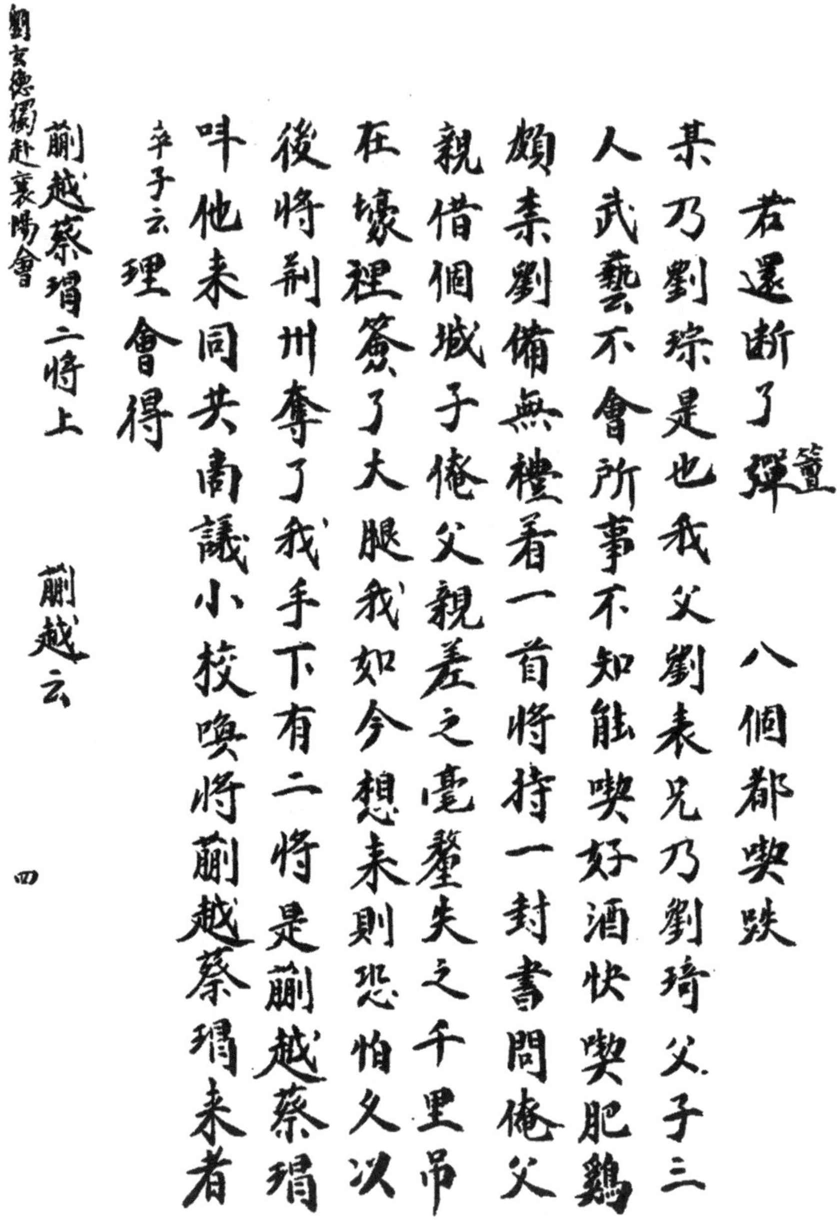

若還斷了彈篁　八個都喫跌
某乃劉琮是也我父劉表兄乃劉琦父子三
人武藝不會所事不知能喫好酒快喫肥鷄
頗奈劉備無禮着一首將持一封書問俺父
親借個城子俺父親差之毫釐失之千里吊
在懷裡簽了大腿我如今想來則恐怕久以
後將荊州奪了我手下有二將是蒯越蔡瑁
叫他來同共商議小校喚將蒯越蔡瑁來者
卒子云　理會得
蒯越蔡瑁二將上　蒯越云
劉玄德獨赴襄陽會　四

Fig. 3. Page 4a from the Ming palace edition of *Liu Xuande Goes Alone to the Xiangyang Meeting,* showing changes in stage direction notations

> If the towing line should break,
> Down will fall all of the eight.

I am Liu Cong, and my father is Liu Biao. There are three of us, including my elder brother Liu Qi. We are incompetent in the martial arts, don't know about anything we do, but we can—and love to—drink and gobble up fat chickens. Now, that Liu Bei lacks all knowledge of the rites. He's dispatched a general here to deliver a letter, asking my father for the loan of a walled city. My father, missing it by an inch here, will wind up losing it by a mile; if he falls into this moat, it'll cost him a leg. I've been thinking: I have two generals under my command, Kuai Yue[9] and Cai Mao,[10] and I should summon them to discuss this together. Sergeant, summon General Kuai and Cai Mao. SOLDIER *speaks:* Understood.

The two generals, KUAI YUE *and* CAI MAO, *enter.* — KUAI YUE *speaks:*

> I am always the general in the front of the front,
> But my old daddy was a leatherworker
> And my elder brother was Lun Ban the woodworker,[11]
> And his little brother . . . sesame sauce.[12]

I am Kuai Yue and this is my little brother Cai Mao.

> I am worthless,
> He's no use,
> I do somersaults,
> And him? A few little skits.

---

9. Kuai Yue, known as Yidu (d. 214), was instrumental in establishing Liu Biao as the uncontested ruler of Jingzhou by laying out a plan by which Liu Biao killed all of his major rivals. He later persuaded Liu Biao not to aid Yuan Shao in the battle at Official Ford against Cao Cao, and when Liu Biao died, Kuai Yue and Cai Mao persuaded his son Liu Cong to surrender to Cao. Kuai Yue then became an important minister in Cao Cao's campaign.

10. Cai Mao (c. 180–220), like Kuai Yue, was instrumental in Liu Biao's pacification of the Jingzhou area. Liu Biao was partial to his elder son Liu Qi, but when Cai Mao's niece was made Liu Cong's wife, Cai Mao began praising Liu Cong and wanted him to succeed his father. He flattered Liu Cong so much and reviled Liu Qi so roundly that the latter decided to take a post away from the capital. After Liu Cong switched sides to Cao Cao, Cai Mao was falsely revealed as a turncoat in the "the plot that sacrifices the body." See Appendix 1, item 11.

11. The last word of the term *lunbanjiang,* which could mean something like "leader of a shift section" (of bureaucrats, workers, etc.) is altered in the palace edition to *jiang,* "craftsman." Lun Ban *jiang,* Master Craftsman [Gong]lun, was an ancient master carpenter.

12. All of the lines rhyme on the phoneme *jiàng.* In the first line, it is the word "general," and in the second two, craftsman (which we have translated as "worker"). The listener clearly expects that this line will either be another kind of worker or a general.

The lord's son has called us for something. We should go see him. Here we are, already. Report that Kuai and Cai are here at the gate. SOLDIER *speaks:* Understood. Oyez! I would like to report to you, lord, that Kuai and Cai are at the gate. — LIU CONG *speaks:* Tell them to come in.[13] TWO CLOWNS [*enter,*] *act out performing greeting.* — CAI MAO *speaks:* I have my sword and armor on; I can't perform the correct rituals. — KUAI YUE *speaks:* — For what duty have you summoned us? — LIU CONG *speaks:* — Kuai Yue and Cai Mao, I've asked you here precisely to discuss Liu Bei's request of my father to borrow a walled city. My father is certain to cede Jingzhou to Liu Bei after a while; this is why I called you. — KUAI YUE *speaks:* — I have a plan. Let's plan a fine feast here, with lots of light food and several dishes to accompany the rice, then get several bowls of sweet sauce ready. We'll make him drunk and so stuffed with food he can't even move, and when he topples over at the bursting point, then we'll capture him and make him die without a place to bury his body. My lord, what do you think about this plan? — LIU CONG *speaks:* — Marvelous! Marvelous! This plan is just too great! It's a fine plan, but if it gets to such a point, you won't be able to prop me up first! — KUAI YUE *speaks:* But the plan is already set; why do we need to keep discussing it? — LIU CONG *speaks:* — Well, now it is what it is, so let's keep to this plan. "If a plan works, you can snatch the jade hare in the moon; / If a plot is successful, you can capture the golden raven in the sun!" — KUAI YUE *speaks:* "Let each sweep the snow before his own gate." — CAI MAO *speaks:* —"Don't worry about the frost on someone else's roof."

Exit together.

LIU BIAO *enters, leading* SOLDIERS, *and speaks:*

A proud steed, a carved saddle, purple brocaded robes,
My whole breast weighed down by the pressure of "Five Tumuli bravado";[14]
And if anyone wants to know my name,
Those who "cling to the phoenix and clamber on the dragon"[15] are old friends.

I am Liu Biao, known as Jingsheng, and have been made prefect here. I've poked around in the classics and histories, and when young I whipped my horse on into Yicheng, the old capital of Ba. Using the plottings of Kuai from Liangzhou, I occupied Jiangling in the south where I guard Xiangyang, Fanzhou, and

---

13. Here the earlier pattern of centered stage directions separated from the text above and below by extended spaces is reinstated.

14. Many rich and powerful families lived near the five tumuli of the Han emperors on the outskirts of Chang'an. By the Yuan, this was simply a metaphor for important and powerful young dandies, a polite way of saying, "You look like you've made it."

15. This means, roughly, "cling to those in power in hopes of advancement" or "make their name on the shirttails of someone in a higher position."

Jingzhou in the north. I have two sons, the elder Liu Qi and the younger, Liu Cong. For those who know how to use troops, I have Kuai Yue and Cai Mao. I've occupied Jingzhou for a long time now, and have held it without problem. Recently Liu Xuande, defeated soundly at Xuzhou by Cao Cao, has stationed his army at Old City. He sent a general here with a letter, asking to borrow a walled city from me where he can station his army and get his horses into shape. It's the third of the third month right now, and I've asked Noble Xuande to come to a meeting in Xiangyang. If Noble Xuande comes, I have my own idea about what to do. Tell me when he arrives. — LIU BEI *enters, speaks:*

This humble official is Liu Bei. I sent Jian Yong to ask my elder brother, Prefect of Jingzhou, if I could borrow a walled city. I never expected my brother to actually assent to it and send someone to fetch me to a meeting at Xiangyang. Here I am, already. Servants, take my horse. Sergeant, report to your master that Liu Bei is at the gate. — SOLDIER *speaks:* Oyez. My lord, I wanted to tell you that Liu Bei is at the gate. — LIU BIAO *speaks:* Well, brother is here. Tell him he's welcome. — SOLDIER *speaks:* — Please come in. — *Act out performing the rituals of greeting.* — LIU BEI *speaks:* — Brother, it's been several years since we met. Please accept these two respectful bows from your brother. — LIU BIAO *speaks:* Please, dispense with the rituals, brother. Bring that couch over. Brother, please sit. Bring out the small table. — *He acts out taking the cup, speaks:* — It's been several years, brother; please drink this cup to the full. — LIU BEI *speaks:* — Brother, I will get drunk if I finish it; please let me put it back. — LIU BIAO *speaks:* — I have two sons, the elder Liu Qi, and younger Liu Cong. Call them out for me.

MALE LEAD *enters with* LIU CONG *and speaks:*

I am Liu Qi, and my brother is Liu Cong. Here in Jingzhou my father leads an army of four hundred thousand armor-clad troops and occupies the nine commanderies of Jingzhou. He is known now as the Prince of Xiangyang. Liu Xuande has come to request a loan of a walled city from my father that he can use temporarily as a place to reside. My father then sent someone to ask Xuande to come to Jingzhou and stay for a few days. Today is the Xiangyang meeting on the third of the third month, and father has asked Noble Xuande to a banquet. He sent someone to summon the two of us, so we'd better get going. — LIU CONG *speaks:* — Brother, when I think how we, father and sons, have held this place "without worries," well then . . . if we're "without fish" then we can eat mutton.[16] — MALE LEAD *speaks:* — Think back, brother, to the time that the

---

16. This is a nice pun that unfortunately does not work well in English. The phrase *wuyu*, "without worries," is an exact homophone for "without fish."

Qin "lost their deer"[17] and all of the brave and eminent rose up, but in three years the Exalted Ancestor of the Han destroyed Qin, and in five years he had destroyed Chu. To last this long as an empire was no easy task.

(XIANLÜ MODE: *Dian jiangchun*)[18]
Consider those days when the Ancestor of Han created the
    foundation,
Ascending to emperor in five short years,
Bringing days without worry,
Sitting in repose, letting his sleeves drop loosely—
It was because his right-hand men could rescue the world.

(*Hunjiang long*)
But after the Restoration the liege lords were strong in their power
And both local custom and civilizing education gradually eroded away.
First, that Dong Zhuo was exterminated
And then Lü Bu met his peril.
Then that Yuan Shao raised up his troops and became intransigent
    with power
And Cao Cao went for the way of power and loosed his perfidy.
Now, for prosperous people and a wealthy state, we must speak of
    Sun Quan,
And truly, for encompassing benevolence and deep virtue, we must
    talk of Liu Bei.
At his disposal he has his second general, Guan Yu,
And his younger brother, Zhang Fei.

LIU CONG *speaks:* Here we are, already. — MALE LEAD *speaks:* — Let's go on in and see father. — *They act out greeting their father.* — LIU BIAO *speaks:* — Liu Qi. Liu Cong. Perform the rituals for your uncle with all due honor. — MALE LEAD *speaks:* — Understood. — *They act out greeting* LIU BEI.

(*You hulu*)
Here I clasp my hands before my chest, bow my body, and finish up
    the ritual.
We are separated by tens of years.

17. From the phrase "When the Qin lost their deer, the whole world chased after it" derives the metaphor of the "lost deer" as the "lost empire."

18. The stage direction "*Sings*" is missing before each new song. The word "sing" occurs whenever a song is interrupted by dialogue and then continues. This may be an artifact of the Yuan edition, when the singer's role type was uniformly left out since the editions were created only for the lead singer. In this case, the direction would be more properly translated in the imperative form, "Sing." See West and Idema 2010, pp. xxi–xxii.

LIU BEI *speaks:* Nephew, we haven't seen each other for many years . . . since we battled with Cao Cao. — *Sing:*

> Separated east from west, all because of bitter campaigning and
> terrible battles.

LIU BEI *speaks:* — Liu Qi, your father and I are both descendants of the Han house. — *Sing:*

> We are of the same relation, separated by form but linked by *qi*;
> You are a direct descendant of Emperor Jing of a former reign.

LIU BEI *speaks:* — Elder brother, I really didn't come for a feast. The walled city is crucial. — *Sing:*

> Uncle, you wish to borrow a commandery or prefecture
> And there collect your men and horses.

LIU BEI *speaks:* — Nephew, your uncle does not have an inch of land. How am I to do battle with Cao Cao? — *Sing:*

> Uncle, you say, "At the present moment I do not have an inch of land
> to give my body peace,"
> But all under Heaven belongs to the empire of Han.
>
> (*Tianxia le*)
> The saying goes, "When a person is in trouble, he draws near a
> relative." This I know.

LIU BIAO *speaks:* — Noble Xuande, please make Xinye and Fancheng your brothers' temporary refuge. — LIU BEI *speaks:* Thank you, brother! — *Sing:*

> Make Xinye and Fancheng your temporary refuge.

LIU BIAO *speaks:* — Noble Xuande, why can't you train your troops and officers, accumulate fodder and store your grain at Xinye or Fancheng, and from there restore the house of Han? — *Sing:*

> If you again polish the sun and moon to aid our altars of state,
> Pacify all within the seas so that it is secure,
> And those war beacons cease—
> On that day we shall sort out all our relations
> And carry out the grand ritual.

LIU BIAO *speaks:* Liu Qi, offer your uncle a cup of wine. MALE LEAD *speaks:* Yes, sir. Bring the wine forward. Uncle, please drink a cup. — LIU BEI *speaks:* Elder son of the duke, please have my elder brother drink first. — LIU BEI *acts out offering a cup of wine.* — *After* LIU BIAO *acts out drinking wine, speaks:* Liu Cong, offer your uncle a cup of wine. — LIU CONG *speaks:* Uncle, please drink this cup to the full. — LIU BIAO *speaks:* Play some music! — LIU BEI *speaks:* Brother, I've had plenty of wine.

> (*Nezha ling*)
> We have a lavish spread of precious viands and beautiful flavors,
> Have raised high the chalcedony liquor and this jade ambrosia,
> Arranged in close order singers and these dancing beauties.
> It's no less than the Eastern Gallery feast of Gongsun Hong,[19]
> But it is certainly no Goosegate meeting by Xiang Yu of Chu,[20]
> So enjoy yourself and drink fully from these golden cups.

LIU BEI *speaks:* — Brother, I can't drink anymore. — LIU BIAO *acts out taking his plaque and seal of office and ceding them to* LIU BEI, *speaks:* — Noble Xuande, I'm getting old now and can't maintain control over these nine commanderies of Jing and Xiang. I'm going to turn the plaque and seal for these nine commanderies over to you to take charge of. Is this satisfactory with you? — LIU BEI *speaks:* Brother, how dare I take them? You have two sons here, who should assume the position of Prefect of Jingzhou through hereditary right. — LIU CONG *speaks:* Look, father, drink if you will, but this plaque and seal . . . Uncle is a man who understands principle. He's not willing to accept this plaque and seal.

> (*Que ta zhi*)
> I bear this plaque and seal aloft to your position on the mat,
> But he is so modest and begs off with all his might.
> We desire to take the nine commanderies of Jing and Xiang
> And have uncle manage them and keep them on the right path.

LIU BEI *speaks:* — My brother, this is a territory that was divided up and given out as fiefs by our ancestors; as descendants, we must preserve them [as family fiefdoms]. — *Sing:*

---

19. Gongsun Hong (200–121 BC), aiding Han Wudi, built a lodge to house worthy men who were seeking employment. He held banquets for these worthies in the Eastern Gallery (*dongge*) where he would discuss political issues with them.

20. This refers to a feast given for Liu Bang by Xiang Yu, who planned to kill Liu Bang but hesitated and lost the opportunity and subsequently the empire as well. This well-known story is derived from the "Basic Annals of Xiang Yu," in the *Records of the Historian.* See "The Basic Annals of Xiang Yu," in Sima Qian 1993, pp. 17–48. A "Goosegate meeting" has come to mean any treacherous or otherwise unpleasant meeting where someone will metaphorically be killed.

You say that the great enterprise of our ancestors is passed down to
   posterity,
But have you not heard that Shun and Yao thought the realm should
   be continued by the worthy and the Sage?[21]

LIU BIAO *speaks:* — Noble Xuande, I am old now. You take control of this
plaque and seal. — LIU BEI *speaks:* — Brother, I definitely dare not accept it.
Release it, brother, to your two sons. — LIU BIAO *speaks:* — You don't understand; these two little ones of mine cannot manage it. Don't even mention
my giving it to them. Should they take control of it now, who would carry it on
[after I die]? — LIU BEI *speaks:* — I've heard many times that the eldest son,
Liu Qi, is a person of complete martial and civil talent, a man of encompassing
benevolence and deep virtue; he can carry it on as a hereditary office. — LIU
CONG *speaks in an aside:* — Such an affront! He just refused the plaque and seal
and said my brother was fine. What damn business is it of yours if we brothers
inherit it or not? I'm upset that I can't bite him.[22]

> (*Jisheng cao*)
> Don't exaggerate about this,
> And don't beg off anymore.
> You say I am loyal to my lord, filial to my father, practice benevolence
>   and righteousness,
> You say I spur on my horse, lead other generals, am full of plans and
>   stratagems,
> You also say I can "regulate the house, order the world"[23] and can
>   create benefit.

LIU BEI *speaks:* — I am just saying that the eldest son of the lord has the talent
to rescue the people and the state and the virtue of Yan Hui and Min Ziqian.[24]
— *Sing:*

> How can I have that "roof-beam talent" to weave heaven and earth
>   together?
> I am of that kind "of a wall of dung and a piece of rotten wood."[25]

---

21. Sage kings who passed their thrones to the most worthy men of the empire rather than
their own sons.

22. I.e., do him harm.

23. Have the ethical power to rule; from the "Great Learning." See Chan 1963, p. 86.

24. *Analects* 11.3: "Those [disciples of Confucius] known for virtuous conduct: Yan Hui, Min
Ziquan, Boniu, and Zhonggong" (trans. Slingerland 2003, p. 112).

25. *Analects* 5.10: "Zai Wo was sleeping during the daytime. The Master said, 'Rotten wood
cannot be carved, and a wall of dung cannot be plastered. As for Zai Wo, what would be the use
of reprimanding him?'" (trans. Slingerland, 2003, p. 43).

LIU BIAO *speaks:* — Since you are determined not to accept it, brother, then let's start the drinking rounds. — LIU CONG *acts out angrily going out of the door and speaks:* — That big-eared jerk is completely rude. We politely ask you to drink, our father loans you a walled city, and you still dare to discourse on which of us brothers is fit and which isn't. You vaunt someone else's awesome presence to squelch my ambition. Servant! Call Kuai Yue and Cai Mao here. — SOLDIER *speaks:* Understood. KUAI YUE, CAI MAO *enter together, speak:* The young lord is calling us, so we'd better go. Hey, soldier, what's happening? — SOLDIER *speaks:* — Generals, sirs, the second young lord has asked you to come. — KUAI YUE *speaks:* Where is he? We'll go see him. *They act out greeting him, speak:* Why did you call us, young master? — LIU CONG *speaks:* — Alas, that big-eared jerk was completely rude. He bamboozled my father at the feast, discoursed on the good and bad points of us two brothers. You get up on your two saddled horses, with weapons in your hands, and get after capturing that Liu Bei. Send Wang Sun out to steal Liu Bei's horse, Rogue. When he steals Liu's horse, have him report back to me. — KUAI YUE *speaks:* — Got it. On the basis of the young lord's orders, let's go on out and capture Liu Bei.

Exit.

MALE LEAD *speaks:* — Hai! What am I going to do about this? If I don't say anything to Uncle to let him know, he's certain to fall into the trap of those two bandits. Brother, offer Uncle another cup of wine. Uncle! Drink another cup! — LIU BEI *acts out reviving, speaks:* — I just can't drink anymore. — MALE LEAD *speaks:* — Uncle, if you don't drink any wine, then at least have some fruit. — LIU BEI *speaks:* — I don't want any.

> (*Zui fu gui*)
> Uncle, you know the taste of these fine jujubes.[26]

LIU BEI *speaks:* I've had enough. — *Sing:*

> Good peaches are also worth eating;[27]

LIU BEI *speaks:* I can't eat anymore. — *Sing:*

> To sober up, well then, pears are better;[28]

LIU BEI *acts out sobering up, speaks:* — Can't eat! — *Sing:*

> These fruits were originally all from the same root;

---

26. This line, *zhe hao zao zhi ziwei,* is also a pun for "you should know this taste as early as possible," i.e., "you should figure this out as quickly as possible."
27. This line, *hao tao ye ken shi,* is a pun for "this is the right time to flee."
28. The last three words of the line, *geng hao li,* are a pun for "it's better if you leave."

He's going to hurt the branches and leaves[29] and skin off the covering!

> — *continued in speaking* — Uncle is drunk! He doesn't understand what I'm saying! — *Acts out shaking him from his stupor, speaks:* Uncle, look at this table: good jujubes, good peaches, good pears![30]

LIU BEI *acts out sobering up, speaks:* — I get it! I get it! I know! — *Sing:*

How can you not know what I'm really saying?

LIU BEI *acts out saying his goodbyes, speaks:* — Elder brother, I've received the great fortune of a walled city, your fine banquet, but now I must bid adieu and go back. LIU BEI *acts out making obeisances.* — LIU BIAO *speaks:* — Stay, brother! Don't go back. Stay a few more days. — LIU CONG *speaks:* Father, don't bother with him. You go and rest. — *He supports* LIU BIAO, *and they exit.* — MALE LEAD *speaks:* — Uncle, Liu Cong has asked Kuai Yue and Cai Mao to lay an ambush to try to capture you. When you leave this place, please, for my sake, flee as fast as you can. LIU BEI *acts out running, speaks:* — Ah, nephew, if you hadn't said something, how would I have known?

> (Jinzhan'er)
> Leave this feast;
> Don't be bewildered.
> Here, I am spitting out the real truth, "letting news of spring leak."[31]
> Quickly lead out your warhorses and change into battle clothes.
> I am afraid that for you: "When your mind is afire, the boat travels too slowly,
> When your heart is agitated, the horse trots too slow."
> Don't look for a "hole to go underground,"
> I just want you to search out that "ladder that rises to heaven."

LIU BEI *speaks:* — If I had known you brothers weren't getting along, I never would have said what I did. — MALE LEAD *speaks:* — Be careful, uncle, and go steadily down the road ahead.

> (Coda)
> We part with suffering,
> Sadly take our leave,
> Who knows what year and day we may see each other again?
> Go quickly now down the road to Xinye and Fancheng,

---

29. "Branches and leaves" is a common designation for scions of a royal family.
30. I.e., "Quick! Flee! Leave!"
31. I.e., "letting the cat out of the bag."

For I want you to round up and drill troops to firmly guard your
    walled city;
I want you to use your cleverest wiles to train those troops and
    horses,
Preparing all the while a force that can extinguish the bandits and
    make the Lius rise again.
And when those spears and bucklers are put to rest,
I will make the whole world at peace,
And when that happens—like winds and clouds, civil and military
    officers alike will prostrate themselves at the cinnabar steps.

Exits.

LIU BEI *speaks:* — Liu Bei, you were at fault. Thanks to the clever plan of the
Field Marshal, I can depart this Xiangyang meeting, and I dare not tarry or
linger, but today return to Xinye and Fancheng.

Exits.

[Act 2]

KUAI YUE, CAI MAO *enter together, speak:* — We are Kuai Yue and Cai Mao, and
we're bearing the order of the young lord. Now, Liu Bei should never have discussed setting up the elder and not the one from the lateral wife. Bearing the
order of the younger lord, we are going to send our personal general, Wang Sun,
to go on ahead to the posthouse and steal Liu Bei's horse, Rogue. Here we are
already at Wang Sun's gate. — *They act out calling him, speak:* — Wang Sun!
The younger lord orders you to go ahead on this night and steal the ass that Liu
Bei is riding and then report back to the younger lord when it is done. Be careful, but carry this out successfully.

Exit together.

MALE LEAD, *costumed as* WANG SUN, *enters, speaks:* — I am the personal general
of the Prince of Jing. Because Liu Xuande requested a loan of a walled city from
the Prince of Jing, he was asked to come to the Xiangyang meeting, where he
got drunk at a feast and asked us for the plaque and seal for Jingzhou. I have
received an order from the younger lord to go and steal the ass Liu Bei rides
tonight, so I'd better get going.

(YUEDIAO MODE: *Dou anchun*)
I've waited until the clepsydra is finished and the night has halved,
And the streets are still and quiet.
I see the Dipper turn and the stars make their transit,
And right at this time no one has yet awakened their dreaming soul.

I enter the main gate of this posthouse hostel,
And circle around these empty eaves and corrugated ramps
Lest I run into a retainer
Or bump into a stable boy.
This Rogue among stallions
Is better than any bayard or magic steed.

(*Zihua'er xu*)
What one wants is well tamed and purely good,
What one fears is a kicker or a spooked runner,
Neither yelling nor angry outburst work.
The horse is controller of the general's destiny,
And after a horse is stolen, it's hard to endure going on foot.
I've weighed it out.
This is no simple thief who bores holes or leaps over walls,
If I am sent out on an assignment, how dare I refuse?
You truly are in this spot: "When a person is in trouble, he draws
    near a relative,"
But what does "He is good at making friends" offer him?

(*Jin jiaoye*)
They just mixed up a trough of fodder,
And fed him until he's completely full.
I'll tiptoe here with silent tread, making no sound,
And release the bridle rope and halter line.

Acts out stealing the horse. — LIU BEI *rushes on, speaks:* Here I am in the posthouse. Ostler, lead out my horse! There's no one here. Well, I will lead out my
horse myself. Hey, who are you? — MALE LEAD *speaks:* — Before I steal his
horse, I'll first behead Liu Xuande! — LIU BEI *speaks:* You, general, why are you
so violent? Why do you have a mind to kill me with your sword?

(*Sai'er ling*)
You tell me, "Don't be so violent,
Display such crude heroism,
Or pull out your shining red sword and take it in hand."

LIU BEI *speaks:* What crime have I committed? *Sing:*

Well, you say I have broken the law, turned away from the rules,
Stolen a horse, led him away from the trough,
Which makes your life as easy to take as lighting swan's down afire.[32]

---

32. Tentative translation of *he ni xingming si liao hongmao*, understanding to be equivalent to
liao mao or *liao fa*, "to catch hair on fire": something easy to do.

LIU BEI *speaks:* — Why are you stealing my horse? — MALE LEAD *speaks:* — Because you asked for the plaque and seal for Jingzhou at the banquet and I am under orders from the younger lord. He wanted me to steal your horse. LIU BEI *speaks:* — You aren't aware that because I wanted to borrow a walled city, I was asked to this banquet. The Prince of Jing voluntarily told me, "I am old now. Who can I have take over the plaque and seal?" I said, "Set up your elder son, not the son from your concubine." This is why the second young lord is bearing a grudge and wants to kill me. — MALE LEAD *speaks:* — Well, if this the case, our young lord is in the wrong. — LIU BEI *speaks:* — General, I am a direct descendant of the house of Han and a younger cousin of the Prefect of Jingzhou.

> (*Reprise*)
> Your argument is that as a direct relative you stem from the Exalted
>   Ancestor of the Han
> And, in terms of fraternal relatives, are a close friend of Liu Biao.
> You had great success in smashing the Yellow Turbans,
> And established your merit in slaying Dong Zhuo—
> A person can figure out in their own mind what is right and what is
>   wrong.

LIU BEI *speaks:* — My life is in your hands, general. — MALE LEAD *speaks:* — Don't worry, my Prince of Xiang, I will escort you out of the city. — LIU BEI *speaks:* — "Today's act of grace will surely be requited tomorrow."

> (*Tiaoxiao ling*)
> No need to dwell on it,
> For we must flee quickly.
>   Ai!
> Don't count again on "Meeting an old friend far away from home."

LIU BEI *speaks:* — Where does this road lead, general? *Sing:*

> Look far off at the road to Xinye and Fancheng.
> Go like a shooting star through the whole night long, night after
>   night.
> Stay on the main road! Don't wander off on any little byways
> Or beg off the travails of distant waters and far-off mountains.

LIU BEI *speaks:* — There are rivers in the way ahead of me. What shall I do?

> (*Shua ci'er*)
> Gazing far off, we see fuzzy and furzy green carpets of sedge and
>   fragrant grasses,

Rolling and boiling waves and breakers of snow and silver.
On the great dike at Sandalwood Creek the water circles in closure,
No boat to cross, no long bridge,
Nearly frightening this hero to death.

LIU BEI *acts out praying to Heaven, speaks:* — August Heaven itself I beseech. If Liu Bei rises to prominence sometime far off—horse, my fate lies with you; your fate lies in water.

> (*Sheng Yaowang*)
> He prays there to Heaven and Earth,
> Invokes his heartfelt desires,
> Adjusts his tiger body, arranges his brocade campaign robes,
> Cinches up his jade belt,
> Lifts up the golden stirrups,
> And on the horse's rump smashes the tip of his rattan whip to
> smithereens.

LIU BEI *acts out jumping over Sandalwood Creek.* — *Sing:*

> And one leap is like a bunted phoenix aflight, a hidden dragon
> running.

LIU BEI *acts out turning back to look at* MALE LEAD, *speaks:* General, we will meet again!

Exits.

KUAI YUE *and* CAI MAO *enter and speak:* We are Kuai Yue and Cai Mao. We are bearing the order of the younger lord to overtake Liu Bei. We are riding fast horses, but we can't catch up to him. This horse—if I don't run, it doesn't either. We've reached Sandalwood Creek. Hey, aren't you Wang Sun? Where is Liu Bei? — MALE LEAD *speaks:* — Liu Bei is innocent of anything and he is furthermore a relative of our Lord. Because of these facts, I have set him free. — KUAI YUE *speaks:* — This good-for-nothing lacks any sense of respect. You have become someone who understands what is proper respect and what isn't, so you have done it willfully. — CAI MAO *speaks:* Will . . . won't . . . won't you dance, won't you dance, won't you dance?[33] — KUAI YUE *speaks:* — Take him and bind him up, brother, and we'll go and see the younger lord. — MALE LEAD *speaks:* — I am not afraid, not afraid, not afraid!

---

33. This is a bit of nonsense, in which Cai Mao makes a pun on the phrase Kuai Yue has just uttered: *ni zuode ge zhili wuli gu wuli,* converting "without ritual" into *wuli,* "dance + emphatic particle." The term "dance" is also used as a verb to mean to "perform rituals."

(*Coda*)
You take the loyal and good and destroy those who accord with the
    Way of Heaven,
His single mount whisked by as though pushed by the wind or swept
    by lightning.
He saved his life and avoided disaster,
But this has sent what's left of my shitty life to its final act.

Exit together.

Wedge

SIMA HUI *enters and speaks:*

My precious sword leaves its sheath; the deviant ghosts are scared;
One strum on my jasper zither and all the spirits are alarmed.

This humble Daoist is Sima Hui, known as Decao, and bearing the Daoist sobriquet of Master Water Mirror. I am working at the Way and perfecting my
actions here on Deergate Mountain. I have seven friends, and we are called the
Eight Extraordinary Talents of the Jiang Xia region. Now Liu Xuande, under
duress from Liu Cong after going to the Xiangyang meeting, has ridden alone
by mistake into Deergate Mountain and is completely lost. I'll just wait here for
him. LIU BEI *enters and speaks:* — I am Liu Bei. Because I went to that Xiangyang meeting, Liu Cong wanted to harm me. So, I secretly fled on a single
mount and leapt over that Sandalwood Creek, and now am completely lost.
I don't know which road takes me on to Xinye and Fancheng. — SIMA HUI
speaks: Say, aren't you Liu Xuande? Now, Noble Xuande, that Xiangyang meeting was really scary. — LIU BEI *speaks:* — How could this transcendent elder
know about this? — SIMA *speaks:* — Perhaps you don't recognize me, Noble
Xuande. But I recognize you. — LIU BEI *speaks:* — Elder, I have lost my way,
and I don't know which road goes on to Xinye and Fancheng. — SIMA *speaks:*
— It's getting late. There's a Daoist residence ahead on this Deergate Mountain; why not go on there and spend the night? Noble Xuande, I observe that
although you have capable generals under your command, you still lack a strategic planner. — LIU BEI *speaks:* — Might I ask, master, what is a strategic
planner? — SIMA *speaks:* — Haven't you heard of the recumbent dragon in the
south and the phoenix fledgling of the north? — LIU BEI *speaks:* — Who are
recumbent dragon and phoenix fledgling? — SIMA *speaks:* — Okay, enough.
— LIU BEI *speaks:* — Might I ask your illustrious name sir? — SIMA *speaks:*
— Okay, enough! Don't ask me. Go ask that guy.

Exits.

LIU BEI *speaks:* — Whom am I supposed to ask? How come I don't see that transcendent elder anymore? Who knows if he was a person or a ghost? It's getting dark and late. I see a lamplight way off there. I'll go there and see if I can spend the night.

Exits.

PANG DEGONG *enters, leading a* DAOIST ACOLYTE. PANG DEGONG *speaks:*

I nurture my nature, perfect the authentic, and discuss the Way and its virtue,
　The patterns of heaven and the structure of earth I lecture on with detail
　　　　and subtlety;
　My sword commands the planets and the constellations—I can lead them
　　　　forth;
　One thrum on my jasper zither can move the hidden mysteries.

This humble Daoist is Pang Degong, and I live here on the south side of Pinnacle Peak. I have never been in a city or in a government office in my life. I do not covet extravagant and lavish things, and I take my pleasure only in pure tranquility. I lecture to my students on the secret path to the Subtlety of the Grand Clarity, and I practice the techniques of refining drugs for long life. I completely understand the Great Way, and through study have reached the quadrant of the immortals. I hide my traces here in the mountains and bury my fame in the forest. We friends in the Way here in Jiang Xia have been named the Eight Extraordinary Talents, and it is I, alone, who am the head, and we work at the Way and cultivate our actions here on Deergate Mountain. Today Xuande leapt over Sandalwood Creek and got lost here on Deergate Mountain after he met up with difficulties at the Xiangyang meeting. Later today I will give Xuande directions to the place where he will rise to glory. I have a plan in mind when he comes. Acolyte! Stand guard at the gate of the residence. Noble Xuande should show up sometime soon. — LIU BEI *speaks:*[34] — When I withdrew from that Xiangyang meeting, I was pressured by one of Liu Cong's generals, and came to Sandalwood Creek where I was blocked. I relied on the protection and aid of Heaven above and my horse Rogue jumped right across the river. But I lost my way and wound up here on Deergate Mountain. I didn't know how to get out, but I saw a Daoist elder who said, "The southern recumbent dragon, the northern phoenix fledgling, okay, that's enough!" and then rose rapidly into the void, and it was hard to determine if he was a spirit or a ghost. Now it's late and getting dark, and I'll see if I can stay overnight at that homestead there. — *Acting out calling at the gate, speaks:* — Is anyone inside? — PANG DEGONG *speaks:* — Acolyte! Liu Xuande has arrived. Go open the door

---

34. There seems to be a stage direction missing that would bring Liu Bei back on stage.

and tell him he is welcome. — ACOLYTE *speaks:* — Understood. Let me open this door. . . . Liu Xuande, my master invites you in. — LIU BEI *speaks:* — I've never met anyone at this Daoist hermitage, but they already know my name. This is certainly out of the ordinary! — *Acts out greeting rituals.* — PANG DE-GONG *speaks:* — Noble Xuande, from the time you left Xinye to the time you went to the Xiangyang and there became the object of Liu Cong's schemes must have been a frightening time! — LIU BEI *speaks:* — I must report to you, master, that my luck has been rotten and I've been very unfortunate. So, I hope with all my heart, respected master, that you have some instructions. Shall we exchange names? — PANG DEGONG *speaks:* — I am Pang Degong, nourishing my artlessness here on Deergate Mountain. Noble Xuande, there must be some kind of karmic affinity that has brought you here to my hermitage tonight. — LIU BEI *speaks:* — I met another master when I reached Deergate Mountain, who spoke about some southern recumbent dragon and northern phoenix fledgling. I asked him his name, but he kept saying, "Okay, enough," and then leapt up into the air and disappeared. I don't know if he was a spirit or a ghost. — PANG DEGONG *speaks:* — Noble Xuande, this was Sima Hui, known as Decao, no one else but Mr. Okay. — LIU BEI *speaks:* — Master, have pity on my lonely and destitute state—what instructions do you have for me in terms of the Way and its virtue, or transcendents' methods? — PANG DEGONG *speaks:* — Noble Xuande, there are two people here in the Jiang Xia area. One is the southern Recumbent Dragon, the other is the northern Phoenix Fledgling. But for those two, their time is not here yet. I will first give you a son. Where is Kou Feng? — KOU FENG *enters and speaks:* — Here I am. — *Acts out greeting rituals.* — PANG DEGONG *speaks:* — Kou Feng, meet the Noble Xuande. Xuande, I give you Kou Feng as a son. Make your obeisances to Noble Xuande. — KOU FENG *speaks:* — I will. — *Acts out making obeisances.* — LIU BEI *speaks:* — I am poor and destitute, and I do not know when I will rise to success. I am deeply moved and accept the revered master's deep virtue. — PANG DEGONG *speaks:* — How about I also recommend another person to you? — LIU BEI *speaks:* — Where is this person, master? — PANG DEGONG *speaks:* — This person is a man from Dushu Village in Yingchuan. He is named Xu Shu and is known as Yuanzhi. — LIU BEI *speaks:* — Master, how does he compare to the Recumbent Dragon and the Phoenix Fledgling? — PANG DEGONG *speaks:* — He's no less of a man. — LIU BEI *speaks:* — Many thanks for my master's instructions. It is getting light, and I should go back. Liu Feng, come back with me to Xinye and Fancheng.

> Campaign battles need their heroes,
> And today I've gotten Liu Feng;
> Not yet visiting Xu Yuanzhi,
> I have already encountered Pang Degong

Exits with LIU FENG.

PANG DEGONG *speaks:* — Acolyte, is Liu Xuande gone? — ACOLYTE *speaks:*
— Liu Xuande is gone. — PANG DEGONG *speaks:* — Xuande will visit Xu Shu
first and then Kongming. It is indispensable that these two men are under the
aegis of Noble Xuande. I am going off now to wander through the mountains
and enjoy the rivers.

> In each and every territory he will govern with authority.
> Xuande is man of harmonious nature who calls out to Sichuan:
> Fifty-four prefectures, a land bold and strong,
> Forty-three years of perfect peace.

Exit together.

OLD WOMAN *enters with* MALE LEAD *and* ACOLYTE. OLD WOMAN *speaks:* —

> I abide by my ambitions with a happy heart, I delight in pristine poverty,
> I instruct my son to hit the books, I lecture on canons of the Way;
> Waiting upon his mother, living in peace, he lives according to his
> predestined lot.
> For many years in this mountain village he has labored hard.

I am Madam Chen, and my husband, surnamed Xu, was a man of Dushu Village in Yingchuan. He left behind only this one son, Xu Shu, known as Yuanzhi, who has completely mastered military and civil knowledge, which he has
practiced to perfection. He is not willing to go out and earn success or fame, but
he perfects his actions and works at the Way, supporting me in my old age. Son!
You should consider success and fame important! You can exert all your energies to exhaust your loyalty.[35] — MALE LEAD *speaks:* — Mother, I am deeply in
debt to your rigorous instruction. But if I am to exhaust my loyalty, then I cannot exhaust my filial feelings; if I exhaust my filial feelings, I cannot exhaust my
loyalty. OLD WOMAN *speaks:* But, won't this get in the way of your success and
fame? MALE LEAD *speaks:* I only want to be in service to you, mother, and to
perfect my authentic self and nourish my nature. Is it not said, "If mother and
father are still at home, far away one cannot roam, but if you roam you must
have a direction!"[36] OLD WOMAN *speaks:* All you want to do, child, is roam
through the mountains, delight in the waters, work on the Way, perfect your
authentic self and nourish your nature, and take care of me. When will you rise
to prominence? — MALE LEAD *speaks:* — Acolyte! Keep watch at the door and

---

35. Following Zhao Qimei's emendation of *jin,* "advance," to *jin,* "exhaust."

36. A colloquial rephrasing, first found in the transformation tale (*bianwen*) "The Transformation Tale of Qiu Hu," of a quote in the *Analects* 4.19: "The Master said, 'While your parents
are alive, you should not travel far, and when you do travel, you must keep to a fixed direction.'"
Altered, in accordance with Zhu Xi's note, from Slingerland 2003, p. 36.

tell me when someone comes. — ACOLYTE *speaks:* — All right! — ZHAO YUN *enters and speaks:*

<blockquote>
From my youth I worked hard at the martial arts,
In younger years I bought horses and went off to the Western Rong;
All heroes within the four seas quail when they hear my name—
For only I am
Zhao Zilong from Changshan in Zhending!
</blockquote>

I am Zhao Yun, and I bear Noble Xuande's command to request Xu Yuanzhi participate in the war of vengeance against Cao Cao and thus be awarded the rank of Field Marshal. I asked someone and they told me this hermitage is his place. Sergeant, take my horse. Acolyte, go report and say that Zhao Yun, one of Noble Xuande's men, is here to make a formal visit. — ACOLYTE *speaks:* — All right! Master, Zhao Yun, one of Noble Xuande's men, is outside at the door. — OLD WOMAN *speaks:* — Son! There's a general here from somewhere. — MALE LEAD *speaks:* — Mother, this Zhao Yun is a general under Liu Xuande. — OLD WOMAN *speaks:* — Son, since a guest is here, I'll make myself scarce. — *Makes a false exit.* — MALE LEAD *speaks:* — Acolyte. Tell him he's welcome. — ACOLYTE *speaks:* — General, my master has invited you in. — ZHAO YUN *acts out making a formal greeting.* — MALE LEAD *speaks:* — Your noble feet, general, have come to tread on this base earth here. Please sit, general. — ZHAO YUN *speaks:* — I have long heard that my respected master's Way and virtue are without end. I am so fortunate to be able to meet you today. — MALE LEAD *speaks:* — Why have you come, general? — OLD WOMAN *acts out entering to see what is going on, speaks:* — I want to listen to what this general from somewhere has to say about things. — ZHAO YUN *speaks:* Master, I am bearing the general order of our Noble Xuande. He has heard that you, master, have the talent to order the world and the abilities of Yi Yin[37] and Lü Wang.[38] So he has sent me especially to request that you come out of the mountains and accept the position of Field Marshal. How do you feel about this, master? — MALE LEAD *speaks:* — General, I am just a lay-about; moreover, I know nothing about treatises on weapons or armor. — ZHAO YUN *speaks:* — Our Noble Xuande has long heard of your deep knowledge of treatises on warfare and broad overview of the tactics of warfare. He has dispatched me especially to invite you. — MALE LEAD *speaks:* — Who recommended this humble Daoist? — ZHAO YUN *speaks:* — Our Noble Xuande by chance encountered Mr. Okay! —Okay!— and Pang Degong, both of whom recommended you. — MALE LEAD *speaks:* Sima Hui is Mr. Okay. He, along with Pang Degong, Zhuge Liang, Pang Shi-

---

37. See *Tripartite Oath,* n. 45.
38. See *Tripartite Oath,* n. 21.

yuan, Cui Zhouping, Shi Guangyuan, Meng Guangwei, and I are known as the Eight Extraordinary Talents of the Jiang Xia region. — ZHAO YUN *speaks:* — Master, you have mysterious ways that even the spirits and ghosts cannot fathom, and strategies to bring peace to the state and move troops around with skill. Please, take pity on us and come down the mountain. — MALE LEAD *speaks:* — You are unaware that in my younger days I only perfected my actions and worked at the Way, and that I truly do not know anything of the texts of weapons and armor. — ZHAO YUN *speaks:* — Master, our Noble Xuande is a man of encompassing benevolence and deep virtue. And he is a seventeenth-generation descendant, a great-great-grandson of Emperor Jing, the offspring of Liu Sheng, the Quiet Prince of Zhongshan. But alas, he has a paucity of troops and a scarcity of generals. Come down the mountain! — MALE LEAD *speaks:* — In your arguments you bring up the prestige of the Han house and the urgency of saving humankind. I do have the inclination to do this, general, but I have an old mother here in the house, and is it not said, "While your parents are alive, you should not travel far, and when you do travel, you must keep to a fixed direction"? — OLD WOMAN *enters, acts out formal greeting, speaks:* — Xu Shu, my son, you have misspoken. Consider that Noble Xuande is a scion of the Han royal family about whom I have often heard that he is a man of encompassing benevolence and deep virtue. Since the lord has sent General Zilong to ask you,[39] how can you make the argument that you have an old mother at home? Son, don't let me get in the way of you making a pure name for yourself for a whole generation! Don't worry about me, son, worry about yourself. — ZHAO YUN *speaks:* — Ai! Ai! Ai! Your mother has it right. Is it not said, "Follow the intent of your parents' words"?[40] This is the greatest act of filial piety. Since your mother has spoken thus, what need to ask you? If you come to Xinye, then we will send someone to fetch your mother to Xinye. What's to stand in the way of you sharing wealth and glory together? — MALE LEAD *speaks:* — Enough! Enough! Since mother has ordered me to go . . . Acolyte, get our luggage ready. Today we will start out on that long journey after we have bid mother adieu. — OLD WOMAN *speaks:* — On this trip, son, I want you to exhaust your mental and physical energies to support Noble Xuande. — ZHAO YUN *speaks:* — Rest easy, mother. As soon as we reach Xinye, I'll come back to fetch you.

([XIANLÜ MODE:] *Shanghua shi*)
Originally, I wanted to nurture my nature, perfect my authentic self,
    avoid the dust of the world,

---

39. Following Zhao Qimei's emendation of *que,* "but on the contrary," to *ni,* "you."
40. Here emending *yanqing* (look on their faces) to *yanqing* (sentiments of their words).

But today these humble words and rich gifts have made the invitation pressing.
All I wanted to do was take care of my mother, provide her fine
delicacies.

ZHAO YUN *speaks:*[41]— Once you have gone there, my lord will surely make
important use of you, master.— *Sing:*

Who envies your high post and top rank?

OLD WOMAN *speaks:* — Son, apply yourself. — MALE LEAD *speaks:* — Don't
worry, mother. — *Sing:*

Just look to me to support the altars of state and establish heaven and
earth!

[ZHAO YUN *and* MALE LEAD] *exit together.*

OLD WOMAN *speaks:* He's gone now.

My eyes will be on the lookout for his banners of office.
My ears will listen for good news!

[Act 3]

CAO CAO *enters, leading* SOLDIERS, *and speaks:*

I am skilled at transforming wind and clouds[42] and am versed in the Six
Secret Teachings;[43]
I lead my army and select my generals using only the brave and heroic;
The battle standards are lightly furled, the dust of campaign retreats,
And when cavalry arrives, we strike drums of victory.

I am Cao Cao, known as Mengde, and am a man from Qiao Commandery in
the state of Pei. When young I practiced the civil arts and when mature, the
military. In text I completely comprehend the *Three Strategies of Master Yellow
Stone,*[44] and in battle the *Six Secret Teachings.* After I destroyed that Great General Lü Bu, I created extraordinary success. I must thank

---

41. The stage direction here in the original reads "ZHAO YUN *enters and speaks,*"—a clear
mistake, since he never exited.

42. "Wind" and "cloud" are the names of two battle formations.

43 The *Six Tactics*; see *Tripartite Oath,* n. 21.

44. See *Tripartite Oath,* n. 4.

THE SAGE[45]

for taking pity on me and awarding me the position of Prime Minister of the Left. I now have a million brave soldiers at my command as well as a thousand seasoned generals. But Liu Bei, Guan Yu, and Zhang Fei were so rude. After I smashed Lü Bu, right in front of

THE SAGE

they took it upon themselves to recommend Liu Bei for office. He did not accept my compromise and fled out to Xudu, where he wrested away Xuzhou. I appointed Xiahou Dun as my point general to battle them at Xuzhou, and they were greatly defeated. I led Guan Yunchang to Xudu, where I appointed him Marquis of Shouting. I never thought the Marquis of Shouting would depart without taking his proper leave of me and would meet up again with them at Old City. I sent Cai Yang to capture Guan Yunchang but didn't anticipate that Guan Yunchang would wind up beheading him. Now the three—Liu, Guan, and Zhang—have stationed their army in Fancheng in Xinye, and I want this over and done with! Now I've summoned Generals Cao Ren and Cao Zhang to go off and capture the three of them. Sergeant, summon Generals Cao Ren and Cao Zhang here. — SOLDIER *speaks:* — Understood. Generals, you are summoned. — CAO REN *enters and speaks:*

When in my youth, I practiced the martial arts,
　Itching for a fight when I campaigned south or quelled rebels to the north;
Approaching an army and looking at their dust, I knew the number on the ground.
　Facing a rampart, I sniffed the earth and recognized their battle plans.

I am Cao Ren. I am good at kenning military texts and have deeply penetrated battle tactics. I've earned merit each time I have faced a foe, and I'm right on the training field, training troops and disciplining officers. I don't know why father called, but I should go see. Report! Say that Cao Ren has come. — SOLDIER *speaks:* — Oyez. I want to inform the Grand Marshal that Cao Ren has arrived. — CAO CAO *speaks:* — Tell him to come in. — SOLDIER *speaks:* — Go in! — *Act out greeting.* — CAO REN *speaks:* — What did you have in mind for me when you called me, father? — CAO CAO *speaks:* — I have something I want to

---

45. In the original text "The Sage," which refers to the emperor, is raised one character above the highest lines in the rest of the text and begins a new line. Since the play (and perhaps even the script) is presented to the emperor before it is performed, any text must abide by court protocol to elevate any of the imperial designations above the rest of the text. This indicates that this play was to be performed before the Ming Emperor.

discuss with you. For the moment, you are only a part of it. Call in General Cao Zhang. — CLOWN, *costumed as* CAO ZHANG, *enters and speaks:* —

I am indeed[46] Cao Zhang,
Body forbidding, countenance dignified;
I'm no use when it comes to killing.
I just eat a stick of candy!

I am Cao Zhang, and I understand well Zhao, Qian, Sun, and Li and have brought into the fold Jiang, Shen, Han, and Yang. If the grand army should be defeated, then Jin, Wei, Tao, Jiang, and if I'm still caught, then Pi, Bian, Qi, Kang.[47] I was just practicing somersaults in a vacant space when my father called me. I'd better go. Report that Cao Zhang is here. — SOLDIER *reports, speaks:* — Oyez. Cao Zhang has arrived. — CAO CAO *speaks:* — Send him in. — SOLDIER *speaks:* Go in. — CAO ZHANG *speaks:* — Why did you call me father? Oh, elder brother Cao Ren is here too. — CAO CAO *speaks:* — Come closer, you two. Now Liu, Guan, and Zhang are in Xinye and Fancheng and have enlisted an army to do battle with me. Cao Ren, I'm going to partition off a hundred thousand troops to give you. You act as general commander of the army. Cao Zhang, you be the point general. Go today and select brave troops and set out on that long journey. I only hope you'll be successful. You be careful out there. Afterward I'll bring a larger army to meet up with you.

The army follows the transfer of the seal of office, discerning what is true,
If an offense needs to be judged, nail it down first;
When at court, do not mistake the Son of Heaven's command,
And do not turn your back on the orders of generals in the field.

CAO REN *speaks:* I am bearing the personal order of my father: now Liu, Guan, and Zhang have stationed their army at Xinye and want to do battle with us. I've been given a hundred thousand brave troops, and I am the general com-

---

46. Following Zhao Qimei's emendation of an unrecognizable blacked-out character to *nai*, "indeed."

47. Each of these sets of four names are individual lines from an early primer, *One Hundred Surnames*. Clearly the first level of meaning is that, in contrast to other's statements about being versed in books on military and political strategy, he has mastered only one of two or three primers with which students began to learn to read. At another level, however, there may be puns that we cannot completely identify. For instance, the four names Jin, Wei, Tao, Jiang may also be understood as *jin wei tao jiang*, "Now I slip across the river," and the fortuitous combination of Pi, Bian can also be read as a homophone for *pibian* (leather whip). But these are simply conjectures. He is, of course, citing this text completely anachronistically. The text was written in the Song (which explains the first two surnames: Zhao, the surname of the royal family of the Song, and Qian, that of the royal family of the preceding Wu Yue kingdom).

mander and my brother Cao Zhang is the point general. Today we have picked out our aides and we're off to do pitched battle with those three. You three ~armies,[48] great and small, listen to my orders. After three beats of the drum, pull up stakes and break camp.

> Major generals pay special heed to stern orders and commands;
> Seasoned campaign generals strap on their armor, set out on the long
>   road;
> Hair-splitting swords hit the whetstone; the doubled blade is keen;
> White-shining spears naturally attract moonlight's brightness.
> Axes clad in bronze—where they are raised, souls fly off on the wind,
> Cudgels with wolves' teeth—where they fall, skulls are crushed.
>   What we sit in are
> Seven-layered lotus tents with golden peaks
>   That crush
> Zhou Yafu's fine-willow camp[49] with his stationed army.

CAO ZHANG *speaks:* — Cao Ren is gone now. I'm going to pick out troops and horses in my command, and go off and do pitched battle with Yunchang.

> This morning for one day, I draw together spears and lances.
> I reckon that Yunchang has already snapped one tally;[50]
> Because his body is nine feet, two inches tall,
> And he can open wide those cinnabar[51] phoenix eyes and stare—
> And when those three armies see this, they all will be terrified.
> If he uses his knife, fresh blood will flow—
> If he twirls his knife and tries to hack my neck,
> As cool as can be, I'll just pull in my head.[52]

> [*Exits.*]

LIU BEI *enters with* GUAN, ZHANG FEI, ZHAO YUN, *and speaks:* — I am Liu Xuande. We have stationed our troops temporarily here in Xinye and Fancheng after we borrowed Jingzhou. I sent Zhao Yun to ask Master Xu Shu to come, and

---

48. A general term for army, it originally meant the left, right, and center armies.

49. Zhou Yafu (d. 143 BC) was a renowned general who helped Emperor Jing pacify seven major principalities. He was a man of great integrity who expected the highest form of disciplined response from troops under his command. He encamped at Fine Willows to ward off Xiongnu attacks from the north. He demanded such discipline that any tightly run, disciplined army base became known as a "fine-willow camp."

50. This metaphor is unclear to us; perhaps it means, "is already one step ahead."

51. Here emending *dan,* "single," to *dan,* "cinnabar."

52. I.e., like a turtle.

today is a propitious day to appoint him general commander of the army.[53] Prepare wine and food and you general officers follow me straightaway to the Grand Marshal's headquarters, where we will fête the general commander.

Exit together.

MALE LEAD *enters with* LIU BEI, GUAN, MALE LEAD ZHANG, MALE LEAD ZHAO, GONG GU, LIU FENG, JIAN YONG, MI ZHU, MI FANG. LIU BEI *speaks:* — Today is a propitious day to appoint you general commander. All of the lower and higher ranking generals have come today to pay their respects to you, master. — MALE LEAD *speaks:* — I have calculated: what virtue and ability do I, Xu Shu, have to be able receive such a weighty gift as this from my lord? — LIU BEI *speaks:* — Master, take pity that Liu Bei has no place to call his own, has been pressured by Cao Cao, and can now temporarily station my army here at Xinye. I have heard that you, master, have bored through the five canons of the classics, that you know well the three mainstays that bind lord to minister, father to child, and husband to wife, that you hide within your breast the sun and the moon, and conceal heaven and earth up your sleeves. You can summon the wind and call the rain so that armies are defeated—master, these spiritual and mysterious secrets and marvelous tactics will smash Lord Cao. — MALE LEAD *speaks:* — I, this untalented Xu Shu, do not seek to be known far and wide and hope for no success and fame. I abide by my pristine poverty to perfect my authentic self and nurture my nature, and I serve and care for my mother in a filial manner from morning to night. Because the Grand Marshal has all-encompassing benevolence and deep virtue, you have enlisted worthy men on behalf of the house of Han. Today I reside in an interior compartment in the Grand Marshal's headquarters where I plan battle strategy away from the front lines, acting as general commander to guide generals and dispatch armies. Just watch as I will sweep away ten thousand miles of campaign dust so that all is peaceful, and protect this brocade and embroidered heaven and earth of four hundred years. It was no easy task for everything that the Exalted Ancestor of the Han gave rise to—sweeping away the various brave contenders, making everything within the four seas calm and pure—to last until today.

([ZHONGLÜ MODE:] *Fendie'er*)
In those days Chu and Han were locked in struggle.
He employed the worthy—a convergence of clouds from every
  direction—
Swept away the many contenders, settled chaos, rooted out danger.
He went on to extinguish powerful Qin,

---

53. In earlier sections, he was due to be appointed as Field Marshal.

Extirpate robust Chu,

Before he was able to universally save the living.

If the three eminences of the Han[54] had not exerted their power to support him,

How could he have ever expanded his borders and brought calm peace to the world?

(*Zui chunfeng*)

Marshal Han Xin settled heaven and earth, relying on secret plans and strategies;

Minister Xiao He made the altars of state secure by use of hidden stratagems.

Zhang Liang planned battle strategy in the rear, reading books of martial kind,

And all supported the rise, the rise of the Duke of Pei.

Only in this way could the house of Han rise to glory,

And could sons and grandsons enjoy it in perpetuity,

Protecting it from harm for myriad years, for a thousand generations.

---

54. The three great men who helped Liu Bang: Han Xin (d. 196 BC), Xiao He (d. 193 BC), and Zhang Liang (d. 186 BC). In his youth Han Xin, who eventually would become one of Liu Bang's most effective generals, survived by begging. After Liu Bang had defeated all his opponents and established the Han dynasty, he began to be paranoid about those around him who posed a threat to his rule. Liu Bang's wife, the cruel Empress Lü, sent the powerful minister Xiao He to summon Han Xin to the capital, where he was relieved of his command and beheaded. Xiao He had also been instrumental in Han Xin's rise to prominence. This curious reversal has given rise to a common saying in Chinese, "Success by Xiao He, defeat by Xiao He" (*cheng ye Xiao He, bai ye Xiao He*), which is used to indicate the fickle and inconstant nature of the world and the foolishness of counting on current circumstances. Han's biography is found in English in "The Marquis of Huai-yin, Memoir 32," in Sima Qian 2008, pp. 61–98, and Sima Qian 1993, pp. 91–98. Zhang Liang was descended from one of the ministerial families of the state of Hann (the double consonant here indicates it is the preimperial state of Han, and not the imperial dynasty). After the First Emperor had annihilated Hann, Zhang Liang tried to have him murdered but failed in this attempt. Later Zhang Liang served Liu Bang in establishing the Han dynasty. But once the dynasty had been established and Liu Bang grew suspicious of his erstwhile supporters, Xhang retired from court, according to legend, to become a hermit. By the end of the Western Han his identity as a Daoist was firmly established, and in his eulogy to the "Marquis of Liu, Hereditary House 25" (*Liuhou shijia ershiwu*) in the *Records of the Historian*, Sima Qian expresses some skepticism about the prevailing idea that Zhang received the texts of the *Laozi* from Laozi himself, which was firmly part the tradition by that time. See Sima Qian 1993, pp. 99–114. One of the commentarial notes to this passage cites a work that declares, "The Lord of the Wind was the commander of the Yellow Emperor's army, and he later transformed into Laozi, who bestowed his text on Zhang Liang." In later religious traditions Zhang Liang became a Daoist immortal. He once displayed his humility by retrieving a slipper that Master Yellow Stone had thrown down a bridge and the latter instructed him in military strategy (the *Three Strategies*).

LIU BEI *speaks:* — Right now there are brave heroes and eminent champions, master, expound on them. — MALE LEAD *speaks:* — My ruler, right now the brave heroes are powerful and rule by force, each occupying part of the territory. North of the river is Yuan Shao, in Jingzhou, Liu Biao, and Sun Quan in the Yangzi East region. In Xudu, Cao Cao leads an army of a million, eyeing the liege lords of the empire like a hungry tiger. You, my lord, are a scion of the Han, but your troops are insignificant and your generals are few. For the moment, let us hold our troops back for self-defense, and then make visits to the worthy eminences, knitting ourselves together as broadly as possible with these brave heroes. Sometime later will emerge those personalities who can aid the ruler. — LIU BEI *speaks:* — Consider, master, that Cao Cao attacked and defeated me at Xuzhou. It has been several years now, and I still have no place to call my own. But now I have fortunately encountered your face, venerated master, and I now request to appoint you commander of the army. We can view Cao Cao now as being as easy as turning over the hand, smashed on a day we specify; we will be successful in no more time than pointing to the sun.

> (*Hongxiuxie*)
> You just said it has been several years without a place to call your
>   own,
> And at this time your generals are few and your troops are
>   insignificant;
> But go and seek out the heroic and worthy, and they will support
>   you.

LIU BEI *speaks:* But your talents, master, are on a par with others. — *Sing:*

> "When human affairs go well, worthy men appear;
> When the mind of heaven is supportive, all favorable signs are
>   equal" —
> And at that time "gather together the wind and clouds"[55] to make the
>   altars of state secure.

Act out making the wind arise. — MALE LEAD *speaks:* — My ruler, did you see that gust of wind? — LIU BEI *speaks:* — Master, what does this gust of wind foretell about my fortune? — MALE LEAD *speaks:* — This wind does not go by the characteristics of the four seasons[56] but is a reliable trade wind that simply indicates that at high noon today some affair relating to the condition of the army will appear. — LIU BEI *speaks:* — My two brothers, stand guard at the

---

55. This is a metaphor for a meeting of prominent figures at a time of crisis.

56. Literally, "pleasant [spring], hot [summer], realm of metal [in the five phases = autumn], northern direction [= winter]" (*he yan jin shuo*).

headquarters' gate and if there is a military report, let me know. — GUAN *speaks:*
Understood. I'll wait here at the gate and see if anyone comes along. — XU CHU
enters and speaks:

> The measure of my gall is powerful, the force of my aura heroic.
> I once studied martial arts, but not all that well;
> I can travel on a warhorse, but can't get on it.
> Altogether I try to mount it forty times.

I am "Strong as Nine Buffalo" Xu Chu,[57] currently in service to Minister Cao.
I received orders from my minister to go to Xinye and Fancheng and deliver a
challenge to do battle to Liu Bei. And here I am, already. I'll get off this horse.
— *Acts out making formal greeting.* — GUAN *speaks:* — Where are you coming
from? — XU CHU *speaks:* — Brother, you don't recognize me. I am "Strong as
Nine Buffalo" Xu Chu, currently in service to Minister Cao. He dispatched
me to deliver this challenge to battle. — GUAN *speaks:* — Give me the letter.
— *Acts out greeting* [MALE LEAD], *speaks:* — Master, Xu Chu has come to deliver a challenge to battle. *Acts out reading it.* — MALE LEAD *speaks:* — Minister
Cao has dispatched an army of one hundred thousand with Cao Ren as general
commander and Cao Zhang as point general to do battle with us. Acolyte!
Bring me a brush. Let me note here on the back, "Pick the day to begin the
battle," and send that challenge to battle back. — XU CHU *speaks:* — I'm going
out the door now. I saw Uncle Guan and I delivered the battle challenge. I don't
dare tarry or linger, but will go back and report to Minister Cao.

Exits.

LIU BEI *speaks:* — Master, Cao Cao sent one of his generals, none other than
Xu Chu, to deliver a battle challenge. What did you write on the back of that
letter? — MALE LEAD *speaks:* — Come forward here, all of you generals. Minister Cao just sent that "Strong as Nine Buffalo" Xu Chu to deliver a letter
challenging us to do battle. Cao has ordered the generals under his command
thusly: Cao Ren is to be the marshal and Cao Zhang is to be point general.
They are leading an army of a hundred thousand brave troops to attack Xinye.
— LIU BEI *speaks:* — What shall we do, master? Right now I have just a few
more than ten thousand troops while he has a hundred thousand men and a

---

57. Xu Chu (fl. 190–220) was one of the two men in charge of Cao Cao's personal guard,
called the Tiger Bodyguards (*huweijun*). He was so ferocious in battle that he earned the nickname "The Insane Tiger" (*huchi*). The nickname here, which means "equal in strength to nine
buffalo," may stem from an early story in which his village was trading one of its buffalo for grain
with a bandit group. The buffalo kept returning to the village. Finally Xu Chu dragged the buffalo backward by its tail for more than two hundred paces, and the bandits were so amazed that
they left without the beast.

thousand battle-tested generals. He has ordered Cao Ren to lead them in order
to face off in battle with me. How can I repulse him? — MALE LEAD *speaks:* —
Here our troops do not number ten thousand. The manuals of warfare say, "A
few cannot match up to many; if you have strength, then battle with that
strength; if you do not have strength, you can take them through tactical
knowledge." Where is Zhang Fei? — ZHANG FEI *speaks:* — Master, you have
called me; what are your orders? — MALE LEAD *speaks:* — Cao Cao has just
sent Xu Chu to deliver a letter challenging us to battle. He wants to fight to the
death with us. I'll partition off three thousand cavalry to you, and you shall be
the point general. Listen to my orders.

> (*Shang xiaolou*)
> He relies on the bravery of his troops and the awesomeness of his
>   generals.
> See how I deftly plot to create a definite plan.
> I just want you to be ready for battle and right at the front,
> Your long spear in your hand,
> Astride Ravenblack.
> I just want you to reveal the momentum of your power,
> Dare to repulse the enemy,
> And immediately display your martial artistry.
>> *Continues in speech:* This time out, be careful.
> Take that army left after defeat, slay them quickly and force them to
>   retreat.

ZHANG FEI *speaks:* I have my orders and I'm on my way out of the headquarters'
gate. I'll lead three thousand men with horses to do battle with Cao Ren.

> Leopard head and round eyes display awesome violence,
>   My person like a fierce tiger, my mount like a dragon;
>   I'll seize Cao Zhang and personally bring his death,
>   And thus take revenge for the loss and flight at Xuzhou.

Exits.

MALE LEAD *speaks:* — Summon Mi Zhu, Mi Fang, and Liu Feng. You three
generals draw close. I am going to portion out a thousand men to each of you,
and you take a route on the left flank. If Cao's army breaks and retreats to the
rear, then your left flank army can slay your way into them. Employ your troops
in accordance with the plan.

> (*Reprise*)
> The left flank army must be put in regular order,
> I want you to work in concert.

Lead the ambush for me,
Observe at a distance who is winning, who is losing,
Look close at hand for the real situation.
You three generals are really an awesome presence—
Each apply the plans and use your knowledge according to your own
   abilities.
Lead these three armies for me, and intensely attack his left flank.

LIU FENG *speaks:* — We have your orders. Bearing the master's command, the
three of us brothers will go off and join the battle with Cao Ren.

Bearing the command we drive forth our troops to display our awesome
   appearance,
Our persons like flood dragons from the deep, our horses like bears;
With red hearts we three generals will support the altars of state,
And prove our merit once by capturing Cao Ren alive.

[*Exit together.*]

MALE LEAD *speaks:* Summon Gong Gu and Jian Xianhe. — GONG GU *speaks:*
Master, why did you call us two generals? — MALE LEAD *speaks:* — I'm portion-
ing off one thousand men to you. Go the right flank and cut off their retreat
and kill them. Employ your troops in accordance with the plan.

(*Bai hezi*)
You employ the right flank squadrons,
And display your virile and dominant power.
With your long-handled knife split them, shoulders and all.
With your great patterned axe, smash their skulls to smithereens.

GONG GU *speaks:* — We have your order. We two generals are going out of this
headquarters' gate on our way to do battle with Cao Ren.

Approaching an army, facing battle, we will spread our fame;
Corralling men and capturing generals, we will be the stronger;
Let enemy soldiers see us just once and their souls are already lost.
Bravely we join the enemy for one round of battle.

Exit together.

MALE LEAD *speaks:* — Summon Zhao Yun and Guan Yu. — ZHAO YUN *speaks:*
Master, you've called me here; how will you use me? — MALE LEAD *speaks:* —
Zhao Yun, I am going to portion out one thousand men to you. First go and
draw Cao's army in. Hide your thousand men in ambush along the road to
Xudu. Then wait until Zhang Fei sends Cao's army into retreat so that the army

lying in wait can catch up to him and attack. On the road in front you block his soldiers. All I want is you to come back a success.

> (*Shi'er yue*)
> I have now given my orders to these three armies,
> And you group of generals must be attuned at heart.
> Completely rely on the vanguard of Yide,
> For true it is that his martial skills are the best.
> On the left and right flanks they will be prepared and lying in
>   ambush,
> And I'm sending you, Zhao Zilong, to pursue them with a surprise
>   attack.

> (*Yaomin ge*)
> Aiya! Who is the match of this Yunchang in heroic bravery?
> You lead these troops out for me and arrange battle standards in a
>   row,
> Make the fierce bravery of a mere thousand seem like clouds covering
>   the sky.
> Here by me the echo of explosions will reach heaven's edge like
>   rumbling thunder,
> And we'll kill until they suffer loss,
> Returning without a shred of armor on their bodies.
> How could they possibly know anything about my spirit immortal
>   plan?[58]

ZHAO YUN *speaks:* — I have received your order. I am out the headquarters' door and, leading an army of a thousand, on my way to have a fierce battle with Cao Ren.

> With long spear of canine tooth and horn, I contest for this world;
> With leather knobs and golden staves I will establish mountain and river;
>   Amidst an army of a million I will employ by heroic bravery,
> And drive back Cao's army with a coldness that penetrates their gall.

> *Exits.*

GUAN *speaks:* — Three armies great and small, heed my order. Bearing our Field Marshal's order and leading one thousand brave soldiers we will head straight for the road to Xudu, where we will wait for Cao's army, and we'll capture that treacherous general.

---

58. I.e., both in the sense that it is devised by a Daoist immortal, but also simply as a "superhuman" plan.

Putting troops in order, arraying formations, I display my virile, dominating
power.
On the left and right they will form into squadrons of equal size;
Wresting away battle drums, tearing up battle flags—a thousand kinds of
bravery,
And from my third-of-the-length blade bloody rays of light will fly.

Exits.

LIU BEI *speaks:* — All of the generals are gone, and following the master's hidden secrets and divine plans, they will surely win glory. — MALE LEAD *speaks:* — Each of the generals is gone, leading their troops away. My ruler, by this battle I will make the gall of the soldiers of Cao grow cold, and from a high peak tomorrow, I'll watch your generals' battle with Cao Ren. My lord, you lead a thousand soldiers and guard Xinye well.

(*Coda*)
Come tomorrow the drums that send them to battle at that first fray
Will bolster the army's morale; they will issue their battle cries in
unison.
Watch as, with one round of battle, I cause one thousand of Cao's
men to retreat,
And then, winning the victory and recalling our army, it will become
a field of joy.

Exit.

Wedge

CAO REN, CAO ZHANG *enter, leading* SOLDIERS, *and* [CAO REN] *speaks:* — I am Cao Ren. This is my brother Cao Zhang. We are bearing our minister's order to capture Liu, Guan, and Zhang, and we've reached Xinye and Fancheng. That cloud of dust way off in the distance must signal the approach of Liu Bei's own army. — ZHANG FEI *enters and speaks:* — I am Zhang Fei. I'm leading an army of three thousand men and their horses to do battle with Cao's troops. Who is that coming? — CAO REN *speaks:* — I am the strapping Cao Ren, under the command of Minister Cao. Who is that coming? — ZHANG FEI *speaks:* — I am Zhang Fei. You're not even worth mentioning. Sound the drums, and I'll do battle with you. — *Act out one battle scene.* — LIU FENG *enters, leading* MI ZHU *and* MI FANG, *and speaks:* — I am Liu Feng and my two brothers are Mi Zhu and Mi Fang. I am leading an army of three thousand[59] to capture Cao Ren and

---

59. The character *qian* (thousand) has been restored to the phrase *sanjun* (three armies) to make "an army of three thousand."

Cao Zhang. Three armies great and small, arrange your formations in a neat and orderly way. Aren't you Zhang Fei? Let us do battle together! — *The four generals act out a confusing battle sequence.* — CAO REN *speaks:* — Cao Zhang, I can't get close to them. It's not working; let's withdraw our shields and spear, and I'll flee with you.

Exit in defeat.

ZHANG FEI *speaks:* — Cao Ren and Cao Zhang have lost. I'll pursue them now, no matter where they go.

Exit together.

GONG GU, JIAN YONG *enter together.* — GONG GU *speaks:* — I am Gong Gu, and we're waiting here on the road to Xudu for Cao's army. There's a cloud of dust stirred up over there. They are coming! — CAO ZHANG *enters and speaks:* — I am Cao Zhang, and I was fighting with Liu, Guan, and Zhang when Zhao Yun split apart my formations. I've chased after Cao Ren to the point I don't know where I am. What shall I do? There is more cavalry coming from my front. — *Act out seeing* MALE LEAD *and* GUAN. — GUAN *speaks:* — Isn't this the junior officer Cao Zhang? Take him! Master, I've taken Cao Zhang. — MALE LEAD *speaks:* — Put him in the jail cart. Let us go to our ruler's presence and report our success!

> ([XIANLÜ MODE:] *Shanghua shi*)
> He should not have poked at the scorpion or stirred up the wasps to seek a battle,
> For here I have stretched out my nets and set my snares to strike the tiger.
> Here, our soldiers are fierce,
> Our generals brave and heroic:
> I've taken him alive in his own formation;
> This is my first success in my very first battle!

All the generals exit together.

Act 4

LIU BEI *enters, leading* SOLDIERS, *and speaks:* —

> There is no joy to match this morn's,
> No happiness like today's!

Who would have thought that Master Xu Shu could muster such divine plans to smash Cao Cao's army. Now our troops are on their way home. Set out a

feast, and we will wait for the master. Soldier, keep watch at the headquarters'
gate, and tell me when he arrives. MALE LEAD *enters and speaks:* — I am the
humble Daoist Xu Shu. Cao Ren, defeated in one battle by me, has been captured alive to be beheaded. This was no ordinary battle!

> (SHUANGDIAO MODE: *Xinshui ling*)
> In mighty order our supporting armies went out from Xiangyang:
> A triumphant army returns, singing a song of victory in unison.
> Battle standards wave, capturing the color of the song;
> Drums resonate, stirring the empty welkin.
> Glinting and glittering radiant swords, halberds, knives, and spears
> Slew until the generals, leftovers of defeat, lost their five souls.

MALE LEAD *speaks:* — Well, here I am. Take my horse! Report that the Field
Marshal has dismounted. — LIU BEI *acts out greeting him,* [*speaks:*] — Welcome.
MALE LEAD *acts out greeting him:* — LIU BEI *speaks:* — You have put out effort,[60]
master, and taken pity on Liu Bei's lonely and destitute state, casually applied a
little of your tactical knowledge, and used your hidden plans to defeat one hundred thousand of Cao's troops, who have all fled without a shred of armor. Indeed, you rank up there with Guan Zhong and Yue Yi![61] The truth is that I am
deeply fortunate. — MALE LEAD *speaks:* — I have relied on your "tiger's authority," my ruler.[62] We have simply made Cao's troops retreat in a single battle,
captured the generals alive for beheading, and returned to the base victoriously.
— LIU BEI *speaks:* — Master, how did you form up your troops, use your divine
strategies and unknown secrets, to capture Cao Ren and Cao Zhang alive?

> (*Yan'er luo*)
> There, they led their brave troops and approached the battlefield,
> Here, I first sent out a vanguard general—
> I relied on your long spear, the absence of your match in battle,
> As well as that black horse that was difficult to stop in its tracks.

> (*Desheng ling*)
> Ah! It was Cao Zhang who faced our formations there
> While here I secretly hid away an ambush on the left flank and right.

---

60. This phrase, *youlao*, can mean both "I have put you to great trouble" and "you have earned
much merit."

61. Guan Zhong was the prime minister of Qi during the Spring and Autumn era, and Yue
Yi was a famous general of the state of Yan during the Warring States period. Liu Bei is saying,
"You are a complete policy maker for the civil government and a great general as well."

62. From an ancient anecdote in which a fox persuades a tiger that other animals are more
frightened of the fox than they are of the tiger. He does this by walking through the forest with
the tiger right behind him.

Greatly defeated, suffering its aftermath, the troops of Cao fled,
And there was Zhao Zilong grasping his canine-tooth and horn
   spear.
They had no place to run and hide,
And looked with hope to the mountain valleys where they fled to
   forests deep.
But there they ran into that Yunchang, just like the heroic hegemon-
   king of Chu.

LIU BEI *speaks:* — Master, our generals have triumphed here. But where is that
Cao Zhang? — MALE LEAD *speaks:* — We slew all but a few hundred cavalry of
that army of one hundred thousand, and they escorted Cao Ren off. But we
captured that point general Cao Zhang alive. — LIU BEI *speaks:* — Set the army
aflight, chased off Cao Ren, and captured that point general, Cao Zhang. He's
been tied up securely. Bring him out to me.

GROUP OF GENERALS *act out taking* CAO ZHANG *and greeting* LIU BEI. — LIU BEI
speaks: — So this is Cao Zhang! Executioner, behead him! — LIU BEI *acts out
investing* GROUP OF GENERALS *with feudal ranks,* [*speaks:*] In this one battle, you
have killed Cao's troops, who are greatly defeated and have lost. Because we
have received the master's application of tactics when sending troops, and because of the dauntless bravery of our generals we have returned in triumph this
time. Set out a feast to celebrate our army, and reward all of our generals. Yet,
why?

Because Cao Cao commanded spear and lance
Xu Yuanzhi broadly applied his secret planning;
Liu Xuande's troops were scarce, his generals few,
But he was greater than Yi Yin aiding Tang or Lü Wang establishing
the Zhou!
Generals under his command exerted their loyalty and exhausted their
strength,
Their persons like tigers, their horses like krakens and dragons;
We raised the master to the position of Field Marshal
And now enfeoff as Marquises our battle-ready generals.

(*Gu meijiu*)
Today they are officials raised twice in rank,
By grace given rewards;
To celebrate, we hold a banquet;
To drink, we have chalcedony liquor.
Our military commanders' awesome presence displays a robust
   appearance;

Each and every one has the gall capacity of a true hero—
Guan Yunchang, who can stir up any battle . . .

(*Taiping ling*)
Zhao Zilong to send out troops and lead generals,
General of Horse and Conveyance Zhang with his horse Ravenblack
    and his long spear.
The officers are brave, each and every man stout and virile,
Sweeping away those who staked their claim as braves, expelled to
    the west, flying east.
Here at this feast pavilion
The various generals receive their rewards.
The Imperial Design[63]—may it thrive for tens upon tens of
    thousands of years![64]

LIU BEI *speaks:* Heed these words, my assembled generals:

    All because
We had been scattered for several years after the loss at Xuzhou,
We gather in righteousness at Old City, have a second reunion.
I took a letter far away, to ask about Jingzhou territory;
    He
Detained me to go to a meeting where he set out a bountiful feast.
    All because that
Second son Liu Cong wanted to harm my life,
Wang Sun led me down to the river's edge.
With a single leap Rogue jumped across Sandalwood Creek,
And I entered the mountains by accident to meet the two
    transcendents.
A revered master was recommended, a man of many plans and
    strategy.
How fortunate, on this day, to encounter heroic worthies;
One hundred thousand of Cao's troops were defeated in an instant.
For a thousand antiquities[65] [my men's] names will be spread and
    carried on,
As they support the altars of state for hundreds upon hundreds of
    generations.

---

63. In the manuscript the two characters for IMPERIAL DESIGN (*huangtu*) have been raised two characters above the surrounding text.

64. This would serve the double purpose of wishing the restoration of the Han a long dynastic reign, but also a direct praise of the current emperor.

65. I.e., for an infinite future.

We pray that

OUR EMPEROR

Will live ten thousand upon ten thousands of years![66]

TITLE: Xu Yuanzhi uses a plan to smash Cao Ren:

NAME: Liu Xuande goes alone to the Xiangyang meeting.

Editorial note: Collated palace archive edition on the second day of the mid-autumn month, the yimao year of the Wanli reign [August 2, 1615]. Recorded by Pure Constancy.

---

66. See note 45.

5

Zhuge Liang Burns the Stores at Bowang

Anonymous

Zhuge Liang Burns the Stores at Bowang (Zhuge Liang Bowang shaotun) first appears—as an anonymous play—in the *zaju* catalogues of the early fifteenth century: Zhu Quan's *Formulary of Correct Sounds for an Era of Great Harmony* (*Taihe zhengyin pu*) and Jia Zhongming's *Continuation of the Register of Ghosts* (*Lugui bu xubian*), a fact that suggests that the play was written during the second half of the fourteenth century. The play has been preserved both as one of the *Thirty Yuan Plays* (translated here) and as a late sixteenth-century manuscript that derives from the Ming palace repertoire. A translation of the fourth act of the Ming palace version is included here to allow a more detailed comparison of the two versions.

The play details how Liu Bei persuades Zhuge Liang to join his cause in the role of primary adviser and how Zhuge Liang then handles relations with Liu Bei's sworn brothers Guan Yu and Zhang Fei. Whereas Guan Yu is willing to accept the presence of Zhuge Liang for the benefit he can bring to their military success, the impetuous Zhang Fei is much less happy with Zhuge Liang's presence and his approach to warfare. The play concludes with Zhang Fei submitting to the superiority of Zhuge Liang's wisdom over his own brute violence. In the various renditions of stories of the Three Kingdoms, at this point in the stories' development the relationship of the three sworn brothers with Cao Cao, with whom they had collaborated in the past while fighting Dong Zhuo and others, has definitely soured. Leaving Northern China, the three brothers move south into Hubei, where Liu Bei holds the office of Prefect of Xinye. Looking for a means to strengthen his power, Liu Bei, who earlier had made Xu Shu his Field Marshal, tries to attract Zhuge Liang to his cause on the basis of Xu Shu's high recommendation. Before the play begins, Liu Bei and his brothers have already twice visited Recumbent Dragon Ridge to meet with Zhuge Liang, but in both cases Zhuge Liang has refused to see them. The first act of this play is devoted to Liu Bei's third and successful visit. Knowing that Liu Bei is destined to become emperor of the Shu-Han dynasty for only three years, Zhuge Liang makes his decision to join Liu Bei after he has recognized, through the physiognomy of Liu Bei's infant son, that the boy will reign as emperor for forty years.[1] Zhuge Liang also realizes that he will have to bully Zhang Fei into submission if he is going to be successful as Field Marshal.

At the beginning of the second act, Cao Cao dispatches Xiahou Dun to Hubei with a large army to wipe out Liu Bei once and for all. Zhuge Liang takes countermeasures by deputing each of Liu Bei's major generals (Zhao Yun, Liu Feng, Mi Zhu and Mi Fang, and Guan Yu) with highly specific instructions to counter the attack. Zhang Fei, eager to fight, is deliberately ignored for each mission. When Zhang Fei eventually is given the mission to capture the fleeing Xiahou Dun, and when Zhuge Liang at the same time predicts that he will fail in that mission, Zhang Fei wagers his head that he will succeed. If so, Zhuge Liang promises to cede his office to him. By the third act, all generals have successfully accomplished their missions, resulting in the utter defeat of Xiahou Dun's army. The only exception is Zhang Fei, who presents himself in shackles and is saved from beheading only by the intervention of Liu Bei. This act closely resembles Act 3 of *Liu Xuande Goes Alone to the Xiangyang Meeting*, where Xu Shu also sends his generals off with specific assignments. What such acts may have lacked in plot they probably compensated for by spectacle as each of the dispatched generals paraded across stage in his elaborate costume.

The fourth and final act introduces the character of Guan Tong, an old friend of Zhuge Liang, whom Cao Cao dispatches to try to convince Zhuge Liang to abandon Liu Bei and switch sides. To his underlings, Zhuge Liang greatly vaunts the supernatural power of Guan Tong to know what is hidden from sight. Once Guan Tong has been seduced into showing off these skills by correctly guessing which *go* stone (chess piece) is held in which hand, Zhuge Liang asks him to physiognomize Liu Bei's generals, Liu Bei, and Liu Bei's infant son in that order, thereby convincing Guan Tong of Liu Bei's imperial destiny. The play concludes with a scene in which Cao Cao is captured and brought on stage—most likely by Zhang Fei, who in this way redeems his earlier failure.

Burning the Stores is a regular *zaju*. It consists of four long sets of songs, which are all sung by the leading male. This role type plays the character of Zhuge Liang in each act, dressed in the first act in the gown of a Daoist priest and in the later acts in the military garb of the Field Marshal. The play contains neither wedges nor final demi-act. If the play is somewhat exceptional, it is in its use of a large cast and in matters of staging—the final act requires a number of "rooms" that are successively opened (but perhaps the backdrop was pulled back again and again to reveal these "rooms"). If it is indeed Zhang Fei who captures Cao Cao at the end, the outline of the plot shows a remarkable simi-

---

1. This central importance of Liu Bei's infant son to the plot, both in this and the final act, is highly unusual since in historical records the boy is usually described as a fool of an emperor who was a mere tool in the hands of the court eunuchs.

larity to *Li Kui Carries Thorns* (*Li Kui fu jing*) by the playwright Kang Jinzhi (late thirteenth century). In that play, the impetuous Li Kui, a heavy like Zhang Fei, finds out he has wrongly accused his leader Song Jiang of abducting a girl and makes amends for his faux pas by capturing the bandits who were responsible for the kidnapping.[2]

The contents of the first three acts show a remarkable similarity to the story of the first meeting of Liu Bei and Zhuge Liang and the latter's victory over Xiahou Dun as told in the *Records of the Three Kingdoms in Plain Language*, as will become immediately clear from a comparison with the relevant section of that text (see Appendix 1, item 9). In the *Records in Plain Language*, Zhang Fei repeatedly gives expression to his antagonism toward Zhuge Liang, but when it comes to a description of Xiahou Dun's doomed campaign, the action is very much described as observed from the perspective of Xiahou Dun. It is not at all clear from the *Records in Plain Language* whether Zhang Fei is under strict orders to capture or to kill Xiahou Dun. And while Zhang Fei on the one hand is described as a drunk (his common vice), on the other hand he is said to inflict a heavy defeat on Xiahou Dun. In the *Records in Plain Language*, Xiahou Dun's defeat through the superior strategy of Zhuge Liang and Xu Shu's consequent praise for that strategy goad Cao Cao into invading Central China himself with an army of a million. The campaign is initially successful but finally ends in utter failure when Cao Cao's attack results in bringing about a coalition of Liu Bei and Sun Quan. Eventually Cao Cao's mighty fleet is destroyed by fire at the battle of Red Cliff. This use of fire as a weapon of mass destruction by Zhuge Liang as found in the *Records in Plain Language* may very well have inspired the much greater emphasis on the use of fire in Zhuge Liang's victory over Xiahou Dun in *Burning the Stores*. Whereas the *Records in Plain Language* describes the rich stores in Bowang primarily as bait to entice Xiahou Dun to enter the walled city, the play waxes lyrical in its description of the conflagration and the huge number of its victims. The play is also more detailed in its description of the destructive power of the unleashed flood of river water after the breaching of a dam.

The fourth and final act of *Burning the Stores* would appear to be the anonymous playwright's original contribution to the Three Kingdoms legend. The character of Guan Tong may well be his own invention since Guan Tong appears nowhere else in Three Kingdoms literature. Guan Tong is portrayed as much as a wizard as a charlatan, since Zhuge Liang draws so much attention to the theatrical elements of his spectacular display of his guessing skills. The addition of Guan Tong may have been motivated by a desire to round out the characterization of Zhuge Liang. Zhang Fei is hardly a match for Zhuge Liang

---

2. See West and Idema 2010, pp. 317–18, and translation by J. I. Crump in Crump 1980.

in terms of guile and trickery, but Guan Tong allows a theatrical space for Zhuge Liang to show off his own talents in competition with a (supposedly superior) fellow student. Once Zhuge Liang has been shown to be able to outwit Cao Cao's ablest generals and advisers, it is only logical that the play should end with the capture of Cao Cao, as much as this act of poetic justice may be in conflict with historic fact.[3]

Burning the Stores must have enjoyed a certain popularity. Not only was it printed in the fourteenth century, but it was also included in the Ming palace repertoire. The sixteenth-century manuscript deriving from the Ming palace repertoire provides a fully written out version of the play. As is common in Ming palace versions, the number of songs in each set has been reduced and other characters in addition to the male or female lead have been given extensive lines—in this case, very elaborate dialogues indeed. All lines in the prose and songs of the *Thirty Yuan Plays* edition that suggest that Liu Bei is an emperor (or at least an emperor-to-be) have been carefully removed as it was not allowed to portray an emperor on stage at the Ming palace. Any doubt expressed on the part of Zhuge Liang about putting himself in service to Liu Bei has also been removed with equal care. This means that there is no role for Liu Bei's infant son as a deus ex machina anymore. As the play most likely had to function at court within a more extensive series of Three Kingdoms plays, there was no place for Cao Cao's capture at the end of the play even if it might have pleased the audience, and it is now Guan Tong instead who is carted off in a prison wagon.

In the *Romance of the Three Kingdoms*, Liu Bei's third visit to Zhuge Liang is described in the first part of chapter 38, and Zhuge Liang's defeat of Xiahou Dun is described in the second half of chapter 39. The novel has Guan Yu, as well as Zhang Fei, chafing at Zhuge Liang's new authority and his place within the formerly closed circle of brotherhood.

---

3. Some modern editors are so uneasy about this blatant "historical mistake" that they insist on replacing the name of Cao Cao with that of Xiahou Dun or Guan Tong, even though the characters in the fourteenth-century woodblock edition are very clear and allow no doubt. Apparently these editors never have read Pu Songling's (1640–1715) ballad, *A Happy Song* (*Kuaiqu*), in which Cao Cao, following his defeat at Red Cliff, is blocked from escaping back to Northern China and instead is captured and killed. Chinese authors were creative enough to not slavishly be bound by transmitted history and to be able to imagine how it might have been.

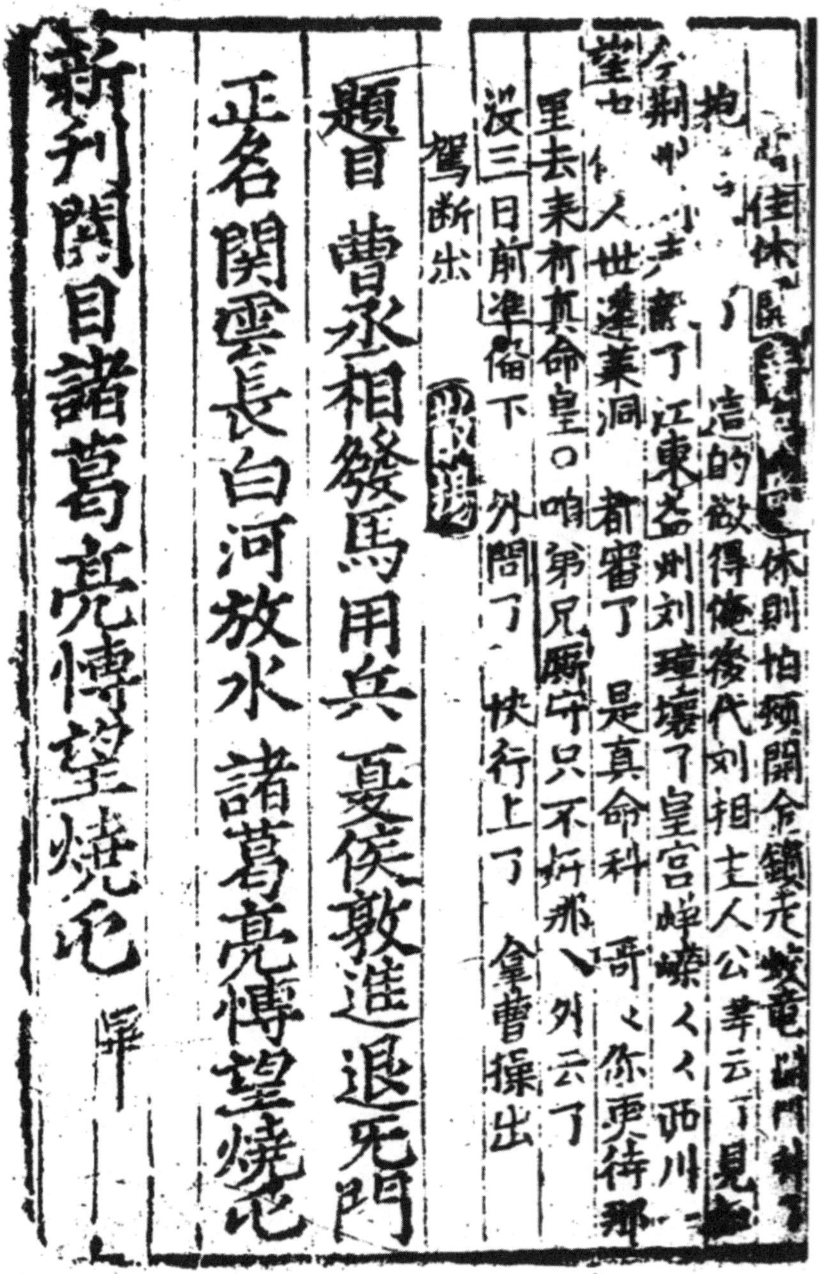

正名　関雲長白河放水　諸葛亮博望燒屯

題目　曹丞相發馬用兵　夏侯惇進退無門

駕斷出

沒三日前準備下外問了快行上了拿曹操出

里去來有真命皇○咱第兄厮守只不折那哥与尔更待那外云了

堂也…人世蓬萊洞都審了是真命科

令荊州…赢了江東益州劉璋壞了皇宮岑嶺人人西川

抱了…這的敵得俺後代刈相主人公苧云了見如

佳休則怕頻開倉鎖老鼠竜…門…

FIG. 4. Page 9b of the *Thirty Yuan Plays* edition of *Zhuge Liang Burns the Stores at Bowang*

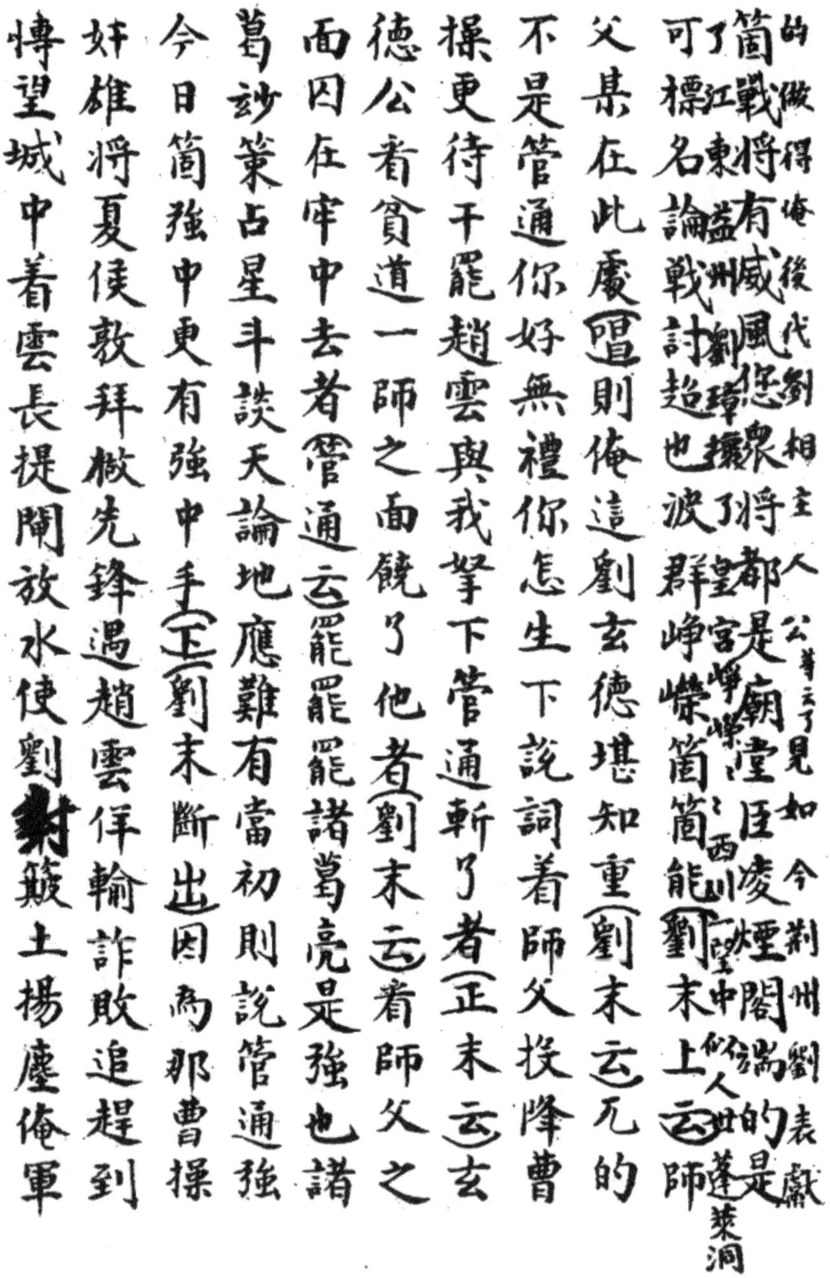

博望城中着雲長提閘放水使劉封簇土揚塵俺軍

奸雄將夏侯敦拜徹先鋒遇趙雲佯輸詐敗追趕到

今日簡強中更有強中手（正）劉末斷出因為那曹操

葛妙策占星斗談天論地應難有當初則說管通強

面囚在牢中去者管通云罷罷罷諸葛亮是強也諸

德公者貧道一師之面饒了他者劉末云者師父之

操更待干罷趙雲與我拏下管通斬了者（正末云）玄

不是管通你好無禮你怎生下說詞着師父投降曹

父基在此處匣則俺這劉玄德堪知重（劉末云）兀的

可標名論戰討超也波群峥嶸簡能劉末上云師

的做得俺後代劉相主

人公筆三字見如今荆州劉表獻的是廟堂匡凌煙閣端西川望中似人如蓬萊洞

FIG. 5. Page 36b of the Ming palace edition of *Zhuge Liang Burns the Stores at Bowang* with Zhao Qimei's collations from the *Thirty Yuan Plays* edition

Dramatis personæ in order of appearance

Role type	Name and family, institutional, or social role
Male lead	Zhuge Liang
Acolyte	Zhuge Liang's boy servant
Imperial Uncle	Liu Bei
Zhang Fei	Zhang Fei
Guan Yu	Guan Yu
Zhao Yun	Zhao Yun, general under Liu Bei's army
Liu Feng	Liu Feng, Liu Bei's adopted son and general in Liu Bei's army
Extra	role unspecified—Servant?
Baby	Liu Bei's infant son
Cao Cao	Cao Cao
Xiahou Dun	Xiahou Dun, general under Cao Cao's command
Extra	role unspecified—Messenger?
Mi Zhu	Mi Zhu, general in Liu Bei's army
Mi Fang	Mi Fang, general in Liu Bei's army
Extra	Guan Tong, trusted adviser of Cao Cao
Messenger	Messenger
Emperor	Emperor Xian

Newly Cut with Plot Prompts

Zhuge Liang Burns the Stores at Bowang
From a *Thirty Yuan Plays* Edition

[Act 1]

MALE LEAD, *costumed as* ZHUGE LIANG, *enters, opens:*

I, this poor Daoist, am Zhuge Liang, also known as Kongming. My Daoist sobriquet is Recumbent Dragon. In a place called Longzhong, twenty miles west of Xiangyang, in Deng County of Nanyang, there is a ridge called Recumbent Dragon Ridge, a place perfect for plowing and hoeing. Recently the Prefect of Xinye, Liu Bei, came to visit me twice, but I've never had anything to do with him. And just because the affairs of this world are in such chaos—dragons and tigers all mixed up and unclear which is which—I lie under the pine-shaded window of my thatched shack and read books on military strategy. Ai! Zhuge Liang, when will you make your appearance in the world?

> ([XIANLÜ MODE:] *Dian jiangchun*)
> I count down the *August Ultimate*,[4]
> Consult the *Changes of Zhou*,
> And I comprehend the [apparent] principles of Heaven.
> I fully nourish its unseen mysteries,
> In anticipation of a "cloud-and-wind meeting of dragon and tiger."[5]

> (*Hunjiang long*)
> A morning will come,
> When I come out of this hut to point out and rectify the confusion
>   of men of this age.

---

4. The *August Ultimate* refers to the *Book of the August Ultimate and the Ordering of the World* (*Huangji jingshi shu*) by Shao Yong (1011–77). This book, published by his son Shao Bowen (b. 1046), provides a summary of Shao Yong's numerological speculations on cosmological and historical cycles of development.

5. The emperor is a dragon; his ministers and generals are tigers; a "cloud-and-wind meeting" is a grand meeting of heroes or important men.

I rely on my guts, stuffed with stars and planets;
If I fulfill my ambition to follow on these great changes like wind and
thunder,
I'll establish that Son of Heaven within the Dragon and Phoenix
Pavilions of a Ninefold Palace,
And display to the eight directions my tiger- and wolf-like might as a
commander.

Act out being startled:

I see the wind winnow the shadow of the bamboo,
The sun penetrate the pine-shaded window.
I begin casting fortunes in my sleeves,[6]
And peek outside the door.
Acolyte,
Prepare to receive his imperial majesty; get some tea ready.
This is that as-yet-to-rise-to-prominence hidden dragon of an
emperor.

Act out pondering:

No, don't lay out the rattan mats,
But for the time being just close the brushwood gate.

Act out reading — wait until IMPERIAL UNCLE[7] *enters with retinue. —* ZHANG
FEI *yells out, stops. — After* ACOLYTE *reports two times, SPEAK:*[8] Since he's come
to visit me three times in a year, and since it is his fated lot to become emperor,
let me see him. What's to fear? Tell that general named Liu to come over. — *Act
out greeting him — after* LIU BEI *makes his obeisances:*

(*Zui zhong tian*)
Let me rise to my feet as fast as fire,
And descend those steps with quickened pace—
"You have truly worn out your body these two or three times!
Forgive my fault in this for just a time,
Please, Imperial Uncle,[9] please sit down in peace."

---

6. I.e., by counting his fingers in his sleeves.

7. In the stage directions Liu Bei most often is simply designated as "Liu," less often as "Liu
Bei," and once or twice as "Imperial Uncle" (*huang shu*).

8. The stage directions on occasion provide the direction "speak" in large characters in a black
cartouche. When this happens, we reproduce such a stage direction in uppercase letters. Usually,
however, the lines spoken by the male lead are not introduced by a direct instruction to speak.

9. When Liu Bei early on in his career was received in audience by the emperor, the latter
politely addressed him as "Imperial Uncle."

Wait until he finishes speaking:

> From his mouth every sound is "this lonely and exhausted Liu Bei."
> Don't speak so crazily,
> What poor village yokel would have the eyes of Shun and the brows
>   of Yao?[10]

Act out having IMPERIAL UNCLE *sit — wait until* IMPERIAL UNCLE *refuses to sit,*
SPEAK: May I ask why you have come to visit me? — *After* LIU BEI *speaks:*
Please forgive me. This humble hermit is just a farmer from Nanyang, temporarily hiding away from the world. How can I even begin to concern myself with
the rise and fall of that human world of yours? I can't go, I can't go.

> (*You hulu*)
> All I want is to imitate Chaofu and Xu You[11] and wash right and
>   wrong from my ears,
> Practice the Way and its virtue,
> And happily ascend the jetty where Lü Wang did his fishing.[12]
> Who wants to squabble over fame and profit between the horns of a
>   snail?[13]
> Who wants to seek an official post in the middle of a spider's web?

After LIU BEI *speaks:*

> Just let me wear my clothes of straw and linen;
> Just let me eat my meals of goosefoot and pulse leaves.
> When the sun has risen three rods high, I still soundly sleep—
> Unconcerned that crow and hare rush on to east and west.[14]

> (*Tianxia le*)
> This poor Daoist
> Knows to do nothing of the world of men except sleep.

---

10. Yao and Shun both were emperors who ruled in a mythic past. Shun was renowned for
having two pupils in each eye.

11. Chaofu ("Nestman") and Xu You were famous hermits who lived during the time of Yao.
When Xu You told Chaofu that Yao had offered him the empire, Chaofu answered, "Why didn't
you hide your body and cover your brilliance? You are not my friend!" He thereupon went to a
brook and rinsed out his ears. According to another legend, Xu You rinsed his ears after Yao had
offered him the empire.

12. See *Tripartite Oath*, n. 21.

13. The *Zhuangzi* contains a passage about two kingdoms that fight a war of attrition between the horns of a snail. This little story became a common metaphor for the fruitlessness of
human conflict or desire in a limitless world. See Zhuangzi 1891, p. 119.

14. The sun is inhabited by a three-legged crow, and the moon is the home of a hare that is
pounding the medicine of immortality.

After LIU *speaks:*

> In truth,
> I have no wisdom.
> All you wanted was to tell me to go down the mountain
> And exert some energy on your behalf.
> In truth this will not forestall the cold,
> Or save anyone from hunger,
> So why do you want me to go down this Recumbent Dragon Ridge?

After LIU *speaks:* —[15] When I consider it, it seems that none of those worthies you have sought have been used to the end. None of them had a good outcome. — *After* LIU *speaks:*

> (*Nezha ling*)
> When I think of presenting a jade, as Bian He did—[16]
> I'd rather beg for food like Han Xin.
> All in vain you are like Zhang Liang presenting a sandal.[17]
> When you want to use someone, you track them down in rivers and
>   marshes,
> Spy them out in mountain forests,
> And behave like a subservient inferior.

> (*Que ta zhi*)
> But as soon as you have settled the Flowery Kingdom and
>   Barbaria,[18]
> You stop treating everyone as an equal,
> Never thinking about when you were in dire straits
> And when you needed them!
> You quickly exercise your cunning plan
> To strip them of their office, shut down their positions.

---

15. All spoken or sung lines are by the male lead, here Zhuge Liang. A colon (or a colon and a dash to indicate spacing in the original text) marks the point at which the lead singer speaks or sings. Since only the arias and speech of the lead singer are included, the text omits stage directions indicating that the lead should sing or speak.

16. Bian He discovered a rock containing an excellent piece of jade, but when he presented the rock to King Li of Chu, the king's jade workers rejected the rock and the king, thinking that Bian He had tried to cheat him, punished Bian He by removing the knee cap of his left leg. Later, Bian He presented the same rock to King Li's successor, King Wu, who had his right knee cap removed. When King Wu's successor, King Wen, eventually had Bian He's rock split, the jade was discovered.

17. See *Xiangyang Meeting*, n. 54.

18. I.e., the Chinese empire and foreign lands; the known world.

And just as quick, inside Weiyang Palace,
You sentence them to slow slicing by ten thousand cuts!

After LIU *speaks:* I won't go! I won't go!

> (*Jisheng cao*)
> I'd rather plow some untamed land,
> Or weed a vegetable patch.
> I'll be a companion of aged gibbons and wild deer,
> Master to disciples who are mountain lads and gatherers of wood,
> And the closest of friends with the fresh breeze and the bright moon.
> For me, this familiar existence of medicine stove and scrolls of the
>   classics
> Will be lived in a human habitat of bamboo fences and thatched
>   cottages.

After LIU *speaks — act out laughing sarcastically:* General, you look down too easily on others!

> (*Reprise*)
> Zhang Liang comprehended rise and fall;
> Yan Guang understood when to advance or retreat.[19]
> At sunrise, one helped to enthrone the High Ancestor,[20]
> At high noon, another established the Restoration Emperor,
> Now at eventide, how can you prop up the state of Lius?
> Isn't it true: "One cock crows as soon as another dies—
> There are only those who come afterward, none ever come before!"

After LIU *speaks:* I was just joking. *After* ACOLYTE *speaks, yell:* Shut up! *After* LIU *speaks:* Since your two brothers have come with you, ask that one named Guan to come in. *After* GUAN *greets you:* This is a liege lord with qualities of the Five Hegemons.[21] He really has an extraordinary appearance!

---

19. Yan Guang was a friend of Liu Xiu who, following the interregnum of the usurper Wang Mang's short-lived Xin dynasty, restored the Han dynasty, becoming the first emperor of the Eastern Han. When Liu Xiu had ascended the throne, Yan Guang went into hiding. Liu Xiu went to great effort and eventually succeeded in bringing Yan Guang to court, but the latter stubbornly refused all appointments and soon left to spend his final years as a farmer and fisherman.

20. Liu Bang, the founder of the Han dynasty, is known to history as Gaozu, or Exalted Ancestor. For his biography, see "The Exalted Emperor, Basic Annals 8," in Sima Qian 2002, pp. 1–91, and "Basic Annals of Emperor Gaozu," in Sima Qian 1993, pp. 51–88.

21. During the Eastern Zhou dynasty, the power of the kings of Zhou gradually declined while the power of their liege lords continued to increase. In the sixth to fifth century BC a succession of five of these liege lords temporarily achieved a preeminent position among the liege lords by their military power, and they are known to history as the Five Hegemons (*wuba*).

(*Jinzhan'er*)
He has a rising-oh-so-high nose of a noble eagle,
Oh-so-long brows like molting silkworms,
A pair of fragrant red cheeks as crimson as rouge,
And a three-braided luxuriant black beard hanging down.
Inside—hiding away the aura of a lord,
Outside—displaying a terrifying awesomeness.
This general:
A general and minister while alive,
A venerated god after he dies!

After LIU *speaks* — *after* ZHANG FEI *speaks:* — Ask that one named Zhang to come over. — ZHANG FEI *shouts, stops.* This is another general with qualities of the Five Hegemons' liege lords. But he is so fierce!

(*Zui zhong tian*)
So without reason, so without shame,
He has no sense of superior or inferior, ignores all hierarchies.
Who are you staring at with those round and bulging eyes?
His ochre sideburns bristle
As he displays the kingly aura of those five liege-lord hegemons.
He keeps calling on Heaven and shouting to Earth.
          General,
You really can play the part of "a rude and rash Zhang Fei."

After LIU *speaks:* — Ask them to come in. *After you greet* ZHAO YUN: — Is this a family general or one who surrendered? — *After* LIU *speaks* — *after you greet* LIU FENG: — Is this general the son of your main wife or a concubine? *After* LIU *speaks:*

(*Jinzhan'er*)
This one is "an adopted son who is full of plans";
And this, "a surrendered general displaying his loyalty and
          uprightness."
Both will live up to their jobs when they are placed amidst the liege
          lords.
Zhao Yun is capable of executing a plan while engaging in battle;
Liu Feng can also defeat the enemy.
On the field of battle, this general will test warhorse against warhorse;
And in the front lines, this general will wave the battle banner.
So we can surely prepare "whips to beat out the rhythm on golden
          spurs,
And men to sing songs of victory as they return."

After LIU *speaks, SPEAK:* Now if I, this poor hermit, would come with you, with whom will you vie to win the world? — *After* LIU *speaks:* — Let's talk about Cao Cao: he already oversees a multitude of millions and commands the liege lords because he controls the Son of Heaven. His power is so great that you cannot go to war against him! — *After* LIU *speaks:* If you want to discuss Sun Quan: he is the third generation to firmly possess the land Left of the River. While his kingdom is difficult to attack, his people are devoted to him, and he employs wise and capable men. His power is so great that you cannot go to war against him. He can be your support, but not the object of your plans. — *After* LIU *speaks:* — There is a kingdom you should scheme for: you should take Jingzhou for your principal and Yizhou for your interest.[22] — *After* LIU *asks a question:* — Let's first talk about Jingzhou. To the north it controls the Han and the Mian, and it collects all profits from the Southern Seas; to the east it is connected to Suzhou and Shaoxing, and to the west it trades with Shu and Ba. This is a kingdom with which one can go to war. There, lord Liu Biao is unable to guard it, and this must be why Heaven grants it to you, my general. Next let me talk about Yizhou. It is protected by natural barriers. With its thousand miles square of fertile fields this land is Heaven's Storehouse. Liu Zhang is stupid and weak and Zhang Lu rules in the north. The population is prosperous and the kingdom is wealthy, but the rulers have no idea how to preserve the people and succor them. The smart and capable officers there seek an enlightened ruler. General, you are not only a scion of the house of Han, but your reliability and righteousness are renowned throughout the world. If you can take possession of Yizhou and maintain its mountainous borders, keep peace with the barbarians and conclude an alliance with Sun Quan, perfect the administration inside your kingdom, and keep a close eye on developments outside your country, you can achieve a hegemon's enterprise and the house of Han can be restored!

(*Houting hua*)
By strategy I can subdue Huang Hansheng;[23]

---

22. Jingzhou here refers both to the city of Xiangyang and the area of Hubei more generally. Yizhou corresponds to modern Sichuan.

23. Huang Hansheng is Huang Zhong (d. 220). Huang Zhong hailed from Nanyang, and initially served under Liu Biao. Huang Zhong joined Liu Bei following the battle at Red Cliff. He played a major role in Liu Bei's later conquest of Yizhou. He is one of the so-called Five Tiger Generals (*wuhujiang*) who fought on the side of Shu Han. This group also includes Ma Chao (176–226) and Zhao Yun (d. 229). These generals were first grouped together in Chen Shou's *Records of the Three Kingdoms* in a single biography.

With power I can defeat Ma Mengqi,[24]
But I truly cannot go to battle against Zhou Gongjin,[25]
And I truly cannot achieve victory over Cao Mengde.[26]

After examining LIU:

I finish completely physiognomizing his features—
Alas! He will be emperor for barely three years.

Act out letting it go:

Let's not go to war!
The proverb says: "To cede to others is not idiocy."

After LIU *speaks — act out refusing to go — after* EXTRA, *holding a baby in his arms, greets you — act out being flabbergasted:* Acolyte, get ready to leave. There is here, after all, a Son of Heaven who will reign for forty years! *Wait until* LIU BEI *and his party express their gratitude:*

(*Zhuansha*)
I will take your Sun, Liu, and Cao,
And establish from them the Wu, Shu, and Wei.
Then it will be a tripartite empire, resembling the feet of a tripod.

After LIU *speaks:*

Even though they have stolen the best of land's benefit and Heaven's
    timing,
Relying on our mutual harmony, we will create our enterprise and
    establish a foundation.
Acolyte, quickly get things ready!
We will travel together as dragon and tigers,
First occupying the four thousand miles of Shu![27]

---

24. Ma Chao originally served Zhang Lu, but he was slandered and surrendered to Liu Bei.

25. According to the *Records of the Three Kingdoms*, Zhou Yu (175–210) died at thirty-five years of age a year after being seriously injured by an arrow and on the verge of launching a major campaign against Shu. The Ming novel, the *Romance of the Three Kingdoms*, attributes his final demise to his being thrice frustrated by Zhuge Liang's superior skills and dying as a result. A man of great success and brilliant strategy and the hero of the battle of Red Cliff, Zhou Yu was destined to be always in the shadow of Zhuge Liang. In the novel, he asks on his deathbed, "Once Heaven gave birth to Zhou Yu, why did it allow Zhuge Liang to be born?" (*jisheng Yu he sheng Liang?*)

26. Cao Cao.

27. Shu is another designation for the area of modern Sichuan.

After ZHANG FEI *speaks, sing facing* GUAN:

> I face Yunchang[28] to explain,
> "I must have it out with Zhang Fei, who made me angry."

After LIU BEI *speaks:* My lord, have no worries,

> Just watch as I casually[29] hand you that Coiling Dragon Robe![30]

Exit.

[Act 2]

After CAO CAO *and* XIAHOU DUN *speak*[31] — *with* LIU BEI, *enter as the* MALE LEAD, *costumed as* FIELD MARSHAL — *after* LIU BEI *speaks:* I, Zhuge Liang, lack any capacity, but thanks to your generous blessing, my lord, and the tiger-like power of your generals, I have been allowed to become a successful man.

([NANLÜ MODE:] *Yizhi hua*)
Multicolored banners obscure the sky,
Floral-patterned drums shake the earth.
A green dragon—the moon-sickle blade,
A silver serpent—a tempered-steel poison.
Arrayed in rows: stirrups, cudgels, spears, and whips,
Lacquered vermilion red: crossbows with decorated bow tips.
Beasts swallowing heads: battleaxes of tempered metal.
We have fifty officers—ridge-leaping racing tigers,
And twenty thousand fierce predatory catamounts that climb the
    mountains.

(*Liangzhou* [*diqi*])
The fact that I'm sitting in this military tent with its seven layers of
    encircling guards
Is all due to your visits to my thatched cottage on Recumbent
    Dragon Ridge.
I regard all the bandits of this realm as nothing,
For my skills in manipulating the cosmos
Are my very techniques to stabilize the empire.
Relying on this single marvelous scheme of mine,

---

28. Guan Yu is also known as Guan Yunchang.
29. More literally: while laughing and bantering.
30. In this play the end of the "act" is marked by a long dash.
31. This conversation will have constituted a short, independent scene.

And three scrolls of heavenly writings,
I will manifest a divine strategy and concentrate alone on Wu in the
    east,
Then rely on your humane way to single-handedly occupy Shu in
    the west.
Banking on General Guan and Zhang Fei at your side, my lord,
What need to fear Zhang Liao and Xu Chu under Cao Cao's
    command?
Or Sun Quan's use of Lu Su and Zhou Yu!

After EXTRA *reports, after* LIU BEI *speaks, act out smiling coldly:*

I was just wondering what kind of matter
Was reported,
When it turned out to be that blind hero Xiahou Dun who drives
    his troops
And considers me, this poor Daoist, just so much mud.
That damnable nobody may command an army,
But how dare he rile up this plow boy?

After LIU BEI *speaks:* My lord, do not worry!

(*Muyang guan*)
We are protected by your virtue that shines in the sky like sun and
    moon
In this imperial abode, redoubtable as mountains and rivers—
Please, my lord, relax your furrowed brow.
Watch this poor Daoist take in hand the mists and grab the clouds;
Watch this poor Daoist summon the wind and call down the rain!
Like a child's game I will first conquer Wei,
And just as casually gobble up all of Wu.
I will make sure my merit caps that of the Three Dukes,[32]
And that "my fame will be completed by the Eightfold Battle Array."[33]

---

32. The Three Dukes is a collective reference to the paramount aides to the ruler, holding the
highest ranks in the bureaucracy.

33. Zhuge Liang is credited with the design of eight different battle arrays. Rock formations
outside Fengjie in Sichuan were believed to represent his eight formations. In the Tang, the poetic master Du Fu (AD 712–70) eulogized Zhuge Liang in his famous poem "The Diagram of
Eight Formations" (trans. Owen 1996, p. 432):

His deeds overshadowed a land split in three;
    his fame was achieved in these Eight Formations.
The river flows on, the rocks do not budge,
    pain surviving from failure to swallow Wu.

After ZHANG FEI *speaks — act out shouting him down:* Off to the side; I am not going to use you! Zhao Yun, come here and listen to my orders.

> (*Sikuai yu*)
> I order you, Zhao Yun.
> Do not tarry or stay:
> Put on your armor and battle dress and command your fighting
>   men—
> Quickly now, with lance athwart, mount your horse and become my
>   vanguard.

After ZHANG FEI *speaks:* Zhao Yun,

> Follow my orders and listen to my commission.
> Pay no attention to whatever others say:
> My order to you is not to win but only to lose.

After ZHANG FEI *speaks:* I am not using you! Liu Feng, listen to my orders.

> (*Muyang guan*)
> I want you to set out your battalions like the scales of a fish,
> Form your squadrons like a flock of geese:
> Execute your plans and unroll your strategies according to me.
> I only want you to raise your voices and wave the banners;
> I only want you to beat the gongs and pound the drums.
> When he flees from you, dash into the middle of his army;
> But if he chases you, hide away in ambush on grassy slopes.
> Battle him straightaway until that miscreant is filled with fear;
> Keep scaring him until that traitor's gall is gone!

After ZHANG FEI *speaks:* Off to the side! I am not using you! Mi Zhu and Mi Fang,[34] listen to my orders.

> (*He xinlang*)
> Prepare plenty of fire gourds[35] in Bowang town,
> And after you trick him to enter, first set fire to his carts and cut off
>   supplies,
> And when you get the chance, put the torch to their encampment.
> Have bombs of fire as big as cartwheels dance in the sky—
> Let the fire close on them until the gods cry and ghosts weep;
> Burn them with fire until the horses die and the men disappear.
> Make them all flee for their lives from the central fire;
> Make them all lose their miserable bodies in that phalanx of fire!

After ZHANG FEI *speaks:*

> General Zhang, there's no use getting angry at the bottom of the
>   steps—
> This is a method from the *Three Strategies of the Yellow Lord;*
> And is described in the *Six Tactics* of Lü Wang!

After ZHANG FEI *speaks:* To one side! I am not going to use you. Call Guan forth to heed my general's command.

> (*Ma yulang*)
> Lord Guan, hold the ford at White River for me
> And dispatch your troops to dam the river and lake.
> In night's depth rein in your horse and look down from a high ridge.
> Harness the river's flow,
> And if their army crosses
> And arrives at the deepest spot,

---

34. These are two brothers, Mi Zhu the elder, who were early supporters of Liu Bei. Mi Fang, in particular, followed Liu Bei on several campaigns. When Liu began his campaign to take Yizhou (modern Chengdu), Mi Fang and a second person, Shi Ren, shared governance of Jingzhou with Guan Yu. But the two men both felt slighted by Guan Yu and did not get along well with him. In the historical record, Mi Fang is forced to surrender Jingzhou to the armies of Wu. In the *Tale of Hua Guan Suo* and the *Romance of the Three Kingdoms*, they are chastised for allowing stores to be burned (or destroyed, depending on which story) and are upbraided by Guan Yu. They then offered up Jingzhou to Wu. In the historical records, Mi Zhu, apologizes to Liu Bei for his brother's actions, is pardoned, and dies soon after from illness. In the vernacular renditions, he is with his brother in Jingzhou and aids in the surrender. Their actions are thought to lead indirectly to the death of Guan Yu.
35. Gourds filled with easily combustible materials that will help spread a fire.

(*Gan huang'en*)
Then open up every ditch and channel
And drown all their troops!
In the billowing waves,
Aloft on the waves,
They will lie on their bellies like dogs.
So let you not brag of being stalwart heroes—
Because all of you will feed the fishes and shrimps!
And even if you flee from this disaster,
Or escape with your life,
You still will fall into my trap!

(*Caicha ge*)
Half of them will be burned away,
Half drowned and gone—
How much better than one hook of scented bait catching a giant
    turtle!

After ZHANG FEI *speaks:*

There's no need for any display of martial valor to catch them,
When I will get them, I will not spend any effort at all.

After ZHANG FEI *protests loudly* — *after* LIU BEI *intervenes* [*on his behalf*] —
SPEAK: Out of respect for our lord I will employ you, so listen to my orders.
Wait until Zhao Yun has seduced them into battle, Liu Feng has chased them
into Bowang, Mi Fang and Mi Zhu have torched the town, and Lord Guan has
flooded them, then—when his huge army of four hundred thousand is win-
nowed down to some twenty defeated soldiers who have fought until they are
worn out and wounded by arrows and swords—I will use you to engage them
in battle. I'll do thus and so:

(*Hong shaoyao*)
I don't want you to bare your fists, roll up your sleeves, and let your
    careless temper out;
I don't want you to shout out loudly or cry at the top of your voice.
I only want you to hold your tongue, suppress your rage, and not
    blabber away;
I only want you to secretly lie in waiting.
Wait until the wind has cleared after the second watch,
And when those fewer-than-twenty troops who are left from the
    defeat—
And, after all the fighting are reeling left and right, wounded by
    barbed arrows—

Are barely, just barely able to force themselves to stand. . . .

(*Pusa Liangzhou*)
When their desire is set solely on the trek ahead,
And they just happen at that moment to cut across the escape route,
They will run right into you as they pass—
How will you answer me if you fail to nab them?

Wait until he speaks: — I'm afraid you will not be able to arrest those twenty or so fleeing troops! — *After* ZHANG FEI *speaks:*

General Zhang, the two of us will establish a contract:
If you are personally able to capture that Xiahou Dun . . .

After ZHANG FEI *speaks:*

I'm sure he'll remain unfound, even though you wear out a pair of
    iron-soled shoes.

After ZHANG FEI *speaks:*

If you disobey my orders, I will not lightly forgive you!

After ZHANG FEI *speaks:*

If you are victorious,
I'll have the tiger tally attached to your belt.
But if you do not win you'll learn my crafty plan to have you
    beheaded!

After LIU *speaks:* — My lord, let's see how this battle will go. Generals, be careful and alert!

(*Sui shawei*)
Because these thousands of tigers and leopards now depart from
    hidden valleys,
It will turn out four hundred thousand jackals and wolves will lie
    along the roadside.
I call Zhao Yun:
"Remember your duty";
I summon Liu Feng:
"Make no mistakes by not being decisive";
I dispatch Lord Guan
And send off Mi Zhu.
It's only Zhang Fei who needs instruction:
"Stage it all just as I said,

And heed my words.
If by any chance you screw up this military situation,
Don't think that I will bear the blame!
I, Zhuge Liang, have my eyes and ears,
No room here for your 'Brothers are like hands and feet.'"
         Zhang Fei, listen! If you don't nab him . . .
I'll make sure you're not the master of what's left of your rude and
    rash life.

[Act 3]

Wait until THE GENERALS *have each done one scene. — After* ZHANG FEI *speaks*[36]
— enter as MALE LEAD. *— After* IMPERIAL UNCLE *speaks,* SPEAK: They have
all surely been victorious this time. My lord, please do not worry.

([SHUANGDIAO MODE:] *Xinshui ling*)
I command two thousand officers, men clad in iron, ready for battle,
Except for that rash Zhang Fei who will not submit to me.
To wrest away the Flying Phoenix Pylons,
You asked me to leave Recumbent Dragon Ridge.
This time's success or failure, rise or fall,
Will all come clear in an hour.

After ZHAO YUN *enters and greets you:* A great general who *did* execute my plan!
Bring in the wine!

(*Bubu jiao*)
How could this general out on point, willing to risk his life,
Control the horse he was riding—like a dragon emerging from the
    waves?
He employed an ivory-tipped, green-lacquered lance.
         Oh,
A hero capable of executing a plan—you really are strong!
One day you will be in charge of the rules of the court;
You will become the minister heading the chancellery.

After pouring him wine — [after LIU FENG *enters and greets you]:* Liu Feng, how
did my plan work out? *After* LIU FENG *speaks and after handing him a cup:*

---

36. As becomes clear from the text below, Zhang Fei and the other generals now leave the
stage, before the male lead enters with Liu Bei. The other generals will each have reported how
they accomplished their mission, while Zhang Fei will have told how he failed to capture Xiahou
Dun.

(*Feng ru song*)
Who can compete in martial arts with Liu Feng?
By nature his physique is most awe-inspiring!
Whenever there was an opening, he fiercely dashed into the center of
    the troops,
Like a raving tiger scattering a herd of sheep.
This time the wine you drink is well won;
If you will not be an emperor, you will certainly be a king!

After pouring wine — after MI FANG *and* MI ZHU *enter and greet you — after
pouring wine:*

> (*Shuixianzi*)
>   Oh,
> Mi Fang and Mi Zhu securely guarded the borders;
> To my delight they went into battle without deliberation.
> In the town of Bowang they blocked the roads with deer antlers;[37]
> And, luring them into the city, just as they drew near,
> Burned the piled-up straw and stores of grain on all four sides.
> The fire's bright glare closed in on troops and officers;
> Its flaring flames scorched the vault of heaven,
> And in this way, "horses died, the men lost their lives."

After GUAN *enters and greets you:* General, you have worn yourself out controlling the floods.[38] *After* LORD GUAN *speaks:*

> (*Chuan bo zhao*)
> I did not summon Yunchang in vain:
> This even surpasses his attacking Che Zhou and beheading Cai
>   Yang![39]
> As I asked, the water was blocked with sand bags
> And the long stream was dammed up,
> So the water of White River steadily rose higher and higher.
> Xiahou Dun was in deep agitation,
> The remnant of his defeated army in a panic.
>
> (*Qi dixiong*)

---

37. "Deer antlers" are pointed multi-branch stakes, planted in the ground. They are used to
block (or at least hinder) the attack of enemy troops; here they were used to close off certain
roads so that the army had to follow a precise route to the predetermined site where they would
be trapped by fire.

38. A joking reference to Yu's work in controlling the floods.

39. Two famous earlier victories of Guan Yu. See Appendix 1, items 6 and 7.

Here, you released the water,
There, you breached the dam:
How, you say, could they defend themselves?
Like a boundless ocean the force of the water flowed down from
    heaven,
And horses and men all bobbed amidst the flowering reeds!

(*Meihua jiu*)
With deepest feelings I offer you this jade flagon,
And sincerely thank you for extending our borders.
Because you saved His Majesty and supported your king,
In later times you will enter the temple and ascend the hall.[40]
You depended on your Green Dragon blade to pacify the empire,
Relied on Red Hare, your mount, to stabilize house and state.
I remember how after Xuchang,
How after Xuchang, you submitted to Cao Cao;
Having submitted to Cao Cao, you were received by the emperor;
Once received by the emperor, you were gifted with court robes;
Once gifted with court robes, you took your seat in the executive
    office.
Seated in the executive office, you became a Prime Minister;
Having become Prime Minister, you led your private officers,
Led your private officers to ascend a high hillock;
Having ascended the high hillock, you espied the enemy troops;
Espying the enemy troops, you did not weigh your options;
Without weighing your options you gave your horse free rein;
Giving your horse free rein, you entered the battlefield;
Entering the battlefield, you confronted the warriors;
Confronting the warriors, your spirits were high!

(*Shou Jiangnan*)
In high spirits you reined in your horse and stabbed Yan Liang;
And, stabbing Yan Liang, you were bruited about throughout the
    world.[41]

Servants, prepare the wine. General Zhang will surely have merit to reveal.
Sing:

---

40. This is a reference to the fact that Guan Yu will become apotheosized later and will be the object of worship in temples dedicated to him, where his image will be installed.

41. While Guan Yu served Cao Cao, he killed Yuan Shao's general Yan Liang (d. 200), who had inspired fear in Cao Cao's troops by his quick victories over a number of Cao's generals. See Appendix 1, item 7.

My lord, be ready to present a cup of the finest wine.
General Zhang is rude and rash:
When he arrives, we'll see who wins, who loses.

After ZHANG FEI *enters and greets you:* — General Zhang, how come you look like this?[42] *After* ZHANG *speaks:*

(*Yan'er luo*)
> General,
> Since you don't "beat out the rhythm on golden stirrups with your
>   whips"—
> Shouldn't you "sing a song of victory in unison"?
> But you have tightly bound your arms crisscross, I see,
> And you stretch out your neck as straight as can be.

(*Desheng ling*)
> Aren't you that purple-gold pillar erected over the ocean?[43]
> Such a general surely is no Pagoda-Lifting Heavenly King Li![44]
> Didn't you earlier say, "If I lose, you win my head!"
> Didn't you say, "If I don't win, my name is not Zhang!"
> When you left, you were all ferocity,
> Upset you couldn't jump three thousand rods in one go.
> But today you are in a panic.
> General,
> Isn't it said that a real man should rely on himself?

Servants, take him outside and report once you have beheaded him.

(*Gu meijiu*)
> I order the soldiers to prepare the execution grounds;
> I command the servants to arrange the swords and lances in a row.
> Take him out of the headquarter gates and don't ask any questions!
> Is it not the case, "A person cannot pass from this existence,
> Though his dead body lies on the field of execution."[45]

---

42. As a defeated general, Zhang Fei may have entered the stage in shackles or carrying thorns as a sign of attrition.

43. From the phrase common in colloquial literature for a mainstay of the court or the army: "A white jade pillar that holds up heaven, a purple gold beam that stretches across the ocean" (*chengtian baiyu zhu jiahai zijin liang*).

44. Li Jing, a fierce divine warrior and protector of Buddhism.

45. A tentative translation for the lines *ren bude miexiang / sishihai wo yunyang chang*. The term *miexiang* has two basic meanings: "to look lightly on a person" (i.e., to obliterate his image) and "to pass from the present to extinction" (Buddhist).

(*Taiping ling*)
Grisly and frightening, stick his head on the end of a spear—
That's so much better than when you tried to one-up everyone at the
    steps.

After LIU BEI *intervenes:*

Here I have Zhang Yide's writ acknowledging his crimes:
Now let him know the courage of this country yokel who runs the army!

Order the beheading — after intervention:

Zhang Fei,
After you go through this event
In front of me
You'll have to bow in submission.

After ZHANG *speaks:*

I will let you off this time on behalf of our lord!

After IMPERIAL UNCLE *speaks — after offering* ZHANG FEI *a cup of wine to sup-press his fright:* Since I have won this round, do not dare look upon me like you
did then.

(*Yuanyang wei*)
Today I sit in the golden-tipped lotus-flower tent, of a commander of
    three armies,
Wrapped in an embroidered brocade clouds-and-cranes gown of the
    seven stars.[46]
As soon as I have pacified Shu in the west,
This poor Daoist will return to Nanyang.
I loudly proclaim, "I view Cao Cao and Sun Quan
Like the passing of a breeze or the scratching of an itch."

After LIU *speaks:*

Please, my lord and Guan and Zhang—
Stop! Stop! There's no need for such praise!
Our lord's generous blessing is without bounds
But wait with your rewards until I have established the house of Liu!

---

46. The seven stars are the stars of the Dipper (Ursa Major) and hold great magical power. The crane that soars through the clouds is an image of the immortal, and therefore of the perfect Daoist master.

[Act 4]

CAO CAO *and* GUAN TONG *do one scene.* — LEADING MALE *and* IMPERIAL UNCLE *and his party enter.* — IMPERIAL UNCLE *opens. After a banquet has been laid out:*

([ZHONGLÜ MODE:] *Fendie'er*)
This battle with Cao Cao to lay first claim
Resembles nothing so much as a spring dream:
How could he contain this band of the finest heroes of the land?
Each of them is good at engaging in battle,
Capable of inciting a fight.
Out of the ordinary, above the masses,
All have accomplished great deeds,
They truly are supporting roof beams of this age, setting up the
　　cosmos!

(*Zui chunfeng*)
In those days the Son of Heaven of Zhou dreamt "not of a bear,"[47]
In these days our lord invited me, Recumbent Dragon.
But why did I thrice refuse to leave my thatched cottage?
I truly was weary of the hustle
And bustle.
To hold power in the age of the Three Kingdoms,
To be the leader responsible to only the Single Man,[48]
Cannot compare with sowing my fields on the hillside.

After seeing the wind rise up and considering the matter: — My lord, don't drink your wine. Today we will be visited by a secret agent. *After* ZHANG FEI *speaks — after* LIU *speaks:* — He will be here before noon. — *After* LIU *speaks:* — Generals, act according to my instructions. *After instructing* ZHAO YUN *and he speaks — after you summon* LIU FENG *and he speaks — after you call* ZHANG FEI *and* LORD GUAN *and they speak:* — My lord, you should leave this place. I will act in such and such a way. — *After you whisper in his ear — after you summon* LIU *back and speak to him a second time:* Don't forget that one item! *They all exit:* — Mi Fang and Mi Zhu, you two stay here at my side! — *After you whisper once again:* — Keep watch at the front gate of the camp. In case someone ar-

---

47. Once, when King Wen planned a hunting party, he performed an osomancy and was told, "What you will capture will be neither a horned dragon nor an unhorned dragon, neither a tiger nor a brown bear. What you will capture will be the assistant of the Hegemon to the King." What he encountered, of course, was Lü Wang. See "T'ai-kung of Ch'i, Hereditary House 2," in Sima Qian 2006, pp. 36–37.
48. The Single Man is the highest ruler, the Son of Heaven.

rives, report his arrival to me. *Wait until* GUAN TONG *enters and speaks — after* EXTRA *reports — act out hurrying to welcome him:* This is my elder brother. Bring him some wine!

> (*Ying xianke*)
> Quickly set out the jade goblets,
> Bring out the golden flagons:
> This is my sworn brother from twenty years ago when we were only students!

Act out bowing:

> Have you lived in the area of River's East these last few years?
> Or did you reside in Hanzhong?

After EXTRA *speaks:*

> I never expected we would meet each other today.
> Dear brother, you've gone to such trouble to make this journey!

Generals, do not treat this man with any disrespect. He is my elder brother. He is unique in this whole wide world. He knows everything I have learned, but I do not know all that he has mastered. Bring more wine! We brothers should celebrate all day! *After* EXTRA[49] *speaks:*

> (*Zhulü qu*)
> Who among your brothers wanted to follow the dragon king and get in this mess?
> Who intended to move tiger generals around to vie for glory?[50]
> It's all the fault of that Xu Shu[51]
> Who praised me far too highly to these people!
> They had not yet managed to find a Pang Tong,[52]
> And when they finally invited this dragon lying low,[53]
> I surpassed that Old Lord Jiang[54] on the banks of the Wei!

Act out requesting EXTRA *to show his tricks — act out telling* EXTRA *to point at* MI FANG *and* MI ZHU: — Whatever the two of you hold to your chest or grasp in

---

49. Here the extra plays the part of Guan Tong.
50. On dragons and tigers, see note 5.
51. Xu Shu was a friend of Zhuge Liang. When Liu Bei settled in Xinye, Xu Shu joined Liu Bei and recommended Zhuge Liang to him. Soon afterward Xu Shu had to leave Liu Bei and join up with Cao Cao because Cao Cao had captured his mother.
52. Pang Tong (179–214) would join Liu Bei following the battle of Red Cliff and become one of his most valuable aides.
53. "Dragon lying low" (*fulong*) here refers to Zhuge Liang.
54. See *Tripartite Oath*, n. 21.

your hands, no matter what it is, my brother will guess right ten out of ten times! — *Wait until* MI FANG *and* MI ZHU *act out having him guess:* Brother, please guess!

> (*Ti yindeng*)
> It is not that I am showing off here in front of the steps;
> Or that you are watching sleights of hand on the stage.
> You generals show no alarm, afraid that he might guess wrong:
> Just watch my brother's magical art, supernatural power!

After ordering him to guess:

> This is a true skill;
> Don't say it's just a simple trick:
> Open your eyes as wide as you can and look closely!
>
> (*Manjingcai*)
> You must ball your fists so tightly no seam can be seen;
> You truly must carefully hide the black and white stones.
> My elder brother definitely has given this quite some effort.

After seeing the go stones:

> Generals, our lives and our deaths
> Are there in the palm of his hand,
> So it's reasonable to say, "If he's not wiped out, then what's the use?"

Act out getting on your feet and calling for rice. After MI FANG *has asked a question:*

> (*Kuaihuo san*)
> His intentions really displeased me,
> But my own intent was even harder to take.
> He intended to set out a snare, install a hidden bow,
> But he was led by my plan into this cave of spells.
>
> (*Baolao'er*)
>   For us
> "Generalship depends on planning, not on courage":
> He's a cinnabar mountain phoenix, halted by me.

Stop the tricks:

> Don't show off your tricks in front of these generals, brother;
> I too am up to earning the emperor's pay.
> In truth, when it comes to discussing Heaven and stirring Earth,
> Moving the stars or switching the Dipper,
> I have supernatural powers not of the ordinary kind!

> When it comes to snatching banners and stealing drums,
> Staging the troops and arranging arrays,
> I have my own and special family tradition!

Wait until all speak: My brother, you just displayed your little tricks, but by the time the rice is here, I will have you see a technique that will shake the gates of heaven! — *Lead* GUAN TONG *by the hand and speak:* Let's leave this tent and have a look at the house in which I live. — *Act out taking a turn around the stage:* — This place is much better than that thatched cottage. — *After* GUAN TONG *asks a question — act out ordering the two generals to leave you alone:* — Brother, what is locked up in the southernmost room on the western side? Please guess! — *After he guesses and speaks — after you open the door — after* ZHAO YUN *enters:* Isn't this general a liege lord like one of the Five Hegemons? — *After* EXTRA *speaks:* — Does Cao Cao have generals like him? *After* EXTRA *speaks — ask him the question, pointing out the two rooms of your brothers — after* EXTRA *speaks — after you ask the same question in the same way one after another — after he examines each in the same way — point at the fifth room and ask* EXTRA MALE: What is in the first room on the west? — *After* EXTRA *guesses — after you open the door — after* IMPERIAL UNCLE *enters:* — This is a Son of Heaven holding the true mandate. — *Wait until he has asked his question:* I will explain it to you, with one line for each person. *Point at* EXTRAS:[55]

> (*Shi'er yue*)
> This is Zilong from Changshan,[56]
> This is the adopted son Liu Feng,
> This is the hero Yide,[57]
> And this is the righteous and courageous Lord Guan.

After GUAN TONG *speaks:*

> If you recognize the true mandate, my dear brother Guan Tong,
> How come this Liu Bei is still "lonely and destitute"?

After EXTRA *physiognomizes him — after* EXTRA *orders the eastern room to be opened:* Don't open that room on the east!

> (*Yaomin ge*)
> Stop, lest you break the golden chain and allow the dragon to escape!

After the door has been opened — after BABY *is carried on stage:*

---

55. The "extras" here are the actors performing as the generals.
56. Zhao Yun.
57. Zhang Fei.

This one will act as lord of the future house of Liu!

*After [*GUAN TONG*] speaks:*

> At present Liu Biao of Jingzhou has offered up the lands in River's
>   East,
> And Liu Zhang of Yizhou has destroyed the imperial palace.
> Lofty and high,
> So high and lofty!
> I envision the western streams
> Like a fairyland on earth!

After scrutinizing all — act out confirming him as the true emperor: — Brother, where do you want to go? Here is the true emperor. Wouldn't it be best if we brothers stayed together? — *After* EXTRA *speaks:* — I already prepared no more than three days ago. *After* EXTRA *asks a question —* MESSENGER *arrives — take* CAO CAO *outside —* EMPEROR *sends him off with a judgment.*[58]

DISPERSAL SCENE

TITLE: Prime Minister Cao dispatches his horses and troops;
             Xiahou Dun can neither advance nor retreat.

NAME: Guan Yunchang releases the waters of White River;
             Zhuge Liang burns the stores at Bowang.

Newly Cut with Plot Prompts: *Zhuge Liang Burns the Stores at Bowang*

Finished

---

58. It is not quite clear how the play ends in the *Thirty Yuan Plays* edition. It is clear that the play departs from history (to the great unease of modern editors) in ending with the capture and beheading of Cao Cao. The text does not specify which general captured Cao Cao, but most likely Zhang Fei redeems himself by doing so. The emperor role could refer to Liu Bei, but he is otherwise never designated in this manner in the stage directions of our text, so perhaps Emperor Xiandi comes on stage to praise Liu Bei and his supporters for their loyalty to the house of Han. The phrase "sends off with a judgment" (*duanchu*) appears in several other dramas; here it is clearly used to dispatch Cao Cao to his execution.

Zhuge Liang Burns the Stores at Bowang
(From a Ming Palace Edition)

Act 4

(CAO CAO *enters, leading soldiers, speaks:*)

> One who lacks righteous hatred is no gentleman;
> One without poison is no real man.

I am Cao Cao. I really hate that Zhuge Liang who is so disrespectful, and I want ever more to be done with him because of what he did to the million troops of Xiahou Dun—he destroyed them all with fire and water in Bowang City. Now that my Commander in Chief Guan Tong is over his illness, I've asked him to come here so that I can honor him as Commander in Chief. Then what's to prevent me from battling with Liu Xuande? Captain, keep watch at the gate and if the old master comes along, report it to me. (SOLDIER *speaks:*) Understood. (GUAN TONG *enters and speaks:*)

> As soon as my precious sword leaves its scabbard, demons and devils are
> in fear;
> My jasper lute is thrummed but once, and ghosts and spirits are frightened.
> After finishing my lecture on the *Scripture of the Yellow Court*, my mind is at
> ease and pure;
> In silken headdress and with feathered fan, I discuss literature with finesse.

I, this poor Daoist under the aegis of Minister Cao, am Guan Tong. I was originally from Deng County in Nanyang, and when young I studied the same arts in the same place with Pang Degong and Zhuge Liang. We all became complete talents in both the civil and military arts. Now this Minister Cao has brought me here to the land of Wei and made me Commander in Chief to train his three armies. I

> Rely on my tricks to open the gates of heaven,
> And establish my merit without shrinking away in fear.

I was just in my private residence when a soldier came to report that Cao Cao requested my appearance. Here I am, already. Captain, report that Guan Tong is at the door. (SOLDIER *speaks:*) Understood. Reporting! I want to let you know that Guan Tong is at the door. (CAO CAO *speaks:*) Invite him in. (SOLDIER *speaks:*) Understood. Please come in! (GUAN TONG *acts out performing a formal greeting, speaks:*) Minister, what did you have to discuss with me? (CAO CAO *speaks:*) The only reason I have invited you here, master, is that I cannot endure that that disrespectful Zhuge Liang completely annihilated the million troops of Xiahou Dun. I have asked you here today so I may honor you as Commander in Chief. How can we plan to smash those three brothers and take Zhuge Liang alive? What ideas do you have? (GUAN TONG *speaks:*) Rest easy on this matter, my minister. I am an old friend and fellow disciple of Zhuge Liang. Before we battle with Liu, Guan, and Zhang, I'll go to Xinye first and persuade him to join us in the space of a single banquet. Then with joined hearts and united strength, we'll smash Liu, Guan, and Zhang—there's time yet. What do you think, sir? (CAO CAO *speaks:*) This is a marvelous plan! Commander, you go on first to Xinye, and persuade Zhuge Liang; if he is willing to join under my aegis, and take those three brothers alive, I will award you with noble rank. (GUAN TONG *speaks:*) I'd better set off today for this long journey.

> There's no need to drive forth armies and generals.
> A marvelous plan quickly puts all in order;
> I'll just lightly, slightly drop the hook,
> And make him rise gradually to the bait.

(Exits.)

(CAO CAO *speaks:*) Master Guan Tong is gone now. This trip will surely be a success. If Zhuge Liang can indeed submit to me, I have my own plan.

> Today Guan Tong has begun his journey,
> Straightaway to Xinye to visit the Recumbent Dragon;
> If he gets that plower and planter from Nanyang,
> I'll take Liu Bei and the other two.

(Exits.)

(MALE LEAD, *with* MALE LEAD LIU, MALE LEAD GUAN, ZHANG FEI, ZHAO YUN, MI ZHU, MI FANG, LIU FENG, *enters, leading troops.*) (MALE LEAD LIU *speaks:*) Master, it is clear that all the generals owe their success in this fierce battle, when we burned the stores at Bowang, to your careful planning. Let's have a banquet today to celebrate you, master. (MALE LEAD *speaks:*) Noble Xuande, arrange the host of generals in orderly ranks. I just cast a fortune in my sleeves and today, right at noon, there will be a "persuader" guest arriving here. All of you generals, I want you to put on your most awesome display. (*Sings:*)

(ZHONGLÜ MODE: *Fendie'er*)
Ever since the battle with Cao Cao to lay first claim,
It has resembled nothing so much as a spring dream:
Now arrange in rank these finest heroes of the land:
Each of them good at engaging in battle,
Capable of inciting a fight.
Out of the ordinary, above the masses,
All have accomplished great deeds;
They truly are supporting roof beams of this age, setting up the
    cosmos!

(*Zui chunfeng*)
I recall in olden days he dreamt "not of a bear";[59]
In these days you have invited me, Recumbent Dragon.
But why was I thrice so loathe to leave my thatched cottage?
I truly worried about the hustle
And bustle.
But today, I have the power,
And hold the title of Field Marshal—
But this cannot compare with nurturing my nature halfway up the
    slope.

(*Speaks:*) Noble Xuande, prepare a feast and make sure it is all in perfect order.
In less than an hour a "persuader" guest will be here. I will keep Mi Zhu and Mi
Fang here. The rest of you generals, listen to my orders: Zhao Yun, bring your
ears closer so I might whisper . . . you are to do thus and so. (ZHAO YUN *speaks:*)
Master is even making our lord himself absent. You generals, listen to the mas-
ter's orders. Mi Zhu and Mi Fang, you stay closely by the master and keep at-
tentive. (MALE LEAD *speaks:*) Right! (MALE LEAD LIU *speaks:*) Master is even
making our lord absent himself. You generals, listen to the master's orders. Mi
Zhu and Mi Fang, you stay closely by the master and keep attentive. (ZHAO
YUN *speaks:*) Let's all disappear.

(*Exits with the group.*)

(GUAN TONG *enters, speaks:*) I am the humble Daoist Guan Tong. I've left the
area of Wei and am already here in Xinye. Captain, report my arrival and say,
"There is a cloud-roving master, none other than Guan Tong, who has come
especially to pay his respects." (SOLDIER *speaks:*) Understood. Reporting! I want
to inform the Field Marshal that there is a cloud-roving master, Guan Tong, at
the door. (MALE LEAD *speaks:*) I'd better go welcome my brother myself. (*Acts out*

---

59. See note 47, to the corresponding passage in the *Thirty Yuan Plays* edition.

greeting him, speaks:) Welcome, brother. (GUAN TONG *speaks:*) I dare not enter![60] (MALE LEAD *speaks:*) Brother, from the time we parted you have been constantly on my mind. Never a day goes by that I don't remember you. I never thought you would actually be here today. This is truly all to the good fortune of Zhuge. (GUAN TONG *speaks:*) My worthy brother has been in my thoughts since we parted long ago, a constant source of concern and worry. I sigh that there are not many beautiful prospects and that time so easily flows by. When I think of your voice and face, then I am distraught at heart and when I ponder your great virtue, then you are always in my thoughts. Since we parted from our little hut, I have always kept you in mind, and that I am able to encounter your venerable visage today is truly all to the good fortune of Guan Tong. (MALE LEAD *speaks:*) Please sit, brother. Captain, bring out the snack table. (SOLDIER *speaks:*) Understood. (MALE LEAD *speaks:*) Bring out the wine. (*Acts out presenting wine, speaks:*) Please, brother, drink fully of this cup. (GUAN TONG *speaks:*) I cannot. Brother, you first. (*Acts out drinking wine.*) (MALE LEAD *sings:*)

> (*Ying xianke*)
> Today we drink cups of the finest wine,
> And here I offer up a golden flagon. . . .

(GUAN TONG *speaks:*) I came because I had been thinking of the feelings of our old friendship that stretches back several decades. (MALE LEAD *sings:*)

> From twenty years ago when we were only students,
> Students in plain gowns and long-sworn brothers.

(GUAN TONG *speaks:*) I have come directly to see you. (MALE LEAD *sings:*)

> Can you be serving in the area of River's East?

(GUAN TONG *speaks:*) I am an adviser under the aegis of Minister Cao. (MALE LEAD *sings:*)

> Oh, so you reside in Hanzhong.

(GUAN TONG *speaks:*) We haven't seen each other for decades, but here we are now. (MALE LEAD *sings:*)

> I never expected we would meet each other today.

(GUAN TONG *speaks:*) I have come such a long way, yet never begged off because of weariness or fear. (MALE LEAD *sings:*)

> Dear brother, you've gone to such trouble to make this journey!

---

60. Not out of fear, but out of humility.

(*Speaks:*) Bring on the wine. (SOLDIER *speaks:*) Understood. (MALE LEAD *acts out toasting him, speaks:*) Drink this cup to the full, brother. (GUAN TONG *speaks:*) Brother, I see you're Field Marshal under Noble Xuande's banner. Glory of this kind is not to be held in vain! (MALE LEAD *speaks:*) Since your brother left you, I have been remiss in my studies, and am just uselessly passing the time as Field Marshal; nothing more. (GUAN TONG *speaks:*) Don't be so modest! (MALE LEAD *speaks:*) Since we've met today, brother, we ought to drink a few. Bring on the wine! Brother, drink to your full. (GUAN TONG *speaks:*) You first, brother! (MALE LEAD *speaks:*) Mi Zhu, Mi Fang. My brother is hard to compare to others, and he can work the magic of guessing hidden items. Anything here in these headquarters, no matter what it is, and no matter where you hide it, he will know what it is. (GUAN TONG *speaks:*) Brother, this bit of magic is no real capability or knowledge, but since these two generals would like to see it—anything here in these headquarters, no matter what it is, and no matter where you hide it, I'll find out what it is. (MALE LEAD *speaks:*) Do you understand? (MI ZHU *and* MI FANG *act out hiding go stones.*) (MALE LEAD *speaks:*) Generals, watch this. (*Sings:*)

> (*Ti yindeng*)
> It is not that I am showing off here in front of the steps;
> You generals don't make fun of him.
> If he guesses it, show no alarm;
> Just watch my brother's magical art, supernatural power!
> This is a true skill,
> Not some simple trick:
> Open your eyes as wide as you can and don't move!
>
> (*Manjingcai*)
> You must ball your fists so tightly no seam can be seen!

(MALE LEAD *speaks:*) Mi Zhu, Mi Fang! Each of you stand on one side and extend your hands. (MI ZHU, MI FANG *act out taking go stones.*) (GUAN TONG *speaks:*) There is something in your hands. Let me guess what it is. Ah! I know now. Think: can you deceive this poor Daoist?

> The two of you have plied your ruse in secret,
> But I comprehend all Daoist mysteries and subtly use my ability to calculate
> the difficult.
> Your hand has two stones, one white and one black—
> The affairs of the entire cosmos, Heaven and Earth, are in that one palm.

You have nine black stones and he has nine white stones. If you don't believe it, then open your two hands, generals. (MALE LEAD *sings:*)

> These black and white stones were carefully hidden,
> And my elder brother has definitely demonstrated his skill.

(GUAN TONG *speaks:*) Open up your hands, generals! (MALE LEAD *sings:*)

> Our lives and our deaths are right here in the palms of our hands;
> If we don't carry it out to the end, then what's their use?

(GUAN TONG *speaks:*) I observe the aura of these two generals, and they have no particular ability or tactical knowledge! Rely on me, for if you have audience with Noble Cao he will certainly make you a Field Marshal. There are a million red-blooded soldiers under the minister's command as well as a thousand battle-tested generals. His fame is spread throughout the cosmos and his majesty overawes all of the states. I have brought your name up many times. Follow me! What are your thoughts? (MALE LEAD *speaks:*) You said just the right thing. But I have several rooms in which I have locked some things. If you manage to get them right, I will follow you, brother. (GUAN TONG *speaks:*) Each of these five rooms of yours contains an object. Let this poor Daoist calculate. Aha! Aha! I already know. What's so hard about figuring this out? (MALE LEAD *speaks:*) Brother, what do you figure is inside this door? (GUAN TONG *speaks:*) Isn't this a general who markets himself around to others? (MALE LEAD *speaks:*) Have you guessed it right, brother? (GUAN TONG *speaks:*) Open the door! (*Act out opening the door.*) (ZHAO YUN *enters, speaks:*) Did you recognize me, Guan Tong? (MALE LEAD *speaks:*) Brother, how about the second room? (GUAN TONG *speaks:*) Doesn't this room hold a general with two surnames?[61] (MALE LEAD *speaks:*) Captain, open the door. (*Act out opening the door.*) (LIU FENG *enters, speaks:*) Guan Tong, did you recognize me? (MALE LEAD *speaks:*) Brother, how about the third room? (GUAN TONG *speaks:*) In this room is a general, as strong as a tiger, as fierce as a fabled lion beast; he is a brave and battle-tested general. (MALE LEAD *speaks:*) I'm afraid you might have foretold it incorrectly. (GUAN TONG *speaks:*) I haven't foretold it incorrectly. You open the door! (MALE LEAD *speaks:*) Captain, open the door. (*Act out opening the door.*) (ZHANG FEI *enters, speaks:*) Guan Tong, I am right here. (MALE LEAD *speaks:*) How about figuring out what is in the fourth room. (GUAN TONG *speaks:*) In this room is a general with a bearing of spiritual majesty, whose aura combines goodness and loyalty, whose intent matches the mind of Heaven; he is a general of majestic power. (MALE LEAD *speaks:*) Couldn't you guess this one, brother? (GUAN TONG *speaks:*) Open the door! (*Act out opening the door.*) (GUAN YU *enters, speaks:*) I, a certain Guan, am here. (GUAN TONG *speaks:*) These generals are innately possessed of a red-blooded awesome presence, an eagle-like courage of tiger generals. They are all commanding generals. But I don't know them. What are their names? Brother, give me each and every name. I am listening. (MALE LEAD *speaks:*) I'll tell you each one by one, brother. (GUAN TONG *speaks:*) Who is this one? (MALE LEAD *sings:*)

---

61. Both his patrilineal surname and his adopted surname. On Kou Feng's adoption by Liu Bei, see the first wedge in *Xiangyang Meeting*.

(*Shi'er yue*)
This is Zhao Yun from Changshan.

(GUAN TONG *speaks:*) Who is this one? (MALE LEAD *sings:*)

This is the adopted son Liu Feng.

(GUAN TONG *speaks:*) Who is this one? (MALE LEAD *sings:*)

This is the man from Yan, Yide.[62]

(GUAN TONG *speaks:*) Who is this one? (MALE LEAD *sings:*)

And this is the righteous and courageous Lord Guan.

(GUAN TONG *speaks:*) I got them all right! (MALE LEAD *sings:*)

Ai! Brother Guan Tong, so capable of the methods of extrasensory
    knowing:
It's hard to see you the same as others.

(*Speaks:*) Well, you've figured out all of the four rooms. But what's in this room,
brother? (GUAN TONG *speaks:*) In this room, the aura is completely different.
Look how it is enwrapped in a globe of auspicious clouds, its purple auras
pulsing higher and higher. This is the image of a noble person, who completely
overwhelms these generals. If you don't believe me, open the door and have a
look. (MALE LEAD *acts out being angry, speaks:*) Don't open the door! (GUAN
TONG *speaks:*) Open it! (MALE LEAD *speaks:*) Don't open it! (GUAN TONG *speaks:*)
Why not? (MALE LEAD *speaks:*) If your brother opens this door, then . . . (*Sings:*)

(*Yaomin ge*)
Ai, I fear you will break the golden chain and allow the dragon to
    escape!
These generals truly possess an awesome air.
You generals are all close court officials,
And your names are fit to be inscribed in Lingyan Gallery,[63]
For you surpass all others in terms of waging battle or suppressing
    bandits—
Each of you a gifted and capable man.

(MALE LEAD LIU *enters, speaks:*) Master, I am right here. (MALE LEAD *sings:*)

And this Liu Xuande of ours is worth thinking of highly!

---

62. Zhang Fei.
63. A gallery in the palace of the founding emperor of the Tang, where he had portraits
painted of twenty-four people who aided him in his establishment of the dynasty .

(MALE LEAD LIU *enters, speaks:*) So, you are Guan Tong. How disrespectful you are! How dare you ply your persuasive words to try to make Master [Zhuge] surrender to Cao Cao? I really want to be done with you. Zhao Yun, take Guan Tong away and cut off his head. (MALE LEAD *speaks:*) Noble Xuande, pardon him for my sake! (MALE LEAD LIU *speaks:*) Out of regard for you, take him away and incarcerate him. (GUAN TONG *speaks:*) Enough! Enough! Zhuge Liang is the stronger.

> Zhuge's marvelous plans can auger the very constellations,
> A hard match when discussing heaven and discoursing on earth;
> In the very beginning I would have said Guan Tong was the stronger,
> But now there is a stronger hand among the strong.

(*Exits.*)

(MALE LEAD LIU *sends everyone from the stage:*)

> Because that Cao Cao was master of intrigue,
> He made Xiahou Dun his general on point;
> But meeting Zhao Yun's feigned loss and false defeat,
> He was chased into Bowang City.
> He ordered Yunchang to lift the water gates and let the water flow,
> And had Liu Feng winnow dirt to stir up dust.
> Our Field Marshal thus plied his crafty scheme,
> And shooting fire arrows, he burned the stores at Bowang.
> But today we gather in our armies and cease battle,
> And will not let weapons or soldiers be used again.

TITLE: Guan Yunchang raises the water gates and lets the water flow:

NAME: Zhuge Liang burns the stores at Bowang.

6

The Great King Guan and the Single Sword Meeting

Guan Hanqing

The Great King Guan and the Single Sword Meeting (*Guan dawang dandao hui*) is one of the finer dramas by the great playwright Guan Hanqing (c. 1245–1322). Guan is the author of some sixty-seven plays, eighteen of which are extant. Whereas he is most noted for his plays about women, *Single Sword Meeting* is a superb historical drama, well conceived and executed, about one of the final brave acts of Guan Yu.[1] Two versions of the play are preserved: a fourteenth-century printing (called the *Thirty Yuan Plays* edition), and a manuscript from the Maiwang Studio collection deriving from the archives of the Ming court (called the Ming palace edition).

Single Sword Meeting appears to be one of a pair of *zaju*, the other being *In a Dream Guan and Zhang, a Pair, Rush to Western Shu*. The latter play recounts the dream visit of the ghosts of Zhang Fei and Guan Yu to their elder brother, Liu Bei, to seek vengeance for their deaths. The staging of both plays is similar: in both, the main character—Guan Yu in the first and Zhang Fei in the second—does not appear until the third act. In each play the male lead in the first two acts portrays two different characters: Qiao Guolao and Sima Hui in *Single Sword Meeting* and the messenger and Zhuge Liang in *Dream of Western Shu*. The plays are mirror plays also in the sense that it is Guan Yu who sings the last two acts of *Single Sword Meeting* and Zhang Fei (or at least his ghost) who sings the last two acts of *Dream of Western Shu*. The plays are alike in that these two brothers portray their basic temperaments through songs: Guan Yu, brave, righteous, and over-awing; Zhang Fei, impetuous, angry, and quick to demand revenge.

The "single-sword meeting" takes place some time after the famous battle of Red Cliff and in the same general area: the Yangzi River just above and below its confluence with the Han River (near modern Wuhan).[2] In the play Lu Su, a minister of Wu (and in the *Thirty Yuan Plays* text, Sun Quan, the Emperor of

---

1. On Guan Hanqing, see West and Idema 2010, pp. 1–5, and sources cited there.
2. In the *Romance of the Three Kingdoms*, the "single-sword meeting" is the subject of the first part of chapter 66.

Wu), wants to reclaim Jingzhou[3] from Liu Bei. When Wu earlier joined forces with Liu Bei to fend off Cao Cao, Sun Quan, King of Wu, had temporarily granted Liu Bei Jingzhou as a place to base his army in the Hubei area. Liu Bei promised to return it after he had conquered Yizhou, which is roughly the area of modern Chengdu in Sichuan. When Liu Bei departed on his campaign, he had installed Guan Yu as the prefect of Jingzhou. Now that Liu Bei is safely installed in Chengdu Lu Su, Sun Quan's adviser, has devised three strategies to make Guan Yu relinquish Jingzhou. He plans to invite Guan Yu to a banquet and ask him, with all due ritual, to return the prefecture; failing that, he will capture all of the boats along the Yangzi and detain Guan Yu until he releases it; and when these two strategies fail, he will detain Guan Yu by force, certain that the troops in Jingzhou, once bereft of their leader, will revolt and thus be easy to overwhelm.

In the first act Lu Su asks Qiao Guolao's opinion about the plans, and Qiao Guolao (a retired prime minister) responds that they surely will end in disaster because of the bravery and martial acumen of Guan Yu. But Qiao Guolao's attempts to stop Lu Su are unsuccessful, and in the second act Lu Su calls on the Daoist master Sima Hui, a former acquaintance of Guan Yu, whom he tries to enlist as a "matching guest" (*peike*), a third person to fill out the relational ties of the banquet. When asked about Guan Yu's temper when drinking, Sima Hui warns Lu Su that the slightest affront to Guan Yu when he has been drinking is just a summons to one's own execution. Not only does Sima Hui refuse to go, but he also warns Lu Su that he may wind up dead.

In Act 3, Huang Wen delivers a message from Lu Su, inviting Guan Yu to the feast. Guan Yu accepts, over the objection of his sons, and goes to the feast. Guan Yu crosses the Yangzi River with a small group of men, and his sons Guan Ping and Guan Xing arrange to meet him on his return. Act 4 is clearly the high point of the drama. The act begins with Guan Yu's sailing across the river at precisely the spot where the battle of Red Cliff raged, to meet with Lu Su. Lu praises Guan Yu's humanness, righteousness, and military acumen but tells him he is untrustworthy because he has not returned Jingzhou. Guan Yu replies that all of the empire belongs to the Emperor of Han, not to Sun Quan. When the attempt to seize Guan Yu by force is thwarted, Guan takes Lu Su hostage and makes him escort him back to his boat.

The play is roughly based on historical realities. Liu Bei had promised to return Jingzhou after he had conquered Chengdu, but Sun Quan did not believe him and pressed for the return of several commanderies from the portion

---

3. The area of Jingzhou roughly covered the modern provinces of Hubei and Hunan. The capital of the area was Jiangling, but Liu Biao had moved his residence to Xiangyang. As Liu Bei's governor of Jingzhou Guan Yu once again resided at Jiangling.

of Jingzhou he had previously given to Liu Bei. Guan Yu thwarted Sun's attempt to send his general, Lü Meng, to reclaim three of the commanderies, and Lu Su then decided that he needed to discuss the matter with Guan Yu. Lu Su's biography in the third-century *Records of the Three Kingdoms* simply says,

> Lu Su stationed his army in Yiyang, where he was in a standoff with Guan Yu. Su invited Yu to a meeting, and each stationed their cavalry a hundred double-paces away and simply requested that the generals meet, each carrying only a single sword. Su took advantage of the situation to criticize and reprove Yu, saying, "The reason our state agreed to originally grant your side land to use was because your army was defeated and had retreated here over a long distance, and because it had nothing to supply itself. Now you have already taken Yizhou but have no intention of returning [the land we granted you]. You merely seek the three commanderies and again will not abide by our orders." Before he had finished speaking, someone in a seat at the mat said, "Now land is merely where virtue exists—it cannot be kept constantly [in one person's hands]." Su barked at the person with severe words and looks. Yu took his sword, arose, and said, "This is a matter of our state— what does this person know?" And he signaled with his eyes for him to leave.

In his comments to this passage, Pei Songzhi adds supplementary material from a work entitled the *Documents of Wu* (*Wushu*):

> Lu Su desired to meet with Guan Yu to discuss the matter, but his various generals, fearful of some extraordinary turn of events, held the opinion that he could not proceed. Su said, "We should open up discussions to persuade him. Liu Bei has turned his back on our state, and with right and wrong of the situation yet to be decided, how would Yu dare desire, on top of this, to violate our mandate." He then invited Yu to meet with him. Each stationed his cavalry outside of one hundred double-paces, and only the various generals assembled for the meeting, each bearing one sword. Su then criticized and reproved Yu for not returning the three commanderies. Yu said, "In the campaign at Wulin, the General of the Left[4] was in the ranks himself, he slept in his armor, and joined his power with yours to smash the enemy. How can it be that he labored there for nothing, not even a clod of dirt, and you now come wanting to take back this land?" Su said, "This is not the case. When I first met [the Prefect] of Yu[5] at Changban, his armies did not even amount to a battalion. His plans were exhausted and his deliberations at their end; his ambition was destroyed and his power was weak; his plan was

---

4. I.e., Liu Bei.
5. Liu Bei.

to hide far away. We hoped it would not come to this. His Highness commiserated and felt sympathy for the fact that the Prefect of Yu had no place to claim as his own, and, without being stingy with his own land or the energies of the worthy and common citizens, made him a place to protect him in order to alleviate his troubles. Yet the Prefect of Yu privately and alone shrouded his emotions in pleasant guise while violating ethical behavior and our friendly relations. He has already brought the western prefecture into his own hands as [an aid to his expansion] and now he wants to trim off and annex the lands of Jingzhou. This is an action that even a common person could not stand, much less a ruler who leads his citizens in the right way." Yu had nothing with which to reply.

Despite the differences of this passage with the play, we can see a common historical source. But the "reproving" by Lu Su occurs in Act 4 of the drama under completely different circumstances and with quite a different outcome. The play more closely follows the later *Records of the Three Kingdoms in Plain Language* (see Appendix 1, item 12), which clearly shares a narrative source with the play, one from which scenes about music at the feast (and the dropping of one of the notes of the scale), as well as the ending in which Lu Su cowers when threatened by Guan Yu, have been added.

One of the features shared by both the *Thirty Yuan Plays* print edition and the Ming manuscript drama is that the fourth act incorporates a famous and quite popular lyric by the famous Song poet Su Shi, called "Recalling Antiquity at the Red Cliff" (*Chibi huaigu*): the first three songs in the *Thirty Yuan Plays* edition and the first two in the Ming palace edition both cite lines from this old chestnut.[6] While it is not uncommon to cite lines from poems written eight hundred years after the event (anachronisms do not bother the authors of *zaju*), it is rather rare to find a poem so thoroughly embedded in the text. It is an interesting process, since Su Shi's poem was written as a meditation on the heroes of the Three Kingdoms, and to have his poem partially recited from the mouth of one of the main figures of the era is quite stunning in its originality. The poem reads:

"Recalling Antiquity at the Red Cliff"

The Great River flows east,
Waves washing clean away
The heroes of a thousand antiquities.
The western edge of the ancient rampart,

---

6. The Ming palace edition omits the third song in its version.

People say,
Is the Red Cliff of Young Zhou[7] of the Three Kingdoms.
Chaotic stones crumble clouds;
Startled waves split the bank,
Rolling up a thousand mounds of snow.
River and mountains like a painting—
So many young braves in that one time.

Pondering far back, to the days of Gongjin,[8]
Just after he married Younger Qiao,
His vigorous form like a flower bursting—
A feathered fan, black headscarf—
In a moment of laughing banter
His powerful enemy flew away in ash, disappeared in smoke.[9]
Such spiritual roaming in an ancient state—
So full of sentiment—they should laugh at me
Turning gray so early.
Human life is like a dream.
With one flagon I will pour out a libation to the River's[10] moon.

All modern print editions of this play are derived from one of two versions: the early printed edition, the full title of which is *A New Edition Newly Published in Hangzhou: The Great King Guan and the Single Sword Meeting*, and a Ming palace edition, entitled simply *The Single Sword Meeting*, but with a longer title at the end of the play, *The Great King Guan Goes Alone to the Single Sword Meeting*.

The first is a typical *Thirty Yuan Plays* text, with little dialogue, no act markers, no indication of musical mode, and no separation between acts. The prose dialogue is set roughly one character space lower than the arias, which run to the top of the marked page. The titles of the songs are in black cartouches, and stage directions are separated by a one-character space. Leaving the end of a line blank after the action of one scene concludes usually marks the end of that scene, although a space can also be left if the cartouche for the next song title is too long to fit into an existing line. Fig. 6 shows the first page of this edition. The very large type is the title; the stage directions and prose are in characters the same size as those in the arias, but are set lower on the page. Unfortunately, page 5, recto and verso, have been torn away. However, since the Ming palace edition is closely related to this edition, these lines can be restored with some

---

7. Zhou Yu.
8. Zhou Yu.
9. Cao Cao's boats were burned.
10. "River" uppercase signifies the Yangzi River.

accuracy. The Ming palace edition provides full dialogue for all characters in the play.

There are some signal differences between the *Thirty Yuan Plays* text and its Ming counterpart. The most obvious is in the opening scene. The *Thirty Yuan Plays* text has a role called "Emperor" (*jia*) who, as in the historical records, is the one who wants to press for Jingzhou, and who is the one engaged in conversation with Qiao Guolao. Because emperors could not be portrayed on the court stage, this scene was rewritten to place Lu Su in the foreground and Sun Quan was removed. The Ming palace edition has removed a total of eight songs from the older printed version: two from Act 1, one from Act 2, two from Act 3, and one from Act 4, as well as two songs that in the fourteenth-century printing constitute a final demi-act—probably a dispersal scene—in which Guan Yu gives a summary of the punishments he levies on Lu Su, who has wound up in his custody. In some later plays, Guan Yu is a god and revenant who appears with his six Ding spirits to recreate order in the human world. This ending could either be a "case reversal" (*fan'an*) play, like the ending of *Zhuge Liang Burns the Stores at Bowang*, in which an alternate ending is presented as a "what if" scenario in which all the evildoers receive their due; or it could possibly be a netherworld scene, in which Guan Yu, in charge of punishments, gets his final vengeance on Lu Su. And not for just this single-sword meeting, but for his death at the hands of a general under Lu Su's command. There are also a number of small but significant changes in the wording of the lines of the two versions.

The manuscript of the Ming palace edition is unique in many ways. First, it not only contains annotations by Zhao Qimei, but also has been collated very closely with the *Thirty Yuan Plays* text by a Qing scholar, He Huang (1668–after 1741); the colophon to the text indicates that his collation was finished on the tenth day of the eighth month in the *yisi* year of the Yongzheng Emperor (September 16, 1725). As Fig. 7 shows, we have a rare instance when a copy of the Yuan printed edition has undergone rewriting at the hands of people associated with court performances, and then is re-collated perhaps two hundred years later with its source.

The manuscript of the Ming palace edition of *Single Sword Meeting* itself is part of a small group of plays in the Maiwang Studio collection that may have an origin in the Court Entertainment Bureau (*Jiaofang si*) rather than in the Office of Drum and Bell (*Zhonggu si*), the eunuch agency for theatricals, which is the source of the majority of court plays in the Maiwang Studio collection. The plays in this group in most cases stem from the manuscripts of Yu Xiaogu, who may have been an adopted son of Yu Shenxing (1545–1607), a late Ming scholar-bureaucrat. The endings of plays that were performed by the Court Entertainment Bureau are different from palace editions from the Office of

Drum and Bell. The latter all have a stereotypical ending in which the players and characters kneel and a "decision" is rendered by one of the players that ends in a paean to the court (see the endings of *Tripartite Oath* and *Xiangyang Meeting* for examples). Several of the plays from the Yu Xiaogu manuscripts end with some variation of a different type of ending. An example is the ending found in the anonymous play *Sima Xiangru Inscribes His Name on the Bridge* (*Sima Xiangru tiqiao ji*). After the final coda has concluded the play proper, the manuscript continues with the following lines:

ENSEMBLE *speaks:* This *zaju* play is finished. BACKSTAGE *speaks:* What did you say? ENSEMBLE *responds:*

> On this fairy isle we set a feast, array our fine guests,
> We celebrate our August Emperor: tens of tens of thousands of Springs!
> Military officers lift their blades and support the altars of state,
> Civil officials grasp their brushes to help with the silken edicts.

We see in the Ming palace edition of *Single Sword Meeting* a remnant of this type of ending in the residual line, "This *zaju* play is finished." This would mark the play as possibly stemming from the Yu Xiaogu collection of manuscripts.

Like the Ming palace edition of *Single Sword Meeting*, none of the known Yu Xiaogu manuscripts have the acts marked with divisions. This is typical of early fifteenth-century plays (Zhu Youdun's plays, for instance), which seem to follow closely the *Thirty Yuan Plays* texts in this respect. Moreover, the spacing between stage directions in the Ming manuscript closely follows the practice of the *Thirty Yuan Plays*. Since Yu Xiaogu's plays were noted as having "come from the Court Entertainment Bureau," we can surmise that perhaps they were collected in a different place and a different time than those in the Office of Drum and Bell, which was staffed primarily by eunuch performers. Komatsu Ken has placed these plays in the mid-fifteenth century. As such, they bear a different relationship both to Yuan printed editions and to later texts as well. They are much more closely related in terms of staging and language to the Yuan texts. As for later editions, if there were indeed alternative versions stemming from two separate times and places, it may account for the wide variation of later editions based on Ming palace editions: *Interlocking Rings* is a good example. Both the Xijizi and Zang Maoxun versions probably stem from the court, but they are clearly completely different versions of the same play, and this difference may reflect their provenance from within the body of Ming court materials.

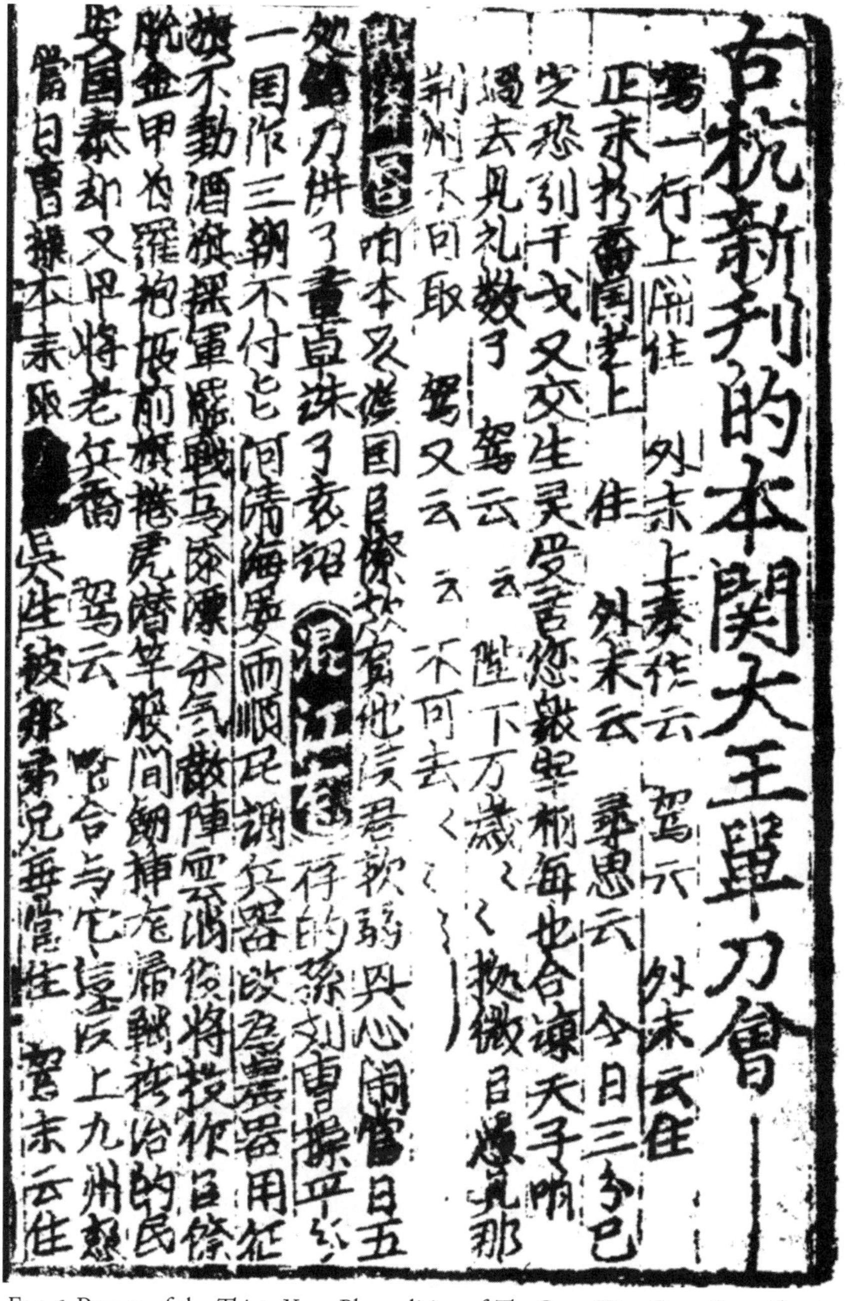
古杭新刊的本関大王單刀會
駕一行上開住 外末上奏住云 駕云 外末云住
正末扮喬國老上住 外末云 尋思云 今日三分已
定恐引干戈又交生灵受苦您微臣怕每也合諫天子咱
過去見礼數了 駕云 云 陛下万歲々々 拠微臣愚見那
荆州不可取 駕又云 云 不可去々々々
仙呂 点絳唇 咱本是漢国臣僚漢皇軟弱興心閙當日五
處鎗刀併了董卓誅了袁紹 混江龍 存的孫劉曹操平分
一国作三朝不付它河清海晏雨順風調兵器改為農器用征
旗不動酒旗搖軍罷戰馬添膘殺氣散陣雲消役將校作臣僚
脫金甲着羅袍帳前旗捲虎潛竿腰間劍插龍歸鞘的民
安国泰却又早將老兵消 駕云 咱合與它追復上九州慰
當日曹操本未取[illegible]吳住被那弟兄每當住 駕末云住

Fig. 6. Page 1a of the *Thirty Yuan Plays* edition of *The Great King Guan Goes Alone to the Single Sword Meeting*

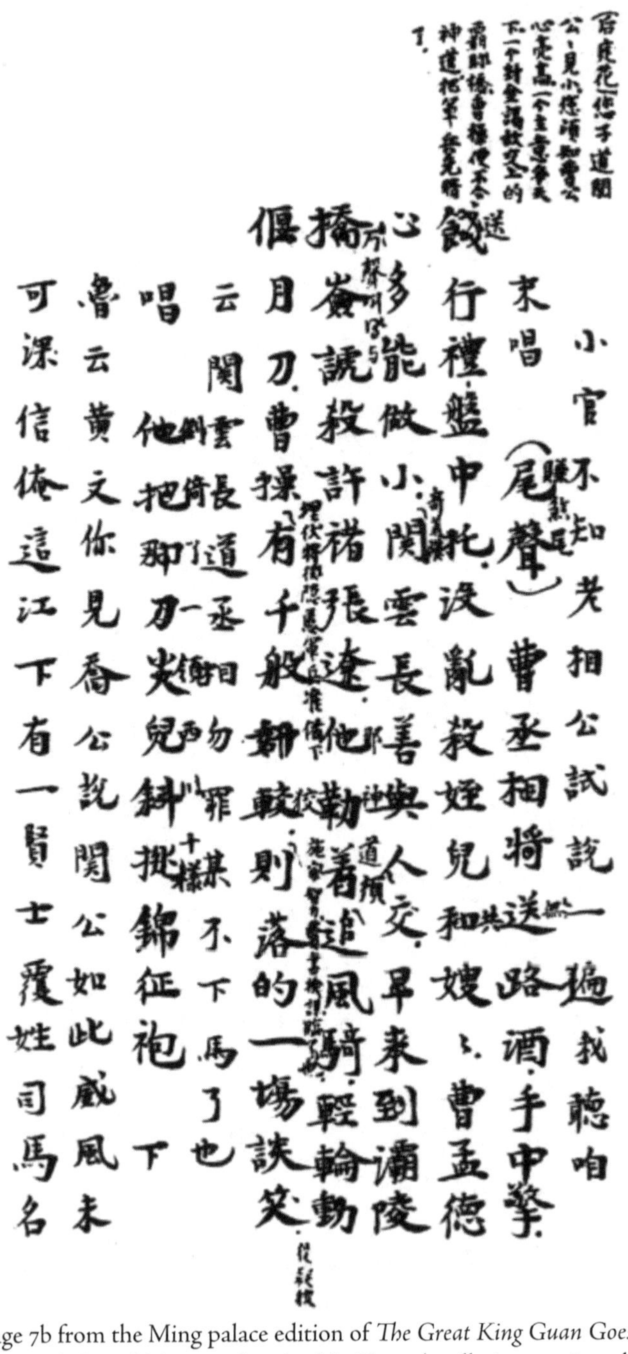

心先惡意下二个對意馮故爻的
公．見小懥濱和意爻
官虎花他乎道朋
秫蓴脈線會樣便不各．送
神道恬筆會見晴

偃搐
所蔡明字
心多嶽嵩讀殺許褚有千般勦較則落的一場談笑
閃雲闊雲長遼他勒著這風馬兒輕輪動
唱他把那刀尖兒斜挑錦征袍下
云他倒荷着道丞日勿罪十樣不下馬了也
月刀．曹操
行禮盤中托沒亂救姪兒和嫂
末唱 (尾聲) 曹丞相把將送路酒．手中擎．曹孟德
能做小關雲長善與人交早来到灞陵
小官不知老相公試說一遍咱聽咱

可深信俺這江下有一賢士覆姓司馬名
魯云黃文你見喬公說閃公如此戚風未

FIG. 7. Page 7b from the Ming palace edition of *The Great King Guan Goes Alone to the Single Sword Meeting,* showing He Huang's collations against the *Thirty Yuan Plays* edition

Dramatis personæ in order of appearance

Role type	*Name and family, institutional, or social role*
Emperor	Sun Quan, Emperor of Wu
Extra male	Lu Su
Male lead	Qiao Guolao
Male lead	Sima Hui, Daoist master
Acolyte	Daoist Acolyte
Comic	role unspecified—Huang Wen?
Aide Guan	Guan Ping, Guan Yu's son and aide
Male lead	Guan Yu (identified as a god)
Soldiers	role unspecified—Zhou Cang and others who accompany Guan Yu?

A Complete Edition Newly Printed in Old Hangzhou

The Great King Guan and the Single Sword Meeting (From a *Thirty Yuan Plays* Edition)

[Act 1]

EMPEROR *and entourage enter, open, stop.* — EXTRA MALE *enters, makes a formal request, stops.* — EMPEROR *speaks.* — EXTRA MALE *speaks, stops.* — MALE LEAD, *costumed as* QIAO GUOLAO, *enters, opens, stops.* — EXTRA MALE *speaks.*[11] *Speak as if pondering a question:* The tripartite partition is already set now; I fear pulling out the shield and spear will cause the people's lives more bitterness. You group of ministers should remonstrate with the Son of Heaven.

After going over to have an audience and performing the proper ritual. — EMPEROR *speaks.* — *Speak:* Myriad years, my lord, myriad years! This insignificant official's own stupid opinion is that Jingzhou cannot be taken. EMPEROR *speaks.* — *Speak:* You cannot go![12] You cannot go!

> ([XIANLÜ MODE:] *Dian jiangchun*)
> We were originally bureaucrats in service to the state of Han
> But bullied that weak and ineffectual lord of the Han,
> Which triggered minds to create trouble.
> Five places of spear and sword in those days
> Swallowed up Dong Zhuo and finished off Yuan Shao,
>
> (*Hunjiang long*)
> Leaving Sun, Liu, and Cao Cao
> To split one state equally into three separate courts.

---

11. All spoken or sung lines are by the male lead. A colon (or a colon and a dash to indicate spacing in the original text) marks the point at which the lead singer either sings or speaks. Since only the arias and speech of the lead singer are included, the text omits stage directions indicating that the lead should sing or speak.

12. The text here reads, *bu ke qu.*[4] Lan 2006, p. 313, following Xu 1980, p. 62, changes it to *bu ke qu,*[3] understanding it to refer to the preceding line, "Jingzhou cannot be taken," and having the unstated object as Jingzhou. We retain the original reading, understanding it as a direct address to Lu Su, warning him not to go to the banquet.

The rivers are just now clear, the seas peaceful;
The rains are timely and the winds just right.
Weapons have been turned to use as farming tools,
Battle standards no longer wave, the wineshop flags flutter.
The armies have ceased warfare,
The horses grow fat and sleek;
The ethers of killing have all dispersed;
The clouds of formations have disappeared;
Now generals and colonels are dispatched
To become civil officials,
Shedding their metal armor
To don robes of silk.
In front of their tents, banners are furled—the tiger curls about the
  flagstaff;
At their waists swords are put away—the dragon returns to its
  sheath.
They have soothingly ruled until the people are secure and the state
  prosperous,
But already the generals are seasoned and the soldiers arrogant.

EMPEROR *speaks:* We should have given him these nine regions on the Han River. Remember that Cao Cao had then taken our Eastern Wu[13] and was turned back strongly by those brothers. — EMPEROR *speaks, stops.*

(*You hulu*)
"Although his brothers are many, his troops and generals are
  few"—
In truth he put the cities of Xiakou and Hanyang in straits.[14]
By chance Zhou Yu and Jiang Gan were friends in their days of
  poverty,
But that right-hand minister Zhuge Liang put his military tactics
  into play,
And in the "plot that sacrifices one's body," Huang Gai augmented
  food and fodder.
Better than half of Cao's army was burned in the fire
And another three of ten floated away on the water;

13. In the original text there is a black space the equivalent length of two characters. It appears from the reproduced text that the two characters, which modern editors agree should be "our eastern" (*zan dong*), were simply left uncut by mistake.
14. "He" here refers to Cao Cao.

If it were not for the fact that "Heaven dispatches those who possess
   the Way to attack those who don't,"[15]
Then in this moment the state of Wu would also belong to Cao,

(*Tianxia le*)
And in Bronze Sparrow, deep in spring, he'd have locked away the
   two Qiaos![16]
Now these three states
Have just established friendly relations.
Not only will "Our mistake of a single day turn into a mistake for an
   entire generation!"
You want to exercise the Way of rule by force,[17]
Start a new war,
And look lightly on Guan Yunchang for being on in years.

(*Nezha ling*)
He took in White Emperor City in Western Shu[18]
And sent Zhou Yu to his death.
Then alongside the Han stretch of the river, Zhang Yide
Blocked the corpse's return[19]
And Grandee Lu, in the prow of the boat, was almost felled by fright.
Contest for that stretch of earth that is Jingzhou
And Guan Yunchang will raise hell when he hears about it
And then wind and hailstones will fall where they may![20]

---

15. Derived from Dong Zhongshu's *Luxuriant Dew of the Spring and Autumn Annals* (*Chun-qiu fanlu*): "Those with the Way attack those without the Way; this is the principle of Heaven" (*youdao fa wu dao, ci tianli ye*).

16. According to the *Records in Plain Language*, Cao Cao had planned to defeat Sun Quan and then capture the lovelies, Qiao Guolao's two daughters who were married to Sun Quan and Zhou Yu, and imprison them in the Palace of the Bronze Sparrow at Ye (modern Linzhang district in Hebei).

17. The phrase *xing badao*, which we have translated as "exercise the Way of the rule by force," is also a much more colloquial phrase usually written as *hengxing badao*, which means "to act rashly without thinking of the consequences."

18. White Emperor City (*Baidi cheng*), located on the Eastern White Emperor Peak in modern Fengjie district in Sichuan, held a commanding position at the Qutang Gorge (*Qutang xia*), effectively guarding Western Shu and also providing a launching point for an attack against Eastern Wu. It is ironic that this was also where Liu Bei was later halted in his attack on Eastern Wu and where he died in Yong'an Palace. This was also the site of the famous "Eightfold Battle Array." See *Burning the Stores*, n. 33.

19. According to the *Records in Plain Language*, Zhang Fei stopped Zhou Yu's advance into Western Shu, but it was Zhuge Liang who blocked Zhou Yu's corpse from returning to Wu.

20. The rest of this line is left blank and the stage directions are moved to begin the next line. This usually indicates a clear demarcation between scenes on stage.

EXTRA *speaks, stops.* [*Speak:*] You ask what General Guan is capable of?

(*Que ta zhi*)
He slew Wen Chou, displaying his rash temperament,
Stabbed Yan Liang, displaying his heroic bravery.[21]
Off toward that million-man army—
On his pike he lightly lifted aloft the heads of those he slew.
And at the battle of Red Cliff he seemed just fine.
> It isn't the same now as then—they had to ingratiate themselves
> with us
And they all seemed filled with joy but hid knives in their smiles.

(*Jisheng cao*)
It's always been the case that "Heaven has no calamities,"
"Men bring disaster upon themselves."
If you are completely unwilling to exercise benevolent government,
    effect the Way of the true ethical king,
Can you hope to compare to that heroic Cao Cao, so full of plans and
    wisdom?
Don't you know that Zhuge Liang from Nanyang will be hard to
    figure out?
You just want to confront a thousand armies and ten thousand
    horses in some awful standoff,
And have absolutely no concern for the millions of souls who will
    stumble into this terrible violence.

(*Jinzhan'er*)
When he goes into formation, his three-braid beautiful beard is
    tossed in the wind,
His nine-foot lion-tiger body shakes mightily,
And he's just like a living god surrounded by five hundred damned
    Guanxi bodyguards.
After the enemy armies see him,
They are so scared that their seven earthly souls disperse
And their five cloud souls vanish.
You all had better pull on several suits of armor
And pile on several layers of battle robes.
And even then can you run into and fell his thousand-mile courser
Or avoid his third-of-the-length blade shaped like the crescent
    moon?

---

21. See Appendix 1, item 7.

(*Zui fu gui*)
In the beginning you were careless enough to make guarantees about
    him
And wrapped yourself up in a bag of courage—
Are you going to lie secretly in ambush or meet him head-on?
If you ask him to come,
Once you see that visage, full of real courage and majesty,
Then you won't even be able to bring yourself to demand Jingzhou.

(*Jinzhan'er*)[22]
You say, "These three plans are truly hard to escape,"
But if a single sentence he will not countenance—
You can use neither a military officer's crudeness nor a civil official's
    craftiness.
That guy is afflicted with an angry nature but manifests a heroic
    bravery;
Snicker-snack he'll grab that jeweled belt at your waist,
And rest that steel blade on the back of your neck.
Even though you hide away war boats along the bank,
They will only serve him as a floating bridge across the river's
    surface.

(*Houting hua*)
You just say, "Lord Guan is a man of little knowledge";
You must know Lord Cao is a man of much capacity.
One has a mind to contest for the empire;
The other sealed everything up and went back to old friends.
When he got on Baling Bridge,
Then Cao Cao did not accord with the ways of heaven
And first hid his troops away.

(*Coda*)
He offered a stirrup cup to send him on his way;
The gifts for his trip were piled in a platter,
And it worried both nephew and sister-in-law to death.
Cao Cao was guileful and could make himself humble,
But was Guan Yunchang "good at gracious interaction"?
He called out in a loud voice
And scared Xu Chu and Zhang Liao to death.

---

22. This aria is repeated in the Chinese text, which is certainly a mistake; it has been
omitted.

That god[23] followed his wind-chasing steed,
And casually twirled his crescent-moon blade.
> Cao Cao put his generals and officers in an ambush, and his army into hiding—

He had indeed prepared a thousand cunning and crafty plans,
> He exhausted every bit of his knowledge and used up all of his plots—

But when time was at hand, he became the butt of history's jokes
And had to fork over fine brocade campaign robes from Western Shu to boot.[24]

Finish speaking.[25]

[Act 2]

MALE LEAD, *costumed as a* DAOIST MASTER, *enters, leading* DAOIST ACOLYTE, *sits in fixed position. Speak:* — I, this humble Daoist, am Sima Decao. From the time when I had met Imperial Uncle Liu after the Xiangyang meeting,[26] I found him to be a person of the same aura as the founding emperor of the Han. The disciple Kou Feng was given to the Imperial Uncle as an adopted son and the Recumbent Dragon of Nanyang was raised up as Field Marshal, and they took Western Sichuan as their share. In my forest retreat amid the mountains

---

23. Guan Yu.

24. The gift of the brocade robe is discussed in Appendix 1, item 7.

25. This simple stage direction is placed in reduced characters between the end of the first act and the beginning of the second with no intervening spaces above or below it to indicate a new scene. Nor is the first act concluded with the stage direction, "exit" (*xia*). The end of Act 2 includes "exit" as a stage direction, but the last lines of Act 3 are missing in the original edition. Moreover, since the conclusion of the suite in Act 4 is immediately followed by two added songs, no "exit" is marked there. Thus there is no clear way to determine the actual point at which Act 1 ends and the prose dialogue of Act 2 begins. Some editors have placed this phrase at the end of Act 1, assuming they represent the dialogue spoken between Huang Wen and Lu Su; others have placed them at the beginning of Act 2, implying that they are an action that takes place on stage before the male lead enters. It is also common that the beginning lines of prose dialogue are at the upper margin and all remaining lines of prose are set two characters below the upper margin, which is not the case here. One intriguing possibility is that they indicate a special relationship between these two acts: that they are not to be interrupted by comic or acrobatic interludes that seem to have been common between acts.

26. When Liu Bei first began his ascent to power, he sought patronage from Liu Biao. Liu Biao's brother-in-law Cai Mao arranged a feast for Liu Bei in Xiangyang in the third month, in which he planned to kill Liu Bei. Liu Bei, recognizing it was a plot, fled. On the way back, he encountered Sima Hui (also known as Sima Decao), who sent him off to Pang Degong. Pang Degong, in turn, introduced him to Kou Feng, whom Liu Bei made an adopted son, renaming him Liu Feng. See *Xiangyang Meeting* and chapter 37 of the *Romance of the Three Kingdoms*.

I have observed ten years of contesting dragons and fighting tigers. I have cut off any thought of name or fame and have been neither favored nor shamed. Isn't this a pure joy indeed!

([ZHENGGONG MODE:] *Duanzheng hao*)
I was originally a man who "fished out giant turtles,"[27]
But then turned into a codger who grasps the plow—
I sigh over Ying Bu,[28] Peng Yue,[29] and Marquis Han.
From outside my body I gather my two cloud-supporting hands,[30]
And will never let them out of the sleeves of my hempen gown again.

(*Gun xiuqiu*)
                    And right now I[31]
Get together with old village codgers,
Meet up with poetic friends;
What we consume are fresh fish and new wine—
Don't care if there are roof-tile plates, rough pottery bottles, or
      ceramic mugs.
We push the stemmed cups forward, never changing the cups,
And clap our own hands for loud songs.
Let time pass in its day and night, shadows and sunlight;
I'll just drink until I'm drunk, and slumber with the patchy quilt
      covering my head,

---

27. A man of great ambition.

28. Ying Bu (d. 196 BC), also known as Qing Bu, was one of the leaders of peasant rebellions at the end of the Qin. He joined Xiang Yu, rose to prominence, and was enfeoffed as the Prince of Jiujiang. Later he reverted his allegiance to Liu Bang. After seeing Peng Yue and others executed, he rebelled against Liu Bang but was duped by the Prince of Changsha and executed. His biography is found in English, "Ch'ing Pu, Memoir 31," in Sima Qian 2008, pp. 45–65.

29. Peng Yue (d. 196 BC) was a renowned general during the war between Chu and Han, and was one of the meritorious officials who helped found the Han. He was enfeoffed as Prince of Liang. Along with Han Xin and Ying Bu, he is known as one of the Three Great Generals of the Early Han (*Han chu san damingjiang*). He was originally a fisherman in the lakes and marshes of Juye who fell in with some bandits. After some urging by a group of youths, he became their leader and then rose to prominence in the wars with Chu. Following the establishment of the Han dynasty, he was killed by Liu Bang through the treacherous action of one of his underlings, who had falsely reported that Peng was planning to rebel; although this was not true, Empress Lü realized that Peng had the possibility of posing a threat, so she persuaded Liu Bang to kill him and his entire family anyway. See "Wei Pao and P'eng Yüeh, Memoir 30," in Sima Qian 2008, pp. 35–39.

30. I.e., "I restrain my naturally brilliant talent."

31. While all modern edited texts represent the three words *wo ru jin* as a sung line, the three characters are clearly in reduced size in the original; therefore they are padding words.

Sleep until the sun reaches three notches high on the staff outside
  the window—
True enough, this is a completely free and happy wandering
That far surpasses those ten thousand tax-right marquisates among
  the world of men.

(*Tang xiucai*)
Beneath mountain springs, fine wine pleases the mouth,
In imperial banquets, high-class food stains the hands—
With the life that's left I'll drink down wine.
But you say this coarse old man
And that Marquis of Shouting[32]
Are old friends.

(*Gun xiuqiu*)
You want me to go to the banquet
And urge him to drink several cups;
Can that guy's despicable nature "lose even half a tally"?[33]
No need to ask about what happens after your preparations,
For when he's angry, fresh blood will flow right before our eyes.
You—because of the Nine Prefectures up the Han—[34]
And I—because of one drunken bout at the feast mat—
Both of us will wind up as corpses with separated heads.
If you and I are to be matching guests, then "we'll share the problem
  and worry together,"
You may have ten years of vexation as the guarantor for two separate
  courts,
But what has the old saw, "a single drunk erases an eternity of
  sorrows," to do with me?
As soon as you start to talk about it, my souls fly far, far away.

(*Tang xiucai*)
You might as well bow and welcome him politely,
Kneel down and urge him once and again to drink—
Wait until he eats, then eat; he tilts, then you tilt; he enjoys it, you
  enjoy it.
If he says "east," then you follow him to the east,

---

32. Guan Yu.

33. I.e., "allow even the slightest loss of face, the slightest insult, the slightest loss at
drinking?"

34. I.e., all of the cities held by Guan Yu and Liu Bei that are in the area of the Han and
Yangzi confluence. This is not an actual number, but "nine" often means "several" or "many."

If he says "west," then flow with him to the west.
When he gets drunk, then you flee.

(*Gun xiuqiu*)
He'll utter half a word while he drinks,
And be a quarter of the way drunk by banquet time;
That guy's drunken nature is violent and best not riled up,
Keep your mouth shut and don't press for Jingzhou.
He'll open wide those man-killing eyes,
Lightly stretch out those general-grabbing hands;
He will wrinkle up those recumbent silkworm brows across his face
And then the fierce fire from his five-*skandahs* mountain[35] will be
    hard to contain.
If his body, that mountain of jade, begins to tilt low, then hurriedly
    pour out more wine;
If that precious sword of his leaves its case,
Then get ready to offer up your head—
You will turn over to him those eighty commanderies and prefectures
    of Wu for free.

(*Tang xiucai*)
You say that Grandee Lu of Eastern Wu, benevolent elder brother,
    will strike,
But all that is needed is for Master Zhuge Liang of Western Shu to
    open his mouth
And petition that Imperial Uncle of Han[36] whose benevolent
    compassion is as deep as the sea.
With a strum of his zither, that master can cause the frost and snow
    to fall,
And, thrumming his sword, fill with sorrow the ghosts and spirits—
I'm afraid under those dire circumstances you will be unable to act.

(*Gun xiuqiu*)
Huang Hansheng is as fierce as a tiger;[37]
Zhao Zilong's gall is as big as a peck measure;
Ma Mengqi is a leader who knows how to kill;

---

35. The five components of a sentient being: form, perception, consciousness, action, knowledge. The first is the physical act of perception; the others are mental qualities related to the heart and mind. Here, of course, the metaphor is one of a volcano of emotions exploding under the influence of drink.

36. Liu Bei.

37. See *Burning the Stores*, n. 23.

One boorish fellow mightily battled nobles from the eighteen routes
    at Tigerkeep Pass,[38]
Riding only a single mighty steed,
Wielding only one eighteen-foot lance.
At Dangyang Slope he roared like thunder,
Scaring into retreat a million savage and armored men of Minister
    Cao.
He shouted one shout and the heavens filled with dust, the bridge
    broke asunder;
He yelled out one yell and violent waves slapped the shore, the water
    flowed backward.
Don't think that group will let you off!

(*Daodao ling*)
If you converge on him with the thumping and pounding sound of
    war drums,[39]
And race on ahead with warhorses with sounding hooves,
Fiercely brutal and vicious he will lift up the sleeves of his battle
    gown,
And it will be hard to rescue yourself from crossing him as his anger
    climbs.
You might as well just go ahead and die,
You might as well just go ahead and die.
Wherever that Green Dragon blade falls, it will slice right through.

(*Coda*)
The bamboo slivers of the feast mat I fear will scratch my hand,
And those tree leaves must be stopped from smashing my head.
He traveled a thousand miles to seek out his two friends,[40]
One horse, a single blade—he occupied the Nine Prefectures;
His person is like a tiger climbing mountains and crossing ranges.
For his horse, he sits astride a dragon that roils the Yangzi and
    muddies the seas.
Lightly lifting Dragon Spring he slew Che Zhou,
Angrily drawing Kunwu he destroyed Wen Chou;
Under the banners and parasols Yan Liang's head was hoisted on a
    sword,
And Cai Yang the hero lost his head in a moment's time.

---

38. The remainder of this song discusses Zhang Fei.
39. This song describes Guan Yu.
40. See Appendix 1, item 7.

My brother,
That man-killer Lord Guan—there's no doubting he will set his hand
    to it.

Exits.

[Act 3]

COMIC *opens one scene.* — AIDE GUAN *opens for one scene.* — COMIC *enters. All exit.*

MALE LEAD, *costumed as* THE GOD[41] *in an informal setting, costumed carrying a horsetail whisk, enters, sits in a fixed position, speaks:*

Just now the empire is split in thirds like a tripod: Lord Cao occupies the Central Plain, the King of Wu occupies the Eastern Part of the Yangzi, and my esteemed elder brother, the Imperial Uncle, occupies Sichuan. I, Guan, was enfeoffed as the King of Jing and I now keep the peace and hold Jingzhou. I have been silently thinking about how swift are the days and months. It has been more than three hundred years since the time of the First Emperor of Qin, and when I begin to ponder about the contestation of Chu and Han, and the plotting of the Grand Enterprise, whether of true king or hegemon, I would never have thought that we would see this day!

    ([ZHONGLÜ MODE:] *Fendie'er*)
    The whole empire was in chaos,
    When Zhou and Qin had just attached themselves to Liu and Xiang:
    To determine the ruler and the minister, far off they pointed to
        Xianyang.[42]
    One "had strength to uproot mountains,"[43]
    One had magnanimity to hold the sea,[44]
    And they both founded their empires at the same time,
    But in those days one ended in the halls of state, the other at Rook
        River,

---

41. This is still Guan Yu; the designation here shows that, at the time the drama was written, he was already apotheosized and worshipped as a god.

42. At the beginning of the campaign to replace the Qin empire, King Huai of Chu told his generals (who included Liu Bang and Xiang Yu), "The first to enter the area Within the Passes will rule as true king there." In other sources, this is written as, "The first to enter Xianyang will rule as true king there." The area Within the Passes is the area west of Hangu Pass, and included Xianyang, the capital of the Qin (northwest of later Chang'an and modern Xi'an).

43. Xiang Yu.

44. Liu Bang.

Because one used the three eminences
And the other quickly executed his eight generals.

(*Zui chunfeng*)
One—a short sword, one body lost;[45]
One—the quieting whip cracked, three times sounded.[46]
I think to myself how ancestor and heirs passed it on to sons and
　　grandsons,
But it was all in vain, in vain.
Xiandi had nothing on which to rely or trust—
Dong Zhuo was neither humane nor righteous
And Lü Bu was too aggressive and impetuous.

(*Shi'er yue*)
In those days, younger brother was in Fanyang[47]
And the elder at Lousang.[48]
I was at Xieliang in Puzhou,
And Zhuge was in Nanyang.
At one moment in time heroes were produced in the four quadrants,
And bound in righteousness were the Imperial Uncle, Guan, and
　　Zhang.

(*Yaomin ge*)
Three visits in a single year to Recumbent Dragon Ridge,
And then the country of the Han was split into three, like a tripod's
　　feet.
My elder brother, designating himself as "The One of Little Virtue,"
　　became the King of Shu,
And I, Guan, with one horse and a single sword, hold Jingzhou and
　　Xiangyang.
This Yangzi—now it's seen many battles,
Just like "The waves behind push those in front,"

(*Shiliu hua*)
As two courts are separated by the Yangzi at Hanyang.[49]
On it is written, "Lu Su invites Yunchang."

---

45. Xiang Yu committed suicide.
46. The whip cracked thrice at the beginning of court to silence all in attendance.
47. Fanyang, also known as Zhuo Commandery, was Zhang Fei's home of registry.
48. Liu Bei's birthplace.
49. This first line is the end of Guan Yu's review of the history leading up to the current moment. The next line probably occurs after a courier delivers the invitation. Stage directions become fewer as the text proceeds.

They will lay out the feast in no ordinary way:
Don't think their "painted hall will be an unusual scene of splendor."
Don't think the phoenix cups will be raised, full of chalcedony-flower
     brew.
He will determinedly set out ricin and arsenic,
And at that tortoiseshell mat he will have his heroic generals arrayed
     in rows—
Don't think he'll let "those dressed up and rouged come forth when
     the feast begins."[50]

(*Dou anchun*)
He is preparing to strike the phoenix and dredge up the dragon,
By setting up nets for the heavens and seines for the earth;
This will be no banquet to treat a guest;
It will be a battlefield for committing murder.
And don't imagine any sincere feelings or a sincere heart,
For he fears nothing about what posterity might say.
But now he has invited me with all due respect,
I will do him the honor of going there in person.

(*Shang xiaolou*)
You say, "He has many soldiers and a wide field of generals,"[51]
That "his men are strong and his horses sturdy."
A real man has a full pair of fists—
If such a man will wager his life,
Ten thousand others together cannot be his match.
You say, "We're separated by the Yangzi,
So when the battle starts,
It will be hard to be by your side when you need us."
I'll have that guy bowing and scraping to escort me onto the boat!

(*Reprise*)
You say, "Strong is the one who strikes first;
Disaster comes to the one who strikes last."
My one hand will grasp his precious belt tight,
My arms I will extend like a gibbon or lemur,
And for a sword I'll pull out my "autumn's frost."
If he has an ambush secretly hidden,

---

50. I.e., the usual accompaniment at the banquet, female entertainers, will be supplanted by
the generals.
51. The reader is directed here to the parallel passage in the palace edition, in which the song
is interlarded with several comments and questions from Guan Yu's son Guan Ping.

I will strongly ward it off.
They are nothing but a passel of foxes and a pack of hounds.
They pale in comparison to that trip alone over a thousand miles,
When I beheaded those generals at the five passes.[52]

(*Kuaihuo san*)
They pale in comparison to taking his nephew to pay respects to the
    King of Ji,
Or leading the August One of Shu's two wives to see him.[53]
At Baling Bridge my spirit swelled mightily
As I sat astride my carved saddle.[54]

(*Baolao'er*)
I had just beheaded Cai Yang in three booms of the drum,
And his blood soaked into the sandy battlefield.
With my sword I plucked up the battle robes and departed from
    Xuchang,
And with one shout I nearly intimidated Minister Cao to death.
To this banquet I go,
Where facing his civilian and military sections
Will be no more than [Liu Bei's] third-month feast at Xiangyang.[55]

(*Ti yindeng*)
Even if he's bravely and mightily staging a scene for battle,
Or has awe-provoking warriors stationed in his tiger tent,
My own courage is more redoubtable than anyone's in Wu.
I will rely on the fact that my horse is like a dragon
And my person like the fierce adamantine guard at temple's gate;
I am not being overweening,
Or overly stubborn,
But just mention a fight and I rub my palms.

(*Manjingcai*)
Let him have capable campaign generals prepared to respond,
Spears and halberds at the ready,

---

52. During his trip after leaving Cao Cao from Yuan Shao's camp to his meeting with Liu Bei and Zhang Fei in the Old City, Guan Yu crossed five major passes and beheaded six generals. The phrase "cross five passes and behead six generals" (*guo wuguan zhan liujiang*) is still an idiom that means "to surmount all difficulties."

53. These two lines still refer to the same trip. The "August One of Shu" refers to Liu Bei by a title he did not yet have at the time of Guan Yu's thousand-mile trek.

54. See Appendix 1, item 7.

55. See note 26.

Flags and lances all aligned,
Ready to fight—
I am the hero of the Three Kingdoms, Yunchang of the Han,
And true it is my powerful spirit stretches for three thousands
     leagues.

(*Liu Qingniang*)
All he will be able to do is to arrange six ranks of golden hairpins,
And have the Court of Transcendents' Sounds[56] play the reeds of
     their ocarina;
They will match the musical patterns of "Music to Bear Up the
     Clouds"[57]
And have the Court of Imperial Entertainments prepare some
     chalcedony liquor.
We will take the hundred flavors of his precious viands . . .[58]
. . . golden cups and jade goblets,
And secretly hide away broad swords and long lances.
I won't even use my third of a blade . . . ,
. . . those esquires clothed in armor.

(*Daohe*)
I estimate,
I estimate,
That Zijing[59] of Eastern Wu has . . .
. . .
He will not yield politely to us, to us,
And will uselessly torment, torment, us.
This Dragon Spring of mine . . .
. . .
. . . all because we contest over the border,
You'll see my obstinate visage,
That makes anyone scared to come close.
. . .
I'll make his, make his spirit die,

---

56. The Court of Transcendents' Sounds (*Xianyin yuan*) was established in the early part of
the Yuan dynasty as an administrative office for musicians. Its name was changed later to the
Court of the Jade Palace (*Yuchen yuan*); here it is used anachronistically as a general term for the
office that administers court music.

57. The name of a song from the most ancient times, attributed to the time of the Yellow
Emperor.

58. The ellipsis marks indicate where the original edition has torn-away portions of the page.

59. Lu Su.

And that clump of gauzy silks as bloody as the stew pot of torture.
Look . . .
And slay so long that the corpses of the dead will fill up the Yangzi at
   Hanyang.

(*Coda*)
This will surely be no Duke Mu of Qin and the meeting of Lintong,[60]
Or that hegemon-king of Chu at the meeting at Goosegate.[61]
Even if those guests who fill the seats are all generals "first to the
   front,"
It will be no match for that round of brawling when I dismounted to
   stab Yan Liang in the midst of myriad troops.[62]

[Act 4]

AIDE GUAN *speaks, stops.* — COMIC *enters, speaks.* — . . . — MALE LEAD, *costumed as* THE GOD *in an informal setting,* [*enters,*] *leading* SOLDIERS, *and* [*acts out*] *sitting on the boat.* — . . . — You are nothing! [*Sings:*]

([SHUANGDIAO MODE:] *Xinshui ling*)
"The Great River flows east," *waves piled a thousand high,*[63]
Leading on these tens of men, plying this little leaf of a boat.
It cannot compare to the dragon-and-phoenix pylons of the nine
   rings of the imperial capital.
Truly it is a *deep cave full of thousands of tigers and wolves.*
But a real man's heart is different than others—
I see this single-sword meeting simply as a local village sacrifice at the
   altar of earth.

(*Zhuma ting*)
Water surges, mountains rise in layers—
Where is young Zhou Lang now?
Don't you sense how the "ashes fly and the smoke disappears?"

60. An incident that occurs only in popular literature, this is the story of Duke Mu of Qin who desired to take into possession the land of seventeen liege lords. Under the pretext of a competition of each state's treasures, he assembled the seventeen lords at Lintong (in Shaanxi). The Chu envoy, Wu Zixu, overawed the duke by lifting a heavy bronze tripod. The duke then ordered his soldiers to seize the liege lords. Wu Zixu drew his sword and threatened the duke, who was forced to reconcile with the lords.

61. See *Xiangyang Meeting,* n. 20.

62. See Appendix 1, item 7.

63. Sections are missing due to torn pages in the Yuan edition; italicized text indicates portions that have been recovered from the palace edition.

Poor Huang Gai, who has become only painful sighs!
The masts and prows of the defeated Cao were all destroyed at once,
And the River's water that bore that heavy battle is still hot.
This makes me heartfelt miserable:
The blood of heroes that has flowed without cease for twenty years.[64]

(*Feng ru song*)
Literary skill, ethical action and ...
...
... state can be told without cease.
Speak of "So many heroes from that single time."
In the hundred years of a man's life ...
... is no exaggeration.

(*Hushiba*)
As soon as one state arises,
Another reign just disappears:
Where are the five ministers of Shun?[65] The three eminences of Han?
Our two courts have been separated these many years,
And when we finally see each other
We have already grown old.
Let us drink a few cups to our hearts' content.
And hope with whole heart to laugh the night long.

(*Qing dongyuan*)
You have treated me well
And set out this feast—
But forcing past into present and present into past *like this*
Idly brings on unexpected frustration.
High-blown phrases and "Confucius says" or "the Odes read"—
Talking like this you should have your *mouth split open and your*
       tongue cut out!
Speaking of Sun and Liu like this
Turns them quickly into Wu and Yue![66]

---

64. The song provides a description of the famous battle at Red Cliff at which Cao Cao was vanquished.

65. Confucius, *Analects* 8.20, mentions that Shun had five ministers (see Slingerland 2003, pp. 84–85). According to tradition as represented in Zhu Xi's commentary to the *Four Books*, and in the Yuan daily life common book, *The Expansive Record of a Forest of Things* (*Shilin guangji*), these were the legendary, semimythical figures, Yu, Ji, Qi, Gaoyao, and Boyi.

66. Two states in constant conflict during the Spring and Autumn era; the phrase is commonly used to indicate lifelong bitter adversaries.

(*Chenzui dongfeng*)
When I consider how our Exalted Progenitor of the Han plotted the
    enterprise of true king and hegemon,
How Guangwu of the Han held fast to the upright and expelled the
    deviant,[67]
How the August Emperor of Han slew Dong Zhuo,
And the August *Uncle of the Han extinguished the Marquis of*
    Wen—[68]
By all that's right, an imperial relative should carry on the founding
    enterprise of the Han.
And more simply, how is that Son of Heaven of Wu, *Sun Quan*
Related in any way to our house of Liu?
Please, Mr. Lack of Manners, explain it yourself!

(*Yan'er luo*)
All because of your three-inch never-tiring tongue,
You've angered my three feet of unfeeling steel.
         This steel—
Hungry, it feasts on the heads of major generals;
Thirsty, it drinks the blood of enemies.

(*Desheng ling*)
It's a dragon hibernating in the scabbard,
A tiger slumped at the banquet mat.
We old friends have just met;
Don't cause a rift between us brothers now.
         I'm here,
Listening.
You, Grandee Lu, don't be so cowardly!
Indeed, you are seduced by evil. . . .
Don't take it amiss that I'm so drunk.

(*Jiao zhengpa*)
Noisy soldiers are arranged in ranks—
Don't block those rushing on; don't intercept them!
I'll make everything red beneath my sword
And blood will flow before your eyes.
You may be as treacherous as Zhao Dun

---

67. He defeated the troops of the Xin dynasty, a short-lived interregnum established by the usurper Wang Mang, and restored the house of Liu as the Eastern Han dynasty.

68. I.e., Lü Bu, defeated not just by Liu Bei, but by Liu Bei and Cao Cao together.

But I will end up as satiated as Ling Zhe.[69]
You can't use that long tongue and lying mouth of yours;
You've said everything you have to say.
> When a real man gets angry, there's nothing else to bring up. Come on,[70]
Escort me to my boat with all your heart,[71]
And I will take my leave from you, at ease.

(*Li tingyan dai xiepo Coda*)
I see my men lined up with their purple robes and silver belts;
The evening is cool, the wind chill; reed flowers fall,
And I am completely delighted
To see how the dark and gloomy evening sunset gathers in,
Cold and whistling the River's wind picks up,
Snapping and flapping the sails quicken.
You have treated us most graciously,
So please accept our lavish gratitude.
Tell the sailors to go slowly for a while;
Already the tether is released to set adrift the clouds beside the bank;
As the boat splits the waves among the billows
The oars rend asunder the moon in the River's heart.
Conversations of dispute never end,
But drinking parties last day and night.
The affairs of these two states should be done with.
You failed to soothe your elder brother's heart;
You can't do away with the standard of the house of Han.

---

69. Once when Zhao Dun, a minister who was a thorn in the side of an evil usurper named Tu'an Gu, made a trip to the countryside, he observed a large man lying on his back beneath a mulberry tree with his mouth open. The man explained that he was a farmhand but that he had such a voracious appetite that no one was willing to hire him. As a result he was starving, but because he did not want to be accused of stealing, he had laid himself down under the tree, waiting for the mulberries to drop into his mouth. Zhao Dun thereupon provided him with a decent meal. Later, Tu'an Gu trained a dog, the Demon Mastiff, to attack Zhao Dun in court. When the attack came, Zhao Dun tried to flee, but the Duke had earlier arranged to have one of Zhao's chariot wheels loosened. When the wheel came free, Ling Zhe jumped forward to carry the axle on his shoulder, allowing Zhao Dun to escape for the moment.

70. We have deviated from our normal practice here. The characters in this line are full size, but they are clearly inserted speech.

71. Perhaps here Guan Yu has grabbed Lu Su and forces him to come with him on his boat as his prisoner. That would have been the only way to ensure a safe escape. There is no indication here that Guan Ping and others come to his rescue as in the palace edition. This may explain the final scene: as soon as Guan Yu has arrived safely on the other side of the river, he proceeds to have Lu Su executed.

❄❄[72]

(*Gu meijiu*)
You, Lu Zijing, are a man without reason:
When you invited me to come to your feast,
Who thought you—with cur-like actions and wolf-like heart—
  would ply your plans?
You had robbed me of my armed horsemen that charge the enemy
  lines. . . .
I have him now, and how shall I deal with him?

(*Taiping ling*)
Bind him tightly with a hempen rope and submit him to an
  investigation,
Then turn him over to those violent Guanxi bodyguards, who love to
  kill,
Use knife- and axe-men and carry out the execution out as fast as you
  can.
Prepare now that bronze cudgel, as big as a peck measure,
And hold the hair on his head tight.
Wait until [his shins] have been broken apart
Then pound his thighs into a pulp—
That still won't cut off this rancor in my heart!

THEME: Old Lord Qiao remonstrates with the Emperor of Wu;
    Sima Hui quits his position and lives in retirement;
    Lu Zijing presses for the return of Jingzhou:
    The Great King Guan and the single-sword meeting.

A Complete Edition Newly Published in Old Hangzhou: *The Great King Guan
and the Single Sword Meeting*

---

72. What follows is a short set of songs that constitute a final demi-act. The exact function
of the section is discussed in the introduction to this play.

Dramatis personæ in order of appearance

Role type	Name and family, institutional, or social role
Opening male	Lu Su
Male lead	Qiao Guolao
Soldier	Gate guard at Lu Su's headquarters
Male lead	Sima Hui
Acolyte	Sima Hui's apprentice and servant
Male lead	Guan Yu
Guan Ping	Guan Ping, Guan Yu's elder son and aide
Guan Xing	Guan Xing, Guan Yu's younger son
Zhou Cang	Zhou Cang, general under Guan Yu's command
Huang Wen	Huang Wen, messenger from Lu Su
Zang Gong	Zang Gong, Lu Su's music master
Armored soldiers	Soldiers lying in ambush at the banquet by Lu Su's order
Group of generals	Guan Yu's generals under Guan Ping's command

A Single Sword Meeting
Guan Hanqing of the Yuan
(From a Ming Palace Edition)

[Act 1]

OPENING MALE, [*costumed as*] LU SU, *enters, speaks:*

> Three feet of Dragon Spring, ten thousand documents,
> Heaven gave me birth, but for what reason?
> Ministers from Shandong, generals from Shanxi,[73]
> They are stout fellows, O, but I am too.[74]

I am Lu Su, also known as Lu Zijing, and hold the position of Central Grandee under the aegis of our King of Wu.[75] In those days, I recall, after lord Sun Quan occupied the lower reaches of the Yangzi, Cao Cao, King of Wei, occupied the Central Plain, and Liu Bei, King of Shu, occupied central Sichuan, he occupied our Jingzhou—precisely the place where intersecting military forces are always in play[76]—and held it firmly without worry. This is how the subcelestial realm

---

73. From the eulogy (*zan*) to "The Biographies of Zhao Chongguo and Xin Qingji" (*Zhao Chongguo Xin Qingji zhuan*) in the *Documents of the Han*, "From the time of the Qin and Han, east of [Hua] mountain has produced ministers; west of the mountain has produced generals." Huashan is located thirty-five miles east of Xi'an. This has, of course, a secondary reference to Lu Su, a minister from east of Huashan and Guan Yu, a general from west of Huashan. See Ban Gu 1962, vol. 4, p. 2998.

74. From *Mencius* 5.4: "They are stout fellows; I am also a stout fellow; what do I have to fear from them?"

75. Sun Quan (182–252) was from Fuchun, modern Fuyang in Zhejiang. Known first as the King of Wu, he proclaimed himself Emperor of Wu in 229 at Wuchang (modern Echeng in Hubei). He moved the capital quickly to Jinling (modern Nanjing).

76. From the "Biography of Zhuge Liang" (*Zhuge Liang zhuan*) in the *Records of the Three Kingdoms* (*Sanguo zhi*): "To the north Jingzhou occupies the Han and Mian rivers [i.e., the middle and lower reaches of the Han River], for its benefit it exhausts all of the southern seas, in the east it connects to Wu and Kuai [the southern part of modern Jiangsu and the northern part of modern Zhejiang], and west it connects to Ba and Shu [modern Sichuan]; this is a state where military power can be used." Jingzhou, one of the thirteen provinces of the Eastern Han, covered all of modern Hubei and Hunan, and portions of modern Henan, Guizhou, Guangzhou, and

is turned into the legs of a tripod vessel. I reflect on how Zhou Yu died on that day at Jiangling[77] and I persuaded our ruler to temporarily give Jingzhou to Liu Bei, vouching for him, so that we might join forces to repel Cao Cao. In addition, our ruler also married off his younger sister to Liu Bei. I never expected that fellow to pretend to be close but inside be so distant from us, to take Yizhou[78] by his clever plan and so swallow up all of the middle reaches of the Han River. He certainly has the ambition of ruling by force to rise to power. Now I want to ask for the return of Jingzhou, but considering that Lord Guan now occupies the place, it is certain that he will not be willing to turn it over. I've sent Huang Wen to first lay out three plans in order to enlighten our ruler by telling him this: Lord Guan has military acumen that goes far beyond others, he has a desire to incorporate Jingzhou into Shu and, because he occupies the River upstream from our state, we had better ask for Jingzhou's return. The first plan: taking advantage of the fact that Sun Quan and Liu Bei are now related through marriage and are to each as other as teeth to lips, we should set out a feast on the bank of the River, compose a letter, and ask Lord Guan to come to the feast on the bank of the River to celebrate our recent defeat of Cao Cao, Liu Bei's recent claim to be ruler of Central Han, and to praise the beauty of his own merit. This man will suspect nothing and while we are in the midst of the feast, we will press for Jingzhou's return with all due ritual respect. If he returns it to us, then this is the perfect plan. The second plan: we will confiscate all of the warships on the River and not let Lord Guan return across the River. As his detention grows longer and longer, he will come to realize that he has fallen into my trap, and filled with silent regret, he will return Jingzhou to us with a sincere heart. And if he still doesn't return it. . . . The third plan: I will conceal armored soldiers among the arras, and when he is tipsy, I will strike a metal gong as a signal, and the troops lying in ambush will all arise and capture Lord Guan and place him in captivity here on the bank of the River. This man is Liu Bei's right hand, and if Jingzhou is returned to River's East, then we can let Lord Guan go back to Yizhou. If he doesn't, then once the lord and his general have both been lost, the leaderless armies will surely revolt, and we can seize this opportunity to begin a great campaign, and Jingzhou will be taken in a single drumbeat. What possible difficulty could there be in this? Even though these three plans are set, I had better have Huang Wen invite Lord Qiao to come and discuss it with me.

Guangxi. The major city of Jingzhou was Xiangyang, but the action of the play is set at Jiangling, located on the Yangzi close to the confluence of the Yangzi and the Han.

77. See *Burning the Stores*, n. 25.
78. The area of Sichuan around modern Chengdu.

MALE LEAD, [*costumed as*] QIAO GUOLAO, *enters and speaks:* — I am the aged Lord Qiao. It appears that now the three-way split of tripod legs is all set: Cao Cao has occupied the Central Plain, Sun Quan has occupied River's East, and Liu Bei has occupied Western Shu. But consider that, before Liu Bei had become successful, he asked us, the house of Eastern Wu for the loan of Jingzhou to be his base, and he hasn't returned it yet. Lu Su is always thinking about getting it back, but he is still mired in doubt and hasn't started anything yet. He sent someone today to summon me for some reason. I'd better go. Just think about it; who could have considered that the subcelestial realm of the house of Han would have ever deteriorated to this point? — *Sings:*

> (XIANLÜ MODE: *Dian jiangchun*)
> I was originally a minister of the state of Han.
> The August One of Han was weak and ineffectual,
> Which triggered minds to create trouble
> And stirred up weapons of war:
> We swallowed up Dong Zhuo and finished off Yuan Shao,
>
> (*Hunjiang long*)
> And left behind Sun, Liu, and Cao
> To split one state equally into three separate courts.
> The rivers are just now clear, the seas peaceful;
> The rains are timely and the winds just right.
> Weapons have been turned to use as farming tools,
> Battle standards no longer wave, the wineshop flags flutter.
> Armies have ceased warfare
> And horses grow fat and sleek;
> The ethers of killing have all dispersed;
> The clouds of formations now rise high,
> Those who were generals and colonels
> Became civil officials,
> Shedding metal armor
> And donning robes of silk.
> In front of their tents, banners are furled—the tiger curls about the
>   flagstaff;
> At their waists swords are put away—the dragon returns to its sheath.
> Men are strong, horses sturdy,
> But the generals are seasoned, the soldiers proud.

Speak: — Here I am, already. Servants, report that Father of the State Qiao has arrived. — SOLDIER *reports, speaks:* I am reporting to you, sir: Lord Qiao has arrived. — LU *speaks:* Tell him he is welcome. — SOLDIER *speaks:* Venerable

sir, please. MALE LEAD *greets* LU, *speaks:* — What have you summoned me for
today, sir? LU *speaks:* — I have asked you here today for nothing else but to
discuss this affair of claiming Jingzhou. MALE LEAD *speaks:* By no means can
Jingzhou be claimed. Just think how fierce Guan Yunchang is. If you press for
Jingzhou, how will his brothers ever let you so sweetly off? — LU *speaks:* His
brothers may be many, but his troops are insignificant and his generals few and
far between. — MALE LEAD *sings:*

> (*You hulu*)
> You say, "His brothers might be many, but his troops and generals are
> few."

Speak: Sir, do you know about that affair of burning the stores at Bowang? —
LU *speaks:* — No, I don't. Tell me about it.

> Seriously, he* put Xiahou Dun in real straits there.[79]

Speak: Sir, do you know about matching wits across the River? — LU *speaks:*
— Well, I know about matching wits across the River, but I don't know it well.
Try me out. MALE LEAD *sings:*

> Know that Zhou Yu and Jiang Gan were friends as commoners,
> But that right-hand minister Zhuge put into play his military tactics,
> And completely destroyed that "plot that sacrifices one's body" when
>   Huang Gai augmented Cao's grain and fodder.

Speak: That fierce battle at Red Cliff was a field of slaughter. LU *speaks:* — I
know it was, but tell it all once again. MALE LEAD *speaks:*

> They burned and broke bow and crossbow like tattered reeds,
> Torched all of the flags and banners like so much firewood;
> Half-clear, half-concealed the flower-patterned drums,[80]
> Hither and thither the crouching-animal shields.
> Still saddled and bridled, horses burnt to their deaths,
> Robed and armored, corpses of the dead.
> Alas! O, the million troops of Cao Cao all defeated,
> So hard for each and every one to escape the calamity of fire or water!

Sings:

> Better than half of that army was burnt in the fire
> And another three of ten floated away on the water;

---

79. An asterisk signals that the corresponding line has a note in the *Thirty Yuan Plays* edition.
This text has emended the line from that edition, and here "he" refers to Guan Yu.

80. I.e., drums to signal during battle.

If it were not for the fact that "Heaven dispatches those who possess
the Way to attack those who don't."*
Then in this moment the state of Wu would have belonged completely to Cao.

LU *speaks:*

Cao Cao a hero, his wisdom and tactics high above the mark,
Suppressed a rebellion but overstepped his authority to usurp the court
of Han;
He wished to capture Liu Bei in the Palace of Eternal Peace,[81]
And lock away the two Qiao lovelies in the Palace of the Bronze
Sparrow.

[MALE LEAD *sings:*]

(*Tianxia le*)
You say, "Spring grows deep in Bronze Sparrow where he wanted to
lock away the two Qiaos";*
But these three states have just established relations.
Let it not be "A mistake of a single day becomes a mistake for an
entire generation!"

LU *speaks:* We have a million heroic troops here and a thousand battle-tested
generals. I see nothing to worry about with him! [MALE LEAD *sings:*]

You want to exercise the Way of rule by force,*
And start a new war.

LU *speaks:* I calculate that Guan Yunchang is on in years; he may be brave, but
he is ineffectual. MALE LEAD *sings:*

Don't chide Guan Yunchang because he is on in years. . . .

Speaks: Let me tell you how he gathered in Western Shu. LU *speaks:* I haven't
heard about how he gathered in Western Shu; go ahead. MALE LEAD *sings:*

(*Nezha ling*)
He took in White Emperor City in Western Shu
And sent Zhou Yu to his death.
Then alongside the Han stretch of the river was Zhang Yide,
To block Zhou's corpse from return,*

---

81. The Palace of Eternal Peace, or Yong'an Palace (*Yong'an gong*), was constructed in White
Emperor City by Liu Bei in 222. Liu had been defeated in a major battle and withdrawn to
Yong'an, where he built a palace. He passed away from illness the next year.

And Grandee Lu, in the prow of the boat, was almost felled by fright.
If you want to contest for that stretch of earth that is Jingzhou,
Guan Yunchang will raise hell when he hears about it
And then he'll let the wind and hailstones fall where they may!

LU *speaks, stops:* What skills does he have to rely on? MALE LEAD *sings:*

> (*Que ta zhi*)
> He slew Wen Chou, displaying his rash temperament,
> Stabbed Yan Liang, displaying his heroic bravery.*
> He went into that army of a million men
> And on his pike lightly lifted aloft the heads of those he slew.

LU *speaks:* But, consider the favor I showed Liu Bei at the battle of Red Cliff.
MALE LEAD *sings:*

> At that time he looked just fine,
> But in his eager joy a knife was hidden in his smile.

LU *speaks:* If he gives me Jingzhou, then all's fine; but if he doesn't give me Jingzhou, then I'll fell him in a single drumbeat. MALE LEAD *speaks:* And should
you raise your troops . . .

> (*Jisheng cao*)
> It's always been the case that "Heaven has no calamities,"
> "Men bring disaster upon themselves."
> If you are completely unwilling to bestow grace, display virtue, effect
>   the Way of the true ethical king,
> How can you hope to compare to that heroic Cao Cao, so full of
>   plans and wisdom?
> You have to know that Zhuge Liang from Nanyang will be hard to
>   figure out.

LU *speaks:* If he doesn't give it to me, then I'll take Jingzhou by force with an
overpowering strike by men and horse. MALE LEAD *sings:*

> You just want to confront a thousand armies and ten thousand
>   horses to grapple in some awful fight
> And have absolutely no concern for the millions of souls who will
>   suffer this terrible violence.

LU *speaks:* I've never met this man. Venerable sir, please tell me what his fero-
ciousness is like. MALE LEAD *speaks:* Well, when he goes into battle, he relies
on that horse beneath him, the sword in his hand, and the generals in their
saddles—he has a bravery that ten thousand men dare not confront. — *Sings:*

(*Jinzhan'er*)
When he goes into battle, his three-braid beautiful beard whistles in
  the wind,
His ten-foot lion-tiger body shakes mightily,
And he's just like a living god held aloft in a crowd of the six Ding
  spirits.[82]
And if the enemy armies see him,
They are so scared that their seven earthly souls disperse
And their five cloud souls vanish.

MALE LEAD *speaks:* And if you are going to fight him to the death . . . — *Sings:*

You had better pull on several suits of armor
And add on several layers of battle robes.
Had you even an army of a million,
You could not withstand his racing thousand-mile courser that
  chases the wind,
And had you a thousand generals
You could not avoid his third-of-the-length blade shaped like the
  crescent moon.

LU *speaks:* — Venerable sir, you do not know that I have three marvelous plans
to press for Jingzhou. — MALE LEAD *speaks:* Which three? — LU *speaks:* — The
first plan: taking advantage of the fact that Sun Quan and Liu Bei are now
related through marriage and are to each as other as teeth to lips, we should set
out a feast at on the bank of the River, compose a letter, and ask Lord Guan to
come to the feast on the bank of the River to celebrate our recent defeat of Cao
Cao, Liu Bei's recent claim to be ruler of Central Han, and to praise the beauty
of his own merit. This man will suspect nothing and while we are in the midst
of the feast; we will press for Jingzhou's return with all due ritual respect. If he
comes across the river to the feast, then with all ritual respect, I will press for
it during the banquet. If he returns it to us, then this is the perfect plan. If he
doesn't, then there's the second plan: we will confiscate all of the warships on
the River and not let Lord Guan return across the River. As his detention grows
longer and longer, he will come to realize himself that he has fallen into my
trap, and filled with silent regret, he will return Jingzhou to us with a sincere
heart. And if he still doesn't return it . . . The third plan: I will conceal armored
soldiers among the arras, and when he is tipsy, I will strike a metal gong as a

---

82. The six Ding spirits of the sexagenary cycle: *dingmao, dingsi, dingwei, dingyou, dinghai,*
and *dingchou.* These are six yin spirits sent by the heavenly thearc when summoned by Daoist
talismans to dispel evil influences.

signal, and the troops lying in ambush will all arise and capture Lord Guan and place him in captivity here on the bank of the River. This man is Liu Bei's right hand, and if Jingzhou is returned to River's East, then we can let Lord Guan go back to Yizhou. If he doesn't, then once the Lord and his general have both been lost, the leaderless armies will surely revolt, and we can seize this opportunity to begin a great campaign. Jingzhou will be taken in a single drumbeat. How hard can it be? These three plans are truly hard to escape. — MALE LEAD *speaks:* — You give three plans, but even if you had a thousand you couldn't come close to him. — *Sings:*

> (*Jinzhan'er*)
> You say, "These three plans are truly hard to escape,"
> But a single sentence is hard to countenance—
> You can use neither a military officer's crudeness nor a civil official's
>   craftiness.

LU *speaks:* What is Lord Guan like when he's drunk? — MALE LEAD [*sings:*]

> When he's drunk, that guy's violent nature manifests a heroic
>   bravery;
> Snicker-snack he'll grab your jeweled belt
> And quick as a blink raise up his steel blade.

LU *speaks:* I'll tie up all of the war boats along the bank. — MALE LEAD *sings:*

> You say you'll tie up the war boats along the bank.

Speaks: If he wants to go back, well then on his behalf . . .

> You might as well use them to make a floating bridge across the
>   river's surface.

LU *speaks:* — Venerable sir, there's no need to keep on going from argument to argument. I have my own wonderful tactics and marvelous tricks to take advantage of this opportunity; there's no way Jingzhou won't be returned. — MALE LEAD *speaks:* Sire, how do these three plans compare with those three of Cao Cao at Baling Bridge? No way could he escape from Guan Yunchang's hands. — LU *speaks:* I don't know about that, tell me the story. — MALE LEAD *sings:*

> (*Coda*)
> Minister Cao held up the stirrup cup to send him on his way;
> The gifts for his trip were piled in a platter,
> And it worried both nephew and sister-in-law to death.
> Cao Cao was guileful and could make himself humble,
> But was Guan Yunchang "good at gracious interaction"?

He got to Baling Bridge early,
And nearly scared Xu Chu and Zhang Liao to death.
He reined in his wind-chasing steed,
And casually twirled his crescent-moon blade.
Cao Cao may have had a thousand kinds of ideas,
But they turned into no more than a joke.

Speaks: Guan Yunchang said, "Please forgive me, Prime Minister Cao, but I am not going to get off my horse." — *Sings:*

With the tip of his blade he plucked up that brocade travel robe.*

Exits.

LU *speaks:* Huang Wen, did you see how Lord Qiao explained the overweening awesomeness of Lord Guan? I am not ready to believe it yet. There is a worthy man here in Jiang Xia, named Sima Wei, also known as Decao. He has a passing acquaintance with Lord Guan. Go and ask him to be a "pairing guest" at our banquet so we can inquire about Lord Guan's wisdom, bravery, tactics, and strategies as well as what he is like when he is drunk. Huang Wen, go with me now to Sima's hut to make our visit.

Exits.

[Act 2]

MALE LEAD, *costumed as* SIMA HUI, *enters, leading* DAOIST ACOLYTE. MALE LEAD *speaks:* I, this humble Daoist, am Sima Hui, known as Decao, and I bear the Daoist sobriquet of Master Water Mirror. Now the subcelestial realm of the house of Han has been split into three, each a leg of a tripod. Since I departed from Imperial Uncle Liu, many years have passed. I have knotted together a hut of grass here in Jiang Xia where I cultivate my actions and work on Daoist techniques. It's such freedom!

([ZHENGGONG MODE:] *Duanzheng hao*)
I was originally a man who "fished out giant turtles,"*
But have turned into a codger who grasps the plow—
I scoff at Ying Bu,* Peng Yue,* and Marquis Han.
Now I tightly clasp my two cloud-supporting hands,*
And will never let them out of the sleeves of my hempen gown again.

(*Gun xiuqiu*)
I just want to assemble all the old village codgers,
Meet up with poetic friends;

I enjoy fresh fish and new wine,
Even in earthenware begging bowls and ceramic mugs.
We push the stemmed cups forward, never changing the cups,
And clap our own hands for loud songs.
Let time pass in its day and night, shadows and sunlight;
For when I'm drunk that patchy quilt will cover my head.
Under that low little window I'll sleep until the sun is three notches
    high on the staff—
True enough, this is a completely free and happy wandering
That far surpasses those ten thousand tax-right marquisates among
    the world of men.

Speak: Acolyte, keep watch at the gate and see if anyone comes by. — ACOLYTE *speaks:* Understood. — LU SU *enters, speaks:* Here I am, already. Take my horse. *Acts out greeting the* ACOLYTE. — LU *speaks:* Is your master here, acolyte? — ACOLYTE *speaks:* My master is here. — LU *speaks:* Go say that Lu Zijing has come especially to pay him a visit. — ACOLYTE *speaks:* You are Mr. Rattan?[83] You are always in a clump with Pinewood. I'll go report to the master. — *Sees* MALE LEAD, *speaks:* You, master, you son of a . . .[84] — MALE LEAD *speaks:* Where does this scoundrel get off cursing me? ACOLYTE *speaks:* — I'm not cursing you. The master is the master and the disciple, just like his real son. Master, son of a disciple . . . — MALE LEAD *speaks:* This scoundrel is full of nonsense. Who is at the door? — ACOLYTE *speaks:* Lu Zijing has come especially to pay you a visit. — MALE LEAD *speaks:* Tell him to come in. — ACOLYTE *speaks:* Understood. — ACOLYTE *goes out to see* LU, *speaks:* Come in. — LU *acts out greeting* MALE LEAD. MALE LEAD *speaks:* Accept my bow. — LU *speaks:* I have been too long in the vulgar bustle, and have not heard your instructions for a long time. — MALE LEAD *speaks:* — We haven't seen each other in years; where are you off to today? — LU *speaks:* — I wouldn't have come for nothing. I want to personally invite you to a meeting at Jiang Xia. — MALE LEAD *speaks:* — I have been cultivating my actions here in Jiang Xia, just a man beyond the human realm. What virtue or capability do I have to bring you so much trouble as to setting out a feast? — *Sings:*

(*Tang xiucai*)
I never dropped my hook on the bank of Panxi Stream,
    Grandee;

83. Making a pun on his name, Zijing, which is a homophone for the rattan vine.
84. The word *dizi* was the common term for "disciple," but in the theater world that term was used to refer to prostitutes. So the term *dizi hai'er* was understood to mean that particular kind of bastard raised by a prostitute and was directed more at a person's mother than the person.

How can I be lucky enough to taste your high-class food and fine
  wine?
I just want to emulate Xu You[85] amid streams and mountains.

Speaks: — Grandee, who else have you invited besides me? — LU *speaks:* —
There are no other guests, except for your old friend the Marquis of Shouting,
Guan Yunchang. MALE LEAD *speaks:* — Sings:

You say that my old acquaintance the Marquis of Shouting* and I are
  good friends.

Speaks: — If Lord Guan is going to be there, then I've got a quick case of the
crazies. I'm not able to go! Can't go! LU *speaks:* — When you first learned of Lu
Su's invitation, you already assented. Now that you know Lord Guan will be
there, you decline with all your strength. Why won't you go? You have a slight
friendship with Lord Guan; it's just to help toast him at the feast. — MALE
LEAD *sings:*

(*Gun xiuqiu*)
    Sire,
You want me to urge on several cups at the banquet.
Will that guy's despicable nature "allow even the loss of half a tally"? *

LU *speaks:* — To entreat someone with wine carries no evil intent. MALE LEAD
sings:

Well then, don't bring up setting out wine and meat,
For when he's angry, fresh blood will flow right before our eyes.
You—because of the Nine Prefectures up the Han—*
And I—because of one drunken bout at the feast mat—
    You, sir, and I—
Both of us will wind up as corpses with separated heads.

LU *speaks:* — You'll be a guest; what do you have to worry about? — MALE LEAD
sings:

If I'm to be a guest, won't I have to share the same problems and
  anxieties as you?

LU *speaks:* — I have three plans by which to press for Jingzhou. — MALE LEAD
sings:

Just because of your three plans to establish a thousand years of
  personal merit,

---

85. See *Burning the Stores*, n. 11.

That old saw, "a single drunk erases an eternity of cares," won't apply
   to me—
When you bring this up, my souls fly far, far away.

LU *speaks:* Since he's an old friend, what's the problem with sharing a banquet?
— MALE LEAD *speaks:* Sire, if you are set on inviting Yunchang, then invite him
only on these three conditions of mine. If you won't abide by them, then don't
invite him. — LU *speaks:* — Spell them out and I'll listen. — MALE LEAD *speaks:*
According to my explanation, when Yunchang gets off his horse . . . — *Sings:*

(*Tang xiucai*)
You and I should bow and welcome him politely.

Speaks: — Can you do that? — LU *speaks:* When Yunchang gets off his horse,
I'll bow and welcome him politely. No problem. I can do it. — MALE LEAD
sings:

Sire, we should kneel down and urge him once and again to drink—
When he drinks, we drink; he eats, we eat; he enjoys it, we enjoy it.
If he says "east," then follow him east,
If he says "west," then flow with him to the west.

Speaks: And this is most important:

If he gets drunk, then you and I will run off together.

LU *speaks:* — Master, what is Lord Guan's conduct like after he gets drunk?
— MALE LEAD *sings:*

(*Gun xiuqiu*)
He'll have but a word before he drinks,
And be a quarter of the way drunk by banquet time;
His drunken nature is violent and best not riled up.
If you open your mouth, then don't press for Jingzhou.

LU *speaks:* — What's to keep me from pressing for Jingzhou? — MALE LEAD
speaks: — If he hears you are asking for Jingzhou . . . — *Sings:*

He'll open wide those cinnabar phoenix pupils,
Lightly stretch out those general-grabbing hands;
He will wrinkle up those recumbent silkworm brows
And the fierce fire from his five-*skandahs* mountain* will be hard to
   contain.
If his body, that mountain of jade, begins to tilt low,
Then prepare yourself to flee;
If that precious sword of his leaves its case,

Then get ready to offer up your head.
And for nothing you will turn over to him those eighty-one commanderies and prefectures of Wu.

LU *speaks:* — You shouldn't worry so much about it; I reckon he is more than
brave, but his thinking is lacking. When he gets here, I'll have armored soldiers
hidden between the arras to catch Lord Guan. Even if he glues on wings, he
won't be able to fly across the Yangzi. I am just after "the first one to strike is the
stronger." — MALE LEAD *speaks:* Sire, I don't think you'll ever get close to him.

(*Tang xiucai*)
When it comes time that you, Grandee Lu of Eastern Wu, strike,
All that is needed is for Master Zhuge Liang of Western Shu to open
his mouth
And petition that Imperial Uncle of Han whose virtuous actions are
compassionate and humane.
With a strum of his zither, that master can cause the frost and snow
to fall,
And, thrumming his sword, make the ghosts and spirits sorrowful—
I'm afraid under those dire circumstances you will be unable to act.

LU *speaks:* I don't think much of Zhuge Liang. Besides him, there's no one else
to go to war. — MALE LEAD *speaks:* Those five brothers, Guan Yunchang and
the others . . . if they find out, there's no letting you off. — LU *speaks:* Which
five? (MALE LEAD *sings:*)

(*Gun xiuqiu*)
One is Huang Hansheng, fierce as a tiger;*
One, Zhao Zilong, whose gall is as big as a peck measure;
There's one Ma Mengqi, a leader who knows how to kill;
One boorish Zhang Fei,
Who mightily battled nobles from the eighteen routes at Tigerkeep
Pass,
Riding only one New Moon Black,
Wielding only one eighteen-foot lance.
At Dangyang Slope he roared like thunder
And scared into retreat a million savage and armored men of
Minister Cao.
He had only to blink, the heavens filled with dust, the bridge broke
asunder;
To yell out once, violent waves slapped the shore, the water flowed
backward.
Don't think that group will let you off!

LU *speaks:* If you are willing to come to the feast, it won't matter if you're together with Lord Guan for a while. — MALE LEAD *speaks:* — Sire. No! It won't work. It won't work. Don't say I didn't try to persuade you! (*Sings:*)

(*Coda*)
I fear the tip of his knife, just scraping, will lightly scar your hand,
And those tree leaves must be stopped from smashing my head.
Guan Yunchang traveled a thousand miles to seek out his two
    friends,*
One horse, a single blade—he occupied the Nine Prefectures,
His person like a tiger climbing mountains and crossing ranges;
For his horse, he sits astride a beast that roils the Yangzi and muddies
    the seas.
Lightly lifting Dragon Spring he slew Che Zhou;
Angrily drawing Kunwu he destroyed Wen Chou;
Under the banners and parasols Yan Liang's head was hoisted on a
    sword,
And Cai Yang the hero lost his head in a moment's time.
This master, for whom there is no right or wrong, will certainly carry
    out what he says,
And that man-killer Yunchang—
            Farewell to you, sir—
There's no doubting he will set his hand to it.

MALE LEAD *exits.*

ACOLYTE *speaks:* — Lu Zijing, you are really blinded by the coarse world, and do not recognize this poor Daoist. If you wanted to take Jingzhou, why didn't you ask me? Guan Yunchang is a good-time buddy of mine. I'll just have him turn over Jingzhou to you as a gift. — LU *speaks:* Well, if your master won't go, you go ahead and go. — ACOLYTE *speaks:* I'll go on down the mountain to the feast. I'll have old Guan offer up Jingzhou to you with both hands. — *Sings:*

(*Gewei*)
All I want is to drag my quinoa staff as I go house to house,
Wear a pair of hempen sandals as I roam from place to place.

Speaks: If I go this time, *Sings:*

I'll cross that Yunchang, that source of everything bad—
Brother Zhou Cang, so keen at combat,
Will come twirling his blade to split my head asunder,
And scare me so much I'll be just like a tortoise tucking in my head
    as I flee into the Bian River.

Exits.

LU *speaks:* — It has made me a little frightened, listening to what that master had to say. But, now that the three plans are set, what do I really have to fear? Huang Wen, take this invitation for me, go straight to Jingzhou, and ask Lord Guan to come. Go and come back as fast as you can, and keep me in the know.

[Act 3]

MALE LEAD, *costumed as* LORD GUAN, *enters, leading* GUAN PING, GUAN XING, ZHOU CANG, *speaks:* I am named Guan Yu, known as Yunchang, and am a man from Xieliang in Puzhou. I am in service to Liu Xuande as his superior general. From the time the empire was divided in three, its shape became like the feet of a tripod: Cao Cao occupied the Central Plain, Sun Ce occupied East of the Yangzi, and my elder brother, Noble Xuande, occupied Western Shu. He had me hold Jingzhou, and I have long fortified it without any problem. I think back to the beginning when Chu and Han vied to see who would come out ahead, and our August One of Han was humane and righteous and used the three eminences; the hegemon-king was brave and heroic but relied on a single man of courage. The three eminences were Xiao He, Han Xin, and Zhang Liang. That courageous one "bellowed out loud and fierce," "lifted tripods and uprooted mountains," and "won seventy or more battles." But still that hegemon ruler found himself in such dire straits that he slit his own throat at Rook River.[86] Gaozu later ascended the throne and the dynasty was passed on until today. But the dynasty fell on hard times and now even finds itself in this state!

> ([ZHONGLÜ MODE:] *Fendie'er*)
> At that time the whole empire was in chaos,
> Zhou and Qin had just attached themselves to Liu and Xiang,
> And ruler and minister would be determined by "the first to reach
>   Xianyang."*
> One "had strength to uproot mountains,"*
> One had magnanimity to hold the sea,*
> And they both founded their worlds at the same time.
> In those days, in the halls of state, at Rook River,
> One made full use of the three eminences,
> And the other slew eight generals.

---

86. The passages in quotations are lifted verbatim from the "Biography of Xiang Yu," in the *Records of the Historian.*

(*Zui chunfeng*)
One—a short sword applied, one body lost;*
One—the quieting whip cracked,* three times sounded,
Ancestor and heirs passing it on to sons and grandsons,
To be enjoyed, today, to be enjoyed.
Xiandi had nothing on which to rely or trust—
Dong Zhuo was neither humane nor righteous.
And Lü Bu was too aggressive and impetuous.

Speaks: — In those days we three brothers bound ourselves in righteousness in the Peach Orchard. We sacrificed a white horse to Heaven, and a black buffalo to Earth. We cannot ask that we were born on the same day, but we all desire to perish at a single moment. — *Sings:*

(*Shi'er yue*)
In those days, younger brother was in Fanyang*
And the elder at Lousang.*
I was at Xieliang in Puzhou,
And Zhuge was in Nanyang.
Simultaneously heroes were produced in the four quadrants,
And bound in righteousness were the Imperial Uncle, Guan, and
    Zhang.

(*Yaomin ge*)
Three visits in a single year to Recumbent Dragon Ridge,
And then the country of the Han house was split like a tripod, three
    feet.
My elder brother claimed to be "The Orphan One," "The One of
    Little Virtue," a peerless man,
And I, Guan, with one horse and a single sword, hold Jingzhou and
    Xiangyang.
This Yangzi—now it's seen many battles,
But true it is, "The waves behind push those in front."

Speaks: — Son, keep watch at the door to see if anyone comes. GUAN PING *speaks:* Understood. — HUANG WEN *enters, speaks:* I am Huang Wen, and I've brought this invitation to Jingzhou, to invite Lord Guan to a banquet. Here I am, already. Servants, report that Huang Wen, the superior general, the "ground-dragging gall"[87] sent by Lu Zijing of Jiang Xia, is here. — PING *speaks:* Wait here. I'll go report. — PING *sees* MALE LEAD, *speaks:* — I wanted to report to you, father, Lu Zijing from River's East has sent a commanding general here

---

87. I.e., his gall, the seat of courage, is so large that it drags on the ground.

with an invitation. — MALE LEAD *speaks:* — Send him in. — PING *speaks:* He wants you to go in. HUANG WEN *acts out greeting him.* — MALE LEAD *speaks:* — Just who are you? HUANG WEN *speaks in a fluster:* — This humble general is Huang Wen. Lu Zijing of River's East has sent me here with an invitation. — LEAD *speaks:* — You go on back. I'll come along later. — HUANG WEN *speaks:* — I'm out the door now. Now that I have seen the godlike countenance of that hero Lord Guan, I feel sad for you, Lu Zijing.

> This humble general Huang Wen
> Came just to invite Lord Guan,
> His beard as long as a foot or two,
> His face as red as the jujube's hue.
> If Green Dragon blade, crescent moon thin
> —Nine times nine, eighty-one *jin*—
> Comes down on this neck of mine,
> Then where would you find Huang Wen?
> If he comes, then we'll have a feast;
> If not, then tofu and wine, three catties each.

Exits.

MALE LEAD *speaks:* Son, Lu Zijing has invited me to a single-sword meeting. I'm going to go. — PING *speaks:* Father, there's no friendly meeting in store at that banquet. Aren't you worried about it? — MALE LEAD *speaks:* — It's not a problem. *Sings:*

(*Shiliu hua*)
Two courts separated by the Yangzi at Hanyang:*
On top is written, "Lu Su invites Yunchang."
He's laid the feast in no ordinary way,
So don't think this "painted hall will be an unusual scene of splendor"
For it will have no phoenix cups raised, full of chalcedony-flower
   brew.
He will have set out ricin and arsenic,
And at that tortoiseshell mat he will have his heroic generals arrayed
   in rows—
Don't think he'll let "those dressed up and rouged come forth when
   the feast begins."*

(*Dou anchun*)
He has prepared to strike the phoenix and capture the dragon,
And has set up nets for the heavens and seines for the earth;
It is no banquet to treat a guest,

But is a battlefield to slay a man.
And don't imagine any deep feelings or a sincere heart,
For he fears nothing of what posterity might say.
But now he has invited me with all due respect,
And I must go there myself.

PING *speaks:* That Lu Zijing is a man of much wisdom and a plethora of plans. Moreover, he has many soldiers and a wide field of generals, and his men are strong and his horses sturdy. I just fear if you go, father, you will fall into his arrow's ambit. — LEAD:

> (*Shang xiaolou*)
> You say, "He has many soldiers and a wide field of generals,"
> That "his men are strong and his horses sturdy."
> A real man dares to be brave, should be right in front:
> For such a man to wager his life alone
> Will pose more than a myriad of the common kind can match.

PING *speaks:* — The Yangzi is so wide; how can we, who are supposed to, render assistance? — MALE LEAD *sings:*

> You say, "Separated by the Yangzi,
> When the battle starts,
> It will be hard to be by your side when things are in peril."
> I'll have that guy bowing and scraping as he escorts me onto the
>   boat!

PING *speaks:* — When your son gets to eastern side of the Yangzi, I'll place horses and infantry along the dry routes, and place warships along the waterways, and simply slay until it's all turned into a bloody alleyway. To my thinking, the first one to strike will be the strongest. — LEAD *sings:*

> (*Reprise*)
> You say, "Strong is the one who strikes first;
> Disaster for the one who strikes last."
> My one hand will grasp his precious belt tight,
> My arms I will extend like a gibbon or lemur,
> And for a sword I'll pull out "autumn's frost."

PING *speaks:* — Father, I'm afraid he will have an ambush there. — LEAD *sings:*

> If he has an ambush secretly hidden,
> I will strongly ward it off.
> They are nothing but a passel of foxes and a pack of hounds.

Speaks: — If I don't go to this single-sword meeting? — *Sings:*

> Well, this is no match to that trip alone over a thousand miles,
> Or the beheadings of generals at five passes.*

Speaks: — Son, what kind of high opinion do you have of him? — PING *speaks:* I don't know about your secret escape from Xuchang; why don't you explain it to me? — LEAD *sings:*

> (*Kuaihuo san*)
> It was no more than taking his nephew to pay respects to the King
>   of Ji,
> Or leading August Liu's two wives to see him.*
> At Baling Bridge my spirit swelled mightily
> And I sat astride my carved saddle.*
>
> (*Baolao'er*)
> I had just beheaded Cai Yang in three booms of the drum,
> And his blood soaked into the sandy battlefield.
> With my sword I plucked up the battle robes and departed from
>   Xuchang,
> Yelling, nearly intimidating Minister Cao to death.
> To this banquet I go,
> Where facing his civilian and military sections
> Will be no more than [Liu Bei's] third-month feast at Xiangyang.*

PING *speaks:* — Father, he's bravely and mightily staging a scene for battle. — LEAD *sings:*

> (*Ti yindeng*)
> Even if he's bravely and mightily staging a scene for battle,
> Or has awe-provoking warriors stationed in their tiger tents,
> My own wisdom rises above that of both Sun Wu and Wu Qi.
> My horse like a dragon
> My person like the fierce adamantine guard at temple's gate,
> I am not being overweening,
> Or overly stubborn,
> But just mention killing him and I rub my palms and fists.
> Spears and halberds will be at the ready,
> Flags and lances all aligned,
> Ready to fight—
> I am the hero of the Three Kingdoms, Yunchang of the Han,
> And true it is my powerful spirit stretches for thousands of leagues.

Speaks: — Prepare a boat for me, and I will take Zhou Cang and go off to the single-sword meeting. — PING *speaks:* Since you are going, please be careful. — LEAD *sings:*

> (Coda)
> This will surely be no Duke Mu of Qin and the meeting of Lintong,*
> Or that hegemon-king of Chu at the meeting at Goosegate.*
> Even if those guests who fill the seats are all generals "first to the
>   front,"
> It will be no match for that round of brawling when I stabbed Yan
>   Liang in the midst of his myriad troops.*

Exits.

ZHOU CANG *speaks:* — Lord Guan is off to the single-sword meeting, and I'd better go too.

> A spirit and ambition to soar across the clouds and penetrate to the
>   Ninth Empyrean,
> Today Zhou Cang gets to manifest his heroic spirit.
> Each and every one will draw his bow, mount his nags side by side;
> One by one they will don their armor and their battle robes.
> Flags and banners will whip and snap, dragons and snakes will shake,
> For this violent battle all the heroes have a courage high and mighty.
> And should we grant Lu Su his thousands of plans,
> They are no match for this single blade of Lord Guan.

Exits.

GUAN XING *speaks:* Brother, father has gone off to the single-sword meeting. I'll go with you to meet him. Three armies, great and small, go with me now to aid my father. And when we get there . . .

> Flapping and snapping—colored [silks] wave the campaign banners;
> Booming and banging—painted drums signal to campaign tambours.
> Level and even, the lances and swords are like flowing water;
> Closely packed, the men are as quick as the northern winds.
>   We will kill
> Until, whelmingly bitter, corpses and skeletons cover the near-city
>   wilds,
> And, wailingly weeping, fathers and sons split forever apart.
>   And at that time
> Buzzingly happy our whips will strike and metal stirrups will echo,

As loudly laughing we all harmonize with a song of victory as we
    return.

Exits.

GUAN PING *speaks:* My father and brothers have all left; I'll follow along behind
to meet him. Three armies, great and small, listen to my commands:

Armored horses—you are not allowed to spur them ahead;
Metal drums—you are not allowed to sound them at random;
No whispering is allowed
Nor laughing banter or other commotion.
Nock your bows and crossbows;
Bring your knives and swords out of their scabbards.
Man after man must be brave;
Each and every one must be awesome.
        And when I get there:
A single-edged knife,
A double-edged sword,
Arrayed as level as the pinions of geese;
Three-tined pitchforks,
Four-sided batons,
Each brighter than the other in the radiant sun;
Flags of the five directions,
Six-barbed spears,
Covering the sky, reflecting the sun;
Seven re-curved bows,
Eight-sided cudgels,
To smash a skull to smithereens;
Nine heavy chains,
And red lassoes.
We cover our heads and then we rise—
We'll battle to the tenth power and slay to the tenth to show our
    brilliance, vaunt our strength.
        And here,
Virile warriors, brave and stout, cross the Long River;
On the two banks at Hanyang are arrayed blades and spears.
Our marines do not fear the waves in River's midst,
Our army troops feel no terror before ironclad braves.
Lord Guan goes a'killing to the single-blade meeting,
Displaying his brilliant heroism in a single battle.

On a lone horse with lance athwart, my father will slay Lu Su—
A much better show than when he stabbed Yan Liang to death!*

Three armies, great and small, follow me across to meet my father.

Exits.

[Act 4]

LU SU *enters, speaks:*

There has been no happiness like this morn's
And never a joyful day like today.

I am Lu Zijing, and I sent Huang Wen with a letter to invite Lord Guan, and he happily consented to come to the meeting today. The land of Jingzhou and Xiangyang should be restored to our River's East. Heroic armored troops are already concealed behind the arras, and I've sent someone to keep watch at the River and report to me when the boat arrives.

MALE LEAD, *costumed as* LORD GUAN, *enters, leading* ZHOU CANG — *speaks:* Zhou Cang, where have we reached? — ZHOU *speaks:* We have reached the center current of the Great River. — LEAD *speaks:* — Look at this Great River, what a fine body of water! *Sings:*

(SHUANGDIAO MODE: *Xinshui ling*)
"The Great River flows east," waves piled a thousand high,
Leading on these tens of men, plying this little leaf of a boat.
It cannot compare to the dragon-and-phoenix pylons of the nine
    rings of the capital,
Truly it is a deep cave full of thousands of tigers and wolves.
But a real man's heart is different than others—
I see this single-sword meeting as a local village sacrifice at the altar
    of earth.

Speaks: What fine River scenery! *Sings:*

(*Zhuma ting*)
Water surges, mountains rise in layers—
Where is young Zhou Lang now?
Don't you sense how the "ashes fly and the smoke disappears"?
Poor Huang Gai, who has become only painful sighs;
The masts and prows of the defeated Cao were destroyed all at once,
And the River's water that bore heavy battle is still hot,
And this makes me heartfelt miserable.

Speaks: This is no River's water! *Sings:*

> This is the blood of heroes that has flowed without cease for twenty
> years.*

Speaks: Well, here I am, already. Announce my arrival. SOLDIER *acts out an-nouncing — act out greeting each other —* LU *speaks:* For this little meeting on the bank of the River, the wine is not "Eternal Spring" from fairy caves, and the music no more than the meager talent of the mortal world of dust. I have shamed you, my lord, to lower your status, make you descend from your ex-alted state to approach this humble one of mine. This is all indeed to the great fortune of me, Lu Su! — LEAD *speaks:* I do not see that I have any virtue or ability to make your lordship set out such a fine feast. Once you invited me, I had to come. — LU *speaks:* Huang Wen, bring the wine. Let us drink to the full to your two lordships![88] LEAD *speaks:* Your lordship, please drink this cup. *Acts out handing cup —* LEAD *speaks:* Thinking on what has passed from ancient times to now, the two of us have spent our days and months too quickly! LU *speaks:* Indeed we have passed the days and months too fast:

> Daylight and darkness like a magnificent steed given the whip,
> This floating world like fallen blossoms on flowing water.

LEAD *sings:*

> (Hushiba)
> From those of ancient past to present,
> Who established merit at state's founding:
> Where are the five ministers of Shun?* The three eminences of Han?
> Our two courts have been separated these many years,
> And when we finally see each other
> We have already grown old.
> Let us drink a few cups to our hearts' content.

Speaks: Bring some wine! *Sings:*

> And hope with whole heart to be drunk the night long.

Holding the cup — LEAD *speaks:* Do you know the phrase, "Requite injury with uprightness, and kindness with kindness"?[89] — LU *speaks:* — Since you, my general, have said, "Requite injury with uprightness and kindness with kind-ness," then what is called injury is borrowing something and not returning it. I consider, my lord, that you are the complete talent of both military and civilian

---

88. Zhou Cang and Guan Yu.
89. *Analects* 14.34 (trans. Slingerland 2003, pp. 167–68).

virtues, that you have understood and have practiced all of the books of military strategy, and that you exemplify through practice what is in the *Springs and Autumns* and the *Chronicle of Master Zuo*. You have rescued those deep in peril, have supported the altars of state—can this not be called benevolent? You treat Liu Bei as your own flesh and blood, look upon Cao Cao as a mortal enemy— can this not be called righteous? You bade Cao Cao goodbye, cast away your seal of power, sealed away the gold—can this not be called proper ritual? Without moving you made Yu Jin surrender, waters covered the seven battalions— can this not be called tactical wisdom?[90] Moreover, general, your benevolence, righteousness, propriety, and wisdom are all replete. Alas, you lack only a single word—trustworthiness—that keeps your virtues from being complete. If you were capable of filling out these virtues with this one word, "trustworthiness," you would rise above all the lords. — LEAD *speaks:* — And how have I lost trustworthiness? — LU *speaks:* — It is not that you, general, have lost trustworthiness personally, but you have lost it because of your elder brother, Liu Bei. — LEAD *speaks:* — How has my brother lost trust? — LU *speaks:* Recall in the past when Liu Bei was defeated at Dangyang and had no where to turn—he was able to station his troops at Xiakou and Three Rivers because of me, Lu Su. And I, Lu Su, together with Zhuge Liang, had an audience together with my own lord, and we raised an army on that very day, we appointed generals, and we smashed Cao Cao's troops at Red Cliff. Eastern Wu spent millions on this campaign and moreover lost its head general, Huang Gai. Because your noble elder brother did not possess a single inch of land, we temporarily loaned him Jingzhou in order to provide him with a place to restore his army. He has not returned it all these years. Today, I must go against my own wishes and temporarily reclaim Jingzhou in order to alleviate our people's distress. When the granaries and storehouses are once again filled to the brim, then we will present it again to you, general, to control. I dare not presume on my own authority in this manner, and defer to you, general, to make an informed judgment about it. — LEAD *speaks:* You invited me to a feast for this? To lay a claim on Jingzhou? — LU *speaks:* No! No! I'm just saying: The Sun and Liu families are bound by marriage, and are as "lips and teeth to each other";[91] the two states are in perfect harmony. — LEAD *sings:*

---

90. In 219 Yu Jin joined with Cao Ren to attack Guan Yu. Autumnal floods from the Han River inundated the area and the Wei armies were mostly drowned. Yu Jin and other generals escaped onto a high hill, but were unable to escape. Guan Yu attacked them by boat and Yu Jin surrendered to him, much to the consternation of Cao Cao, who had trusted Yu Jin for thirty years.

91. A famous saying from the *Zuo Commentary*, which here means that while they may be in "perfect harmony," both are dependent on each other. This may be seen as a circumlocutive warning to Guan Yu that Shu-Han could not survive without Wu. Thus Guan Yu's retort two lines below about "high-blown" citations from the classics.

(*Qing dongyuan*)
You have treated me well
And set out this feast—
But forcing past into present and present into past like this
Does not "distinguish stems and leaves."[92]
Don't use any of your high-blown phrases here, any "Confucius says"
   or "the *Odes* read . . ."
Lest you have your mouth split open and your tongue cut out!
You are purposely stirring up Sun and Liu;
Don't turn them into arch-enemies like Wu and Yue!*

LU *speaks:* — All this time, general, you have been overbearing and care nothing for trust. — LEAD *speaks:* And how have I been overbearing and cared nothing for trust? — LU *speaks:* — On that day Zhuge Liang himself said that after Cao Cao had been smashed Jingzhou would be given back to Eastern Wu immediately. I personally vouched for it. You don't think about the favors of former days, and have turned favor now into enmity. Still you say, "requite kindness with kindness, and requite injury with uprightness." The Sage himself said, "Trustworthiness comes close to righteousness in that your words can be counted upon."[93] He said you can dispense with food and armaments, but not with trust,[94] as well as, "a large ox-drawn cart without a linchpin for its yolk, or a small horse-drawn cart without a linchpin for its collar: how could they possibly be driven?"[95] Now you, general, lack any heart of benevolence and righteousness and therefore vainly act the class of "hero." You have not returned Jingzhou now for a very long time. Is it not commonly said, "Without trustworthiness, a person cannot stand"? — LEAD *speaks:* Lu Zijing, do you hear this sword sounding? — LU *speaks:* — What's with the sword sounding? — LEAD *speaks:* — When this sword first sounded, it slew Wen Chou; the second time it beheaded Cai Yang. Lu Su, will the third to run afoul of it be you? — LU

---

92. I.e., brings superfluous matter into the discussion, talks about stems and leaves rather than about the main trunk of the matter.

93. *Analects* 1.13 (trans. Slingerland 2003, pp. 5–6).

94. *Analects* 12.7: "Zigong asked about governing. The Master said, 'Simply make sure there is sufficient food, sufficient armaments, and that you have the trust of the common people.' Zigong said, 'If sacrificing one of these three things became unavoidable, which would you sacrifice first?' The Master replied, 'I would sacrifice armaments.' Zigong said, 'If sacrificing one of the next two remaining things became unavoidable, which would you sacrifice next?' The Master replied, 'I would sacrifice the food. Death has always been with us, but a state cannot stand once it has lost the trust of its people.'" Translation slightly altered from Slingerland 2003, p. 128.

95. *Analects* 2.22: "The Master said, 'I cannot see how a person devoid of trustworthiness could possibly get along in the world. Imagine a large ox-drawn cart without a linchpin for its yolk, or a small horse-drawn cart without a linchpin for its collar: how could they possibly be driven?'" (trans. Slingerland 2003, p. 15)

speaks: — No! No! I was just saying. . . . — LEAD *speaks:* — Who does Jingzhou belong to? — LU *speaks:* Jingzhou is ours! — LEAD *speaks:* Since you don't get it, listen to me explain. — *Sings:*

(*Chenzui dongfeng*)
When I consider how our Exalted Progenitor of the Han plotted the
    enterprise of true king and hegemon,
How Guangwu of the Han held fast to the upright and expelled the
    deviant,[96]
How Emperor Xuan slew Dong Zhuo,
And the August Uncle of the Han extinguished the Marquis of
    Wen—[97]
By all that's right, my brother should carry on the founding enter-
    prise of the Han.
And more simply, how is Sun Quan of this Eastern Wu
Related in any way to our house of Liu?
Please, Mr. Lack of Manners, explain it yourself!

LU *speaks:* What's that ringing? LEAD *speaks:* That was the second warning of my sword. — LU *speaks:* Well then how can I explain? LEAD *speaks:* This sword relies on

The noumenal force of heaven and earth,
The refined essence of metal and fire,
The ethers of yin and yang—
The very forms of the sun and the moon.
Store it, then ghosts and spirits hide away;
Pull it out and sprites and goblins make their traces disappear;
Happy—it loves its scabbard, never moving from deep inside;
Angry—it leaps from its case, sounding out ringing and
    singing.
Should an armed contest arise at this morning's feast—
Now I'm afraid you might not believe me,
So let me pull out the sword to show it off.
Let me grasp my sword—
Lu Su, don't be afraid.
This sword indeed possesses spiritual power that cannot be
    withstood,

---

96. He defeated the troops of the Xin dynasty, a short-lived interregnum established by the usurper, Wang Mang, and restored the house of Liu as the Eastern Han dynasty.

97. I.e., Lü Bu, defeated not just by Liu Bei, but by Liu Bei and Cao Cao together.

It cannot be compared to any old implement from the ancestral
halls.[98]

And for this morning's demand for Jingzhou's return,

[Before that happens,] this single sword will first cause Lu Su's death.

Sings:

> (*Yan'er luo*)
> All because of your three-inch never tiring tongue,
> You've angered my three feet of unfeeling steel.
> This sword—hungry, it feasts on the heads of major generals;
> Thirsty, it drinks the blood of enemies.

> (*Desheng ling*)
> It's a dragon hibernating in the scabbard;
> I'm a tiger slumped at the banquet mat.
> Today old friends have just met;
> Don't cause a rift between us brothers now.
> Listen, Lu Zijing,
> Don't be so cowardly!
> Indeed, you have no mind of your own;
> Don't take it amiss that I'm so drunk.

LU *speaks:* — Zang Gong, start the music. ZANG GONG *enters, speaks:* — Heaven
displays the five moving stars,[99] earth has the five marchmounts; a person has
the five virtues, music is set to the five tones. The five stars are metal (Venus),
wood (Jupiter), water (Mercury), fire (Mars), and earth (Saturn); the marchmounts are Mount Chang, Mount Heng, Mount Tai, Mount Hua, and Mount
Song. The five virtues are warmth, goodness, respect, parsimony, and conces-
sion. The five tones are *gong, shang, jiao, zhi,* YU! ARMORED SOLDIERS *act out
rushing on stage.* LU *speaks:* Back into hiding! LEAD *strikes the table, angrily speaks:*
Is this an ambush? LU *speaks:* No! Certainly not. LEAD *speaks:* If there is an
ambush, a single swoosh of my sword cuts you in half! *Acts out striking table.*
— LU *speaks:* You've broken the mirror! — LEAD *speaks:* I came precisely to
smash the mirror![100] *Sings:*

> (*Jiao zhengpa*)
> Now why would these noisy soldiers be arranged in ranks?
> Don't get in my way; let no one cut me off.

---

98. I.e., a weapon that establishes or safeguards the ancestral temple.

99. In China in the past, the planets were considered "stars" (*xing*), a term used collectively
for stars and planets.

100. The word for mirror (*jing*) is an exact homophone for part of Lu Zijing's name.

Speaks: — Anyone who confronts me, well . . .

> I'll make him perish under my sword;
> Blood will flow before your eyes.
> Had you the mouth of Zhang Yi,
> The tongue of Kuai Tong . . .[101]
> Don't just shrink away there or hide.
> Escort me to my boat with all your heart,
> And I will take my leave from you, at ease.

LU *speaks:* — If you leave, it will wind up well. HUANG WEN *speaks:* — General, is there an ambush? — LU *speaks:* — I'm too late with mine. GUAN PING *leads a* GROUP OF GENERALS *and enters, speaks:* Father, please get on the boat; we have come to meet you and escort you back. — LEAD *speaks:* — Lu Su, don't lament that all your troops now are my rear guard!

> (*Li tingyan dai xiepo Coda*)
> I see my men lined up with their purple robes and silver belts;
> The evening is cool, the wind chill; reed flowers fall,
> And I am completely delighted.
> Dark and gloomy the evening sunset gathers in,
> Cold and whistling the River's wind picks up,
> Snapping and flapping the sails quicken.
> You have treated us well, treated us well,
> And I thank you and thank you once again.
> Summon the sailors slowly;
> The tether is loosed to set adrift the dragon beside the bank;
> As the boat splits the waves among the billows
> The oars rend asunder the moon in the River's heart.
> I am truly happy and pleased, for there is no danger,
> And for the time let us chat and laugh with no regard to day or
>   night.
> I'll tell you two things you should remember well, sir:
> Amidst all of the turmoil you could not get the best of my heart,

---

101. These are two famous rhetoricians. Zhang Yi (d. 310 BC) was one of the strategists of the Warring States period who helped Qin in its rise to power. Kuai Tong, attached to Han Xin, tried to persuade Han Xin to rebel against Liu Bang, first emperor of Han. Han Xin did not rebel, but he was killed anyway. Liu Bang later pardoned Kuai Tong who, when sentenced to death, remarked that a dog barks at others not because they are bad, but because they are not its master. So, he had aided Han Xin, not out of malice toward Liu Bang, but because he was in his service.

And for all your pressure you could not overturn the standard of the house of Han.

THIS ZAJU PLAY IS FINISHED

TITLE: Sun Zhongmou solely occupies the territory of River's East.
Duke Qiao is asked to discuss setting three plans.

NAME: Lu Zijing sets out a feast to request Jingzhou.
The Great King Guan goes alone to the single-sword meeting.

7

In a Dream Guan and Zhang, A Pair, Rush to Western Shu

[Guan Hanqing]

In a Dream Guan and Zhang, A Pair, Rush to Western Shu (*Guan Zhang shuang fu Xi Shu meng*) recounts the visit of the spirits of Guan Yu and Zhang Fei to Liu Bei after their deaths to persuade him to take vengeance for them. Although their actual deaths were separated by nearly two years, the tale compresses them so that their unavenged spirits can be released from a form of limbo through sacrifice of their enemies' blood. The play's focus is on the close personal bond between the three sworn brothers and is, in starkest terms, in Liu Bei's decision to seek vengeance, a completion of the oath they took to "die on the same day." Although they do not literally die on the same day, they finish their lives as they lived them: as true brothers willing to die for each other. The play dramatizes an episode that is not found in the *Records of the Three Kingdoms*, the *Records of the Three Kingdoms in Plain Language*, or the novel, the *Romance of the Three Kingdoms*. It is found, however, in the *Tale of Hua Guan Suo* (*Hua Guan Suo zhuan*). This prosimetric narrative of the heroic life of Guan Yu's son Guan Suo, discovered in a sixteenth-century grave near Shanghai in 1967, has been preserved in a printed edition from the Chenghua reign (1465–88) but may well have been composed much earlier. As we already noted in the introduction to *Liu, Guan, and Zhang: The Tripartite Oath of Brotherhood in the Peach Orchard*, its story derives from a Three Kingdoms tradition that often is quite different from that represented by the *Records in Plain Language* and the other plays in this volume. This alternative tradition dates back, however, at least to the second half of the thirteenth century as is proven by this play (see Appendix 2, where we have translated excerpts from the *Tale of Hua Guan Suo*). In the corresponding scene from the *Tale of Hua Guan Suo*, the emphasis is very much on the death of Guan Yu and the appearance of his ghost to Liu Bei. This makes sense in the context of the story as a whole because Liu Bei would set out on his ill-fated campaign against Wu in order to avenge the death of Guan Yu. The playwright, who was not obligated to take the larger story into consideration within the limits of his one play, rather chose to focus on the death of Zhang Fei and the subsequent journey of his ghost to Chengdu. Guan Hanqing, the purported author, may have been inspired to make this change since he conceived of *Single Sword Meeting* and *Dream of Western Shu* as a set, with Guan Yu the lead in the first and Zhang Fei the lead in the second.

Some scholars have argued that this particular story might already have been current in the ninth century. They base their arguments on a line in a poem by Li Shangyin (c. 813–c. 853), which they would render as "The wronged ghost of Yide eventually alerted his lord," but which more likely should be understood as "The wronged ghost of Yide eventually repaid his lord."

The play exists only in a Yuan edition, shorn of all stage directions and dialogue. It is made up of four suites of arias. The first is sung by an imperial envoy dispatched to summon Zhang Fei and Guan Yu back to the capital in Shu; the second by Zhuge Liang, who receives the news of their death after seeing portents of disaster in the skies; and the third and fourth by Zhang Fei's spirit.

In Act 1, Liu Bei has been moved by recurring visions of his brothers and acts to summon them back to the capital to be with him. He dispatches an envoy who discovers, first, that Guan Yu has been killed and then, second, that Zhang Fei has fallen victim to treacherous subordinates. The act ends with his quick return and the first voiced desire for vengeance. Act 2 opens with Zhuge Liang taking his daily reading of heavenly portents, which are proven true when the messenger delivers the news of the deaths. Zhuge Liang is here shown as a fallible astromancer, and his dismay at learning of the deaths of Guan and Zhang is soon supplanted by his awareness that, as soon as he tells Liu Bei, any hope of uniting the empire will be lost. In Act 3 Zhang's soul encounters that of Guan Yu on the road, and in Act 4 it appears to Liu Bei in a dream.

The focus of the story is the desire and the need for revenge. China, like most societies, was intellectually and emotionally governed by separate modes of thinking and feeling that depended on the level of society and period of history involved. Classical Confucian ideology, which underlies historical writing and elite cultural values, stressed the force of a cosmic morality of which human relationships were both a mirror and an integral part. This ideology emphasized a moral mind that was committed to right action and that was immovable in the face of danger or ethical particularism.[1] It provided a model to extend that moral nature, through the virtue of human-heartedness, to others in a vertical hierarchical structure from elder to younger and superior to inferior, as well as horizontally in carefully defined spatial gradations from the closest relationships to the farthest—from the family to the world at large. At the center of this is the belief that the individual owed, above all, allegiance to the moral nature of Heaven, part of which was the refinement of moral goodness through

---

1. A set of ethics that gives priority to family, close friends, or colleagues and does not need to make reference to an ethical universalism.

right action. In politics this was reified in the concept of "Heaven's mandate," a political ideology based on the belief that Heaven granted the most moral person under Heaven the mandate to rule as king or emperor. A leader must obey that mandate, even to the exclusion of all other values, must do what was right rather than expedient or comfortable, and must assure that the greater morality was carried out even at the expense of personal obligations or desires.

Popular society, however, was ruled by the law of *bao*, a Chinese term that, in English, can run a gamut of meanings from retribution to reciprocity to simple response. This was an individualized (or familial) virtue; it was what one person, one family, one village owed another. Each action by one side demanded a reciprocal action from the other. This concept, which lies, for instance, at the heart of the idea of *guanxi*, a relational system of reciprocal favors and obligations that still powers Chinese society, also lies at the root of the terrible rounds of retribution and vengeance that saw people and families exterminated throughout history. In religious terms it meant that a person or a family would either suffer or enjoy the fruits of their own, their families', or their ancestors' actions. Though congruent in some ways with the Buddhist idea of *karma*, this form of retribution was distinctly Chinese. As early as the earliest classic, the *Book of Changes*, there appeared the clear concept that an individual or a family will reap the benefits of merciful acts or will suffer the calamity of evil deeds done by its members or forbears. In terms of conventional justice it also meant that an eye must be taken for an eye and a tooth for a tooth.

This is one of the fundamental issues underlying our play. When Zhuge Liang assesses the brothers' relationship in Act 2, he sings,

> Were these two ministers ever really ministers
> Or the Lord and King indeed the lord and king?
> From their time as commoners they kept always the hearts of brothers!

While we may read these words as praising the strength of their relationship, we may also read them as a criticism. The brothers' personal bond, an oath that bound them together as a founding force, kept them from assuming proper roles in the kingdom they founded. Liu Bei, by rights, should have assumed the mantle of Heaven's mandate; the two brothers should have acted as loyal generals and ministers. But they did not. Instead, they demanded the fulfillment of the personal obligation of vengeance. Liu Bei, in avenging his brothers, essentially gave up his claim to the throne. Zhang Fei and Guan Yu, by demanding vengeance, forsook their proper roles as ministers who should vouchsafe the existence of the imperial entity above all else. Zhuge Liang procrastinates telling Liu Bei of the deaths of the brothers, for he knows that the bond of brotherhood will mean that Liu will commit all of the kingdom's soldiers in a blood revenge.

In the final act of the play, the spirits arrive at the palace on the ninth day of the ninth month, normally a festival day when the palace hummed with feasts and song. Also the day of Liu Bei's birthday celebration, the ambience the spirits find when they return—sober, depressive, and gloomy—is compared with happier days at court. Liu Bei, asleep on his couch, sees them in a dream and questions them. At first reluctant to answer, Zhang Fei's ghost finally winds up pleading for retribution, which we know in the normal course of the legend will take place after the action shown in the play. Thus the blood oath in the Peach Orchard will be kept, but at the cost of empire.

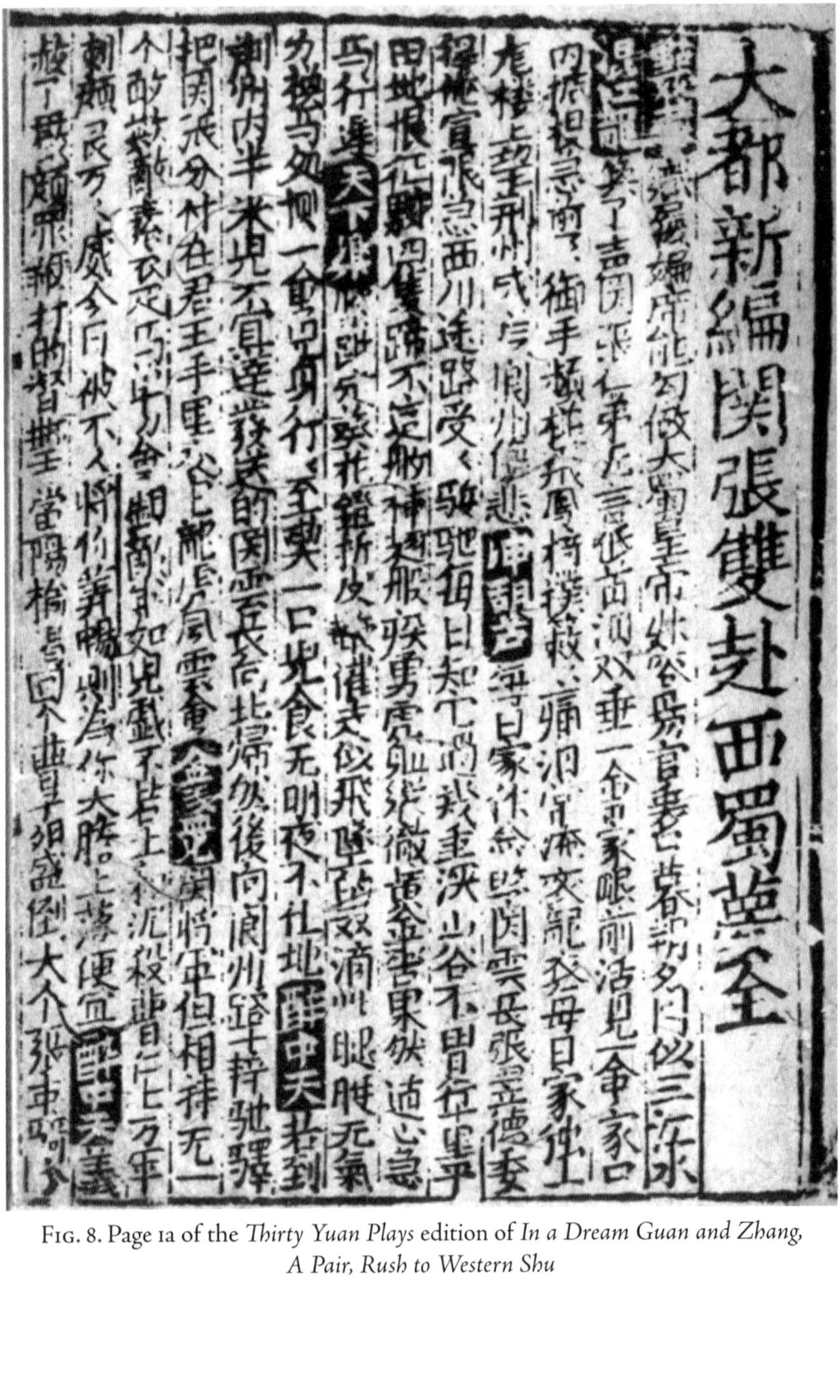

FIG. 8. Page 1a of the *Thirty Yuan Plays* edition of *In a Dream Guan and Zhang, A Pair, Rush to Western Shu*

Dramatis personæ in order of appearance

Role type	Name and family, institutional, or social role
Male lead	Envoy from Liu Bei to Guan Yu and Zhang Fei
Male lead	Zhuge Liang
Male lead	Zhang Fei

Newly Compiled at the Capital

In a Dream Zhang and Guan, A Pair, Rush to Western Shu Complete

[Act 1]

[ENVOY *sings:*]

([XIANLÜ MODE:] *Dian jiangchun*)
"From plaiting sandals and weaving mats,"[2]
Able to become the Emperor of Greater Shu—
No easy task.
But now—dawn and dusk, morning and eve—His Highness'
Depression runs like the waters of the three rivers.[3]

(*Hunjiang long*)
He calls out, "O my brothers Guan and Zhang,"
And then, silent, lowers his head—tears course down.
One moment they appear alive before his eyes;
The next, their names rise to his lips.
Worried and anxious—again and again the imperial fist pounds the
     flying-phoenix throne,
Constant and copious—tears of pain saturate his Coiling Dragon Robe.
Each and every day, all alone, he climbs the dragon loft—
Looking toward Jingzhou, he sighs with feeling;
Toward Langzhou, he laments with pain.

---

2. A common aphorism to capture the early part of Liu Bei's life; see *Xiangyang Meeting*, n. 4.

3. The three rivers are the Minjiang, the Fujiang, and the Tuojiang, all of which empty into the Yangzi. This is a particularly apt metaphor. Perhaps the most common trope for describing sorrow is a couplet from a lyric poem by Li Yu (937–78), "I ask you sir, 'How much sorrow can there be?' / 'Just like a whole Yangzi of spring's waters, flowing to the east'" (*wen jun neng you jiduo chou / qiasi yijiang chunshui xiang dong liu*). So his current sorrow at being parted, as great in its depth as the three great rivers of Shu, only presages that which will come later, just as the three rivers become the much larger Yangzi.

(*You hulu*)
Each and every day he was obsessed by thoughts of Guan Yunchang
    and Zhang Yide,
Until he dispatched me to give a deadline to hurry their return.
Along the roads of Shu I galloped on and on without rest,
Crossing daily through mountains countless, valleys deep—
Never traveling over more than a few miles of level land.
How I wished that the hooves of my battle steed
Would fly as fast as if they had sprouted wings.
I give free rein to this golden-bridled leaping tiger—
Truthfully spoken: "Where the heart hurries, the horse can only
    slowly follow."

(*Tianxia le*)
My feet push firmly down on the sunflower stirrups.[4]
My flailing whip urges the horse on.
He flies and drops like a doubled arrowhead in flight;
My legs have no strength left.
When changing horses, I can lean my body for a moment and rest,
Eat a mouthful now and then while on the run,
Stopping my journey neither day nor night.

(*Zui fu gui*)
And when I reach Jingzhou,
I cannot fall half a second behind
But must accompany Guan Yunchang part of the way back north,
Then spur on, posthouse by posthouse, up the road to Langzhou,
And so bring Guan and Zhang into the embrace of our king—
Then, dragon and tigers, as wind and clouds, will congregate.[5]

(*Jinzhan'er*)[6]
O General Guan, you had only to appear in battle,
And not a single person dared slight you as a foe.
Unarmed, on a lone horse, you went to the meeting of the single
    sword,
And there looked upon the enemy's army as no more than child's
    play,
Less than dirt and mud.

---

4. The pattern on the round plate of the stirrup.
5. See *Burning the Stores*, n. 5.
6. In the intervening scene, the envoy has discovered that Guan Yu has been killed.

You killed Cao Ren's seventy thousand troops,[7]
Skewered Yan Liang, whose might welled up ten thousand leagues.[8]
But today you've been done in by devious men—[9]
And in truth it was your great courage that finally brought you
  down.

(*Zui zhong tian*)[10]
Your righteousness pardoned the crime of Yan Yan,[11]
But you horsewhipped the Inspector General until he died.[12]
On Dangyang Slope a single shout sent Cao Mengde into retreat—[13]
O, you were so magnificent, Marshal Zhang,
But now some nobody has chopped off your head like a dead goat's.
No sign of Stone Pavilion Posthouse in this![14]

(*Jinzhan'er*)
I have never left the saddle;
Would I even dare loosen my uniform?
Barely gone from court, just two months and ten days,
Worn out for nothing, I have galloped in vain.
One went out: whip driving his spirit away.[15]
One returned: people joining in sounds of lamentation.

---

7. There is no mention of Guan Yu defeating Cao Ren's armies in any source, though the incident itself is referred to twice in *Xiangyang Meeting*. The *Records in Plain Language* indicates that Zhao Yun and Xu Shu were responsible for the defeat. See Appendix 1, item 8.

8. While in service to Cao Cao, Guan Yu slew Yuan Shao's great general, Yan Liang. See Appendix 1, item 7.

9. According to the *Records in Plain Language*, at a critical juncture in the battle for Jingzhou, Liu Feng and Meng Da refused to deliver a request for reinforcements to Zhuge Liang or Liu Bei, who were in Yizhou.

10. By now the envoy has arrived in Langzhou and has learned that Zhang Fei has been killed.

11. When Zhang Fei reached Jiangzhou, he imposed a humiliating defeat on Yan Yan, Grand Protector of Ba Commandery and Liu Zhang's general. He also captured Yan alive. Zhang Fei scorned him derisively and ordered his head chopped off. But Yan never showed the slightest sign of fear and Zhang Fei wound up releasing him. See Appendix 1, item 13.

12. The inspector general has been dispatched to arrest Liu Bei who, in the *Records of the Three Kingdoms*, kills him. But in fiction and drama it is always Zhang Fei who intercedes at the moment the inspector general orders the arrest of Liu, and then kills the inspector general. See Appendix 1, item 2.

13. See Appendix 1, item 10.

14. See Appendix 1, item 5.

15. These lines are problematical. It may refer to Zhang Fei's whipping of Zhang Da, the person who eventually killed him. Another possible readings is, "I go out, my whip stirring up their spirits [to return to appear to Liu Bei], I return while others join in lamentation."

All I summoned was fine-bearded Guan Yu in his memorial hall,
And Zhang Fei of the Han, hovering by his spirit banner.

(*Coda*)
We will slay the house of Eastern Wu until their corpses stop up the
    water in the Yangzi's heart,
And its lower reaches are aflood with blood,
Make our thick rain capes dyed with red through and through,
And turn them into the scarlet pelts of a lion cape.
We will murder until they drip with blood,
And so make Wu and Yue break and flee.
In the wink of an eye, we'll turn them into Taihu rocks.[16]
On riverbanks black as pitch,
In fields brown as clay,
The hooves of our horses will trample them into a pepper paste.[17]

[Act 2]

[ZHUGE LIANG *sings:*]

([NANLÜ MODE:] *Yizhi hua*)
This very morning I cast the *Book of Changes*,
And last night observed the celestial signs.
The star of traitors has grown in brilliance,
And the star of true generals has shortened its rays.
Just as I was measuring these signs against our empire's earthly
    analogs,[18]
Over the southern reaches a white rainbow has pierced the sun.[19]
I lower my head to ponder this—
What's the reason for these portentous signs?

(*Liangzhou* [*diqi*])
It can only signify that one brave general of Eastern Wu[20]
Has cut down the two golden roof beams of our Western Shu.

---

16. Rocks with large holes in them, usually used for decoration in gardens.

17. I.e., a paste as thick as ground fagara.

18. He is referring here to "distribution of the wilds" (*fenye*), a system of astronomical obser-vation and divination in which heavenly portents are directly connected to a predetermined geo-graphical area on earth and, by correlation, to political and personal activity taking place within those realms.

19. A sign of disaster, as that which results from the slaying of a great man.

20. That is, Lü Meng (178–220), who led the final assault that defeated Guan Yu.

Who could have expected this bitter grief?
Who now to capture men and nab generals?
Who now to expand our lands and open up new frontiers?
Were these two ministers ever really ministers
Or the Lord and King indeed the lord and king?
From their time as commoners they kept always the hearts of loving
    brothers!
We'll see no more: Yan Liang stabbed with a sword at Official
    Ford,[21]
Cai Yang punished with the blade at Old City,[22]
Or Yuan Xiang hurled with force at Stone Pavilion Posthouse.
In his palace hall the emperor longs for them while walking, thinks
    of them when seated.
Right now he gazes to the south,
Unaware that disaster descended from heaven.
If I am summoned and questioned at court,
How shall I answer?

(*Gewei*)
I, this rustic farmer from Nanyang, this Zhuge Liang,
Am assisting this emperor of Han, whose blessings match heaven.
From the time I became minister, I have never deceived my lord,
But this time, in this case,
I had best, before my lord, concoct a lie.

(*Muyang guan*)
That traitor, that beast Zhang Da,[23]
Won't be hard to get to;
No escape for Mi Zhu, Mi Fang![24]
With the mighty power of our Western Shu
We will obliterate all traces of Eastern Wu.
Let our golden drums thunder to quell their bravery.
A rain of dust will saturate the sky until the sun has no light.

---

21. See Appendix 1, item 7.
22. See Appendix 1, item 7.
23. In the *Records of the Three Kingdoms* it simply says that Zhang Fei failed to heed Liu Bei's counsel about treating his underlings better. When Liu Bei went on campaign against Eastern Wu and Zhang Fei's army left Langzhong, Zhang Da and a person named Fan Jiang stabled Zhang Fei, cut off his head, and took it to Wu as a token of surrender. Zhang Fei's treatment of Zhang Da and the resulting murder are fleshed out in the *Tale of Hua Guan Suo*, and particularly in chapter 81 of the *Romance of the Three Kingdoms*.
24. See *Burning the Stores*, n. 34.

The hooves of our horses will trample Jinling to pieces.[25]
The tips of our whips will dip the Yangzi dry.

(*He xinlang*)
Wherever he walks, wherever he sits, His Highness says only, "Guan
    and Zhang,"
So it always is, "What is on the tip of the tongue is never far from the
    heart."
Each and every day, he is obsessed by them as though his heart
    itches;
Not a single day passes that he does not worry and fret.
So it always is, his inner thoughts are grieved and sad.
By daytime, he recites their names over and over,
And late in the night, he longs for them even more.
Truly it is said, "Dreams are the imaginings of the heart."
He needs only close his eyes to meet with Yide;
As soon as he dreams, he sees Yunchang.

(*Muyang guan*)
Like Fu Yue of the Shang, [slaving on] the construction of earthen
    walls,[26]
And Lü Wang of Jiang, fishing with a [hookless] line—[27]
Those two dreams that moved lords of antiquity to virtue,
These dreams were foreknown and foretold.
But I blundered, I bungled—
The butterfly confused Master Zhuang,[28]
Song Yu went up to Gaotang—[29]
Affairs of this world are a thousand clouds changing,
Our floating life but a single dream.

(*Shouwei*)
That pine and that cedar, unable to reach the sky, grew only thirty
    feet,[30]

---

25. Sun Quan had established his capital at Jinling, modern Nanjing.

26. See *Tripartite Oath*, n. 46.

27. See *Tripartite Oath*, n. 21.

28. Zhuangzi once dreamt he was a butterfly, flying about as happy as could be. When he awoke, then he was Zhuangzi again, but he did not know if he were Zhuangzi, having dreamt that he was a butterfly, or if he were still a butterfly, dreaming that he was Zhuangzi.

29. This particular allusion is usually used for a sexual tryst. Here, it is used to mean a confusing dream.

30. That is, their growth was stopped short; they were killed before their time. Both the pine and the cedar are symbols of enduring and unflinching integrity.

And became nothing more than half a page of paper on which was
    written peerless fame and success.
General Guan, of fine manly build,
General Zhang, of fierce disposition—
When will we ever face each other again?
"Heroes have returned to the Nine Springs below"[31]
And become nothing but: Driving a mooring pin into the earth of
    the river dike,
Or sitting on the carrying pole—
Nothing but gist for a tale told by fishermen and woodcutters over
    dreggy wine.

[Act 3]

[ZHANG FEI'S GHOST *sings:*]

([ZHONGLÜ MODE:] *Fendie'er*)
Fortune has turned and the time is past.
Who could have expected this fatal disaster?
I recall those years, the horses armored in iron, the golden lance.
From the time we first swore our oath of brotherhood in the Peach
    Orchard,
I have assisted my worthy brother:
Against enemy armies we beat our drums, sounded our gongs—
Who did not fear us, we brothers three?

(*Zui chunfeng*)
Horsewhipping the Inspector General in Anxi District,
Shouting Cao Cao into retreat at Dangyang Bridge,
Joining in a battle of ninety bouts with Lü Bu, Marquis of Wen—[32]
That was me then, me!
My robust will has been ground away,
My evening years broken and crushed—
Today I have submitted to a nobody.

(*Hongxiuxie*)
How huge that nine-foot body in those dark clouds![33]

---

31. "Nine Springs" and its homophone "Wine Springs" mean the world of the dead.

32. Lü Bu, also known as the Marquis of Wen, first served Dong Zhuo, regent to the last Han emperor. Lü later killed Dong and then began a protracted campaign against Cao Cao who, along with Liu Bei (then in the employ of Cao Cao), eventually captured and executed him.

33. He sees Guan Yu's ghost and mistakes it for the live Guan Yu.

Three plaits of beard hang below his jade belt—
It really is my second brother from Jingzhou!
But I am a ghost from the darkness;
How can I follow him?
So scared that I can't hide even in these clouds of darkness.

(*Ying xianke*)
If he were in the world of men
Then he should be passing by on *that* road.
Why is he treading *here* in clouds of darkness?
In the past those damned Guanxi bodyguards
Would be all around him,
But today, his sergeants are few,
No more than a dozen in retinue.

(*Shiliu hua*)
In the past, enjoying himself, he would often laugh heartily.
His cinnabar cheeks, crimson clouds, looked like apples;
But today, under eyebrows thick as recumbent silkworms, he stares
    with wooden face.
Now why do his tears
Fall as fast as a shuttle thrown?
I'll throw caution aside, go ahead and chase after him,
But if he sees me, I'm afraid he'll stop.
Rushing on, I'm really afraid to make myself known,
Lest I stir his tiger-like body to action.

(*Dou anchun*)[34]
Brother, if you say you are a ghost from the darkness,
Well, what am I?
Everything that happened
I'll tell you from beginning to end:
Because I got into a row with my underling Zhang Da,
Your brother let his anger flare even more.
I originally wanted to pardon him;
How could I know he would be roused to kill me?

(*Shang xiaolou*)
Because of my ungoverned bravery in years gone by,
I crushed everyone.

---

34. In the scene between these two songs, Zhang Fei's ghost questions Guan Yu's ghost and
discovers they both have been killed.

Just what was the outcome
With Yuan Xiang at Stone Pavilion Posthouse?
He pissed me off.
I grabbed him
And smashed his brain box to smithereens.
Could I have let him off after he wronged me?

(*Reprise*)
Brother, you ponder it.
This was no small affair,
All the way to the point that, with Cao Cao and Sun Quan,
We divided the kingdom like three legs of a tripod,
And the altars of earth and grain, and mountains and rivers,
Were held tenuously together, linked by tendon only.
The three of us
Walked together, sat together.
So why have we two preceded our brother in death?

(*Shaopian*)
Now you've mentioned how Jingzhou was smashed,
But, alas, your younger brother also lies dead in a ditch.
In these cloudy vapors I ask myself,
How can Liu Feng excuse his actions?
We'll slice that bastard to pieces.
Mi Fang, Mi Zhu,
My underling Zhang Da,
Have clearly gone to hide in Eastern Wu.
First we will rouse up Field Marshal Zhuge Liang, make him aware,
And then enter into the palace
And appear in a dream to our elder brother.
As our army draws near the Han River, horses will whinny into the
     wind,
As corpses fill up the Yangzi, it will billow with blood.
Don't think you can escape;
There's no place to hide.
How can you get away?

(*Shua hai'er*)
The awe and might of Western Shu is like a mighty wind.
Assisted by us, ghost soldiers, there will be no obstacle in the road.
Mi Fang, Mi Zhu, and Zhang Da
Couldn't flee if they wanted.

Only after we have taken the upper reaches of the Han River will we
    return to our state.
Unless we kill the traitors, there'll be no peace.
And if all of them are caught,
We will guard them closely—
Brook no delay!

(*San*)
Our lord and king, so full of anxious grief,
Will rejoice after taking vengeance.
After we've rooted out Liu Feng,
We'll lock the other three in a prison cart.
But no joy we'll feel to strike our golden stirrups,
And have no heart to sing our song of victory.
If we smash these traitorous ministers,
Our lord and king will make sacrifice to us—
We'll have no need of the clanging and banging of a funeral mass.

(*Er*)
We'll burn half a mound of firewood,
And prop up the nine tripod cauldrons,[35]
And hack off those bastard's limbs with a steel knife—joint, by joint,
    by joint,
After we gut them, empty their bellies—let the cocks and crows peck
    away.
When we're finished with their fat and marrow—let fierce tigers drag
    it off.
We'll sit in state on our funeral seats,
Having no need for the incantations of Buddhist monks
Or the prayers of Daoist priests.

(*Shouwei*)
Nor will we need incense and candles,
Wine, or fruit.
We need only the hot blood from their breasts spurting into the air,

---

35. This is a conflation (found only in Yuan editions of dramas) of two terms, "nine tripods"
(*jiuding*) and the common phrase "tripod and cauldron" (*dinghuo*), which is used for the punishment of being boiled alive. The "nine tripods" are the ritual tripods of state (each holding earth of
one of the ancient divisions of China). The *huo* is a torture implement, a pot used for boiling
people alive. In both cases, the phrase occurs in a context in which the instruments of the state
are used to satisfy personal interests.

And my brother will be reborn and I will have received proper
  sacrifice.

[Act 4]³⁶

[ZHANG FEI'S GHOST *sings:*]

  ([ZHENGGONG MODE:] *Duanzheng hao*)
  So beset with care,
  Suffering in vain,
  Our dead souls have no state to take us in.
  Murdered before our time by the hands of three traitors;
  Not a single relative came to our rescue.

  (*Gun xiuqiu*)
  My brother's cinnabar phoenix eyes
  And my tiger-like leopard head
  Fell into others' snares
  And died a death less than that of shrimps or loaches.
  I once horsewhipped the Inspector General,
  My brother executed Wen Chou,³⁷
  Obliterated Che Zhou,³⁸
  And fought fiercely with Marquis of Wen at Tigerkeep Pass.
  Our three inches of vital breath was used in a thousand ways,
  But a sudden death brought all affairs to a close,
  And our life's ambitions could not be realized.

  (*Tang xiucai*)
  In the past, when the true guardians of the gates saw us, they saluted
    with arms across their breasts,
  But now, seeing the paper door guards, we hesitate, starting and
    stopping.³⁹
  So it turns out being a ghost is less free than being a man in the
    world of light.
  We stand before the cinnabar steps,

---

36. In this act they arrive at Liu Bei's palace.
37. See Appendix 1, item 7.
38. Cao Cao, fearful of the power of the three brothers, had dispatched Liu Bei to be Grand
Protector of Xuzhou. He also secretly sent Che Zhou, with an order from Cao Cao to assume
that position, to lay prior claim to the post. Guan Yu caught up with him and easily killed him.
See Appendix 1, item 6.
39. The paper door guards on the palace gates protect the palace by refusing entry to ghosts.

And before I can stop it, tears flow,
For my pack of old friends is seen no more.

(*Gun xiuqiu*)
Then, too, it was the end of autumn,
The ninth of the ninth month,
The birthday of our emperor.
Ministers and nobles lined up on the cinnabar steps,
And in the crowd I raised my jade goblet,
Offering the imperial wine.
All together we shouted, "May you live forever!"
And His Highness answered us, "A thousand autumns for my
   ministers!"
In the past, women of the palace thronged the courtyard,
But today, I ride a single sorrowful cloud at the corner of the hall,
With tears of grief flowing freely.

(*Daodao ling*)
Rippling and emerald, furrowed waves wrinkle in green waters;
Soughing and sighing, fragrant breezes penetrate the jade hall.
The footfalls of black court boots are silent on the glazed tiles;
The striking of white ivory tablets makes no sound against the golden
   animal.[40]
So, we really are dead,
So, we really are dead.
What we hear are the silver arrows in the dripping clepsydra.[41]

(*Tang xiucai*)
From his dragon couch, His Highness questions me in a loud voice,[42]
And I nervously kowtow in the shadow of the candle's light.
Avoiding my lord and king I quickly retreat,
As he continues to ask me what happened.
And I force out a smiling face.

(*Dai guduo*)
In the end we harbor sorrow for thirty years of friendship lost—
We loved each other and were of a single mind.

---

40. These are tablets carried by officials as they go to court. The "striking against the golden animal" is unclear. "Golden animal" can refer to either an incense censer or a door handle. Morning court in China occurred at daybreak.

41. The silver arrows rose with the water in the pot of the water clock, marking off time by the notches in their side as they cleared the rim.

42. The ghosts appear to Liu Bei in a dream.

I was always around you two brothers,
And you never left my side.
One was an unyielding phoenix amid the clouds,
The other an awesome beast from the mountains;
Gloomy and dark—now oil lamps in the wind,
Empty and windblown—now froth on the water.

(*Tang xiucai*)
Your Highness' body was here, in dragon lofts and phoenix lofts,[43]
But your soul hurried to Jingzhou and Langzhou,
Knowing not that these two brick-walled cities had turned to earthen
    mounds.[44]
Heaven will not accept us;
The underworld cannot contain us;
We have nowhere to go.

(*Gun xiuqiu*)
His Highness' anger does not cease,
His resentment does not cease,
For fear we do not understand the depth of your friendship,
Or why our dead souls pay no attention to you.
He recalls our old friendship,
Asks us how we are.
He recalls the former oath we once spoke,
When we butchered a white horse and black bull in the Peach
    Orchard.
Becoming brothers, you, the elder, kept the pact to the end,
But we have not seen our service to our lord and king through,
To our eternal regret.

(*Sansha*)
Tomorrow let Zhuge Liang bring our two stupid sons
To recount all in detail,
And then you will cry without end.
His Highness desperately asks us to stay,
And surely we would like to tarry here awhile.
But we can't stop the drip, drip, dripping vase of bronze,
Or the tick, tick, ticking of the watch's pointer.
We stay, we remain,

---

43. I.e., the capital.
44. Referring to the emperor's state in the first act, when he had a premonition that they
were dead.

We go and come again,
We grow sadder, more sorrowful.
When we came, the jade toad rose from the Eastern Sea,
Now when we leave, the hook of that moon sinks by the western loft.

(*Ersha*)
Together, we race as a wild wind along the ancient road,
We follow close on the whitecap flow of the Yangzi.
Weeping bitterly, bereft and forlorn,
Increasing our painful sorrow little by little.
Having bid the dragon countenance adieu,
We will suffer through our springs and autumns.
If we had not spoken this time,
It would have been impossible to come later,
And it would have been all over.
We have explained it all with urgency,
That you must avenge our wrongs for all the world to see.

(*Coda*)
"One who has had his fill of the world is loathe to open his mouth;
One who understands human beings simply nods his head."
Quick as fire, dispatch your officers and troops,
Station your horses by the whitecap flow of the Yangzi.
Take Mi Fang and Mi Zhu alive,
In Langzhou, lock Zhang Da into the prison cart.
Arrange their four heads in a row on the points of the pike.
Let the blood from their breasts flow in the Chengdu marketplace—
How much better than a thousand cups of the finest imperially
    sealed-and-sanctioned sacrificial wine!

Newly Compiled at the Capital: *In a Dream Guan and Zhang, A Pair, Rush to Western Shu*

Complete

Appendix 1

The *Records of the Three Kingdoms in Plain Language*
In Summary with Selected Passages Fully Translated

The *Records of the Three Kingdoms in Plain Language* belongs to a small group of texts from the thirteenth and fourteenth century that offer an exciting narrative of a major episode in Chinese history. As a genre, these texts are known as "plain tales" (*pinghua*). In traditional canonical historiography, the preferred modes of writing were the annalistic chronicle, the biographical sketch, and the institutional compendium. These writings relied heavily on the official documents produced by the imperial bureaucracy, and the compilation of historical writings became increasingly a responsibility of that same bureaucracy. Plain tales, however, prefer to treat the interregna between the major dynasties and they also weave written and oral sources together into one coherent narrative of the past. In twentieth-century Chinese scholarship the plain tales have often been characterized as the precursors of vernacular fiction as it would flourish from the sixteenth century onward, but from a Western perspective the plain tales probably are best understood as popularized historiography and not as historical fiction.

As in the case of the *Records in Plain Language*, most of the narrative of plain tales is usually taken up by a description of the many battles that accompanied the collapse of one dynasty and the founding of the next. Most of the plain tales are written in a simple standard written Chinese that incorporates only a few vernacular elements. But occasionally passages are written in a more outspoken vernacular idiom; the text is interrupted by couplets and poems quoted from a wide variety of sources, and may also include letters, proclamations, and other genres of formal prose. Many scholars have argued that the plain tales derived from the professional storytellers of the Song and Yuan dynasties, and that these texts served as their promptbooks. Others have argued—more convincingly, in our opinion—that these texts were printed primarily for a reading public. One element that enhanced the attractiveness of these texts as books in some editions was their continuous illustration of the narrative with carefully designed and executed woodblock prints on the upper one-third of the page. By the sixteenth century, the plain tales disappeared from public view as they were replaced by the vernacular novels of the time that greatly expanded upon the plain tales' simple narratives, often cannibalizing their predecessors in the process.

The *Records in Plain Language* is the only plain tale that has been preserved in two contemporary editions. We have one independent printing, which is usually dated to 1294 and has rather crudely executed illustrations. The second printing dates to 1324 and is part of an incompletely preserved series nowadays known as the *Five Completely Illustrated Plain Tales* (*Quanxiang pinghua wu-zhong*). This set is available in a number of photographic facsimile editions. Following earlier modern typeset editions of the individual texts in this series, Zhong Zhaohua prepared a critical, annotated edition in 1989. Our translation of selected passages is based on this edition.[1] Our summary of the narrative is based on the summary provided in the *Comprehensive Catalogue, with Summaries, of Chinese Popular Fiction*.[2]

---

1. *Quanxiang pinghua Sanguozhi*, in Zhong Zhaohua 1989, pp. 371–501.
2. *Zhongguo tongsu xiaoshuo zongmu tiyao*, in Jiangsusheng shehui kexueyuan and Ming Qing xiaoshuo yanjiu zhongxin 1990, pp. 26–28.

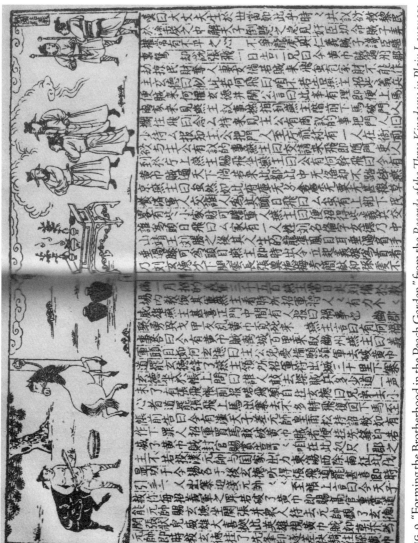

FIG. 9. "Forming the Brotherhood in the Peach Garden," from the *Records of the Three Kingdoms in Plain Language*

PART I

The Judgment by Sima Zhongxiang

When Emperor Guangwu of the Eastern Han (r. 25–57) ascends the throne, he issues an edict allowing the common people to enjoy spring with him in the imperial gardens. The imperial gardens are crowded with people, and when a student named Sima Zhongxiang arrives too late, he can find no place to sit and must sit down on the grass to read his book and drink his wine. When he comes across the description of the violent government of the First Emperor of Qin in his book, he denounces the First Emperor as a ruler bereft of the Way. He also states that the Lord of Heaven made a mistake in choosing the First Emperor to be the ruler. Sima Zhongxiang is then invited to go to the underworld and decide the sentencing of legal cases. There, he redresses the injustices suffered by the meritorious ministers Han Xin, Peng Yue, and Ying Bu—who had been instrumental in the founding of the Han but who had been murdered by the Exalted Ancestor of the Han, Gaozu, and his wife, Empress Lü—by having them reborn on earth in order to exact revenge. Han Xin will be reborn as Cao Cao and occupy the Central Plain; Peng Yue will be reborn as the emperor of Sichuan, Liu Bei; and Ying Bu will become the King of Eastern Wu, Sun Quan. The Exalted Ancestor of the Han will live in Xuchang as the feckless Emperor Xian, and Empress Lü will become Emperor Xian's wife, Empress Fu. Han Xin's injustice is redressed when, as Cao Cao, he seizes the right moment to imprison Emperor Xian and kill Empress Fu. Sun Quan of Eastern Wu will have the advantage of terrain, and Liu Bei of Sichuan will enjoy the advantage of social harmony. Kuai Tong, originally adviser to Han Xin, is reborn as Zhuge Liang. Sima Zhongxiang himself is reborn at the command of Heaven as Sima Yi (179–251), whose grandson will become the first ruler of the Jin dynasty (266–420) when the Three Kingdoms are reunited.

The Miraculous Revelation

When Emperor Ling of the Han (r. 156–89) ascends the throne, a hole opens up at the foot of Mount Tai. When Teacher Sun enters that hole, he finds a celestial book, which he later uses to cure diseases, and attracts disciples. Among his five hundred students there is one named Zhang Jiao (d. 184), who obtains one scroll of famous prescriptions. Zhang, one of the leaders of the later Yellow Turban revolt, cures the diseases of the whole world, and travels through the four directions. He certifies more than ten thousand disciples. At an agreed-upon time they assemble in Guangling and rise in rebellion. They invade many regions, finally occupying two-thirds of the Han empire.

The Suppression of the Yellow Turbans

Emperor Ling appoints Huangfu Song (d. 195) as commander and orders him to mobilize troops. Guan Yu, Zhang Fei, and Liu Bei meet in the Peach Or-chard of Zhang Fei's farm and become sworn brothers.

1. The Oath in the Peach Orchard

The story goes that there was a man named Guan Yu, also known as Yun-chang. He hailed from Xieliang in Puzhou in Pingyang. From birth he had the eyebrows of a god and the eyes of a phoenix, a curly beard and face like purple jade; he was nine feet, two inches tall[3] and loved to read the *Springs and Autumns* and *Zuo's Commentary*. When he studied the biographies of rebellious vassals and evil sons, he was filled with a furious hatred. He killed the district magistrate because the latter coveted wealth and loved kickbacks

---

3. During the final decades of the Han a foot measured roughly twenty-four centimeters. Ten inches made one foot, and ten feet made one *zhang*.

and greatly harmed the common people. Fleeing for his life he became a fugitive and went to Zhuo Prefecture.

> If he would not have fled for his life, drifting and roaming about,
> How would he have met friends who prized righteousness over gold?

The story goes that there was a man named Zhang Fei, also known as Yide, who hailed from Fanyang in Zhuo Prefecture, in the princedom of Yan. From birth he had the head of a panther and round eyes, the jowls of a swallow, and the whiskers of a tiger; his body was more than nine feet tall, and his voice resounded like a huge bell. He came from a very rich family. Because he was idly standing outside, he saw Lord Guan pass through the streets: his physique was extraordinary, but his clothes were in tatters—he was not a local man. So he stepped forward and greeted Lord Guan with a bow, which the latter returned.

Fei asked him, "Sir, where are you going? And where are you from?" As Lord Guan was being questioned by Fei, he saw that Fei too had an exceptional physique, and said: "I hail from Xiezhou in Hedong. Because the local magistrate treated the people most cruelly, I killed him. Not daring to stay in my village, I came to this place to seek safety." When Fei had heard this tale, he realized that Lord Guan had the ambition of a true man, and invited him to a wineshop. Fei ordered up some wine, "Bring us two hundred coins worth of wine." The owner brought it promptly.

Lord Guan saw that Fei was a serious person. As they were talking and speaking, they were in complete harmony. When the wine was finished, Lord Guan wanted to buy the next round, but he had no money with him and looked uncomfortable about it. Fei said, "How could that be?" And he ordered the owner to bring more wine. The two of them toasted each other, and as they were talking found themselves in such harmony that they resembled old friends. Indeed:

> The day that dragon and tiger meet with each other
> Is the time when lord and vassal happily gather.

Let us begin to speak about a man named Liu Bei, also known as Xuande. He hailed from Fanyang in Zhuo Prefecture and was the worthy seventeenth-generation great-grandson of Emperor Jingdi of the Han and a descendant of Liu Sheng, the Quiet Prince of Zhongshan. From birth he had a dragon [face], aquiline [nose], the eyes of a phoenix, the back of Yu, and the shoulders of Tang;[4] his body was seven feet, five inches tall, and his hands hung

---

4. Yu was the mythic founder of the Xia dynasty (twentieth–sixteenth century BC); Tang was the founder of the Shang dynasty (fifteenth–eleventh century BC).

down below his knees. When he was speaking, joy or anger never showed on his face, and he loved to befriend heroes. As a child he had lost his father; he lived with his mother and made a living by weaving mats and plaiting sandals. At the southeastern corner of his house a mulberry tree grew above the fence. It was more than five *zhang* tall. If you had a look at it from close up you saw the various layers [of leaves] resembled the canopy of a little carriage. Passersby all marveled at the exceptional nature of this tree, which was bound to produce a man destined for greatness. When Xuande was still a child he would play below this tree with other children in the family, [and say,] "I am the Son of Heaven, and this is the Great Audience Hall." When his uncle Liu Deran noticed him uttering these words, he said, "Don't wipe out our family with light-hearted words!" Deran's father was Yuanqi, and [Yuan]qi's wife said, "He has his own family. Chase him away from our gates." But Yuanqi said, "If our family has such a boy, he is not a common person. Don't speak such words!" When the boy turned fifteen, his mother had him travel and study, and he studied at the house of Lu Zhi, the former Prefect of Jiujiang, whom he honored as his teacher. But Lord Liu did not like the study of books very much; he loved dogs and horses and fine clothes, and was fond of music.

That day, when he had plaited his sandals and gone to the market and sold them, he also came into this wineshop to buy a drink. When Guan and Zhang saw the extraordinary physique of Lord Liu and his thousand kinds of indescribable blessings, Lord Guan offered him a drink. When Lord Liu saw that these two people also had exceptional physiques, he was very pleased and did not reject the offer, but took the cup and promptly drank it. When he had finished it, Zhang Fei offered him a cup, which he also accepted and finished. Fei invited him to sit with them, and after they had finished three cups of wine, the three of them stayed together as old friends, united in harmony.

But Zhang Fei said, "This is no place for us to sit. If you two gentlemen have no objection, let's go to my place and have a drink." When the two of them heard this, they promptly followed Fei to his house. In the back there was a peach orchard, and in that orchard there was a little pavilion. Fei thereupon invited the two of them and brought wine to the pavilion, where the three of them happily drank. While they were drinking, each told his age: Lord Liu was the eldest, Lord Guan was the next, and Fei was the youngest. And so the eldest became the eldest brother, and the youngest the youngest brother. They slaughtered a white horse in sacrifice to Heaven, and killed a black ox in sacrifice to Earth. They did not find it necessary to be born on the same day, but they vowed to die on the same day. The three of them would be inseparable in walking, sitting, and sleeping. They swore to be brothers.

Lord Liu saw that the situation of the Han dynasty was as perilous as piled-up eggs: robbers and bandits arose in swarms and the common people suffered distress. He said with a sigh, "Should a real man live like this in this world?" Time and again they discussed how they could save the common people from this terrible situation, and how they could free the Son of Heaven from his powerless situation. They saw traitorous ministers ignore orders and bandits manipulate power, and were filled with indignation!

> Because dragon and tigers are filled with love and righteousness,
> Evil sons and slanderous ministers are startled from their sleep.

Now let us speak about that one day Zhang Fei informed his two elder brothers, "At present the Yellow Turban rebels are spreading everywhere, plundering the people's money, and stealing their wives and daughters. If these rebels come here, I may be very rich, but I won't be able to do anything about it." Xuande said, "So what should we do in such a situation?" Fei said, "The best for us is to inform the Prince of Yan and hire some volunteer soldiers. Then what do we have to fear even if these rebels show up?" Xuande and Lord Guan said, "Such an action makes sense." And so they got on their horses, left [Zhang's] home, and came to discuss the situation with the Prince of Yan.

They collect troops, buy horses, and serve under the command of Huangfu Song in the war of suppression against the Yellow Turbans. After Liu Bei, Guan Yu, and Zhang Fei have played a major part in pacifying the rebellion, they follow Huangfu Song to court to receive their rewards. One of the Ten Constant Attendants (the court eunuchs), Duan Gui, unsuccessfully tries to shake the three down, and then blocks their rewards. With the support of the emperor's father-in-law Dong Cheng (d. 200), Liu Bei is appointed as defender of Wenxi in Ding Prefecture. Yuan Qiao, the prefect of Ding, first chastises Liu Bei for arriving too late at the prefecture and wishes to punish him, but later orders him to go to his own office and to be very careful in handling his duties. When Zhang Fei hears how Liu Bei was treated, he kills the prefect under the cover of night. The court dispatches an inspector general to investigate the murder of the prefect. Upon arrival at Dingzhou he determines that the prefect must have been killed by one of the men under the command of Liu Bei and tells his underling to arrest Liu Bei. Zhang Fei becomes furious, scares them away, strips the inspector general of his clothes, ties him to a hitching pole for horses, and lashes him a hundred times with a huge cudgel—the corpse is dismembered.

2. Zhang Fei Kills the Inspector General

Zhang Fei also killed the Prefect Yuan Qiao. There was a concubine in the lamplight who cried out, "Murderer!" So he also killed the concubine. Because of this, the yamen night guard was aroused, and about thirty men rushed in to seize Zhang Fei. Fei slew more than twenty archers, leapt over the rear wall, and escaped, returning to his own [i.e., Liu Bei's] offices.

At dawn the next day all of the officials, high and low, called on the District Defender, Liu Bei, to discuss the situation. Liu Bei was determined to pursue the killer and to immediately notify the court. The Court Remonstrator offered the opinion, "The murderer who killed the prefect had to be someone in the District Defender's group."

The court dispatched the Inspector General Cui Lian as an envoy in the capacity of Censor to go and settle in at Dingzhou Posthouse. The officials high and low paid a visit to the envoy and asked him, "Sir, what assignment do you have?" The Inspector General replied, "They have sent me here to question you because of the murder of the magistrate. Is there a District Defender here?"

"The District Defender is outside, but he dares not visit you." The envoy then summoned the District Defender, who entered with three hundred soldiers, among whom were Guan, Zhang, and twenty or thirty of the defender's entourage, to make a formal visit. The envoy said, "Are you the District Defender?" "I am," replied Liu Bei. "Did you kill the magistrate?" asked the envoy. Liu Bei replied, "The magistrate was in his rear apartments; it was lit by lamps and candles, and there was a night guard of thirty or so men. If you insist that the man who killed twenty or so of the magistrate's men and then escaped from such a well-lit place must have been Liu Bei, then of course it has to be Liu Bei."

The Inspector General spoke angrily, "In the past you were the reason your sworn brother Zhang Fei knocked out Duan Gui's two front teeth. Today the sage's directive has sent me here to question you about the magistrate's killer. In the former case, the Prefectural Administrator went beyond the statute of limitations. You should have been sentenced for that crime, but out of respect for all of the officers, you were not. Because of this incident you bore resentment and killed the magistrate. So don't try to worm your way out of it!" He shouted to his attendants, "Take him!"

On either side, Guan Yu and Zhang Fei were enraged, and each ran up into the hall carrying a blade, scaring the host of officials who all fled. They captured the envoy and stripped him. Zhang Fei helped Liu Bei sit on a chair, and then they bound the envoy to a hitching post at the front of the hall, where he died after being bastinadoed more than a hundred times. The corpse was split into six sections, the head was hung outside the north gate, and the feet [and hands] hung from the four corners. Then Liu Bei, Guan Yu, Zhang Fei, and all of the generals and troops went to ground in the Taihang Mountains.

After Liu, Guan, and Zhang take their troops with them and become bandits in the Taihang Mountains, Dong Cheng proposes that Liu Bei can be made to surrender if the Ten Constant Attendants are killed. Emperor Ling accepts the proposal and has them killed. Dong Cheng goes to the Taihang Mountains with the heads of the Ten Constant Attendants and induces Liu Bei to surrender. When Liu Bei accompanies Dong Cheng to Chang'an, he is appointed as assistant magistrate of Pingyuan in Dezhou. While in Pingyuan, Liu Bei's virtuous administration benefits the local population.

The Death of Dong Zhuo and the Execution of Lü Bu

When Emperor Xian (r. 189–220) ascends the throne, he orders the high minister Dong Zhuo (138–92) to defeat the Yellow Turbans of Xiliang. When they have been defeated, Dong Zhuo enters the capital with his army and monopolizes power. Emperor Xian secretly summons Dong Cheng and asks him how to get rid of Dong Zhuo. Cao Cao is sent an edict to contact all liege lords of the empire so they can cooperate in an attack on Dong Zhuo. Cao Cao especially recommends Liu, Guan, and Zhang for this operation. But the liege lords despise Liu, Guan, and Zhang because their positions are so lowly. Instead, they order Cao Bao and Sun Jian to battle Dong Zhuo's adopted son Lü Bu, but the two are defeated. Later Liu, Guan, and Zhang fight Lü Bu together, and Zhang also fights Lü all by himself. After Zhang Fei fights to a standoff, Lü Bu is sufficiently wary enough not to emerge again to carry on the fight.

3. The Battle at Tigerkeep Pass and the Defeat of Lü Bu

With thirty riders, Cao Cao waited outside the gates of the district yamen, and had his servants report to [Liu] Xuande. The gate guard said, "There is an imperial envoy of the Han outside of the yamen gate. You, sir, should hurry out to receive him." The various officers greeted Cao Cao and led him into the yamen, and had him sit at the head of the hall. When the ritual greetings were finished, each took their place at the feast mat.

After they had gone through several courses, each accompanied by wine, Cao said, "I bear the Sage's directive to summon the liege lords of the twenty-eight garrisons. Now Dong Zhuo wields the power of the throne and has long plotted to seize the world of Han. I am to direct all the liege lords to protect His Majesty, pacify the empire, and smash Dong Zhuo. Then there are Lü Bu and Li Su, each of whom has unmatched courage—no one can match them. Because I was going to inform Han Fu of the Henghai Command in Cangzhou, I passed by Pingyuan District, and heard that Xuande was here. So I came particularly to pay my respects. Please don't distance yourself from this, Lord Xuande. Think of the world of Han; should you go to Tigerkeep Pass and smash Dong Zhuo and Lü Bu, I will recommend you, sir, to be invested as a Myriarch liege lord and be entered into the ministerial offices."

Cao Cao took up his cup and toasted Liu Bei. Bei said, "I, this humble officer, have no skill in the martial arts and am unfamiliar with bow and horse; I fear I will ruin this affair of state."

At his side Zhang Fei spoke up, "Brother! From the time we bound ourselves in righteousness at the Peach Orchard, together we have smashed the Yellow Turbans and made a name for ourselves in history. Now, for the state, this is precisely the juncture to utilize men. Let us follow all of the liege lords to Tigerkeep Pass to do battle with Dong Zhuo and Lü Bu. Relying on the emperor's great beneficence, after we kill Dong Zhuo and Lü Bu we will have our names inscribed in the Lingyan Pavilion, and that is so much better than being a magistrate in Pingyuan District. We will be able to wear golden belts and be robed in purple, to offer protected privilege for our sons, and to have our wives invested with a noble title. If you don't go, brother, I want to."

Cao Cao thanked him as soon as he heard the utterance. When the feast was done, Cao Cao reminded them twice and then again, "General Zhang has promised to go. But if he arrives late, I will send an envoy to request the three of you." Cao Cao withdrew and started down the road.

Xuande returned to his lodgings where he discussed it thoroughly with his brothers. He explained, "If we go and we wind up unused when we get there, where will we go back to?"

"Relax, brother," said Zhang Fei, "I'll go alone to smash Dong Zhuo and execute Lü Bu."

Xuande said, "Wait until the envoy comes before you leave."

Let us now speak about Emperor Xian in Luoyang, who was weak and incompetent as a ruler. The Grand Preceptor Dong Zhuo wielded the power. He weighed three hundred pounds and was set on usurping the state. He carried his sword when he entered the palace and everyone—civil and military—was terrified of him. He constantly bullied and suppressed the liege lords of the empire, relying on these subordinates: his adopted son Lü Bu, the civilian Li Su, the four bandits, and the eight strong generals.

Let us speak instead, now, of the Grand Protector of Qiao Commandery, Cao Cao, who had gone to court a second time to have an audience with the emperor. Seeing how Dong Zhuo used his power to bully others, he found it even more unbearable. When the court was finished, he again memorialized the emperor and discussed how he might, in a hidden way, put a secret edict into effect to assemble all of the liege lords in the empire in front of Tigerkeep Pass, and together smash Dong Zhuo. The emperor decreed that on the third day of the third month of the fifth year of Zhongping [April 15, 188] the multitude would assemble before Tigerkeep Pass. Immediately he ordered him to summon the liege lords of all of the garrisons in the subcelestial realm, to arrive early in front of the pass. The soldiers of Changsha were the first of all and the Grand Protector of Changsha, Sun Jian, was the first to reach the pass. Yuan Tan of Qingzhou did not go. When all the armies and horses of the subcelestial realm were in front of the pass, they lacked fodder and provisions. In order to press for grain, Cao Cao went to pressure Yuan Tan to go. In a few days, he had reached as far as Pingyuan District, and when he finished greeting Xuande, Cao Cao said, "All of the liege lords are at Tigerkeep Pass, what about you three generals?"

Xuande did not say anything, but Zhang Fei spoke, "I see that the world of Han is now without a ruler, and that we should slay that traitorous official, the Grand Preceptor, and reestablish the house of Han." The First Ruler [Liu Bei][5] finally relented. Cao said, "The Prince of Ji, Yuan Shao, is now the generalissimo, and you can take a letter to him." The Prime Minister then wrote a letter and turned it over to the First Ruler. After Lord Cao departed, he went straight to Qingzhou.

But let us now speak about Guan, Zhang, and Liu, who had selected three thousand tiger cavalry from their subordinates, and who had selected a day on which to begin their journey to go off to the southwest. They had been on the road for several days when they set up their tents about five or six miles from the main camp at Tigerkeep Pass. On the next day the three put their battle raiment in order and went first to see the generalissimo, arriving at the gate of the camp.

But let us return to Yuan Shao, Prince of Ji, who had assembled the liege lords in his tent, and asked them, "The house of Han is now without a ruler and a traitorous official is wielding power. Emperor Xian is in Luoyang, and

---

5. Liu Bei is often referred to as the First Ruler, as eventually he would become the first ruler of Shu-Han. He is distinguished in this way from his son, the second and last ruler of Shu-Han, who is often called the Young Ruler or Later Ruler.

is an incompetent and weak ruler. Dong Zhuo is at Tigerkeep Pass, where
he has a hundred noted generals. The best of those is the Marquis of Wen,
Lü Bu, who is nine feet, two inches tall, and employs a "square heaven halberd," and who has no match. You many liege lords: how can you set a plan
to execute the traitorous minister to repay the court and leave a name for
those who follow?" The whole group of officers was silent.

Suddenly they heard the sound of a commotion outside the camp gates.
The gate guard reported, "There are three generals outside the camp gate to
see you." The Prince of Ji quickly ordered them to be brought before him.
The host of officers all looked at the general who was their leader. His face
was like a full moon, his ears hung past his shoulders, his arms drooped
below his kneecaps, and he had an aquiline nose and dragon face. He truly
had the features of an emperor and king. The general below and to his left
was nine feet, two inches tall, a man of Xieliang in Puzhou, called Guan Yu,
also known as Yunchang. Below and on his left was a man of Zhuojun in
Youzhou, Zhang Fei, also known as Yide, who had a leopard head and round
eyes, the neck of a sparrow, and the whiskers of a tiger.

The Prince of Ji asked, "Who are you three generals?"

The First Ruler replied, "This useless one is a man of Dasang Village in
Zhuo Prefecture, in Youzhou. I am Liu Bei, currently District Magistrate in
Pingyuan."

"Are you a 'green robed one with the sophora screed'?"[6] "Yes," replied the
First Ruler. "Because the Grand Protector of Qiao Commandery passed by
and left a letter for me, I've now come to the pass to smash Dong Zhuo together with you." The Prince of Ji was elated.

The First Ruler took out the letter and turned it over to Yuan Shao. After
Yuan Shao finished reading it, he asked the host of liege lords, "What about
this?" In a thundering voice one of the generals in the tent shouted out, "The
liege lords have assembled here at Tigerkeep Pass and will cut off the heads
of that traitorous minister Dong Zhuo and Lü Bu within days." The officers
looked and it turned out to be the Grand Protector of Changsha, Sun Jian.
Song Wenju said, "We don't need any 'green-robed esquire' to help us kill
Dong Zhuo at the pass." When the host of officers heard this, they were all
happy. The Prince of Ji asked again, but none of the officers spoke.

The three generals bade goodbye to the Prince of Ji and went out of the
camp to their own bivouac about five or six miles to the northeast. "If we had
been in Pingyuan," said Zhang Fei, "we would never have suffered anxiety
because of another."

---

6. A lower-level official, so named because of the green robe and official plaque made of sophora wood.

They had an audience with Yuan Shao at dawn on the following day, but the host of officers expressed their displeasure again. The three generals went back out again, and the next day they hit the road to go directly back to Pingyuan. They had gone but a few miles when they encountered Cao Cao, and they told him truthfully everything that happened.

Cao Cao laughed and said, "Follow me back again. If you smash this traitorous official and establish great merit, no office is out of your reach."

The next day they returned with their army and reached the grand camp of Yuan Shao.

Two days later, Cao Cao spoke in the camp, "Xiao He recommended Han Xin three times, and this gave rise to the Han for four hundred years." The Prince of Ji was setting out a grand feast and invited Prime Minister Cao and the liege lords. Just as the main banquet was progressing, someone reported that the Marquis of Wen, Lü Bu, was challenging them to battle at Tigerkeep Pass.

The Prince of Ji asked, "Who dares battle to death with Lü Bu?" He hadn't finished speaking when everyone saw a general come forth, and they recognized him as the Infantry General Cao Bao, who was in the employ of Tao Qian, the Grand Protector of Xuzhou.

He spoke of his own volition, "I will battle to death with Lü Bu, and I want to capture him." The assembled officers were all delighted. He got on his horse and arrayed his troops against Lü Bu, but he was quickly taken by Lü. In less than two hours his defeated troops had returned, explaining that the Marquis of Wen had seized Cao Bao after a single round. The Prince of Ji was alarmed.

Someone then said, "But they have released Cao Bao to return!" When Cao Bao entered the camp, the host of officers all said that Lü Bu was undefeatable and only wanted to capture the liege lords of the eighteen garrisons. Every one of the officers was filled with fear.

At dawn of the next day, a spy reported, "Lü Bu has left Tigerkeep Pass with an army of thirty thousand and challenges us to battle." The Prince of Ji asked the host of officers, "Who will do battle with the Marquis of Wen?" Before he had finished speaking, Sun Jian, Grand Protector of Changsha, had led out his army and horse to face off with Lü Bu. He and Lü Bu had only fought for three rounds before Sun Jian was mightily defeated. Lü Bu chased him into a great forest and launched an arrow that struck Sun Jian. Sun Jian then employed "the golden cicada husks off its shell" stratagem— that is, he hung his armor and clothes on a tree and fled. Lü Bu sent the strong general Yang Feng off to Tigerkeep Pass with Sun Jian's helmet and battle garb to turn over to Dong Zhuo. But on his way, he ran smack into Zhang Fei, who wrestled the helmet and battle garb away from him.

At day's light, Zhang Fei reached Yuan Shao's great camp and got off his horse. He went to see the First Ruler and Lord Guan. Xuande explained, "Sun Jian said that we were nothing but cats and dogs, just sacks to stuff with food and bone racks on which to hang clothes." The First Ruler said, "He is the Grand Protector of Changsha, and I am just a green-robed esquire. How can I even hope to get the best of him?"

Zhang Fei laughed and shouted, "A real man doesn't worry about life or death, but plans a name for later generations!"

Neither the First Ruler nor Lord Guan could stop him, and Zhang Fei took off straight for the Prince of Ji's tent, where he presented the helmet and battle garb to the prince. The Grand Protector Sun Jian and the other officers were silent. In a voice like a huge bell, [Zhang said], "Before the Grand Protector called us the likes of cats and dogs. But when Lü Bu came out of the pass, the Grand Protector managed to escape by husking off his battle garb."

Sun Jian was outraged when he heard this, and pushed Zhang Fei out with the intent of cutting off his head. All of the liege lords stood up, but Yuan Shao, Prince of Ji, Liu Biao, Prince of Jing, and Cao Cao of Qiao Commandery said, "Lü Bu's might can't be matched. If we behead Zhang Fei, who will smash Dong Zhuo?"

Sun Jian was silent, and Zhang Fei offered, "When Lü Bu comes out of the pass, we three brothers will cut off the head of that slave." The host of officers was delighted and Zhang Fei managed to get out of it.

On the third day, Lü Bu came out to battle again, and all of the liege lords went out of the encampment to face off with Lü Bu.

The Three-Battle Lü Bu

Zhang Fei rode out holding his spear, and battled with Lü for more than twenty rounds, but there was no clear winner. Lord Guan flew into a rage, let his horse run free, and twirling his blade battled twice with Lü Bu. The First Ruler couldn't stand it anymore and employed his double blades, riding three times against Lü Bu, who was greatly defeated and fled, returning back up Tigerkeep Pass to the northwest.

The next day Lü Bu came down out of the pass and shouted, "Send out the big-eyed fellow!" Zhang Fei, greatly enraged, came out on his horse, holding his eighteen-foot supernatural spear, and with round eyes glaring went straight away to seize Lü Bu. The two horses met for more than thirty rounds, but there was no clear winner.

Zhang Fei Battles Lü Bu Alone

Zhang Fei had always loved battle and he smashed into his opponent and battled him for thirty more rounds, and in that fight Lü Bu's battle flags covered his face. Zhang Fei was like a god and Lü Bu quailed in his heart, and spurred his horse back up into the pass, closed it tightly, and did not come out again.

Wang Yun presents Lü Bu's wife Diaochan (with whom Lü had lost contact) to Dong Zhuo, and later also arranges a meeting of Lü Bu and Diaochan. When Lü Bu sees how Dong Zhuo dallies with Diaochan, he promptly kills Dong Zhuo.

4. The Story of Diaochan and the Interlocking Rings

But let us speak of Grand Preceptor Dong, who intercepted the royal chariot in Luoyang and [took the emperor] and went west into Chang'an. The emperor took a seat in the Palace of Eternal Peace and ordered the Grand Preceptor to lay a banquet. When it got late the emperor, feeling the effects of the liquor, returned to his rear chambers. Dong Zhuo spied Consort Four, and began to flirt with her in suggestive language. There was a Prime Minister there, Wang Yun, who in pique said to himself, "There is no ruler in the empire!"

Wang Yun went back to his residence and dismounted, and sat glumly in a small courtyard. He told himself that Emperor Xian was weak and powerless and now that Dong Zhuo was manipulating power, the empire was in deep peril. Suddenly he saw a woman burning incense, saying that she would not be able to return home and see her master again. She burned incense and made two bows. Wang Yun said to himself, "I am troubled by state affairs, so what's this woman praying for?" He had no other recourse but to go out and ask her, "Why are you burning incense? Tell me the truth."

He scared Diaochan so much that she fell quickly to her knees, daring not to prevaricate. She told her truthful reasons, "This humble concubine was originally surnamed Ren, and my child name was Diaochan. My master was Lü Bu, but we were separated at Lintao and haven't seen each other since. This is why I'm burning incense."

The Prime Minister was overjoyed, "This woman is the one who will bring peace to the Han empire." He returned to a hall and summoned Diaochan, "I will look upon you and treat you as my own child." He then gave her gold, pearls, and bolts of silk and sent her on her way.

Several days later, the Prime Minister invited the Grand Preceptor Dong Zhuo to a banquet. As the day drew later the Grand Preceptor was feeling the effects of the wine and the candles and lamps appeared to be flickering and shimmering. Wang Yun ordered up tens of beautiful women, and put Diaochan in the middle with the others around her. In her chignon were stuck short golden pins with green-tinted white jade; on her body she wore a chemise of crimson silk woven with golden threads. She was a veritable state-toppling, city-toppling beauty! Dong Zhuo was greatly taken aback, and his gaze moved over her awhile and then he said to himself, "My own home simply lacks a woman like this!" Wang Yun had her sing, and the Grand Preceptor was delighted. Wang Yun said, "She's a person from Lintao, west of the passes;[7] her surname is Ren, and her child's name is Diaochan." The Grand Preceptor became infatuated with her, and the Prime Minister assented [to the match]. When the feast finished, the Grand Preceptor also arose.

At dawn the next day, the Prime Minister thought to himself, "I have eaten my lord's salary as a minister, and now I have come up with a plan to make the house of Han secure once again. If I am not successful, I will earn a name with my death." Immediately he invited Lü Bu to a meeting and fêted him until late in the day, when the minister once again had Diaochan come out and sing at the banquet. Lü Bu looked at her and thought to himself, "Ding Jianyang rebelled at Lintao in those days past, and I didn't know where my wife Diaochan ended up. But here she is today!" Wang Yun took up a cup and spoke, "Marquis of Wen, your face has taken on a look of anxiety, but why?" Lü Bu rose from his seat and told everything in precise detail. The Prime Minister was overjoyed, "Now there is a ruler in the empire of Han!" The Prime Minister spoke again, "I didn't know she was your wife. There's nothing happier in the world than the reunion of husband and wife." And then he went on, "I have treated her as if she were my own daughter. Let's select an auspicious and propitious hour, and I will send Diaochan to the residence of the Grand Preceptor, where she can become your wife again." Lü Bu was extremely happy, and as it drew late, he announced he was going home.

Within a few days he sent Diaochan, accompanied by a young serving girl, in a four-in-hand and with rich gifts to the Grand Preceptor's residence. That day, the third day of the third month of the seventh year of the Zhongping reign,[8] the Grand Preceptor was sitting silently when someone reported, "Prime Minister Wang Yun has sent someone here in his four-in-hand and with rich gifts." The Grand Preceptor scurried out and welcomed him at the reception hall, remarking, "Is it Diaochan?" "Yes, it is," said Yun. The Grand Preceptor had someone put out wine. Wang Yun spoke, "I am feeling a little ill, so I won't tarry here." He bade the Grand Preceptor goodbye and left.

---

7. In modern Gansu.

8. This date does not in fact exist. The Zhongping reign ended in the sixth year. If this is the first year of the subsequent reign, it would be April 25, 190.

Late that night, Dong Zhuo and Diaochan drank together. Now Dong Zhuo was a lecher and a drunk. About two days later, when Lü Bu returned from the Serpentine,[9] he dismounted at the front of the residence, and the eight strong generals all scattered. Late that night the Marquis of Wen heard the sound of music tinkling and ringing in the residence, and he asked his attendants what was happening. All of them explained, "[He's got] a woman of the Prime Minister; it's that Diaochan!" Lü Bu was greatly shaken and walked to a place underneath the gallery corridor, but there was no way he could see inside. Suddenly he saw Diaochan push aside the curtain and come out. Lü Bu was incensed and asked, "Where is that miscreant?" "He's already drunk," replied Diaochan. Lü Bu raised his sword and went into the hall, where he saw Dong Zhuo snoring like thunder, lying there like a mountain of flesh, and cursed him, "You, miscreant, have no morals!" A single swipe of the sword cut his neck, and the fresh blood spurted out. He stabbed Dong Zhuo, who then died.

Lü Bu went quickly out of the house and fled to the Prime Minister's residence. Wang Yun hurriedly asked him what was going on. Lü Bu told him the whole story from the start. The Prime Minister, overjoyed, said, "You will be the most famous man of this age! If you had not slain Dong Zhuo, the Han empire would be in as much danger as a stack of eggs!" As they were speaking, a gate guard reported, "Li Su is outside, sword raised, looking for Lü Bu." The Prime Minister went outside with the speed of fire and saw Li Su approach, who said, "Lü Bu has killed the Grand Preceptor. If I see Lü Bu, a thousand slices will cut his body to shreds." Wang Yun said, "You are mistaken, general. The house of Han has lasted for four hundred years. Your ancestor Li Guang supported the house of Han. Lately, Dong Zhuo has monopolized power and Lü Bu has extirpated him. You say you 'will slay Lü Bu,' but if you do your name will be cursed all through the world—unlike your ancestors'. One who can dismiss the dark to let light shine is truly a great man." Li Su threw his sword on the ground, clasped his hands, and bowed, saying "You are right, Prime Minister. I request to speak with the Marquis of Wen." When the two met, Lü Bu told him all about Dong Zhuo's immorality. Li Su said in a rage, "I did not know the truth of the matter!"

Lü Bu had taken his leave of Wang Yun and returned to his house when the gate guard reported, "Defender-in-Chief Wu Zilan has surrounded the residence with ten thousand soldiers." Lü Bu thought to himself, "I cannot

---

9. This was a park with a twisting waterway that was called the Plain of Happy Wandering during the Han (formally named the Serpentine later, in the Tang), and was the site of outings for the *Shangsi* festival, an ancient ablution rite of the third of the third month that had, by this time, become primarily a festival to celebrate spring's return.

stay in Chang'an any longer." He summoned the eight strong generals, and with three thousand men, he took the eastern gate and then left. Behind him, Defender-in-Chief Wu Zilan was catching up and another ten thousand men blocked the way ahead. But when the dead Dong Zhuo's four Grand Marshals—Li Jue, Guo Si, Fan Chou, and Zhang Ji—cursed him as a "slave," the Marquis of Wen gave no response and smashed through their formation.

After Lü Bu flees from Chang'an, he requests that Liu Bei, who is at that moment the prefect of Xuzhou, grant him Xiaopei as a temporary abode. When Liu Bei and Guan Yu temporarily leave Xuzhou, and while Zhang Fei is dead drunk, Lü Bu captures Xuzhou.

5. Zhang Fei Slays Yuan Xiang at Stone Pavilion Posthouse

Half a year later, more or less, someone reported to the First Ruler, "There is a certain Yuan Shu in Shouchun, in a region four hundred miles south, who has sent out his Crown Prince Yuan Xiang at the head of an army on its way to take Xuzhou. The First Ruler immediately appointed Zhang Fei as a reception envoy to welcome Yuan Xiang in the south. Some thirty miles of travel brought him to a pavilion called Stone Pavilion Posthouse, where he received Yuan Xiang. When the two had exchanged ritual greetings, Zhang Fei set out three rounds of wine, and when this was finished, Yuan Xiang discussed the matter of Xuzhou. Zhang Fei did not accede to his demands, so Yuan Xiang rudely swore, "Xuande is a hick who weaves mats and plaits sandals!"

Enraged, Zhang Fei cursed, "My brother is the son of a whole line of emperors and kings, the seventeenth-generation grandson of Emperor Jing of the Han, and a descendant of the Quiet Prince of Zhongshan. When you curse him as 'a hick who weaves mats and plaits sandals!' you insult my brother. Truly, it's your ancestors who are nothing but farm boys."

Zhang Fei was about to make a ready return when Yuan Xiang began to strike him. Zhang Fei grabbed him tight, lifted him up with his hands, and hurled him down to the ground at the Stone Pavilion. None of the officers exhorted him not to, so he killed Yuan Xiang by smashing him on the ground.

Zhang Fei requests supporting troops from Cao Cao. By the time that Zhang Fei has defeated Lü Bu in battle, Xu Chu (at the behest of Cao Cao) has already occupied Xuzhou. Zhang Fei captures Lü Bu and presents him to Cao Cao who, following the advice of Liu Bei, beheads Lü Bu.

PART II

The Rift between Cao Cao and Liu Bei

Cao Cao brings Liu Bei, Guan Yu, and Zhang Fei with him to the capital and they restore Emperor Xian to the throne. Because the decapitation of Lü Bu shows the merit of Liu, Guan, and Zhang, Emperor Xian treats the three of them in a very friendly manner, and appoints Liu Bei as Warden of Yuzhou and General of the Left. He also begins to address him as Imperial Uncle of the Han. But Cao Cao claims to be ill and refuses to come to court because he secretly harbors rebellious intentions. Emperor Xian issues a handwritten edict ordering Dong Cheng, Liu Bei, and others to do away with Cao Cao. The medical doctor Ji Ping wants to kill Cao Cao with poison when Cao Cao suffers an attack of "tiger-head epilepsy." Cao Cao discovers Ji Ping's intentions and Ji dies during interrogation. Cao Cao proposes to the emperor that Liu Bei be appointed protector of Xuzhou. Cao's troops then make a surprise attack on Xuzhou.

6. Guan Yu Kills Che Zhou

Cao Cao beat Ji Ping to death, and then became deeply suspicious of the Imperial Uncle. He said to himself, "My mistake. I should never have brought Liu Bei to court. These three brothers are like tigers and wolves; there is no plan by which to outwit them."

In a few days Minister Cao invited Xuande to a feast, which he called "A Meeting to Discuss Heroism." That scared the Imperial Uncle so much he dropped his chopsticks. The meeting was disbanded.

Suddenly one day Cao Cao made a request of the emperor, "The traitors in the east are too widespread." The emperor responded, "How can we control this?" Cao said, "Send the Imperial Uncle off to guard Xuzhou." The emperor assented to the request.

Xuande had been on the road for a month, and was just thirty miles from Xuzhou, having reached the inn at Tiekou. All of the officials and yamen personnel from Xuzhou, along with civilians, had come to greet him.

Let us speak now of how Cao Cao deliberately had sent off Che Zhou to be the Grand Protector of Xuzhou, with the intent of wresting away the First Ruler's position. Che Zhou also reached the inn, and he asked the First Ruler, "Do you have a proper letter from the Prime Minister?" The Imperial Uncle said, "I only have the order of the August Emperor; why should I be bearing Lord Cao's letter?"

Che Zhou hurried down the stairs and fled by himself to Xuzhou. The First Ruler said, "If Che Zhou gets to Xuzhou first and does not come out, what shall we do about it?" Lord Guan said, "I will go on ahead."

Lord Guan got on his horse and applied the whip, and just before reaching Xuzhou, he attacked Che Zhou from the rear. Che Zhou tried to avoid him, but "as soon as the blade chopped, the head fell off." When the First Ruler arrived, the host of officers and the aged seniors all welcomed him into the grand yamen. After the banquet given by the officers was over, Xuande said, "Guan, Zhang, and you officers, prepare your battle garb and armor. Sooner or later Lord Cao's troops will arrive." The host of officers discussed this, and then each of them put their garb, armor, and military weapons in order.

Liu Bei and Zhang Fei fail in their surprise attack on Cao's camp and their whole army is destroyed, with the exception of Guan Yu, who guards Liu Bei's family at Xiapi. When Cao's general Zhang Liao urges Guan Yu to surrender to Cao Cao, Guan Yu has three conditions: (1) the house will be divided into two courtyards; (2) when he obtains information about the Imperial Uncle he will visit him; and (3) he surrenders to the Han, not to Cao. Guan Yu follows Cao Cao back to Chang'an, where Emperor Xian ennobles him as Marquis of Shouting. Liu Bei has nowhere to flee. When he stays with Yuan Tan in Qingzhou, he meets Zhao Zilong in the guesthouse, and together they flee to Yuan Shao. Yuan Shao mobilizes his troops and attacks Cao, and Cao mobilizes a hundred thousand troops to oppose him. On behalf of Cao Cao, Guan Yu beheads Yuan Shao's major generals Yan Liang and Wen Chou.

When pressured by Yuan Shao, Liu Bei flees Yuan's camp and sets out for Jingzhou to join Liu Biao. Zhao Zilong follows him. When Guan Yu learns that Liu Bei is at Yuan Shao's camp, he hangs up his seal of office, seals up the gold he was given, returns all gifts to Cao Cao, and leaves with Liu Bei's family to find Liu Bei. When he arrives at Yuan Shao's camp, he learns that Liu Bei has left for Jingzhou, and he promptly sets out for Jingzhou with Liu Bei's family. While on the road Liu Bei and Zhao Zilong run into a highwayman, and this highwayman leads them to Old City, where they are unexpectedly reunited with Zhang Fei. When Guan Yu arrives at Old City, a furious Zhang Fei, who earlier had heard that Guan Yu had surrendered to Cao Cao, wants to kill him, but at exactly that moment Cai Yang, who has received Cao Cao's order to pursue and kill Guan Yu, arrives on the scene, and Guan Yu beheads Cai Yang.

7. Guan Yu Kills Yan Liang, Slays Wen Chou, and Goes to Seek His Sisters-in-Law; Lord Cao Bestows the Robe; Lord Guan Travels Alone for a Thousand Miles, and Beheads Cai Yang

Sighing, Lord Cao said, "Yan Liang is a hero. What's to be done about him?" In the midst of his depression someone reported, "Lord Guan has arrived." Lord Cao hurriedly received him and brought him to the hall, where he explained the awesome power of Yan Liang.

Lord Guan laughed, "This guy is a nothing."

Lord Guan Skewers Yan Liang

Lord Guan went out of the camp, got on his horse with his broad blade, and from a high position observed all of the flags and canopies of Yan Liang until he recognized Yan Liang's own parasol. Seeing that a hundred thousand soldiers surrounded and guarded the camp, Yunchang spurred toward the encampment on a single horse, brandishing his blade. Seeing Yan Liang in the middle of the camp, he caught him completely unaware, and with one swing of the blade he chopped off Yan Liang's head, which fell to the earth. Then he used the tip of his blade to pluck up Yan Liang's head and went out of the encampment and back to his base camp.

He met with Lord Cao who was completely taken with him and stroked Yunchang's back, and said, "You plucked Yan Liang's head right out of an army of a hundred thousand as though you were looking at the palm of your hand. You are the bravest of brave generals."

"I am not strong," said Yunchang. "My brother could pluck a person's head from an army of a million, just like looking at the palm of his hand!" Lord Cao said, "So Zhang Fei is even stronger!" There is an encomium for his shrine that says:

> His brave aura traversed the clouds;
> Truly he was called "A Tiger Officer";
> His bravery equaled that of an entire state of men;
> For a match, call ten thousand men.
> Shu and Wu were like wings,
> And yet Wu finished off this magic beast.
> Alas! Such bravery—
> Before and after, without a match.

But let us speak of Yuan Shao. When the defeated army returned to camp and explained that Lord Guan had slain Yan Liang, Yuan Shao was enraged and cursed the Imperial Uncle, "You and Lord Guan were in communication to make this plan to behead my beloved general Yan Liang. You have destroyed one of my arms!"

He ordered someone to take the Imperial Uncle out and behead him. Wen Chou reported, "Cease your anger, my lord. I want to go and battle Lord Guan in order to repay this injustice to Yan Liang."

Wen Chou led his army out and went forward to face off with Cao's army. Wen Chou shouted, "Come out, bearded one!"

Lord Guan made no reply but went to seize Wen Chou. Wen Chou was defeated in less than ten rounds of battle, and he spurred his horse to flee. Angrily, Lord Guan said, "How can you not give me battle!" He pursued him for thirty miles or more until they reached a ford called Official Ford. As they approached it Lord Guan twirled his blade. . . .

Lord Guan Slays Wen Chou

. . . [A]nd as soon as he spied Wen Chou he hacked, cutting him in two pieces, arms and all. Wen Chou fell from his horse and died. Minister Cao led his troops in an all-out attack, and seventy or eighty percent of Yuan Shao's army was lost. The defeated army returned to see Yuan Shao and they related in detail how Lord Guan had slain Wen Chou.

Yuan Shao was mightily shaken, "They have taken away my two arms. That damned Liu Bei intentionally said that he did not know where Lord Guan was, and now he's destroyed my two generals." He sent someone to round up Liu Bei with the intent of cutting his head off.

But unexpectedly someone approached to kneel before him and it was that man from Changshan, Zhao Yun (known as Zhao Zilong), who said, "In reality, Lord Guan does not know Liu Bei is here. If he knew the First Ruler were here, he would come straight away to join you, great king. The three brothers once swore an oath, 'We need not be born on the same day, but we wish to die on the same day.'" And he went on, "I will guarantee that if Liu Bei and I appear together in front of Cao's battle formation, Lord Guan will immediately cast his lot with us should he see Liu Bei." Yuan Shao was silent. "If you do not believe me, my king, let me leave my family as pawn."

Only then did Yuan Shao assent and spare the life of the First Ruler. The First Ruler and Zhao Yun mounted up and went out of the camp. "If it were not for Zhao Yun," thought the First Ruler to himself, "my life would not have been vouchsafed. Now that brother Yunchang has received a noble title as Marquis of Shouting and has a Han official title, he must have lost his fraternal heart. I have nowhere to turn now. I know that Liu Biao is now the Prince of Jing in Jingzhou; should I get there, it would be a place to find some security."

Without looking back at Zhao Yun, he gave his horse its head and applied the whip to flee off to the southwest. Zhao Yun pursued him aggressively and asked him, "Where are you going?" Liu Bei was silent. "You have but to say where," said Zhao Yun, "and I will follow." Zhao Yun thought to himself, "The First Ruler is not the image of a common man; he will eventually rise to an eminent position. And he is also the seventeenth-generation descendant of Gaozu. How can I abandon him?" He caught up with him again and asked him once more. Seeing how aggressively Zhao Yun was pursuing him, the First Ruler told the whole truth and said, "Now there is Yunchang, but he has accepted a salary from the Han without even considering the heart that bound us in righteousness. Now the Prince of Jing, Liu Biao, is residing in Jingzhou."

"Since you will stay in Jingzhou," said Zhao Yun, "I will go there with you." "But your family are held as ransom by the King of Ji," said the First Ruler. "How can you bear to leave them?" "You are a man of humane virtue," replied Zhao Yun, "and will rise to an eminent position in future days." They went on toward the southwest.

Let us now speak of how delighted Cao Cao was, "In a rare act Lord Guan went out on a single horse into an army of one hundred thousand to skewer Yan Liang, and he caught up with Wen Chou at Official Ford. If I can get him to help me, then it's nothing to take the empire." Cao Cao treated Lord Guan with profound courtesy, giving him a small banquet every three days and a major one every five. He was gifted with gold when he mounted his horse and with silver when he dismounted. He also gave ten beautiful girls to Lord Guan as his personal servants.

Lord Guan, upright as always, never paid any attention to them, but lived in the same compound, in two separate courtyards, with sisters-in-law Gan and Mi. Lord Guan performed morning and evening rituals every day in front of the spirit tablet of the First Ruler. As that day drew toward evening, he went into the compound of his sisters-in-law where he saw them wailing as they burned incense and offered up sacrificial wine. He laughed, saying, "Don't cry, sisters; my elder brother is alive." "Are you drunk?" said ladies Gan and Mi. But Lord Guan replied, "I have just heard that brother is at Yuan Shao, the Prince of Ji's place. Pack up your luggage now, sisters. We will bid Minister Cao adieu tomorrow and head off to Yuan Shao's camp." Lord Guan then returned to his own quarters.

The next day Lord Guan went to take his leave from Minister Cao, but when he got to his headquarters, this sign was hung out—Tenth Day: At Rest.[10] Lord Guan returned to his quarters, but when he went back on the second day, the same plaque was hanging there, so he returned to his quarters. When he went on the third straight day and the plaque was still there,

---

10. The work and rest cycle in ancient China was one day of rest in every ten.

he became angry, "Minister Cao is purposely keeping me from seeing him." So he returned to his quarters again, packed away and sealed up all of the gold and silver he had been given, and together with his seals, he turned all this over to the ten beautiful girls. He had someone gather up all of his saddles and horses for use in war, and then requested that his two sisters-in-law get on a cart, and he went out of Chang'an bound for the northwest.

Let us now speak of how angry Minister Cao was, "I can't believe, after I showed Lord Guan how much I relied on and valued him, that he would be unwilling to stay with me and go off instead to Yuan Shao." The reason that Minister Cao did not open up his office for three days was because he knew that Lord Guan wanted to go to Yuan Shao's camp to find Liu Bei. He had trusted spies in Guan's quarters, all of who acted as Cao Cao's eyes and ears. In the few days that the office was not open, Cao Cao deliberated with his officers.

One of his advisers, Zhang Liao, a real bag of tricks, said, "First set out troops in ambush on both sides of Baling Bridge. If Lord Guan reaches there, you offer him a stirrup cup. Lord Guan has but to dismount and you can have "Strong as Nine Bulls" Xu Chu take Lord Guan into custody. If he doesn't get off his horse then, minister, give him a gift of a ten-patterned brocade silk robe. He has to get off his horse to thank you properly for the gown. Then Nine Bulls Xu Chu can seize him."

Cao Cao was overjoyed, and first sent a troop of soldiers to wait in ambush at Baling Bridge. Then Cao Cao, Xu Chu, and Zhang Liao all went to Baling Bridge to wait.

Lord Cao Bestows the Robe

Lord Guan soon arrived, and the minister offered him a stirrup cup. Lord Guan said, "Please do not take offense, minister, but I am not going to drink." Nor did he get off his horse. Then the brocade robe was brought out, and Xu Chu was ordered to present it. Again, he did not get off his horse, but Lord Guan used the tip of his blade to pluck it up, and then he left, saying, "Thanks for the robe! Thanks for the robe!" Although there were less than a hundred men in Guan's retinue, it frightened Lord Cao so much that he dared not strike. Yunchang escorted the carts of sister Gan and sister Mi and went off to the Prince of Ji's camp.

In a few days he had reached the Prince of Ji's camp. The gate guards reported, "A Lord Guan is at the gates." The King of Ji was alarmed, "First he destroys my two generals and then he comes here!" Then he thought to himself, "Well, Lord Guan has shown up here, and if I should attain his services then what worry do I have that Xindu will not be secure?" He ordered someone to ask Lord Guan to enter the camp.

When Yuan Shao met him, he received Lord Guan in the headquarters' tent. The Prince of Ji pressed wine on him, but Lord Guan would not drink it, saying, "I do not see my brother. Where is he?" "He is drunk," replied the King of Ji. Lord Guan thought to himself, "My brother isn't here." Then he said, "I have my two sisters-in-law outside the gate, we will still have time to drink after they enter the camp." The Prince of Ji was delighted by this.

Lord Guan went out of the camp, mounted up, and then quickly summoned the gate guard. He grabbed the guard's hair with one hand and brandished his sword with the other. "Is the First Ruler here?" he said. "If you don't answer truthfully, I'll kill you." He scared the gate guard so much he repeated over and over, "Not here! Not here!" And when Lord Guan asked where he had gone, the gate guard replied, "He went off to Jingzhou with Zhao Yun." Only then did Lord Guan release him.

Let us now speak of how Lord Guan, with his two sisters-in-law, went south into the Taihang Mountains in order to go to Jingzhou. It was Lord Guan, alone, who led sister Gan and sister Mi over a thousand mountains and ten thousand rivers.

Lord Guan Travels Alone for a Thousand Miles

Let us now speak of how the First Ruler and Zhao Yun, leading three thousand troops, suddenly heard the sound of gongs and drums and saw a band of robbers. The one in front wore a crimson headscarf, had armor of tempered brass, and held a "mountain-splitting" axe. He cried out, "You'll have to leave behind a toll for this road." The First Ruler approached him on horseback and said, "What is your name?" When the bandit saw the First Ruler, he quickly dismounted and performed a ritual obeisance, saying, "Xuande! You have been well since our last parting? I am the Han official Gong Gu. I became a brigand here because Dong Zhuo has usurped power." Then he invited the First Ruler, Zhao Yun, and all of their troops to return to his mountain stronghold, where he treated them to buffalo meat and wine.

They were just drinking a round when a lieutenant reported, "An envoy from the grand king is here." Gong Gu went out to meet with the envoy. The envoy said, "Now receive the sagely command of the grand king. Since you have offered no payment for three months, I originally wanted your head gone, but I'm temporarily letting you off this time. If you do not send payment again, I will certainly carry it out to the end. But for the time being, I am letting you off."

When Gong Gu went back to the tent and saw the First Ruler, the First
Ruler asked, "From which state did this envoy come?" Gong Gu replied, "If
you reach to the dead center of the mountains ahead, it can be said that I
control the area. But there is another, recently, who came with ten horses and
defeated me, so I have to pay a monthly offering. He is in Old City south of
the mountains; he calls himself 'The Grand and Nameless King,' he has built
a palace in the city, called Palace of the Prime Musical Mode, and has insti-
tuted a reign title named 'A Bang-up Time.' He uses a magic spear eighteen
feet long that ten thousand men cannot match." When the First Ruler heard
this, he thought to himself, "Must be Zhang Fei!"

Now Zhao Yun employed a spear that was named "Corners of the Sea
Spear," and it was unmatched to the very corners of the sea or to the edge of
heaven. Except for that spear of Zhang Fei's, this was the number one spear
mentioned in the *Records of the Three Kingdoms*. Zhao Yun wanted to see
this Grand and Nameless King, and he rode down the mountain with the
First Ruler and all of their troops. When they drew near Old City, Zhao
Yun purposely had the gongs and drums sounded.

Let us now speak of how Zhang Fei was sitting in his palace in Old City,
when a foot soldier reported, "Someone is outside the walls, challenging you
to battle." As soon as Zhang Fei heard this, he gave out a shout, "Who?
Which one wants to die?" He quickly ordered his horse prepared, and as fast
as fire he donned his armor, and then took his spear and mounted his horse.
He led several of his cavalry out of the northern gate and saw the First Ruler's army far off. He flew closer until they were squared off, and Zhang Fei
said, "What person dares challenge me to battle?"

Zhao Yun came out on his horse holding his spear and Zhang Fei, enraged, wielded his eighteen-foot steel spear to take on Zhao Yun. The two
horses joined together and the two spears went back and forth like pythons
as they joined in hard battle for thirty rounds. Angrily, Zhang Fei said, "Now
I've seen plenty of people wielding a spear. But this guy really is a tough one."
They joined in battle for thirty more rounds when Zhao Yun had no more
energy, and he quit the field to return to his battle line.

Zhang Fei spoke angrily, "We were just getting to the fiercest part of the
battle; how could he leave off so early?" And giving his horse its head and
holding his spear, he chased Zhao Yun. When he reached the front of the
army, and the First Ruler recognized that it was Zhang Fei, he shouted,
"Brother Zhang Fei." Zhang Fei looked at him, and it was his elder brother,
so he rolled off the saddle and dismounted, lowered his head, and offered
obeisance, saying, "Brother, why did you come here?" Then he remounted

and welcomed him, "Come on in the city and be emperor." Everyone entered the city together.

Zhang Fei invited the First Ruler to sit in the main hall, and they held a banquet. Zhang Fei asked, "Where is elder Brother Two?"

The First Ruler spelled it out in detail, "Lord Guan aided and abetted Cao Cao, he was enfeoffed as the Marquis of Shouting, he slew two generals of Yuan Shao, and he nearly caused my death. He just has no feelings left for our Peach Orchard oath."

After Zhang Fei had listened, he grew enraged, "That good for nothing bastard! He said, 'We do not seek to be born on the same day, but we seek to die together.' And now he receives honor and nobility from Cao Cao! If I see him, there's no way he'll get away with it." He urged more wine on the First Ruler.

But let's not speak anymore of the First Ruler at Old City, but talk instead about Lord Guan coming nearer Old City, and sending someone to report to Zhang Fei. Zhang Fei listened and then shouted, "You bastard barbarian! You have some kind of nerve!" He then ordered men to prepare the horses and strap on armor, and he issued forth with the First Ruler and all the rest.

When Zhang Fei saw Lord Guan, he set his horse galloping, seized his spear, and went straight for Lord Guan. Lord Guan said, "Brother Zhang Fei!" But Zhang Fei didn't heed him and used his spear to thrust at Lord Guan, who quickly parried and blocked it.

Seeing that Lord Guan was not going to fight, Zhang Fei pulled up his horse and said, "You are a man of no trust, for you have forgotten the heart that bound us together in righteousness."

"Brother," said Lord Guan, "you don't understand. I have come a thousand miles, bringing my two sisters-in-law and Adou, to find you two brothers. Why do you want to slay me now?"

Replied Zhang Fei, "You have received riches and nobility from Cao Cao but have purposely hidden it from us to pursue the First Ruler."

Just as the two were talking, they saw that dust was covering the sun just like rain obscures the sky. As it drew nearer, there were also battle standards with a family name, on which was written "The Han General Cai Yang."

Cai Yang transmitted an order to his multitude to open in formation and strike, then he rode out on horseback and said, "You ungrateful soul. I have received the Prime Minister's order and have come to track you down."

Enraged, Lord Guan said, "I forgot no grace, but led my relatives back to find my brother. The great merit that I established for Minister Cao is enough to repay his grace." Then he ordered his men to wave their flags and sound their drums. Cai Yang took up his spear to take Lord Guan, but Lord Guan gave his horse its head while twirling his blade.

(Lord Guan Beheads Cai Yang)

By the time the drum had sounded once, Cai Yang's head had been lopped off by Lord Guan's single blade. Cai's army fled in disarray. This was called "Beheading Cai Yang in a single drumbeat."

Zhang Fei, seeing that Lord Guan had beheaded Cai Yang, rolled off his saddle and dismounted, performed the proper rituals, and came forward, saying, "You were not at fault, Brother Two. When I said you were in league with Cao Cao, I never considered your chaste and incorruptible heart."

The Arrival in Jingzhou

Zhang Fei invites Guan Yu to Old City, and the three brothers are reunited. Together they arrive in Jingzhou, where they are welcomed by Liu Biao. But Liu Biao's generals Cai Mao and Kuai Tong ask Liu Biao to order Liu Bei to leave Xiangyang and garrison Xinye. At Xinye, Liu Bei obtains the services of Xu Shu. When Cao's troops arrive, Xu Shu attacks them with fire and forces them to flee.

8. The First Ruler Leaps across Sandalwood Creek; Cao Ren Barely Gets Out Alive

One day the First Ruler said, "Old City is no place to linger long. What would we do if Cao Cao's armies would arrive? But now there is Liu Biao in Jingzhou, who is at present Prince of Jing. If I would visit the Prince of Jing and get a prefecture from him, we could settle there." Guan and Zhang replied, "You are absolutely right!" So they promptly gathered their luggage and selected a day to start on their journey.

Let's not talk about the ten days spent on the road. Soon they had arrived in Jingzhou and had someone go ahead and report their arrival. The Prince of Jing, Liu Biao, came out of the city to welcome the First Ruler and invited them inside, where they were accommodated in a hostel. The Prince of Jing laid out a banquet and said, "I had never expected that you, Imperial Uncle, would come here. Here in Jingzhou I have no other relatives, but now I have you, Imperial Uncle, and Guan and Zhang to be my bulwarks."

Also present were Liu Biao's in-laws, Kuai Yue and Cai Mao, who were very much displeased. When the Prince of Jing had gone inside and the officials had all dispersed, Kuai Yue and Cai Mao deliberated, "This First Ruler

Liu will wrest away our power, so we have to do away with him!" Cai Mao said, "Let's dispatch him to the border." The two of them therefore promptly went to court to see the prince, and said, "At present Xinye lacks a warden. We fear that if Cao Cao's armies arrive, they will first take Xinye and next take Fancheng, and that it will be difficult to stop them. Our advice is to have the Imperial Uncle with Guan and Zhang defend Xinye as warden, so Cao Cao will not dare cross the borders." The Prince of Jing followed their advice.

The two of them delivered a royal command to the Imperial Uncle and Guan and Zhang that ordered them to choose a day for their departure. Kuai and Cai said, "First have Guan and Zhang go there with the members of your family. You, Imperial Uncle, should stay here for a while. Tomorrow is the third day of the third month. First enjoy with us the banquet at the riverside." The First Ruler indeed stayed behind while the two generals left with the members of his family.

Now tell that these two royal in-laws had designed a plan to murder the First Ruler. The two men had decided on a plan to invite the Imperial Uncle to the feast and have him killed by strongmen halfway through the banquet. When the two of them had settled on this plan, they invited the Imperial Uncle because on the third day of the third month all people in the city would go out and enjoy a riverside banquet. Kuai Yue and Cai Mao took the Imperial Uncle along with them to a banquet outside the walls of Xiangyang. When Kuai Yue secretly gave his orders to the strongmen, one of them noticed that the Imperial Uncle had a face like the full moon, with a high nose and the countenance of a dragon, so he secretly hurried to the Imperial Uncle and whispered in his ear. Frightened, the Imperial Uncle had people bring his horse to a thicket of willows. Feigning that he had to relieve himself, the Imperial Uncle left the banquet and mounted his horse behind the willows. When people shouted, "The Imperial Uncle is fleeing!" Kuai Yue and Cao Mao were greatly surprised. They quickly ordered their men to bring their horses and set out in pursuit with their troops.

Fleeing, the First Ruler arrived at a river, namely Sandalwood Creek. The First Ruler looked up to heaven and cried, "Behind of me are those enemy soldiers, and in front of me is this big river—I'm bound to die here in this river!" The First Ruler's horse was called Rogue. The First Ruler leaned forward on his horse and said, "My fate depends on you; your fate depends on this river. If fate is with us, then jump across this river!" The First Ruler whipped his horse forward, and in one jump it leapt across Sandalwood Creek. When Kuai Yue and Cao Mao arrived there in their pursuit and saw how the First Ruler jumped across Sandalwood Creek, they exclaimed, "A true Son of Heaven!" There is a poem that describes this:

In the third month in Xiangyang the grasses spread evenly;
Grandsons of princes take each other to Sandalwood Creek.
Where now are the dragon bones of Rogue buried?
The flowing stream as before circles the great dike.

Another poem goes:

On both banks of Sandalwood Creek green rushes grow;
Passersby coming and going all sing praises of Rogue.
But don't believe that even the best of horses could jump across:
A sagely bright Son of Heaven was supported by the gods.

Now tell that when the First Ruler had arrived in Xinye as its warden, he dined and feasted each day with Xu Shu. One day, Xu Shu remarked, "Based upon my observation, Xinye will turn any time now into a mountain of corpses, an ocean of blood!" Zhang Fei didn't believe it and said, "How could that be?" In a matter of days Cao Ren, the noble son deputed by Cao Cao, led a huge army of a hundred thousand down the road from Xuchang. He had hundreds of noted generals and had come to seize Fancheng and Xinye. The Imperial Uncle was greatly alarmed.

Zhang Fei laughed and said, "Let's see, master, how you will deal with them!"

"Rest easy, Imperial Uncle," said Xu Shu. "I'll send Cao Ren back without a single piece of armor."

Xu then summoned Zhao Yun and whispered into his ear, explaining a plan to him. Then he invited the Imperial Uncle to the southern gate, saying, "This is a propitious spot."

The master then disheveled his hair, took of his shoes, and, using a plate of food and fragrant potage, he performed a sacrifice until it stirred up a whirlwind. Zhao Yun led all of the armies out to encircle the walled city and had them shoot fire arrows into it. Fire arose on all sides. The forces of Cao Ren were badly defeated, and no one can even guess the number burned to death. Cao Ren, with less than a thousand men, escaped with his life and went back.

Because Xu Shu's mother and family are in Xuchang, which had been held by Cao Cao, he wants to go there to protect them. Liu Bei finds it hard to accept his departure, and when he sees Xu Shu off, the latter recommends Zhuge Liang to him.

The Retreat South

Liu, Guan, and Zhang thrice visit Zhuge Liang, and the latter leaves his hermitage to be appointed Field Marshal. When Cao Cao dispatches Xiahou Dun to attack Xinye, Zhuge Liang uses a trick and inflicts a major defeat on Xiahou Dun.

9. The Third Visit to Zhuge Liang and the Battle at Bowang

The Third Visit to Zhuge

The story says that the First Ruler throughout the four seasons of a single year had thrice gone to the thatched cottage to pay his respects to Recumbent Dragon, but that he had not succeeded in seeing him. Zhuge was originally a divine immortal who had studied his craft from his early youth. Now that he had reached middle age, there was no book he had not read; he understood the mysteries of Heaven and Earth and the inscrutable will of gods and ghosts; he could call up the wind and commandeer rain, create soldiers by scattering beans, and create rivers by waving his sword. Sima Zhongda once remarked, "Coming, he cannot be stopped; going, he cannot be held back; and even when in dire straits he cannot be captured—I do not know whether he is a man, a god, or a ghost!" Now, since Xu Shu had recommended Zhuge Liang to Liu Bei, the First Ruler was unshakable in his determination and arrived once again at the thatched cottage.

The First Ruler was accompanied by his two younger brothers Guan and Zhang and brought his troops with him. In front of the hermitage they dismounted but he still did not dare announce their arrival. After a while an acolyte came out and the First Ruler asked, "Is your master at home?" The acolyte replied, "My master is reading his texts." Accompanied by Guan and Zhang, the First Ruler entered the Daoist hermitage and, reaching the thatched cottage, performed the rituals of greeting. Zhuge continued to pay attention only to his books. Enraged, Zhang Fei said, "Our brother is the seventeenth-generation descendant of Liu Sheng, the Quiet Prince of Zhongshan. Now he is bending his back in front of your thatched cottage. You deliberately humiliate our brother!" With all his authority Yunchang ordered him to shut up. Zhuge lifted his eyes and looked at them, and then came outside to greet them.

When they had finished the formalities, Zhuge asked, "Who might you gentlemen be?" Xuande replied, "I am the seventeenth-generation descendant of Liu Sheng, the Quiet Prince of Zhongshan, and I currently serve as Prefect of Xinye." After Zhuge heard this, he invited the Imperial Uncle into his hermitage, where they sat down. Zhuge said, "I am not really at fault—my acolyte failed to report your arrival." The First Ruler said, "Master, Xu Shu recommends you as an expert in strategy whose skillful schemes surpass those of Lü Jiang.[11] I have now come for the third time in these four seasons to invite you to leave your thatched cottage; I want you to become my Field General." Zhuge replied, "Imperial Uncle, will you annihilate Cao Cao and

---

restore the house of Han?" "Yes," replied Xuande, and he continued to speak, "I have heard that Zhao Gao, chief eunuch, abused his prerogatives, that Dong Zhuo has usurped all power, that Cao Cao is a master of cunning, and Emperor Xian is a fearful weakling. Before long the empire will be mastered by many hegemons, each in his own area. I, Liu Bei, have come here for this reason, to invite you, master, to leave your hermitage and campaign against Cao—but it would be enough if we can simply obtain a single prefecture where we can settle in peace!"

"Ever since Emperor Heng and Emperor Ling lost control of the government," replied Zhuge, "the common people have found it hard to survive. And treacherous ministers usurped all of the high positions within the Gates of the Golden Horse.[12] As a result men of virtue have had to flee to mountain and field. Alas! Cao Mengde commands a million troops and thousands of fierce generals. Because he controls the power of the Son of Heaven, there are no liege lords who do not fear him! By guile Sun Zhong occupies the geographical advantage of the mountains and rivers of Changsha. His state is wealthy, its people haughty. He rules as the third generation, succeeding his father and elder brother, and its rivers can hold back a million troops. And then there is you, Imperial Uncle, one who relies on love and righteousness and who builds on heroic action. But also one who lacks even ten thousand troops or a hundred officers! If you wish to restore the empire, Imperial Uncle, you will first have to grasp the opportunity to borrow Jingzhou as your capital, and then later set your eyes on Xichuan[13] as your interest. Now the area of Jing and Chu has the Great River to its north and to its south the southern barbarians; to its east are Suzhou and Shaoxing, and to its west Ba and Shu. Haven't you heard about that Liu Zhang, who starves his people? He is a fearful weakling as a ruler. As soon as you give the signal to your troops to attack, you can conquer [that region] in a single day! Once that has happened, you place Guan in command of the armies of Shu, and if you march eastward through Sword Pass to conquer everything west of Hangu Pass it will be as easy as picking up a mustard seed from the floor—why wouldn't the common people welcome you with plates of rice and jugs of brew?"

When the Imperial Uncle had found Zhuge, he was as happy as a fish that had found water! Let's not talk about outstanding courage, let's not speak about the loftiest hero—heaven's timing, the advantages of topography, or the harmony of people: each of the three kingdoms utilized one of these virtues to establish its state. Xuande thereupon appointed Zhuge as his Field General. When Zhuge left his thatched cottage, he was twenty-nine.

---

12. Metonymy for the central palaces of government.
13. Modern Sichuan.

Zhuge Leaves His Thatched Cottage

When he went to Xinye, he was treated each day to a banquet. One day the Imperial Uncle suddenly asked the Field General to train the troops. Zhuge proclaimed, "When I train the troops, whoever disobeys my commands will be beheaded!" Now Zhang Fei had long wanted to get the best of Kongming, so he loudly shouted in front of the hall, "Imperial Uncle, that's impossible! How can a hick country cowherd give orders to the troops?" Lord Guan covered Zhang's mouth with his hand and said, "Zhang Fei, you are too crude! The Imperial Uncle treats the Field General as the Great Duke!"[14] The First Ruler said, "To me, finding Kongming was like a fish finding water!" The Imperial Uncle invited Zhuge to his office and treated him to a banquet each day.

A few days more than a month later, someone came to report, "Cao Cao has appointed Xiahou Dun as Great Marshal and he is going to take Xinye with a hundred thousand troops." Zhang Fei shouted loudly, "Imperial Uncle, for you, finding Kongming was like a fish finding water. My martial prowess is crude and blunted, so let's see how the Field General will deal with this situation." Immediately Zhuge called out to Lord Guan, "Use my plan!" And he also ordered Zhao Yun, "Act according to my plan!" The other generals too all received their instructions. Zhang Fei asked, "Field General, you haven't employed me, so what am I supposed to do?" The Field General quickly responded, "General, here are my instructions for you." When Zhang Fei had looked them over, Zhuge said, "General, give it your best!" Within a few days these officers had all dispersed [as ordered by] the Field General.

The Field Marshal Executes His Plan

Let us now tell how Xiahou Dun set up camp at a distance of thirty miles[15] from Xinye and ordered his men to explore the situation there. They heard the sound of drums and music, and reported to the Great Marshal, "The Field General, executing his plans, has ascended the top of a mountain, and has asked the Imperial Uncle to have a banquet there with music." Xiahou Dun said, "That country hick arrogantly treats me too lightly!" He led fifty thousand troops to the high slope. He wheeled to face south, and hoisted his marshal's banner. The Imperial Uncle and the Field General, accompanied by the officials, fled to the western side. From the upper slope, stones from

---

14. The Great Duke is yet another name for Lü Jiang.

15. For convenience, we have translated the *li*, a Chinese distance measure that equals approximately one-third of an English mile, simply as "mile." Since the Chinese time segment (*shi*) was the equivalent of two modern hours, in cases where the text reads "half a *shi*," we translate as "an hour."

catapults and rolling tree trunks hit the hillside. Xiahou Dun's horse never had any rest, for he was pursued from behind by two generals. As soon as Zhao Yun emerged from the flank with three thousand troops, Xiahou Dun wanted to return to his camp—but during his absence Ma Gou and Liu Feng had already captured it. Xiahou Dun fled then toward the north, and when evening fell, he arrived at Old City. He sent out spies who reported, "There is a limitless supply of grain and straw, wagons, and oxen inside the walls." Everyone explained to Xiahou Dun that these were supplies bound for Xinye, but that [the guards there], learning of the impending battle, had fled.

Xiahou Dun and his troops entered the town and dismounted at the government office. The marshal told them to cook food. But when the rice was done and they wanted to eat, troops that had been lying in ambush attacked and surrounded them on all four sides. Xiahou Dun wanted to flee, but the rope holding together his armor had been cut. A hundred horsemen emerged to make a direct assault on his formation, and wounded who knows how many. Xiahou Dun realized, "This must be the scheme of that cowherd country hick!" Not even thirty thousand of his troops remained as they fled toward the east. He had gone no more than twenty miles from the city—it was just a little after midnight—when they all dismounted by the banks of Sandalwood Creek. Xiahou Dun once again told them to make food since the men were exhausted and the horses worn out. Officers and soldiers all were lying on their backs. When the rice was done, they asked the marshal to eat before any of the officers. Suddenly they heard a sound that echoed like thunder and someone reported to Xiahou Dun, "The water of Sandalwood Creek is billowing down like a bank of massive white clouds!" The marshal ordered his men to hasten to the top of a hillock, from where he watched as the corpses of men and horses were swept downriver by the water. The marshal wept bitterly—not even ten thousand of his troops were left.

When morning came, Xiahou Dun once again went on in a northerly direction, and arrived at a bridge across Sandalwood Creek. Between east and west it exactly faced south, and he crossed the bridge straight to the north. But hidden troops emerged to block his way, and he was trapped between Jian Xianhe behind and Lord Guan in front. Xiahou Dun attacked the formations head on and got past, but saw that now he had fewer than three hundred troops left. Xiahou Dun said, "First rocks rained down all over the hillside, next my camp was occupied, then there was the battle in the old town, and in the end I had to flee because a flood was released to drown my troops." And Xiahou Dun went on, "If there is yet another body of troops waiting for me, I will not be able to return to Xuchang!" Before he had finished saying this, less than three miles ahead of him three thousand troops appeared below the willow trees. Amongst them a drunken general shouted, "The Field General, the Imperial Brother, and the other generals all abided by the plan and they shoved me off to this place. And the Field General said, 'After Xiahou Dun is defeated, he will pass through your hands!'"[16] When Zhang Fei fell silent, someone hurried up to inform him, "Those defeated troops are coming straight east; they're less than three hundred men!" "Who is it?" asked Zhang Fei. "Xiahou Dun," came the reply. Zhang Fei said with a smile, "That Field General truly is smart!" As soon as his words were finished, Zhang Fei mounted his horse to block Xiahou Dun. The two sides engaged in battle, and Xiahou Dun was soundly defeated.

Let us now tell how Cao Cao had taken his seat in the hall and inquired of his officers, "Xiahou Dun left with a hundred thousand troops and a hundred generals to take Fancheng and Xinye. He has been gone for three months now and there's been no news." Before he had finished these words, one of his underlings reported, "Xiahou Dun and his army have returned." "What," asked Cao Cao, "was the outcome?" The soldier said, "Only twenty or thirty people have made it back." Cao Cao was shaken and ordered Xiahou Dun to present himself. He saw that his armor was covered in blood and that his body betrayed multiple wounds. Xiaohou Dun prostrated himself on the ground and said, "Please spare my wife and children; I beg to die." Xiahou Dun went on, "A hundred thousand troops beheaded by five generals! Immolated by fire, drowned by a flood, ambushed again and again! And eventually I was bitterly defeated by that Zhang Fei!"

When Cao Cao heard this, he flew into a rage, "Take Xiahou Dun out and behead him in front of the steps." He heard someone loudly call out before he finished speaking. He recognized that it was Xu Shu, who said, "Prime Minister, Dun has the courage of a prince!" Minister Cao spoke, "What about this Zhuge?" Xu Shu replied, "That man has the skill to fathom Heaven. The whole world is as clear to him as the ten fingers of his hands. If Xiahou Dun managed to escape from Zhuge with his life, he is an outstanding general!" Cao Cao said with a smile, "In my eyes that country hick is nothing. Xu Shu, I will prove you wrong! Leading a million of troops and a thousand of fine officers, I will trample Fancheng and Xinye to pieces and even take Jingzhou!" Immediately he mobilized the troops.

When Liu Bei goes back to Jingzhou, Liu Biao has died, and Liu Zong refuses to let him enter the city. As he continues his retreat in a southerly direction, the

---

16. The expression has a double meaning, "will pass your way" and "will slip through your fingers." In this text, however, the emphasis is not so much on Zhang Fei's failure as on Xiahou Dun's defeat.

common people follow him while weeping because Liu Bei is such a humane and virtuous ruler. During Liu Bei's retreat toward the south, he is separated from his family. When Zhao Yun (Zilong) goes back to look for them, he finds Liu Bei's infant son Adou and brings him back. With a single shout at Dangyang Slope, Zhang Fei scares Cao Cao's troops into retreating. Liu Bei continues his southward journey and is welcomed by Sun Quan's official, Lu Su, into Xiakou. Zhuge Liang travels with Lu Su to Jinling (Nanjing) to visit Sun Quan, carrying a letter by Liu Bei requesting aid from Sun Quan. Cao Cao now raises a million troops and a thousand generals to attack Xinye, Fancheng, and Jingzhou.

10. Zhang Fei Halts Cao Cao's Advance at Dangyang Slope and Zhao Yun Saves Adou

Thirty miles further was a river with a large bridge over it. The mountain grade was particularly steep and it was known as "the long slope of Dangyang." When the Imperial Uncle passed by this long slope of Dangyang, Commander General Zhuge Liang noted how high and precipitous this peak was, and he thought that if he could find one stalwart general and a hundred horse to occupy the top, he could hold off the entire million men of Cao Cao's army.

"I am wrong," said Kongming. "I sent Lord Guan to the River yesterday to tie up the boats [on the bank opposite Cao Cao], and he won't reach here by today."

He heard someone shout out loudly, and recognized it to be Zhang Fei. "Do you acknowledge that the bearded Lord Zhang Fei can hold them off?"

"I have heard," said the Field Marshal, "that his eminence's great battle at Tigerkeep Pass and the three exits from Minor Pei were all due to the virtue of Yide. Anyone who is brave and staunch today and can block the progress of that traitor Cao, winning fame in history, is surely a great man."

Let us then speak of Zhang Fei, who summoned twenty men to go out with twenty battle flags and went off north to the long slope at Dangyang.

Later we will speak of Zhao Yun, who went into Cao's encampment with a single mount. He said, "We are now over a hundred miles from the battlefield, so let me search for the Imperial Uncle's relatives." He made a circuit several times until he suddenly saw Lady Gan, with her right hand clutching her ribs and her left holding Adou. Zhao Yun got off his horse and when Consort Gan saw him, tears coursed down without cease as she explained, "All relatives were slain by the berserk troops of Lord Cao." She went on, "Zhao Yun, you have come at just the right time."

Her right ribs had been struck by an arrow and when she lifted her hand, her guts came out. "Our Imperial Uncle is already old but still has no place 'to stand an awl on end.' I'm finished now. You take Adou and turn him over to uncle."

When her words were finished, she went south to the base of a wall and bade goodbye to Zhao Yun and Adou, and then she died there below the wall. Zhao Yun pushed the wall over to cover her body. Zhao Yun said, "I will save Adou for our lord from the clutches of Cao's millions!" This instant of bravery won Zhao Yun recognition in history. He held the crown prince as he raced southward, smashing directly through the enemy's formations. There was a later poem:

> How marvelous was this Zhao Zilong:
> A whole heart of loyalty that puts others in awe;
> The First Ruler had been defeated in Jingzhou,
> And his family was unable to follow him.
> With a lifelong disregard for death
> Zhao plunged again into the thicket of tigers and wolves;
> Loyal and filial, he protected the weak little child,
> Daring to challenge a million brave men.
> In the Spring and Autumn era was a Minister Wu,[17]
> And the reign of Han has its Zilong—
> A thousand generations from this point on,
> Who will not look up to these high moral actions?

Zhao Zilong Carries the Baby in His Arms

Zhao Zilong flees toward the south.

But let us speak of Cao Cao, watching from a high vantage point, who thought, "Must be some officer in the hands of Liu Bei!" He then dispatched a host of officers to take Zhao Yun, and their leader, Guan Jing, blocked his way. Zhao Yun twirled his blade and spurred his horse, breaking directly through the formation until, as he reached the bridge, his horse lost its footing and lord and minister were on the ground tightly clutching each other. Behind, Guan Jing was in hot pursuit and drawing near, so Zhao Yun used his stout bow and with a single arrow shot and killed Guan Jing.

Carrying the heir apparent in his arms, Zhao Yun then fled southward. A mile or so away from the long slope at Dangyang, he saw Zhang Fei far off.

---

17. Minister Wu is Wu Zixu, whose father and elder brother had been killed by the King of Chu. Despite great deprivation he persisted in his determination to take revenge. Eventually he rose to high position in the state of Wu and inflicted a devastating defeat on his old home state.

"Grand Defender," said Zhang Fei, "you have to save Adou!" Zhao Yun said, "As for the Imperial Uncle's family, the two wives are dead. The crown prince is the only one to survive, and I will take him to the Imperial Uncle." Zhang Fei wept and said, "As a real hero, I just told the Imperial Uncle that I would hold the long slope at Dangyang, to assure that His Majesty makes his escape."

Zhao Yun went on south, and when he had finished the greeting rituals when he saw the Imperial Uncle, he said, "Consort Gan and Consort Mi were both killed by Lord Cao. I was able to rescue the heir apparent from the berserk troops and escape." Zhao Yun then went to see the Imperial Uncle holding the heir apparent. The Imperial Uncle took the child and threw him to the ground. His officers were all startled and remonstrated with the Imperial Uncle. Xuande said, "Because of this 'shameful child of mine,'[18] I almost lost my great general Zhao Yun." When the Imperial Uncle finished speaking, they all praised his goodness. The Imperial Uncle went on southward.

Now let us speak of Zhang Fei reaching the long slope at Dangyang to the north. Zhang Fei ordered his soldiers to take fifty flags[19] and make a formation of a long horizontal line on a high place to the north. Twenty-some cavalry were to keep lookout to the river to the south. Lord Cao arrived with an army of three hundred thousand. "Respected Sir, why are you not avoiding me?" Zhang Fei laughed, "I see no huge army; all I see is Cao Cao." When Cao's cavalry let out a continuous yell, he then shouted out, "I am Zhang Yide from Yan, who dares fight to the death with me?" His shout was like thunder in the ears, and the bridge broke completely asunder. Cao's army withdrew some thirty miles away. There is a eulogy for the shrine to Yide:

> The First Ruler plotted to be king;
> The vessel, torn in three, bubbled over;
> He resisted at the bridge and sent the troops in flight;
> His overpowering shout sundered the water.
> The liege lords trembled in terror;
> The soldiers traveled in the most terrifying place.
> Stern and awesome like a god,
> He had the aura of a hegemon!

The Alliance of Liu Bei and Sun Quan

Sun Quan's men, Zhang Zhao and Wu Wei, strongly argue that Wu should rely on the River for defense and not help Liu Bei. Cao Cao sends a messenger with

---

18. Humble way of referring to one's child.
19. Each flag signified a unit of troops.

a letter to Sun Quan, demanding his surrender. When Zhuge Liang kills the messenger with his own hands, Zhang Zhao has him arrested, but Zhuge Liang asks Sun Quan to read the letter carefully, and tells him that Cao Cao had already killed quite a number of the liege lords. When Lu Su informs Sun Quan that Cao Cao will wield the power of life and death, Sun Quan orders Zhuge Liang released. Sun Quan tells his mother that Zhuge Liang has come to borrow troops, and that Cao's army is encamped on the northern bank of the River. His mother reminds him to follow his father's command to appoint Zhou Yu as commander in times of crisis. Sun Qun makes up his mind and cuts a table in two with his sword, saying that if anyone again opposes the mobilization of troops, they will suffer the fate of that table. He orders Lu Su and Zhuge Liang to go to Yuzhang, but Zhou Yu does not want to become involved. Zhuge Liang informs him that Cao Cao is building the Bronze Sparrow Terrace and is searching for the most beautiful girls of the world—including the two daughters of Lord Qiao, one of whom is engaged to Zhou Yu. Zhou Yu then goes and visits Sun Quan.

Cao Cao's Defeat and Escape

Zhou Yu becomes commander and sails westward. When Cao's troops shoot their arrows, Zhou Yu protects his boats with heavy curtains. He first lets them shoot at his left side, and then at his right side, and within an hour he has obtained a million arrows. The next day Zhou Yu attacks Cao's army with catapults and defeats him. Cao Cao, seeing that Sun Quan has Zhou Yu and Liu Bei has Zhuge Liang, also wants to appoint a Field Marshal. He finds an elderly Daoist priest, Jiang Gan, and appoints him as Field Marshal. Cao considers Jiang Gan as someone of the same ilk as Lü Wang or Zhang Liang.[20] Jiang Gan crosses the River, and falls for a ruse claiming that Huang Gai wants to surrender, which he reports upon his return to Cao Cao. Zhou Yu and his generals all decide to use fire to attack Cao Cao's fleet, but Zhuge Liang writes on his hand the character "wind." Huang Gai falsely surrenders and enters Cao's camp, which is destroyed by a conflagration.

11. The Plot That Sacrifices One's Body and the Battle of Red Cliff

"If it were just on dry land," Cao Cao said, "I would defeat Zhou Yu. But battling on the water I can find no way to get an advantage."

---

20. Lü Wang was the wise adviser of King Wen and King Wu, the founders of the Zhou dynasty. Zhang Liang was an adviser of Liu Bang.

Then Cao Cao had an idea, and thought, "Sun Quan has his Zhou Yu, Liu Bei has his Zhuge Liang, but I'm all alone." He discussed it with his officials and decided to raise up a Field Marshal. Followed by a thousand or so men, riding in one unadorned cart, he took his officials to the Yangzi, where he saw a Daoist elder sitting and strumming a zither.

"Well," Cao Cao thought to himself, "King Wen found Jiang Taigong and established the Zhou for eight hundred years." Cao Cao quit his conveyance and greeted the man, then invited him to return to his car for a conversation.

"Master," asked Cao Cao. "Are you not one of the Eight Eminences of the Lower Yangzi?"

"Yes," replied the master.

Cao Cao Appoints Jiang Gan as Marshal of the Army

Cao Cao was elated and took him back to his stronghold, where he fêted him for several days.

Cao asked him, "Master, what's to be done about making Zhou Yu withdraw?"

Jiang Gan then launched into a discussion, "Zhou Yu is from Fuchun, in the Jiangnan area, from the same village as me. Let me have an audience with Zhou Yu, ply my words to persuade him, and make him give up on setting his troops in action. Then, at Xiakou on the north bank of the Yangzi, you first behead Liu Bei and afterward drive your troops to the south across the River and take Wu. It can be had in any amount of time you stipulate."

Cao Cao was elated, and looked upon Jiang Gan as a man of the same ilk as Jiang Taigong or Zhang Liang. The next day Jiang Gan crossed the river.

Zhou Yu, Lu Su, and Zhuge Liang were engaged in conversation together when someone reported, "An elder is here to see the Grand Marshal." Someone was deputed to ask Jiang Gan to enter the camp and all of the officials received him into the tent and offered him a seat.

Zhou Yu began, "My old friend, we have been parted many years, and today we meet again." And he went on, "One who 'leaves the family' does not covet name or benefit. Now Zhou is a Grand Marshal in Eastern Wu, with a rugged army of three hundred thousand, and a hundred noted generals, and has encamped at the ford at Chaisang. Master, please explain the rights and wrongs of the two states!" With this one sentence Jiang Gan was stumped for a way to reply.

Now let us speak about how Zhou Yu was in his cups and had asked his host of officers, "Minister Cao is encamped at Xiakou with thirteen hundred thousand troops, and sooner or later Xiakou has to fall. Which of you officers has a plan that can lead to the withdrawal of Cao's army?" From their midst, Huang Gai came forth and said, "Grand Marshal! Send three officers with fifty thousand men to secretly cross at Chaisang, and then follow a small path to a keep some sixty miles north of Xiakou. There cut off noble Cao's supplies; then Cao will kill himself in less than a month. This is called 'the plan to cut off the road and stop supplies.'" "Huang Gai," said Zhou Yu angrily, "this plan is worthless!" Lu Su had no plans and the other officers were silent. "Huang Gai is a flatterer and should be put to death!" The host of officers all urged him to be tolerant and Huang was spared death, but he received sixty blows from the bastinado.[21]

That night the Grand Marshal got drunk and his officers dispersed. In his tent, Jiang Gan said to himself, "From the start, Zhou Yu stopped me from speaking." Huang Gai, full of grief and resentment, went to Jiang's tent and said, "Thank you, sir, for being one of the first to urge the marshal to spare me." The master said, "Zhou Yu is not fit to be Grand Marshal." Huang Gai then opined, "Now there is no true mandate to help him." Seeing that they were alone, Jiang Gan spoke of the virtue of Cao Cao. [Huang Gai] said, "Who can believe that from afar? I should be able to see the noble Cao." Jiang Gan explained, "Minister Cao has appointed me Field Marshal. I came to persuade Zhou Yu to a different course of action, but he cut me off so that I could not speak about it. Are you, notable one, willing to cast your lot with Cao?" Jiang Gan went on, "There's no need to worry, general, because you would receive a high post or commission."

Going on in the same vein, Huang Gai offered, "You are probably not aware that Kuai Yue and Cai Mao have already sent letters and surrendered to Zhou Yu." Jiang Gan was greatly taken aback. Huang Gai said, "The Grand Marshal gave me the letter." Jiang Gan wanted to read the letter, and after he did he was alarmed, saying, "Minister Cao needs to know about this. I should give the letter to Cao Cao and have those two men executed, so that there is no need for later regret." Huang Gai himself wrote out a letter of surrender, and he said, "When I surrender to Cao Cao, I will offer up five hundred [carts] of food and fodder to the minister." They spoke until very late. The next day, Jiang Gan was sent off.

Let us now speak about how how Jiang Gan got on the boat and reached Lord Cao's stronghold that night. On the next day, he had audience with Minister Cao and explained the whole affair in detail. After Cao Cao read Huang Gai's letter of surrender, he was ecstatic. Jiang Gan then informed him of how Kuai Yue and Cai Mao had surrendered to Zhou Yu and, after he gave the letter to Lord Cao to read, Cao was greatly alarmed.

---

21. Jiang Gan does not know that the bastinado is part of a plot to make Huang Gai's (feigned) defection to Cao Cao look convincing.

Let us speak instead of Cao Cao's army of thirteen hundred thousand men, for whom being on the boat was like climbing onto level land. Cao Cao was delighted, and he said, "I have heard of Huang Gai's virtue, but I've never seen him face to face. If he comes, I will certainly rely on him heavily."

Yu Fan went back to the southern bank and had an audience with Zhou Yu, and told him everything that had come to pass. He was also carrying a letter from Cao Cao to Huang Gai. Zhou Yu said, "This great venture is now complete." He gave rewards to Yu Fan and promoted him in rank. The Grand Marshal ordered his close top-ranking officials and the general officers to look at him, and Zhou Yu said, "There is a brief window to destroy the million-man army of Cao Cao. I have a plan. If all of you are of the same mind, then bring out a brush and inkstone and write in the palm of your hand. If we all agree, then this plan is the right one. If we don't, then we will discuss it in more detail." "What you say, marshal," said the general officers, "is sure to be right." So they wrote in the palm of their hands, and when finished the general officers followed him and ordered the other soldiers to move to the back. The general officers looked at their palms and the palm of the marshal's hand, and every character was "fire." All of them were overjoyed. Then Zhou Yu stared at Field Marshal Zhuge, and said to him, "This plan is 'flaming fire.' It comes from Guan Zhong's 'Pacify the People with Slight Parching Military Strategy.'" But only the Field Marshal's hand had the character "wind" written on it.

"This," said Zhuge, "is a marvelous plan of yours. On the day that the fire will be set, our stronghold will be on the southeast, and Cao Cao's on the northwest. How will we defeat Cao Cao if the wind is not in our favor when the time comes?" The Grand Marshal said, "Why did you write the word 'wind'?" The Field Marshal repeated, "If all of the general officers employ the word 'fire,' I can aid them with the wind." Zhou Yu said, "Wind and rain are creations of the interaction of yin and yang in the heavens. Are you capable of raising the wind?" Again the Field Marshal explained, "From the time heaven and earth came into existence, there have been three people who are capable of invoking the wind through sacrifice. The first was the Yellow Emperor, Xuanyuan. He made the Lord of the Wind his marshal and had Wind defeat Chi You. I also heard that Emperor Shun made Gao Yao his marshal and he employed Wind to pin down the San Miao peoples. I have received diagrams and texts, and when the day comes, I will aid with a southeasterly wind." None of the general officers were happy and Zhou Yu thought to himself, "I employ a marvelous plan that will allow not a sliver of Cao's army to return, and Zhuge Liang steals my thunder!" The general officers began to get rowdy.

A gatekeeper reported, "There is a gentleman outside who says he would like to see his friend Zhuge." The general officers went out to greet him. Let us turn to Zhuge Liang, when he met him and escorted him up the stairs where they sat according to their rank. This was Zhuge Liang's cousin, Zhuge Jin. They feasted until late and the general officers all left.

Zhou Yu welcomed Zhuge Jin into his own tent to sit, and he said, "Do you know that Zhuge is not loyal? The general officers all raised up 'fire' and he talked about sacrificing to the wind." "This Recumbent Dragon of our house," replied Zhuge Jin, "has techniques beyond comprehension." Zhou Yu laughed, "If it makes Cao Cao withdraw and rescues Liu Bei, then I am a prisoner under his aegis!" He departed after speaking.

Some days later—tell that Zhuge built a high terrace of rammed earth, with its north side bordering on the River. Three days later—tell that Huang Gai had loaded a lot of grain and fodder, and there were three boats outside. On that day several tens of Zhou Yu's officers led a group of marines to rush outside Xiakou city. When Huang Gai's boats arrived at Xiakou, someone reported to Cao Cao, "Huang Gai is carrying grain and fodder to the stronghold." Cao Cao welcomed them with smiles and laughter.

Finally let us speak of how the Field Marshal calculated when the full army would reach Xiakou, and how Zhuge ascended the terrace where he saw fire starting in the northwest. Let us speak of how Zhuge donned his yellow cape, and with disheveled hair and bare feet, holding a sword in his left hand and clacking his teeth, performed a Daoist ritual, and the wind rose up mightily. There is a poem:

> Violent battles at Red Cliff, mighty from antiquity,
> Men of those days all were in awe of Lord Zhou;
> But Heaven knew that what came after the separation into thirds
> Was all due to the loyalty of the humble Huang Gai!

Let us now speak of how the Martial Marquis [Zhuge Liang] crossed the River to Xiakou. On his boat, Cao Cao cried out, "I am dead!" His general officers said, "It's all Jiang Gan's fault." And in a flurry of knives they hacked Jiang Gan into ten thousand pieces. Cao Cao got on a boat, and hurriedly sought out a road by which to flee out of Jiangkou, and he saw that every boat, on all four sides, was aflame. He saw tens of boats. On those was Huang Gai, who said, "Behead the traitor Cao and make the empire as secure as Mount Tai!" The hundred officers of Minister Cao were ignorant of water battle, and the army was shooting arrows at them. It was too late for Cao Cao to do anything about it—there was fire on four sides and in front

was a barrage of arrows. Cao Cao wanted to flee, but Zhou Yu was to the
north, Lu Su to the south, Ling Tong and Gan Ning to the west, and Zhang
Zhao and Lü Fan to the east. Death lay on all four sides. The Office of
Scribes says, "If it weren't for the fact that Lord Cao's family had the fated
outcome of the Five Emperors,[22] he would not have been able to escape."

Cao Cao did escape this peril alive and fled to the northwest. When he
reached the bank of the River, his men surrounded Lord Cao as he mounted
up. It is said that the fire broke out at dusk and it was noon the next day
before he got out. Cao Cao turned around to look and he could still see the
smoke and flames from the boats at Xiakou spreading across the sky—not
ten thousand men were left from his own army.

Cao has no way to escape, but he manages to break through and leave in a
northwesterly direction. His way is blocked by Zhao Yun with five thousand
troops, but he manages to dash through. Then his way is blocked by Zhang Fei
with two thousand troops. After he fights his way through, he runs into Guan
Yu with his troops. Cao begs Guan Yu to let him pass, but Guan Yu answers
that he is under strict orders of the Field Marshal. But suddenly a dust cloud
arises, and Cao Cao makes his escape.

The Battle of Wits of Zhou Yu and Zhuge Liang

Zhou Yu observes that Liu Bei has the features of a king or emperor, and invites him to a banquet at Yellow Crane Tower where he hopes to kill him. Liu
Bei adopts a stratagem of Zhuge Liang and escapes safely to the other side of the
River while Zhou Yu is drunk. Zhang Fei inflicts a defeat on Cao Zhang and
offers Xiakou and three other prefectures to Zhou Yu to repay him for his help
and assistance. But when Zhou Yu discovers that Liu Bei has already occupied
Jingzhou, he raises an army and attacks him. Actually Liu Bei had assisted the
eldest son of the Prince of Jing, Liu Qi, to occupy Jingzhou, and Zhou Yu is
so enraged that his old battle wounds open up again. When Liu Qi dies, Zhou
Yu once again attacks Jingzhou, but Zhuge Liang presents him with already
approved documents, according to which the emperor has appointed Liu Bei
as Area Commander in Chief of the Three Rivers and Warden of Yuzhou and
Commander in Chief of the Fleet and Governor of the Thirteen Prefectures of
the Lower Reaches of the River. Zhou Yu is so enraged that his battle wounds
erupt again. Zhou Yu then has Sun Quan marry his younger sister to Liu Bei
so she may kill Liu Bei at a suitable moment. But when Lady Sun sees a golden
snake curled up on Liu Bei's breast, she cannot bring herself to do it. Liu Bei

---

22. That is, because his family would go on to establish the Wei dynasty, he was fated to live.

comes with Lady Sun to Jinling, and Zhou Yu tries in many ways to kill Liu Bei, but without success. Zhou Yu sends tens of thousands of loads of grain to Jingzhou, borrowing passage for his army on its way to conquer Sichuan. But as Zhou Yu travels forward, fighting all the way, Zhang Fei follows behind him and reoccupies all those cities without a fight. Zhou Yu realizes that he has been outwitted by Zhuge Liang, and finally dies.

Part III

Liu Bei's Conquest of Sichuan

Pang Tong is not utilized by Sun Quan to the extent of his abilities and he goes over to Liu Bei, who makes him magistrate of Liyang. This is against Pang's wishes, and for half a month he mishandles public affairs. When Zhang Fei is ordered to investigate, Pang Tong has already left. Four prefectures rise in rebellion, and Zhuge Liang dispatches people to subjugate and recover the four prefectures of Changsha, Guiyang, Wuling, and Jinling, and obtains the services of the surrendered Wei Yan and Huang Zhong. Cao Cao orders Ma Teng to come to the capital, where he kills him. Ma Teng's sons Ma Chao and Ma Dai want to take revenge for their father and fight with Cao Cao. They put so much pressure on Cao Cao that he can only escape by cutting of his beard and leaving behind his coat. But Cao Cao sows dissension among Ma Chao's officers and defeats Ma Chao through this stratagem. In Sichuan, Liu Zhang sends Zhang Song to present maps of Sichuan to Cao Cao, but when the latter sees how short and ugly Zhang Song is, he ignores him. Zhang Song then proceeds to Jingzhou and presents the maps to Liu Bei. Liu Bei and Pang Tong now lead an army to conquer Sichuan. Liu Bei meets with Liu Zhang at Fujiang, but cannot bring himself to kill Liu Zhang. Arriving at Luocheng, Pang Tong is struck by an arrow and dies.

Zhuge Liang's Defense of Sichuan

When Zhuge Liang receives the information that Pang Tong is dead, he mobilizes men and horses and enters Sichuan by three routes. When Liu Bei takes Yizhou, he also wins over Ma Chao. Liu Bei ennobles the five great tiger generals: Guan Yu is ennobled as Marquis of Shouting, Zhang Fei as Marquis of Xichang, Ma Chao as Dingyuan Marquis, Huang Zhong as Dingluan Marquis, and Zhao Yun as Liguo Marquis. While Guan Yu is governor of Jingzhou, Lu Su invites him to dinner, and Guan Yu goes to the meeting with a single sword.

12. Guan Yu Goes to the Single Sword Meeting

One day a spy offered this report: Lu Su, Grandee of Jiang Wu, was leading a huge army across the River, and had dispatched someone with a letter inviting Lord Guan to go to a "single-sword meeting." Lord Guan said, "There is surely some plot afoot in this single-sword meeting, but what do I fear?"

When the day arrived Lord Guan, with a light bow and short arrows, and with good mounts and trusted men bearing swords—no more than fifty in all—went south to Lu Su's encampment. The generals of Wu saw that Lord Guan was clothed in absolutely no armor and had but a single sword hanging from his waist. Lord Guan saw that there were three thousand men in Lu Su's retinue, all in armor, and that each of the officers was wearing a "heart-protecting bronze mirror" on his chest. His lordship thought to himself, "What is this traitor's objective?" When the feast was spread and wine brought forward, Lu Su ordered the army to play music to accompany the feast. The flute made no sound three times in a row and the Grandee shouted out the five notes of the scale, "*gong, shang, jue, zhi, yu!*" And then, three times in a row, he said, "*Yu* did not sound." Lord Guan was enraged and clutched Lu Su. Lord Guan said, "You traitor; you set up this feast for no reason and called it a 'single-sword meeting,' then had your troops play music that did not sound the note *yu*. You said, '*Yu* does not sound / *Yu* is clueless,'[23] but today I'll make 'the mirror' be the first to break this sound."[24] Lu Su prostrated himself on the ground and said, "I would not dare." Lord Guan spared his life, got on his horse, and returned to Jingzhou.

Lu Su asks the commander in chief Lü Meng to take Changsha and three more prefectures, and Guan Yu requests aid from Zhuge Liang. Zhuge Liang leads the tiger generals in their fight with Lü Meng, and inflicts a major defeat on the army of Wu. Zhuge Liang returns with the army to Sichuan. Cao Cao has incorporated the army of Zhang Lu, and invades Sichuan as far as Yangping Pass, but Zhuge Liang raises an army of fifty thousand troops and repulses Cao Cao. After Zhuge Liang has returned to Chengdu, Cao Cao once again occupies Yangping Pass, but Zhuge Liang defeats Cao's troops yet another time.

13. Zhang Fei Releases Yan Yan out of Righteousness

Let us speak of Zhang Fei who, after ten days on the road, finally reached Baqiu County, only to find that all of the civilians had fled. He went on to

---

23. This is a pun on the homophonic line *yu buming* (the tone *yu* [the same character as Guan Yu's given name] does not sound) and *yu buming* (*Yu* is clueless).

24. A pun on the syllable *jing*, which can mean both "mirror" and part of Lu Zijing's given name; i.e., "you'll die first."

the southwest until he reached Ba Prefecture, where he set up his stronghold some forty miles away. One day, Zhang Fei led his army of thirty thousand off to Ba, but about five miles outside the prefectural city he came to a small confluence of two rivers, where he ordered someone to probe how deep the water was. Zhang Fei crossed the river, which was about five miles wide, and was about to reach the bank on the other side. The Grand Protector of Ba Prefecture, Yan Yan, laughingly asked him, "Zhang Fei! Haven't you read Master Sun's *Art of War*? In there it said, 'Those who are halfway through a river crossing may be attacked.'" Zhang Fei replied, "Haven't you heard about my actions at the long slope of Dangyang? Seeing the million-man army of Cao Cao, I just let out a single shout and they were no more than little recruits. How much less is this little ditch? It doesn't cause me any worry." Zhang Fei spurred his horse up the bank to fight, and Yan Yan fell off his horse in the middle of the panicked army and was captured by Zhang Fei. When they reached a forest, Zhang Fei dismounted.

Zhang Fei Overawes Yan Yan with Righteousness

He shouted in a loud voice, "I have heard that Yan Yan was a famous general of Shu, and now I have him. Behead him! Behead him!" When the Major General heard him he laughed, "Zhang Fei might consider me nothing. I fell off, lost my horse, and was captured by him. A great man risks his life as if it were nothing. What's the reason you're beheading me?" Zhang Fei stopped the executioners and said, "Yan Yan is a real hero!" So he ordered someone to release his ropes and he set him free.

When Cao Cao orders Xiahou Yuan to occupy Mount Dingjun, Zhuge Liang has Huang Zhong kill Xiahou Yuan, and when Huang takes Mount Dingjun, he captures five hundred loads of provisions and stores.

The Death of Guan Yu

Cao Cao returns to Chang'an and kills the Emperor Xian's crown prince. When Xian raises Cao's title to that of Great King of Wei, Sun Quan in Wu assumes the title of Great King of Wu, and Liu Bei in Sichuan assumes the title of Prince of Hanzhong. Liu Bei also establishes [his son] Liu Shan (also known as Aji or Adou) as Lord of Sichuan. When people from Wu propose to Guan Yu a marriage with the daughter of the King of Wu, Guan Yu, who is drunk, replies, "I am the son of dragons and tigers—how could I ever marry the grandchild of a melon grower?" When armies of Wei invade Jingzhou, Guan Yu fights the generals of Wei and kills General Pang De. He also drowns the seven armies of Yu Jin. But when Lü Meng of Eastern Wu and the Wei general Zhang Liao team up to attack Jingzhou, Guan Yu dies. Cao Cao wants Emperor Xian to establish Cao's son, Cao Pi, as emperor, and Cao Cao builds a terrace for the abdication ceremony. When [following the death of Cao Cao] Cao Pi ascends the throne, he adopts the reign title Huangchu. Sun Quan in Eastern Wu now declares himself Emperor of Wu, and adopts the reign title Huanglong, while in Sichuan Liu Bei becomes the Emperor of Shu, and adopts the reign title Jianwu.

The Murder of Zhang Fei and the Death of Liu Bei

When Liu Bei learns that Lü Meng has killed Guan Yu, he ignores Zhuge Liang's advice and leads five hundred thousand troops in a campaign against Wu. Zhang Fei serves as commander of the vanguard. When they arrive at Baidicheng (White Tiger City), they establish five interlocked camps. When the chief commander of Wu, Lü Meng, arrives, Zhang Fei asks permission to fight him, but Liu Bei, noticing his advanced age, tells him not to sally forth. While drunk, Zhang Fei administers a beating to the standard bearer Wang Qiang as well as the kitchen officers Zhang Shan and Han Bin. Wang Qiang, Zhang Shan, and Han Bin kill Zhang Fei while he is drunk and take his head to surrender to Wu. The enraged Liu Bei has to keep to his bed for a few days with some illness. When the Wu commanders Lü Meng and Lu Xun attack him, Liu Bei is heavily defeated. He retires to Baidicheng, and as his end is drawing near he has the crown prince, the Field Marshal, and Zhao Long summoned from Sichuan. Liu Bei asks Zhuge Liang to assist Liu Shan, and also says: "Aji is still very young. If he is fit to be placed on the throne, then do so. If he is not fit for the job, then you should do it yourself." He orders Liu Shan in all policy matters to follow the advice of Zhuge Liang. Upon Liu Bei's death, Zhuge Liang sets up the Eightfold Battle Array and inflicts a defeat on the army of Wu, whereupon he leads the army back to Chengdu.

Zhuge Liang's Campaigns to the South and the North

The king of the southern barbarians, Meng Huo, rebels, and Zhuge Liang leads an army of fifty thousand troops against him. After Zhuge Liang has captured him for the seventh time, Meng Huo surrenders, and Zhuge Liang returns to Chengdu. In the fourth year of the reign period Qinglong (236) of the Wei emperor Ming, Meng Da is appointed as commander (to lead the campaign) against Shu, and Zhuge Liang leads an army of fifty thousand men against him. Meng Da, who had hoped to subjugate Shu, finds himself unable to do so and commits suicide. Sima Yi then leads fifty thousand troops to confront Zhuge Liang, but when Cao Fang ascends the throne, Sima Yi retreats. Zhuge Liang constructs "wooden oxen" and "streaming horses"[25] to transport provisions and conquers the plains of Qin. Jiang Wei surrenders and honors Zhuge Liang as his father. When Zhuge Liang returns to Chengdu, he orders Jiang Wei to command the camp. When the Wei general Xiahou Dun attacks at night, Jiang Wei inflicts a heavy defeat on Xiahou Dun and captures Jieting. Upon his return to Chengdu, Zhuge Liang sees the Young Lord and the eunuch Huang Hao sitting side by side having fun. Weeping, he reports this to the spirit tablet of the First Ruler, and, having killed Huang Hao, he again marches from Mount Qi. Sima Yi tries to capture Jieting but is badly defeated by Zhuge Liang. In Chengdu it is reported that Zhuge Liang has rebelled, but when he is recalled and questioned by the Later Lord, he explains that it is a plot of Sima Yi. Zhuge Liang again marches from Mount Qi. When he learns that Ma Su has lost Jieting, he has Ma Su beheaded, and then recaptures Jieting. Summoned back to Chengdu, Zhuge Liang dispatches people to Eastern Wu [upon the death of Sun Quan] to offer condolences, and then once more marches from Mount Qi. When Sima Yi sees that Zhou Cang uses the wooden oxen and streaming horses to transport provisions, he steals some and imitates them, but they move very slowly. When Zhou Cang arrives to deliver a challenge to battle, he inquires about these wooden oxen and streaming horses, and Zhou Cang tells him that in order to make these oxen and horses run, you have to recite the Classic of Wooden Oxen and Streaming Horses. Zhuge Liang writes a letter poking fun at Sima Yi, but even so, this famed general of Wei does not understand the operation of these wooden oxen and streaming horses.

When the Brocade River overflows in Chengdu and creates a disaster, Zhuge Liang is summoned back to Chengdu. He orders all useless stuff in the palace sold in the market in order to buy grain, and in a few days he has bought a limitless supply. Zhuge Liang orders an iron chain constructed at the Qutang Gorge to block the River as a defense against Eastern Wu. Zhuge Liang contracts a disease, but still goes to Jieting to confront Sima Yi. Zhuge Liang dies of this disease at Wuzhang Plains. Sima Yi tries to attack during the mourning period, but he suffers a heavy defeat at the hands of Jiang Wei, and in Chang'an people say, "A dead Zhuge Liang can still make a living Zhongda flee!" Zhuge Liang's coffin is taken back to Chengdu for burial. When Sima Yi observes the fortifications of Zhuge Liang's camp, he exclaims, "This was the most exceptional talent of this world!"

---

25. The "wooden oxen" may have been wheelbarrows, and the "streaming horses" probably were four-wheeled pushcarts.

The End

Sima Yi executes Cao Shuang and his army; he deposes the ruler of Wei, making him Duke of Gaoguixiang. As the power of the Sima family expands, the Young Emperor of the Wei abdicates in favor of the Simas. When the Prince of Chenliu, the former Emperor Xian of the Han, hears this, he dies laughing. The King of Jin annihilates Shu, and also annihilates Wu.[26] Liu Yuan, a distant cousin of the Han emperor, escapes, and founds the state of Han at Pingyang.[27] Following the demise of the Western Jin, he sacrifices to the ancestors of the Han and proclaims an amnesty for the empire.

---

26. The Jin dynasty, which earlier had conquered Shu-Han, achieved the unification of the Chinese world in 280 when it annexed the kingdom of Wu. In the beginning of the fourth century, the Jin was ripped apart by civil war. It survived in Southern China, while Northern China was ruled by non-Chinese warlords.

27. This is a reference to the Cheng-Han regime, which maintained an independent government in modern Sichuan throughout the first half of fourth century. The ruling family was originally surnamed Li, but had adopted the surname Liu in order to be able to claim kinship with the imperial family of the Han.

Appendix 2

Excerpt from the *Tale of Hua Guan Suo*

The *Tale of Hua Guan Suo* (*Hua Guan Suo zhuan*) belongs to a group of texts that was discovered in 1967 on the outskirts of Shanghai in the grave of the wife of a lowly official. These texts turned out to be heretofore unknown examples of prosimetric narratives (*chantefables*) that had been printed during the Chenghua reign (1467–87) of the Ming dynasty in Beijing. On the basis of the rhymes in the verse sections of the texts, some scholars have concluded, however, that these texts must have been written earlier in a Wu-dialect area (the city of Suzhou and its surrounding countryside). There they must have enjoyed a considerable popularity before they were reprinted in Northern China, and it seems safe to conclude that the actual composition of these texts may date from any year in the two centuries before their printing. This period, from the middle of the thirteenth century to the middle of the fifteenth century, saw the first flourishing of drama and narrative in the vernacular. Many of the texts that were discovered in 1967 are advertised on their front page as "ballad-stories for singing and narrating" (*shuochang cihua*). The majority of these ballad-stories retell famous court cases of the incorruptible Judge Bao, a few other texts are moral fables, and three of the texts deal with historical subjects.

The *Tale of Hua Guan Suo* is one of the three ballad-stories dealing with a historical subject. It tells the story of the heroic career of Guan Yu's son Hua Guan Suo, whose life is spared when Zhang Fei kills Guan Yu's relatives following the oath in the Peach Orchard. The boy is raised by his mother's family (he joins their surname Hua to his own), and goes out into the world to find his father once he is grown up.

The text is divided into four "scrolls" (*juan*): "The Early Career of Hua Guan Suo," "How Hua Guan Suo Met His Father," "How Hua Guan Suo Subdued Xichuan," and "Hua Guan Suo Exiled to Yunnan." The fragment presented here is from the last scroll.[1] The *Tale of Hua Guan Suo* reflects a tradition of Three Kingdoms narratives that, at the time, was quite different from that represented by the *Records of the Three Kingdoms in Plain Language*. Both its account of the oath in the Peach Orchard (quoted in the introduction to the *Tripartite Oath*)

---

1. The translation is based on the text as provided in Zhu Yixuan, ed. *Ming Chenghua shuochang cihua congkan.* Zhengzhou: Zhongzhou guji chubanshe, 1997, p. 56.

FIG. 10. "Liu Bei, Guan, and Zhang Form the Brotherhood," from the *Newly Compiled, Completely Illustrated, Full Version of Hua Guan Suo's Life*

and its account of the death of Guan Yu and Zhang Fei are conspicuous examples of the extent to which these traditions could diverge.

From *The Story of Hua Guan Suo Exiled to Yunnan*
A Complete Edition of *Chantefables* Newly Compiled with Complete Pictures

(The text begins as Guan Yu is besieged in Jingzhou by the army of the King of Wu.)

[*Sung:*]

> [Lord Guan hastily wrote a letter to his dear brother:
> "Now go to Sichuan and request additional troops!"
> The two soldiers were in a hurry to leave, and said;
> "Today we will take your letter as your messengers."
>
> When the letter had been written and quickly sealed,
> The couriers left the city of Jingzhou, and raced across
> Deserted lands and grassy plains as fast as they could:
> Along the road they flew like clouds before the wind.
>
> Let's not speak of the stages of journey along the way—
> They tracked on forward till they saw a mountain forest.
> They decided to make their way beneath Mount Beiyin,
> Where the adopted son Liu Feng stopped them short.
>
> He demanded the letter from the messengers, and saw
> It spoke of seeking a relief army from Western Shu.
> When Liu Feng saw this, his heart burned with rage
> And he arrested the two messengers there on the spot.
>
> He ripped that letter from brother to brother to shreds
> And he killed those two lads [as he thought to himself:]
> "Let Lord Guan in Jingzhou keep lookout with hope—
> No men and horses will ever be dispatched from Shu!"

[*Spoken:*]

Liu Feng said, "Your son Guan Suo treated me without respect, and then you had me taken in chains to my father to explain the situation,[2] and for that I was

---

2. When, following the conquest of Sichuan, Guan Yu returned to Jingzhou, Liu Bei had Liu Feng take a cart full of treasure to Jingzhou for Guan Yu to distribute to the troops. When Guan Yu's sons Guan Ping and Hua Guan Suo were drinking with Liu Feng, Liu Feng felt slighted when Guan Suo first offered a cup to Guan Ping and only then to him. Liu Feng claimed that he

banished to this defile here in Mount Beiyin and cannot go home. Well, I've suppressed your request for an army, so let them hope in vain at Jingzhou."

Let's not talk about Liu Feng's perfidy, but about Lord Guan waiting for a rescue that never came. He said, "Why don't we get any news from them? Why doesn't my brother send relief troops?" He wrote another letter and sent another soldier on his way, but still nothing. He sent thirteen requests for relief, but Liu Feng intercepted them all and killed all thirteen messengers. Lord Guan said, "What should I do?" Guan Ping said, "Father, I'll go." "All right," said Lord Guan. On that very day Guan Ping left Jingzhou.

Because Jingzhou had been besieged for so long by the armies of the King of Wu, Mi Zhu and Mi Fang put one over on Lord Guan and offered up Jingzhou, casting their lot with the King of Wu, and from all four gates Wu's army poured in to slaughter the city's inhabitants. Lord Guan and Zhou Cang fled, leading what was left of their army as well as their defeated officers, fleeing directly to the foot of Jade Fount Mountain. But again Lord Guan's men and horse were intercepted by the King of Wu, and blocked for a full day and night.

Lord Guan said, "Zhou Cang, the three armies are collapsing from hunger, and my own stomach is empty." "I'll go out and hunt some game to stave off the hunger," said Zhou Cang. He made a complete circuit, but there was nothing to be seen. He said to himself, "My lord is hungry." He cut off a piece of his left thigh and grilled it over a fire. Because Zhou Cang had had nothing at all to eat, he fainted for lack of energy. Lord Guan waited a long time, but only saw a soldier who reported, "Zhou Cang is dead." "How did he die?" asked Lord Guan. The soldier said, "Because his lord was hungry, he hacked off a piece of meat from his thigh, passed out, and died." Lord Guan cried out bitterly, "Isn't anything working?" And then he saw his horse Red Hare jump into the river trailing his knife, and the knife fell into the water.

[Sung:]

> After Lord Guan had watched this, he bitterly lamented:
> Both died of hunger, the young esquire and the horse.
> Zhou Cang hacked off his flesh and passed out to die:
> Red Hare trailed the knife and jumped into the river.
>
> No troops have come from Sichuan to bring us relief—
> How on earth could Prince Liu be such a man?

---

as son of Liu Bei was bound to inherit the throne, but Guan Suo countered that Guan Yu would succeed to the throne. When Guan Yu learned of their fight, he had Guan Suo and Liu Feng locked in chains and sent to Chengdu. When the two of them appeared before Liu Bei, the latter banished Guan Suo to Yunnan and appointed Liu Feng to the lowly position of pass commander at Mount Beiyin. The story is told at the beginning of the fourth and final scroll of the *Hua Guan Suo zhuan*.

How could he forget their common bond of loyalty?
Lord Guan was in trouble, yet there was no reunion!

"Horse and men of King Wu surround us so tightly,
But who will be able to stand up against my might?"
His three cloud souls sailed off far away into the void,
And his seven spirits forced their way out of the camp.

The King of Wu captured his troops and his horses,
He snatched away all of that walled city of Jingzhou.
Now that he had died, Lord Guan went off into the void
Leading an army of a million of strong souls.

As he was making his way to Chengdu in Sichuan
To appear in dreams to King Liu, ruler of Han,
He came to pass beneath Mount Beiyin, and there
Thirteen strong souls reported to their leader, saying

They had been killed, robbed of their lives by Liu Feng,
And so had never made it to Sichuan to ask for relief.
Then Lord Guan that very moment shouted out sadly,
"How could I have known Liu Feng would trap me?"

His traveling soul hurried down the road to Sichuan
To show itself in a dream to King Liu, the ruler of Han.
But when he got to Chengdu city, there in Sichuan
He ran smack into Zhang Fei, his own younger brother!

[*Spoken:*]

Zhang Fei said, "Brother, where are you going?" "I was cheated by King Wu in Jingzhou," said Lord Guan, "and he trapped me below Jade Fount Mountain, where I too soon died. My purpose in coming here is to appear in a dream to our elder brother." "When I was in Langzhou," said Zhang Fei, "Colonel Zhang Da was planning rebelling against me, and I made the mistake of giving him a beating. He waited until I was drunk and then stabbed me to death. I want to appear in a dream to my brother too. The two of us died in truly miserable ways!"

[*Sung:*]

When Lord Guan heard what he said, he shed tears like pearls,
"The two of us, elder and younger brothers, so wrongly killed!"
The two were waiting for dusk to fall, as only then they might
Appear in a dream to their brother to explain what had happened.

Let's not sing of how these two waited outside his gate,
But sing instead of the First Ruler, that King Liu.
Everyday he pined so much for his younger brothers
That he was loath to sit on his throne in the palace hall.

Late that night he returned to his private bedchamber
Where alone, in the palace, he pined for his brothers.
"Since I've lost sight of their faces, Guan and Zhang,
We, this person of little virtue, lack all energy here at court."

The very moment that King Liu was thinking of them,
The two of them, Guan and Zhang, arrived at the gate.
There, beneath the lamplight stood the pair,
And saw that their brother's eyes were filled with tears.

"The King of Wu laid waste to the area of Jingzhou;
Inside the city I had no provisions and no army either.
My thirteen letters asking for relief, again and again,
Were intercepted by Liu Feng, who killed the couriers.

Thus I lost my life at the foot of Jade Fount Mountain,
And now appear to you in your dream here at court."
Zhang Fei then told him that he had died in Langzhou,
"A nobody stabbed me, and my life went into the shades."

"We hope, elder brother, that you will requite our injustice
And forget not the loyal hearts of the Peach Orchard oath."
When the elder brother Liu Bei witnessed this dream
He called out in his sleep and woke up full of fright.

On and on he wept through the night until the sky grew bright,
Then summoned Zhuge Liang to explain its causes.
Liu Bei told him everything right from the beginning,
And the Field Marshal came and said: "Bright ruler,

In general, dreams are only that which is on our minds,
But this time around, this dream just has to be real."
And just as the Field Marshal finished speaking,
The audience usher reported to the bright ruler,

"Now Guan Ping and Zhang Yi have both arrived
At the palace gate, dressed in mourning clothes."
King Liu, the First Ruler, ordered them called in
And there in court these two saw the bright ruler:

"We will tell you everything right from the start."
So, King Liu, this single man, wept uncontrollably
And from the Field Marshal's eyes fell tears like pearls—
"The traces of heroes now vanished forever from this world!"

Appendix 3

A Selection of Yuan Plays Version of The Plan of Interlocking Rings

*T*he *Plan of Interlocking Rings* (*Jinyun tang anding Lianhuan ji*) found in Zang Maoxun's *Selection of Yuan Plays* differs in several respects from the Xijizi edition, translated earlier in this volume as *The Story of the Interlocking Rings*. The differences are due both to different sources and to Zang's editorial practices. As we noted in the introduction to *The Story of the Interlocking Rings*, the most likely provenance of Zang's version is a late Ming palace edition from the eunuch agency, the Office of Drum and Bell. This would have been a play performed before the emperor and as such was subject to the constraints that this imposed. Some fundamental differences in the play—the substitution of Yang Biao for Wu Zilan for instance—may well stem from earlier court rewritings. While Wu Zilan's name occurs very occasionally in historical texts, briefly in the *Records of the Three Kingdoms in Plain Language* as a general in service to Dong Zhuo, and in the *Romance of the Three Kingdoms* as a co-conspirator in the assassination of Cao Cao, Yang Biao (141–225) is a much more prominent figure. He is best known for his early opposition to Dong Zhuo's decision to move the capital to Chang'an and his quick change of heart after Dong Zhuo assassinated two other officials who opposed the move. He appears not at all in the *Records in Plain Language*, and, in the *Romance of the Three Kingdoms*, whereas he is not mentioned in relationship to the strategy of interlocking rings, he is cashiered by Dong Zhuo and made a common citizen after his objection to moving the capital to Chang'an. In historical and literary texts, Yang goes on to hold high ceremonial rank in the Wei.

One major difference between the two versions is the Gate of the Silver Dais, which is mentioned in both plays, but which is very much emphasized through repetition in Zang's *Plan of Interlocking Rings*. The place itself is an anachronism: it was a name for a gate in Tang dynasty Chang'an where judgments of crimes were carried out. Its appearance early on in the *Selection of Yuan Plays* version not only provides a focal point for the action to culminate in Dong Zhuo's death but is linked constantly through the play with his increasing desire for ascension to the throne. It provides a concrete site from the beginning of the play, a specific point toward which both Dong Zhuo's desires and

Wang Yun's conniving are aimed, and intensifies the final resolution of these two desires in frustration and joy.

This version of the play is far more severe in its treatment of Dong Zhuo, and it portrays Wang Yun as far more conniving. Dong consistently uses the imperial eidetic pronouns and laughs heartily at nearly every instance of flattery. His political ambitions are more naked and, coupled with his susceptibility to sycophancy, make him easy prey for Wang Yun. In the *Selection of Yuan Plays* version, Wang Yun is far more capable of feigned flattery and much more direct in propelling the eventual conflict between Dong Zhuo and Lü Bu by more strongly substantiating their individual claims to Diaochan through rhetoric and persuasion. In both versions the plot is the same, and composed of the same series of events, but Zang Maoxun's version highlights the naked cunning and duplicity of Wang Yun.

We have no way of knowing whether the above differences between the *Selection of Yuan Plays* and *Anthology of Northern Dramas New and Ancient* versions are due to Zang Maoxun, or to differences in the court plays that were their respective sources. Other changes are clearly wrought by Zang's own hand to make a reading version that would fit well with an educated elite's vision of what makes a literary text. He shows a tendency to rewrite arias to fit the sensibility of the *ci* lyric, he uses many more classical allusions, and he stresses political personality over emotional longing. He has muted all references to Diaochan's status in Wang Yun's household, stressing the bond of "father and daughter" instead of that of entertainer and perhaps sexual partner of master of the house.

Zang Maoxun clearly sees the play as a reading text, not a performing script. He has expanded the stage directions so that they provide a clear narrative guide, functioning in some ways like the role of an intrusive third-person narrator. And, as he nearly always does, he has fleshed out the fourth act of the play with two extra songs and an extended closing poem. This shows the influence of the "grand reunion" (*da tuanyuan*) scenes found in later *chuanqi* drama. In this case, it allows the two co-conspirators, Yang Biao and Wang Yun, an opportunity to summarize the play and to parcel out rewards to each of the main characters in the drama. This last scene is called a "judgment" (*duan*) in the later sixteenth-century court plays, and is performed kneeling toward the emperor (here both the Han emperor in the play, and the Ming emperor in the audience). Zang has extended the scene, as he does in other dramas (for instance in his version of Guan Hanqing's famous *Injustice to Dou E*), so that each person receives the correct reward or punishment for their actions, and social and political order is restored.

There are good reasons why Zang Maoxun's plays are so popular. They are literary, easy to read, shorn of the occasional distractions and dead-ends of earlier texts of performing literature, and they fit well into the domain of what might be called "elite colloquial" literature that dominated the scene in the seventeenth century and beyond. It also explains why the plays are used with such frequency as the texts of choice in scholarly literature on "Yuan" drama. But if we are to avoid an anachronistic reading of these Northern dramas, we must realize that Zang's plays definitely to a large extent reflect the language and ideology of his time and his social class.

The Northern Drama

In the Hall of Brocade Clouds They Secretly Set the Plan of Interlocking Rings

Yuan Dynasty Anonymous
Collated by Zang Jinshu of the Ming dynasty, from Wuxing

Act 1

(CLOWN, *costumed as* DONG ZHUO, *enters, leading* EXTRAS, *costumed as* LI RU *and* LI SU, *and* SOLDIERS, *and speaks:*)

> Leading my troops into the palace to protect the emperor, I established
> extraordinary merit.
> All the officials, civil and military, hid from the downflowing wind;
> The emperor's grace was deep in the Nine Bestowals, but I am still not
> satisfied;[1]
> My own desire is to not grow old in the Han court.[2]

I am Dong Zhuo, a man from Lintao in Longxi.[3] I have been a general since youth and have had much success along the border. But when the Ten Constant Attendants created trouble, He Jin recommended that I enter the court, and after that I was appointed to the post of Grand Commander. And now I have been awarded the Nine Bestowals: (1) horses and carts, (2) clothing, (3) musical instruments, (4) vermilion gates, (5) inset steps,[4] (6) a bodyguard, (7) axes and broadaxes, (8) bows and arrows, and (9) sweet sacrificial wine. When I go out, a personal guard surrounds me; when I enter, they clear the road in front.[5] For proclamations, I send out imperial edicts; for sending down commands, I call them imperial orders; for discussions, I call them imperial

---

1. For Nine Bestowals, see *Interlocking Rings*, n. 5.
2. By deposing the Han and establishing his own dynasty.
3. In modern Gansu.
4. For inset steps, see *Interlocking Rings*, n. 10.
5. Usually done only for emperors.

proclamations; and for reports, I call them imperial rescripts.[6] Each time I go into court I allow this precious sword at my waist to show the tiniest glint of its blade, making all the officials civil and military blanch with fear. And there's no need to discuss all of the able ministers who join in planning or battle-tested generals. Just these two—Li Ru and Li Su—are braver than Meng Ben and Xia Yu[7] and are more strategically attuned than either Sun Wu or Wu Qi.[8] Thousands of herds of famous horses, hundreds of thousand of brave troops— by these I do as I will in the capital district and my power shakes the city of Chang'an. I see that wresting away the empire of Han is as easy as turning over one's palm. But, there's that Wang Yun who always has some crafty plan. He's set against me with his whole heart, and I'm constantly on guard against him. No matter what he does—walk, stop, sit, or lie down—I have someone follow him, observe his actions, and quickly report them to me. I was sitting in the Prime Minister's office doing nothing today when someone came to tell me that he had gone out of the palace gate and went straightaway to Yang Biao's house instead of going home. Afraid they might be cooking up some plan, I'd best go straight to Yang Biao's house myself and put an end to that.

> This miscreant has always been full of treacherous tricks,
> So I have no choice but to be on guard;
> Even though a man has no heart to harm the tiger,
> Still the tiger has a mind to injure the man!

(*Exits.*)

(EXTRA, *costumed as* YANG BIAO, *enters, leading an* ATTENDANT, *speaks:*) This old man before you named Yang Biao and also known as Wenxian is from Hua-yin in Hongnong.[9] I am now Defender-in-Chief in the palace. Right now Emperor Xian of the Han is on the throne, but he is being manipulated by that Dong Zhuo, who has usurped his power over life or death, which now stems from Dong alone. All of the officials, civil and military, tremble in fear and dare not look him straight in the eye. Alas, because of this the Sage is anxious and depressed. It is truly said, "The ruler's anxiety is the shame of the minister; the shame of the ruler is the death of the minister." If we do not share His Highness' anxiety, how can we complete the way of minister and son? I want to seize the opportunity to eliminate this treacherous brave. But that household slave

---

6. That is, he sends these out under the emperor's name. He is the real power.

7. Two legendary brave strongmen.

8. Two famous military strategists, including Master Sun, most famous in the West as the author of *The Art of War*. See Ralph D. and Mei-chün Sawyer, *The Seven Military Classics of Ancient China.* Boulder: Westview Press, 1993.

9. The area around modern Xinxiang in Henan.

of his, Lü Bu, is more heroic and brave than others and it's just too hard to set my hand to it right now. I am thinking that this needs the Minister of Instruction, Wang Yun, who is full of plans and strategies and is someone I can work with. I've asked him to come and discuss this with me. I sent someone to invite him earlier, but it doesn't appear he is here yet. Servants, keep watch at the door, and if Minister Wang arrives, report to me. (ATTENDANT *speaks:*) Understood. (MALE LEAD, *costumed as* WANG YUN, *enters and speaks:*) I am Wang Yun, also known as Zishi. I am a man of Qi in Taiyuan. From the time I was recommended to the court in the category of the filial and those with integrity,[10] I have been thankful for the favor and love of the Sage, who has awarded me the rank of Minister of Instruction. But that Dong Zhuo is manipulating authority, putting the house of Han in peril; all of the officials are terrified and in awe and dare not ask "Who?" or "Why?" Defender-in-Chief Yang Biao sent someone to summon me. I don't know why, but I'd better go. I am ashamed to be so old and useless, eating on my salary and giving nothing in return!

> (XIANLÜ MODE: *Dian jiangchun*)
> I pass my springs and autumns now for nothing,
> Forcing myself to endure the nights and days;
> For nothing I enjoy
> Fat horses and light sables.
> For what reason do I bear this haggard form?

> (*Hunjiang long*)
> It's the universe of the Han
> That has caused my two thin brows to be locked by sorrows for the
>   dynasty.
> It's just like an opening blossom encountering rain
> That does not last to evoke leaves dropping in return to autumn.
> I just want to ask, "How can thieving miscreants be allowed in 'the
>   ranks of mandarin drakes and egrets'?[11]
> Just what kind of 'dukes and marquises'[12] are painted on the walls of
>   the Unicorn Gallery?"[13]
> When they are to "act the official," they are all full of energy, waiting
>   to leap over others and scramble to the front,

---

10. One man from each commandery in the empire was recommended to the court on the basis of his filial piety and integrity.

11. Waterbirds that come to rest in groups and stand in a line: a metaphor for assembly of officials at morning court.

12. A metaphorical reference to high officials.

13. A gallery within Weiyang Palace in the Han where notable officials' portraits were painted.

But when they have to establish some merit, they quickly shrink
   back, happy to be in the rear.
If I can just find one man to settle this state,
   I will have not left in vain a name to endure for a ten thousand
   epochs.

(*Speaks:*) I've reached his gate. Servant! Report that I am here. (ATTENDANT
acts out reporting.) (YANG BIAO *speaks:*) Tell him he is welcome. (ATTENDANT
speaks:) Please go in. (*Act out greeting each other.* MALE LEAD *speaks:*) Defender-
in-Chief, you have asked me over. What do you want to discuss? (YANG BIAO
speaks:) I have asked you, Minister of Instruction, for the express purpose to
discuss something I've been thinking about: from the time that Chu and Han
were locked in struggle, and our state was established, it has been more than
four hundred years. Now it has been passed down to our ruler Emperor Xian;
the dynasty is in danger of extinction! Dong Zhuo monopolizes all authority
and bullies and suppresses all of the officials at court. We need a plan. I have
exhaustively looked through the whole court and no one is as clever and re-
sourceful as you, sir, when it comes to ideas and plans. There must be some way
to come up with a clever strategy for us to establish great merit together—what
do you think? (MALE LEAD *sings:*)

> (*You hulu*)
> Consider Chu and Han in those days, when it was the autumn that
>   their armies contested in battle,[14]
> Lord and minister were still not split apart into identifiable
>   categories,
> And they had once divided the empire in the middle by pointing to
>   Goose Channel.[15]

(YANG BIAO *speaks:*) Once they divided the empire down the middle, why did
Han alone complete its work and last four hundred years? Whose energy was
this due to? (MALE LEAD *sings:*)

> In this, we owe everything to that persuasive rhetoric of Zhang
>   Liang,[16]
> And Marshal Han Xin's innate ability to grasp battlefield
>   circumstances.[17]

---

14. Autumn in the sense of the critical time as the year moves toward its end; meant to link
the solar cycle of renewal with the political concept of dynastic cycle, itself based on the biologi-
cal metaphor of a plant's life.

15. For Goose Channel (Honggou), see *Interlocking Rings*, n. 14.

16. Literally, "a mouth that discusses heaven and talks about earth" (*shuotian tandi kou*).

17. Literally, "a hand that can grab fog and take hold of clouds" (*wowu nayun shou*).

That one was able to do battle with the enemy;

This one was able to perfect plots and plans.

They aided the completion of the fundamental enterprise that would last a thousand years;

Truly, they shared and thereby destroyed the worries of their emperor.

(YANG BIAO *speaks:*) Now Dong Zhuo monopolizes authority, and his power shakes everyone, inside the court and out. I begin to think about that time when the liege lords from every place controlled a million-man army but never got so much as a broken arrow from him at Tigerkeep Pass.[18] How can we ever root out this kind of violent power? (MALE LEAD *sings:*)

(*Tianxia le*)

I fear "problems will come from sticking your nose in where it does not belong,"[19]

For when you consider those liege lords from the eighteen circuits,

Just bringing it up fills my face with shame.

(YANG BIAO *speaks:*) If it had not been for the fact that Liu, Guan, and Zhang had once smashed Lü Bu, then all of the liege lords in the empire would find it hard to die without shame. (MALE LEAD *sings:*)

When I consider how hard it was to handle Tigerkeep Pass at once back then . . .[20]

Nowadays all of the civil officials all bow in submission,

And all of the military officers have fled in fear,

Making that guy accustomed to unrestrained freedom and total power.

(YANG BIAO *speaks:*) I have received the Sage's order to ask you here to come up with a plan and by some means to capture Dong Zhuo. (MALE LEAD *speaks:*) Silence, sir! That treacherous official Dong Zuo is a man of much power and authority; it will be no easy task to get rid of him. Moreover, his eyes and ears are spread throughout the court. If our plans and deliberations should leak out, wouldn't that just summon disaster on us? (YANG BIAO *speaks:*) That may be so, but we have been ministers of the Han for generations, and I swear I will not stand next to this scoundrel. If there is any possibility to get at him, I will be happy to risk my life for the sake of the dynasty—there is nothing I fear! (DONG

---

18. I.e., never reached a conclusion in which an arrow was snapped to indicate agreement between parties.

19. Literally, "forcing oneself to stick out one's head" (*qiang chutou*).

20. For handling Tigerkeep Pass, see *Interlocking Rings*, n. 18.

ZHUO *makes a sudden entrance, leading* SOLDIERS, *and speaks:*) I am Dong Zhuo.
I've come directly to Yang Biao's house today to catch this old devil. Servant!
Report that Grand Preceptor Dong is at the gate. (ATTENDANT *acts out reporting:*) Master, Grand Preceptor Dong is here. (YANG BIAO *acts out being startled
and speaks:*) Just as you predicted, Minister, the Grand Preceptor is here. We
should go out and greet him. (*They go out together to greet him.* DONG ZHUO
acts out greeting them and speaks:) Aha! Minister Wang is here too. What have
you been discussing here? (YANG BIAO *speaks:*) Because we happened to run
into each other when court was over, Minister Wang and I have just been chat-
ting about nothing in particular. (DONG ZHUO *speaks:*) Wang Yun—it seems
that the two of you looked startled and frightened when you saw me at the door.
Could it be that you want to do some harm to me? (MALE LEAD *speaks:*) All of
our lives are in your control; would I dare do such a thing? (*Sings:*)

> (*Houting hua*)
> Not at all; it's just that you now control great authority.

(DONG ZHUO *acts out laughing and speaks:*) Yes, my authority is no small thing.
(MALE LEAD *sings:*)

> And Lü Bu, the Marquis of Wen, is also head of the army.
> So we wanted to discuss this together with him,
> Wanting to pick out a propitious day.

(DONG ZHUO *speaks:*) So, you were picking out an auspicious day. Were you
discussing inviting me to a banquet? (MALE LEAD *speaks:*) Indeed no, we want
to invite the Grand Preceptor to ascend the grand position.[21]

(DONG ZHUO *acts out laughing and speaks:*) I am afraid that this lonely person[22]
will never reach such a position. (MALE LEAD *sings:*)

> I see by what you say we are on the same page.

(DONG ZHUO *speaks:*) If this day comes, then all you have to do is mention it
and I will act completely in accord with what you propose. (MALE LEAD *sings:*)

> Since you have said you act in accordance with our proposal,

(*Acts out speaking in an aside and sings:*)

> I just fear that will be the end to your evil machinations.

---

21. I.e., as emperor.
22. "This lonely person" is the Chinese equivalent of the royal "We" and therefore inappropriate for Dong Zhuo to use as a self-designation.

(DONG ZHUO *speaks:*) Defender Yang, let me ask you, from ancient times to the present has there ever been anyone who was willing to let another wear the emperor's cap? (YANG BIAO *speaks:*) There is an ancient saying, "Those with the Way go to war against those who don't. This is why Tang banished Jie and King Wu slew Zhou. Those without virtue yield to those who have it. This is why Yao invested Shun and Shun invested Yu." (DONG ZHUO *speaks:*) Looking at it like this, Minister Wang, the current situation is clear. (MALE LEAD *sings:*)

> (*Nezha ling*)
> There once was the sage king Shun,
> Who received Yao's throne and protected it with warmth and respect.
> There once was a First Emperor of the Qin,
> Who unified all the warring states[23] of the Zhou, but not for long.
> There once was that Grand Lord of the Xin,
> Who usurped the house of Han but whose crafty deceit was exposed
>   to all.[24]

(DONG ZHUO *speaks:*) It is precisely this for which We have spent much time trying to devise a clever plan. But it can't be accomplished in a single moment, and this very thing keeps me upset all the time. (MALE LEAD *sings:*)

> In the current situation, what plan do you fear will not be successful?
> What scheme do you fear will be hard to carry off?
> All it takes is one brave act to rebel and raise up spear and lance.

(DONG ZHUO *speaks:*) In Our opinion, only I am revered both inside the court and out. Should I want to start something, who dares to say, "No!"? I'll cause him disaster and misfortune in a snap, his life and his family will be hard to protect, and none of the nine mourning grades of his family shall be left.[25] (MALE LEAD *speaks:*) When I look at the heavenly phenomena at night, the fated numbers of the house of Han are almost at their end. Grand Preceptor, your merit and virtue are towering and dominating, so you should replace the Han and take possession of the empire. (*Sings:*)

> (*Que ta zhi*)
> You can force yourself to take this responsibility—
> Open wide your eyes.

---

23. The Chinese expression used here (*qiangliang*) is more commonly used of bandits, but here refers to the violent battles between warring states in the last few centuries of the Zhou dynasty.

24. Referring here to the usurpation of Wang Mang, who initiated the very short-lived Xin or "New" dynasty between the Western and Eastern Han. But Dong Zhuo seems to take it in reference to himself and understand "a new minister lord" to refer to himself.

25. For nine grades of mourning, see *Interlocking Rings*, n. 22.

How can you miss the heavenly signs and the four stars of Dipper's bowl?[26]

Good luck is flowing all around them.

(DONG ZHUO *acts out laughing and speaks:*) Even though the heavenly signs are like this, I'm afraid that this portion of luck is not for Us. (MALE LEAD *speaks:*) You might not have known, but a high platform is being constructed right now inside the Gate of the Silver Dais—if this is not for the abdication of the current emperor and the investiture [of a new emperor], what is its purpose? (*Sings:*)

> The tall platform is already under construction for the abdication ceremony.
> Don't forget the two of us, Wang Yun and Yang Biao.

(DONG ZHUO *speaks:*) If We decide to plot for the grand affair,[27] then those grand officials in the civil and military branches who go along with me will receive benevolent treatment, but those who oppose me will become my enemies. Why don't you mark this very well in your heart? (MALE LEAD *sings:*)

> (*Jisheng cao*)
> All along this is about submission to virtue; it is not a matter of power.
> Do not misconstrue kindness for hatred.
> All that's desired is that you rely on your Dragon Spring[28] to settle the dust and filth now flying on the wind;
> Use the Dragon Stratagems[29] to patch up where heaven and earth have leaked away,
> And occupy the Dragon Throne, stabilizing our glorious rivers and mountains.[30]

(DONG ZHUO *speaks:*) This is something that needs doing sooner than later. (MALE LEAD *sings:*)

> All we hope is that you will act in accord with the harmony of people: "a musk that has a natural odor,"[31]
> Don't go against the mind of Heaven—"Who can be without disaster?"[32]

---

26. For Dipper, see *Interlocking Rings*, n. 23.
27. I.e., the establishment of a new dynasty.
28. The name of a precious sword; i.e., "your magnificent sword."
29. The *Six Tactics* of Lü Wang; see *Tripartite Oath*, n. 21
30. "Rivers and mountains" is a metonymy for the state.
31. I.e., it is naturally attractive; it does not need a wind to carry it to others' noses.
32. No one wins against the will of Heaven.

(DONG ZHUO *speaks:*) All this needs is the unanimous support of you high officials; when there is support, We will reward you handsomely. (YANG BIAO *speaks:*) Rest easy, Grand Preceptor. In four or five days, we will pick out a propitious day and the host of high officials will come to welcome you. (DONG ZHUO *speaks:*) Defender, minister, since I have come to court I have controlled important military units that number several millions. And for fierce and brave generals like Lü Bu, there are more than one. Life or death as well as dismissal and appointment all rely on one word from Our mouth. To wrest away the empire of Han will be just like plucking something out of a sack—what's hard about it? Since a platform is already being constructed inside the Gate of the Silver Dais for ceding the throne, I will return to my offices and there prepare my own emperor's cap and wait. Even so, I feel we should do it a few days earlier to avoid the possibility of any incidents during the intervening period. (*Recites:*)

> Observing cosmic signs: the Han has already lost Heaven,
> And We have long held the hawsers of court in Our own hands;
> Yet We should make sure nothing happens in between:
> Don't bring calamity on yourself by drawing this out!

(*Exits.*)

(YANG BIAO *speaks:*) This fellow is so presumptuous; he wants with all his heart to wrest away the empire of the house of Han. Minister, what about our plan? (MALE LEAD *sings:*)

> (*Jinzhan'er*)
> Originally I was just a single layer of sorrow,
> But now it is turned into two!
> Only now do I believe, "All problems come from opening your mouth too much!"

(YANG BIAO *speaks:*) Minister, how can we set a plan to capture this miscreant so that we can secure the rivers and mountains of the Han? (MALE LEAD *sings:*)

> You want me to painstakingly search through all my secret plans and divine strategies,
> But how I can become a Jiang Ziya who was capable of attacking Zhou[33]
> Or a Zhang Liang who could help the Lius rise as emperors?

(YANG BIAO *speaks:*) Minister, I believe you are the equal of former worthies. We have to take care of Lü Bu first, and then Dong Zhuo can be easily apprehended. (MALE LEAD *sings:*)

---

33. The evil last ruler of the Shang dynasty.

You want to root out Preceptor Dong,
But by what method shall we deal with Lü, the Marquis of Wen?

(YANG BIAO *speaks:*) In this we must rely completely on the plan you decide to use. (MALE LEAD *acts out thinking deeply and speaks:*) Defender! Rest easy for now. Let me carefully consider it. (*Sings:*)

(*Coda*)
To get control of this episode of difficult days
I've brought some idle torture on myself—
This will require at least four or five nights of "haggard face and
  hoary head."[34]

(YANG BIAO *speaks:*) "A man's years will not reach one hundred, / but he's constantly beset with anxieties enough for a thousand years."[35] Minister, when will our vexation ever cease? (MALE LEAD *sings:*)

Because of those anxieties of a thousand years one constantly carries
  during one's own hundred,
I will have to search throughout the four great areas of the
  heartland.[36]
We can put a clever plan in action,
But any meritorious accomplishment from it will be hard to realize—
Alas, these rivers and mountains that extend for tens of thousands of
  miles will cease in a single morning.

(YANG BIAO *speaks:*) Well, it so happened that we agreed right in front of this old miscreant that everything would be clear in four or five days. Minister, you must plan this early, and you must get it right! (MALE LEAD *sings:*)

I see the raven fly and the hare run,[37]
But alas this contest of dragons and battle of tigers[38]
Has put a heavy draw-weight bow smack into my heart.[39]

---

34. Deep worry.

35. The first couplet of one of the "Nineteen Old Poems," followed by: "Days are short, the bitter nights long, / Why not take up a candle and roam?" Here, however, they seem to be taking "anxieties of a thousand years" to refer to a concern for what will happen in the future. See note 36.

36. The term here (*si da shenzhou*) in Buddhism means the four great worlds that make up the world of being. In more common parlance in Chinese, it means the four of the nine traditional areas (*jiuzhou*) that make up the Chinese world that comprise the Central Plain, the heartland of Chinese civilization.

37. For the raven and the hare, see *Interlocking Rings*, n. 32.

38. For the dragon and tigers, see *Interlocking Rings*, n. 33.

39. For draw-weight bow, see *Interlocking Rings*, n. 34.

(*Exits.*)

(YANG BIAO *speaks:*) Once Wang Yun leaves here, he'll employ a trick to capture Dong Zhuo and protect the empire of the house of Han. I'll now go secretly to reply to the Sage and be done with it. (*Recites in verse:*)

> The rivers and mountains of the house of Han we have sworn to support
> together;
> Can we agree to tolerate a miscreant having crazy plans?
> When the scheme is perfect, you can nab the jade hare in the moon;
> When plots work out, you can capture the metal raven in the sun.

(*Exits.*)

Act 2

(DONG ZHUO *enters with* LI RU, LI SU, *and* SOLDIER *and recites:*)

> I have not seen those civil and military court officials,
> So what's happening with the event at the Gate of the Silver Dais?
> Just because it is difficult to sit on the dragon throne,
> My heart has burned throughout the night, turning my hair all white.

Damn, Wang Yun and the other assembled officials are so disrespectful. They said they would soon pick an auspicious day and come to welcome me to ascend that grand position. I see propitious days all over the yellow calendar,[40] so why haven't they come to ask me yet? Servant, keep watch at the gate, and if Wang Yun and the other officials come, let me know. (SOLDIER *recites:*) Understood. (EXTRA, *costumed as* SPIRIT OF GREAT WHITE,[41] *enters holding a piece of cloth and speaks:*) Laymen of the world, follow me and leave your homes; I'll make each and every one become a transcendent, all of you, person by person, come to know the way! Oh, there's no one here. Well, this humble Daoist is Great White from the upper realm. Born to reside in the territory of metal, I issue forth from the western quadrant. I make no mistakes when I observe the good and bad among the world of men and have a set standard for discriminating success and failure in the mortal world. I was coming back from the court of the heavenly emperor, and I looked down and saw Dong Zhuo manipulating power in the lower realm as a way to scheme for the empire of the Han house. The Upper Welkin[42] was exercised in its anger, and all of the spirits were

---

40. These were almanacs that contained, among other information, a list of days that were auspicious for certain events.

41. For Great White, see *Interlocking Rings*, n. 35.

42. Where Buddhist and Daoist immortals dwell.

unhappy, so they sent me down to convert this person by a hint and see if he can get the message. Here's Dong Zhuo's house. (*Acts out laughing three times and speaks:*) Grand Preceptor Dong, you have an incredibly large ambition. (*Acts out weeping three times and speaks:*) Grand Preceptor Dong, you will soon die! (SOLDIER *acts out reporting and speaks:*) I want to report to Daddy Preceptor that there is a crazy priest at the door who looked inside the gates of the residence and laughed three times then wept three times. I beat him but he won't go away, so I've come to report it to you. (DONG ZHUO *speaks:*) No way! Let me go out and take a look myself. (*Acts out looking.*) (GREAT WHITE *speaks:*) Ah, ah, ah! Dong Zhuo you will soon die! (DONG ZHUO *speaks:*) This really is a crazed Buddhist monk or lunatic Daoist priest! Catch him! (*Act out trying but being unable to catch him.*) (DONG ZHUO *speaks:*) I'll catch this guy myself! ([GREAT WHITE] *acts out throwing the cloth to the ground and exits.*) (DONG ZHUO *speaks:*) Aiyo! He beat the hell out of me! How did he disappear? Did you see what it was that beat me? (*Acts out picking it up and inspecting it, speaks:*) It's just a piece of cloth, with two mouths, one on each end,[43] and two lines of writing in the center, which read, "A thousand miles of grass oh green, so green, / Prognostication says that ten will live forever." Li Ru, can you figure it out? (LI RU *speaks:*) Grand Preceptor, I will examine it carefully. . . . I don't know what it means. Only Academician Cai Yong can understand it. (DONG ZHUO *speaks:*) You are right, my son. Li Su, go fetch Cai Yong for me. (LI SU *speaks:*) Where is Academician Cai?

(EXTRA, *costumed as* CAI YONG, *enters and speaks:*) I am Cai Yong, known as Bojie, and my hereditary home is Chenliu.[44] I now hold the post of Academician. The Grand Preceptor has just summoned me for some reason, so I'd better go. (*Acts out reporting and performing greeting rituals.* CAI YONG *speaks:*) What instructions do you have for me, Grand Preceptor? (DONG ZHUO *speaks:*) I was just sitting quietly in my residence when a crazed priest looked inside my door and wept three times, then laughed three times. I went out to take a look at him, and I was struck on the head by something that he was carrying. I had just ordered people to catch him, but he had already disappeared in a shaft of golden light. I have that thing with me here now. But I don't understand what it means, so I've called you to take a look. (CAI YONG *speaks:*) If that's it, let me have a look. (*Acts out looking at it and speaks:*) Huh! It's a piece of cloth, ten feet in length, with two lines written on it. (*Acts out speaking in an aside:*) This old miscreant will die by Lü Bu's hands in the future; that's all there is to it. (*Turns back and speaks:*) Grand Preceptor, my opinion is this: the two lines of charac-

---

43. For interpreting the characters on the cloth, see *Interlocking Rings*, n. 38–40.
44. Located just south of modern Kaifeng.

ters are, "A thousand miles of grass oh green, so green, / Prognostication says that ten will live forever." Underneath the character "thousand" is the character "mile" and on top of the character "thousand" is a grass radical. Isn't this the character Dong?[45] Under the character "prognostication" is the character "speak," and under "speak" is the character "ten." Isn't this the character Zhuo? These lines conceal your honorable taboo name.[46] This piece of cloth also has the character "mouth" on either end, and when you fold them doesn't it make the character Lü? This conceals the name of Lü Bu. The cloth is ten feet long, to report that the Grand Preceptor will enjoy perfect happiness and that it will all be due to Lü Bu's bravery. This is both the will of Heaven and the power of men. (DONG ZHUO *acts out laughing and speaks:*) You've got it right, sir. If I am successful in carrying off this grand affair, the position of Prime Minister of the Left is yours to occupy. (CAI YONG *speaks:*) I'm just afraid you will forget, preceptor. (DONG ZHUO *speaks:*) You are absolutely right. The common saying is, "Important people often forget things." You take this cloth with you, and if I complete this grand affair, bring it back out and this office of Prime Minister of the Left is yours. (CAI YONG *speaks:*) Many thanks, Grand Preceptor. I am leaving now. Here I go out the door. I had no choice but to attach myself to Dong Zhuo because of my father and mother. I'm going to secretly take this cloth to Minister of Instruction Wang's residence to discuss this with him.

(Exits.)

(DONG ZHUO *speaks:*) Is Cai Yong gone? Well, this just tickles me to death! *(Recites:)*

Relying on my son Lü Bu
On this day, right now I will complete the grand affair;
If a man who understands the Way has desire for good,
It is certain that Heaven must follow along!

(Exits with group.)

(MALE LEAD *enters and speaks:*) I am Wang Yun. Yesterday Defender-in-Chief Yang orally transmitted a secret edict to me, ordering me to come up with a plan to take Dong Zhuo. But when I think about it, he has enormous authority and power, and at the same time Lü Bu has a bravery that ten thousand men together cannot match. I've thought and thought but I still don't have a plan. What shall I do? It's getting dark and I should close up my compound gate. Then I will ponder it some more. (CAI YONG *enters and speaks:*) This is the

---

45. The lines would be read vertically on the cloth.
46. For taboo name, see *Interlocking Rings*, n. 47.

minister's house. I'll call out at the door. (*Acts out calling out at the door.*) (MALE LEAD *comes out to look and speaks:*) Who's calling at the door? (CAI YONG *speaks:*) Cai Yong. (*Acts out exchanging greetings.* MALE LEAD *speaks:*) Why have you come, academician? (CAI YONG *speaks:*) Minister, I wouldn't have come if I didn't have something important. That Grand Preceptor Dong was sitting in leisure at his home when a mendicant priest suddenly looked inside the gates and laughed three times, then wept three times. The Grand Preceptor was enraged and ordered someone to grab him. The priest then hit him with something, transformed into a shaft of golden light and disappeared. This is what he hit him with, minister; please examine it. (MALE LEAD *acts out taking it to examine, then speaks:*) It turns out to be a piece of cloth with two lines of characters, "A thousand miles of grass oh green, so green, / Prognostication says that ten will live forever." Let's see: "grass," connected to "a thousand" and "mile"; "prognostication" connected to "says" to "ten": doesn't this make Dong Zhuo? (CAI YONG *speaks:*) That's correct. (MALE LEAD *acts out examining it again and speaks:*) Two "mouth" characters on the cloth clearly is a coded reference to Lü Bu. But this cloth is neither nine nor eleven feet; what does that mean? I can't figure it out. (CAI YONG *speaks:*) There's nothing difficult about interpreting it. This is precisely ten feet long, which clearly means that Dong Zhuo's number is up[47] and that he will soon die. And if he dies, it must be by Lü Bu's hand. (MALE LEAD *speaks:*) You are mistaken. Lü Bu is Dong Zhuo's adopted son—would he be willing to kill Dong Zhuo? (CAI YONG *speaks:*) What is Dong Zhuo compared to Ding Jianyang?[48] You stand beneath the one man, sit above ten thousand, "mix perfect fixings in the tripod,"[49] and "put yin and yang in proper order";[50] but if you can just put the idea in Lü Bu's mind, then Dong Zhuo no longer is worthy of considering. I have little talent, but I want to offer up a plan, called "A plan of interlocking rings." It's already late, though, and I must go home.

(*Exits.*)

(MALE LEAD *speaks:*) He's gone. He did have a good point. But how do we carry off this plan of interlocking rings? He's left me with a something I can't even guess at. This just drives me mad! (*Sings:*)

(NANLÜ MODE: *Yizhi hua*)
    In this moment of pressure, nothing goes according to my wishes:

---

47. I.e., the number ten designates "completion" and therefore it means that his luck has run out.

48. For Ding Jianyang, see *Interlocking Rings*, n. 50.

49. "You govern by making everything work in harmony"; metaphor for a wise minister.

50. Regulate government by making sure everything works by abiding by the synchronic tie between cosmic forces and human affairs; to aid the emperor in governing.

I cannot redeem the grace of our sovereign;
I cannot capture that Grand Preceptor Dong,
I cannot establish the mountains and rivers of the Han.
I'm simply driven to calculate what will happen later, ponder what
    went on before,
Search through a hundred different plots—
All, alas, hard to unravel at a moment's notice.
It has made me so anxious that my mental powers are gone,
I'm silent and wordless,
And it made me so sad that my spirit and bravery have shrunk
    away,
Now too tremulous to do battle.

(MALE LEAD *speaks:*) When will this worry and sorrow ever end? (*Sings:*)

(*Liangzhou diqi*)
What I worry about is that preventing disastrous chaos is like
    preventing Heaven from falling;
What I sorrow over is that being next to these usurping braves is like
    sleeping next to a tiger.
True it is; flying and tumbling human affairs are a thousand trans-
    formations of clouds,
A ruddy face easily transforms in a single second,
And a hoary head becomes our curse.
It makes me so angry I am struck dumb—
Just as if I had gone mad.
They are like a heavy draw-weight bow simmering and bubbling in
    my heart,
Like a keen knife twisting and turning in my belly.
And so this Minister Wang has supported both loyalty and filial
    piety with all his might but to no avail,
For how can I face that Grand Preceptor Dong who, as evil as can be,
    monopolizes power and authority as his own?
Or that Marquis of Wen Lü who, with overarching spirit, has both
    strategic wisdom and bravery?
Several times
I've called on Heaven;
But Heaven is far from the world of men
And is not inclined to grant us ease.
How sad that my single point of vermilion heart, solid as iron or
    stone,
Will result in nothing.

(MALE LEAD *speaks:*) My heart and mind are troubled and tired. I'll go into the rear garden for a while to wile away some time. Here we are at the Peony Pavilion. Houseboy, bring me my zither. (HOUSEBOY *enters, acts out handing him the zither, and speaks:*) Here is the zither. (MALE LEAD *acts out sighing and speaks:*) Alas! The house of Han will start to fall and it cannot be pulled up by human effort! The only thing I can do is face the moon, play my zither, and sing a tune. (*Acts out strumming the zither.*) (*Sings the lyrics:*)

> Ah, the fiery Han, the last of its luck ill-starred:
> Vile ministers manipulate power and buckler and spear arise.
> Lü Bu is quick and powerful; he is the claws and fangs.
> At the single battle at Tigerkeep, the multitude all quailed.
> The emperor moved the capital, went into Chang'an
> Like a bird out of the nest, a fish out of water.
> Three hundred years and more, the foundational enterprise begins
>   to fall,
> Twenty-four royal emperors; today they come to an end.
>
> This old man brave and forbearing, embosoms the state's very enmity;
> Angry that I cannot pull my sword, hoist his head on its tip.
> Nothing can be done as the flowering years encounter their declining
>   evening,
> And those officials in the court, all incapable of plans.
> In vain I received the secret edict; it is in the belt of my clothes—
> In the end void of clever plots, can I share His anxieties?
> The days and nights hesitantly come to a halt; my heart is about to
>   break.
> Facing the wind I sigh so deeply, my tears flow across my face.

(FEMALE, *costumed as* DIAO CHAN, *enters, leading* MEIXIANG, *and speaks:*) I am Diaochan. After I was separated from Lü Bu, I never thought I'd wind up here. Fortunately, old Minister Wang treats me like his own daughter.[51] But this affair in my heart is truly hard to reveal. But now the moon is bright and the people are asleep, so I have led Meixiang out into the rear garden to burn incense. (MEIXIANG *speaks:*) Faster, sister! (MALE LEAD *acts out seeing and hiding from them, sings:*)

> (Gewei)
> I would have said that, rustling and swooshing, a roosting bird was
>   slipping through the flower's shadows,

---

51. For the position of Diaochan, see *Interlocking Rings*, n. 54.

But it turned out to be a charming and winsome beauty gliding along
the bamboo path.
Let her tread over this jade dew and green moss.

(MEIXIANG *speaks:*) Sister, shall I put this incense table here by the railing
around the tree peonies? (MALE LEAD *sings:*)

I will hide behind this Taihu rock,
While she walks to the railing around the peonies.

(FEMALE *acts out sighing.*) (MALE LEAD *sings:*)

I see her delicate little hand propped against the lilac tree.

(FEMALE *speaks:*) Meixiang, bring the incense here. (MEIXIANG *speaks:*) Sister,
please raise the incense. (FEMALE *speaks:*)

Pond's bank keeps apart double-stemmed lotuses;
How can they stand another year's separation?
For two single winged birds to fly as one is no easy task,[52]
With this one stick of pure incense, I pray to Heaven.

I, Diaochan, was originally Lü Bu's wife. Since I was separated from my husband at Lintao Prefecture, I have wandered to Minister Wang's residence,
where I have had the fortune of being treated like his own daughter. Unfortunately, I do not know where Lü Bu is. I burn this stick of nighttime incense in
the rear garden now and pray to heaven. I want us—husband and wife—to be
whole again and together soon.

Willow shadows and flowers' shade—the moon is high in the void;
The censer beast's incense vapor is dispersed by the wind;
So many heartbreaking feelings in my heart
Are expressed to the full in these two deep, deep bows.

(MEIXIANG *speaks:*) I'll burn another stick on your behalf, sister. Heaven, we
have heard people say, "Among men there is Lü Bu; among women, Diaochan."
Do not do this fine marriage match wrong. If they can be a pair again soon, they
can also take Meixiang along.[53] (MALE LEAD *sings:*)

(*Sikuai yu*)
I would have said that she was sickly thin, suffering some lingering
illness,

---

52. For single winged birds, see *Interlocking Rings*, n. 56.
53. For "take Meixiang along," see *Interlocking Rings*, n. 57.

But all the time she was quietly silent, preoccupied with "boudoir
    resentment."[54]
Now I admit the truth of the saying, "Desire for sex is as great as
    heaven!"

(FEMALE *acts out weeping.*) (MALE LEAD *sings:*)

Just look at the tear tracks breaking their boundary to streak her
    made-up face.
I am not one "who rules the family like ruling the state,"
And she cannot "protect ritual like she was protecting her life."
We both look to the past and not the future.

(*Speaks:*) Diaochan, what are you doing here? Do you dare to be so bold as
this?[55] (MEIXIANG *speaks:*) It's all over! The minister has heard everything.
(FEMALE *speaks:*) I never said anything here; I just came to burn some incense
because I am not well. (MALE LEAD *speaks:*) Silence! (*Sings:*)

(*Ma yulang*)
Do you still want to deceive me with flowery words and clever lies?
You just burned incense and made an oath while pointing at blue
    heaven,
Kneeled and bowed your head and yourself professed an oath.
A heart as brave as this, a willed intent this firm—
Was it really just to protect your body from illness?

(FEMALE *speaks:*) I had no other oath. Seeing it was such a fine night, my whole
intent was to burn incense to celebrate the moon. I never said anything wrong!
(MALE LEAD *sings:*)

(*Gan huang'en*)
Ai! Didn't you say you "wanted to hand over the silken whip"[56] a
    second time?
To put in order your fine predestined lot once more?
But who was it who drove these embroidered mandarin ducks
    apart?[57]
Who split up this pair of flying swallows?
And who hacked down the double-headed lotus?

---

54. Lovesickness.

55. I.e., be out alone at this time of night.

56. In traditional lore, a woman gives a man a soft silken whip to symbolize her attachment
to him. Here, of course, her wish is to bind herself to Lü Bu once more in a reunion.

57. Mandarin ducks were thought to mate for life; hence, they are a symbol of a married
couple.

What hurt you enough to stir up a lifetime of hatred
Was seeing this pair being dragged around by their emotions.

(FEMALE *speaks:*) I never said these words. (MALE LEAD *speaks:*) You still won't admit it! (*Sings:*)

> I will just ask you this: troubles were encountered,
> Separation occurred
> In precisely what year?

(FEMALE *speaks:*) Your child prayed to the moon and burned incense only because I was not feeling well. That was truly the only reason. (MALE LEAD *sings:*)

> (*Caihua ge*)
> But the injustice in your belly became words in your mouth,
> And sound after sound said, "Lord of Heaven, why will you not pity me?"

(MEIXIANG *speaks:*) My sister never said such a thing. If I am lying, then turn me into a Pekingese pup. (MALE LEAD *speaks:*) Shush! (*Sings:*)

> You said, "Lü Bu is the most handsome and elegant among men,
> And Diaochan the most gorgeous in the all the world."

(FEMALE *speaks:*) Your child really didn't say anything. (MALE LEAD *speaks:*) Diaochan, I heard you say, "I pray that husband and wife will soon be reunited." Which one is your husband? Tell me the complete truth. If a single word is untrue, I'll beat to you to death, you little hussy. I will never let you off. (FEMALE *kneels and speaks:*) I beg you, father, still your anger and stop your rage; set aside for a moment your tiger- and wolf-like presence, and listen to your child slowly tell you all. I am not from here, but a person from Mu'er Village in Xinzhou, the daughter of Ren Ang, and my child name was Hongchang. Because Emperor Ling of the Han made a thorough search for women for his seraglio, I was selected and sent to the palace, where I became Lady in Charge of Sable and Cicada Hats.[58] Emperor Ling gave me to Ding Jianyang, and in those days Lü Bu was Ding Jianyang's adopted son. Ding then arranged for me to marry Lü Bu. But during the chaos of the Yellow Turban revolt we were separated from each other in the fighting, and I don't know where Lü Bu is. I was fortunate enough to wind up in your house, father, where you treat me like your own daughter. This is truly an act of grace that has given me a second life, and I am incapable of repaying it correctly. Yesterday mother and I were on the Loft for Watching the Mainstreet, and we saw the head of a ceremonial guard

---

58. For sable and cicada hats, see *Interlocking Rings*, n. 62.

prance by, and it was surely Lü Bu on that Red Hare steed. This is why I was
burning incense and praying—I want husband and wife to be reunited. I never
expected to be overheard by you, father, and I should die a thousand deaths for
this affront. (MALE LEAD *speaks:*) Diaochan, is this the truth? (FEMALE *speaks:*)
Father, I would not dare lie to you. (MALE LEAD *speaks:*) Hai! Academician Cai,
you are truly a capable man. Doesn't the plan of interlocking rings rest on this
girl's shoulders? (*Sings:*)

> (*Xu hama*)
> This is truly a case of "the will of Heaven changes to accommodate
>   man,"
> And reveals how my loyal heart will be concentrated on behalf of the
>   state.
> In secret I am overcome with happiness—
> There's no need to search out another expedient plan,
> No need to calculate exigent changes.
> I need not face off with him,
> Need not do battle with him.
> This marvelous plan of mine will last forever,
> This marvelous plan of mine will be long effective.
> The common folk will be released from their dire straits,
> And the altars of state will be preserved whole from this point on.
> But that rebellious official Dong Zhuo manipulates authority—
> Truly his power flares enough to infuse Heaven with smoke.
> If the slightest hint of this were to leak out and spread,
> Would he not extinguish everyone high and low within my gates?
> I worry so much,
> I worry so much my thinking ceases, my passions turn upside down—
> My heart seems to be fried in oil.
> Who would have ever thought that right here, in my house,
> I would come up with this beautiful charmer?
> And on that day when we set the feast,
> In that bevy of rouge and powder a battle campaign will be secretly
>   hidden away.
> How could he ever escape
> From this crafty plan?
>   (*Continues in speech:*) Diaochan,
> I will have husband and wife be whole and complete,
> Forever reunited.

(*Speaks:*) Child, if you can just do one thing for me, I will unite you and your
husband. (FEMALE *speaks:*) Father, not one, but ten things would I do for you. I

will comply, but what is it? (MALE LEAD *speaks:*) I was just thinking that back in the Spring and Autumn era, there was a wife of a certain Zhuan Zhu[59] who had the strength to help her husband and aid him in the completion of his great success. In our own reign there is the also the mother of Wang Ling who fell on a sword to kill herself, leaving her son behind to be of service to the house of Han without a mind torn in two.[60] Later both of these women's names were entered into the historical records and they are now passed down and eulogized by everyone. If you can carry out this one plan for your father, and allow me to secretly plot against Dong Zhuo to restore proper order to our reign, then I will see to it that you and your husband are reunited forever. Child, don't be concerned about a moment of "spring's defilement" from that fat Dong Zhuo and win for yourself an eternity of a vaunted name for rescuing your emperor. (FEMALE *speaks:*) Father, I will do as you say; what is it you want me to do? (MALE LEAD *speaks:*) Now that you've agreed, child, return to the rear chambers for the moment. (FEMALE *speaks:*) I understand.

> If I want my traces to be found in the green chronicles,[61]
> Dare I begrudge serving someone else with my rouged face?

> (*Exits.*)

(MALE LEAD *speaks:*)[62] Ji Lü, where are you? (CLOWN, *costumed as* JI LÜ *enters and speaks:*) I am no one else but the majordomo of Minister Wang's house. The old master has called me, and I'd better go find out why. (*Acts out greeting him and speaks:*) What use do you have for me, master, now that you've summoned me. (MALE LEAD *speaks:*) Ji Lü, I want you to tell those in charge of banquets to get a feast prepared to lavish on our guest, and also go to the personal quarters of the Marquis of Wen just beside the Grand Preceptor's residence, and ask Lü Bu to come. (JI LÜ *speaks:*) I understand.

> (*Exits.*)

(MALE LEAD *speaks:*) Ji Lü is on his way. I reckon that Lü Bu will certainly come to the feast. When he gets here, I have an idea of what to do. True it is:

59. For Zhuan Zhu, see *Interlocking Rings*, n. 63.

60. According to the *Documents of the Han*, Wang Ling had joined Liu Bei's armies in their attack on Xiang Yu. Ling's mother had been taken captive by Xiang Yu and when she had a chance to speak to an envoy from her son, she told him to tell her son to serve the "King of Han well" and not be worried about her. She then fell on her sword and died.

61. So called because the records of the court scribes were originally written on staves made from freshly cut bamboo.

62. The *Anthology of Northern Dramas New and Ancient* version of the play indicates here that the night has passed and the sky has brightened.

If you don't employ a plan that reaches to the bottom of a ten-thousand-foot
lake,
How can you ever get a leviathan to take the bait?

(*Exits.*)

(OPENING MALE, *costumed as* LÜ BU, *enters, leading* SOLDIERS, *and recites:*)

I am a true hero; my horse is a coursing stallion;
The Grand Preceptor has given me a crimson unicorn gown.
When people of the world ask me, "What are you named?"
I answer, "Once you saw me rush to battle, coming out of Tigerkeep Pass."

I am Lü Bu, known as Fengxian. I once drove the army of eighteen liege lords
into retreat at Tigerkeep Pass; my might shook the empire and I was enfeoffed
as the Marquis of Wen. I now am an aide in the house of Grand Preceptor
Dong, where I am named The Adopted Son, and am shown favor surpassing all
other officials. If not engaged in battle, I do nothing but drink and play around.
There's nothing going on in camp today, so let's see if anyone comes to invite me
somewhere. (JI LÜ *enters and speaks:*) I am Ji Lü, and I've come to invite the
Marquis Lü of Wen. Here I am, already. Doorkeeper, please report that Ji Lü,
messenger from Minister of Instruction Wang, would like to have an audience.
(SOLDIER *acts out reporting.*) (LÜ BU *speaks:*) Tell him to come in. (SOLDIER
speaks:) Messenger, enter. (JI LÜ *acts out greeting rituals.*) (LÜ BU *speaks:*) Ji Lü,
why did you come? (JI LÜ *speaks:*) I am bearing the command of Minister of
Instruction Wang, who says that there have been few reports from the border
these days and so he has especially prepared a small banquet in order to catch
up on things with the Marquis of Wen. (LÜ BU *laughs and speaks:*) This old fellow is not to be bested! Go ahead. I will come later. (JI LÜ *speaks:*) I will go back
and report. I just hope that you will start out soon.

(*Exits.*)

(LÜ BU *speaks:*) Ji Lü has left. Servants, saddle up my horse, and I will go off to
Wang Yun's residence for a banquet.

(*Exits.*)

(MALE LEAD *enters, leading* JI LÜ *and* SERVANTS, *speaks:*) I am Wang Yun. I sent
Ji Lü off to invite Lü Bu. He said he'd come right away. Servants! Keep watch
outside the door and report to me when the Marquis of Wen is here. (JI LÜ
speaks:) Understood. (LÜ BU, *leading* SOLDIERS, *enters and speaks:*) Here is Minister Wang's residence. Servants, take my horse. (JI LÜ *acts out reporting.*) (MALE
LEAD *acts out rushing to receive him, speaks:*) I knew earlier you were coming and
I should have met you at a distance from the house. Please don't hold me at

fault for this lack of proper reception. (LÜ BU *speaks:*) You are an elderly official from the court, so why do you need to be so formal? Isn't it a little inappropriate to be so modest and humble? (MALE LEAD *speaks:*) Not at all; I am the one who receives the radiance of the Marquis' heartfelt visit. Servants, bring out the table. (*Act out bringing the table and having the* MALE LEAD *offer wine.*) Fengxian, please drink this cup to the full. (LÜ BU *speaks:*) What virtue or ability do I have that can make you, elderly minister, set out wine and spread a banquet? Such a proper welcome as this—how can I respond correctly? (MALE LEAD *sings:*)

> (*Muyang guan*)
> Wang Yun's official title is so small,
> My talents and arts so shallow—
> How can I play the part of "A man of rank goes to a feast?"[63]

(LÜ BU *speaks:*) Old minister, what was on your mind when you invited me? (MALE LEAD *speaks:*) I don't have anything else on my mind except to pay respects to Fengxian's awesome reputation. (*Sings:*)

> I hope that the Marquis of Wen's household will be given an escort
>   of a thousand soldiers,
> That the Marquis of Wen's status will be invested with tax rights to
>   eight districts.
> I hope that the Marquis of Wen soon controls the Field Marshal's
>   seal of office,
> That the Marquis of Wen will soon be summoned by the emperor.
> I hope for the Marquis of Wen that the black parasol will fly above
>   his head,
> That for the Marquis of Wen those vermilion robes will be aligned
>   before his horse.[64]

(LÜ BU *laughs and speaks:*) Thank you for such refulgent wishes, old minister. But I am afraid my luck does not lie here. (MALE LEAD *speaks:*) When I was young, I studied the patterns of heaven, and I now see that the fated years of the Han are over. The Grand Preceptor's meritorious virtue climbs high to the sky, and in the time it takes to point to the sun, he will inevitably ascend the exalted position. I am just hoping that the Marquis of Wen will raise Wang Yun to a high position when this happens. (LÜ BU *speaks:*) Minister, don't worry. If the Grand Preceptor carries off this grand affair, at least a position like Prime Minister of the Left is yours. (MALE LEAD *acts out pouring him wine and speaks:*) Thank you! Thank you! Please, Fengxian, drink this cup to the full. (LÜ BU

---

63. For this phrase, see *Interlocking Rings*, n. 65.
64. These are all carefully graded symbols of office; see *Interlocking Rings*, n. 66.

speaks:) This is too much wine too soon. Let me drink several cups at a leisurely rate. (MALE LEAD *speaks:*) It is well said, "If there is no music at a feast, then it does not become a happy affair." Servants, send my words to the rear chambers and please ask Diaochan to come out. (FEMALE *acts out entering, leading* MEI-XIANG, *and speaks:*) Father, why did you call your daughter? (MALE LEAD *speaks:*) My child, Lü Bu is now out in the front hall. When you take him wine, pretend that you don't recognize him. Give him a cup and then sing a song, and let's see what he says. (FEMALE *speaks:*) I understand. (MEIXIANG *speaks:*) Here is the wine. (FEMALE *acts out giving him wine and speaks:*) Marquis of Wen, please drink this cup to the full. (LÜ BU *acts out taking and drinking the wine and speaks:*) Elderly minister, I am already drunk and not acting correctly. That's enough wine. (MALE LEAD *speaks:*) Fengxian, please relax, enjoy yourself, and drink. What's the problem, even if you are drunk? Child, sing a tune as you offer the Marquis wine. (FEMALE *sings:*)

> SHUANGDIAO MODE: (*Zhegui ling*)[65]
> I once served my lord the ruler when I was young,
> And had just been given to a real hero,
> Who paired with me like mandarin ducks,
> But because of those windblown waves halfway down the road,
> We have now been separated for three years,
> Split apart in two separate places.
> I remember how in the beginning when we fled from war, buckler
>   and spear caused trouble,
> While now at present, in years of peace, the black-haired people are
>   safe and at peace.
> I kept on hoping for a beautiful fulfillment as a pair once again,
> So we could pay our thanks to that arching welkin.
> I never would have expected that now when we meet again face to
>   face,
> You would have so swiftly forgotten Hongchang!

(LÜ BU *acts out recognizing her and speaks:*) Isn't this Diaochan? How did she get here? (MALE LEAD *speaks in an aside:*) So they really are what they say. That guy has fallen for my plan! (*Sings:*)

> (*Gewei*)
> One covers her hibiscus face in embarrassment while her eyes
>   transmit her feelings;
> One cannot sit still, and finds it hard to keep going at the tortoise-
>   shell mat!

---

65. This is an inserted performance text (like zither lyrics, poems, etc.), and is not the beginning of a new suite.

I see how he feigns drunkenness, pretends to go to the privy, to temporarily let the situation ease.

(LÜ BU *speaks:*) Old minister, please forgive my wild and rude behavior! (MALE LEAD *sings:*)

Please be at ease, Marquis.

(LÜ BU *acts out vomiting and speaks:*) I am really drunk! I have made a mess of this fine banquet; how can you not be upset with me? (MALE LEAD *sings:*)

What mess?

(*Speaks:*) Fengxian, please sit back down. I have a few things to arrange. (*Sings:*)

While I am speaking
I will withdraw further away.

(*Makes a false exit.*)

(LÜ BU *speaks in a soft voice:*) The old minister has left. Diaochan! (FEMALE *acts out responding.*) (LÜ BU *speaks:*) Wife, how did you come to be here? (FEMALE *speaks:*) I drifted to the minister's residence after we were separated at Lintao. I never thought I'd have to wait until today to see you. Fengxian, you have caused me so much pain. (FEMALE *acts out crying.* LÜ BU *acts out stifling his weeping and speaks:*) Diaochan, don't make me pine so much it hurts. (MALE LEAD *rushes on and speaks:*) What are the two of you saying? (LÜ BU *and* FEMALE *kneel.*) (MALE LEAD *sings:*)

(*Ku huangtian*)
You have already been discovered by my prying eyes.

(LÜ BU *speaks:*) It's just that I'm drunk! (MALE LEAD *sings:*)

The two of them are so willful because of love.

(FEMALE *speaks:*) I did not dare say anything! (MALE LEAD *speaks:*) Silence! (*Sings:*)

You, base woman, have no dowry to offer!

(LÜ BU *speaks:*) This is all my fault; she's innocent in this! (MALE LEAD *sings:*)

You, a new bridegroom, want to save your money.[66]
You look at me as if I were as insignificant as a blade of grass.
With all good intentions I spread this banquet,

---

66. In traditional marriages, the money the male's family pays to the female's family as a bride price.

But you strode in and flaunted your handsomeness to get her in the
   sack.
You really have stepped in it this time, Lü Fengxian!

(LÜ BU *speaks:*) You don't understand. Let me explain it to you. She's originally
a girl from Mu'er Village in Xinzhou, the daughter of Ren Ang, and her child
name is Hongchang. She was selected for Emperor Ling's seraglio, where she
was Lady in Charge of Sable and Cicada Hats, and so was called Diaochan.
Later Emperor Ling gave her as a gift to Ding Jianyang. I was his adopted son
in those days, and he gave Diaochan to me in marriage. We were split apart in
the battles of the Yellow Turban revolt, and this whole time I haven't known
where she was. She's been here in your house all this time, elderly minister, and
I just couldn't overcome my feelings about having been apart. I just hope you
will find it in your heart to take pity on us, and allow us—husband and wife—
to be together again. I would not forget such great virtue until the day I die, and
will serve you as a horse or a dog serves its master. (MALE LEAD *speaks:*) Child,
what do you have to say for yourself? (FEMALE *speaks:*) It's just as he says. I just
hope you will be able to forgive us. (MALE LEAD *speaks:*) Well, since this is the
case, please rise, Marquis. (*Sings:*)

> You don't have to tell me a singe thread cannot make a string—
> I will make your waning moon whole again!

(*Speaks:*) Child, go on back to your quarters!

(FEMALE and MEIXIANG exit.)

(MALE LEAD *sings:*)

> (*Wu ye ti*)
> We can simply say, "Once you enter the gate of a noble, it is like
>   heaven."[67]

(MALE LEAD *speaks:*) This isn't my private residence. (LÜ BU *speaks:*) If it isn't
your private residence, then what is it? (MALE LEAD *sings:*)

> Who would ever think that Liu Chen of the Han would stumble into
>   his Peach Blossom Fount?[68]
> For nothing has your beauty endured such lovesick longing;
> We should quickly have you hand in hand, shoulder pressed to
>   shoulder,
> Sleeping together on a shared pillow.

---

67. A common saying about how well the rich have it.
68. For Peach Blossom Fount, see *Interlocking Rings*, n. 71.

All I want is this bejeweled Hualiu[69] to receive the purple silken
    whip once more;[70]
How could I make those brocaded mandarin ducks be locked deeply
    away in a golden hall?
A beautiful road is ahead,
A new marriage bond.
Let all those spring winds enter into the courtyard dwellings
And let the night moon shine on their balustrades.

(MALE LEAD *speaks:*) If you hadn't said anything, Marquis, how would I have
known? I could never have found such a match as proper as this. I will select an
auspicious day, and will also provide a dowry of three strings of a thousand
cash to make Diaochan your wife. How does that sit with you? (LÜ BU *speaks:*)
Many thanks, minister. Diaochan's father is my father. Such grace as this must
be repaid with equal weight. (MALE LEAD *speaks:*) There is just one thing, Marquis, I just fear that if the Grand Preceptor should find out, won't he see it as an
offense I've committed? (LÜ BU *speaks:*) This is not a problem. When my father
knows, we'll be even happier. (MALE LEAD *speaks:*) If this is the case, then have
no worries, general. I will invite the Grand Preceptor tomorrow and lay out
another banquet. On the one hand we will be able to discuss the grand affair,
and on the other bring up this marriage business. There's nothing standing
in the way. (LÜ BU *speaks:*) Father-in-law, to have exercised your mind so to aid
your child is something that I will not forget until the day I die. I've had enough
wine, so I'll take my leave. (MALE LEAD *speaks:*) Forgive me for any breaches of
protocol, general. (LÜ BU *speaks:*) I dare not presume![71] I'm out the door now
and on the way back to my private residence. (*Recites:*)

> By chance I went to a nobleman's feast,
> Where I met my old wife, as I had met her before;
> Again in accord as a pair of phoenix mates
> We do not resemble those five goat hides.[72]

(*Exits.*)

---

69. A famous steed of strength and power.

70. To receive a silken whip was to accept a marriage proposal from a woman's family.

71. These last two lines are formulaic utterances for departing a feast.

72. This refers to the story of Baili Xi, as told in two versions. One is that he sold himself to
Qin to a herdsman for five goat hides in order to get close to the Duke of Qin. The second is that
the Duke of Qin had heard that Baili Xi, then detained in Chu, was a worthy man, and he offered
to ransom him for five goat hides. In any case, the term "five goat hides" came to refer to a person
of very low standing or a thing of no value.

(MALE LEAD *speaks:*) Lü Bu has left. Ji Lü, go to the Grand Preceptor's residence again and say that Wang Yun especially invites the Grand Preceptor to a banquet. If he will not come for that, tell him that I am inviting him to discuss the grand affair. I hope there are no other obstacles. (JI LÜ *speaks:*) I understand. (MALE LEAD *speaks:*) I reckon Dong Zhuo is a simple soldier. He's surely willing to come if he sees we're discussing the grand affair. (*Sings:*)

> (*Huangzhong Coda*)
> Tomorrow, I'll arrange a Goosegate feast,[73] set out Double Pupil's
>   banquet,[74]
> Prepare a trap for catching phoenixes, Empress Lü's feast.[75]
> I'll use my innate cleverness,
> Employ shrewd plans.
> These expedient tactics
> Must be clever and facile.
> We will play the ocarina, sing,
> Set out pipes and string.
> The flowers will seem like embroidery,
> The wine like rivers.
> I will be even more humble,
> Act the meek and good one.
> Grand Preceptor Dong
> Will be undone by a drunken nature:
> Seeing that rouged face,
> He will certainly fall in love.
> Then I will fake offering him that beautiful face of Diaochan
> And secretly speak my desires to Heaven.
>> (*Continues in speech:*) And should you say, "What is it you desire?"
> I just desire to quickly exterminate this rebellious minister,
> And let the sagely brilliance shine for all to see.[76]

> (*Exits with* JI LÜ *and* SERVANTS.)

---

73. This refers to a feast given for Liu Bang by Xiang Yu, who planned to kill Liu Bang but hesitated and lost the opportunity and subsequently, the empire as well. See *Xiangyang Meeting,* n. 20.

74. Xiang Yu was said to have double pupils in his eyes like the sage king Shun.

75. For Empress Lü, see *Interlocking Rings,* n. 76.

76. For sagely brilliance, see *Interlocking Rings,* n. 79.

Act 3

(DONG ZHUO *enters, leading* ATTENDANT, *and speaks:*) I am Dong Zhuo. A few days ago Defender-in-Chief Yang Biao and Minister of Instruction Wang Yun told me that a tall platform was under construction at the Gate of the Silver Dais and that they would come request me to take the throne in four or five days. Why have I had no response in these past few days? That old miscreant Yang Biao has always been a stiff-necked man. Well, be that as it may, would Wang Yun deceive me? Servant, keep watch at the gate and should a group of high officials come, inform me right away. (ATTENDANT *speaks:*) Understood. (JI LÜ *enters and speaks:*) I am Ji Lü, and I've come to invite Grand Preceptor Dong. Here I am, already. Doorkeeper, please report that Ji Lü, messenger from Minister of Instruction Wang, is at the door. (ATTENDANT *acts out reporting.*) (DONG ZHUO *speaks:*) Tell him to come in. (ATTENDANT *speaks:*) Messenger, enter. ([JI LÜ] *acts out greeting rituals.* DONG ZHUO *speaks:*) Ji Lü, why have you come? (JI LÜ *speaks:*) Grand Preceptor, my Wang Yun has ordered me, Ji Lü, to come and invite the Grand Preceptor to a banquet. (DONG ZHUO *speaks:*) Ji Lü, I am totally occupied by thoughts of the grand affair, which I want to discuss with the ministers and high officials. I couldn't care less about that banquet of yours! You go back and tell that old geezer Wang that I don't want his wine. (JI LÜ *speaks:*) Grand Preceptor, Wang Yun has spoken to me and said that he is setting out a banquet for no other reason than to discuss the grand affair with the Grand Preceptor. (DONG ZHUO *speaks:*) Oh, he's here to invite me to discuss the grand affair. Ji Lü, go back first, and I will come later. (JI LÜ *speaks:*) Understood. Now out of the door, I dare not tarry or delay, but go back and report to the master.

(*Exits.*)

(DONG ZHUO *speaks:*) Ji Lü is gone now. Servant, get my carriage ready, and I will go personally to Wang Yun's residence to attend a banquet. (*Acts out laughing and speaks:*) Should anything happen during this banquet, then I'll just finish off this old fellow.

(*Exits.*)

(MALE LEAD *enters, leading* ATTENDANT, *and speaks:*) I sent Ji Lü off to the Grand Preceptor's residence to invite Dong Zhuo. I think that old miscreant must come soon. (*Sings:*)

> (ZHENGGONG MODE: *Duanzheng hao*)
> Depending on my talent and ability,
> Relying on my capacity to plan,

There will be no need to stir broad swords and long lances;
It's all about "cuddling a red and drawing near a green," like a painted
    wind screen—
Everything is all in place now.

(*Gun xiuqiu*)
In the censer I will burn precious seal-script incense,[77]
For wine I will pour a liquor of liquid jade;
During the playing of pipes and singing, the sound of the music will
    be crisp and concordant. Today there is a different atmosphere in
    this painted hall.
It might seem like a land of brocade and embroidery,
But it secretly conceals a battlefield,
But one without tiger-mighty generals who fight to win—
At the tortoiseshell mat I shall lead out one who is rouged with red.
I just expect to take the wolves and tigers with hidden bows and
    poisoned arrows,
And to snare the phoenix with snares unrolled and nets stretched
    tight.
It will be no ordinary feast.

(JI LÜ *enters and speaks:*) I am Ji Lü. I just took an invitation to the Grand Preceptor and now I'm going back to inform the old master. (*Acts out greeting.*)
(MALE LEAD *speaks:*) Ji Lü, how did it go with the invitation? (JI LÜ *speaks:*) I
used your exact words to go and invite the Grand Preceptor. Originally he was
very unhappy, but his expression changed just as soon as I mentioned discussing the grand affair. He said, "You go back first. I will come later." (MALE LEAD
speaks:) Ji Lü, go and keep watch at the door, and when you see the Grand
Preceptor's outriders far off in the distance, you come quickly to inform me.
(JI LÜ *speaks:*) Understood. (DONG ZHUO, *enters, leading* EXTRAS, *costumed as*
LI RU *and* LI SU, *and* SOLDIERS, *and speaks:*)

The house of Wang has set out a banquet—don't get suspicious.
        I am aware of every hidden plan;
        If half a word should sound out wrong,
        I'll trample his residence until it's a muddy bog.

I am Grand Preceptor Dong. Wang Yun has invited me to a banquet today.
Generals—station yourselves outside the door. (GENERALS *act out responding
affirmatively.*) (JI LÜ *hurriedly reports and speaks:*) I want to let you know, old

---

77. For seal-script incense, see *Interlocking Rings*, n. 81.

master, that Grand Preceptor Dong has arrived. (MALE LEAD *speaks:*) I'll go out personally to greet him. (*Acts out kneeling, speaks:*) I have troubled the Grand Preceptor's noble feet to tread on this base ground. Please pardon me for not going out afar to greet you, a crime that deserves death. (DONG ZHUO *speaks:*) Minister Wang, you have such a high rank yourself, people outside will see you kneeling in the street and think it is vulgar. Please rise. (MALE LEAD *speaks:*) This humble office should act in this way! I early on wanted to invite you here today; if we had put it off four or five more days, then the Grand Preceptor would already have taken the imperial position. Then the denotative names of "ruler" and "minister" would have been as surely separated as heaven and earth. We would no more be able to enjoy the happiness of colleagues. So, I simply hope that the Grand Preceptor not find me wrong for such a presumptuous invitation. (DONG ZHUO *acts out laughing heartily and speaks:*) I'm just afraid I will never reach this position. (MALE LEAD *speaks:*) Servant, bring out the table for me. (JI LÜ *acts out bringing out the table and serving wine.* MALE LEAD *speaks:*) Preceptor, please drink this cup to the full. (DONG ZHUO *speaks:*) Stop! I want to drink and I want to say clearly what I have to say. As for that affair at the Gate of the Silver Dais, precisely which day will it be? (MALE LEAD *speaks:*) I can report to the Grand Preceptor, this affair has now been set by deliberation, and it will be more than three days hence. (DONG ZHUO *speaks:*) Well, if it is just a matter of three days, it's not important. Minister, bring on the wine, and I will drink and drink. (*Acts out receiving the wine and drinking.* MALE LEAD *offers him more wine, speaks:*) Please, Grand Preceptor, please drink three full cups to set the banquet in motion. (DONG ZHUO *acts out drinking three times, speaks:*) When I observe those high court officials, there are many I find wanting. I will pluck out their eyes and cut out their tongues in light cases, but for more serious cases I will cut off their heads, and for the most severe, I'll extinguish their clans. Only you, old fellow, are humble and respectful when you conduct yourself, are modest and yielding when you speak, and this really pleases me. The ancients have a saying, "The humble man has a good end, it will be propitious."[78] This certainly is in reference to you, Minister. (MALE LEAD *speaks:*) Thank you for your praise, Grand Preceptor. (*Sings:*)

(*Ban dushu*)
I see your words are clear, Grand Preceptor,
And make me decide clearly when I hear them.
What you have said is, "I will immediately take control of court, and
    spread prosperity.

---

78. Based on Zhang Zai's (1020–77) commentaries to the hexagram *qian,* "humble," from the *Book of Changes.*

The hundred officials, civil and military, will each be raised in rank
and rewarded.
When that happens, do not incline toward either new emotions or
old feelings!"
I desire the Grand Preceptor to live a long and happy life without
end.

(DONG ZHUO *speaks:*) Minister, after We carry off the grand affair, I will make
certain your grade is at the highest level and that your position is above all of
the liege lords. (MALE LEAD *sings:*)

(*Xiao heshang*)
I desire that the Grand Preceptor ascend the hall of the Son of
Heaven toward evening,

(DONG ZHUO *speaks:*) If this day should happen, what should Li Su be given as
an office? (MALE LEAD *sings:*)

Li Su should be made Vanguard General.

(DONG ZHUO *speaks:*) Right! And my son, Lü Bu? What rank should we give
him? (MALE LEAD *sings:*)

Lü Bu should sit in a lotus-blossom tent with a golden peak.[79]

(DONG ZHUO *speaks:*) This is appropriate. (*Acts out laughing and speaks:*) Minister, what about you? (MALE LEAD *sings:*)

I've only been in charge of charts and documents to aid the court,
For I never strapped on armor to fight on the sandy battlefield.

(DONG ZHUO *speaks:*) Even so, what position do you really want? (MALE LEAD
sings:)

I hope the Grand Preceptor will make me a top minister.

(DONG ZHUO *speaks:*) I would say that the reason you invited me was because
you wanted this position all along. No matter. If I complete this grand affair in
three or four days, the office of Prime Minister of the Left is yours to take.
(MALE LEAD *acts out bowing to thank him and speaks:*) I just hope the Grand
Preceptor will not forget what he has said here today. Servant, bring out more
wine. (JI LÜ *speaks:*) Here is the wine. (MALE LEAD *acts out presenting him wine
and speaks:*) Grand Preceptor, please drink this cup to the full. (DONG ZHUO
speaks:) Stop! The wine is coming too fast. The weather is really hot and I'm

---

79. The tent used by the Field Marshal, the highest military post.

feeling tired right now. Let me rest a bit. (*Acts out nodding off.*) (MALE LEAD *speaks:*) Ji Lü, the preceptor is passed out. Send a message to the rear apartments, and have Meixiang bring Diaochan out to fan the Grand Preceptor. (JI LÜ *acts out summoning them.*) (FEMALE *enters, leading* MEIXIANG *holding a fan, and speaks:*) Father, why did you call me? (MALE LEAD *speaks:*) Child, Dong Zhuo is now passed out in hall and is sleeping. Go fan him! (FEMALE *speaks:*) Yes, sir. (MALE LEAD *sings:*)

(*Gun xiuqiu*)
Her chignon, brushed with oil, shines;
Her face, newly made up, is fragrant,
And drawn in the new fashion of moon-curve brows,
And she wears newly woven immortals skirts as soft as lotus threads.
If this gorgeous made-up face
Presses on the jade goblets,
And diligently sings in a low voice as she fills the cups,
Her ten fingers will reveal, long and delicate, springtime bamboo
     shoots.
I simply want to expel the Han emperor's sickness of heart's anxiety,
And should you possess a spiritual recipe to cure traitorous treachery,
It's not worth discussing![80]

(DONG ZHUO *acts out reviving and speaks:*) Ya! This cool breeze penetrates to the very bone. Who is fanning me? (*Acts out seeing* FEMALE *and speaks:*) What a fine girl! The human world seldom sees such a face as this. Is she an immortal? A fine girl! A fine girl! Come closer, and let's drink a few cups together. (FEMALE *acts out being* embarrassed.) (MALE LEAD *speaks in an aside:*) This guy is already in the trap! (*Sings:*)

(*Daodao ling*)
I see Dong Zhuo himself set the wine cups down with a clatter,

(DONG ZHUO *speaks:*) What a beautiful woman. I have over a thousand hussies in my residence, but not one of them can match her. How come this old geezer has such a fine one? (MALE LEAD *sings:*)

He looks over her charming and gorgeous form from head to toe.

(DONG ZHUO *acts out pulling the* FEMALE *and speaks:*) Come closer to me. What's the harm in that? (MALE LEAD *sings:*)

I see Diaochan hesitate to get near him, flustered and embarrassed,

---

80. I.e., it will not be as effective as sex.

(DONG ZHUO *speaks:*) What a fine girl! (MALE LEAD *sings:*)

> That old miscreant is stealing looks at her with drooling eyes.

(DONG ZHUO *speaks:*) What a fine girl! Come nearer (MALE LEAD *sings:*)

> This guy has fallen into my trap,
> Into my trap.
> I will make the excuse of giving orders in the kitchen and leave this
> feast.

(DONG ZHUO *speaks:*) I look at this girl, who has a countenance to make fish sink to the depths and geese fall from the sky, a face to close off the moon and put flowers to shame. What a fine girl. Oh, what a fine breeze. Miss, come closer and fan a little harder.

> (FEMALE *acts out trailing the fan on the ground and exits.*)

(DONG ZHUO *acts out running after her and speaks:*) Wang Yun! Who was that young girl just fanning me a minute ago? (MALE LEAD *speaks:*) That's my daughter, whom I've yet to grant in betrothal. (DONG ZHUO *speaks:*) Oh, so it turns out to be your daughter. In this case, why did you have her come fan me? (MALE LEAD *speaks:*) When the ancients wanted to show respect to their guests they often brought out their wives and children and thought it no shame. How much more so since I have already granted you my own body;[81] why should I begrudge a daughter? (DONG ZHUO *speaks:*) Minister, after completing that grand affair in a few days, all I will lack is just such a fine wife. Minister, if you are willing to give her to me, then won't both of us fulfill our desires? (MALE LEAD *speaks:*) Well, if you aren't ashamed of my little daughter's ugly face with its unkempt makeup, I would very much desire to give her to you as a concubine. (DONG ZHUO *speaks:*) Why do you say concubine? Were she a main wife I fear that I would not be worthy enough for her. (*Acts out looking at and taking his jade belt, speaks:*) Having received the minister's assent, I dare take this jade belt as a betrothal gift. (MALE LEAD *speaks:*) Thank you very much, preceptor. (DONG ZHUO *speaks:*) Minister, today is hard to compare to days past. Now that you have given me your beloved daughter as wife, you will later on become an imperial relative and elder of the state. I will be your son-in-law, which is the same as a son, so you are my father. Father, please sit and receive your son's obeisances. (*Bows.* MALE LEAD *hastily bows back.*) (DONG ZHUO *speaks:*) I have something to say I have not completely thought out. Dare I say it? (MALE LEAD *speaks:*) What instructions do you have, preceptor? (DONG ZHUO *speaks:*) Since you have granted me your daughter, she is now a person of my own family.

81. In service.

Wouldn't it be great if you summoned her back out to pass about a round of wine? (DONG ZHUO *speaks:*) Since you have ordered it, dare I not heed? Ji Lü, take a message to the rear chambers and quickly summon Diaochan out. (FEMALE *enters.* MALE LEAD *speaks:*) Child, please pass a cup of wine to the Grand Preceptor with the utmost respect. (FEMALE *acts out passing the wine.*) (DONG ZHUO *laughs and speaks:*) If this wife were to send the wine cups about, I'd drink it whether it was wine or piss. Bring out a large flagon, and if you don't have a large flagon, a foot-washing basin will do. What a fine girl! What a fine girl! The more I look at her the finer she becomes. Father-in-law, today is different than earlier times. I have received so much from you. I've already drunk enough, I can't drink anymore. I judge that tomorrow is an auspicious day, so send your precious daughter over "to cross the threshold."[82] I will be sitting in the Grand Preceptor's residence, just to wait for father-in-law to bring my wife. I will also prepare a little feast in honor of father-in-law. Don't mess up this wonderful tryst and make me anxiously wait! (MALE LEAD *speaks:*) Since you have observed that tomorrow is an auspicious day, I will bring my daughter to your residence, and throw in a dowry of three thousand cash. (DONG ZHUO *speaks:*) Father-in-law, I heard you tell the majordomo to go get some little girl with a glib tongue. I saw that she spoke very properly, and wasn't the slightest bit glib-tongued.[83] (MALE LEAD *speaks:*) That wasn't glib-tongued [*diaoshe*], but Diaochan [*diaochan*], which is her childhood name. (DONG ZHUO *laughs and speaks:*) All the high nobles wear sable and cicada hats, and since you call her that, it is clear that she should be my wife! (MEIXIANG *speaks:*) Since my sister is going to be the preceptor's wife, and since he is going to wear the "cap equal to heaven"[84] she won't be called Diaochan anymore! (DONG ZHUO *speaks:*) I'll be waiting in my residence tomorrow for you to bring Diaochan to cross the threshold. I'm leaving now.

(Exits.)

(MALE LEAD *speaks:*) Dong Zhuo is gone. Ji Lü, prepare my cart. Tomorrow toward evening we will take Diaochan to the Grand Preceptor's residence.

(Exit together.)

(DONG ZHUO *enters, leading* LI RU, LI SU, ATTENDANT, FEMALE SERVANT, *and speaks:*) Li Ru and Li Su, is the banquet I asked you to prepare yesterday all in

---

82. To come into the house as a bride.

83. The term *diaoshe* may be a contraction of the term *diaozui youshe* (artful lips and an oily tongue). But *diao* also occurs in terms that mean to "speak unkindly," "to be sharp tongued," and to stammer.

84. *Pingtian guan*, worn by the emperor.

order? (LI RU *speaks:*) It has been prepared for some time. (DONG ZHUO *speaks:*) Minister Wang is going to bring Diaochan here today, who will become my wife—and this made me excited. I couldn't sleep all night. I've already prepared the gifts for the ceremonies of "making obeisances in the ancestral hall"[85] and "crossing the threshold." Everything is in proper order. It's getting late, so they should be here soon. (MALE LEAD *enters, leading* FEMALE *and with drum music being played.*) (MALE LEAD *speaks:*) While the drum music is playing, servant, go and report to the preceptor that Wang Yun is at the door. (LI RU *acts out reporting and speaks:*) Grand Preceptor, Minister Wang has arrived, bringing his daughter. (DONG ZHUO *speaks:*) Invite him in, quickly! (MALE LEAD *acts out entering and performing greeting rituals.*) (DONG ZHUO *speaks:*) Father-in-law, you didn't break your trust and I confess you are a good man. Where is my wife now? (MALE LEAD *speaks:*) She's in the cart. (DONG ZHUO *speaks:*) Please get out of the cart. Headmistress, please go and help my wife into the back rooms so that she can do her hair and put on her jewelry.[86]

(FEMALE SERVANT *goes out, welcomes* FEMALE. *They exit.*)

(DONG ZHUO *speaks:*) Servant, bring out the wine. Today is not the same as earlier for you are now my father-in-law. (*Acts out delivering the wine, speaks:*) Father-in-law, please drink this cup to the full. (MALE LEAD *speaks:*) I dare not. Please sir, you drink first. (DONG ZHUO *speaks:*) Father-in-law, please drink. (MALE LEAD *acts out drinking, speaks:*) I have drunk now. (*Acts out offering a return cup, speaks:*) Please, Grand Preceptor, drink a full cup. (DONG ZHUO *speaks:*) Bring it here. Normally I'd drink a flagon, offer a flagon, and we could just drink until dawn. But I have a little bit of business tonight, so please allow me to offer another banquet on some other day. (MALE LEAD *speaks:*) The wine has been sufficient. I will return now.

(*Exits.*)

(DONG ZHUO *speaks:*) Please forgive me, father-in-law. Li Ru, spread the banquet in the rear quarters, and I will go and drink the "exchange cups" with my wife.[87]

(*All exit.*)

(LÜ BU *enters and speaks:*) I am Lü Bu. Minister Wang said that he was going to bring Diaochan tonight to present to me as a wife. I didn't expect that when I got to the residence gate, the little cart, the carrying poles loaded with boxes,

---

85. The new couple makes an offering to Heaven, to their ancestors, and to their parents.
86. That was given to the bride's family as betrothal gifts.
87. For exchange cups, see *Interlocking Rings*, n. 90.

and the drum music would already have gone inside [the Grand Preceptor's residence]. Even Minister Wang hasn't come back out. Could that old miscreant have been putting one over on me? I'll just wait for Wang Yun to come out here at the gate and see what he has to say! (MALE LEAD *enters and speaks:*) That old miscreant has gone back into the rear chambers. (*Sings:*)

> (*Kuaihuo san*)
> I've seen Dong Zhuo go off happy as a spring breeze into the rear chambers.

(LÜ BU *speaks:*) Old minister, I've been waiting here a long time. (MALE LEAD *speaks:*) Silence! (*Sings:*)

> In vain you and the nighttime moon have "waited at the Western Wing."[88]
> Father and son both have worn "hats bright and shiny,"[89]
> To act out in this silly way.

(LÜ BU *speaks:*) Your daughter, minister, was originally *my* wife who had wound up in your residence. You personally granted her to Lü Bu yesterday at the banquet, but today you have sent her into the Grand Preceptor's residence. What's the meaning of this? (MALE LEAD *sings:*)

> You can drum your tongue and flap your lips here, talk about who's right, who's wrong,
> But when that new bride on the cart
> Failed to see her old-time lover with his painted halberd and carved saddle,
> She roundly cursed on Minister Wang.
> To nothing have you paraded your military prowess and awesome presence,
> And exhausted your loyalty, offered up all your integrity,
> Settled the state and made our land secure.
> Wrongly have we allowed that vile owl to stir up trouble with its tongue,
> That black rook to spread its wings
> And force a match with a magical bird.

(LÜ BU *speaks:*) Old minister, in truth, where is your daughter? (MALE LEAD *speaks:*) You can't know that yesterday when I invited the Grand Preceptor to a

---

88. For *Western Wing*, see *Interlocking Rings*, n. 92.
89. This is a direct quote from *The Injustice to Dou E* (see West and Idema 2010, p. 16). In the original scene, Donkey Zhang and his father believe that they both will become bridegrooms.

feast and brought up this affair of the wedding, he was extraordinarily happy and said, "Call the girl out and let me have a look at her." I should never have called Diaochan out to bow to the Grand Preceptor four times. Who could have expected that, as soon as that old miscreant saw Diaochan's face, it would stir up his animal desires? Today when the cart arrived, he dispatched a bunch of female servants to welcome Diaochan as she got out of the cart and whisked her into the back chambers. Marquis, this makes it moot that you are a husband—if you can't be an advocate for your wife, what's your purpose? When has a father ever taken an intended daughter-in-law and forced her to become his concubine? Bah! This makes me so embarrassed. (LÜ BU *speaks:*) If you hadn't said something, minister, how would I have known? That this old fellow would carry out such an inhumane act—this really infuriates me. (MALE LEAD *sings:*)

> (*Shua hai'er*)
> I think that you, Marquis of Wen, are a brave and heroic general.
> Who can stand against your "square heaven" double-bladed halberd?
> Moreover, once at Tigerkeep Pass you spread your name far and
>   wide,
> Frightening the assembled liege lords, whose galls shrank and souls
>   fled.
> You have always been a pillar holding up heaven in your support of
>   the altars of state,
> A beam arcing across the ocean that secures the peace of the
>   cosmos.
> You have benevolence and righteousness, but he has no sense of
>   yielding or concession—
> How can he twist that minister's residence linked to the clouds above
> Into a Gaotang where rains are made to fall?[90]

(LÜ BU *speaks:*) That boorish Dong Zhuo has no sense of shame. Diaochan and I were husband and wife who had been matched in youth. Once that old boor has recognized me as his adopted son, how can such behavior be the established

---

90. Gaotang, also known as Yang Terrace, is a common metaphor for a site of a lovers' tryst. This is a common reference to the story of King Huai of Chu and the spirit of Shamanka Mountain, recounted in Song Yu's "Rhapsody on the High Terrace." While visiting Shamanka Mountain the king took a noontime nap; a woman appeared to him, offering him a pillow, and the two made love. As she was leaving, she bade him goodbye with the following words: "I live on the sunny side of Shamanka Mountain, at the dangerous point of the highest hill. At sunrise I am the morning clouds, and at sunset, the traveling rains. Morning after morning, sunset after sunset, I am below the Yang Terrace." From this story come many expressions—clouds and rain, Gaotang, Shamanka Mountain, spirit of Shamanka Mountain, Yang Terrace, even the name of the poet, Song Yu—that denote romance and the act of physical love.

household tradition? (MALE LEAD *speaks:*) Of course there is no such household tradition! (*Sings:*)

> (*Second from Coda*)
> He has been to every corner of the empire to collect his yellow gold.
> Doesn't he have enough red faces to fill his bedchambers?
> How can he be capable of such unleashed desire just like an animal?
> In the beginning at the feast, you wept and spilled your sorrows of
>   separation,
> But now today that intimate love has been split in half without a
>   thought.
> What "benevolent father's love" can you still regard?
> If you can't think of a "minister repaying the state,"
> At least you should want that basic human link between husband
>   and wife!

(LÜ BU *speaks:*) Old minister, I've been waiting here a long time. If sometime
tonight I get to see Diaochan, I will ask her the reason for all of this. I cannot
say that I will let that old miscreant off. (MALE LEAD *sings:*)

> (*Coda*)
> Although women don't have the stuff to put up a fight,
> It has always been the case that "a real man should find strength in
>   himself."
> If we desire your thundering anger to soar three thousand rods into
>   the air,
> Then you must, yourself, this very night, carefully question Diaochan
>   fair.

(Exits.)

(LÜ BU *speaks:*) This old miscreant is completely off base, and he has stolen
away my Diaochan. I'll see it done and over with. I'll go straightaway into the
rear chambers and find that old miscreant.

(Makes a false exit.)

(DONG ZHUO *enters, leading* FEMALE, FEMALE SERVANT, *and speaks:*) I am so
happy. Headmistress, bring out the table, then wait until my wife and I have
passed a few cups between us, and when we have gotten sodden drunk, that
may aid our "spring arousal" a bit. (FEMALE *acts out passing wine to him.* DONG
ZHUO *drinks several cups in a row and speaks:*) I'll have another cup. Wife, you
have one too. Headmistress, go get our bedding ready. I'm going to rest a while
with my wife. (*Acts out sleeping.*) (LÜ BU *enters and speaks:*) I'm in front of the

old miscreant's bedroom, but how can I get Diaochan to come out? It would be better if I could actually see her. (FEMALE *speaks:*) This old miscreant is drunk. I've heard people say that there is a little corner gate in the rear garden that leads to Lü Bu's private residence. I'll go have a look. There really is a gate here! Let me open it up. (LÜ BU *speaks:*) Isn't that Diaochan coming here? I'll call her name. Diaochan! (FEMALE *speaks:*) Aren't you Fengxian? (*Act out meeting.* LÜ BU *speaks:*) Aren't you Diaochan? (FEMALE *speaks:*) Lü Bu, this embarrasses me to death. When my cart reached your residence gate, I was whisked away into the preceptor's residence by a bunch of people sent by him. When has a man's father ever taken his betrothed? Fengxian, you are a real man, with heaven above and earth below, teeth in your mouth, and hair on your head. But if you cannot even protect your own wife, then what's the use of your heroism to you? Bah! Aren't you embarrassed? (*Recites:*)

> I am only a young girl in the spring of her youth,
> And now I have told you what happened;
> Even if you scooped out all of the water from the Western River,
> Shit! It would never wash away the embarrassment on your face today.

(LÜ BU *speaks:*) Wife, I already know the whole story. Just turn inside this gate and my private residence is right over there. Let's go there and talk. (DONG ZHUO *acts out waking up and speaks:*) Wife! Wife! Why don't I see my wife? Where did she go? (*Acts out looking for her and speaks:*) Yah! Why is this corner gate open? This direction is the private residence of my son, Lü Bu. I'll take a look to see if I can find her. Wife, where are you? (FEMALE *speaks:*) Fengxian! Isn't that the old miscreant coming? (LÜ BU *speaks:*) No problem, I'll hide beside this shade wall and see what he says.[91] I'll give him a taste of my fist! (DONG ZHUO *speaks:*) Wife! Why did you go into Lü Bu's residence? Was it because that little beast was flirting with you? (*Acts out seeing him and speaks:*) So, that little beast was here. Lü Bu, if I don't kill you then my name is not Dong! (LÜ BU *acts out striking* DONG ZHUO *and speaks:*) I've knocked down this old miscreant. This is no good. I have to flee, flee, flee.

(Exits.)

(DONG ZHUO *acts out falling.*) (FEMALE *acts out hurriedly helping* DONG ZHUO *get up and* [DONG ZHUO] *speaks:*) That little beast gave me a whipping. Where is Li Su? (LI SU *enters and speaks:*) You've called me, Grand Preceptor, what are your orders? (DONG ZHUO *speaks:*) Li Su, for some reason this beastly Lü Bu has completely overstepped what is proper. He flirted with my wife in public, and when I happened to see it, he knocked me down to the ground. He's fled now.

---

91. For the shade wall, see *Interlocking Rings*, n. 99.

Go nab that little beast for me. Be careful, and make haste. (LI SU *speaks:*) I have received your orders. How could something like this happen? I'll go on and capture Lü Bu now. True it is, "A man with no hatred is not a gentleman;[92] a man without poison in his sting is no real man at all!"

(Exits.)

(DONG ZHUO *speaks:*) Li Su has gone off to nab that little beast. He'll bring him back for sure. Wife, my whole body aches from falling down. Please help me back to the rear chambers. (FEMALE *speaks:*) Fortunately you came in time, Grand Preceptor, before that fellow could sully me. You just take care of yourself now, preceptor.

(Exit, with her supporting him.)

Act 4

(LI SU *enters in battle garb and recites:*)

> The top of Mount Tai has been ground down by blades I have sharpened;
> The waves of the Northern Sea have been drunk dry by my warhorses;
> > If a man at thirty has yet to realize his ambition,
> > Then it's for naught that he is a strapping great man.

I am the white-robed Li Su. Wang Yun gave Diaochan to the Grand Preceptor as a wife. Who would have expected that little beast Lü Bu to have noticed her beauty and flirted with her right out in the open? Our Grand Preceptor ran into them, and Lü Bu gave him a beating and then fled. He doesn't have any sense of hierarchy—his behavior is unacceptable by any accounts! The Grand Preceptor has now sent me to put on my battle robes and wriggle into my armor, to stick arrows in my quiver and bend my bow to go out and capture Lü Bu, so that this hatred can be cleansed away. I'll have to catch up by following his horse's tracks along this road.

(Exits.)

(MALE LEAD *enters and speaks:*) I am Wang Yun, and I set up this plan of interlocking rings, but I don't know how it is going. (*Sings:*)

> (SHUANGDIAO MODE: *Xinshui ling*)
> In vain I may have used my heart's clever designs in double-trap
>   plans,

---

92. This particular use of the word *hen* here means a hatred for some act carried out against one that was ethically wrong.

But it was because someone had designs they shouldn't have on the
state of Han.
Now the brass pot of the clepsydra transmits sounds of dripping that
never end
And the hoary moon is slow to rise on the window's silken screen.
I paced incessantly the whole night long,
For sleep never came to my eyes.

(*Speaks:*) It's almost midnight. Why is there no news? (*Sings:*)

(*Zhuma ting*)
Grand Preceptor Dong was set for a tryst of swallows and orioles,
Overjoyed he was, a groom whose flesh weighs in at a thousand pounds.
Lü Bu, the Marquis of Wen, was an orphaned simurgh and lonely
phoenix cock,
Driven to distraction over a former winsome wife whose passions are
now split in two.
Pearls of Diaochan's tears drip until they fill the phoenix cup.
And storms from Lü Bu's anger have blown apart a mandarin-duck
rendezvous.
And because of all of this I am apprehensive and in doubt,
For I feared a "single branch completely leaked all of the news of
spring."[93]

(LÜ BU *enters and speaks:*) I knocked down that old miscreant with a single
punch, and he's surely sent someone to capture me. I'll hide out for the time
being in Minister Wang's residence and talk it over with him. I will have to kill
that old miscreant and get my Diaochan back before my life's ambitions are
fulfilled. This is Minister Wang's gate. Let me call out. Open the gate! Open the
gate! (MALE LEAD *speaks:*) That sounds like Lü Bu calling at the gate. He's fallen
into my plan. (*Sings:*)

(*Bubu jiao*)
I am so satisfied and happy to suddenly hear the sound of a voice
outside my gate.
If he hasn't fallen right into my plan,
Why would he be knocking so loudly over and over?

(*Acts out listening again and sings:*)

Now who is it, on such a quiet night and so late?
I'll hustle out and go ask for the real truth.

---

93. For this phrase, see *Interlocking Rings*, n. 101.

(*Speaks:*) I'm opening the door. Let me see who it is. (LÜ BU *speaks:*) Minister, it's your son, Lü Bu. (MALE LEAD *sings:*)

> All I see is him puffing and panting, standing and leaning against the
>   door.

(*Speaks:*) Marquis, please come in and we can talk. Why have you come here now? (LÜ BU *speaks:*) Because that old miscreant was so inhumane, I knocked him down with a single punch, and I've come to tell you about it. This kind of treacherous official and miscreant is of no use to anyone. We'd be better off if we came up with a plan that would allow me to be able to take vengeance on him. (MALE LEAD *sings:*)

> (*Hushiba*)
> According to what I think,
> How can I not get angry on your behalf?
> To no avail did you help him and support him.
> No one in all the world is as ignorant as him,
> To act in such a way—the so-called
> Intelligence of a donkey or a horse.
> This is what comes from working so hard,
> Working so hard for him.

(LÜ BU *acts out getting angry and speaks:*) Now that it's started, I have to go through with it. This old miscreant must die by my hand. (MALE LEAD *speaks:*) Still your irritation for the moment, and let's talk it over a bit longer. (LI SU *enters and speaks:*) I am bearing the order of the Grand Preceptor to go and capture Lü Bu. I've tracked him the whole way to here. This is Minister Wang's personal residence; he must be hiding here. I'll call out at the door. Minister! Open the gate! Open the gate! (LÜ BU *speaks:*) Minister, isn't that Li Su calling at the gate? That old miscreant has certainly sent him here to take me. What shall we do? (MALE LEAD *speaks:*) It's not a problem. Hide here behind the arras and let me go open the door. (*Acts out going out and meeting him.*) (LI SU *speaks:*) Minister Wang, what were you thinking? If you sent your daughter to the Grand Preceptor, then give her to the Grand Preceptor. If you are going to give her to Lü Bu, then give her to Lü Bu. Why did you leave it so unclear, and cause father and son to fight it out all night long? Lü Bu knocked the Grand Preceptor down, and it took a long time for him to get up again. I am now bearing the Grand Preceptor's orders and am leading troops to capture Lü Bu. I've been on his tail the whole road, and I can see that he's gone into your house. Hurry up and hand him over. Don't protect him. You don't need to worry about the Grand Preceptor never easing up; even I won't let you off, old man. (MALE LEAD *speaks:*) Still your anger, general! I recall that your ancestor Li Tong gathered together twenty-eight generals at Cloudy Terrace[94] and executed Wang Mang on Jian Terrace, thereby restoring the Later Han and its twelve emperors. The last two hundred years of the empire owes a great debt to your ancestor Li Tong. You are the progeny of loyal officials, what are you doing in the employ of that treacherous official? When you later are the object of foul cursing from ten thousand generations, won't that also tarnish the name your ancestor Li Tong earned for his loyalty and filial piety? Won't everyone be stained? Consider that Diaochan was originally Lü Bu's wife, but Dong Zhuo, seeing she was a real looker, took her in as a concubine by force. General, if your wife was forcibly snatched away by Dong Zhuo, how would you react? (LI SU *speaks:*) If you hadn't explained it, minister, how would I have known? So it was this old miscreant all the time who was the one without shame and it was Lü Bu who, unexpectedly, was the one with forbearance. If it were me, the white-robed Li Su, that old miscreant would have been dead a long time. Where is Lü Bu now? Let me give him a hand, and we'll go kill that old miscreant together. (MALE LEAD *speaks:*) Marquis, if you haven't come out yet, what are you waiting for? (LÜ BU *emerges and greets him with bows, speaks:*) Brother, I am overcome with anger. (LI SU *helps him up and speaks:*) Brother, it was this old miscreant all the time who was completely out of order. I'll lend you a hand and we'll go kill him ourselves. (MALE LEAD *speaks:*) General, since you are thinking this way now, go with me to see the Sage.

(*Exit together.*)

(YANG BIAO *enters, leading* SOLDIER, *and speaks:*) I am Yang Biao. All because Dong Zhuo has monopolized power and has plans to remove the house of Han, I have been constantly thinking day and night, but no plan has appeared. I haven't even seen Minister Wang these last few days; this really vexes. (MALE LEAD *enters, together with* LÜ BU *and* LI SU, *and speaks:*) This is Defender-in-Chief Yang's gate. Servant! Go report that Minister of Instruction Wang wants to see him. (SOLDIER *acts out reporting and sending him to see* [YANG].) (YANG BIAO *speaks:*) Minister, why have you hurried here in such an agitated state? (MALE LEAD *speaks:*) Lü Bu and Li Su are now enlisted and willing, together, to capture Dong Zhuo. I have come precisely to discuss this with you. The two generals are at this moment outside the gate. (YANG BIAO *speaks:*) Since it's come to this already, why not ask them in? (LÜ BU *and* LI SU *act out entering and being greeted.*) (YANG BIAO *speaks:*) We are fortunate that you two generals have such loyal and righteous hearts. If you are willing to support the house of Han and capture Dong Zhuo, I will immediately report it to the Sage, and reward and higher rank will naturally follow. (LI SU *speaks:*) I beg to report to you, de-

94. For Cloudy Terrace, see *Interlocking Rings*, n. 102.

fender, that my brother Lü Bu has given Dong Zhuo a few blows and is already "riding a tiger"; there is no possibility now that the two can stand together in the same state. But Dong Zhuo is extraordinarily powerful, and the court is full of his minions, his talons and fangs. If we don't carry this off perfectly, then we are going to feel the disaster of it. Defender, you and Minister Wang must immediately come up with a final plan—one like a thunderclap so quick there's no time to cover the ears—before this affair can be finished. The two of us are nothing but two men with a singular bravery, but if there is a place we can exert that bravery, we will do so to the point of our own lives. (YANG BIAO *speaks:*) You are absolutely correct, general. We already have a secret plan. Please go ahead of us and hide in ambush at the Gate of the Silver Dais. Wait until the edict is issued and then you come forward together and attack that miscreant. Then you will have established merit and success unmatched and a name that will never decay.

(LI SU *and* LÜ BU *exit first.*)

(YANG BIAO *speaks:*) I'm so happy that there is now a rift between Lü Bu and Dong Zhuo. Isn't it actually Heaven who is defeating him? Now we have only the matter of investiture at the Gate of the Silver Dais. We need to send someone to request Dong Zhuo to enter court. Whom should we choose from the officials to do this? (MALE LEAD *speaks:*) It has to be Academician Cai Yong if this miscreant is not going to get suspicious. (YANG BIAO *speaks:*) Right! Servant, quickly go and summon Academician Cai Yong. (SOLDIER *speaks:*) Academician Cai Yong, I have an invitation. (CAI YONG *enters and recites:*)

> From my early life on, I have loved to strum the zither;
> "High mountains and flowing waters" called out for "one who knows my music";
> In those days I could not see those "praying mantis events,"[95]
> And I wrongly blamed the Lord of Spring for having a murderous heart.

I am Cai Yong. Defender-in-Chief Yang has summoned me and I must hasten there. (SOLDIER *announces him.*) (CAI YONG *acts out greeting them and speaks:*) Why have you two distinguished officials summoned me? (YANG BIAO *speaks:*) Today we are specifically bearing a secret edict to send you off to bring Dong Zhuo to court to be invested. If you can lure him inside the court you will have earned great merit after we have captured him. (CAI YONG *speaks:*) Rest easy, sir. I'll rely on the three inches of my glib tongue and persuade Dong Zhuo to enter the court. There will surely be no problems. I simply want you two distinguished officials to be very careful so that we may all earn great merit. (MALE

---

95. When the cicada is singing its song, the praying mantis is about to devour it, not knowing that it itself will end up being eaten by the sparrow, which will be become the prey of the hawk.

LEAD *speaks:*) We are very happy you are willing to go and invite Dong Zhuo. We should inform the Sage about what is going on, so that he can disseminate the edict. It cannot be delayed.

(*Exits with* YANG BIAO.)

(CAI YONG *acts out walking and speaks:*) I'm crossing the main street and turning into these short pathways. Here is the Grand Preceptor's residence. I'll call out at the door. Is anyone there? (DONG ZHUO, *leading* LI RU *and* ATTENDANT, *enters and speaks:*) Li Ru, who is calling at the door? (LI RU *acts out listening and speaks:*) It's Academician Cai at the door. (DONG ZHUO *speaks:*) Since it is Cai Yong, Li Ru, open up this corner gate and let him in. (LI RU *speaks:*) I'll open the door. Academician, please come in. (*Acts out performing greeting rituals.*) (DONG ZHUO *speaks:*) Cai Yong, why have you come this time? (CAI YONG *acts out kneeling and speaks:*) I am reporting to the Grand Preceptor: This is an auspicious day when the fixed stars are lined up on the ecliptic, and all the officials who fill the court are waiting at the Gate of the Silver Dais, and we sincerely invite the Grand Preceptor to enter the court and be invested as emperor. (DONG ZHUO *acts out laughing and speaks:*) Good! Good! Good! I have my day too! Academician, you have the first merit. Servant, bring my court robes. (LI RU *acts out inspecting the court robes and speaks:*) You can't go to court today. These court robes have all been chewed to pieces by bugs and mice. If you go into court in these, it will be very disadvantageous to you. (DONG ZHUO *speaks:*) Cai Yong, I won't go to court. These court robes of mine have all been chewed to pieces by bugs and mice. Aren't they inappropriate? (CAI YONG *speaks:*) Preceptor, this is the time to establish the new and discard the old. Don't you simply want to change into the Coiling Dragon Robe?[96] (DONG ZHUO *speaks:*) Cai Yong, you are a man after my own heart. You are right. When I get inside the Gate of the Silver Dais, I will change into the Coiling Dragon Robe. What use will I have for these old court clothes? Cai Yong was right; Li Ru was wrong. Servant, open the central gate. (LI RU *acts out investigating and speaks:*) Preceptor, you cannot go out the gate today. It has been sealed up inside and out by spiderwebs. If you go this time, I fear you will encounter the disaster of being trapped in a net. (DONG ZHUO *speaks:*) Cai Yong, I'm not going. There must be something dishonest afoot which is why we have seen this unpropitious sign. (CAI YONG *speaks:*) Preceptor, this is also called establishing the new and discarding the old. Once you have ascended the precious throne inside the Gate of the Silver Dais, then you should cover the empire as a net, and you won't need this private residence anymore. (DONG ZHUO *speaks:*) You are right, Li Ru is

96. The emperor's robe.

wrong. Servant, bring out my cart. (LI RU *acts out investigating and speaks:*) Ai! Why is one wheel broken on this four-horse cart? This is a very inauspicious event. Grand Preceptor, you cannot get on the cart today. You can leave on this trip today, but you will not come back. (CAI YONG *speaks:*) When you reach the Gate of the Silver Dais, all of the high officials will greet you, and you will mount the imperial chariot. Why stop with this four-in-hand? This is also called establishing the new and discarding the old. (DONG ZHUO *speaks:*) You are right; Li Ru is wrong. Say one more thing and your head will roll. (LI RU *speaks:*) Enough! Enough! Enough! All of my attempts to halt him have gone unheeded. This journey will wind up with you dead and your clan exterminated. Don't say then that I did not warn you! (*Acts out sighing and speaks:*) If you are to be ruined, what is the point of my life? I will bid you adieu today, Grand Preceptor. It's better to die by banging my head against the cart than meet death at the hands of rebels. (*Acts out banging his head and dying.*)

(*Exits.*)

(ATTENDANT *reports and speaks:*) I am informing you that Li Ru smashed his head against the cart and died. (DONG ZHUO *speaks:*) Huh? Li Ru smashed his head against the cart and died? Li Ru, my son, you are so unlucky. So unlucky! (*Acts out traveling and speaks:*) Cai Yong, we have arrived at the gate outside the court. Why don't I see the hundred officials welcoming my chariot? (CAI YONG *speaks:*) All of the officials, civil and military, are waiting inside the Gate of the Silver Dais to receive you. (DONG ZHUO *speaks:*) Well, in that case, I'll get out of the cart and walk on to the Gate of the Silver Dais. (CAI YONG *speaks:*) Let me go ahead and announce you, then bring out the minor officials to welcome you. (DONG ZHUO *speaks:*) Right, right. (CAI YONG *speaks:*) I'll go on in. Servant, close up the gate.

(*Exits.*)

(DONG ZHUO *speaks:*) Why did Cai Yong go in and then have the gate closed? This affair has taken a turn for the worse. I'll go back for the time being. (MALE LEAD, YANG BIAO, CAI YONG *enter, leading* SOLDIERS.) (MALE LEAD *speaks:*) Dong Zhuo, you traitorous official, where do you think you're going? Do you understand your crimes? (DONG ZHUO *speaks:*) Wang Yun, what have I done wrong? (MALE LEAD *speaks:*) Cai Yong, you read out that edict in a loud voice, and you, you traitorous official, you listen. (CAI YONG *reads the edict out loud and speaks:*) The edict of the August Emperor reads:

> We, because of Our slight virtue, have shamed the great enterprise as its heir, and it is precisely the state's plummeting down as a fallen star that We

fear. In the past the Commanding General He Jin planned to extirpate those castrated eunuchs,[97] and mistakenly summoned this treacherous minister, who immediately rushed into court with his troops, and snatched away the great controls[98] of authority. We are truly remorseful and pained at heart. By fortune We can rely on the spirits of Our ancestors; Heaven will kill the evil. We decree that his corpse shall be burned in the main street[99] in order to warn those inside and outside the court.[100] As for other members of his faction, they are all pardoned without interrogation. We make this clear through this edict.

(DONG ZHUO *speaks:*) This is not right! I had better flee and save my life. (LI SU *enters, leading* SOLDIERS, *and speaks:*) Where are you going, you old miscreant? Eat my spear. (DONG ZHUO *speaks:*) Good Li Su, good Li Su, how can you stab me? Where is my son, Lü Bu? (LÜ BU *rushes on and speaks:*) Don't flee, you old miscreant! Eat my halberd! (LÜ BU *acts out stabbing* DONG ZHUO, *who acts out stumbling and falling down and speaks:*) Shit! What bad luck to have two such unfilial sons. The whole group! Might as well call my wife Diaochan to come and tie me up! (LI SU *and* LÜ BU *act out binding* DONG ZHUO.) (YANG BIAO *speaks:*) That we have been able today to punish Dong Zhuo and secure the stability of the House of Han is all due to the old minister's miraculous plan. (MALE LEAD *sings:*)

> (*Yan'er luo*)
> He had the guts, but you had them too;
> But you are righteous, and he was not.
> "A man may not have a desire to kill the tiger,
> But the tiger is intent on killing that man!"

(YANG BIAO *speaks:*) Dong Zhuo himself said that the power and authority were in his hands, and he looked upon the empire of the house of Han as something that could be had in a single day. Who knew this day would come? (MALE LEAD *sings:*)

---

97. In 189 the young emperor assumed the throne but his mother, Empress Dowager He, ruled in his stead. He Jin, in contest to control the government, went to Luoyang to kill all of the eunuchs, asking Dong Zhuo and other generals to join in his campaign.

98. The rights to grant feudal titles, to grant emolument, and to establish, give, take away, do away with, and carry out executions.

99. In traditional Chinese legal thinking, the destruction of the corpse is the ultimate punishment.

100. This reflects the historical account, in which fat flows from Dong's corpse in the hot weather. According to the "Biography of Dong Zhuo" in the *Documents of the Later Han*, "the persons guarding his corpse lit a wick and placed it in Zhuo's belly button, and it gave light until dawn. It was like this for days and days."

(*Desheng ling*)
Now I understand the sayings, "The net of heaven is all
     encompassing";[101]
"If the perfidy is heavy, the calamity it summons follows in kind."
He assumed that power and good fortune could forever be borrowed,
But how could he know that rivers and mountains could not be
     moved?[102]
Now this burning navel today
Is a sentence he brought down on himself that will fill all of heaven.
You and I can now be pleased, our eyebrows raised;
It was not in vain that we wagered what was left of our life to save
     our ruler from peril.

(YANG BIAO *speaks:*) How could we have ever have successfully carried off what we did today if it were not for your certain plan? I will immediately inform the Sage, and your feudal ranks shall be raised and you shall be given heavy reward. (MALE LEAD *speaks:*) We simply relied on the huge good fortune of the Son of Heaven; what merit do I have? (*Sings:*)

(*Gua yugou*)
This was all the hidden protection and support of the spirits of
     Heaven and Earth,
That, because of this, stirred our heroes to action.

(YANG BIAO *speaks:*) I thought that Dong Zhuo was relying on Lü Bu, whom he bound to him as an adopted son. How could he have reverted his allegiance to the court to help quell this traitor? What was the reason? (MALE LEAD *sings:*)

Who could have hoped that my adopted daughter Diaochan was
     truly Lü Bu's wife?
He[103] never should have flirted with her.

(YANG BIAO *speaks:*) I know all about this already. So Lü Bu wanted revenge. But Li Su was also Dong Zhuo's adopted son. Why was he willing to go along with us? (MALE LEAD *speaks:*) Because of that contretemps over Diaochan, Dong Zhuo sent Li Su to capture Lü Bu. When he got to my residence, I stirred

---

101. From the *Zhuangzi*, "The net of heaven is all encompassing; its mesh is wide but nothing falls through." Originally a philosophical statement, it was later used politically to refer to the law of the state which, while lax, would let no evil man escape.

102. That is, he always assumed he could arrogate imperial power to himself forever. He never expected that the actual transfer of the state ("rivers and mountains") could not be accomplished.

103. I.e., Dong Zhuo.

him up with a few words about loyalty and righteousness. So even Li Su could not forgive this affair. So he pulled his knife to help us. The success that is a result of all of this is all owed to the strength of these two men. (*Sings:*)

> Lü Bu has a prestige that rises above his age,
> And Li Su, a courage that assails Heaven itself.
> If they had not reverted to our august court,
> Who else would have joined us to exterminate this treacherous
>   miscreant?

(YANG BIAO *speaks:*) Since it all comes to this, I will go and report it all to the Sage and he will distribute rewards according to each person's merit.

(*Exits.*)

(CAI YONG *speaks:*) I said myself back then that Dong Zhuo would die by Lü Bu's hand. If you were to cause a rift between father and son, it was necessary to use the plan of a beautiful woman and the interlocking rings. I don't know if you still remember, old minister. (MALE LEAD *speaks:*) It turned out just as you calculated. (*Sings:*)

> (*Shuixianzi*)
> In the beginning it was a transcendent's prognostication when that
>   crazy Daoist threw down the cloth,
> And Academician Cai, you already knew when you made your plan.
> Grand Preceptor Dong was indeed finished off by the plan of
>   interlocking rings;
> Lü, the Marquis of Wen, had courage and strength;
> And now Defender-in-Chief Yang is making his report at the
>   Cinnabar Steps.

(YANG BIAO *enters and speaks:*) All of you officials face the imperial palace and kneel. Heed now the order of the Sage. (MALE LEAD *and others kneel.*) (YANG BIAO *speaks:*)

> Zhuo was originally a mounted warrior from west of the passes,
> Who thought so highly of his bravery he felt it could soar over the age;
> He personally led his stout soldiers into the court,
> Under his eyes there was no August Emperor of the Han.
> He grabbed power, usurped authority, acted against the Way,
> He took in children and wives to use like dogs and pigs.
> Now his minions with talons and fangs have crumpled and fled,
> Already aware that Heaven has rejected this caitiff.
> Right now he has been beheaded at the Gate of the Silver Dais,
> And his corpse is burned in Chang'an to carry out his punishment.

Academician Cai Yong had many strategic plans,
Going back and forth between the parties, using the persuasions of the
   itinerant;
He is extraordinarily raised to the rank of Esquire-in-Waiting in Ritual
   Section,
And Drafter of Proclamations in the Central Secretariat.

Lü Bu quelled the rebel, establishing the highest merit:
He is enfeoffed as a prince and sent to guard the areas of You and
   Yan;[104]
His wife Diaochan is also made Lady of the State[105]
And in accordance with her husband's feudal title will be noble and
   rich.

Li Su once was a lackey in the house of Zhuo,
But in the end plucked himself out and returned to righteousness;
He can be made Major General of the Flying Cavalry,
And will still lead the Feathered Forest[106] and be a private guardian of
   the emperor.

The elderly official Wang Yun internalized the anxieties of our ruler,
And at the feast cleverly employed the plan of the interlocking rings;
For this he is rewarded a high post as Prime Minister of the Left,
To end only with the state and never to be replaced!

(*They all offer thanks for the favor given them.*) (MALE LEAD *speaks:*) I am already
old, and I suspect that I will not be head of the court for long to aid our ruler,
His Highness. (*Sings:*)

   I wish our sagely ruler a long life of a thousand years,
      That he will protect the imperishable foundation of the imperial
      house.
   May he allow Wang Yun to fold up his sleeves and go into retirement.

(*The group exits.*)

TITLE: They pretend to transmit the documents of investiture at the Gate
   of the Silver Dais:

NAME: In the Hall of Brocade Clouds they secretly set the plan of
   interlocking rings.

---

104. Roughly equivalent to the area of modern Beijing, portions of Liaoyang and Hebei.
105. A rank just below royal princess.
106. The imperial guard.

Bibliography and Suggested Readings

Primary Sources

Thirty Yuan Plays Editions

Dadu xinbian Guan Zhang shuangfu Xi Shu meng 大都新編關張雙赴西蜀夢. Vol. 1. *Yuankan zaju sanshizhong* 元刊雜劇三十種. Collection 4, *Guben xiqu congkan* 古本戲曲叢刊: 1a–3b.

Gu Hang xinkan diben Guan dawang dandao hui 古杭新刊的本關大王單刀會. Vol. 1. *Yuankan zaju sanshizhong* 元刊雜劇三十種. Collection 4, *Guben xiqu congkan* 古本戲曲叢刊: 11a–17b.

Xinkan guanmu Zhuge Liang Bowang Shaotun 新刊關目諸葛亮博望燒屯. Vol. 3. *Yuankan zaju sanshizhong* 元刊雜劇三十種. Collection 4, *Guben xiqu congkan* 古本戲曲叢刊: 43a–47b.

Zhu Youdun

Xinbian Guan Yunchang yiyong cijin 新編關云長義勇辭金. Reproduction of original woodblock in Chen Wannai, ed. 1979, vol. 4, 2163–2212.

Ming Manuscript Editions

Dandao hui 單刀會. Vol. 6. *Maiwangguan chaojiaoben gujin zaju* 脈望館抄校本古今雜劇. Collection 4, *Guben xiqu congkan* 古本戲曲叢刊: 1a–25b.

Liu Guan Zhang taoyuan sanjieyi zaju 劉關張桃園三結義. Vol. 52. *Maiwangguan chaojiaoben gujin zaju* 脈望館抄校本古今雜劇. Collection 4, *Guben xiqu congkan* 古本戲曲叢刊: 75a–94b.

Zhuge Liang Bowang Shaotun zaju 諸葛亮博望燒屯雜劇. Vol. 20. *Maiwangguan chaojiaoben gujin zaju* 脈望館抄校本古今雜劇. Collection 4, *Guben xiqu congkan* 古本戲曲叢刊: 15a–54b.

Liu Xuande dufu Xiangyang hui zaju 劉玄德獨赴襄陽會雜劇. Vol. 11. *Maiwangguan chaojiaoben gujin zaju* 脈望館抄校本古今雜劇. Collection 4, *Guben xiqu congkan* 古本戲曲叢刊: 28a–68b.

Anthology of Northern Dramas New and Ancient Edition

Jinyun tang meinü lianhuan ji zaju 錦雲堂美女連環記雜劇. Vol. 21. *Maiwangguan chaojiaoben gujin zaju* 脈望館抄校本古今雜劇. Collection 4, *Guben xiqu congkan* 古本戲曲叢刊: 27a–47b.

A Selection of Yuan Plays Edition

Jinyun tang anding lianhuan ji zaju 錦雲堂暗定連環計雜劇. *Yuanqu xuan* 元曲選. Reduced version of 1918 Hanfen lou photoreproduction of 1616 ed. Hangzhou: Zhejiang guji chubanshe, 1998: 694c–705c.

Western Secondary Sources

Allen, Sarah. 1972–73. "The Identities of Taigong Wang in Zhou and Han Literature." *Monumenta Serica* 30: 57–99.

Besio, Kimberly. 1995. "Enacting Loyalty: History and Theatricality in The Peach Orchard Pledge." *CHINOPERL Papers* 18: 61–81.

———. 1997. "Zhang Fei in Yuan Vernacular Literature: Legend, Heroism and History in the Reproduction of the Three Kingdoms Story Cycle." *Journal of Sung-Yüan Studies* 27: 63–98.

———. 2007. "Zhuge Liang and Zhang Fei: *Bowang shao tun* and Competing Masculine Ideals within the Development of the *Three Kingdoms* Story Cycle." In Besio and Tung, eds., 73–86.

Besio, Kimberly, and Constantine Tung, eds. 2007. *Three Kingdoms and Chinese Culture.* Albany: State University of New York Press.

Breuer, Rüdiger Walter. 2001. "Early Chinese Vernacular Literature and the Oral-Literary Continuum: The Example of Song and Yuan Dynasties *Pinghua*," Ph.D. diss., Washington University.

Brewitt-Taylor, C. H. 1925. *San-kuo, or Romance of the Three Kingdoms.* 2 vols. Shanghai: Kelly and Walsh.

Chan, Wing-tsit. 1963. *A Source Book in Chinese Philosophy.* Princeton: Princeton University Press.

Chang, Shelley Hsueh-lun. 1990. *History and Legend: Ideas and Images in the Ming Historical Novels.* Ann Arbor: University of Michgan Press.

Cutter, Robert Joe, and William Gordon Crowell. 1999. *Empresses and Consorts: Selections from Chen Shou's Records of the Three States, with Pei Songzhi's Commentary.* Honolulu: University of Hawai'i Press.

Crump, James I. 1958. "The Elements of Yuan Opera." *Journal of Asian Studies* 17 (3): 417–33.

———. 1980. *Chinese Theater in the Days of Kublai Khan.* Tucson: University of Arizona Press.

De Crespigny, Rafe, trans. 1969. *The Last of the Han: Being the Chronicle of the Years 181–220 A.D. as Recorded in Chapters 58–68 of the Tzu-chih T'ung-chien of Ssu-ma Kuang.* Canberra: Centre of Oriental Studies, Australian National University.

———. 1970. *The Records of the Three Kingdoms: A Study in the Historiography of San-kuo chih.* Canberra: Centre of Oriental Studies, Australian National University.

———, trans. 1989. *Emperor Huan and Emperor Ling: Being the Chronicle of the Later Han for the Years 157 to 189 AD as Recorded in Chapters 54 to 59 of the Zizhi tongjian of Sima Guang.* Canberra: Faculty of Asian Studies, Australian National University.

———. 1990a. *Man from the Margin: Cao Cao and the Three Kingdoms.* Canberra: Australian National University. http://www.anu.edu.au/asianstudies/decrespigny/morrison51.html

———. 1990b. *Generals of the South: The Foundation and Early History of the Three Kingdoms State of Wu.* Canberra: Australian National University. http://www.anu.edu.au/asianstudies/decrespigny/gos_index.html

———. 1991a. "The Three Kingdoms and the Western Jin." *East Asian History* 1: 1–36. http://www.anu.edu.au/asianstudies/decrespigny/3KWJin.html

———. 1991b. "The Three Kingdoms and the Western Jin." *East Asian History* 2: 143–64. http://www.anu.edu.au/asianstudies/decrespigny/3KWJin.html

———, trans. 1996. *To Establish Peace: Being the Chronicle of the Later Han for the Years 189 to 220 AD as Recorded in Chapters 59 to 69 of the Zizhi tongjian of Sima Guang*. Canberra: Faculty of Asian Studies, Australian National University. http://www.anu.edu.au/asianstudies/decrespigny/peace1_index.html

———. 2010. *Imperial Warlord: A Biography of Cao Cao (155–220 AD)*. Leiden: E. J. Brill.

Diény, Jean-Pierre. 2000. *Les poèmes de Cao Cao (155–220)*. Paris: Institut des Hautes Études Chinoises Collège de France.

Diesinger, Günther. 1984. *Vom General zum Gott: Kuan Yü (gest. 220 n. Chr.) und seine "posthume Karriere."* Frankfurt: Haag & Herchen.

Duara, Prasenjit. 1988. "Superscribing Symbols: The Myth of Guandi, Chinese God of War." *Journal of Asian Studies* 47: 778–95.

Forke, Alfred, and Martin Gimm, eds. and trans. 1978. *Chinesische Dramen der Yüan-Dynastie: 10 nachgelassene Übersetzungen von Alfred Forke*. Wiesbaden: Steiner.

Ge Liangyan. 2007. "*Sanguo yanyi* and the Mencian View of Political Sovereignty." *Monumenta Serica* 55: 157–93.

Henry, Eric. 1992. "Chu-ko Liang in the Eyes of His Contemporaries." *Harvard Journal of Asiatic Studies* 52 (2): 589–612.

Hsia, C.T. 1968. *The Classic Chinese Novel*. New York: Columbia University Press.

Hu Ying. 1993. "Angling with Beauty: Two Stories of Women as Narrative Bait in *Sanguo zhi yanyi*." *CLEAR* 15: 99–112.

Idema, W. L. 1974. "Some Remarks and Speculations Concerning *P'ing-hua*." *T'oung Pao* 60: 121–72.

———. 1985. *The Dramatic Oeuvre of Chu Yu-tun (1379–1439)*. Leiden: E. J. Brill.

———. 1990a. "The Founding of the Han Dynasty in Early Drama: The Autocratic Suppression of Popular Debunking." In W. L. Idema and E. Zürcher, eds., *Thought and Law in Qin and Han China*. Leiden: E. J. Brill. 183–207.

———. 1990b. "Emulation through Readaptation in Yüan and Early Ming," *Asia Major*. Third Series 3: 113–28.

———. 1996. "Why You Never Have Read a Yuan Drama: The Transformation of *Zaju* at the Ming Court." In S. M. Carletti et al., eds., *Studi in onore di Lionello Lanciotti* [Studies in Honor of Lionello Lanciotti]. Napoli: Istituto Universitario Orientale, Vol. 2. 765–91.

Idema, W. L., and Stephen H. West. 1982. *Chinese Theater 1100–1450: A Source Book*. Wiesbaden: Steiner.

Johnson, Dale R. 1980. *Yuarn Music Dramas: Studies in Prosody and Structure and a Complete Catalogue of Northern Arias in the Dramatic Style*. Ann Arbor: Center for Chinese Studies, University of Michigan.

Johnson, David. 1980. "The Wu Tzu-hsü *pien-wen* and Its Sources: Parts I and II." *Harvard Journal of Asiatic Studies* 40 (1): 93–119; 40 (2): 466–505.

———. 1981. "Epic and History in Early China: The Matter of Wu Tzu-hsü." *Journal of Asian Studies* 40 (2): 255–71.

King, Gail. 1987. "A Few Textual Notes Regarding Guan Suo and the *Sanguo yanyi.*" *CLEAR* 9: 89–92.

———, trans. 1989. *The Story of Hua Guan Suo*. Tempe: Arizona State University Center for Chinese Studies.

Kroll, Paul W. 1976. "Portraits of Ts'ao Ts'ao: Literary Studies of the Man and the Myth." Ph.D. diss., University of Michigan.

Liu, Jung-en. 1972. *Six Yüan Plays*. Harmondsworth: Penguin.

Liu Ts'un-yan. 1980. "Lo Kuan-chung and His Historical Romances." In Yang and Adkins, eds., 85–114.

McLaren, Anne. 1985 "Chantefables and the Textual Evolution of the *San-Kuo-Chih Yen-I.*" *T'oung Pao* 71: 159–227.

———. 1995. "Ming Audiences and Vernacular Hermeneutics: The Uses of *The Romance of the Three Kingdoms.*" *T'oung Pao* 81: 51–80.

———. 1998. *Chinese Popular Culture and Ming Chantefables*. Leiden: E. J. Brill.

Mansvelt Beck, B. J. 1986. "The Fall of Han." In Denis Twitchett and John K. Fairbank, eds., *The Cambridge History of China*. Vol. 1, *The Ch'in and Han Empires, 221 B.C.– A.D. 220*. Cambridge: Cambridge University Press. 317–76.

Moore, Oliver. 2003. "Violence Un-scrolled: Cultic and Ritual Emphases in Painting Guan Yu." *Arts Asiatiques* 58: 86–97.

Owen, Stephen. 1996. *An Anthology of Chinese Literature: Beginnings to 1911*. New York: Norton.

Plaks, Andrew H. 1987. *The Four Masterworks of the Ming Novel*. Princeton: Princeton University Press.

Roberts, Moss, trans. 1991. *Three Kingdoms: A Historical Novel*. Attributed to Luo Guanzhong. Berkeley: University of California Press.

Ross, Gordon. 1976. "Kuan Yü in Drama: Translation and Critical Discussion of Two Yuan Plays." Ph.D. diss., University of Texas.

———. 1977. "Kuan Yu Travels a Thousand Miles Alone: A Yuan-dynasty *tsa-chü.*" *Literature East and West* 21: 38–50.

Roy, David T. 1990. "How to Read the *Romance of the Three Kingdoms.*" In David L. Rolston, ed., *How to Read the Chinese Novel*. Princeton: Princeton University Press. 152–95.

Sawyer, Ralph D., and Mei-chün, eds. 1993. *The Seven Military Classics of Ancient China*. Boulder, CO: Westview Press.

Sima Qian (Ssu-ma Ch'ien). 1993. *Records of the Grand Historian. Han Dynasty I* (Revised Edition). Trans. Burton Watson. A *Renditions*–Columbia University Press Book. Hong Kong/New York: Research Centre for Translation, Chinese University of Hong Kong, and Columbia University Press.

———. 1994. *The Grand Scribe's Records*. Vol. 7, *The Memoirs of Pre-Han China*. Trans. Cheng Tsai-fa, William H. Nienhauser, et al. Ed. W. Nienhauser. Bloomington: Indiana University Press.

———. 2002. *The Grand Scribe's Records.* Vol. 2, *The Basic Annals of Han China.* Trans. Cheng Tsai-fa, William H. Nienhauser, et al. Ed. W. Nienhauser. Bloomington: Indiana University Press.

———. 2006. *The Grand Scribe's Records.* Vol. 1, *The Hereditary Houses of Pre-Ch'in China.* Trans. Cheng Tsai-fa, William H. Nienhauser, et al. Ed. W. Nienhauser. Bloomington: Indiana University Press.

———. 2008. *The Grand Scribe's Records.* Vol. 8, *The Memoirs of Han China, Part 1.* Trans. Cheng Tsai-fa, William H. Nienhauser, et al. Ed. W. Nienhauser. Bloomington: Indiana University Press.

Slingerland, Edward, trans. 2003. Confucius: *Analects.* Indianapolis: Hackett Publishing Company.

Tillman, Hoyt Cleveland. 1996. "One Significant Rise in Chu-ko Liang's Popularity: An Impact of the 1127 Jurchen Conquest." *Chinese Studies* 14 (2): 1–34.

———. 2002. "Reassessing Du Fu's Line on Zhuge Liang." *Serica: Journal of Oriental Studies* 50: 295–313.

———. 2007. "Selected Historical Sources for *Three Kingdoms*: Reflections from Sima Guang's and Chen Liang's Reconstructions of Kongming's Story." In Besio and Tung, eds., *Three Kingdoms and Chinese Culture,* 53–69.

West, Stephen H. 1991. "A Study in Appropriation: Zang Maoxun's 'Injustice to Dou E.'" *Journal of the American Oriental Society* 101: 282–302.

———. 2003. "Text and Ideology: Ming Editors and Northern Drama." In Paul Jakov Smith and Richard von Glahn, *The Song-Yuan-Ming Transition in Chinese History.* Cambridge, MA: Harvard University Press. 329–73.

West, Stephen H., and Wilt L. Idema. 1995. *The Story of the Western Wing.* Berkeley: University of California Press.

———. 2010 *Monks, Bandits, Lovers, and Immortals: Eleven Early Chinese Plays.* Indianapolis: Hackett Publishing Company.

Yang, Winston L. Y. 1980. "The Literary Transformation of Historical Figures in the *San-kuo chi yen-i*: A Study of the Use of *San-kuo chih* as a Source of the *San-kuo-chih yen-i.*" In Yang and Adkins, eds., 45–84.

———. 1981. "From History to Fiction: The Popular Image of Kuan Yü." *Renditions* 15: 67–79.

Yang, Winston L. Y., and Curtis P. Adkins, eds. 1980. *Critical Essays on Chinese Fiction.* Hong Kong: Chinese University Press.

Yang Xianyi, and Gladys Yang, trans. 1979. *Selected Plays of Guan Hanqing.* Beijing: Foreign Languages Press.

Zhuangzi 1891. *The Texts of Taoism: The Writings of Kwang-dze (Chuang Tzu).* Vol. 40, *The Sacred Books of the East.* Trans. James Legge. Ed. F. M. Müller. Oxford: Clarendon Press.

Chinese and Japanese Secondary Sources

Anon. 1956. *Quanxiang pinghua wuzhong* 全相平話五種. Beijing: Wenxue guji kanxingshe.

———. 1959. *Sanguo zhi pinghua* 三國志平話. Beijing: Zhonghua shuju.

———. 1971. *Quanxiang pinghua Wuwang fa Zhou shu* 全相平話武王伐紂書. Taipei: Guoli Zhongyang tushuguan.

———. 1989. *Quanxiang pinghua Sanguozhi* 全相平話三國志, in Zhong Zhaohua 1989, 371–501.

Ban Gu 班固. 1962. *Hanshu* 漢書. 12 vols. Beijing: Zhonghua shuju.

Chen Shou 陳 壽. 1959. *Sanguo zhi* 三國志. 5 vols. Beijing: Zhonghua shuju.

Chen Wannai 陳萬鼐, ed. 1979. *Quan Ming zaju* 全名雜劇. 12 vols. Taipei: Dingwen shuju.

Dai Shen 戴申, ed. and ann. 2000. *Ming Qing zaju juan* 明清雜劇卷. Beijing: Huaxia chubanshe.

Gao Mingge 高明阁. 1986. *Sanguo yanyi lungao* 三国演義論稿. Shenyang: Liaoning daxue chubanshe.

Guan Siping 關四平. 2009. *Sanguo yanyi yuanliu yanjiu* 三國演義源流研究. 3rd ed. Harbin: Heilongjiang jiaoyu chubanshe.

Hu Ji 胡忌. 2008. *Song Jin zaju kao* 宋金雜劇考. Rev. ed. Beijing: Zhonghua shuju.

Inoue Taizan 井上泰山 et al. 1989. *Ka Kan Saku den no kenkyū* 花关索傳の研究. Tokyo: Kyuko shoin.

Jiangsusheng shehui kexueyuan 江蘇省社會科學院 and Ming Qing xiaoshuo yanjiu zhongxin 明清小說研究中心, eds. *Zhongguo tongsu xiaoshuo zongmu tiyao* 中國通俗小說總目提要. Beijing: Zhongguo wenlian chubanshe, 1990.

Kim Bunkyō 金文京. 1993. *Sankokushi engi no sekai* 三國志演義の世界. Tokyo: Tōhō shohō.

Lan Liming 藍立蓂. 2006. *Huijiao xiangzhu Guan Hanqing ji* 彙校詳注關漢卿集. 1st ed. 3 vols. *Zhongguo gudian wenxue jiben congshu*. Beijing: Zhonghua shuju.

Li Fuqing 李福清. 1997a. Boris Rifkin, *Guangong chuanshuo; Sanguo yanyi* 關公傳說三國演義. Taipei: Hanzhong.

———. 1997b. *Sanguo yanyi yu minjian wenxue chuantong* 三國演義與民間文學傳統. Trans. Yin Xikang 尹西康 and Tian Dawei 田大畏. Shanghai: Shanghai guji chubanshe.

Liu Haiyan 劉海燕. 2004. *Cong minjian dao jingdian: Guan Yu xingxiang yu Guan Yu chongbai di shengcheng yanbian shilun* 從民間到經典：關羽形象與關羽崇拜的聲稱演變史論. Shanghai: Shanghai Sanlian shudian.

Lu Shihua 盧世華. 2009. *Yuandai pinghua yanjiu: yuanshengtai di tongsu xiaoshuo* 元代平話研究：原生態的通俗小說. Beijing: Zhonghua shuju.

Meng Yuanlao 孟元老 et al. 1962. *Dongjing meng Hua lu (wai sizhong)* 東京夢華錄外四種. Beijing: Zhonghua shuju.

Ning Xiyuan 寧希元. 1988. *Yuankan zaju sanshizhong xinjiao* 元刊雜劇三十種新校. 1st ed. 2 vols. *Lanzhou daxue gujisuo guji zhengli congkan*. Lanzhou: Lanzhou daxue chubanshe.

Shanghai bowuguan 上海博物館 and Shanghai wenwu baoguan weiyuanhui 上海文
物保管委員會, eds. 1973. *Ming Chenghua shuochang cihua congkan* 明成化說唱詞
話叢刊. Shanghai: Shanghai bowuguan.

Shen Bojun 沈伯俊 and Tan Liangxiao 譚良嘯, eds. 2007. *Sanguo yanyi dacidian* 三國
演義大辭典. Beijing: Zhonghua shuju.

Sun Kaidi 孫楷第. 1953. *Yeshiyuan gujin zaju kao* 也是園雜劇考. Shanghai: Shangza
chubanshe.

Tan Luofei 譚洛非. 1992. *Sanguo yanyi yu Zhongguo wenhua* 三國演義與中國文化.
Chengdu: Ba Shu shushe.

Wang Jilie 王季烈. 1942, reprinted 1958. *Guben Yuan Ming zaju* 孤本元明雜劇. Beijing: Zhongguo xiqu chubanshe.

Wang Lijuan 王麗娟. 2007. *Sanguo gushi yanbian zhong di wenren xushi yu minjian
xushi* 三國故事演變中的文人敘事與民間敘事. Jinan: Qi Lu shushe.

Wang Xueqi 王學奇. 1994. *Yuan qu xuan jiao zhu* 元曲選校注. 8 vols. Shijiazhuang:
Hebei jiaoyu chubanshe.

Xu Qinjun 徐沁君. 1980. *Xinjiao Yuankan zaju san shi zhong* 新校元刊雜劇三十種.
Beijing: Zhonghua shuju.

Xu Zheng 徐征 and Zhang Yuezhong 張月中. 1998. *Quan Yuan qu* 全元曲. 12 vols.
Shijiazhuang: Hebei jiaoyu chubanshe.

Yan Dunyi 嚴敦易. 1960. *Yuanju zhenyi* 元劇斟疑. 2 vols. Beijing: Zhonghua shuju.

Zeng Yongyi (Tseng Yong-yih) 曾永義. 2003. *Suwenxue gailun* 俗文學概論. Taipei:
Sanmin shuju.

Zhang Shengyun 张生筠 and Wei Chunping 魏春萍. 2006. *Sanguo yanyi yu Zhongguo xiqu* 三國演義與中國戲曲. Changchun: Jilin daxue chubanshe.

Zheng Qian 鄭騫. 1962. *Jiaoding Yuankan zaju sanshizhong* 校訂元刊雜劇三十種.
Taipei: Shijie shuju.

———. 1972. "Zang Maoxun gaiding Yuan zaju pingyi" 藏懋循改訂元雜劇評議.
Jingwu congbian 景午叢編. Vol. 1. Taipei: Taiwan Zhonghua shuju, pp. 408–21.

Zhong Zhaohua 鍾兆華. 1989. *Yuankan quanxiang pinghua wuzhong jiaozhu* 元刊全
相平話五種校注. Chengdu: Ba Shu shushe.

Zhou Yibai 周遺白, Ann. 1958. *Mingren zaju xuan* 明人雜劇選. Beijing: Renmin
wenxue chubanshe.

Zhu Yixuan 朱一玄, ed. 1997. *Ming Chenghua shuochang cihua congkan* 明成化說唱
詞話叢刊. Zhengzhou: Zhongzhou guji chubanshe.

Zhu Yixuan 朱一玄 and Liu Yushen 劉毓深, eds. 1983. *Sanguo yanyi ziliao huibian*
三國演義資料匯編. Beijing: Baihua wenyi chubanshe.

Zuojia chubanshe bianjibu 作家出版社編輯部. 1957. *Sanguo yanyi yanjiu lunwenji*
三國演義研究論文集. Beijing: Zuojia chubanshe.

Classified Glossary

I. Modes and Tune Titles

Modes

BANSHE	般涉
NANLÜ	南呂
SHUANGDIAO	雙調
XIANLÜ	仙呂
YUEDIAO	越調
ZHENGGONG	正宮
ZHONGGONG	中宮
ZHONGLÜ	中呂

Tune Titles

Bai hezi	白鶴子
Ban dushu	伴讀書
Baolao'er	鮑老兒
Bazhuan	八轉
Bubu jiao	步步嬌
Caicha ge	採茶歌
Caihua ge	採花歌
Chenzui dongfeng	沈醉東風
Chuan bo zhao	川撥棹
Dai guduo	帶骨朵
Daodao ling	叨叨令
Daohe	道和
Desheng ling	得勝令
Dian jiangchun	點絳唇
Dianqian huan	殿前歡
Dou anchun	鬥鵪鶉
Duanzheng hao	端正好
Er	二
Ersha	二煞
Erzhuan	二轉
Fendie'er	粉蝶兒
Feng ru song	風入松
Gan huang'en	感皇恩
Gewei	隔尾
Gu meijiu	沽美酒
Gua yugou	掛玉鉤
Gun xiuqiu	滾繡球
He xinlang	賀新郎

Hong shaoyao	紅芍藥
Hongxiuxie	紅繡鞋
Houting hua	後庭花
Huang qiangwei	黃薔薇
Huangzhong	黃鍾
Huangzhong wei	黃鍾尾
Hunjiang long	混江龍
Huolang'er	貨郎兒
Hushiba	胡十八
Jiao zhengpa	攪箏琶
Jin zhan'er	金盞兒
Jinjiaoye	金蕉葉
Jisheng cao	寄生草
Jiuzhuan	九轉
Jiuzhuan Huolang'er	九轉貨郎兒
Ku huangtian	哭皇天
Kuaihuo san	快活三
Li tingyan dai xiesha	離亭宴帶歇煞
Litingyan Coda	離亭宴煞
Liangzhou	梁州
Liu Qingniang	柳青娘
Liuye'er	柳葉兒
Liuzhuan	六轉
Ma yulang	罵玉郎
Malang'er	麻郎兒
Manjingcai	蔓菁菜
Manting fang	滿庭芳
Meihua jiu	梅花酒
Muyang guan	牧羊關
Nezha ling	那吒令
Pingsha zou kaige	平沙奏凱歌
Pusa Liangzhou	菩薩梁州
Qi dixiong	七弟兄
Qiaopai'er	喬牌兒
Qing dongyuan	慶東原
Qing Yuanzhen	慶元貞
Qizhuan	七轉
Que ta zhi	鵲踏枝
Sai'er ling	塞兒令
San	三
Sansha	三煞
Sanzhuan	三轉
Shang xiaolou	上小樓
Shanghua shi	賞花時

Shaobian	哨遍
Sheng Yaowang	聖藥王
Shi'er yue	十二月
Shiliu hua	石榴花
Shou Jiangnan	收江南
Shouwei	收尾
Shua ci'er	耍廝兒
Shua hai'er	耍孩兒
Shuixianzi	水仙子
Sikuai yu	四塊玉
Sizhuan	四轉
Sui shawei	隨煞尾
Taiping ling	太平令
Tang xiucai	倘秀才
Ti yindeng	剔銀燈
Tianxia le	天下樂
Tiaoxiao ling	調笑令
Tusi'er	禿斯兒
Wei (coda)	尾
Weisha	尾煞
Weisheng	尾聲
Wu ye ti	烏夜啼
Wuzhuan	五轉
Xiao heshang	笑和尚
Xiaotao hong	小桃紅
Xinshui ling	新水令
Xu hama	絮蝦蟆
Yan'er luo	雁兒落
Yao (reprise)	幺
Yaomin ge	堯民歌
Ying xianke	迎仙客
Yizhi hua	一枝花
You hulu	油葫蘆
Yuanyang wei	鴛鴦尾
Zhegui ling	折桂令
Zhuan Coda	賺尾
Zhuandiao Huolang'er	轉調貨郎兒
Zhuansha	賺煞
Zhulü qu	朱履曲
Zhuma ting	駐馬聽
Zihua'er xu	紫花兒序
Zui chunfeng	醉春風
Zui fu gui	醉扶歸
Zui zhong tian	醉中天

II. People, Institutions, Spirits, and Horses
(All dates are AD unless otherwise noted.)

Emperors, Kings, and Palace Women

Three Sovereigns and Five Emperors

Shun (23rd–22nd c. BC)   舜
  Yao (c. 2356–2255 BC)   堯
  Yellow Emperor (r. 2696–2598 BC)   黃帝
  Yu (21st c. BC)   禹

Shang
  King Tang (r. 1675–1646 BC)   湯
  King Zhou (r. 1075–1046 BC)   紂王
  Wuding (r. 1250–1192 BC)   武丁

Zhou
  Duke Guang of Wu (r. 514–496 BC)   光
  Duke Huan of Qi (d. 643 BC)   齊桓公
  Duke Mu of Qin (r. 659–621 BC)   秦穆公
  King Li of Chu (r. 757–741 BC)   楚厲王
  King Liao of Wu (d. 515 BC)   吳王僚
  King Ping of Chu (d. 516 BC)   楚平王
  King Wen of Zhou (r. 1099–1050 BC)   周文王
  King Wen of Chu (689–677 BC)   楚文王
  King Wu of Chu (r. 740–690 BC)   楚武王
  King Wu of Zhou (r. 1087–1043 BC)   周武王

Qin
  Qin Shi Huang (Ying Zheng)   秦始皇 (嬴政)

Han
  Emperor Gaozu (r. 202–195 BC)   高祖
  Emperor Guangwu (r. 25–57) (Liu Xiu)   光武帝 (劉秀)
  Emperor Heng (r. 147–67) (Huandi)   桓帝
  Emperor Hui (210–188 BC)   漢惠帝
  Emperor Jing (r. 157–141 BC)   景帝
  Emperor Ling (r. 168–88)   靈帝
  Emperor Ming (r. 58–75) (Mingdi)   漢明帝
  Emperor Shao (r. 189)   少帝
  Emperor Wu (156–87 BC)   漢武帝
  Emperor Xian (r. 189–220)   獻帝
  Emperor Xuan (r. 74–49 BC)   宣帝
  Emperor Zhang (r. 76–88)   漢章帝
  Empress Chen Jiao (r. 141–130 BC)   陳嬌
  Empress Fu (d. 214)   伏壽
  Empress Lü (241–180 BC)   呂雉
  Prince Ding of Changsha (d. 127 BC)   長沙定王
  Prince of Jing (Liu Sheng)   中山靖王

Prince of Jiujiang (Ying Bu)	九江王 (英布)
Prince of Liang (Peng Yue)	梁王 (彭越)
Prince of Qi (r. 201–189 BC) (Liu Fei)	齊悼惠王 (劉肥)
Quiet Prince of Zhongshan (Liu Sheng)	中山靖王(劉勝)
Wang Mang (r. 9–23) (Xin dynasty)	王莽 (新朝)

Tang

Emperor Taizong (r. 626–49) (Li Shimin)	唐太宗 (李世民)

Song

Emperor Renzong (r. 1023–63)	仁宗

Ming

Chenghua Emperor (r. 1465–88)	成化
Exemplary Prince of Zhou (Zhu Youdun)	周憲王 (朱有燉)
Hongwu Emperor (Zhu Yuanzhang)	洪武帝 (朱元璋)
Jianwen Emperor (Zhu Yunwen)	建文 (朱允炆)
Prince Ding of Zhou (Zhu Su)	周定王 (朱繡)
Prince of Ning (Zhu Quan)	寧王 (朱權)
Prince of Yan (Zhu Di)	燕王 (朱棣)
Wanli Emperor (1563–1620)	萬曆

Qing

Yongzheng Emperor (r. 1722–35)	雍正帝

Institutional Names and Official Titles

guanli (clerk)	官吏
Han chu san damingjiang	漢初三大名將
Hongjin (Red Scarves)	紅巾
Hou (marquis)	侯
Huangjin (Yellow Turbans)	黃巾
Jiaofang si	教坊司
Taishuai (Grand Preceptor)	太帥
Taiwei (Defender-in-Chief)	太尉
Tingchang (post station chief)	亭長
Xianyin yuan (Court of Transcendents' Sounds)	仙音院
Yuanshuai (Grand Marshal)	元帥
Yuchen yuan (Court of the Jade Palace)	玉宸院
Zhonggu si (Office of Drum and Bell)	鐘鼓司
Zuo chengxiang (Minister of the Left)	左丞相

Non-Han Peoples

Meng Huo	孟獲
Xiongnu	匈奴

Spirits, Deities, and Mythical People

Boyi	伯益
Chang E	嫦娥

Chaofu (23rd c. BC)	巢夫
Gaoyao	皋陶
Great White (Taibai)	太白
Guanyin	觀音
Huanggong (*Huangshi gong*)	黃公 (黃石公)
Ji	薊
Jiang Shang (Jiang Ziya)	姜尚(姜子牙)
Jiang Taigong (Jiang Ziya)	姜太公
Jiang Ziya (Lü Shang) (c. 1100 BC)	姜子牙 (呂尚)
Li Jing	李靖
Liu Chen (1st–4th c.)	劉晨
Lü Wang (Jiang Ziya)	呂望
Pagoda-Bearing Heavenly King Li (Li Jing)	托塔李天王
Qi	齊
Queen Mother	王母
Ruan Zhao (1st–4th c.)	阮肇
White Emperor (Baidi)	白帝
Xu You (23rd c. BC)	許由
Xuan Yuan (Yellow Emperor)	軒轅
Yu	禹
Zhou Qiongji	周瓊姬

Horses

Chitu ma (Lü Bu's horse, Red Hare)	赤兔馬
Dilu (Liu Bei's horse, Rogue)	的盧
Hualiu (Duke Mu's steed)	驊騮

Personal Names

A'dou (207–71)	阿斗
A'man (Cao Cao)	阿瞞
Bai Juyi (772–846)	白居易
Baili Xi (*Chunqiu*)	百里奚
Bao Shuya (d. 644 BC)	鮑叔牙
Bian He (c. 600 BC)	卞和
Bojie (Cai Yong)	伯喈
Boniu (544–478 BC)	伯牛
Cai Mao (180–220)	蔡瑁
Cai Yang (d. 200)	蔡陽
Cai Yong (132–92)	蔡邕
Cao Cao (155–220)	曹操
Cao Fang (232–74)	曹芳
Cao Man	曹滿
Cao Mengde (Cao Cao)	曹孟德
Cao Pi (187–226)	曹丕

Cao Ren (168–223)	曹仁
Cao Shuang (d. 249)	曹爽
Cao Zhang (d. 223)	曹彰
Cao Zhi (191–232)	曹植
Che Zhou (164–99)	車冑
Chen Shou (233–97)	陳壽
Chen Zhong (Eastern Han)	陳重
Confucius (Kongzi) (551–479 BC)	孔子
Cui Zhouping (late 2nd–early 3rd c.)	崔州平
Decao (Sima Hui)	德操
Diaochan (d. 192)	貂蝉
Ding Jianyang (Ding Yuan)	丁建陽
Ding Yuan (d. 189)	丁原
Dong Cheng (d. 200)	董承
Dong Huang (d. 192)	董璜
Dong Min (d. 192)	董旻
Dong Zhongshu (179–104 BC)	董仲舒
Dong Zhuo (d. 192)	董卓
Dou E	竇娥
Du Fu (712–70)	杜甫
Fan Chou (d. 195)	樊稠
Fengxian (Lü Bu)	奉先
Fu Yue (d. 1246 BC)	傅說
Gan Ning (d. c. 220)	甘寧
Gao Cheng (c. 1080)	高承
Gao Wenxiu (Yuan dynasty)	高文秀
Ganjiang (Chunqiu period)	干將
Geng Gong	耿恭
Gong Gu (late 2nd–early 3rd c.)	鞏固
Gongjin (Zhou Yu)	公瑾
Gongsun Hong (200–121 BC)	公孫弘
Gongsun Sheng	公孫勝
Guan Hanqing (c. 1245–1322)	關漢卿
Guan Ping (d. 219)	關平
Guan Tong	關統
Guan Xing (Han dynasty)	關興
Guan Yu (d. 219)	關羽
Guan Yunchang (Guan Yu)	關雲長
Guan Zhong (c. 720–645 BC)	管仲
Guo Si (d. 197)	郭汜
Han Wang (Liu Bang)	漢王
Han Xin (d. 196 BC)	韓信
He Huang (1668–after 1741)	何煌
He Jin (d. 192)	何進

Hongchang (Diaochan)	紅昌
Hongniang	紅娘
Hu Zeng (9th c.)	胡曾
Hua Guan Suo	花關索
Hua Li Lang (13th c.)	花李郎
Huang Gai (Han dynasty)	黃蓋
Huang Hansheng (Huang Zhong)	黃漢升
Huang Hao (early 3rd c.)	黃皓
Huang Wen	黃文
Huang Zhong (d. 220)	黃忠
Huangfu Song (d. 195)	皇甫嵩
Ji Lü	季旅
Ji Ping (d. 218)	吉平
Jia Zhongming (1343–1422)	賈仲明
Jian Xianhe (Jian Yong)	簡憲和
Jian Yong (c. 180–220)	簡雍
Jiang Gan (Han dynasty)	蔣幹
Jiang Wei (202–64)	姜維
Jin Renjie (d. 1329)	金仁傑
Jingsheng (Liu Biao)	景升
Kang Jingzhi (late 13th c.)	康進之
Kongming (Zhuge Liang)	孔明
Kou Feng	寇峯
Kuai Tong (Han dynasty)	蒯通
Kuai Yue (d. 214)	蒯越
Lady Gan (d. 209)	甘夫人
Lady Mi	糜夫人
Lady Sun	孫妃
Laozi (fl. 6th c. BC)	老子
Lei Yi (Eastern Han)	雷義
Li Jue (d. 198)	李傕
Li Kui	李逵
Li Qujin	李取進
Li Ru (2nd c.)	李儒
Li Shangyin (c. 813–53)	李商隱
Li Shimin (599–649)	李世民
Li Shouqing	李壽卿
Li Su (d. 192)	李肅
Li Tong (Han dynasty)	李通
Li Yu (937–78)	李煜
Ling Tong	凌統
Ling Zhe	靈輒
Liu Bang (r. 202–195 BC)	劉邦
Liu Bei (161–223)	劉備

Liu Biao (142–208)	劉表
Liu Cong (Han dynasty)	劉琮
Liu Deran	劉德然
Liu Feng (d. 220)	劉封
Liu Qi (d. 209)	劉琦
Liu Shan (A'dou)	劉禪
Liu Sheng (d. 113 BC)	劉勝
Liu Xiu (5 BC–AD 57)	劉秀
Liu Yuan (d. 310)	劉淵
Liu Yuanqi	劉元起
Liu Zhang (d. 219)	劉璋
Lü Bu (d. 198)	呂布
Lü Fan (d. 228)	呂範
Lü Jiang (Lü Wang)	呂望
Lü Meng (178–220)	呂蒙
Lü Qianghui (2nd c.)	呂強回
Lu Su (172–217)	魯肅
Lu Zhi (Han dynasty)	盧植
Lun Ban	輪班
Luo Guanzhong (1330–1400)	羅貫中
Ma Chao (176–226)	馬超
Ma Dai	馬岱
Ma Gou	馬垢
Ma Mengqi (Ma Chao)	馬孟起
Ma Teng (d. 211)	馬騰
Madam Chen	陳夫主
Mao Zonggang (1632–1709)	毛宗崗
Master Water Mirror (Sima Hui)	水鏡先生
Meixiang	梅香
Meng Ben (Warring States)	孟賁
Meng Guangwei (late 2nd–early 3rd c.)	孟光威
Meng Ying (Zhou)	孟嬴
Mengde (Cao Cao)	孟德
Mengzi (4th c. BC)	孟子
Mi Fang (late 2nd–early 3rd c.)	麋芳
Mi Zhu (d. 221)	麋竺
Miao Yue (1904–95)	繆鉞
Min Ziqian (536–487 BC)	閔子騫
Mister Okay (Hao Hao xiansheng)	好好先生
Neire (Pi Han)	內熱 (皮寒)
Ningqi (Zhou dynasty)	寧戚
Oriole (Cui Yingying)	崔鶯鶯
Pang De (d. 219)	龐德
Pang Degong (Han dynasty)	龐德公

Pang Shiyuan (179–214)	龐士元
Pang Tong (179–214)	龐統
Pei Songzhi (372–451)	裴松之
Peng Yue (d. 196 BC)	彭越
Phoenix Fledgling	鳳雛
Pi Han (Neire)	皮寒 (内熱)
Pu Songling (1640–1715)	蒲松齡
Qi Biaojia (1602–45)	祁彪佳
Qiao Guolao (109–83)	喬國老
Qing Bu (Ying Bu)	黥布 (英布)
Qiu Hu (Chunqiu period)	秋胡
Recumbent Dragon	臥龍 (竜)
Ren Ang	任昂
Shao Bowen (1057–1134)	邵伯溫
Shao Yong (1011–77)	邵雍
Shi Guangyuan (late 2nd–early 3rd c.)	石廣元
Shi Junbao (d. 1276)	石君寶
Shi Ren (Han dynasty)	士仁
Shisun Rui (d. 195)	士孫瑞
Sima Decao (Sima Hui)	司馬德操
Sima Guang (1019–86)	司馬光
Sima Hui (d. 208)	司馬徽
Sima Xiangru (179–118 BC)	司馬相如
Sima Yi (Sima Zhongxiang) (179–251)	司馬懿
Sima Zhongda (Sima Yi)	司馬仲達
Sima Zhongxiang	司馬仲祥
Song Jiang	宋江
Song Yu (fl. 3rd c. BC)	宋玉
Student Zhang	張生
Su Shi (1037–1101)	蘇軾
Sun Ce (175–200)	孫策
Sun Jian (d. 191)	孫堅
Sun Quan (182–252)	孫權
Sun Wu (c. 544–496 BC)	孫武
Sun Zhongmou (Sun Quan)	孫仲謀
Sun Zi (Sun Wu)	孫子
Tai Jia (Shang dynasty)	太甲
Tang Zhou (2nd c.)	唐周
Tseng Yong-yih (Zeng Yongyi)	曾永義
Wang Can (177–217)	王粲
Wang Ji (1474–1540)	王濟
Wang Jilie (1873–1952)	王季烈
Wang Ling (171–251)	王淩
Wang Mang (d. 23)	王莽

Wang Qiang	王強
Wang Shifu (Yuan dynasty)	王實甫
Wang Sun	王孫
Wang Xiang (185–269)	王祥
Wang Ye (Jin dynasty)	王業
Wang Yun (137–92)	王允
Wang Zhongwen (Yuan dynasty)	王忠文
Wei Yan (d. 234)	魏延
Wen Chou (d. 200)	文醜
Wu Hanchen (Yuan dynasty)	武漢臣
Wu Qi (440–381 BC)	吳起
Wu She (d. 522 BC)	伍奢
Wu Wei	吳危
Wu Yun (d. 484 BC)	伍員
Wu Zilan (d. 200)	吳子蘭
Wu Zixu (Wu Yun)	伍子胥
Xi Chu Bawang (Xiang Yu)	西楚霸王
Xia Yu (Han dynasty)	夏育
Xiao He (d. 193 BC)	蕭何
Xiahou Dun (d. 220)	夏侯惇
Xiang Yu (232–202 BC)	項羽
Xijizi (Ming dynasty)	息機子
Xin Qingji (d. 12 BC)	辛慶忌
Xu Chu (fl. 190–220)	許褚
Xu Shu (late 2nd c.)	徐庶
Xu Yuanzhi (Xu Shu)	徐元直
Xuande (Liu Bei)	玄德
Yan Dunyi (1905–62)	嚴敦易
Yan Guang (late 1st c. BC–AD 1st c.)	嚴光
Yan Hui (521–481 BC)	顏回
Yan Liang (d. 200)	顏良
Yan Yan (Han dynasty)	嚴顏
Yang Biao (142–225)	楊彪
Yang Feng (d. 197)	楊奉
Yang Xiang (Jin)	杨香
Yi Yin (Shang)	伊尹
Yide (Zhang Fei)	翼德
Yidu (Kuai Yue)	異度
Ying Bu (d. 196 BC)	英布
Ying Zheng (259–210 BC)	嬴政
Yingying	鶯鶯
Yu Boyuan (Yuan)	于伯淵
Yu Fan (164–233)	虞翻
Yu Jin (d. 221)	于禁

Yu Shenxing (1545–1607)	于慎行
Yu Xiaogu (Ming dynasty)	于小谷
Yuan Benchu (Yuan Shao)	袁本初
Yuan Haowen (1190–1257)	元好問
Yuan Shao (d. 202)	袁紹
Yuan Shu (d. 199)	袁術
Yuan Xiang	袁襄
Yuanzhi (Xu Shu)	元直
Yue Yi (Warring States)	樂毅
Zai Wo (522–458 BC)	宰我
Zang Gong	臧宮
Zang Jinshu (Zang Maoxun)	臧晉叔
Zang Maoxun (1550–1620)	臧懋循
Zang Yigui	臧一貴
Zhang Da	張達
Zhang Fei (d. 221)	張飛
Zhang Ji (d. 223)	張既
Zhang Jiao (d. 184)	張角
Zhang Liang (d. 186 BC)	張良
Zhang Liao (169–222)	張遼
Zhang Lu (d. 216)	張魯
Zhang Qian	張千
Zhang Song (d. 213)	張松
Zhang Yi (d. 310 BC)	張儀
Zhang Yide (Zhang Fei)	張翼德
Zhang Zai (1020–77)	張載
Zhang Zhao (156–236)	張昭
Zhao Chongguo (d. 52 BC)	趙充國
Zhao Qimei (1563–1624)	趙琦美
Zhao Shanfu (Song dynasty)	赵善傅
Zhao Yun (d. 229)	趙雲
Zhao Zilong (Zhao Yun)	趙子龍
Zheng Dehui (Yuan dynasty)	鄭德輝
Zheng Guangzu (Yuan dynasty)	鄭光祖
Zheng Zhenduo (1898–1958)	鄭振鐸
Zhong Ji (d. 200)	种輯
Zhong Linbin (1937–)	鍾林斌
Zhong Ying (Dong Zhuo)	仲英
Zhonggong (522–466 BC)	仲弓
Zhou Cang	周倉
Zhou Gongjin (Zhou Yu)	周公瑾
Zhou Lang (Zhou Yu)	周郎
Zhou Yafu (d. 143 BC)	周亞夫
Zhou Yu (175–210)	周瑜

Zhu Di (1360–1424)	朱棣
Zhu Kai (Yuan dynasty)	朱凱
Zhu Maichen (d. 115 BC)	朱買臣
Zhu Quan (1378–1448)	朱權
Zhu Su (1361–1425)	朱橚
Zhu Xi (1130–1200)	朱熹
Zhu Youdun (1379–1439)	朱有燉
Zhu Yuanzhang (1328–98)	朱元璋
Zhu Yunwen (1377–1402)	朱允炆
Zhuan Zhu (d. 515 BC)	鱄諸
Zhuangzi (369–286 BC)	莊子
Zhuge Liang (181–234)	諸葛亮
Zijing (Lu Su)	子敬
Zishi (Wang Yun)	子師
Zu Shou	詛授

III. Places Cited in the Text

Architectural Sites and Built Environments

Baling Bridge (*Baling qiao*)	灞陵桥
Bronze Sparrow (*Tongque*)	銅雀
Cloudy Terrace (*Yun tai*)	雲臺
Dragon and Phoenix Pavilions (*Longfeng ge*)	龍鳳閣
Eastern White Emperor Peak (*Dong Baidi feng*)	東白帝峰
Fine Willows (camp)	細柳營
Gate of the Silver Dais (*Yin tai men*)	銀臺門
Great Wall (*Changcheng*)	長城
Hangu Pass (*Hangu guan*)	函谷關
Jian Terrace (*Jian tai*)	漸臺
Lingyan Pavilion (*Linyan ge*)	凌煙閣
Loft for Watching Mainstreet (*Kan jie lou*)	看街樓
Meiwu	郿塢
Ninefold Palace (*Jiu chong*)	九重
Palace of Eternal Peace (*Yong'an gong*)	永安宮
Pavilion of Silk and Ribbon (*Silun ge*)	絲綸閣
Peach Blossom Fount (*Tao yuan*)	桃源
Peach Orchard (*Tao yuan*)	桃園
Phoenix Tower (*Fenghuang lou*)	鳳凰樓
Pomegranate Garden (*Shiliu yuan*)	石榴園
Stone Pavilion Posthouse (*Shiting yi*)	石亭驛
Weiyang Hall (Weiyang Palace)	未央宮
White Emperor City (*Baidi cheng*)	白帝城
Yang Terrace (*Yang tai*)	陽臺
Yellow Crane Tower (*Huanghe lou*)	黃鶴樓

Yellow Pavilion (*Huangge*) 黃閣
Yong'an Palace (Palace of Eternal Peace) 永安宮

Geographical Features

Changshan 常山
Dangyang Bridge 當陽橋
Dangyang Slope 當陽坡
Deergate Mountain(s) 鹿門山
Fujiang 涪江
Goose Channel (Honggou) 鴻溝
Hua Mountain (Huashan) 華山
Hulao guan 虎牢關
Hushan rock (Hushan shi) 湖山石
Jade Fount Mountain (Yuyuanshan) 玉源山
Kunlun Mountains (Kunlunshan) 崑崙山
Minjiang 岷江
Mount Beiyin 北陰山
Mount Dingjun (Dingjunshan) 定軍山
Mount Heng (Hengshan) 衡山
Mount Li (Lishan) 驪山
Mount Mangdang (Mangdangshan) 芒碭山
Mount Qi (Qishan) 祁山
Mount Song (Songshan) 嵩山
Official Ford (*Guandu*) 官渡
Pan Creek (Panxi) 磻溪
Pinnacle Peak (Xianshan) 峴山
Qutang Gorge (*Qutang xia*) 瞿塘峽
Recumbent Dragon Ridge 臥龍(竜)崗
Red Cliff (Chibi) 赤壁
Rook River 烏江
Sandalwood Creek (Tanxi) 檀溪
Shamanka Mountian (*Wu shan*) 巫山
Southern Seas (*Nan hai*) 南海
Taihang Mountains (*Taihang shan*) 太行山
Taihu rock (*Taihu shi*) 太湖石
Tanxi 檀溪
Tiantai Range (*Tiantai shan*) 天台山
Tigerkeep Pass (*Hulao guan*) 虎牢關
Tuojiang 沱江
White River (*Bai he*) 白河
Wuzhang Plains (*Wuzhang yuan*) 五丈原
Yan Ford (*Yanjin*) 延津
Yangping Pass (*Yangping guan*) 陽平關
Yangzi River (*Chang jiang*) 長江

Administrative Place-Names

Anhui	安徽
Anxi	安西
Ba	巴
Baqiu	巴邱
Barbaria	夷
Bazhou (Eight Regions)	八州
Beidi	北地
Beijing	北京
Bingzhou	並州
Bowang	博望
Cangzhou	滄州
Chaisang	柴桑
Chang'an	長安
Changban	長坂
Changsha	長沙
Chengdu	成都
Chenliu	陳留
Dangyang	當陽
Dasang Village	大桑村
Dashu	大樹
Deng County	鄧縣
Dezhou	德州
Ding Prefecture (Dingzhou)	定州
Dingluan	丁欒
Dingyuan	定遠
Dushu Village	獨樹村
Duting	都亭
Echeng	鄂城
Fancheng	樊城
Fanyang	范陽
Fanzhou	樊州
Fengjie	奉節
Fengpei	豊沛
Flowery Kingdom	華夏
Fuchun	富春
Fuyan	傅岩
Fuyang	富陽
Gansu	甘肅
Gaoguixiang	高貴鄉
Gaotang	高唐
Guangling	廣靈
Guangzhou	廣州

Guanxi	關西
Gucheng (Old City)	古城
Guiyang	貴陽
Guizhou	貴州
Hanzhong	漢中
Hangzhou	杭州
Hanyan	寒燕
Hanyang	漢陽
Hedong	河東
Henan	河南
Henghai	橫海
Hongnong	弘農
Huaibei	淮北
Huaiyin	淮陰
Hubei	湖北
Hunan	湖南
Ji (one of the Eight Regions)	冀
Jiang Xia Region	江夏區
Jiangling	江陵
Jiangnan	江南
Jiangsu	江蘇
Jianyang	簡陽
Jieting	街亭
Jing (one of the Eight Regions)	荊
Jingzhou	荊州
Jinling	金陵
Jiuzhou	九州
Julu	鉅鹿
Juye	巨野
Kaifeng	開封
Langzhou	閬州
Liaoyang	遼陽
Liguo	利國
Lintao	臨洮
Lintong	臨潼
Linzhang	臨漳
Liyang	溧陽
Longxi	隴西
Longzhong	隆中
Lousang	樓桑
Lu	魯
Luocheng	羅城
Luoyang	洛陽
Mei	郿

Mu'er	木耳
Nanjing	南京
Nanyang	南陽
Ning	寧
Old City (Gucheng)	古城
Pei	沛
Pingyuan	平原
Puyang	濮陽
Puzhou	蒲州
Qiao Commandery	譙都
Qi	齊
Qing (one of the Eight Regions)	青
Runan	汝南
Ruying	汝潁
Shaanxi	陝西
Shandong	山東
Shanghai	上海
Shanxi	山西
Shaoxing	紹興
Shouchun	壽春
Shouting	壽亭
Shu	蜀
Sichuan	四川
Sishang	泗上
Suzhou	蘇州
Taiwan	臺灣
Taiyuan	太原
Tiekou	帖口
Weihe	渭河
Wenxi	聞喜
Western Rong	西戎
Wuchang	武昌
Wuhan	武漢
Wulin	武林
Wuling	武陵
Wuxing	吳興
Xi'an	西安
Xiakou	夏口
Xianggang	香港
Xiangyang	襄陽
Xiaopei	小沛
Xiapi	下邳
Xichang	西昌
Xichuan	西川

Xieliang	解良
Xiliang	西涼
Xindu	新都
Xinxiang	新鄉
Xinye	新野
Xinzhou	欣州
Xu (one of the Eight Regions)	徐
Xuchang	許昌
Xudu	許都
Xuzhou	徐州
Yamen	崖門
Yan (one of the Eight Regions)	兗
Yan	燕
Yang (one of the Eight Regions)	楊
Yicheng	夷城
Yingchuan	穎川
Yiyang	益陽
Yizhou	益州
You (one of the Eight Regions)	幽
Yu (one of the Eight Regions)	豫
Yunnan	雲南
Yuzhang	豫章
Zhejiang	浙江
Zhending	真定
Zhongguo	中國
Zhuo	涿
Zhuojun	涿郡

IV. Titles of Plays, Poems, and Songs Cited in the Text

Baijia xing	百家姓
Bowang shaotun	博望燒屯
Changmen fu	長門賦
Chibi aozhan	赤壁鏖戰
Chibi huaigu	赤壁懷古
Chunqiu	春秋
Chunqiu fanlu	春秋繁露
Ci Dong Zhuo	刺董卓
Da Liu Bei	大劉備
Dandao hui	單刀會
Diaochannü	貂蟬女
Dongpo zhilin	東坡志林
Ge jiang dou zhi	隔江鬥志
Guan dawang dandao hui	關大王單刀會

Guan Yunchang gucheng juyi	關雲長古城聚義
Guan Yunchang qianli duxing	關雲長千里獨行
Guan Yunchang yiyong cijin	關雲長義勇辭金
Guben Yuan Ming zaju	孤本元明雜劇
Gujin zaju xuan	古今雜劇選
Hei xuanfeng zhangyi shucai	黑旋風仗義疏財
Hou Hanshu	後漢書
Hulaoguan sanzhan Lü Bu	虎牢關三戰呂佈
Hua Guan Suo zhuan	花關索傳
Hua Guan Suo shuochang cihua	花關索説唱詞話
Huanghe lou	黃鶴樓
Huangji jingshi shu	皇極經世書
Huolang dan	貨郎旦
Jinshu	晉書
Kuaiqu	快曲
Laozi	老子
Li Kui fujing	李達負荊
Lianhuan ji	連環計
Lianhuan ji	連環記
Liji	禮記
Liu Guan Zhang Taoyuan san jieyi	劉關張桃園三結義
Liu xianzhu tiao Tanxi	劉先主跳檀溪
Liu xianzhu Xiangyang hui	劉先主襄陽會
Liu Xuande dufu Xiangyang hui	劉玄德獨赴襄陽會
"Liuhou shijia ershiwu"	留侯世家二十五
Liutao	六韜
Lugui bu xubian	錄鬼簿續編
Lunyu	論語
Ma Lü Bu	罵呂佈
Mang Zhang Fei danao Shiliu yuan	莽張飛大鬧石榴園
Mang Zhang Fei danao xiangfuyuan	莽張飛大鬧相府院
Mengqiu	蒙求
Ming Chenghua shuochang cihua congkan	明成化説唱詞話叢刊
Mudan ting (Peony Pavilion)	牡丹亭
Qianli duxing	千里獨行
Quanxiang pinghua Wuwang fa Zhou shu	全相平話武王伐紂書
Quanxiang pinghua wuzhong	全相平話五種
Qiu Hu bianwen	秋胡變文
Sanfen shilüe	三分事略
Sanguo yin	三國因
Sanguo zhi	三國志
Sanguo zhi pinghua	三國志平話
Sanguo zhi tongsu yanyi	三國志通俗演義
Sanlüe	三略

Shilin guangji	事林廣記
Shiwu jiyuan	事物紀原
Sima Xiangru tiqiao ji	司馬相如題橋記
Taihe zhengyin pu	太和正音譜
Tongque ji	銅雀姬
Wei Jin shiyu	魏晉世語
Weishu	魏書
Wu Yue chunqiu	吳越春秋
Wushu	吳書
Xi Shu meng	西蜀夢
Xixiang ji	西廂記
Xiangfuyuan Cao gong kan Ji Ping	相府院曹公勘吉平
Xiangyang hui	襄陽會
Yingxiong ji	英雄記
Yongxi yuefu	雍熙樂府
Yuankan zaju sanshizhong	元刊雜劇三十種
Yuanqu xuan	元曲選
Zaju shiduanjin	雜劇十段錦
Zhan Cai Yang	斬蔡陽
Zhou Xiaolang yueye xi Xiao Qiao	周小郎月夜戲小喬
Zhou Yu ye Lu Su	周瑜謁魯肅
Zhuge Liang Bowang shaotun	諸葛亮博望燒屯
Zizhi tongjian	資治通鑒
Zuozhuan	左傳

V. Terms Cited in the Text

aiya (yayaya)	哎呀 (呀呀呀)
Baidi zhi zi	白帝之子
bao	報
bei	背
bei bu (cloth on back)	背布
bei Bu (rebelling Lü Bu)	背布
bianwen	變文
bingshen	丙申
bu (cloth)	布
bu (prognostication)	卜
bu ke qu (you cannot go)	不可去
bu ke qu (it cannot be taken)	不可取
caimei	猜枚
cao	草
cheng ye Xiao He, bai ye Xiao He	成也簫何，敗也簫何
chengtian baiyu zhu, jiahai zijin liang	撐天白玉柱，架海紫金梁
chenzi	襯字

chide kuzhong ku fang wei renshang ren	吃得苦中苦方為人上人
chongmo	沖末
chuanqi	傳奇
cihua	詞話
da shi	大事
da tuanyuan	大團圓
daishi shoufen	待時守分
dan	旦
dan (cinnabar)	丹
dan (single)	單
diaoshe	刁舌
diaozui youshe	刁嘴油舌
difang (place)	地方
difang (place of work)	地坊
ding	丁
dingchou	丁丑
dinghai	丁亥
dinghuo	頂鑊
dingmao	丁卯
dingsi	丁巳
dingwei	丁未
dingyou	丁酉
diyizhe	第一折
dizi	弟子
dizi hai'er	弟子孩兒
dongge	東閣
duan	斷
duanchu	斷出
dun	惇
duozi	多子
fan'an	翻案
feifu	肺腑
fenye	分野
fu feng pan long	附鳳攀龍
fulong	伏龍
fumo	副末
ganhua	肝花
ganjiang	干將
geng hao li	更好梨
gong, shang, jiao, zhi, yu	宮、商、角、徵、羽
gonglun	工輪
guanghui	光輝
guanxi	關係
guo wuguan zhan liujiang	過五關斬六將

Han	漢
hao tao ye ke kan shi	好桃也可堪食
he ni xingming si liao hongmao	和你性命似燎鴻毛
he yan jin shuo	和炎金朔
hen	恨
hengxing badao	橫行霸道
hua	花
hua (Chinese)	華
huchi	虎痴
huang shu	皇叔
Huangchu	黃初
huo	鑊
Huweijin	虎衛軍
ji sheng Yu he sheng Liang	既生瑜何生亮
jia	駕
jian	鶼
Jian'an	建安
jiang (craftsman)	匠
jiang (sesame sauce)	醬
Jianwu	建武
jiaolong	蛟龍
jin	金
jin (advance)	進
jin (exhaust)	盡
jin wei tao jiang	今為逃江
jing	淨
jing (mirror)	鏡
Jingju	京劇
Jiuding	九頂
juan	卷
kang	炕
kun	昆
Kunwu	昆吾
lang	郎
li	里
liang	兩
liao fa	燎髮
liao mao	燎毛
luan	鸞
lunbanjiang	輪班將
maiqiao xingjian	賣俏行奸
Maiwangguan (Maiwang Studio)	脈望館
mengong	悶弓
mengong'er	悶弓兒

Mian	免
Miexiang	滅相
mo	末
moben	末本
mu	畝
nai	乃
nanke (Southern Branch)	南柯
ni	你
ni zuode ge zhili wuli gu wuli	你做的箇知禮無禮故無禮
nuo	儺
pibian	庇鞭
pinghua	平話
pingtian guan	平天冠
qi	氣
qian ("humble" hexagram)	謙
Qian (surname)	錢
Qian (thousand)	千
qiang chutou	強出頭
qiangliang	強梁
Qinglong	青龍
qiu	虬
quanbin	全賓
que	卻
quehua gong (magpie birch bow)	鵲樺弓
quehua gong (bow with magpie pictures)	鵲畫弓
ren bude miexiang / sishihai wo zai yunyang	人不得滅相 / 死屍骸臥在雲陽
rongjiang (military commander)	戎將
rongjiang (floss and soy sauce)	絨醬
sabache	撒八赤
sanjun	三軍
sanqu	散曲
se	色
shang	商
shangsi	上巳
shen	參
shengming	聖明
shengming zhi jun bi you zhongxian zhi chen	聖明之君必有忠賢之臣
shenming	神明
shi (double-hour)	時
shi (ten)	十
shuochang cihua	説唱詞話
shuotian tandi kou	說天談地口
si (thought)	思
si (thread)	絲

si da shenzhou	四大神州
suan (garlic)	蒜
suan (plan)	算
timu	題目
tongpan	筒判
touzhe	頭折
wai	外
wen jun neng you jiduo chou /	問君能有幾多愁/
qiasi yijiang chunshui xiang dong liu	恰似一江春水向東流
wo ru jin	我如今
wowu nayun shou	握霧拿雲手
wuba	五霸
wuhujiang	五虎將
wuli (dance + emphatic particle)	舞哩
wuling hao	五陵豪
wuyu (without fish)	無魚
wuyu (without worries)	無虞
xia	下
xiang	相
xiehouyu	歇後語
xiezi	楔子
xifang jin zhi jing	西方金之精
xijiu	喜酒
xing	星
xing badao	行霸道
xiwen	戲文
xuesheng	學生
xueshi	學士
yang	陽
yanqing (look on their faces)	顏情
yanqing (sentiment of their words)	言情
yi (barbarian)	夷
yi (measure word)	鎰
yijian	夷堅
yimao	乙卯
yin	陰
yisi	乙巳
yong er wu mou tan er wu yi	勇而無謀貪而無義
Yongle	永樂
youdao fa wu dao, ci tianli ye	有道伐無道，此天理也
youlao	有勞
yu bu ming (fifth note did not sound)	羽不鳴
Yu bu ming (Yu is clueless)	羽不明
yuanben	院本

Yuankan	元刊
yue	曰
zaju	雜劇
zan	贊
zan dong	咱東
zhang	丈
Zhao (surname)	趙
zhaode jiangjun	昭德將軍
zhe hao zao zhi ziwei	這好棗知滋味
zhengdan	正旦
zhengming	正名
zhengmo	正末
zhengtong	正統
zhongguan	種官
Zhongping	中平
zouyu	騶虞

Index

acolyte, 175–79, 205, 208, 211, 251, 275–76, 280, 347

Adou, 319, 343, 352–53, 363

Analects, 11, 110, 167, 177, 262, 289, 291

Anthology of Northern Dramas New and Ancient, xxi, 21, 44, 47

arias, xx, xxii–xxiv, xxviii

Bai Juyi, 62

black ox and white horse, 1–2, 33–34, 322

brotherhood, xx, 1–3

Burning the Stores. See Zhuge Liang Burns the Stores at Bowang

Cai Mao, 138, 154, 161

Cai Yong, 44–46, 50, 62–65, 99–101, 388–90, 421–23, 426–27

canonical historiography, xviii; and popular traditions, x

Cao Cao, vii, x, xii, xv–xvi, xviii, xx–xxi, 182, 194, 117–23, 127, 187, 191, 228, 250, 274, 279, 338–40, 343, 351, 356–57, 359; death of, vii, xii, xvi, xviii, xx–xxi; escape from Red Cliff, 354–60; and Guan Yu, 115–23, 139–43, 146–50, 335–43, 351–57; and Liu Bei, 263, 292, 335; tomb of, x; and Xiahou Dun, 351; and Zhang Fei, 352–54;

Cao Pi, xvi, 364

Cao Ren, 152–56, 181–96, 290, 319, 374–76

Cao Zhang, 181–94, 360

Cao Zhi, xvi

capital cities, xii

capital diaries, xiii

Carnage at Red Cliff, xvii

Causes of the Three Kingdoms, xiii

chantefable, xiv, 367

characterization, xvi, 47, 199; across genre, xvi

Che Zhou, 114, 219, 255, 335–36

Chengdu, vii, 158, 213, 237, 268, 296, 362–65, 370

Chenghua period, xiv, 296, 367

Cheng Tang. See Tang (founder of Shang)

Chen Shou, x–xii

Chibi aozhan. See Carnage at Red Cliff

Chu-Han story-cycle, xiii

chuanqi, xxii, 375

cloud-and-wind meeting, 204

Comprehensive Mirror for Aid in Government, xii

Confucius, 5, 11, 82, 110, 151, 167, 262, 291

Court Entertainment Bureau, 241, 441

crescent-moon, third-of-the-length blade, 5, 20, 251, 271, 275

Cursing Lü Bu, xvii

De Crespigny, xi–xii, xvi

Diaochan, xx, xxii, xxix–xxx, 40, 42, 43–48; status of, 44, 68, 375; and story of interlocking rings, 69–95 passim, 331–34, 391–427 passim

Ding Jianyang. See Ding Yuan

Ding Yuan, 41, 44, 46, 65

dispersal scene, 227, 241

Disturbance at the Pomegranate Garden. See Rude and Rash Zhang Fei Creates a Disturbance at the Pomegranate Garden

Dong Cheng, xxi

Dong Zhuo, 55–56, 61, 66–67, 74, 83–85, 96, 326–31, 382, 388, 390–91, 398, 404–7, 418, 426; acts, inhumane, 91–92, 414, 419; fatness of, 73, 397